Eve

John Grisham

THE CLIENT

THE STREET LAWYER

This edition published in 1999 by Cresset Editions,
an imprint of Random House UK Ltd,
20 Vauxhall Bridge Road, London SW1V 2SA

Printed and bound in Germany

ISBN 0 09187 277 4

THE CLIENT

To Ty and Shea

ONE

Mark was eleven and had been smoking off and on for two years, never trying to quit but being careful not to get hooked. He preferred Kools, his ex-father's brand, but his mother smoked Virginia Slims at the rate of two packs a day, and he could in an average week pilfer ten or twelve from her. She was a busy woman with many problems, perhaps a little naive when it came to her boys, and she never dreamed her eldest would be smoking at the age of eleven.

Occasionally Kevin, the delinquent two streets over, would sell Mark a pack of stolen Marlboros for a dollar. But for the most part he had to rely on his mother's skinny cigarettes.

He had four of them in his pocket this afternoon as he led his brother Ricky, age eight, down the path into the woods behind their trailer park. Ricky was nervous about this, his first smoke. He had caught Mark hiding the cigarettes in a shoe box under his bed yesterday, and threatened to tell all if his big brother didn't show him how to do it. They sneaked along the wooded trail, headed for one of Mark's secret spots where he'd spent many solitary hours trying to inhale and blow smoke rings.

Most of the other kids in the neighborhood were into beer and pot, two vices Mark was determined to avoid. Their ex-father was an alcoholic who'd beaten both boys and their mother, and the beatings always followed nasty bouts with beer. Mark had seen and felt the effects of alcohol. He was also afraid of drugs.

'Are you lost?' Ricky asked, just like a little brother, as they left the trail and waded through chest-high weeds.

'Just shut up,' Mark said without slowing. The only time their father had spent at home was to drink and sleep and abuse them. He was gone now, thank heavens. For five years Mark had been in charge of Ricky. He felt like an eleven-year-old father. He'd taught him how to throw a football and ride a bike. He'd explained what he knew about sex. He'd warned him about drugs, and protected him from bullies. And he felt terrible about this introduction to vice. But it was just a cigarette. It could be much worse.

The weeds stopped and they were under a large tree with a rope hanging from a thick branch. A row of bushes yielded to a small clearing, and beyond it an overgrown dirt road disappeared over a hill. A highway could be heard in the distance.

Mark stopped and pointed to a log near the rope. 'Sit there,' he instructed, and Ricky obediently backed onto the log and glanced around anxiously as if the police might be watching. Mark eyed him like a drill sergeant while picking a cigarette from his shirt pocket. He held it with his right thumb and index finger, and tried to be casual about it.

'You know the rules,' he said, looking down at Ricky. There were only two rules, and they had discussed them a dozen times during the day, and Ricky was frustrated at being treated like a child. He rolled his eyes away and said, 'Yeah, if I tell anyone, you'll beat me up.'

'That's right.'

Ricky folded his arms. 'And I can smoke only one a day.'

'That's right. If I catch you smoking more than that, then you're in trouble. And if I find out you're drinking beer or messing with drugs, then – '

'I know, I know. You'll beat me up again.'

'Right.'

'How many do you smoke a day?'

'Only one,' Mark lied. Some days, only one. Some days, three or four, depending on supply. He stuck the filter between his lips like a gangster.

2

'Will one a day kill me?' Ricky asked.

Mark removed the cigarette from his lips. 'Not anytime soon. One a day is pretty safe. More than that, and you could be in trouble.'

'How many does Mom smoke a day?'

'Two packs.'

'How many is that?'

'Forty.'

'Wow. Then she's in big trouble.'

'Mom's got all kinds of troubles. I don't think she's worried about cigarettes.'

'How many does Dad smoke a day?'

'Four or five packs. A hundred a day.'

Ricky grinned slightly. 'Then he's gonna die soon, right?'

'I hope so. Between staying drunk and chain-smoking, he'll be dead in a few years.'

'What's chain-smoking?'

'It's when you light the new one with the old one. I wish he'd smoke ten packs a day.'

'Me too.' Ricky glanced toward the small clearing and the dirt road. It was shady and cool under the tree, but beyond the limbs the sun was bright. Mark pinched the filter with his thumb and index finger and sort of waved it before his mouth. 'Are you scared?' he sneered as only big brothers can.

'No.'

'I think you are. Look, hold it like this, okay?' He waved it closer, then with great drama withdrew it and stuck it between his lips. Ricky watched intently.

Mark lit the cigarette, puffed a tiny cloud of smoke, then held it and admired it. 'Don't try to swallow the smoke. You're not ready for that yet. Just suck a little then blow the smoke out. Are you ready?'

'Will it make me sick?'

'It will if you swallow the smoke.' He took two quick drags and puffed for effect. 'See. It's really easy. I'll teach you how to inhale later.'

3

'Okay.' Ricky nervously reached out with his thumb and index finger, and Mark placed the cigarette carefully between them. 'Go ahead.'

Ricky eased the wet filter to his lips. His hand shook and he took a short drag and blew smoke. Another short drag. The smoke never got past his front teeth. Another drag. Mark watched carefully, hoping he would choke and cough and turn blue, then get sick and never smoke again.

'It's easy,' Ricky said proudly as he held the cigarette and admired it. His hand was shaking.

'It's no big deal.'

'Tastes kind of funny.'

'Yeah, yeah.' Mark sat next to him on the log and picked another one from his pocket. Ricky puffed rapidly. Mark lit his, and they sat in silence under the tree enjoying a quiet smoke.

'This is fun,' Ricky said, nibbling at the filter.

'Great. Then why are your hands shaking?'

'They're not.'

'Sure.'

Ricky ignored this. He leaned forward with his elbows on his knees, took a longer drag, then spat in the dirt like he'd seen Kevin and the big boys do behind the trailer park. This was easy.

Mark opened his mouth into a perfect circle and attempted a smoke ring. He thought this would really impress his little brother, but the ring failed to form and the gray smoke dissipated.

'I think you're too young to smoke,' he said.

Ricky was busy puffing and spitting, and thoroughly enjoying this giant step toward manhood. 'How old were you when you started?' he asked.

'Nine. But I was more mature than you.'

'You always say that.'

'That's because it's always true.'

They sat next to each other on the log under the tree, smoking quietly and staring at the grassy clearing beyond the shade. Mark *was* in fact more mature than Ricky at the

4

age of eight. He was more mature than any kid his age. He'd always been mature. He had hit his father with a baseball bat when he was seven. The aftermath had not been pretty, but the drunken idiot had stopped beating their mother. There had been many fights and many beatings, and Dianne Sway had sought refuge and advice from her eldest son. They had consoled each other and conspired to survive. They had cried together after the beatings. They had plotted ways to protect Ricky. When he was nine, Mark convinced her to file for divorce. He had called the cops when his father showed up drunk after being served with divorce papers. He had testified in court about the abuse and neglect and beatings. He was very mature.

Ricky heard the car first. There was a low, rushing sound coming from the dirt road. Then Mark heard it, and they stopped smoking. 'Just sit still,' Mark said softly. They did not move.

A long, black, shiny Lincoln appeared over the slight hill and eased toward them. The weeds in the road were as high as the front bumper. Mark dropped his cigarette to the ground and covered it with his shoe. Ricky did the same.

The car slowed almost to a stop as it neared the clearing, then circled around, touching the tree limbs as it moved slowly. It stopped and faced the road. The boys were directly behind it, and hidden from view. Mark slid off the log, and crawled through the weeds to a row of brush at the edge of the clearing. Ricky followed. The rear of the Lincoln was thirty feet away. They watched it carefully. It had Louisiana license plates.

'What's he doing?' Ricky whispered.

Mark peeked through the weeds. 'Shhhhh!' He had heard stories around the trailer park of teenagers using these woods to meet girls and smoke pot, but this car did not belong to a teenager. The engine quit, and the car just sat there in the weeds for a minute. Then the door opened, and the driver stepped into the weeds and looked around. He was a chubby man in a black suit. His head was fat and round and without hair except for neat rows above the ears

5

and a black-and-gray beard. He stumbled to the rear of the car, fumbled with the keys, and finally opened the trunk. He removed a water hose, stuck one end into the exhaust pipe, and ran the other end through a crack in the left rear window. He closed the trunk, looked around again as if he were expecting to be watched, then disappeared into the car.

The engine started.

'Wow,' Mark said softly, staring blankly at the car.

'What's he doing?' Ricky asked.

'He's trying to kill himself.'

Ricky raised his head a few inches for a better view. 'I don't understand, Mark.'

'Keep down. You see the hose, right? The fumes from the tail pipe go into the car, and it kills him.'

'You mean suicide?'

'Right. I saw a guy do it like this in a movie once.'

They leaned closer to the weeds and stared at the hose running from the pipe to the window. The engine idled smoothly.

'Why does he want to kill himself?' Ricky asked.

'How am I supposed to know? But we gotta do something.'

'Yeah, let's get the hell outta here.'

'No. Just be still a minute.'

'I'm leaving, Mark. You can watch him die if you want to, but I'm gone.'

Mark grabbed his brother's shoulder and forced him lower. Ricky's breathing was heavy and they were both sweating. The sun hid behind a cloud.

'How long does it take?' Ricky asked, his voice quivering.

'Not very long.' Mark released his brother and eased on to all fours. 'You stay here, okay. If you move, I'll kick your tail.'

'What're you doing, Mark?'

'Just stay here. I mean it.' Mark lowered his thin body almost to the ground and crawled on elbows and knees

6

through the weeds toward the car. The grass was dry and at least two feet tall. He knew the man couldn't hear him, but he worried about the movement of the weeds. He stayed directly behind the car and slid snakelike on his belly until he was in the shadow of the trunk. He reached and carefully eased the hose from the tail pipe, and dropped it to the ground. He retraced his trail with a bit more speed, and seconds later was crouched next to Ricky, watching and waiting in the heavier grass and brush under the outermost limbs of the tree. He knew that if they were spotted, they could dart past the tree and down their trail and be gone before the chubby man could catch them.

They waited. Five minutes passed, though it seemed like an hour.

'You think he's dead?' Ricky whispered, his voice dry and weak.

'I don't know.'

Suddenly, the door opened, and the man stepped out. He was crying and mumbling, and he staggered to the rear of the car where he saw the hose in the grass, and cursed it as he shoved it back into the tail pipe. He held a bottle of whiskey and looked around wildly at the trees, then stumbled back into the car. He mumbled to himself as he slammed the door.

The boys watched in horror.

'He's crazy as hell,' Mark said faintly.

'Let's get out of here,' Ricky said.

'We can't! If he kills himself, and we saw it or knew about it, then we could get in all kinds of trouble.'

Ricky raised his head as if to retreat. 'Then we won't tell anybody. Come on, Mark!'

Mark grabbed his shoulder again and forced him to the ground. 'Just stay down! We're not leaving until I say we're leaving!'

Ricky closed his eyes tightly and started crying. Mark shook his head in disgust but didn't take his eyes off the car. Little brothers were more trouble than they were worth. 'Stop it,' he growled through clenched teeth.

7

'I'm scared.'

'Fine. Just don't move, okay. Do you hear me? Don't move. And stop the crying.' Mark was back on his elbows, deep in the weeds and preparing to ease through the tall grass once more.

'Just let him die, Mark,' Ricky whispered between sobs.

Mark glared at him over his shoulder and eased toward the car, which was still running. He crawled along his same trail of lightly trampled grass so slowly and carefully that even Ricky, with dry eyes now, could barely see him. Ricky watched the driver's door, waiting for it to fly open and the crazy man to lunge out and kill Mark. He perched on his toes in a sprinter's stance for a quick getaway through the woods. He saw Mark emerge under the rear bumper, place a hand for balance on the taillight, and slowly ease the hose from the tail pipe. The grass crackled softly and the weeds shook a little and Mark was next to him again, panting and sweating and, oddly, smiling to himself.

They sat on their legs like two insects under the brush, and watched the car.

'What if he comes out again?' Ricky asked. 'What if he sees us?'

'He can't see us. But if he starts this way, just follow me. We'll be gone before he can take a step.'

'Why don't we go now?'

Mark stared at him fiercely. 'I'm trying to save his life, okay? Maybe, just maybe, he'll see that this is not working, and maybe he'll decide he should wait or something. Why is that so hard to understand?'

'Because he's crazy. If he'll kill himself, then he'll kill us. Why is that so hard to understand?'

Mark shook his head in frustration, and suddenly the door opened again. The man rolled out of the car growling and talking to himself, and stomped through the grass to the rear. He grabbed the end of the hose, stared at it as if it just wouldn't behave, and looked slowly around the small clearing. He was breathing heavily and perspiring. He looked at the trees, and the boys eased to the ground. He

8

looked down, and froze as if he suddenly understood. The grass was slightly trampled around the rear of the car and he knelt as if to inspect it, but then crammed the hose back into the tail pipe instead and hurried back to his door. If someone was watching from the trees, he seemed not to care. He just wanted to hurry up and die.

The two heads rose together above the brush, but just a few inches. They peeked through the weeds for a long minute. Ricky was ready to run, but Mark was thinking.

'Mark, please, let's go,' Ricky pleaded. 'He almost saw us. What if he's got a gun or something?'

'If he had a gun he'd use it on himself.'

Ricky bit his lip and his eyes watered again. He had never won an argument with his brother, and he would not win this one.

Another minute passed, and Mark began to fidget. 'I'll try one more time, okay. And if he doesn't give up, then we'll get outta here. I promise, okay?'

Ricky nodded reluctantly. His brother stretched on his stomach and inched his way through the weeds into the tall grass. Ricky wiped the tears from his cheek with his dirty fingers.

The lawyer's nostrils flared as he inhaled mightily. He exhaled slowly and stared through the windshield while trying to determine if any of the precious, deadly gas had entered his blood and begun its work. A loaded pistol was on the seat next to him. A half-empty fifth of Jack Daniels was in his hand. He took a sip, screwed the cap on it, and placed it on the seat. He inhaled slowly and closed his eyes to savor the gas. Would he simply drift away? Would it hurt or burn or make him sick before it finished him off? The note was on the dash above the steering wheel, next to a bottle of pills.

He cried and talked to himself as he waited for the gas to hurry, dammit! before he'd give up and use the gun. He was a coward, but a very determined one, and he much preferred this sniffing and floating away to sticking a gun in his mouth.

He sipped the whiskey, and hissed as it burned on its descent. Yes, it was finally working. Soon, it would all be over, and he smiled at himself in the mirror because it was working and he was dying and he was not a coward after all. It took guts to do this.

He cried and muttered as he removed the cap of the whiskey bottle for one last swallow. He gulped, and it ran from his lips and trickled into his beard.

He would not be missed. And although this thought should have been painful, the lawyer was calmed by the knowledge that no one would grieve. His mother was the only person in the world who loved him, and she'd been dead four years so this would not hurt her. There was a child from the first disastrous marriage, a daughter he'd not seen in eleven years, but he'd been told she had joined a cult and was as crazy as her mother.

It would be a small funeral. A few lawyer buddies and perhaps a judge or two would be there all dressed up in dark suits and whispering importantly as the piped-in organ music drifted around the near-empty chapel. No tears. The lawyers would sit and glance at their watches while the minister, a stranger, sped through the standard comments used for dear departed ones who never went to church.

It would be a ten-minute job with no frills. The note on the dash required the body to be cremated.

'Wow,' he said softly as he took another sip. He turned the bottle up, and while gulping glanced in the rearview mirror and saw the weeds move behind the car.

Ricky saw the door open before Mark heard it. It flew open, as if kicked, and suddenly the large, heavy man with the red face was running through the weeds, holding on to the car and growling. Ricky stood, in shock and fear, and wet his pants.

Mark had just touched the bumper when he heard the door. He froze for a second, gave a quick thought to crawling under the car, and the hesitation nailed him. His foot slipped as he tried to stand and run, and the man

10

grabbed him. 'You! You little bastard!' he screamed as he grabbed Mark's hair and flung him on to the trunk of the car. 'You little bastard!' Mark kicked and squirmed, and a fat hand slapped him in the face. He kicked once more, not as violently, and he got slapped again.

Mark stared at the wild, glowing face just inches away. The eyes were red and wet. Fluids dripped from the nose and chin. 'You little bastard,' he growled through clenched, dirty teeth.

When he had him pinned and still and subdued, the lawyer stuck the hose back into the exhaust pipe, then yanked Mark off the trunk by his collar and dragged him through the weeds to the driver's door, which was open. He threw the kid through the door and shoved him across the black leather seat.

Mark was grabbing at the door handle and searching for the door lock switch when the man fell behind the steering wheel. He slammed the door behind him, pointed at the door handle, and screamed, 'Don't touch that!' then he backhanded Mark in the left eye with a vicious slap.

Mark shrieked in pain, grabbed his eyes and bent over, stunned, crying now. His nose hurt like hell and his mouth hurt worse. He was dizzy. He tasted blood. He could hear the man crying and growling. He could smell the whiskey and see the knees of his dirty blue jeans with his right eye. The left was beginning to swell. Things were blurred.

The fat lawyer gulped his whiskey and stared at Mark, who was all bent over and shaking at every joint. 'Stop crying,' he snarled.

Mark licked his lips and swallowed blood. He rubbed the knot above his eye and tried to breathe deeply, still staring at his jeans. Again, the man said, 'Stop crying,' so he tried to stop.

The engine was running. It was a big, heavy, quiet car, but Mark could hear the engine humming very softly somewhere far away. He turned slowly and glanced at the hose winding through the rear window behind the driver like an angry snake sneaking toward them for the kill. The fat man laughed.

11

'I think we should die together,' he announced, all of a sudden very composed.

Mark's left eye was swelling fast. He turned his shoulders and looked squarely at the man, who was even larger now. His face was chubby, the beard was bushy, the eyes were still red and glowed at him like a demon in the dark. Mark was crying. 'Please let me out of here,' he said, lip quivering, voice cracking.

The driver stuck the whiskey bottle in his mouth and turned it up. He grimaced and smacked his lips. 'Sorry, kid. You had to be a cute ass, had to stick your dirty little nose into my business, didn't you? So I think we should die together. Okay? Just you and me, pal. Off to La La Land. Off to see the wizard. Sweet dreams, kid.'

Mark sniffed the air, then noticed the pistol lying between them. He glanced away, then stared at it when the man took another drink from the bottle.

'You want the gun?' the man asked.

'No sir.'

'So why are you looking at it?'

'I wasn't.'

'Don't lie to me, kid, because if you do, I'll kill you. I'm crazy as hell, okay, and I'll kill you.' Though tears flowed freely from his eyes, his voice was very calm. He breathed deeply as he spoke. 'And besides, kid, if we're gonna be pals, you've got to be honest with me. Honesty's very important, you know? Now, do you want the gun?'

'No sir.'

'Would you like to pick up the gun and shoot me with it?'

'No sir.'

'I'm not afraid of dying, kid, you understand?'

'Yes sir, but I don't want to die. I take care of my mother and my little brother.'

'Aw, ain't that sweet. A real man of the house.'

He screwed the cap on to the whiskey bottle, then suddenly grabbed the pistol, stuck it deep into his mouth, curled his lips around it, and looked at Mark, who watched every move, hoping he would pull the trigger and hoping he

12

wouldn't. Slowly, he withdrew the barrel from his mouth, kissed the end of it, then pointed it at Mark

'I've never shot this thing, you know,' he said, almost in a whisper. 'Just bought it an hour ago at a pawnshop in Memphis. Do you think it'll work?'

'Please let me out of here.'

'You have a choice, kid,' he said, inhaling the invisible fumes. 'I'll blow your brains out, and it's over now, or the gas'll get you. Your choice.'

Mark did not look at the pistol. He sniffed the air and thought for an instant that maybe he smelled something. The gun was close to his head. 'Why are you doing this?' he asked.

'None of your damned business, okay, kid. I'm nuts, okay. Over the edge. I planned a nice little private suicide, you know, just me and my hose and maybe a few pills and some whiskey. Nobody looking for me. But, no, you have to get cute. You little bastard!' He lowered the pistol and carefully placed it on the seat. Mark rubbed the knot on his forehead and bit his lip. His hands were shaking and he pressed them between his legs.

'We'll be dead in five minutes,' he announced officially as he raised the bottle to his lips. 'Just you and me, pal, off to see the wizard.'

Ricky finally moved. His teeth chattered and his jeans were wet, but he was thinking now, moving from his crouch on to his hands and knees and sinking into the grass. He crawled toward the car, crying and gritting his teeth as he slid on his stomach. The door was about to fly open. The crazy man, who was large but quick, would leap from nowhere and grab him by the neck, just like Mark, and they'd all die in the long, black car. Slowly, inch by inch, he pushed his way through the weeds.

Mark slowly lifted the pistol with both hands. It was as heavy as a brick. It shook as he raised it and pointed it at the

13

fat man, who leaned toward it until the barrel was an inch from his nose.

'Now, pull the trigger, kid,' he said with a smile, his wet face glowing and dancing with delightful anticipation. 'Pull the trigger, and I'll be dead and you go free.' Mark curled a finger around the trigger. The man nodded, then leaned even closer and bit the tip of the barrel with flashing teeth. 'Pull the trigger!' he shouted.

Mark closed his eyes and pressed the handle of the gun with the palms of his hands. He held his breath, and was about to squeeze the trigger when the man jerked it from him. He waved it wildly in front of Mark's face, and pulled the trigger. Mark screamed as the window behind his head cracked into a thousand pieces but did not shatter. 'It works! It works!' he yelled as Mark ducked and covered his ears.

Ricky buried his face in the grass when he heard the shot. He was ten feet from the car when something popped and Mark yelled. The fat man was yelling, and Ricky peed on himself again. He closed his eyes and clutched the weeds. His stomach cramped and his heart pounded, and for a minute after the gunshot he did not move. He cried for his brother, who was dead now, shot by a crazy man.

'Stop crying, dammit! I'm sick of your crying!'

Mark clutched his knees and tried to stop crying. His head pounded and his mouth was dry. He stuck his hands between his knees and bent over. He had to stop crying and think of something. On a television show once some nut was about to jump off a building, and this cool cop just kept talking to him and talking to him, and finally the nut started talking back and of course did not jump. Mark quickly smelled for gas, and asked, 'Why are you doing this?'

'Because I want to die,' the man said calmly.

'Why?' he asked again, glancing at the neat, little round hole in his window.

'Why do kids ask so many questions?'

'Because we're kids. Why do you want to die?' He could

14

barely hear his own words.

'Look, kid, we'll be dead in five minutes, okay? Just you and me, pal, off to see the wizard.' He took a long drink from the bottle, now almost empty. 'I feel the gas, kid. Do you feel it? Finally.'

In the side mirror, through the cracks in the window, Mark saw the weeds move and caught a glimpse of Ricky as he slithered through the weeds and ducked into the bushes near the tree. He closed his eyes and said a prayer.

'I gotta tell you, kid, it's nice having you here. No one wants to die alone. What's your name?'

'Mark.'

'Mark who?'

'Mark Sway.' Keep talking, and maybe the nut won't jump. 'What's your name?'

'Jerome. But you can call me Romey. That's what my friends call me, and since you and I are pretty tight now you can call me Romey. No more questions, okay, kid?'

'Why do you want to die, Romey?'

'I said no more questions. Do you feel the gas, Mark?'

'I don't know.'

'You will soon enough. Better say your prayers.' Romey sank low into the seat with his beefy head straight back and eyes closed, completely at ease. 'We've got about five minutes, Mark, any last words?' The whiskey bottle was in his right hand, the gun in his left.

'Yeah, why are you doing this?' Mark asked, glancing at the mirror for another sign of his brother. He took short, quick breaths through the nose, and neither smelled nor felt anything. Surely Ricky had removed the hose.

'Because I'm crazy, just another crazy lawyer, right. I've been driven crazy, Mark, and how old are you?'

'Eleven.'

'Ever tasted whiskey?'

'No,' Mark answered truthfully.

Suddenly, the whiskey bottle was in his face, and he took it.

'Take a shot,' Romey said without opening his eyes.

15

Mark tried to read the label, but his left eye was virtually closed and his ears were ringing from the gunshot, and he couldn't concentrate. He sat the bottle on the seat where Romey took it without a word.

'We're dying, Mark,' he said almost to himself. 'I guess that's tough at age eleven, but so be it. Nothing I can do about it. Any last words, big boy?'

Mark told himself that Ricky had done the trick, that the hose was now harmless, that his new friend Romey here was drunk and crazy, and that if he survived he would have to do so by thinking and talking. The air was clean. He breathed deeply and told himself that he could make it. 'What made you crazy?'

Romey thought for a second and decided this was humorous. He snorted and actually chuckled a little. 'Oh, this is great. Perfect. For weeks now, I've known something no one else in the entire world knows, except my client, who's a real piece of scum, by the way. You see, Mark, lawyers hear all sorts of private stuff that we can never repeat. Strictly confidential, you understand. No way we can ever tell what happened to the money or who's sleeping with who or where the body's buried, you follow?' He inhaled mightily, and exhaled with enormous pleasure. He sank lower in the seat, eyes still closed. 'Sorry I had to slap you.' He curled his finger around the trigger.

Mark closed his eyes and felt nothing.

'How old are you, Mark?'

'Eleven.'

'You told me that. Eleven. And I'm forty-four. We're both too young to die, aren't we, Mark?'

'Yes sir.'

'But it's happening, pal. Do you feel it?'

'Yes sir.'

'My client killed a man and hid the body, and now my client wants to kill me. That's the whole story. They've made me crazy. Ha! Ha! This is great, Mark. This is wonderful. I, the trusted lawyer, can now tell you, literally seconds before we float away, where the body is. The body,

Mark, the most notorious undiscovered corpse of our time. Unbelievable. I can finally tell!' His eyes were open and glowing down at Mark. 'This is funny as hell, Mark!'

Mark missed the humor. He glanced at the mirror, then at the door lock switch a foot away. The handle was even closer.

Romey relaxed again and closed his eyes as if trying desperately to take a nap. 'I'm sorry about this, kid, really sorry, but, like I said, it's nice to have you here.' He slowly placed the bottle on the dash next to the note and moved the pistol from his left hand to his right, caressing it softly and stroking the trigger with his index finger. Mark tried not to look. 'I'm really sorry about this, kid. How old are you?'

'Eleven. You've asked me three times.'

'Shut up! I feel the gas now, don't you? Quit sniffing, dammit! It's odorless, you little dumbass. You can't smell it. I'd be dead now and you'd be off playing GI Joe if you hadn't been so cute. You're pretty stupid, you know.'

Not as stupid as you, thought Mark. 'Who did your client kill?'

Romey grinned but did not open his eyes. 'A United States Senator. I'm telling. I'm telling. I'm spilling my guts. Do you read newspapers?'

'No.'

'I'm not surprised. Senator Boyette from New Orleans. That's where I'm from.'

'Why did you come to Memphis?'

'Dammit, kid! Full of questions, aren't you?'

'Yeah. Why'd your client kill Senator Boyette?'

'Why, why, why, who, who, who. You're a real pain in the ass, Mark.'

'I know. Why don't you just let me go?' Mark glanced at the mirror, then at the hose running into the backseat.

'I might just shoot you in the head if you don't shut up.' His bearded chin dropped and almost touched his chest. 'My client has killed a lot of people. That's how he makes money, by killing people. He's a member of the Mafia in New Orleans, and now he's trying to kill me. Too bad, ain't it, kid. We beat him to it. Joke's on him.'

17

Romey took a long drink from the bottle and stared at Mark

'Just think about it, kid, right now, Barry, or Barry The Blade as he's known, these Mafia guys all have cute nicknames, you know, is waiting for me in a dirty restaurant in New Orleans. He's probably got a couple of his pals nearby, and after a quiet dinner he'll want me to get in the car and take a little drive, talk about his case and all, and then he'll pull out a knife, that's why they call him The Blade, and I'm history. They'll dispose of my chubby little body somewhere, just like they did Senator Boyette, and, bam! Just like that, New Orleans has another unsolved murder. But we showed them, didn't we, kid? We showed them.'

His speech was slower and his tongue thicker. He moved the pistol up and down on his thigh when he talked. The finger stayed on the trigger.

Keep him talking. 'Why does this Barry guy want to kill you?'

'Another question. I'm floating. Are you floating?'

'Yeah. It feels good.'

'Buncha reasons. Close your eyes, kid. Say your prayers.' Mark watched the pistol and glanced at the door lock. He slowly touched each fingertip to each thumb, like counting in kindergarten, and the coordination was perfect.

'So where's the body?'

Romey snorted and his head nodded. The voice was almost a whisper. 'The body of Boyd Boyette. What a question. First US Senator murdered in office, did you know that? Murdered by my dear client Barry The Blade Muldanno, who shot him in the head four times, then hid the body. No body, no case. Do you understand, kid?'

'Not really.'

'Why aren't you crying, kid? You were crying a few minutes ago. Aren't you scared?'

'Yes, I'm scared. And I'd like to leave. I'm sorry you want to die and all, but I have to take care of my mother.'

'Touching, real touching. Now, shut up. You see, kid,

18

the Feds have to have a body to prove there was a murder. Barry is their suspect, their only suspect, because he really did it, you see, in fact they know he did it. But they need the body.'

'Where is it?'

A dark cloud moved in front of the sun and the clearing was suddenly darker. Romey moved the gun gently along his leg as if to warn Mark against any sudden moves. 'The Blade is not the smartest thug I've ever met, you know. Thinks he's a genius, but he's really quite stupid.'

You're the stupid one, Mark thought again. Sitting in a car with a hose running from the exhaust. He waited as still as could be.

'The body's under my boat.'

'Your boat?'

'Yes, my boat. He was in a hurry. I was out of town, so my beloved client took the body to my house and buried it in fresh concrete under my garage. It's still there, can you believe it? The FBI has dug up half of New Orleans trying to find it, but they've never thought about my house. Maybe Barry ain't so stupid after all.'

'When did he tell you this?'

'I'm sick of your questions, kid.'

'I'd really like to leave now.'

'Shut up. The gas is working. We're gone, kid. Gone.' He dropped the pistol on the seat.

The engine hummed quietly. Mark glanced at the bullet hole in the window, at the millions of tiny crooked cracks running from it, then at the red face and heavy eyelids. A quick snort, almost a snore, and the head nodded downward.

He was passing out! Mark stared at him and watched his thick chest move. He'd seen his ex-father do this a hundred times.

Mark breathed deeply. The door lock would make noise. The gun was too close to Romey's hand. Mark's stomach cramped and his feet were numb.

The red face emitted a loud, sluggish noise, and Mark

19

knew there would be no more chances. Slowly, ever so slowly, he inched his shaking finger to the door lock switch.

Ricky's eyes were almost as dry as his mouth, but his jeans were soaked. He was under the tree, in the darkness, away from the bushes and the tall grass and the car. Five minutes had passed since he had removed the hose. Five minutes since the gunshot. But he knew his brother was alive because he had darted behind trees for fifty feet until he caught a glimpse of the blond head sitting low and moving about in the huge car. So he stopped crying, and started praying.

He made his way back to the log, and as he crouched low and stared at the car and ached for his brother, the passenger door suddenly flew open, and there was Mark.

Romey's chin dropped on to his chest, and just as he began his next snore Mark slapped the pistol on to the floor with his left hand while unlocking the door with his right. He yanked the handle and rammed his shoulder into the door, and the last thing he heard as he rolled out was another deep snore from the lawyer.

He landed on his knees and grabbed at the weeds as he scratched and clawed his way from the car. He raced low through the grass and within seconds made it to the tree where Ricky watched in muted horror. He stopped at the stump and turned, expecting to see the lawyer lumbering after him with the gun. But the car appeared harmless. The passenger door was open. The engine was running. The exhaust pipe was free of devices. He breathed for the first time in a minute, then slowly looked at Ricky.

'I pulled the hose out,' Ricky said in a shrill voice between rapid breaths. Mark nodded but said nothing. He was suddenly much calmer. The car was fifty feet away, and if Romey emerged, they could disappear through the woods in an instant. And hidden by the tree and the cover of the brush, they would never be seen by Romey if he decided to jump out and start blasting away with the gun.

20

'I'm scared, Mark. Let's go,' Ricky said, his voice still shrill, his hands shaking.

'Just a minute.' Mark studied the car intently.

'Come on, Mark. Let's go.'

'I said just a minute.'

Ricky watched the car. 'Is he dead?'

'I don't think so.'

So the man was alive, and had the gun; and it was becoming obvious that his big brother was no longer scared and was thinking of something. Ricky took a step backward. 'I'm leaving,' he mumbled. 'I want to go home.'

Mark did not move. He exhaled calmly and studied the car. 'Just a second,' he said without looking at Ricky. The voice had authority again.

Ricky grew still and leaned forward, placing both hands on both wet knees. He watched his brother, and shook his head slowly as Mark carefully picked a cigarette from his shirt pocket while staring at the car. He lit it, took a long draw, and blew smoke upward to the branches. It was at this point that Ricky first noticed the swelling.

'What happened to your eye?'

Mark suddenly remembered. He rubbed it gently, then rubbed the knot on his forehead. 'He slapped me a couple of times.'

'It looks bad.'

'It's okay. You know what I'm gonna do?' he said without expecting an answer. 'I'm gonna sneak back up there and stick the hose into the exhaust pipe. I'm gonna plug it in for him, the bastard.'

'You're crazier than he is. You're kidding, right, Mark?'

Mark puffed deliberately. Suddenly, the driver's door swung open, and Romey stumbled out with the pistol. He mumbled loudly as he faltered to the rear of the car, and once again found the garden hose lying harmlessly in the grass. He screamed obscenities at the sky.

Mark crouched low and held Ricky with him. Romey spun around and surveyed the trees around the clearing. He cursed more, and started crying loudly. Sweat dripped

21

from his hair, and his black jacket was soaked and glued to him. He stomped around the rear of the car, sobbing and talking, screaming at the trees.

He stopped suddenly, wrestled his ponderous bulk on to the top of the trunk, then squirmed and slid backward like a drugged elephant until he hit the rear window. His stumpy legs stretched before him. One shoe was missing. He took the gun, neither slowly nor quickly, almost routinely, and stuck it deep in his mouth. His wild red eyes flashed around, and for a second paused at the trunk of the tree above the boys.

He opened his lips and bit the barrel with his big, dirty teeth. He closed his eyes, and pulled the trigger with his right thumb.

TWO

The shoes were shark, and the vanilla silks ran all the way to the kneecaps where they finally stopped and caressed the rather hairy calves of Barry Muldanno, or Barry The Blade, or simply The Blade, as he liked to be called. The dark green suit had a shine to it and appeared at first glance to be lizard or iguana or some other slimy reptile, but upon closer look it was not animal at all but polyester. Double-breasted with buttons all over the front. It hung handsomely on his well-built frame. And it rippled nicely as he strutted to the pay phone in the rear of the restaurant. The suit was not gaudy, just flashy. He could pass for a well-dressed drug importer or perhaps a hot Vegas bookie, and that was fine because he was The Blade and he expected people to notice, and when they looked at him they were supposed to see success. They were supposed to gawk in fear and get out of his way.

The hair was black and full, colored to hide a bit of gray, slicked down, laden with gel, pulled back fiercely and gathered into a perfect little ponytail that arched downward and touched precisely at the top of the dark green polyester jacket. Hours were spent on the hair. The obligatory diamond earring sparkled from the proper left lobe. A tasteful gold bracelet clung to the left wrist just below the diamond Rolex, and on his right wrist another tasteful gold chain rattled softly as he strutted.

The swagger stopped in front of the pay phone, which was near the rest rooms in a narrow hallway in the back of

23

the restaurant. He stood in front of the phone, and cut his eyes in all directions. To the average person, the sight of Barry The Blade's eyes cutting and darting and searching for violence would loosen the bowels. The eyes were very dark brown, and so close together that if one could stand to look directly into them for more than two seconds, one would swear Barry was cross-eyed. But he wasn't. A neat row of black hair ran from temple to temple without the slightest break for the furrow above the rather long and pointed nose. Solid brow. Puffy brown skin half-circled the eyes from below and said without a doubt that this man enjoyed booze and the fast life. The shady eyes confessed many hangovers, among other things. The Blade loved his eyes. They were legendary.

He punched the number of his lawyer's office, and said rapidly without waiting for a reply, 'Yeah, this is Barry! Where's Jerome? He's late. Supposed to meet me here forty minutes ago. Where is he? Have you seen him?'

The Blade's voice was not pleasant either. It had the menacing resonance of a successful New Orleans street thug who had broken many arms and would gladly break one more if you lingered too long in his path or weren't quick enough with your answers. The voice was rude, arrogant, and intimidating, and the poor secretary on the other end had heard it many times and she'd seen the eyes and the slick suits and the ponytail. She swallowed hard, caught her breath, thanked heavens he was on the phone and not in the office standing before her desk cracking his knuckles, and informed Mr Muldanno that Mr Clifford had left the office around 9 a.m. and had not been heard from since.

The Blade slammed the phone down and stormed through the hallway, then caught himself and began the strut as he neared the tables and the faces. The restaurant was beginning to fill. It was almost five.

He just wanted a few drinks and then a nice dinner with his lawyer so they could talk about his mess. Just drinks and dinner, that's all. The Feds were watching, and listening.

24

Jerome was paranoid and just last week told Barry he thought they had wired his law office. So they would meet here and have a nice meal without worrying about eavesdroppers and bugging devices.

They needed to talk. Jerome Clifford had been defending prominent New Orleans thugs for fifteen years – gangsters, pushers, politicians – and his record was impressive. He was cunning and corrupt, completely willing to buy people who could be bought. He drank with the judges and slept with their girlfriends. He bribed the cops and threatened the jurors. He schmoozed with the politicians and contributed when asked. Jerome knew what made the system tick, and when a sleazy defendant with money needed help in New Orleans he invariably found his way to the law offices of W. Jerome Clifford, Attorney and Counselor-at-Law. And in that office he found a friend who thrived on the dirt and was loyal to the end.

Barry's case, however, was something different. It was huge, and growing by the moment. The trial was a month away and loomed like an execution. It would be his second murder trial. His first had come at the tender age of eighteen when a local prosecutor attempted to prove, with only one most unreliable witness, that Barry had cut the fingers off a rival thug and slit his throat. Barry's uncle, a well-respected and seasoned mobster, dropped some money here and there, and young Barry's jury could not agree on a verdict and thus simply hung itself.

Barry later served two years in a pleasant federal joint on racketeering charges. His uncle could've saved him again, but he was twenty-five at the time and ready for a brief imprisonment. It looked good on his résumé. The family was proud of him. Jerome Clifford had handled the plea bargain, and they'd been friends ever since.

A fresh club soda with lime awaited Barry as he swaggered to the bar and assumed his position. The alcohol could wait a few hours. He needed steady hands.

He squeezed the lime and watched himself in the mirror. He caught a few stares; after all, at this moment he was perhaps the most famous murder defendant in the country. Four weeks from trial, and people were looking. His face was all over the papers.

This trial was much different. The victim was a Senator, the first ever to be murdered, they alleged, while in office. *United States of America versus Barry Muldanno.* Of course, there was no body, and this presented tremendous problems for the United States of America. No corpse, no pathology reports, no ballistics, no bloody photographs to wave around the courtroom and display for the jury.

But Jerome Clifford was cracking up. He was acting strange – disappearing like this, staying away from the office, not returning calls, always late for court, always mumbling under his breath and drinking too much. He'd always been mean and tenacious, but now he was detached and people were talking. Frankly, Barry wanted a new lawyer.

Just four short weeks, and Barry needed time. A delay, a continuance, something. Why does justice move so quickly when you don't want it to? His life had been lived on the fringes of the law, and he'd seen cases drag on for years. His uncle had once been indicted, but after three years of exhaustive warfare the government finally quit. Barry had been indicted six months ago, and bam! here's the trial. It wasn't fair. Romey wasn't working. He had to be replaced.

Of course, the Feds had a hole or two in their case. No one saw the killing. There would be a decent circumstantial case against him, with motive, perhaps. But no one actually saw him do it. There was an informant who was unstable and unreliable and expected to be chewed up on cross-examination, if he indeed made it to trial. The Feds were hiding him. And, Barry had his one marvellous advantage – the body, the diminutive, wiry corpse of Boyd Boyette rotting slowly away in concrete. Without it, Reverend Roy could not get a conviction. This made Barry smile, and he winked at two peroxide blondes at a table near the door. Women had been plentiful since the indictment. He was famous.

26

Reverend Roy's case was weak all right, but it hadn't slowed his nightly sermons in front of the cameras, or his pompous predictions of swift justice, or his blustering interviews with any journalist bored enough to quiz him. He was an oily-voiced, leather-lunged, pious US Attorney with obnoxious political aspirations and a thunderous opinion about everything. He had his very own press agent, a most overworked soul charged with the tas of keeping the Reverend in the spotlight so that one day very soon the public would insist he serve them in the United States Senate. From there, only the Reverend knew where God might lead him.

The Blade crunched his ice at the repulsive thought of Roy Foltrigg waving his indictment before the cameras and bellowing all sorts of forecasts of good triumphing over evil. But six months had passed since the indictment, and neither Reverend Roy nor his confederates, the FBI, had found the body of Boyd Boyette. They followed Barry night and day – in fact, they were probably waiting outside right now, as if he were stupid enough to have dinner, then go look at the body just for the hell of it. They had bribed every wino and street bum who claimed to be an informant. They had drained ponds and lakes; they had dragged rivers. They had obtained search warrants for dozens of buildings and sites in the city. They had spent a small fortune on backhoes and bulldozers.

But Barry had it. The body of Boyd Boyette. He would like to move it, but he couldn't. The Reverend and his host of angels were watching.

Clifford was an hour late now. Barry paid for two rounds of club soda, winked at the peroxides in their leather skirts, and left the place cursing lawyers in general and his in particular.

He needed a new lawyer, one who would return his phone calls and meet him for drinks and find some jurors who could be bought. A real lawyer!

He needed a new lawyer, and he needed a continuance or a postponement or a delay, hell, anything to slow this thing down so he could think.

27

He lit a cigarette and walked casually along Magazine between Canal and Poydras. The air was thick. Clifford's office was four blocks away. His lawyer wanted a quick trial! What an idiot! No one wanted a quick trial in this system, but here was W. Jerome Clifford pushing for one. Clifford had explained not three weeks ago that they should push hard for a trial because there was no corpse, thus no case, et cetera, et cetera. And if they waited, the body might be found, and since Barry was such a lovely suspect and it was a sensational killing with a ton of pressure behind its prosecution, and since Barry had actually performed the killing, was in fact guilty as hell, then they should go to trial immediately. This had shocked Barry. They had argued viciously in Romey's office, and things had not been the same since.

At one point in the discussion, three weeks ago, things got quiet and Barry boasted to his lawyer that the body would never be found. He'd disposed of lots of them, and he knew how to hide them. Boyette had been hidden rather quickly, and though Barry wanted to move the little fella, he was nonetheless secure and resting peacefully without the threat of disturbance from Roy and the Fibbies.

Barry chuckled to himself as he strolled along Poydras.

'So where's the body?' Clifford had asked.

'You don't want to know,' Barry had replied.

'Sure I want to know. The whole world wants to know. Come on, tell me if you've got the guts.'

'You don't want to know.'

'Come on. Tell me.'

'You're not gonna like it.'

'Tell me.'

Barry flicked his cigarette on the sidewalk, and almost laughed out loud. He shouldn't have told Jerome Clifford. It was a childish thing to do, but harmless. The man could be trusted with secrets, attorney-client privilege and all, and he had been wounded when Barry hadn't come clean initially with all the gory details. Jerome Clifford was as crooked and sleazy as his clients, and if they got blood on them he wanted to see it.

'You remember what day Boyette disappeared?' Barry had asked.

'Sure. January 16.'

'Remember where you were January 16?'

At this point, Romey had walked to the wall behind his desk and studied his badly scrawled monthly planners. 'Colorado, skiing.'

'And I borrowed your house?'

'Yeah, you were meeting some doctor's wife.'

'That's right. Except she couldn't make it, so I took the Senator to your house.'

Romey froze at this point, and glared at his client, mouth open, eyes lowered.

Barry had continued. 'He arrived in the trunk, and I left him at your place.'

'Where?' Romey had asked in disbelief.

'In the garage.'

'You're lying.'

'Under the boat that hasn't been moved in ten years.'

'You're lying.'

The front door of Clifford's office was locked. Barry rattled it and cursed through the window. He lit another cigarette and searched the usual parking places for the black Lincoln. He'd find the fat bastard if it took all night.

Barry had a friend in Miami who was once indicted for an assortment of drug charges. His lawyer was quite good, and had managed to stall and delay for two and a half years until finally the judge lost patience and ordered a trial. The day before jury selection, his friend killed his very fine lawyer, and the judge was forced to grant another continuance. The trial never happened.

If Romey died suddenly, it would be months, maybe years, before the trial.

THREE

Ricky backed away from the tree until he was in the weeds, then found the narrow trail and started to run. 'Ricky,' Mark called. 'Hey, Ricky, wait,' but it didn't work. He stared once more at the man on the car with the gun still in his mouth. The eyes were half-open and the feet twitched at the heels.

Mark had seen enough. 'Ricky,' he called again as he jogged toward the trail. His brother was ahead, running slowly in an odd way with both arms stiff and straight down by his legs. He leaned forward at the waist. Weeds hit him in the face. He tripped but didn't fall. Mark grabbed him by the shoulders and spun him around. 'Ricky, listen! It's okay.' Ricky was zombielike, with pale skin and glazed eyes. He breathed hard and rapidly, and emitted a dull, aching moan. He couldn't talk. He jerked away and resumed his trot, still moaning as the weeds slapped him in the face. Mark followed close behind as they crossed a dry creek bed and headed for home.

The trees thinned just before the crumbling board fence that encircled most of the trailer park. Two small children were throwing rocks at a row of cans lined neatly along the hood of a wrecked car. Ricky ran faster and crawled through a broken section of the fence. He jumped a ditch, darted between two trailers, and ran into the street. Mark was two steps behind. The steady groan grew louder as Ricky breathed even harder.

The Sway mobile home was twelve feet wide and sixty

feet long, and parked on a narrow strip on East Street with forty others. Tucker Wheel Estate also included North, South, and West streets, and all four curved and crossed each other several times from all directions. It was a decent trailer park with reasonably clean streets, a few trees, plenty of bicycles, and few abandoned cars. Speed bumps slowed traffic. Loud music or noise brought the police as soon as it was reported to Mr Tucker. His family owned all the land and most of the trailers, including Number 17 on East Street, which Dianne Sway rented for two hundred and eighty dollars a month

Ricky ran through the unlocked door and fell on to the couch in the den. He seemed to be crying, but there were no tears. He curled his knees to his stomach as if he were cold, then, very slowly, placed his right thumb in his mouth. Mark watched this intently. 'Ricky, talk to me,' he said, gently shaking his shoulder. 'You gotta talk to me, man, okay, Ricky. It's okay.'

He sucked harder on the thumb. He closed his eyes and his body shook.

Mark looked around the den and kitchen, and realized things were exactly as they had left them an hour ago. An hour ago! It seemed like days. The sunlight was fading and the rooms were a bit darker. Their books and backpacks from school were piled, as always, on the kitchen table. The daily note from Mòm was on the counter next to the phone. He walked to the sink and ran water in a clean coffee cup. He had a terrible thirst. He sipped the cool water and stared through the window at the trailer next door. Then he heard smacking noises, and looked at his brother. The thumb. He'd seen a show on television where some kids in California sucked their thumbs after an earthquake. All kinds of doctors were involved. A year after it hit the poor kids were still sucking away.

The cup touched a tender spot on his lip, and he remembered the blood. He ran to the bathroom and studied his face in the mirror. Just below the hairline there was a small, barely noticeable knot. His left eye was puffy and looked awful. He ran water in the sink and washed a spot of blood from his lower lip. It was not swollen, but suddenly began throbbing. He'd looked worse after fights at school. He was tough.

He took an ice cube from the refrigerator and held it firmly under his eye. He walked to the sofa and studied his brother, paying particular attention to the thumb. Ricky was asleep. It was almost five-thirty, time for their mother to arrive home after nine long hours at the lamp factory. His ears still rang from the gunshots and the blows he took from his late friend Mr Romey, but he was beginning to think. He sat next to Ricky's feet and slowly rubbed around his eye with the ice.

If he didn't call 911, it could be days before anyone found the body. The fatal shot had been severely muffled, and Mark was certain no one heard it but them. He'd been to the clearing many times, but suddenly realized he had never seen another person there. It was secluded. Why had Romey chosen the place? He was from New Orleans, right?

Mark watched all kinds of rescue shows on television, and knew for certain that every 911 call was recorded. He did not want to be recorded. He would never tell anyone, not even his mother, what he had just lived through, and he really needed, at this crucial moment, to discuss the matter with his little brother so they could get their lies straight. 'Ricky,' he said, shaking his brother's leg. Ricky groaned but did not open his eyes. He pulled himself tighter into a knot. 'Ricky, wake up!'

There was no response to this, except a sudden shudder as if he were freezing. Mark found a quilt in a closet and covered his brother, then wrapped a handful of ice cubes in a dish towel and placed the pack gingerly over his own left eye. He didn't feel like answering questions about his face.

He stared at the phone and thought of cowboy and Indian movies with bodies lying around and buzzards circling above and everyone concerned about burying the dead before the damned vultures got them. It would be dark in an hour or so. Do buzzards strike at night? Never saw that in a movie.

The thought of the fat lawyer lying out there with the gun in his mouth, one shoe off, probably still bleeding, was horrible enough, but throw in the buzzards ripping and tearing, and Mark picked up the phone. He punched 911 and cleared his throat.

'Yeah, there's a dead man, in the woods, and, well, someone needs to come and get him.' He spoke in the deepest voice possible, and knew from the first syllable that it was a pitiful attempt at disguise. He breathed hard and the knot on his forehead pounded.

'Who's calling please?' It was a female voice, almost like a robot's.

'Uh, I really don't want to say, okay.'

'We need your name, son.' Great, she knew he was a kid. He hoped he could at least sound like a young teenager.

'Do you want to know about the body or not?' Mark asked.

'Where is the body?'

This is just great, he thought, already telling someone about it. And not someone to be trusted, but someone who wore a uniform and worked with the police, and he could just hear this taped conversation as it would be repeatedly played before the jury, just like on television. They would do all those voice tests and everyone would know it was Mark Sway on the phone telling about the body when no one else in the world knew about it. He tried to make his voice even deeper.

'It's near Tucker Wheel Estates, and – '

'That's on Whipple Road.'

'Yes, that's right. It's in the woods between Tucker Wheel Estates and Highway 17.'

'The body is in the woods?'

'Sort of. The body is actually lying on a car in the woods.'

'And the body's dead?'

'The guy's been shot, okay. With a gun, in the mouth, and I'm sure the man's dead.'

33

'Have you seen the body?' The woman's voice was losing its professional restraint. It had an edge to it now.

What kind of stupid question is that, Mark thought. Have I seen it? She was stalling, trying to keep him on the line so she could trace it.

'Son, have you seen the body?' she asked again.

'Of course I've seen it.'

'I need your name, son.'

'Look, there's a small dirt road off Highway 17 that leads to a small clearing in the woods. The car is big and black, and the dead man is lying on it. If you can't find it, well, tough luck. Bye.'

He hung up and stared at the phone. The trailer was perfectly still. He walked to the door and peered through the dirty curtains, half-expecting squad cars to come flying in from all directions – loudspeakers, SWAT teams, bullet-proof vests.

Get a grip. He shook Ricky again, and, touching his arm, noticed how clammy it was. But Ricky was still sleeping and sucking his thumb. Mark gently grabbed him around the waist and dragged him across the floor, down the narrow hallway to their bedroom where he shoveled him into bed. Ricky mumbled and wiggled a bit along the way, but quickly curled into a ball. Mark covered him with a blanket and closed the door.

Mark wrote a note to his mother, told her Ricky felt bad and was sleeping so please be quiet, and he'd be home in an hour or so. The boys were not required to be home when she arrived, but if they weren't, there'd better be a note.

The distant beat of a helicopter went unnoticed by Mark.

He lit a cigarette along the trail. Two years ago, a new bike had disappeared from a house in the suburbs, not far from the trailer park. It was rumored to have been seen behind one of the mobile homes, and the same rumor held that it was being stripped and repainted by a couple of trailer park kids. The suburb kids enjoyed classifying their lesser neighbors as trailer park kids, the implications being obvious. They attended the same school, and there were daily fights between the two societies. All crime and mischief in the suburbs were automatically blamed on the trailer people.

Kevin, the delinquent on North Street, had the new bike and had shown it to a few of his buddies before it was repainted. Mark had seen it. The rumors flew and the cops poked around, and one night there was a knock at the door. Mark's name had been mentioned in the investigation, and the policeman had a few questions. He sat at the kitchen table and glared down at Mark for an hour. It was very unlike television where the defendant keeps his cool and sneers at the cop.

Mark admitted nothing, didn't sleep for three nights, and vowed to live a clean life and stay away from trouble.

But this was trouble. Real trouble, much worse than a stolen bike. A dead man who told secrets before he died. Was he telling the truth? He was drunk and crazy as hell, talking about the wizard and all. But why would he lie?

Mark knew Romey had a gun, had even held and touched the trigger. And the gun killed the man. It had to be a crime to watch someone commit suicide and not stop it.

He would never tell a soul! Romey had stopped talking. Ricky would have to be dealt with. Mark had kept silent about the bike, and he could do it again. No one would ever know he had been in the car.

There was a siren in the distance, then the steady thump of a helicopter. Mark eased under a tree as the chopper swept close by. He crept through the trees and brush, staying low and in no hurry, until he heard voices.

Lights flashed everywhere. Blue for the cops and red for the ambulance. The white Memphis Police cars were parked around the black Lincoln. The orange-and-white ambulance was arriving on the scene as Mark peeked through the woods. No one seemed anxious or worried.

Romey had not been moved. One cop took pictures while the others laughed. Radios squawked, just like on

35

television. Blood ran from under the body and down across the red-and-white tailights. The pistol was still in his right hand, on top of his bulging stomach. His head slumped to the right, his eyes closed now. The paramedics walked up and looked him over, then made bad jokes and the cops laughed. All four doors were open and the car was being carefully inspected. There was no effort to remove the body. The helicopter made a final pass then flew away.

Mark was deep in the brush, maybe thirty feet from the tree and the log where they had lit the first smokes. He had a perfect view of the clearing, and of the fat lawyer lying up there on the car like a dead cow in the middle of the road. Another cop car arrived, then another ambulance. People in uniform were bumping into each other. Small white bags with unseen things in them were removed with great caution from the car. Two policemen with rubber gloves rolled up the hose. The photographer squatted in each door and flashed away. Occasionally, someone would stop and stare at Romey, but most of them drank coffee from Styrofoam cups and chatted away. A cop laid Romey's shoe on the trunk next to the body, then placed it in a white bag and wrote something on it. Another cop knelt by the license plates and waited with his radio for a report to come back.

Finally, a stretcher emerged from the first ambulance and was carried to the rear bumper and laid in the weeds. Two paramedics grabbed Romey's feet and gently pulled him until two other paramedics could grab his arms. The cops watched and joked about how fat Mr Clifford was because they knew his name now. They asked if more paramedics were needed to carry his big ass, if the stretcher was reinforced or something, if he would fit in the ambulance. Lots of laughter as they strained to lower him.

A cop put the pistol in a bag. The stretcher was heaved into the ambulance, but the doors were not closed. A wrecker with yellow lights arrived and backed itself to the front bumper of the Lincoln.

Mark thought of Ricky and the thumb-sucking. What if he needed help? Mom would be home soon. What if she

36

tried to wake him and got scared? He would leave in just a minute, and smoke the last cigarette on the way home.

He heard something behind him, but thought nothing of it. Just the snap of a twig, then, suddenly, a strong hand grabbed his neck and a voice said, 'What's up, kid?'

Mark jerked around and looked into the face of a cop. He froze and couldn't breathe.

'What're you doing, kid?' the cop asked as he lifted Mark up by the neck. The grip didn't hurt, but the cop meant to be obeyed. 'Stand up, kid, okay. Don't be afraid.'

Mark stood and the cop released him. The cops in the clearing had heard and were staring.

'What're you doing here?'

'Just watching,' Mark said.

The cop pointed with his flashlight to the clearing. The sun was down and it would be dark in twenty minutes. 'Let's walk over there,' he said.

'I need to go home,' Mark said.

The cop placed his arm around Mark's shoulders and led him through the weeds. 'What's your name?'

'Mark.'

'Last name?'

'Sway. What's yours?'

'Hardy. Mark Sway, huh?' the cop repeated thoughtfully. 'You live in Tucker Wheel Estates, don't you?'

He couldn't deny this, but he hesitated for some reason. 'Yes sir.'

They joined the circle of policemen who were now quiet and waiting to see the kid.

'Hey, fellas, this is Mark Sway, the kid who made the call,' Hardy announced. 'You did make the call, didn't you, Mark?'

He wanted to lie, but at the moment he doubted a lie would work. 'Uh, yes sir.'

'How'd you find the body?'

'My brother and I were playing.'

'Playing where?'

37

'Around here. We live over there,' he said, pointing beyond the trees.

'Were you guys smoking dope?'

'No sir.'

'Are you sure?'

'Yes sir.'

'Stay away from drugs, kid.' There were at least six policemen in the circle, and the questions were coming from all directions.

'How'd you find the car?'

'Well, we just sort of walked up on it.'

'What time was it?'

'I don't remember, really. We were just walking through the woods. We do it all the time.'

'What's your brother's name?'

'Ricky.'

'Same last name?'

'Yes sir.'

'Where were you and Ricky when you first saw the car?'

Mark pointed to the tree behind him. 'Under that tree.'

A paramedic approached the group and announced they were leaving and taking the body to the morgue. The wrecker was tugging at the Lincoln.

'Where is Ricky now?'

'At home.'

'What happened to your face?' Hardy asked.

Mark instinctively reached for his eye. 'Oh, nothing. Just got in a fight at school.'

'Why were you hiding in the bushes over there?'

'I don't know.'

'Come on, Mark, you were hiding for a reason.'

'I don't know. It's sort of scary, you know. Seeing a dead man and all.'

'You've never seen a dead man before?'

'On television.'

One cop actually smiled at this.

'Did you see this man before he killed himself?'

'No sir.'

38

'So you just found him like this?'

'Yes sir. We walked up under that tree and saw the car, then, we, uh, we saw the man.'

'Where were you when you heard the gunshot?'

He started to point to the tree again, but caught himself. 'I'm not sure I understand.'

'We know you heard the gunshot. Where were you when you heard it?'

'I didn't hear the gunshot.'

'You sure?'

'I'm sure. We walked up and found him right here, and we took off home and I called 911.'

'Why didn't you give your name to 911?'

'I don't know.'

'Come on, Mark, there must be a reason.'

'I don't know. Scared, I guess.'

The cops exchanged looks as if this were a game. Mark tried to breathe normally and act pitiful. He was just a kid.

'I really need to go home. My mom's probably looking for me.'

'Okay. One last question,' Hardy said. 'Was the engine running when you first saw the car?'

Mark thought hard, but couldn't remember if Romey had turned it off before he shot himself. He answered very slowly. 'I'm not sure, but I think it was running.'

Hardy pointed to a police car. 'Get in. I'll drive you home.'

'That's okay. I'll just walk.'

'No, it's too dark. I'll give you a ride. Come on.' He took his arm, and walked him to the car.

FOUR

Dianne Sway had called the children's clinic and was sitting on the edge of Ricky's bed, biting her nails and waiting for a doctor to call. The nurse said it would be less than ten minutes. The nurse also said there was a very contagious virus in the schools and they had treated dozens of children that week. He had the symptoms, so don't worry. Dianne checked his forehead for a fever. She shook him gently again, but there was no response. He was still curled tightly, breathing normally and sucking his thumb. She heard a car door slam and went back to the living room.

Mark burst through the door. 'Hi, Mom.'

'Where have you been?' she snapped. 'What's wrong with Ricky?'

Sergeant Hardy appeared in the door, and she froze.

'Good evening, ma'am,' he said.

She glared at Mark. 'What have you done?'

'Nothing.'

Hardy stepped inside. 'Nothing serious, ma'am.'

'Then why are you here?'

'I can explain, Mom. It's sort of a long story.'

Hardy closed the door behind him, and they stood in the small room looking awkwardly at one another.

'I'm listening.'

'Well, me and Ricky were back in the woods playing this afternoon, and we saw this big black car parked in a clearing with the motor running, and when we got closer there was this man lying across the trunk with a gun in his mouth. He was dead.'

'Dead!'

'Suicide, ma'am,' Hardy offered.

'And we ran home as fast as we could and I called 911.' Dianne covered her mouth with her fingers.

'The man's name is Jerome Clifford, male white,' Hardy reported officially. 'He's from New Orleans, and we have no idea why he came here. Been dead for about two hours now, we think, not very long. He left a suicide note.'

'What did Ricky do?' Dianne asked.

'Well, we ran home, and he fell on the couch and started sucking his thumb and wouldn't talk. I took him to his bed and covered him.'

'How old is he?' Hardy asked with a frown.

'Eight.'

'May I see him?'

'Why?' Dianne asked.

'I'm concerned. He witnessed something awful, and he might be in shock.'

'Shock?'

'Yes ma'am.'

Dianne walked quickly through the kitchen and down the hall with Hardy behind her and Mark following, shaking his head and clenching his teeth.

Hardy pulled the covers off Ricky's shoulders and touched his arm. The thumb was in the mouth. He shook him, called his name, and the eyes opened for a second. Ricky mumbled something.

'His skin is cold and damp. Has he been ill?' Hardy asked.

'No.'

The phone rang, and Dianne raced for it. From the bedroom, Hardy and Mark listened as she told the doctor about the symptoms and the dead body the boys had found.

'Did he say anything when you guys saw the body?' Hardy asked quietly.

'I don't think so. It happened pretty fast. We, uh, we just

41

took off running once we saw it. He just moaned and grunted all the way, ran sort of funny with his arms straight down. I never saw him run like that, and then as soon as we got home he curled up and hasn't spoken since.'

'We need to get him to a hospital,' Hardy said.

Mark's knees went weak and he leaned on the wall. Dianne hung up and Hardy met her in the kitchen. 'The doctor wants him at the hospital,' she said in panic.

'I'll call an ambulance,' Hardy said, heading for his car. 'Pack a few clothes.' He disappeared and left the door open.

Dianne glared at Mark, who was weak and needed to sit. He fell into a chair at the kitchen table.

'Are you telling the truth?' she asked.

'Yes ma'am. We saw the dead body, and Ricky freaked out I guess, and we just ran home.' It would take hours to tell the truth at this point. Once they were alone, he might reconsider and tell the rest of the story, but the cop was here now and it would get too complicated. He was not afraid of his mother, and generally came clean when she pressed. She was only thirty, younger than any of his friends' moms, and they had been through a lot together. Their brutal ordeals fighting off his father had forged a bond much deeper than any ordinary mother-son relationship. It hurt to hide this from her. She was scared and desperate, but the things Romey told him had nothing to do with Ricky's condition. A sharp pain hit him in the stomach and the room spun slowly.

'What happened to your eye?'

'I got in a fight in school. It wasn't my fault.'

'It never is. Are you okay?'

'I think so.'

Hardy lumbered through the door. 'The ambulance'll be here in five minutes. Which hospital?'

'The doctor said to go to St Peter's.'

'Who's your doctor?'

'Shelby Pediatric Group. They said they would call in a children's psychiatrist to meet us at the hospital.' She nervously lit a cigarette. 'Do you think he's okay?'

'He needs to be looked at, maybe hospitalized, ma'am. I've seen this before with kids who witness shootings and stabbings. It's very traumatic, and it could take time for him to get over it. Had a kid last year who watched his mother get shot by a crack dealer, in one of the projects, and the poor little fella is still in the hospital.'

'How old was he?'

'Eight, now he's nine. Won't talk. Won't eat. Sucks his thumb and plays with dolls. Really sad.'

Dianne had heard enough. 'I'll pack some clothes.'

'You'd better pack clothes for yourself too, ma'am. You might have to stay with him. '

'What about Mark?' she asked.

'What time does your husband get home?'

'I don't have one.'

'Then pack clothes for Mark too. They might want to keep you overnight.'

Dianne stood in the kitchen with her cigarette inches from her lips, and tried to think. She was scared and uncertain. 'I don't have health insurance,' she mumbled to the window.

'St Peter's will take indigent cases. You need to get packed.'

A crowd gathered around the ambulance as soon as it stopped at Number 17 East Street. They waited and watched, whispering and pointing as the paramedics went inside.

Hardy laid Ricky on the stretcher, and they strapped him down under a blanket. Ricky tried to curl, but the heavy Velcro bands kept him straight. He moaned twice, but never opened his eyes. Dianne gently freed his right arm and made the thumb available. Her eyes were watery, but she refused to cry.

The crowd backed away from the rear of the ambulance as the paramedics approached with the stretcher. They loaded Ricky, and Dianne stepped in behind. A few neighbors called out their concerns, but the driver slammed the door before she could answer. Mark sat in the front seat of the police car with Hardy, who hit a switch and suddenly blue lights were fluttering and bouncing off the nearby trailers. The crowd inched away, and Hardy gunned the engine. The ambulance followed.

Mark was too worried and scared to be interested in the radios and mikes and guns and gadgets. He sat still and kept his mouth shut.

'Are you telling the truth, son?' Hardy, suddenly the cop again, asked from nowhere.

'Yes sir. About what?'

'About what you saw?'

'Yes sir. You don't believe me?'

'I didn't say that. It's just a little strange, that's all.'

Mark waited a few seconds, and when it was obvious Hardy was waiting for him, he asked, 'What's strange?'

'Several things. First, you made the call, but wouldn't give your name. Why not? If you and Ricky just stumbled upon the dead man, why not give your name? Second, why did you sneak back to the scene and hide in the woods? People who hide are afraid. Why didn't you simply return to the scene and tell us what you saw? Third, if you and Ricky saw the same thing, why has he freaked out and you're in pretty good shape, know what I mean?'

Mark thought for a while, and realized he could think of nothing to say. So he said nothing. They were on the interstate headed for downtown. It was neat to watch the other cars get out of the way. The red ambulance lights were close behind.

'You didn't answer my question,' Hardy finally said.

'Which question?'

'Why didn't you give your name when you made the call?'

'I was scared, okay. That's the first dead body I ever saw, and it scared me. I'm still scared.'

'Then why did you sneak back to the scene? Why were you trying to hide from us?'

'I was scared, you know, but I just wanted to see what was going on. That's not a crime, is it?'

44

'Maybe not.'

They left the expressway, and were now darting through traffic. The tall buildings of downtown Memphis were in sight.

'I just hope you're telling the truth,' Hardy said.

'Don't you believe me?'

'I've got my doubts.'

Mark swallowed hard and looked in the side mirror. 'Why do you have doubts?'

'I'll tell you what I think, kid. You want to hear it?'

'Sure,' Mark said slowly.

'Well, I think you kids were in the woods smoking. I found some fresh cigarette butts under that tree with the rope. I figure you were under there having a little smoke and you saw the whole thing.'

Mark's heart stopped and his blood ran cold, but he knew the importance of trying to appear calm. Just shrug it off. Hardy wasn't there. He didn't see anything. He caught his hands shaking, so he sat on them. Hardy watched him.

'Do you arrest kids for smoking cigarettes?' Mark asked, his voice a shade weaker.

'No. But kids who lie to cops get in all sorts of trouble.'

'I'm not lying, okay. I've smoked cigarettes there before, but not today. We were just walking through the woods, thinking about maybe having a smoke, and we walked up on the car and Romey.'

Hardy hesitated slightly, then asked, 'Who's Romey?'

Mark braced himself and breathed deeply. In a flash, he knew it was over. He'd blown it. Said too much. Lied too much. He'd lasted less than an hour with his story. Keep thinking, he told himself.

'That's the guy's name, isn't it?'

'Romey?'

'Yeah. Isn't that what you called him?'

'No. I told your mother his name was Jerome Clifford, from New Orleans.'

'I thought you said it was Romey Clifford, from New Orleans.'

45

'Who ever heard of the name Romey?'

'Beats me.'

The car turned right, and Mark looked straight ahead. 'Is this St Peter's?'

'That's what the sign says.'

Hardy parked to the side, and they watched the ambulance back up to the emergency dock.

FIVE

The honorable J. Roy Foltrigg, United States Attorney for the Southern District of Louisiana at New Orleans, and a Republican, sipped properly from a can of tomato juice and stretched his legs in the rear of his customized Chevrolet van as it raced smoothly along the expressway. Memphis was five hours to the north, straight up Interstate 55, and he could've caught a plane, but there were two reasons why he hadn't. First, the paperwork. He could claim it was official business related to the Boyd Boyette case, and he could stretch things here and there and make it work. But it would take months to get reimbursed and there would be eighteen different forms. Second, and much more important, he didn't like to fly. He could've waited three hours in New Orleans for a flight that would last for an hour and place him in Memphis around 11 p.m., but they would make it by midnight in the van. He didn't confess this fear of flying, and he knew he would one day be forced to see a shrink to overcome it. For the meantime, he had purchased this fancy van with his own money and loaded it down with appliances and gadgets, two phones, a television, even a fax machine. He buzzed around the Southern District of Louisiana in it, always with Wally Boxx behind the wheel. It was much nicer and more comfortable than any limousine.

He slowly kicked off his loafers and watched the night fly by as Special Agent Trumann listened to the telephone stuck in his ear. On the other end of the heavily padded back bench sat Assistant US Attorney Thomas Fink, a loyal Foltrigg subordinate who'd worked on the Boyette case eighty hours a week and would handle most of the trial, especially the nonglamorous grunt work, saving of course the easy and high-profile parts for his boss. Fink was reading a document, as always, and trying to listen to the mumblings of Agent Trumann, who was seated across from him in a heavy swivel seat. Trumann had Memphis FBI on the phone.

Next to Trumann, in an identical swivel recliner, was Special Agent Skipper Scherff, a rookie who'd worked little on the case but happened to be available for this joyride to Memphis. He scribbled on a legal pad, and would do so for the next five hours because in this tight circle of power he had absolutely nothing to say and no one wanted to hear him. He would obediently stare at his legal pad and record orders from his supervisor, Larry Trumann, and, of course, from the general himself, Reverend Roy. Scherff stared intently at his scribbling, avoiding with great diligence even the slightest eye contact with Foltrigg, and tried in vain to discern what Memphis was telling Trumann. The news of Clifford's death had electrified their office only an hour earlier, and Scherff was still uncertain why and how he was sitting in Roy's van speeding along the expressway. Trumann had told him to run home, pack a change of clothes, and go immediately to Foltrigg's office. And this is what he'd done. And here he was, scribbling and listening.

The chauffeur, Wally Boxx, actually had a license to practice law, though he didn't know how to use it. Officially, he was an Assistant United States Attorney, same as Fink, but in reality he was a fetch-and-catch boy for Foltrigg. He drove his van, carried his briefcase, wrote his speeches, and handled the media, which took fifty percent of his time because his boss was gravely concerned with his public image. Boxx was not stupid. He was deft at political maneuvering, quick to the defense of his boss, and thoroughly loyal to the man and his mission. Foltrigg had a great future, and Boxx knew he would be there one day whispering importantly with the great man as only the two of them strolled around Capitol Hill.

Boxx knew the importance of Boyette. It would be the biggest trial of Foltrigg's illustrious career, the trial he'd been dreaming of, the trial to thrust him into the national spotlight. He knew Foltrigg was losing sleep over Barry The Blade Muldanno.

Larry Trumann finished the conversation and replaced the phone. He was a veteran agent, early forties, with ten years to go before retirement. Foltrigg waited for him to speak.

'They're trying to convince Memphis PD to release the car so we can go over it. It'll probably take an hour or so. They're having a hard time explaining Clifford and Boyette and all this to Memphis, but they're making progress. Head of our Memphis office is a guy named Jason McThune, very tough and persuasive, and he's meeting with the Memphis chief right now. McThune's called Washington and Washington's called Memphis, and we should have the car within a couple of hours. Single gunshot wound to the head, obviously self-inflicted. Apparently he tried to do it first with a garden hose in the tail pipe, but for some reason it didn't work. He was taking Dalmane and codeine, and washing it all down with Jack Daniels. No record on the gun, but it's too early. Memphis is checking it. A cheap .38. Thought he could swallow a bullet.'

'No doubt it's suicide?' Foltrigg asked.

'No doubt.'

'Where did he do it?'

'Somewhere in north Memphis. Drove into the woods in his big black Lincoln, and took care of himself.'

'I don't suppose anyone saw it?'

'Evidently not. A couple of kids found the body in a remote area.'

'How long had he been dead?'

'Not long. They'll do an autopsy in a few hours, and determine the time of death.'

'Why Memphis?'

'Not sure. If there's a reason, we don't know it yet.'

Foltrigg pondered these things and sipped his tomato juice. Fink took notes. Scherff scribbled furiously. Wally Boxx hung on every word.

'What about the note?' Foltrigg asked, looking out the window.

'Well, it could be interesting. Our guys in Memphis have a copy of it, not a very good copy, and they'll try and fax it to us in a few minutes. Apparently the note was handwritten in black ink, and the writing is fairly legible. It's a few paragraphs of instructions to his secretary about the funeral – he wants to be cremated – and what to do with his office furniture. The note tells the secretary where to find his will. Nothing about Boyette, of course. Nothing about Muldanno. Then, he apparently tried to add something to the note with a blue Bic pen, but it ran out of ink after he started his message. It's badly scrawled, and hard to read.'

'What is it?'

'We don't know. The Memphis Police still have possession of the note, the gun, the pills, all the physical evidence removed from the car. McThune is trying to get it now. They found a Bic pen, no ink, in the car, and it appears to be the same pen he tried to use to add something to the note.'

'They'll have it when we arrive, won't they?' Foltrigg asked in a tone that left no doubt he expected to have it all as soon as he got to Memphis.

'They're working on it,' Trumann answered. Foltrigg was not his boss, technically, but this case was a prosecution now, not an investigation, and the Reverend was in control.

'So Jerome Clifford drives to Memphis and blows his brains out,' Foltrigg said to the window. 'Four weeks before trial. Man oh man. What else can go crazy with this case?'

No answer was expected. They rode in silence waiting for Roy to speak again.

'Where's Muldanno?' he finally asked.

'New Orleans. We're watching him.'

'He'll have a new lawyer by midnight, and by noon

tomorrow he'll file a dozen motions for continuances claiming the tragic death of Jerome Clifford seriously undermines his constitutional right to a fair trial with assistance of counsel. We'll oppose it of course, and the judge will order a hearing for next week, and we'll have the hearing, and we'll lose, and it'll be six months before this case goes to trial. Six months! Can you believe it?'

Trumann shook his head in disgust. 'At least it'll give us more time to find the body.'

It certainly would, and of course Roy had thought of this. He needed more time, really, he just couldn't admit it because he was the prosecutor, the people's lawyer, the government fighting crime and corruption. He was right, justice was on his side, and he had to be ready to attack evil at any moment, any time, any place. He had pushed hard for a speedy trial, because he was right, and he would get a conviction. The United States of America would win! And Roy Foltrigg would deliver the victory. He could see the headlines. He could smell the ink.

He also needed to find the damned body of Boyd Boyette, or else there might be no conviction, no front page pictures, no interviews on CNN, no speedy ascent to Capitol Hill. He had convinced those around him that a guilty verdict was possible with no corpse, and this was true. But he didn't want to chance it. He wanted the body.

Fink looked at Agent Trumann. 'We think Clifford knew where the body is. Did you know that?'

It was obvious Trumann did not know this. 'What makes you think so?'

Fink placed his reading material on the seat. 'Romey and I go way back. We were in law school together twenty years ago at Tulane. He was a little crazy back then, but very smart. About a week ago, he called me at home and said he wanted to talk about the Muldanno case. He was drunk, thick-tongued, out of his head, and kept saying he couldn't go through with the trial, which was surprising given how much he loves these big cases. We talked for an hour. He rambled and stuttered – '

51

'He even cried,' Foltrigg interrupted.

'Yeah, cried like a child. I was surprised by all this at first, but then nothing Jerome Clifford did really surprised me anymore, you know. Not even suicide. He finally hung up. He called me at the office at nine the next morning scared to death he'd let something slip the night before. He was in a panic, kept hinting he might know where the body is and fishing to see whether he'd dropped off any clues during his drunken chitchat. Well, I played along, and thanked him for the information he gave me the night before, which was nothing. I thanked him twice, then three times, and I could feel Romey sweating on the other end of the phone. He called twice more that day, at the office, then called me at home that night, drunk again. It was almost comical, but I thought I could string him along and maybe he'd let something slip. I told him I had to tell Roy, and that Roy had told the FBI, and that the FBI was now trailing him around the clock.'

'This really freaked him out,' Foltrigg added helpfully.

'Yeah, he cussed me out pretty good, but called the next day at the office. We had lunch, and the guy was a nervous wreck. He was too scared to come right out and ask if we knew about the body, and I played it cool. I told him we were certain we'd have the body in plenty of time for the trial, and I thanked him again. He was cracking up before my eyes. He hadn't slept or bathed. His eyes were puffy and red. He got drunk over lunch, and started accusing me of trickery and all sorts of sleazy, unethical behavior. It was an ugly scene. I paid the check and left, and he called me at home that night, remarkably sober. He apologized. I said no problem. I explained to him that Roy was seriously considering an indictment against him for obstruction of justice, and this set him off. He said we couldn't prove it. I said maybe not, but he'd be indicted, arrested, and put on trial, and there would be no way he could represent Barry Muldanno. He screamed and cussed for fifteen minutes, then hung up. I never heard from him again.'

'He knows, or he knew, where Muldanno put the body,' Foltrigg added with certainty.

'Why weren't we informed?' Trumann asked.

'We were about to tell you. In fact, Thomas and I discussed it this afternoon, just a short time before we got the call.' Foltrigg said this with an air of indifference, as if Trumann should not question him about such things. Trumann glanced at Scherff, who was glued to his legal pad, drawing pictures of handguns.

Foltrigg finished his tomato juice and tossed the can in the garbage. He crossed his feet. 'You guys need to track Clifford's movements from New Orleans to Memphis. Which route did he take? Are there friends along the way? Where did he stop? Who did he see in Memphis? Surely he must've talked to someone from the time he left New Orleans until he shot himself. Don't you think so?'

Trumann nodded. 'It's a long drive. I'm sure he had to stop along the way.'

'He knew where the body is, and he obviously planned to commit suicide. There's an outside chance he told someone, don't you think?'

'Maybe.'

'Think about it, Larry. Let's say you're the lawyer, heaven forbid. And you represent a killer who's murdered a United States Senator. Let's say that the killer tells you, his lawyer, where he hid the body. So, two, and only two, people in the entire world know this secret. And you, the lawyer, go off the deep end and decide to kill yourself. And you plan it. You know you're gonna die, right? You get pills and whiskey and a gun and a water hose, and you drive five hours from home, and you kill yourself. Now, would you share your little secret with anyone?'

'Perhaps. I don't know.'

'There's a chance, right?'

'Slight chance.'

'Good. If we have a slight chance, then we must investigate it thoroughly. I'd start with his office personnel. Find out when he left New Orleans. Check his credit cards. Where did he buy gas? Where did he eat? Where did he get the gun and the pills and the booze? Does he have family between here and there? Old lawyer friends along the way? There are a thousand things to check.'

Trumann handed the phone to Scherff. 'Call our office. Get Hightower on the phone.'

Foltrigg was pleased to see the FBI jump when he barked. He grinned smugly at Fink. Between them on the floor was a storage box crammed with files and exhibits and documents all related to *USA vs. Barry Muldanno*. Four more boxes were at the office. Fink had their contents memorized, but Roy did not. He pulled out a file and flipped through it. It was a thick motion filed by Jerome Clifford two months earlier that still had not been ruled upon. He laid it down, and stared through the window at the dark Mississippi landscape passing in the night. The Bogue Chitto exit was just ahead. Where do they get these names?

This would be a quick trip. He needed to confirm that Clifford was in fact dead, and had in fact died by his own hand. He had to know if any clues were dropped along the way, confessions to friends or loose talk to strangers, perhaps notes with last words that might be of help. Longshots at best. But there had been many dead ends in the search for Boyd Boyette and his killer, and this would not be the last.

SIX

A doctor in a yellow jogging suit ran through the swinging doors at the end of the emergency hallway and said something to the receptionist sitting behind the dirty sliding windows. She pointed, and he approached Dianne and Mark and Hardy as they stood by a Coke machine in one corner of the Admissions lobby of St Peter's Charity Hospital. He introduced himself to Dianne as Dr Simon Greenway and ignored the cop and Mark. He was a psychiatrist, he said, and had been called moments earlier by Dr Sage, the family's pediatrician. She needed to come with him. Hardy said he would stay with Mark.

They hurried away, down the narrow hallway, dodging nurses and orderlies, darting around gurneys and parked beds, and disappeared through the swinging doors. The Admissions lobby was crowded with dozens of sick and struggling patients-to-be. There were no empty chairs. Family members filled out forms. No one was in a hurry. A hidden intercom rattled nonstop somewhere above, paging a hundred doctors a minute.

It was a few minutes after seven. 'Are you hungry, Mark?' Hardy asked.

He wasn't, but he wanted to leave this place. 'Maybe a little.'

'Let's go to the cafeteria. I'll buy you a cheeseburger.'

They walked through a busy hallway, down a flight of stairs to the basement where a mass of anxious people roamed the corridor. Another hall led to a large open area, and suddenly they were in a cafeteria, louder and more crowded than the lunchroom at school. Hardy pointed to the only empty table in view, and Mark waited there.

Of particular concern to Mark at this moment was, of course, his little brother. He was worried about Ricky's physical condition, although Hardy had explained that he was in no danger of dying. He said that some doctors would talk to him and try to bring him around. But it could take time. He said that it was terribly important for the doctors to know exactly what happened, the truth and nothing but the truth, and that if the doctors were not told the truth then it could be severely damaging to Ricky and his mental condition. Hardy said Ricky might be locked up in some institution for months, maybe years, if the doctors weren't told the truth about what the boys witnessed.

Hardy was okay, not too bright, and he was making the mistake of talking to Mark as if he were five years old instead of eleven. He described the padded walls, and rolled his eyes around with great exaggeration. He told of patients being chained to beds as if spinning some horror story around the campfire. Mark was tired of it.

Mark could think of little except Ricky and whether he would remove his thumb and start talking. He desperately wanted this to happen, but he wanted to have first crack at Ricky when the shock ended. They had things to discuss.

What if the doctors or, heaven forbid, the cops got to him first, and Ricky told the whole story and they all knew Mark was lying? What would they do to him if they caught him lying? Maybe they wouldn't believe Ricky. Since he'd blanked out and left the world for a while, maybe they would tend to believe Mark instead. This conflict in stories was too awful to think about.

It's amazing how lies grow. You start with a small one that seems easy to cover, then you get boxed in and tell another one. Then another. People believe you at first, and they act upon your lies, and you catch yourself wishing you'd simply told the truth. He could have told the truth to the cops and to his mother. He could have explained in great detail everything that Ricky saw. And the secret would still be safe because Ricky didn't know.

Things were happening so fast he couldn't plan. He wanted to get his mother in a room with the door locked and unload all this, just stop it now before it got worse. If he didn't do something, he might go to jail and Ricky might go to the nuthouse for kids.

Hardy appeared with a tray covered with french fries and cheeseburgers, two for him and one for Mark. He arranged the food neatly and returned the tray.

Mark nibbled on a french fry. Hardy launched into a burger.

'So what happened to your face?' Hardy asked, chomping away.

Mark rubbed the knot and remembered he had been wounded in the fray. 'Oh nothing. Just got in a fight in school.'

'Who's the other kid?'

Dammit! Cops are relentless. Tell one lie to cover another. He was sick of lying. 'You don't know him,' he answered, then bit into his cheeseburger.

'I might want to talk to him.'

'Why?'

'Did you get in trouble for this fight? I mean, did your teacher take you to the principal's office, or anything like that?'

'No. It happened when school was out.'

'I thought you said you got in a fight at school.'

'Well, it sort of started at school, okay. Me and this guy got into it at lunch, and agreed to meet when school was out.'

Hardy drew mightily on the tiny straw in his milk shake. He swallowed hard, cleared his mouth, and said, 'What's the other kid's name?'

'Why do you want to know?'

This angered Hardy and he stopped chewing. Mark refused to look into his eyes, and he bent low over his food and stared at the ketchup.

57

'I'm a cop, kid. It's my job to ask questions.'

'Do I have to answer them?'

'Of course you do. Unless, of course, you're hiding something and afraid to answer. At that point, I'll have to get with your mother and perhaps take the both of you down to the station for more questioning.'

'Questioning about what? What exactly do you want to know?'

'Who is the kid you had a fight with today?'

Mark nibbled forever on the end of a long fry. Hardy picked up the second cheeseburger. A spot of mayonnaise hung from the corner of his mouth.

'I don't want to get him in trouble,' Mark said.

'He won't get in trouble.'

'Then why do you want to know his name?'

'I just want to know. It's my job, okay?'

'You think I'm lying, don't you?' Mark asked, looking pitifully into the bulging face.

The chomping stopped. 'I don't know, kid. Your story is full of holes.'

Mark looked even more pitiful. 'I can't remember everything. It happened so fast. You expect me to give every little detail, and I can't remember it that way.'

Hardy stuck a wad of fries in his mouth. 'Eat your food. We'd better get back.'

'Thanks for the dinner.'

Ricky was in a private room on the ninth floor. A large sign by the elevator labeled it as the PSYCHIATRIC WING, and it was much quieter. The lights were dimmer, the voices softer, the traffic much slower. The nurses' station was near the elevator, and those stepping off were scrutinized. A security guard whispered with the nurses and watched the hallways. Down from the elevators, away from the rooms, was a small, dark sitting area with a television, soft drink machines, magazines, and Gideon Bibles.

Mark and Hardy were alone in the waiting area. Mark sipped a Sprite, his third, and watched a rerun of 'Hill

Street Blues' on cable while Hardy dozed fitfully on the terribly undersized couch. It was almost nine, and half an hour had passed since Dianne had walked him down the hall to Ricky's room for a quick peek. He looked small under the sheets. The IV, Dianne had explained, was to feed him because he wouldn't eat. She assured him Ricky would be all right, but Mark studied her eyes and knew she was worried. Dr Greenway would return in a bit, and wanted to talk to Mark.

'Has he said anything?' Mark had asked as he studied the IV.

'No. Not a word.'

She took his hand and they walked through the dim hallway to the sitting area. At least five times, Mark had almost blurted something out. They had passed an empty room not far from Ricky's and he thought of dragging her inside for a confession. But he didn't. Later, he kept telling himself, I'll tell her later.

Hardy had stopped asking questions. His shift ended at ten, and it was obvious he was tired of Mark and Ricky and the hospital. He wanted to return to the streets.

A pretty nurse in a short skirt walked past the elevators and motioned for Mark to follow her. He eased from his chair, holding his Sprite. She took his hand, and there was something exciting about this. Her fingernails were long and red. Her skin was smooth and tanned. She had blonde hair and a perfect smile, and she was young. Her name was Karen, and she squeezed his hand a bit tighter than necessary. His heart skipped a beat.

'Dr Greenway wants to talk to you,' she said, leaning down as she walked. Her perfume lingered, and it was the most wonderful fragrance Mark could remember.

She walked him to Ricky's room, Number 943, and released his hand. The door was closed, so she knocked slightly and opened it. Mark entered slowly, and Karen patted him on the shoulder. He watched her leave through the half-open door.

Dr Greenway now wore a shirt and tie with a white lab

59

jacket over it. An ID tag hung from the left front pocket. He was a skinny man with round glasses and a black beard, and seemed too young to be doing this.

'Come in, Mark,' he said after Mark was already in the room and standing at the foot of Ricky's bed. 'Sit here.' He pointed to a plastic chair next to a foldaway bed under the window. His voice was low, almost a whisper. Dianne sat with her feet curled under her on the bed. Her shoes were on the floor. She wore blue jeans and a sweater, and stared at Ricky under the sheets with a tube in his arm. A lamp on a table near the bathroom door provided the only light. The blinds were shut tight.

Mark eased into the plastic chair, and Dr Greenway sat on the edge of the foldaway, not two feet away. He squinted and frowned, and projected such somberness that Mark thought for a second they were all about to die.

'I need to talk to you about what happened,' he said. He was not whispering now. It was obvious Ricky was in another world and they were unafraid of waking him. Dianne was behind Greenway, still staring blankly at the bed. Mark wanted her alone so he could talk and work out of this mess, but she was back there in the darkness, behind the doctor, ignoring him.

'Has he said anything?' Mark asked first. The past three hours with Hardy had been nothing but quick questions, and the habit was hard to break.

'No.'

'How sick is he?'

'Very sick,' Greenway answered, his tiny, dark eyes glowing at Mark. 'What did he see this afternoon?'

'Is this in secret?'

'Yes. Anything you tell me is strictly confidential.'

'What if the cops want to know what I tell you?'

'I can't tell them. I promise. This is all very secret and confidential. Just you and me and your mother. We're all trying to help Ricky, and I've got to know what happened.'

Maybe a good dose of the truth would help everyone, especially Ricky. Mark looked at the small, blond head with hair sticking in all directions on the pillow. Why oh why didn't they just run when the black car pulled up and parked? He was suddenly hit with guilt, and it terrified him. All of this was his fault. He should have known better than to mess with a crazy man.

His lip quivered and his eyes watered. He was cold. It was time to tell all. He was running out of lies and Ricky needed help. Greenway watched every move.

And then Hardy walked slowly by the door. He paused for a second in the hall and locked eyes with Mark, then disappeared. Mark knew he wasn't far away. Greenway had not seen him.

Mark started with the cigarettes. His mother looked at him hard, but if she was angry she didn't convey it. She shook her head once or twice, but never said a word. He spoke in a low voice, his eyes alternating quickly between Greenway and the door, and described the tree with the rope and the woods and the clearing. Then the car. He left out a good chunk of the story, but did admit to Greenway, in a soft voice and in extreme confidence, that he once crawled to the car and removed the hose. And when he did so, Ricky cried and peed in his pants. Ricky begged him not to do it. He could tell Greenway liked this part. Dianne listened without expression.

Hardy walked by again, but Mark pretended not to see him. He paused in his story for a few seconds, then told how the man stormed out of the car, saw the garden hose lying harmlessly in the weeds, and crawled on the trunk and shot himself.

'How far away was Ricky?' Greenway asked.

Mark looked around the room. 'You see that door across the hall?' he asked, pointing. 'From here to there.'

Greenway looked and rubbed his beard. 'About forty feet. That's not very far.'

'It was very close.'

'What exactly did Ricky do when the shot was fired?'

Dianne was listening now. It apparently had just occurred to her that this was a different version from the earlier one.

61

She wrinkled her forehead and looked hard at her eldest.

'I'm sorry, Mom. I was too scared to think. Don't be angry with me.'

'You actually saw the man shoot himself?' she asked in disbelief.

'Yes.'

She looked at Ricky. 'No wonder.'

'What did Ricky do when the shot was fired?'

'I wasn't looking at Ricky. I was watching the man with the gun.'

'Poor baby,' Dianne mumbled in the background. Greenway held up a hand to cut her off.

'Was Ricky close to you?'

Mark glanced at the door, and explained faintly how Ricky had frozen, then started away in an awkward jog, arms straight down, a dull moaning sound coming from his mouth. He told it all with dead accuracy from the point of the shooting to the point of the ambulance, and he left out nothing. He closed his eyes and relived each step, each movement. It felt wonderful to be so truthful.

'Why didn't you tell me you watched the man kill himself?' Dianne asked.

This irritated Greenway. 'Please, Ms Sway, you can discuss it with him later,' he said without taking his eyes off Mark.

'What was the last word Ricky said?' Greenway asked.

He thought and watched the door. The hall was empty. 'I really can't remember.'

Sergeant Hardy huddled with his lieutenant and Special Agent Jason McThune of the FBI. They chatted in the sitting area next to the soft drink machines. Another FBI agent loitered suspiciously near the elevator. The hospital security guard glared at him.

The lieutenant explained hurriedly to Hardy that it was now an FBI matter, that the dead man's car and all other physical evidence had been turned over by Memphis PD, that print experts had finished dusting the car and found lots of fingerprints too small for an adult, and they needed to know if Mark had dropped any clues or changed his story.

'No, but I'm not convinced he's telling the truth,' Hardy said.

'Has he touched anything we can take?' McThune asked quickly, unconcerned about Hardy's theories or convictions.

'What do you mean?'

'We have a strong suspicion the kid was in the car at some point before Clifford died. We need to lift the kid's prints from something and see if they match.'

'What makes you think he was in the car?' Hardy asked with great anticipation.

'I'll explain later,' his lieutenant said.

Hardy looked around the sitting area, and suddenly pointed to a trash basket by the chair Mark had sat in. 'There. The Sprite can. He drank a Sprite while sitting right there.' McThune looked up and down the hall, and carefully wrapped a handkerchief around the Sprite can. He placed it in the pocket of his coat.

'It's definitely his,' Hardy said. 'This is the only trash basket, and that's the only Sprite can.'

'I'll run this to our fingerprint men,' McThune said. 'Is the kid, Mark, staying here tonight?'

'I think so,' Hardy said. 'They've moved a portable bed into his brother's room. Looks like they'll all sleep in there. Why is the FBI concerned with Clifford?'

'I'll explain later,' said his lieutenant. 'Stay here for another hour.'

'I'm supposed to be off in ten minutes.'

'You need the overtime.'

Dr Greenway sat in the plastic chair near the bed and studied his notes. 'I'm gonna leave in a minute, but I'll be back early in the morning. He's stable, and I expect little change through the night. The nurses will check in every so often. Call them if he wakes up.' He flipped a page of notes

63

and read the chicken scratch,then looked at Dianne. 'It's a severe case of acute post- traumatic stress disorder.'

'What does that mean?' Mark asked. Dianne rubbed her temples and kept her eyes closed.

'Sometimes a person sees a terrible event and cannot cope with it. Ricky was badly scared when you removed the garden hose from the tail pipe, and when he saw the man shoot himself he was suddenly exposed to a terrifying experience that he couldn't handle. It triggered a response in him. He sort of snapped. It shocked his mind and body. He was able to run home, which is quite remarkable because normally a person traumatized like Ricky would immediately become numb and paralyzed.' He paused and placed his notes on the bed. 'There's not a lot we can do right now. I expect him to come around tomorrow, or the next day at the latest, and we'll start talking about things. It may take some time. He'll have nightmares of the shooting, and flashbacks. He'll deny it happened, then he'll blame himself for it. He'll feel isolated, betrayed, bewildered, maybe even depressed. You just never know.'

'How will you treat him?' Dianne asked.

'We have to make him feel safe. You must stay here at all times. Now, you said the father is of no use.'

'Keep him away from Ricky,' Mark said sternly. Dianne nodded.

'Fine. And there are no grandparents or relatives nearby.'

'No.'

'Very well. It's imperative that both of you stay in this room as much as possible for the next several days. Ricky must feel safe and secure. He'll need emotional and physical support from you. He and I will talk several times a day. It will be important for Mark and Ricky to talk about the shooting. They need to share and compare their reactions.'

'When do you think we might go home?' Dianne asked.

'I don't know, but as soon as possible. He needs the safety and familiarity of his bedroom and surroundings.

Maybe a week. Maybe two. Depends on how quickly he responds.'

Dianne pulled her feet under her. 'I, uh, I have a job. I don't know what to do.'

'I'll have my office contact your employer first thing in the morning.'

'My employer runs a sweatshop. It is not a nice, clean corporation with benefits and sympathy. They will not send flowers. I'm afraid they won't understand.'

'I'll do the best I can.'

'What about school?' Mark asked.

'Your mother has given me the name of the principal. I'll call first thing in the morning and talk to your teachers.'

Dianne was rubbing her temples again. A nurse, not the pretty one, knocked while entering. She handed Dianne two pills and a cup of water.

'It's Dalmane,' Greenway said. 'It should help you rest. If not, call the nurses' station and they'll bring something stronger.'

The nurse left and Greenway stood and felt Ricky's forehead. 'See you guys in the morning. Get some sleep.' He smiled for the first time, then closed the door behind him.

They were alone, the tiny Sway family, or what was left of it. Mark moved closer to his mother, and leaned on her shoulder. They looked at the small head on the large pillow less than five feet away.

She patted his arm. 'It'll be all right, Mark. We've been through worse.' She held him tight and he closed his eyes.

'I'm sorry, Mom.' His eyes watered, and he was ready for a cry. 'I'm so sorry about all this.' She squeezed him, and held him tight for a long minute. He sobbed quietly with his face buried in her shirt.

She gently lay down with Mark still in her arms, and they curled together on the cheap foam mattress. Ricky's bed was two feet higher. The window was above them. The lights were low. Mark stopped the crying. It was something he was lousy at anyway.

The Dalmane was working, and she was exhausted. Nine hours of packing plastic lamps into cardboard boxes, five hours of a full-blown crisis, and now the Dalmane. She was ready for a deep sleep.

'Will you get fired, Mom?' Mark asked. He worried about the family finances as much as she did.

'I don't think so. We'll worry about it tomorrow.'

'We need to talk, Mom.'

'I know we do. But let's do it in the morning.'

'Why can't we talk now?'

She relaxed her grip and breathed deeply, eyes already closed. 'I'm very tired and sleepy, Mark. I promise we'll have a long talk first thing in the morning. You have some questions to answer, don't you? Now go brush your teeth and let's try and sleep.'

Mark was suddenly tired too. The hard line of a metal brace protruded through the cheap mattress, and he crept closer to the wall and pulled the lone sheet over him. His mother rubbed his arm. He stared at the wall, six inches away, and decided he could not sleep like this for a week.

Her breathing was much heavier and she was completely still. He thought of Romey. Where was he now? Where was the chubby little body with the bald head? He remembered the sweat and how it poured from his shiny scalp and ran down in all directions, some dripping from his eyebrows and some soaking his collar. Even his ears were wet. Who would get his car? Who would clean it up and wash the blood off? Who would get the gun? Mark realized for the first time that his ears were no longer ringing from the gunfire in the car. Was Hardy still out there in the sitting room trying to sleep? Would the cops return tomorrow with more questions? What if they asked about the garden hose? What if they asked a thousand questions?

He was wide awake now, staring at the wall. Lights from the outside trickled through the blinds. The Dalmane worked well because his mother was breathing very slow and heavy. Ricky had not moved. He stared at the dim light above the table, and thought of Hardy and the police. Were they watching him? Was he under surveillance, like on television? Surely not.

He watched them sleep for twenty minutes, and got bored with it. It was time to explore. When he was a first-grader, his father came home drunk late one night, and started raising hell with Dianne. They fought and the trailer shook, and Mark eased open the shoddy window in his room and slid to the ground. He went for a long walk around the neighborhood, then through the woods. It was a hot, sticky night with plenty of stars, and he rested on a hill overlooking the trailer park. He prayed for the safety of his mother. He asked God for a family in which everyone could sleep without fear of abuse. Why couldn't they just be normal? He rambled for two hours. All was quiet when he returned home, and thus began a habit of night-time excursions that had brought him much pleasure and peace.

Mark was a thinker, a worrier, and when sleep came and went or wouldn't come at all, he went for long secret walks. He learned much. He wore dark clothing and moved like a thief through the shadows of Tucker Wheel Estates. He witnessed petty crimes of theft and vandalism, but he never told. He saw lovers sneak from windows. He loved to sit on the hill above the park on clear nights and enjoy a quiet smoke. The fear of getting caught by his mother had vanished years ago. She worked hard and slept sound.

He was not afraid of strange places. He pulled the sheet over his mother's shoulder, did the same for Ricky, and quietly closed the door behind him. The hall was dark and empty. Karen the gorgeous was busy at the nurses' desk. She smiled beautifully at him and stopped her writing. He wanted to go for some orange juice in the cafeteria, he said, and he knew how to get there. He'd be back in a minute. Karen grinned at him as he walked away, and Mark was in love.

Hardy was gone. The sitting room was empty but the television was on. 'Hogan's Heroes.' He took the empty elevator to the basement.

The cafeteria was deserted. A man with casts on both legs

sat stiffly in a wheelchair at one table. The casts were shiny and clean. An arm was in a sling. A band of thick gauze covered the top of his head and it looked as though the hair had been shaven. He was terribly uncomfortable.

Mark paid for a pint of juice, and sat at a table near the man. He grimaced in pain, and shoved his soup away in frustration. He sipped juice through a straw, and noticed Mark.

'What's up?' Mark asked with a smile. He could talk to anyone and felt sorry for the guy.

The man glared at him, then looked away. He grimaced again and tried to adjust his legs. Mark tried not to stare.

A man with a white shirt and tie appeared from nowhere with a tray of food and coffee, and sat at a table on the other side of the injured guy. He didn't appear to notice Mark. 'Bad injury,' he said with a large smile. 'What happened?'

'Car wreck,' came the somewhat anguished reply. 'Got hit by an Exxon truck. Nut ran a stop sign.'

The smile grew even larger and the food and coffee were ignored. 'When did it happen?'

'Three days ago.'

'Did you say Exxon truck?' The man was standing and moving quickly to the guy's table, pulling something out of his pocket. He took a chair and was suddenly sitting within inches of the casts.

'Yeah,' the guy said warily.

The man handed him a white card. 'My name's Gill Teal. I'm a lawyer, and I specialize in auto accidents, especially cases involving large trucks.' Gill Teal said this very rapidly, as if he'd hooked a large fish and had to work quickly or it might get away. 'That's my speciality. Big-truck cases. Eighteen wheelers. Dump trucks. Tankers. You name it, and I go after them.' He thrust his hand across the table. 'Name's Gill Teal.'

Luckily for the guy, his good arm was his right one, and he lamely slung it over the table to shake hands with this hustler. 'Joe Farris.'

Gill pumped it furiously, and eagerly moved in for the

kill. 'What you got – two broke legs, concussion, coupla puncture wounds?'

'And broken collarbone.'

'Great. Then we're looking at permanent disability. What type of work do you do?' Gill asked, rubbing his chin in careful analysis. The card was lying on the table, untouched by Joe. They were unaware of Mark.

'Crane operator.'

'Union?'

'Yeah.'

'Wow. And the Exxon truck ran a stop sign. No doubt about who's at fault here?'

Joe frowned and shifted again, and even Mark could tell he was rapidly tiring of Gill and this intrusion. He shook his head no.

Gill made frantic notes on a napkin, then smiled at Joe and announced, 'I can get you at least six hundred thousand. I take only a third, and you walk away with four hundred thousand. Minimum. Four hundred grand, tax free, of course. We'll file suit tomorrow.'

Joe took this as if he'd heard it before. Gill hung in mid-air with his mouth open, proud of himself, full of confidence.

'I've talked to some other lawyers,' Joe said.

'I can get you more than anybody. I do this for a living, nothing but truck cases. I've sued Exxon before, know all their lawyers and corporate people locally, and they're terrified of me because I go for the jugular.It's warfare, Joe, and I'm the best in town. I know how to play their dirty games. Just settled a truck case for almost half a million. They threw money at my client once he hired me. Not bragging, Joe, but I'm the best in town when it comes to these cases.'

'A lawyer called me this morning and said he could get me a million.'

'He's lying. What was his name? McFay? Ragland? Snodgrass? I know these guys. I kick their asses all the time, Joe, and anyway I said six hundred thousand is a minimum. Could be much more. Hell, Joe, if they push us to trial, who knows how much a jury might give us. I'm in trial every day, Joe, kicking ass all over Memphis. Six hundred is a minimum. Have you hired anybody yet? Signed a contract?'

Joe shook his head no. 'Not yet.'

'Wonderful. Look, Joe, you've got a wife and kids, right?'

'Ex-wife, three kids.'

'So you've got child support, man, now listen to me. How much child support?'

'Five hundred a month.'

'That's low. And you've got bills. Here's what I'll do. I'll advance you a thousand bucks a month to be applied against your settlement. If we settle in three months, I withhold three thousand. If it takes two years, and it won't, but if it does I'll withhold twenty-four thousand. Or whatever. You follow me, Joe? Cash now on the spot.'

Joe shifted again and stared at the table. 'This other lawyer came by my room yesterday and said he'd advance two thousand now and float me two thousand a month.'

'Who was it? Scottie Moss? Rob LaMoke? I know these guys, Joe, and they're trash. Can't find their way to the courthouse. You can't trust them. They're incompetent. I'll match it – two thousand now, and two thousand a month.'

'This other guy with some big firm offered ten thousand up front and a line of credit for whatever I needed.'

Gill was crushed, and it was at least ten seconds before he could speak. 'Listen to me, Joe. It's not a matter of advance cash, okay. It's a matter of how much money I can get for you from Exxon. And nobody, I repeat, nobody will get more than me. Nobody. Look. I'll advance five thousand now, and allow you to draw what you need to pay bills. Fair enough?'

'I'll think about it.'

'Time is critical, Joe. We must move fast. Evidence disappears. Memories fade. Big corporations move slow.'

'I said I'll think about it.'

'Can I call you tomorrow?'

'No.'

'Why not?'

'Hell, I can't sleep now for all the damned lawyers calling. I can't eat a meal without you guys bargin' in. There are more lawyers around this damned place than doctors.'

Gill was unmoved. 'There are a lot of sharks out here, Joe. A lot of really lousy lawyers who'll screw up your case. Sad but true. The profession is overcrowded, so lawyers are everywhere trying to find business. But don't make a mistake, Joe. Check me out. Look in the yellow pages. There's a full-page, three-colour ad for me, Joe. Look up Gill Teal, and you'll see who's for real.'

'I'll think about it.'

Gill came forth with another card and handed it to Joe. He said goodbye and left, never touching the food or coffee on his tray.

Joe was suffering. He grabbed the wheel with his right arm, and slowly rolled himself away. Mark wanted to help, but thought better of asking. Both of Gill's cards were on the table. He finished his juice, glanced around, and picked up one of the cards.

Mark told Karen, his sweetheart, that he couldn't sleep and would be watching television if anyone needed him. He sat on the couch in the waiting area and flipped through the phone book while watching 'Cheers' reruns. He sipped another Sprite. Hardy, bless his heart, had given him eight quarters after dinner.

Karen brought him a blanket and tucked it around his legs. She patted his arm with her long, thin hands, and glided away. He watched every step.

Mr Gill Teal did indeed have a full-page ad in the Attorneys section of the Memphis yellow pages, along with a dozen other lawyers. There was a nice picture of him standing casually outside a courthouse with his jacket off and sleeves rolled up. 'I FIGHT FOR YOUR RIGHTS!' it said under the photo. In bold red letters across the top, the

71

question 'HAVE YOU BEEN INJURED?' cried out. Thick green print answered just below, 'IF SO, CALL GILL TEAL – HE'S FOR REAL.' Further down, in blue print Gill listed all the types of cases he handled, and there were hundreds. Lawnmowers, electrical shock, deformed babies, car wrecks, exploding water heaters. Eighteen years' experience in all courts. A small map in the corner of the ad directed the world to his office, which was just across the street from the courthouse.

Mark heard a familiar voice, and suddenly there he was, Gill Teal himself, on television standing beside a hospital emergency entrance talking about injured loved ones and crooked insurance companies. Red lights flashed in the background. Paramedics ran behind him. But Gill had the situation under control, and he would take your case for nothing down. No fee unless he recovered.

Small world! In the past two hours, Mark had seen him in person, picked up one of his business cards, was literally looking at his face in the yellow pages, and now, here he was speaking to him from the television.

He closed the phone book and laid it on the cluttered coffee table. He pulled the blanket over him and decided to go to sleep.

Tomorrow he might call Gill Teal.

SEVEN

Foltrigg liked to be escorted. He especially enjoyed those priceless moments when the cameras were rolling and waiting for him, and at just the right moment he would stroll majestically through the hall or down the courthouse steps with Wally Boxx in front like a pit bull and Thomas Fink or another assistant by his side brushing off idiotic questions. He spent many quiet moments watching videos of himself darting in and out of courthouses with a small entourage. His timing was usually perfect. He had the walk perfected. He held his hands up patiently as if he would love to answer questions but, being a man of great importance, he just didn't have the time. Soon thereafter, Wally would call the reporters in for an orchestrated press conference in which Roy himself would break from his brutal work schedule and spend a few moments in the lights. A small library in the US Attorney's suite had been converted to a press room, complete with floodlights and a sound system. Roy kept makeup in a locked cabinet.

As he entered the Federal Building on Main Street in Memphis, a few minutes after midnight, he had an escort of sorts with Wally and Fink and agents Trumann and Scherff, but there were no anxious reporters. In fact, not a soul waited for him until he entered the offices of the FBI where Jason McThune sipped stale coffee with two other weary agents. So much for grand entrances.

Introductions were handled quickly as they walked to McThune's cramped office. Foltrigg took the only available seat. McThune was a twenty-year man who'd been shipped to Memphis four years earlier against his wishes and was counting the months until he could leave for the Pacific Northwest. He was tired and irritated because it was late. He'd heard of Foltrigg, but never met him. The rumors described him as a pompous ass.

An agent who was unidentified and unintroduced closed the door, and McThune fell into his seat behind the desk. He covered the basics: the finding of the car, the contents of it, the gun, the wound, the time of death, and on and on. 'Kid's name is Mark Sway. He told Memphis PD he and his younger brother happened upon the body and ran to call the authorities. They live about half a mile away in a trailer park. The younger kid is in the hospital now suffering from what appears to be traumatic shock. Mark Sway and his mother, Dianne, divorced, are also at the hospital. The father lives here in the city, and has a record of petty stuff. DUI's, fights, and the like. Sophisticated criminal. Low-class white people. Anyway, the kid's lying.'

'I couldn't read the note,' Foltrigg interrupted, dying to say something. 'The fax was bad.' He said this as if McThune and the Memphis FBI were inept because he, Roy Foltrigg, had received a bad fax in his van.

McThune glanced at Larry Trumann and Skipper Scherff standing against the wall, and continued. 'I'll get to that in a minute. We know the kid's lying because he says they arrived on the scene after Clifford shot himself. Looks doubtful. First, the kid's fingerprints are all over the car, inside and out. On the dash, on the door, on the whiskey bottle, on the gun, everywhere. We lifted a print from him about two hours ago, and we've had our people all over the car. They'll finish up tomorrow, but it's obvious the kid was inside. Doing what, well, we're not yet certain. We've also found prints all around the rear taillights just above the exhaust pipe. And there were also three fresh cigarette butts under a tree near the car. Virginia Slims, the same brand used by Dianne Sway. We figure the kids were being kids, took the cigarettes from their mother, and went for a smoke. They were minding their own business when Clifford appears from nowhere. They hide and watch him – it's a dense area and hiding is no problem. Maybe they sneak around and pull out the hose, we're not sure and the kids aren't telling. The little boy can't talk right now, and Mark evidently is lying. Anyway, it's obvious the hose didn't work. We're trying to match prints on it, but it's tedious work. May be impossible. I'll have photos in the morning to show the location of the hose when Memphis PD arrived.'

McThune lifted a yellow notepad from the wreckage on his desk. He spoke to it, not to Foltrigg. 'Clifford fired at least one shot from inside the car. The bullet exited through the center, almost exactly, of the front passenger window, which cracked but did not shatter. No idea why he did this, and no idea when it was done. The autopsy was finished an hour ago, and Clifford was full of Dalmane, codeine, and Percodan. Plus his blood alcohol content was point two-two, so he was drunk as a skunk, as these people say down here. My point being, not only was he off his rocker enough to kill himself, but he was also drunk and stoned, so there's no way to figure out a lot of this. We're not tracking a rational mind.'

'I understand that.' Roy nodded impatiently. Wally Boxx hovered behind him like a well-trained terrier.

McThune ignored him. 'The gun's a cheap .38 he purchased illegally at a pawnshop here in Memphis. We've questioned the owner, but he won't talk without his lawyer present, so we'll do that in the morning, or this morning I should say. A Texaco receipt shows a purchase of gasoline in Vaiden, Mississippi, about an hour and a half from here. The clerk is a kid who says she thinks he stopped around 1 p.m. No other evidence of any stops. His secretary says he left the office around 9 a.m., said he had an errand to run and she didn't hear a word until we called. Frankly, she was not very upset at the news. It looks as though he left New Orleans shortly after nine, drove to Memphis in five or six hours, stopped once for gas, stopped to buy the gun, and drove off and shot himself. Maybe he stopped for lunch, maybe to buy whiskey, maybe a lot of things. We're digging.'

'Why Memphis?' Wally Boxx asked. Foltrigg nodded, obviously approving the question.

'Because he was born here,' McThune said solemnly while staring at Foltrigg, as if everyone prefers to die in the place of their birth. It was a humorous response delivered by a serious face, and Foltrigg missed it all. McThune had heard he was not too bright.

'Evidently, the family moved away when he was a child,' he explained after a pause. 'He went to college at Rice and law school at Tulane.'

'We were in law school together,' Fink said proudly.

'That's great. The note was handwritten and dated today, or yesterday I should say. Handwritten with a black felt tip pen of some sort – the pen wasn't found on him or in the car.' McThune picked up a sheet of paper and leaned across the desk. 'Here. This is the original. Be careful with it.'

Wally Boxx leaped at it and handed it to Foltrigg, who studied it. McThune rubbed his eyes and continued. 'Just funeral arrangements and directions to his secretary. Look at the bottom. It looks as though he tried to add something with a blue ballpoint pen, but the pen was out of ink.'

Foltrigg's nose got closer to the note. 'It says "Mark, Mark where are," and I can't make out the rest of it.'

'Right. The handwriting is awful and the pen ran out of ink, but our expert says the same thing. "Mark, Mark where are." He also thinks that Clifford was drunk or stoned or something when he tried to write this. We found the pen in the car. Cheap Bic. No doubt it's the pen. He has no children, nephews, brothers, uncles, or cousins by the name of Mark. We're checking his close friends – his secretary said he had none – but as of now we haven't found a Mark.'

'So what does it mean?'

'There's one other thing. A few hours ago, Mark Sway

rode to the hospital with a Memphis cop by the name of Hardy. Along the way he let it slip that Romey said or did something. Romey. Short for Jerome, according to Mr Clifford's secretary. In fact, she said more people called him Romey than Jerome. How would the kid know the nickname unless Mr Clifford himself told him?'

Foltrigg listened with his mouth open. 'What do you think?' he asked.

'Well, my theory is that the kid was in the car before Clifford shot himself, and that he was there for some time because of all the prints, and that he and Clifford talked about something. Then, at some point, the kid leaves the car, Clifford tries to add something to his note, and shoots himself. The kid is scared. His little brother goes into shock, and here we are.'

'Why would the kid lie?'

'One, he's scared. Two, he's a kid. Three, maybe Clifford told him something he doesn't need to know.'

McThune's delivery was perfect, and the dramatic punch line left a heavy silence in the room. Foltrigg was frozen. Boxx and Fink stared blankly at the desk with open mouths.

Because his boss was temporarily at a loss, Wally Boxx moved in defensively and asked a stupid question. 'Why do you think this?'

McThune's patience with US Attorneys and their little flunkies had been exhausted about twenty years ago. He'd seen them come and go. He'd learned to play their games and manipulate their egos. He knew the best way to handle their banalities was simply to respond. 'Because of the note, the prints, and the lies. The poor kid doesn't know what to do.'

Foltrigg placed the note on the desk, and cleared his throat. 'Have you talked to the kid?'

'No. I went to the hospital two hours ago, but did not see him. Sergeant Hardy of Memphis PD talked to him.'

'Do you plan to?'

'Yes, in a few hours. Trumann and I will go to the hospital around nine or so and talk to the kid and maybe his mother. I'd also like to talk to the little brother, but it'll depend on his doctor.'

'I'd like to be there,' Foltrigg said. Everyone knew it was coming.

McThune shook his head. 'Not a good idea. We'll handle it.' He was abrupt and left no doubt that he was in charge. This was Memphis, not New Orleans.

'What about the kid's doctor? Have you talked to him?'

'No, not yet. We'll try this morning. I doubt if he'll say much.'

'Do you think these kids would tell the doctor?' Fink asked innocently.

McThune rolled his eyes at Trumann as if to say, 'What kind of dumbasses have you brought me?' 'I can't answer that, sir. I don't know what the kids know. I don't know the doctor's name. I don't know if he's talked to the kids. I don't know if the kids will tell him anything.'

Foltrigg frowned at Fink, who shrank with embarrassment. McThune glanced at his watch and stood. 'Gentlemen, it's late. Our people will finish with the car by noon, and I suggest we meet then.'

'We must know everything Mark Sway knows,' Roy said without moving. 'He was in that car, and Clifford talked to him.'

'I know that.'

'Yes, Mr McThune, but there are some things you don't know. Clifford knew the location of the body, and he was talking about it.'

'There are a lot of things I don't know, Mr. Foltrigg, because this is a New Orleans case, and I work Memphis, you understand. I don't want to know any more about poor Mr Boyette and poor Mr Clifford. I'm up to my ass in dead bodies here. It's almost 1 a.m., and I'm sitting here in my office working on a case that's not mine, talking to you fellas and answering your questions. And I'll work on the case until noon tomorrow, then my pal Larry Trumann here can have it. I'll be finished.'

'Unless, of course, you get a call from Washington.'

'Yes, unless of course I get a call from Washington, then I'll do whatever Mr Voyles tells me.'

'I talk to Mr Voyles every week.'

'Congratulations.'

'The Boyette case is the FBI's top priority at this moment, according to him.'

'So I've heard.'

'And I'm sure Mr Voyles will appreciate your efforts.'

'I doubt it.'

Roy stood slowly and stared at McThune. 'It is imperative that we know everything Mark Sway knows. Do you understand?'

McThune returned the stare and said nothing.

EIGHT

Karen checked on Mark throughout the night, and brought him orange juice around eight. He was alone in the small waiting room. She woke him gently.

In spite of his many problems at the moment, he was falling hopelessly in love with this beautiful nurse. He sipped the juice and looked into her sparkling brown eyes. She patted the blanket covering his legs.

'How old are you?' he asked.

She smiled even wider. 'Twenty-four. Thirteen years older than you. Why do you ask?'

'Just a habit. Are you married?'

'No.' She gently removed the blanket and began folding it. 'How was the sofa?'

Mark stood, stretched, and watched her. 'Better than that bed Mom had to sleep on. Did you work all night?'

'From eight to eight. We're doing twelve-hour shifts, four days a week. Come with me. Dr Greenway is in the room and wants to see you.' She took his hand, which helped immensely, and they walked to Ricky's room. Karen left and closed the door behind her.

Dianne looked tired. She stood at the foot of Ricky's bed with an unlit cigarette in her trembling hand. Mark stood next to her, and she put her arm on his shoulder. They watched as Greenway rubbed Ricky's forehead and spoke to him. His eyes were closed and he was not responding.

'He doesn't hear you, Doctor,' Dianne said finally. It was difficult to listen to Greenway chat away in baby talk. He ignored her. She wiped a tear from her cheek. Mark smelled fresh soap and noticed her hair was wet. She had changed clothes. But there was no makeup and her face was different.

Greenway stood straight. 'A most severe case,' he said properly, almost to himself while staring at the closed eyes.

'What's next?' she asked.

'We wait. His vital signs are stable, so there's no physical danger. He'll come around, and when he does, it's imperative that you be in this room.' Greenway was looking at them now, rubbing his beard, deep in thought. 'He must see his mother when he opens his eyes, do you understand this?'

'I'm not leaving.'

'You, Mark, can come and go a bit, but it's best if you stay here as much as possible too.'

Mark nodded his head. The thought of spending another minute in the room was painful.

'The first moments can be crucial. He'll be frightened when he looks around. He needs to see and feel his mother. Hold him and reassure him. Call the nurse immediately. I'll leave instructions. He'll be very hungry, so we'll try and get some food in him. The nurse'll remove the IV, so he can walk around the room. But the important thing is to hold him.'

'When do you –'

'I don't know. Probably today or tomorrow. There's no way to predict.'

'Have you seen cases like this before?'

Greenway looked at Ricky, and decided to go for the truth. He shook his head. 'Not quite this bad. He's almost comatose, which is a bit unusual. Normally, after a period of good rest, they'll be awake and eating.' He almost managed a smile. 'But, I'm not concerned. Ricky will be all right. It'll just take some time.'

Ricky seemed to hear this. He grunted and stretched, but did not open his eyes. They watched intently, hoping for a mumble or word. Though Mark preferred that he remain silent about the shooting until they discussed it alone, he desperately wanted his little brother to wake up and start talking about other matters. He was tired of looking at him curled up on the pillow, sucking that damned thumb.

Greenway reached into his bag and produced a newspaper. It was the *Memphis Press*, the morning paper. He laid it on the bed, and handed Dianne a card. 'My office is in the building next door. Here's the phone number, just in case. Remember, the moment he wakes up, call the nurses' station, and they'll call me immediately. Okay?'

Dianne took the card and nodded. Greenway unfolded the newspaper on Ricky's bed in front of them. 'Have you seen this?'

'No,' she answered.

At the bottom of the front page was a headline about Romey. NEW ORLEANS LAWYER COMMITS SUICIDE IN NORTH MEMPHIS. Under the headline to the right was a big photo of W. Jerome Clifford, and to the left was the smaller headline – FLAMBOYANT CRIMINAL LAWYER WITH SUSPECTED MOB TIES. The word 'Mob' jumped at Mark. He stared at Romey's face, and suddenly needed to vomit.

Greenway leaned forward and lowered his voice. 'It seems as though Mr Clifford was a rather well-known lawyer in New Orleans. He was involved in the Senator Boyette case. Apparently, he was the attorney for the man charged with the murder. Have you kept up with it?'

Dianne actually put the unlit cigarette in her mouth. She shook her head no.

'Well, it's a big case. The first US Senator to be murdered in office. You can read this after I leave. There are police and FBI downstairs. They were waiting when I arrived an hour ago.' Mark grabbed the railing on the foot of the bed. 'They want to talk to Mark, and of course they want you present.'

'Why?' she asked.

Greenway looked at his watch. 'The Boyette case is complicated. I think you'll understand more after you read the story here. I told them you and Mark could not speak with them until I say so. Is this all right?'

'Yes,' Mark blurted. 'I don't want to talk to them.' Dianne and Greenway looked at him. 'I may end up like Ricky if these cops keep bugging me.' For some reason, Mark knew the police would return with a lot of questions. They were not finished with him. But the photo on the front page of the paper and the mention of the FBI suddenly sent chills over him, and he needed to sit down.

'Keep them away for now,' Dianne said to Greenway.

'They asked if they could see you at nine, and I said no. But they won't go away.' He looked at his watch again. 'I'll be here at noon. Perhaps we should talk to them then.'

'Whatever you think,' she said.

'Very well. I'll put them off until twelve. My office has called your employer and the school. Try not to worry about that. Just stay by this bed until I return.' He almost smiled as he closed the door behind him.

Dianne ran to the bathroom and lit her cigarette. Mark punched the remote control by Ricky's bed until the television was on and he found the local news. Nothing but weather and sports.

Dianne finished the story about Mr Clifford and placed the paper on the floor under the foldaway bed. Mark watched anxiously.

'His client killed a United States Senator,' she said in awe.

No kidding. There were about to be some tough questions, and Mark was suddenly hungry. It was past nine. Ricky hadn't moved. The nurses had forgotten about them. Greenway seemed like ancient history. The FBI was waiting somewhere in the darkness. The room was growing smaller by the minute, and the cheap cot on which he was sitting was ruining his back.

'I wonder why he did that,' he said because he could think of nothing else to say.

'It says Jerome Clifford had ties with the New Orleans mob, and that his client is widely thought to be a member.'

He'd seen *The Godfather* on cable. In fact, he'd even seen

83

the first sequel to *The Godfather*, and he knew all about the mob. Scenes from the movies flashed before his eyes, and the pains in his stomach grew sharper. His heart pounded. 'I'm hungry, Mom. Are you hungry?'

'Why didn't you tell me the truth, Mark?'

'Because the cop was in the trailer, and it wasn't a good time to talk. I'm sorry, Mom. I promise I'm sorry. I planned to tell you as soon as we were alone, I promise.'

She rubbed her temples and looked so sad. 'You never lie to me, Mark.'

Never say never. 'Can we talk about this later, Mom? I'm really hungry. Give me a couple of bucks and I'll run down to the cafeteria and get some doughnuts. I'd love a doughnut. I'll get you some coffee.' He was on his feet waiting for the money.

Fortunately, she was not in the mood for a serious talk about truthfulness and such. The Dalmane lingered and her thoughts were slow. Her head pounded. She opened her purse and gave him a five-dollar bill. 'Where's the cafeteria?'

'Basement. Madison Wing. I've been there twice.'

'Why am I not surprised? I suppose you've been all over this place.'

He took the money and crammed it in the pocket of his jeans. 'Yes ma'am. We're on the quietest floor. The babies are in the basement and it's a circus down there.'

'Be careful.'

He closed the door behind him. She waited, then took the bottle of valium from her purse. Greenway had sent it.

Mark ate four doughnuts during 'Donahue' and watched his mother try to nap on the bed. He kissed her on the forehead, and told her he needed to roam around a bit. She told him not to leave the hospital.

He used the stairs again because he figured Hardy and the FBI and the rest of the gang might be hanging around somewhere downstairs waiting for him to happen by.

Like most big-city charity hospitals, St Peter's had been

84

built over time whenever funds could be squeezed, with little thought of architectural symmetry. It was a sprawling and bewildering configuration of additions and wings, with a maze of hallways and corridors and mezzanines trying desperately to connect everything. Elevators and escalators had been added wherever they would fit. At some point in history, someone had realized the difficulty of moving from one point to another without getting hopelessly lost, and a dazzling array of color-coded signs had been implemented for the orderly flow of traffic. Then more wings were added. The signs became obsolete, but the hospital failed to remove them. Now they only added to the confusion.

Mark darted through now familiar territory and exited the hospital through a small lobby on Monroe Avenue. He'd studied a map of downtown in the front of the phone book, and he knew Gill Teal's office was within easy walking distance. It was on the third floor of a building four blocks away. He moved quickly. It was Tuesday, a school day, and he wanted to avoid truant officers. He was the only kid on the street, and he knew he was out of place.

A new strategy was developing. What was wrong, he asked himself as he stared at the sidewalk and avoided eye contact with the pedestrians passing by, with making an anonymous phone call to the cops or FBI and telling them exactly where the body was? The secret would no longer belong to him. If Romey wasn't lying, then the body would be found and the killer would go to jail.

There were risks. His phone call to 911 yesterday had been a disaster. Anybody on the other end of the phone would know he was just a kid. The FBI would record him and analyze his voice. The Mafia wasn't stupid.

Maybe it wasn't such a good idea.

He turned on Third Street, and darted into the Sterick Building. It was old and very tall. The lobby was tile and marble. He entered the elevator with a crowd of others, and punched the button for the third floor. Four other buttons were pushed by people wearing nice clothes and carrying

85

briefcases. They chatted quietly, in the normal hushed tones of elevator alk.

His stop was first. He stepped into a small lobby with hallways running left, right, and straight ahead. He went left, and roamed about innocently, trying to appear calm, as if lawyer shopping were a chore he'd done many times. There were plenty of lawyers in the building. Their names were etched on distinguished bronze plates screwed into the doors, and some doors were covered with rather long and intimidating names with lots of initials followed by periods. J. Winston Buckner. F. MacDonald Durston. I. Hempstead Crawford. The more names Mark read, the more he longed for plain old Gill Teal.

He found Mr Teal's door at the end of the hall, and there was no bronze plate. The words GILL TEAL – THE PEOPLE'S LAWYER were painted in bold black letters from the top of the door to the bottom. Three people waited in the hall beside it.

Mark swallowed, and entered the office. It was packed. The small waiting room was filled with sad people suffering from all sorts of injuries and wounds. Crutches were everywhere. Two people sat in wheelchairs. There were no empty seats, and one poor man in a neck brace sat on the cluttered coffee table, his head wobbling around like a newborn's. A lady with a dirty cast on her foot cried softly. A small girl with a horribly burned face clung to her mother. War could not have been more pitiful. It was worse than the emergency room at St Peter's.

Mr Teal certainly had been busy rounding up clients. Mark decided to leave, when someone called out rudely, 'What do you want?'

It was a large lady behind the receptionist's window. 'You, kid, you want something?' Her voice boomed around the room, but no one noticed. The suffering continued unabated. He stepped to the window and looked at the scowling, ugly face.

'I'd like to see Mr Teal,' he said softly, looking around.

'Oh you would. Do you have an appointment?' She picked up a clipboard and studied it.

86

'No, ma'am.'

'What's your name?'

'Uh, Mark Sway. It's a very private matter.'

'I'm sure it is.' She glared at him from head to toe. 'What type of injury is it?'

He thought about the Exxon truck and how it had excited Mr Teal, but he knew he couldn't pull it off. 'I, uh, I don't have an injury.'

'Well, you're in the wrong place. Why do you need a lawyer?'

'It's a long story.'

'Look, kid, you see these people? They've all got appointments to see Mr Teal. He's a very busy man, and he only takes cases involving death or injuries.'

'Okay.' Mark was already retreating and thinking about the minefield of canes and crutches behind him.

'Now please go bother someone else.'

'Sure. And if I get hit by a truck or something, I'll come back to see you.' He walked through the carnage, and made a quick exit.

He took the stairs down and explored the second floor. More lawyers. On one door he counted twenty-two bronze names. Lawyers on top of lawyers. Surely one of these guys could help him. He passed a few of them in the hall. They were too busy to notice.

A security guard suddenly appeared and walked slowly toward him. Mark glanced at the next door. The words REGGIE LOVE – LAWYER were painted on it in small letters, and he casually turned the knob and stepped inside. The small reception area was quiet and empty. Not a single client was waiting. Two chairs and a sofa sat around a glass table. The magazines were arranged neatly. Soft music came from above. A pretty rug covered the hardwood floor. A young man with a tie but no coat stood from his desk behind some potted trees, and walked a few steps forward. 'May I help you?' he asked, quite pleasantly.

'Yes. I need to see a lawyer.'

'You're a bit young to need a lawyer, aren't you?'

'Yes, but I'm having some problems. Are you Reggie Love?'

'No. Reggie's in the back. I'm her secretary. What's your name?'

He was her secretary. Reggie was a she. The secretary was a he. 'Uh, Mark Sway. You're a secretary?'

'And a paralegal, among other things. Why aren't you in school?' A nameplate on the desk identified him as Clint Van Hooser.

'So you're not a lawyer?'

'No. Reggie's the lawyer.'

'Then I need to speak with Reggie.'

'She's busy right now. You can have a seat.' He waved at the sofa.

'How long will it be?' Mark asked.

'I don't know.' The young man was amused by this kid needing a lawyer. 'I'll tell her you're here. Maybe she can see you for a minute.'

'It's very important.'

The kid was nervous and sincere. His eyes glanced at the door as if someone had followed him here. 'Are you in trouble, Mark?' Clint asked.

'Yes.'

'What type of trouble? You need to tell me a little about it, or Reggie won't talk to you.'

'I'm supposed to talk to the FBI at noon, and I think I need a lawyer.'

This was good enough. 'Have a seat. It'll be a minute.'

Mark eased into a chair, and as soon as Clint disappeared he opened a yellow phone book and flipped through the pages until he found the attorneys. There was Gill Teal again in his full-page spread. Pages and pages of huge ads, all crying out for injured people. Photos of busy and important men and women holding thick law books or sitting behind wide desks or listening intently to the telephones stuck in their ears. Then half-page ones, then quarter. Reggie Love was not there. What kind of lawyer was she?

Reggie Love was one of thousands in the Memphis yellow pages. She couldn't be much of a lawyer if the yellow pages thought so little of her, and the thought of racing from the office crossed his mind. But then there was Gill Teal, the one for real, the people's lawyer, the star of the yellow pages who also had enough fame to get himself on television, and just look at his office down the hall. No, he quickly decided, he'd take his chances with Reggie Love. Maybe she needed clients. Maybe she had more time to help him. The idea of a woman lawyer suddenly appealed to him because he'd seen one on 'LA Law' once and she had ripped up some cops pretty good. He closed the book and returned it carefully to the magazine rack beside the chair. The office was cool and pretty. There were no voices.

Clint closed the door behind him and eased across the Persian rug to her desk. Reggie Love was on the phone, listening more than talking. Clint placed three phone messages before her, and gave the standard hand signal to indicate someone was waiting in the reception area. He sat on the corner of the desk, straightening a paper clip and watching her.

There was no leather in the office. The walls were papered with light floral shades of rose and pink. A spotless desk of glass and chrome covered one corner of the rug. The chairs were sleek and upholstered with a burgundy fabric. This, without a doubt, was the office of a woman. A very neat woman.

Reggie Love was fifty-two years old, and had been practicing law for less than five years. She was of medium build with very short, very gray hair that fell in bangs almost to the top of her perfectly round, black-framed glasses. The eyes were green, and they glowed at Clint as if something funny had been said. Then she rolled them and shook her head. 'Goodbye, Sam,' she finally said, and hung up.

'Got a new client for you,' Clint said with a smile.

'I don't need new clients, Clint. I need clients who can pay. What's his name?'

'Mark Sway. He's just a kid, ten maybe twelve years old. And he says he's supposed to meet with the FBI at noon. Says he needs a lawyer.'

'He's alone?'

'Yeah.'

'How'd he find us?'

'I have no idea. I'm just the secretary, remember. You'll have to ask some questions yourself.'

Reggie stood and walked around the desk. 'Show him in. And rescue me in fifteen minutes, okay. I've got a busy morning.'

'Follow me Mark,' Clint said, and Mark followed him through a narrow door and down a hallway. Her office door was covered with stained glass, and a small brass plate again said REGGIE LOVE – LAWYER. Clint opened the door, and motioned for Mark to enter.

The first thing he noticed about her was her hair. It was gray and shorter than his; very short above the ears and in the back, a bit thicker on top with bangs halfway down. He'd never seen a woman with gray hair worn so short. She wasn't old and she wasn't young.

She smiled appropriately as they met at the door. 'Mark, I'm Reggie Love.' She offered her hand, he took it reluctantly, and she squeezed hard and shook firm. Shaking hands with women was not something he did often. She was neither tall nor short, thin nor heavy. Her dress was straight and black and she wore black and gold bracelets on both wrists. They rattled.

'Nice to meet you,' he said weakly as they shook. She was already leading him to a corner of the office where two soft chairs faced a table with picture books on it.

'Have a seat,' she said. 'I only have a minute.'

Mark sat on the edge of his seat, and was suddenly terrified. He'd lied to his mother. He'd lied to the police. He'd lied to Dr Greenway. He was about to lie to the FBI. Romey had been dead less than a day, and he was lying right and left to everyone who asked. Tomorrow he would certainly lie to the next person. Maybe it was time to come clean for a change. Sometimes it was frightening to tell the truth, but he usually felt better afterward. But the thought of unloading all this baggage on a stranger made his blood run cold.

'Would you like something to drink?'

'No ma'am.'

She crossed her legs. 'Mark Sway, right? Please do not call me ma'am, all right? My name is not Ms Love or any of that, my name is Reggie. I'm old enough to be your grandmother, but you call me Reggie, okay?'

'Okay.'

'How old are you, Mark? Tell me a little about yourself.'

'I'm eleven. I'm in the fifth grade at Willow Road.'

'Why aren't you in school this morning?'

'It's a long story.'

'I see. And you're here because of this long story?'

'Yes.'

'Do you want to tell me this long story?'

'I think so.'

'Clint said you're supposed to meet with the FBI at noon. Is this true?'

'Yes. They want to ask me some questions at the hospital.'

She picked up a legal pad from the table and wrote something on it. 'The hospital?'

'It's part of the long story. Can I ask you something, Reggie?' It was strange calling this lady by a baseball name. He'd watched a cheap TV movie about the life of Reggie Jackson, and remembered the crowd chanting Reggie! Reggie! in perfect unison. Then there was the Reggie candy bar.

'Sure.' She grinned a lot, and it was obvious she enjoyed this scene with the kid who needed a lawyer. Mark knew the smiles would disappear if he made it through the story. She had pretty eyes, and they sparkled at him.

'If I tell you something, will you ever repeat it?' he asked.

'Of course not. It's privileged, confidential.'

'What does that mean?'

91

'It means simply that I can never repeat anything you tell me, unless you tell me I can repeat it.'

'Never?'

'Never. It's like talking to your doctor or minister. The conversations are secret and held in trust. Do you understand?'

'I think so. Under no circumstances –'

'Never. Under no circumstances can I tell anyone what you tell me.'

'What if I told you something that no one else knows?'

'I can't repeat it.'

'Something the police really want to know?'

'I can't repeat it.' She at first was amused by these questions, but his determination made her wonder.

'Something that could get you into a lot of trouble.'

'I can't repeat it.'

Mark looked at her without blinking for a long minute, and convinced himself she could be trusted. Her face was warm and her eyes were comforting. She was relaxed and easy to talk to.

'Any more questions?' she asked.

'Yeah. Where'd you get the name Reggie?'

'I changed my name several years ago. It was Regina, and I was married to a doctor, and then all sorts of bad things happened so I changed my name to Reggie.'

'You're divorced?'

'Yes.'

'My parents are divorced.'

'I'm sorry.'

'Don't be sorry. My brother and I were really happy when they got a divorce. My father drank a lot and beat us. Beat Mom too. Me and Ricky always hated him.'

'Ricky's your brother?'

'Yes. He's the one in the hospital.'

'What's the matter with him?'

'It's part of the long story.'

'When would you like to tell me this story?'

Mark hesitated a few seconds and thought about a few

92

things. He wasn't quite ready to tell all. 'How much do you charge?'

'I don't know. What kind of case is it?'

'What kind of cases do you take?'

'Mostly cases involving abused or neglected children. Some abandoned children. Lots of adoptions. A few medical malpractice cases involving infants. But mainly abuse cases. I get some pretty bad cases.'

'Good, because this is a really bad one. One person is dead. One is in the hospital. The police and FBI want to talk to me.'

'Look, Mark, I assume you don't have a lot of money to hire me, do you?'

'No.'

'Technically, you're supposed to pay me something as a retainer, and once this is done I'm your lawyer and we'll go from there. Do you have a dollar?'

'Yes.'

'Then why don't you give it to me as a retainer.'

Mark pulled a one-dollar bill from his pocket and handed it to her. 'This is all I've got.'

Reggie didn't want the kid's dollar, but she took it because ethics were ethics and because it would probably be his last payment. And he was proud of himself for hiring a lawyer. She would somehow return it to him.

She laid the bill on the table, and said, 'Okay, now I'm the lawyer and you're the client. Let's hear the story.'

He reached into his pocket again and pulled out the folded clipping from the newspaper Greenway had given them. He handed it to her. 'Have you seen this?' he asked. 'It's in this morning's paper.' His hand was trembling and the paper shook.

'Are you scared, Mark?'

'Sort of.'

'Try to relax, okay.'

'Okay, I'll try. Have you seen this?'

'No, I haven't seen the paper yet.' She took the clipping and read it. Mark watched her eyes closely.

'Okay,' she said when she finished.

'It mentions the body was found by two boys. Well, that's me and Ricky.'

'Well, I'm sure that must've been awful, but it's no crime to find a dead body.'

'Good. Because there's much more to the story.'

Her smile had disappeared. The pen was ready. 'I want to hear it now.'

Mark breathed deeply and rapidly. The four doughnuts churned away in his stomach. He was scared, but he also knew he would feel much better when it was over. He settled deep in the chair, took a long breath, and looked at the floor.

He started with his career as a smoker, and Ricky catching him, and going to the woods. Then the car, the water hose, the fat man who turned out to be Jerome Clifford. He spoke slowly because he wanted to remember it all, and because he wanted his new lawyer to write it all down.

Clint attempted to interrupt after fifteen minutes, but Reggie frowned at him. He quickly closed the door and disappeared.

The first account took twenty minutes with few interruptions from Reggie. There were gaps and holes, none the fault of Mark, just soft spots that she picked through during the second pass, which took another twenty minutes. They broke for coffee and ice water, all fetched by Clint, and Reggie moved the conversation to her desk where she spread out her notes and prepared for the third run-through of this remarkable story. She filled one legal pad, and started another. The smiles were long gone. The friendly, patronizing chitchat from the grandmother to her grandchild had been replaced with pointed questions picking for details.

The only details Mark withheld were the ones describing the exact location of the body of Senator Boyd Boyette, or rather Romey's story about the body. As the secret and confidential conversaton unfolded, it became obvious to Reggie that Mark knew where the body was allegedly buried, and she skilfully and fearfully danced around this information. Maybe she would ask, maybe she wouldn't. But it would be the last thing discussed.

An hour after they started, she took a break and read the newspaper story twice. Then again. It seemed to fit. He knew too many details to be lying. This was not a story a hyperactive mind could fabricate. And the poor kid was scared to death.

Clint interrupted again at eleven-thirty to inform Reggie her next appointment had been waiting for an hour. Cancel it, Reggie said without looking from her notes, and Clint was gone. Mark walked around her office as she read. He stood in her window and watched the traffic on Third Street below. Then he returned to his seat and waited.

His lawyer was deeply troubled, and he almost felt sorry for her. All those names and faces in the yellow pages, and he had to drop this bomb on Reggie Love.

'What are you afraid of, Mark?' she asked, rubbing her eyes.

'Lots of things. I've lied to the police about this, and I think they know I'm lying. And that scares me. My little brother's in a coma because of me. It's all my fault. I lied to his doctor. And all that scares me. I don't know what to do, and I guess that's why I'm here. What should I do?'

'Have you told me everything?'

'No, but almost.'

'Have you lied to me?'

'No.'

'Do you know where the body is buried?'

'I think so. I know what Jerome Clifford told me.'

For a split second, Reggie was terrified he would blurt it out. But he didn't, and they stared at each other for a long time.

'Do you want to tell me where it is?' she finally asked.

'Do you want me to?'

'I'm not sure. What keeps you from telling me?'

'I'm scared. I don't want anybody to know that I know, because Romey told me his client had killed many people

95

and was planning on killing Romey too. If he's killed lots of people, and if he thinks I know this secret, he'll come after me. And if I tell this stuff to the cops then he'll come after me for sure. He's in the Mafia, and that really scares me. Wouldn't it scare you?'

'I think so.'

'And the cops have threatened me if I don't tell the truth, and they think I'm lying anyway, and I just don't know what to do. Do you think I should tell the police and the FBI?'

Reggie stood and walked slowly to the window. She had no wonderful advice at this point. If she suggested that her newest client spill his guts to the FBI, and he followed her advice, his life could indeed be in danger. There was no law requiring him to tell. Obstruction of justice, maybe, but he was just a kid. They didn't know for certain what he knew, and if they couldn't prove it, he was safe.

'Let's do this, Mark. Don't tell me where the body is, okay? For now anyway. Maybe later, but not now. And let's meet with the FBI and listen to them. You won't have to say a word. I'll do the talking, and we'll both do the listening. And when it's over, you and I will decide what to do next.'

'Sounds good to me.'

'Does your mother know you're here?'

'No. I need to call her.'

Reggie found the number in the phone book and dialled the hospital. Mark explained to Dianne that he had gone for a walk and would be there in a minute. He was a smooth liar, Reggie noticed. He listened for a while and looked disturbed. 'How is he?' he asked. 'I'll be there in a minute.'

He hung up and looked at Reggie. 'Mom's upset. Ricky's coming out of the coma and she can't find Dr Greenway.'

'I'll walk with you to the hospital.'

'That would be nice.'

'Where does the FBI want to meet?'

'I think at the hospital.'

She checked her watch and threw two fresh legal pads into her briefcase. She was suddenly nervous. Mark waited by the door.

NINE

The second lawyer hired by Barry The Blade Muldanno to defend him on these obnoxious murder charges was another angry hatchet man by the name of Willis Upchurch, a rising star among the gang of boisterous mouthpieces trotting across the country performing for crooks and cameras. Upchurch had offices in Chicago and Washington, and any other city where he could hook a famous case and rent space. As soon as he talked with Muldanno after breakfast, he was on a plane to New Orleans to, first, organize a press conference and, second, meet with his famous new client and plot a noisy defense. He had become somewhat rich and noted in Chicago for his passionate defense of mob assassins and drug traffickers, and in the past decade or so had been called in by mob brass around the country for all sorts of representation. His record was average, but it was not his won/lost ratio that attracted clients. It was his angry face and bushy hair and thunderous voice. Upchurch was a lawyer who wanted to be seen and heard in magazine articles, news stories, advice columns, quickie books, and gossip shows. He had opinions. He was unafraid of predictions. He was radical and would say anything, and this made him a favorite of the loony daytime TV talk shows.

He took only sensational cases with lots of headlines and cameras. Nothing was too repulsive for him. He preferred rich clients who could pay, but if a serial killer needed help, Upchurch would be there with a contract giving himself exclusive book and movie rights.

Though he enjoyed his notoriety immensely, and received some praise from the far left for his vigorous defense of indigent murderers, Upchurch was little more than a Mafia lawyer. He was owned by the mob, yanked around by their strings, and paid whenever they decided. He was allowed to roam a bit and spout at the mouth, but if they called, he came running.

And when Johnny Sulari, Barry's uncle, called at four in the morning, Willis Upchurch came running. The uncle explained the scarce facts about the untimely death of Jerome Clifford. Upchurch drooled into the receiver as Sulari asked him to fly immediately to New Orleans. He skipped to the bathroom at the thought of defending Barry The Blade Muldanno in front of all those cameras. He whistled in the shower when he thought of all the ink the case had already generated, and how he would now be the star. He grinned at himself in the mirror as he tied his ninety-dollar tie and thought of spending the next six months in New Orleans with the press at his beck and call.

This was why he went to law school!

The scene was frightening at first. The IV had been removed because Dianne was in the bed clutching Ricky and rubbing his head. She hugged him fiercely and wrapped her legs around his. He was moaning and grunting, twisting and jerking. His eyes were open, then shut. Dianne pressed her head to his and spoke softly through her tears. 'It's okay, baby. It's okay. Mommy's here. Mommy's here.'

Greenway stood close by, arms folded, rubbing his beard. He appeared puzzled, as if he hadn't seen this before. A nurse held the other side of the bed.

Mark entered the room slowly and no one noticed. Reggie had stopped at the nurses' station. It was almost noon, time for the FBI and all, but Mark knew immediately that no one in the room was remotely concerned with the cops and their questions.

'It's okay, baby. It's okay. Mommy's here.'

98

Mark inched to the foot of the bed for a closer look. Dianne managed a quick, uncomfortable smile, then closed her eyes and kept whispering to Ricky.

After a few long minutes of this, Ricky opened his eyes, seemed to notice and recognize his mother, and grew still. She kissed him a dozen times on the forehead. The nurse smiled and patted his shoulder and cooed something at him.

Greenway looked at Mark and nodded at the door. Mark followed him outside, into the quiet hallway. They walked slowly toward the end of it, away from the nurses' station.

'He woke up about two hours ago,' the doctor explained. 'It looks like he's coming out of it slowly.'

'Has he said anything yet?'

'Like what?'

'Well, you know, like about what happened yesterday.'

'No. He's mumbled a lot, which is a good sign, but he hasn't made any words yet.'

This was comforting, in a sense. Mark would have to stick close to the room just in case. 'So he's gonna be okay?'

'I didn't say that.' The lunch cart stopped in the middle of the hall and they walked around it. 'I think he'll be okay, but it could take time.' There was a long pause in which Mark worried if Greenway expected him to say something.

'How strong is your mother?'

'Pretty strong, I guess. We've been through a lot.'

'Where's the family? She'll need plenty of help.'

'There's no family. She has a sister in Texas, but they don't get along. And her sister has problems too.'

'Your grandparents?'

'No. My ex-father was an orphan. I figure his parents probably dumped him somewhere when they got to know him. My mother's father is dead, and her mother lives in Texas too. She's sick all the time.'

'I'm sorry.'

They stopped at the end of the hall and looked through a dirty window at downtown Memphis. The Sterick Building stood tall.

'The FBI is bugging me,' Greenway said.

Join the club, Mark thought. 'Where are they?'

'Room 28. It's a small conference room on the second floor that's seldom used. They said they'd be expecting me, you, and your mother at exactly noon, and they sounded very serious.' Greenway glanced at his watch, and started to walk back to the room. 'They are quite anxious.'

'I'm ready for them,' Mark said in a weak effort at boldness.

Greenway frowned at him. 'How's that?'

'I've hired us a lawyer,' he said proudly.

'When?'

'This morning. She's here now, down the hall.'

Greenway looked ahead but the nurses' station was around a bend in the corridor. 'The lawyer's here?' he asked in disbelief.

'Yep.'

'How'd you find a lawyer?'

'It's a long story. But I paid her myself.'

Greenway pondered this as he shuffled along. 'Well, your mother cannot leave Ricky right now, under any circumstances. And I certainly need to stay close.'

'No problem. Me and the lawyer will handle it.'

They stopped at Ricky's door, and Greenway hesitated before pushing it open. 'I can put them off until tomorrow. In fact, I can order them out of the hospital.' He was attempting to sound tough, but Mark knew better.

'No, thanks. They won't go away. You take care of Ricky and Mom, and me and the lawyer'll take care of the FBI.'

Reggie had found an empty room on the eighth floor, and they hurried down the stairs to use it. They were ten minutes late. She closed the door quickly, and said, 'Pull up your shirt.'

He froze, and stared at her.

'Pull up your shirt!' she insisted, and he began pulling at his bulky Memphis State Tigers sweatshirt. She opened her briefcase and removed a small, black recorder and a strip of

100

plastic and Velcro. She checked the micro-cassette tape, then punched the buttons. Mark watched every move. She'd used this device many times before, he could tell. She pressed it to his stomach, and said, 'Hold it right here.' Then she threaded the plastic strap through a clip on the recorder, wrapped it around his mid-section and back, and fastened it snugly with the Velcro ends. 'Breathe deeply,' she said, and he did.

He tucked the sweatshirt into his jeans. Reggie took a step back and stared at his stomach. 'Perfect,' she said.

'What if they frisk me?'

'They won't. Let's go.'

She grabbed her briefcase, and they were out the door.

'How do you know they won't frisk me?' he asked again, very anxious. He walked fast to keep up with her. A nurse looked at them suspiciously.

'Because they're here to talk, not to arrest. Just trust me.'

'I trust you, but I'm really scared.'

'You'll do fine, Mark. Just remember what I told you.'

'Are you sure they can't see this thing?'

'I'm positive.' She pushed hard through a door and they were back in the stairwell, descending quickly on green concrete steps. Mark was one step behind. 'What if the beeper goes off or something and they freak out and pull guns? What then?'

'No beeper.' She took his hand, squeezed it hard, and zig-zagged downward to the second floor. 'And they don't shoot kids.'

'They did in a movie once.'

The second floor of St Peter's had been built many years before the ninth. It was gray and dirty, and the narrow corridors were swarming with the usual anxious traffic of nurses, doctors, technicians, and orderlies pushing stretchers, and patients rolling along in wheelchairs, and dazed families walking to nowhere in particular and trying to stay awake. Corridors met from all directions in chaotic little junctions, then branched out again in a hopeless

101

labyrinth. Reggie asked three nurses about the location of Room 28, and the third pointed and talked but never stopped walking. They found a neglected hallway with ancient carpet and bad lighting, and six doors down to the right was their room. The door was cheap wood with no window.

'I'm scared, Reggie,' Mark said, staring at the door.

She held his hand firmly. If she was nervous, it was not apparent. Her face was calm. Her voice was warm and reassuring. 'Just do as I told you, Mark. I know what I'm doing.'

They retreated a step or two, and Reggie opened an identical door to Room 24. It was an abandoned coffee room now used for haphazard storage. 'I'll wait in here. Now, go knock on the door.'

'I'm scared, Reggie.'

She carefully felt the recorder, and worked her fingers around it until she pushed the button. 'Now go,' she instructed and pointed down the hall.

Mark took a deep breath and knocked on the door. He could hear chairs move inside. 'Come in,' someone said, and the voice was not friendly. He opened the door slowly, stepped inside, and closed it behind him. The room was narrow and long, just like the table in the center of it. No windows. No smiles from the two men who stood on each side of the table near the end. They could pass for twins – white button-down shirts, red-and-blue ties, dark pants, short hair.

'You must be Mark,' one said as the other stared at the door.

Mark nodded, but could not speak.

'Where's your mother?'

'Uh, who are you?' Mark managed to get it out.

The one on the right said, 'I'm Jason McThune, FBI, Memphis.' He stuck out his hand and Mark shook it limply. 'Nice to meet you, Mark.'

'Yeah, my pleasure.'

'And I'm Larry Trumann,' said the other. 'FBI, New

102

Orleans.' Mark allowed Trumann the same feeble hand-shake. The agents exchanged nervous looks, and for an awkward second neither knew what to say.

Trumann finally pointed to the chair at the end of the table. 'Have a seat, Mark.' McThune nodded his agreement and almost smiled. Mark carefully sat down, terrified the Velcro would break away and the damned thing would somehow fall off. They'd handcuff his little butt so fast and throw him in the car and he'd never see his mother again. What would Reggie do then? They moved toward him in their rolling chairs. They slid their notepads on the table to within inches of him.

They were breathing on him, and Mark figured it was part of the game. Then he almost smiled. If they wanted to sit this close, fine. But the black recorder would get it all. No fading voices.

'We, uh, we really expected your mother and Dr Greenway to be here,' Trumann said, glancing at McThune.

'They're with my brother.'

'How is he?' McThune asked gravely.

'Not too good. Mom can't leave his room right now.'

'We thought she'd be here,' Trumann said again and looked at McThune as if uncertain how to proceed.

'Well, we can wait a day or two until she's available,' Mark offered.

'No, Mark, we really need to talk now.'

'Maybe I can go get her.'

Trumann took his pen from his shirt pocket, and smiled at Mark. 'No, let's talk a few minutes, Mark. Just the three of us. Are you nervous?'

'A little. What do you want?' He was still stiff with fear but breathing better. The recorder hadn't beeped or shocked him.

'Well, we want to ask you some questions about yesterday.'

'Do I need a lawyer?'

They looked at each other with perfectly symmetrical

103

open mouths, and at least five seconds passed before McThune cocked his head at Mark and said, 'Of course not.'

'Why not?'

'Well, we just, you know, want to ask you a few questions. That's all. If you decide you want your mother, then we'll go get her. Or something. But you don't need a lawyer. Just a few questions, that's all.'

'I've already talked to the cops once. In fact, I talked to the cops for a long time last night.'

'We're not cops. We're FBI agents.'

'That's what scares me. I think maybe I need a lawyer to, you know, protect my rights and all.'

'You've been watching too much TV, kid.'

'The name's Mark, okay? Can you at least call me Mark?'

'Sure. Sorry. But you don't need a lawyer.'

'Yeah,' Trumann chimed in. 'Lawyers just get in the way. You have to pay them money, and they object to everything.'

'Don't you think we should wait until my mother can be here?'

They exchanged matching little smiles, and McThune said, 'Not really, Mark. I mean, we can wait if you want to, but you're a smart kid and we're really in a hurry here, and we just have a few quick questions for you.'

'Okay. I guess. If I have to.'

Trumann looked at his notepad, and went first. 'Good. You told the Memphis Police that Jerome Clifford was already dead when you and Ricky found the car yesterday. Now, Mark, is this really the truth?' He sort of sneered toward the end of the question as if he knew damned well it wasn't the truth.

Mark fidgeted and looked straight ahead. 'Do I have to answer the question?'

'Sure you do.'

'Why?'

'Because we need to know the truth, Mark. We're the FBI, and we're investigating this thing, and we must know the truth.'

104

'What happens if I don't answer?'

'Oh, lots of things. We might be forced to take you down to our office, in the backseat of the car of course, no handcuffs, and ask some really tough questions. May have to bring along your mother too.'

'What will happen to my mother? Can she get in trouble?'

'Maybe.'

'What kind of trouble?'

They paused for a second and exchanged nervous looks. They had started on shaky ground, and things were getting shakier by the minute. Children are not to be interviewed without first talking to the parents.

But what the hell. His mother didn't know. He had no father. He was a poor kid, and here he was all alone. It was perfect, really. They couldn't ask for a better situation. Just a couple of quick questions.

McThune cleared his throat and went into a deep frown. 'Mark, have you ever heard of obstruction of justice?'

'I don't think so.'

'Well, it's a crime, okay. A federal offense. A person who knows something about a crime, and withholds this information from the FBI or the police, might be found guilty of obstruction of justice.'

'What happens then?'

'Well, if found guilty, such a person might be punished. You know, sent to jail or something like that.'

'So, if I don't answer your questions, me and Mom might go to jail?'

McThune retreated a bit and looked at Trumann. The ice was getting thinner. 'Why don't you want to answer the question, Mark?' Trumann asked. 'Are you hiding something?'

'I'm just scared. And it doesn't seem fair since I'm just eleven years old and you're the FBI, and my mom's not here. I don't know what to do, really.'

'Can't you just answer the questions, Mark, without your mother? You saw something yesterday, and your mother was not around. She can't help you answer the questions. We just want to know what you saw.'

'If you were in my place, would you want a lawyer?'

'Hell no,' McThune said. 'I would never want a lawyer. Pardon my language, son, but they're just a pain in the ass. A real pain. If you have nothing to hide, you don't need a lawyer. Just answer our questions truthfully, and everything will be fine.' He was becoming angry, and this did not surprise Mark. One of them had to be angry. It was the good guy-bad guy routine Mark had seen a thousand times on television. McThune would get ugly, and Trumann would smile a lot and sometimes even frown at his partner for Mark's benefit, and this would somehow endear Trumann to Mark. McThune would then get disgusted and leave the room, and Mark would then be expected to spill his guts all over the table.

Trumann leaned to him with a drippy smile. 'Mark, was Jerome Clifford already dead when you and Ricky found him?'

'I take the Fifth Amendment.'

The drippy smile vanished. McThune's face reddened, and he shook his head in absolute frustration. There was a long pause as the agents stared at each other. Mark watched an ant crawl across the table and disappear under a notepad.

Trumann, the good guy, finally spoke. 'Mark, I'm afraid you've been watching too much television.'

'You mean, I can't take the Fifth Amendment?'

'Lemme guess,' McThune snarled. 'You watch "LA Law," right?'

'Every week.'

'Figures. Are you gonna answer any questions, Mark? Because if you're not, then we have to do other things.'

'Like what?'

'Go to court. Talk to the judge. Convince him to require you to talk to us. It's pretty nasty, really.'

'I need to go to the rest room,' Mark said as he slid his chair away from the table and stood.

'Uh, sure, Mark,' Trumann said, suddenly afraid they'd

made him sick. 'I think it's just down the hall.' Mark was at the door.

'Take five minutes, Mark, we'll wait. No hurry.'

He left the room and closed the door behind him.

For seventeen minutes, the agents made small talk and played with their pens. They weren't worried. They were experienced agents with many tricks. They'd been here before. He would talk.

A knock, and McThune said, 'Come in.' The door opened, and an attractive lady of fifty or so walked in and closed the door as if this were her office. They scrambled to their feet just as she said, 'Keep your seats.'

'We're in a meeting,' Trumann said officially.

'You're in the wrong room,' McThune said rudely.

She placed her briefcase on the table and handed each agent a white card. 'I don't think so,' she said. 'My name is Reggie Love. I'm an attorney, and I represent Mark Sway.'

They took it well. McThune inspected the card while Trumann just stood there, arms dangling by his legs, trying to say something.

'When did he hire you?' McThune said, looking wildly at Trumann.

'That's really none of your business, is it now? I'm not hired. I'm retained. Sit down.'

She eased gracefully into her seat and rolled it to the table. They backed awkwardly into theirs, and kept their distance.

'Where's, uh, where's Mark?' Trumann asked.

'He's off somewhere taking the Fifth. Can I see your ID, please?'

They instantly reached for their jackets, fished around desperately, and simultaneously produced their badges. She held both, studied them carefully, then wrote something on a legal pad.

When she finished, she slid them across the table and asked, 'Did you in fact attempt to interrogate this child outside the presence of his mother?'

'No,' said Trumann.

'Of course not,' said McThune, shocked at this suggestion.

'He tells me you did.'

'He's confused,' said McThune. 'We initially approached Dr Greenway, and he agreed to this meeting, which was supposed to include Mark, Dianne Sway, and the doctor.'

'But the kid showed up alone,' Trumann added quickly, very anxious to explain things. 'And we asked where his mother was, and he said she couldn't make it right now, and we sort of thought she was on her way or something, so we were just chitchatting with the kid.'

'Yeah, while we waited for Ms Sway and the doctor,' McThune chimed in helpfully. 'Where were you during this?'

'Don't ask questions that are irrelevant. Did you advise Mark to talk to a lawyer?'

The agents locked eyes and searched each other for help. 'It wasn't mentioned,' Trumann said, shrugging innocently.

It was easier to lie because the kid wasn't there. And he was just a scared little kid who'd gotten things confused, and they were, after all, FBI agents, so she'd eventually believe them.

McThune cleared his throat and said, 'Uh, yeah, once, Larry, remember Mark said something, or maybe I said something about "LA Law", and then Mark said he might need a lawyer, but he was sort of kidding and we, or at least I, took it as a joke. Remember, Larry?'

Larry now remembered. 'Oh, sure, yeah, something about "LA Law". Just a joke though.'

'Are you sure?' Reggie asked.

'Of course I'm sure,' Trumann protested. McThune frowned and nodded along with his partner.

'He didn't ask you guys if he needed a lawyer?'

They shook their heads and tried hopelessly to remember. 'I don't remember it that way. He's just a kid, and very scared, and I think he's confused,' McThune said.

'Did you advise him of his Miranda rights?'

Trumann smiled at this and was suddenly more confident. 'Of course not. He's not a suspect. He's just a kid. We need to ask him a few questions.'

'And you did not attempt to interrogate him without his mother's presence or consent?'

'No.'

'Of course not.'

'And you did not tell him to avoid lawyers after he asked your advice?'

'No ma'am.'

'No way. The kid's lying if he told you otherwise.'

Reggie slowly opened her briefcase and lifted out the black recorder and the micro-cassette tape. She sat them in front of her, and placed the briefcase on the floor. Special Agents McThune and Trumann stared at the devices and seemed to shrink a bit in their seats.

Reggie rewarded each with a bitchy smile, and said, 'I think we know who's lying.'

McThune slid two fingers down the bridge of his nose. Trumann rubbed his eyes. She let them suffer for a moment. The room was silent.

'It's all right here on tape, fellas. You boys attempted to interrogate a child outside the presence of his mother and without her consent. He specifically asked you if you shouldn't wait until she was available and you said no. You attempted to coerce the child with the threat of criminal prosecution not only for the child but also for his mother. He told you he was scared, and twice he specifically asked you if he needed a lawyer. You advised him not to get a lawyer, giving as one of your reasons the opinion that lawyers are a pain in the ass. Gentlemen, the pain is here.'

They sunk lower. McThune pressed four fingers against his forehead and gently rubbed. Trumann stared in disbelief at the tape, but was careful not to look at this woman. He thought of grabbing it, and ripping it to shreds, and stomping on it because it could be his career, but for some reason he believed with all his troubled heart that this woman had made a copy of it.

Getting slapped with a lie was bad enough, but their problems ran much deeper. There could be serious disciplinary proceedings. Reprimands. Transfers. Crap in the record. And at this moment, Trumann also believed that this woman knew all there was to know about the disciplining of wayward FBI agents.

'You wired the kid,' Trumann said meekly to no one in particular.

'Why not? No crime. You're the FBI, remember. You boys run more wire than AT&T.'

What a smartass! But then, she was a lawyer, wasn't she? McThune leaned forward, cracked his knuckles, and decided to offer some resistance. 'Look, Ms Love, we –'

'It's Reggie.'

'Okay, okay. Reggie, uh, look, we're sorry. We, uh, got a little carried away, and, well, we apologize.'

'A little carried away? I could have your jobs for this.'

They were not about to argue with her. She was probably right, and even if there was room for debate they simply were not up to it.

'Are you taping this?' Trumann asked.

'No.'

'Okay, we were out of line. We're sorry.' He could not look at her.

Reggie slowly placed the tape in her coat pocket. 'Look at me, fellas.' They slowly lifted their eyes to hers, but it was painful. 'You've already proven to me that you'll lie, and that you'll lie quickly. Why should I trust you?'

Trumann suddenly slapped the table, hissed, and made a noisy show of standing and pacing to the end of the table. He threw up his hands. 'This is incredible. We came here with just a few questions for the kid, just doing our jobs, and now we're fighting with you. The kid didn't tell us he had a lawyer. If he'd told us, then we would have backed off. Why'd you do this? Why'd you deliberately pick this fight? It's senseless.'

'What do you want from the kid?'

'The truth. He's lying about what he saw yesterday. We

110

know he's lying. We know he talked to Jerome Clifford before Clifford killed himself. We know the kid was in the car. Maybe I don't blame him for lying. He's just a kid. He's scared. But dammit, we need to know what he saw and heard.'

'What do you suspect he saw and heard?'

The nightmare of explaining this to Foltrigg suddenly hit Trumann, and he leaned against the wall. This is exactly why he hated lawyers – Foltrigg, Reggie, the next one he met. They made life so complicated.

'Has he told you everything?' McThune asked.

'Our conversations are extremely private.'

'I know that. But do you realize who Clifford was, and Muldanno and Boyd Boyette? Do you know the story?'

'I read the paper this morning. I've kept up with the case in New Orleans. You boys need the body, don't you?'

'You could say that,' Trumann said from the end of the table. 'But at this moment we really need to talk to your client.'

'I'll think about it.'

'When might you reach a decision?'

'I don't know. Are you boys busy this afternoon?'

'Why?'

'I need to talk to my client some more. Let's say we'll meet in my office at 3 p.m.' She took her briefcase and placed the recorder in it. It was obvious this meeting was over. 'I'll keep the tape to myself. It'll just be our little secret, okay?'

McThune nodded his agreement, but knew there was more.

'If I need something from you boys, like the truth or a straight answer, I expect to get it. If I catch you lying again, I'll use the tape.'

'That's blackmail,' said Trumann.

'That's exactly what it is. Indict me.' She stood and grabbed the doorknob. 'See you boys at three.'

McThune followed her. 'Uh, listen, Reggie, there's this guy who'll probably want to be at the meeting. His name is Roy Foltrigg, and he's –'

'Mr Foltrigg is in town?'

'Yes. He arrived last night, and he'll insist on attending this meeting at your office.'

'Well, well. I'm honored. Please invite him.'

TEN

The front page story in the *Memphis Press* about Clifford's death was written top to bottom by Slick Moeller, a veteran police reporter who had been covering crime and cops in Memphis for thirty years. His real name was Alfred, but no one knew it. His mother called him Slick, but not even she could remember the nickname's origins. Three wives and a hundred girlfriends had called him Slick. He did not dress exceptionally well, did not finish high school, did not have money, was blessed with average looks and build, drove a Mustang, could not keep a woman, and so no one knew why he was called Slick.

Crime was his life. He knew the drug dealers and pimps. He drank beer at the topless bars and gossiped with the bouncers. He kept charts on the who's who of motorcycle gangs that supplied the city with drugs and strippers. He could move deftly through the toughest projects of Memphis without a scratch. He knew the rank and file of the street gangs. He had busted no less than a dozen stolen car rings by tipping the police. He knew the ex-cons, especially the ones who returned to crime. He could spot a fencing operation simply by watching the pawnshops. His cluttered down-town apartment was most unremarkable except for an entire wall of emergency scanners and police radios. His Mustang had more junk than a police cruiser, except for a radar gun, and he didn't want one.

Slick Moeller lived and moved in the dark shadows of Memphis. He was often on the crime scene before the cops.

113

He moved freely about the morgues and hospitals and black funeral parlors. He had nurtured thousands of contacts and sources, and they talked to Slick because he could be trusted. If it was off the record, then it was off the record. Background was background. An informant would never be compromised. Tips were guarded zealously. Slick was a man of his word, and even the street gang leaders knew it.

He was also on a first-name basis with virtually every cop in the city, many of whom referred to him with great admiration as the Mole. Mole Moeller did this. Mole Moeller said that. Since Slick had become his real name, the added nickname did not bother him. Nothing bothered Slick much. He drank coffee with cops in a hundred all-night diners around town. He watched them play softball, knew when their wives filed for divorce, knew when they got themselves reprimanded. He was at Central Head-quarters at least twenty hours a day, it seemed, and it was not uncommon for cops to stop him and ask what was going on. Who got shot? Where was the holdup? Was the driver drunk? How many were killed? Slick told them as much as he could. He helped them whenever possible. His name was often mentioned in classes at the Memphis Police Academy.

And so it was no surprise to anyone that Slick spent the entire morning fishing around Central. He'd made his calls to New Orleans and knew the basics. He knew Roy Foltrigg and New Orleans FBI were in town, and that everything had been turned over to them. This intrigued him. It was not just a simple suicide; there were too many blank faces and 'no comments'. There was a note of some sort, and all questions about it were met with sudden denials. He could read the faces of some of these cops, been doing it for years. He knew about the boys and that the younger one was in bad shape. There were some fingerprints, some cigarette butts.

He left the elevator on the ninth floor and walked away from the nurses' station. He knew the number of Ricky's room, but this was the psychiatric ward and he was not about to go barging in with his questions. He didn't want to scare anyone, especially an eight-year-old kid who was in shock. He stuck two quarters in the soft drink machine and sipped on a diet Coke as if he'd been there all night walking the floors. An orderly in a light blue jacket pushed a cart of cleaning supplies to the elevator. He was a male, about twenty-five, long hair, and certainly bored with his menial job.

Slick stepped to the elevators, and when the door opened he followed the orderly into it. The name Fred was sewn into the jacket above the pocket. They were alone.

'You work the ninth floor?' Slick asked, bored but with a smile.

'Yeah.' Fred did not look at him.

'I'm Slick Moeller with the *Memphis Press*, working on a story about Ricky Sway in Room 943. You know, the shooting and all.' He'd learned early in his career that it was best to tell them up front who and what.

Fred was suddenly interested. He stood erect and looked at Slick as if to say 'Yeah, I know plenty, but you're not getting it from me.' The cart between them was filled with Ajax, Comet, and twenty bottles of generic hospital supplies. A bucket of dirty rags and sponges covered the bottom tray. Fred was a toilet scrubber but, in a flash, he became a man with the inside scoop. 'Yeah,' he said calmly.

'Have you seen the kid?' Slick asked nonchalantly while watching the numbers light up above the door.

'Yeah, just left there.'

'I hear it's severe traumatic shock.'

'Don't know,' Fred said smugly as if his secrets were crucial. But he wanted to talk, and this never ceased to amaze Slick. Take an average person, tell him you're a reporter, and nine times out of ten he'll feel obligated to talk. Hell, he'll want to talk. He'll tell you his deepest secrets.

'Poor kid,' Slick mumbled to the floor as if Ricky were terminal. He said nothing else for a few seconds, and this was too much for Fred. What kind of a reporter was he? Where were the questions? He, Fred, knew the kid, had just left his room, had talked to his mother. He, Fred, was a player in this game.

'Yeah, he's in bad shape,' Fred said, also to the floor.

'Still in a coma?'

'In and out. May take a long time.'

'Yeah. That's what I heard.'

The elevator stopped on the fifth floor, but Fred's cart blocked the door and no one entered. The door closed.

'There's not much you can do for a kid like that,' Slick explained. 'I see it all the time. Kid sees something horrible in a split second, goes into shock, and it takes months to drag him out. All kinds of shrinks and stuff. Really sad. This Sway kid ain't that bad, is he?'

'I doubt it. Dr Greenway thinks he'll snap out in a day or two. It'll take some therapy, but he'll be fine. I see it all the time. Thinking about med school myself.'

'Have the cops been snooping around?'

Fred cut his eyes around as if the elevator were bugged. 'Yeah, FBI was here all day. The family has already hired a lawyer.'

'You don't say.'

'Yeah, cops are real interested in this case, and they're talking to the kid's brother. Somehow a lawyer's got in the middle of it.'

The elevator stopped on the second floor, and Fred grabbed the handles on his cart.

'Who's the lawyer?' Slick asked.

The door opened and Fred pushed forward. 'Reggie somebody. I haven't seen him yet.'

'Thanks,' Slick said as Fred disappeared and the elevator filled. He rode it to the ninth floor to search for another fish.

By noon, the Reverend Roy Foltrigg and his sidekicks, Wally Boxx and Thomas Fink, had become a collective nuisance around the offices of the United States Attorney for the Western District of Tennessee. George Ord had held the office for seven years, and he did not care for Roy Foltrigg. He had not invited him to Memphis. Ord had met

Foltrigg before at numerous conferences and seminars where the various US Attorneys gather and plot ways to protect the government. Foltrigg usually spoke at these forums, always anxious to share his opinions and strategies and great victories with anyone who would listen.

After McThune and Trumann returned from the hospital and broke the frustrating news about Mark and his new lawyer, Foltrigg, along with Boxx and Fink, had once again situated himself in Ord's office to analyze the latest. Ord sat in his heavy leather chair behind his massive desk, and listened as Foltrigg interrogated the agents and occasionally barked orders to Boxx.

'What do you know about this lawyer?' he asked Ord.

'Never heard of her.'

'Surely someone in your office has dealt with her?' Foltrigg asked. The question was nothing short of a challenge for Ord to find someone with the scoop on Reggie Love. He left his office and consulted with an assistant. The search began.

Trumann and McThune sat very quietly in one corner of Ord's office. They had decided to tell no one of the tape, at least for the moment. Maybe later. Maybe, they hoped, never.

A secretary brought sandwiches, and lunch was eaten amid aimless speculation and chatter. Foltrigg was anxious to return to New Orleans, but more anxious to hear from Mark Sway. The fact that the kid had somehow obtained the services of an attorney was most troublesome. He was afraid to talk. Foltrigg was convinced Clifford had told him something, and as the day wore on he became more convinced the kid knew about the body. He was never one to hesitate before drawing conclusions. By the time the sandwiches were finished, he had persuaded himself and everyone in the room that Mark Sway knew precisely where Boyette was buried.

David Sharpinski, one of Ord's many assistants, presented himself at the office and explained he'd gone to law school at Memphis State with Reggie Love. He sat next to

Foltrigg, in Wally's seat, and answered questions. He was busy and would rather have been working on a case.

'We finished law school together four years ago,' Sharpinski said.

'So she's only practised for four years,' Foltrigg surmised quickly. 'What kind of work does she do? Criminal law? How much criminal law? Does she know the ropes?'

McThune glanced at Trumann. They'd been nailed by a four-year lawyer.

'A little criminal stuff,' Sharpinski replied. 'We're pretty good friends. I see her around from time to time. Most of her work is with abused children. She's, well, she's had a pretty rough time of it.'

'What do you mean by that?'

'It's a long story, Mr Foltrigg. She's a very complex person. This is her second life.'

'You know her well, don't you?'

'I do. We were in law school together for three years, off and on.'

'What do you mean, off and on?'

'Well, she had to drop out, let's say, emotional problems. In her first life, she was the wife of a prominent doctor, an ob-gyn. They were rich and successful, all over the society pages, charities, country clubs, you name it. Big house in Germantown. His and her Jaguars. She was on the board of every garden club and social organization in Memphis. She had worked as a schoolteacher to put him through med school, and after fifteen years of marriage he decided to trade her in for a new model. He started chasing women, and became involved with a younger nurse, who eventually became wife number two. Reggie's name back then was Regina Cardoni. She took it hard, filed for divorce, and things got nasty. Dr. Cardoni played hardball, and she slowly cracked up. He tormented her. The divorce dragged along. She felt publicly humiliated. Her friends were all doctors' wives, country club types, and they ran for cover. She even attempted suicide. It's all in the divorce papers in the clerk's office. He had a truckload of lawyers, and they pulled strings and had her committed to an institution. Then he cleaned her out.'

'Children?'

'Two, a boy and a girl. They were young teenagers, and of course he got custody. He gave them their freedom and enough money to finance it, and they turned their backs on their mother. He and his lawyers kept her in and out of mental institutions for two years, and by then it was all over. He got the house, kids, the trophy wife, everything.'

Describing this tragic history of a friend troubled Sharpinski, and he was obviously uncomfortable telling it all to Mr Foltrigg. But most of it was public record.

'So how'd she become a lawyer?'

'It wasn't easy. The court order prohibited visitation with the children. She lived with her mother, who, I think, probably saved her life. I'm not sure, but I've heard that her mother mortgaged her home to finance some pretty heavy therapy. It took years, but she slowly pieced her life back together. She pulled out of it. The kids grew up and left Memphis. The boy went to prison for selling drugs. The daughter lives in California.'

'What kind of law student was she?'

'At times, very astute. She was determined to prove to herself she could succeed as a lawyer. But she continued to battle depression. She struggled with booze and pills, and finally dropped out halfway through. Then she came back, clean and dry, and finished with a vengeance.'

As usual, Fink and Boxx scribbled furiously on legal pads, trying importantly to take down every word as if Foltrigg would later quiz them on their notes. Ord listened but was more concerned with the pile of past due work on his desk. With each minute, he resented Foltrigg and this instrusion more and more. He was just as busy and important as Foltrigg.

'What kind of lawyer is she?' Roy asked.

Mean as hell, thought McThune. Shrewd as the devil, thought Trumann. Quite talented with electronics.

119

'She works hard, doesn't make much money, but then I don't think money is important to Reggie.'

'Where in the world did she get a name like Reggie?' Foltrigg asked, thoroughly baffled by it. Perhaps it comes from Regina, Ord thought to himself.

Sharpinski started to speak, then thought for a second. 'It would take hours to tell what I know about her, and I really don't want to. It's not important, is it?'

'Maybe,' Boxx snapped.

Sharpinski glared at him, then looked at Foltrigg. 'When she started law school, she tried to erase most of her past, especially the painful years. She took back her maiden name of Love. I guess she got Reggie from Regina, but I've never asked. But she did it legally, court orders and all, and there's no trace of the old Regina Cardoni, at least not on paper. She didn't talk about her past in law school, but she was the topic of a lot of conversation. Not that she gives a damn.'

'Is she still sober?'

Foltrigg wanted the dirt, and this irritated Sharpinski. To McThune and Trumann she appeared remarkably sober.

'You'll have to ask her, Mr Foltrigg.'

'How often do you see her?'

'Once a month, maybe twice. We talk on the phone occasionally.'

'How old is she?' Foltrigg asked the question with a great deal of suspicion, as if perhaps Sharpinski and Reggie had a little thing going on the side.

'You'll have to ask her that too. Early fifties, I'd guess.'

'Why don't you call her now, ask her what's going on, just friendly small talk, you know. See if she mentions Mark Sway.'

Sharpinski gave Foltrigg a look that would sour butter. Then he looked at Ord, his boss, as if to say 'Can you believe this nut?' Ord rolled his eyes and began refilling a stapler.

'Because she's not stupid, Mr Foltrigg. In fact, she's quite smart, and if I call she'll immediately know the reason why.'

120

'Perhaps you're right.'

'I am.'

'I would like for you to go with us at three to her office, if you can work it in.'

Sharpinski looked at Ord for guidance. Ord was deeply involved with the stapler. 'I can't do it. I'm very busy. Anything else?'

'No. You can go now,' Ord suddenly said. 'Thanks, David.' Sharpinski left the office.

'I really need him to go with me,' Foltrigg said to Ord.

'He said he was busy, Roy. My boys work,' he said, looking at Boxx and Fink. A secretary knocked and entered. She brought a two-page fax to Foltrigg, who read it with Boxx. 'It's from my office,' he explained to Ord as if he and he alone had such technology at his fingertips. They read on, and Foltrigg finally finished. 'Ever hear of Willis Upchurch?'

'Yes. He's a big shot defense lawyer from Chicago, lot of mob work. What's he done?'

'It says he just finished a press conference before a lot of cameras in New Orleans, and that he's been hired by Muldanno, that the case will be postponed, his client will be found not guilty, etc., etc.'

'That sounds like Willis Upchurch. I can't believe you haven't heard of him.'

'He's never been to New Orleans,' Foltrigg said with authority, as if he remembered every lawyer who dared to step on his turf.

'Your case just became a nightmare.'

'Wonderful. Just wonderful.'

121

ELEVEN

The room was dark because the shades were pulled. Dianne was curled along the end of Ricky's bed, napping. After a morning of mumbling and thrashing and getting everyone's hopes aroused, he had drifted away again after lunch and had returned to the now familiar position of knees pulled to his chest, IV in the arm, thumb in the mouth. Greenway assured her repeatedly that he was not in pain. But after squeezing and kissing him for four hours, she was convinced her son was hurting. She was exhausted.

Mark sat on the foldaway bed with his back against the wall under the window, and stared at his brother and his mother in the bed. He, too, was exhausted, but sleep was not possible. Events were whirling around his overworked brain, and he tried to keep thinking. What was the next move? Could Reggie be trusted? He'd seen all those lawyer shows and movies on TV, and it seemed as if half the lawyers could be trusted and the other half were snakes. When should he tell Dianne and Dr Greenway? If he told them everything, would it help Ricky? He thought about this for a long time. He sat on the bed listening to the quiet voices in the hallway as the nurses went about their work, and debated with himself about how much to tell.

The digital clock next to the bed gave the time as two thirty-two. It was impossible to believe that all this crap had happened in less than twenty-four hours. He scratched his knees and made the decision to tell Greenway everything that Ricky could have seen and heard. He stared at the blond hair sticking out from under the sheet, and he felt better. He would come clean, stop the lying, and do all he could to help Ricky. The things Romey told him in the car were not heard by anyone else, and, for the moment, and subject to advice from his lawyer, he would hold them private for a while.

But not for long. These burdens were getting heavy. This was not a game of hide-and-seek played by trailer park kids in the woods and ravines around Tucker Wheel Estates. This was not a sly little escape from his bedroom for a moonlit walk through the neighborhood. Romey stuck a real gun in his mouth. These were real FBI agents with real badges, just like the true crime stories on television. He had hired a real lawyer who'd stuck a real tape recorder to his stomach so she could outfox the FBI. The man who killed the Senator was a professional killer who'd murdered many others, according to Romey, and was a member of the Mafia, and those people would think nothing of rubbing out an eleven-year-old kid.

This was just too much for him to handle alone. He should be at school right now, fifth period, doing math which he hated but suddenly missed. He'd have a long talk with Reggie. She'd arrange a meeting with the FBI, and he'd tell them every stinking detail Romey had unloaded on him. Then they would protect him. Maybe they would send in bodyguards until the killer went to jail, or maybe they would arrest him immediately and all would be safe. Maybe.

Then he remembered a movie about a guy who squealed on the Mafia and thought the FBI would protect him, but suddenly he was on the run with bullets flying over his head and bombs going off. The FBI wouldn't return his phone calls because the guy didn't say something right in the courtroom. At least twenty times during the movie someone said, 'The mob never forgets.' In the final scene, this guy's car was blown to bits just as he turned the key, and he landed a half a mile away with no legs. As he took his final breath, a dark figure stood over him and said, 'The mob never forgets.' It wasn't much of a movie, but its message was suddenly clear to Mark.

He needed a Sprite. His mother's purse was on the floor under the bed, and he slowly unzipped it. There were three bottles of pills. There were two packs of cigarettes and for a split second he was tempted. He found the quarters and left the room.

A nurse whispered to an old man in the waiting area. Mark opened his Sprite and walked to the elevators. Greenway had asked him to stay in the room as much as possible, but he was tired of the room and tired of Greenway, and there seemed little chance of Ricky waking anytime soon. He entered the elevator and pushed the button to the basement. He would check out the cafeteria, and see what the lawyers were doing.

A man entered just before the doors closed, and seemed to look at him a bit too long. 'Are you Mark Sway?' he asked.

This was getting old. Starting with Romey, he'd met enough strangers in the past twenty-four hours to last for months.

He was certain he'd never seen this guy before. 'Who are you?' he asked cautiously.

'Slick Moeller, with the *Memphis Press*, you know, the newspaper. You're Mark Sway, aren't you?'

'How'd you know?'

'I'm a reporter. I'm supposed to know these things. How's your brother?'

'He's doing great. Why do you want to know?'

'Working on a story about the suicide and all, and your name keeps coming up. Cops say you know more than you're telling.'

'When's it gonna be in the paper?'

'I don't know. Tomorrow maybe.'

Mark felt weak again, and stopped looking at him. 'I'm not answering any questions.'

'That's fine.' The elevator door suddenly opened and a swarm of people entered. Mark could no longer see the reporter. Seconds later it stopped on the fifth floor, and Mark darted out between two doctors. He hit the stairs and walked quickly to the sixth floor.

He'd lost the reporter. He sat on the steps in the empty stairwell, and began to cry.

Foltrigg, McThune, and Trumann arrived in the small but tasteful reception area of Reggie Love, Attorney-at-Law, at exactly 3 p.m., the appointed hour. They were met by Clint, who asked them to be seated, then offered coffee or tea, all of which they stiffly declined. Foltrigg informed Clint right properly that he was the United States Attorney for the Southern District of Louisiana, New Orleans, and that he was now present in this office and did not expect to wait. It was a mistake.

He waited for forty-five minutes. While the agents flipped through magazines on the sofa, Foltrigg paced the floor, glanced at his watch, fumed, scowled at Clint, even barked at him twice and each time was informed Reggie was on the phone with an important matter. As if Foltrigg was there for an unimportant matter. He wanted to leave so badly. But he couldn't. For one of the rare times in his life he had to absorb a subtle ass-kicking without a fight.

Finally, Clint asked them to follow him to a small conference room lined with shelves of heavy law books. Clint instructed them to be seated, and explained that Reggie would be right with them.

'She's forty-five minutes late,' Foltrigg protested.

'That's quite early for Reggie, sir,' Clint said with a smile as he closed the door. Foltrigg sat at one end of the table with an agent close to each side. They waited.

'Look, Roy,' Trumann said with hesitation, 'you need to be careful with this gal. She might be taping this.'

'What makes you think so?'

'Well, uh, you just never –'

'These Memphis lawyers do a lot of taping,' McThune added helpfully. 'I don't know about New Orleans, but it's pretty bad up here.'

125

'She has to tell us up front if she's taping, doesn't she?' Foltrigg asked, obviously without a clue.

'Don't bet on it,' said Trumann. 'Just be careful, okay.'

The door opened and Reggie entered, forty-eight minutes late.

'Keep your seats,' she said as Clint closed the door behind her. She offered a hand to Foltrigg, who was half-standing. 'Reggie Love, you must be Roy Foltrigg.'

'I am. Nice to meet you.'

'Please be seated.' She smiled at McThune and Trumann, and for a brief second all three of them thought about the tape. 'Sorry I'm late,' she said as she sat alone at her end of the conference table. They were eight feet away, huddled together like wet ducks.

'No problem,' Foltrigg said loudly as if it was very much a problem.

She pulled a large tape recorder from a hidden drawer in the table and sat it in front of her. 'Mind if I tape this little conference?' she asked as she plugged in the microphone. The little conference would be taped whether they liked it or not. 'I'll be happy to provide you with a copy of the tape.'

'Fine with me,' Foltrigg said, pretending he had a choice.

McThune and Trumann stared at the tape recorder. How nice of her to ask! She smiled at the two of them as they smiled at her, then all three smiled at the recorder. She was as subtle as a rock through a window. The damnable micro-cassette could not be far away.

She pushed a button. 'Now, what's up?'

'Where's your client?' Foltrigg asked. He leaned forward and it was clear he would do all the talking.

'At the hospital. The doctor wants him to stay in the room near his brother.'

'When can we talk to him?'

'You're assuming that you will in fact talk to him.' She looked at Foltrigg with very confident eyes. Her hair was gray and cut like a boy's. The face was quite colorful. The eyebrows were dark. The lips were soft red and meticulously painted. The skin was smooth and free of heavy makeup. It was a pretty face, with bangs, and eyes that glowed with a calm steadiness. Foltrigg looked at her, and thought of all the misery and suffering she'd seen. She covered it well.

McThune opened a file and flipped through it. In the past two hours they had assembled a two-inch-thick dossier on Reggie Love, aka Regina L. Cardoni. They had copied the divorce papers and commitment proceedings from the clerk's office in the county courthouse. The mortgage papers and land records on her mother's home were in the folder. Two Memphis agents were attempting to obtain her law school transcripts.

Foltrigg loved the trash. Whatever the case and whoever the opponent, Foltrigg always wanted the dirt. McThune read the sordid legal history of the divorce with its allegations of adultery and alcohol and dope and unfitness and, ultimately, the attempted suicide. He read it carefully, though, without being seen. He did not, under any circumstances, want to make this woman angry.

'We need to talk to your client, Ms Love.'

'It's Reggie. Okay, Roy?'

'Whatever. We think he knows something, plain and simple.'

'Such as?'

'Well, we're convinced little Mark was in the car with Jerome Clifford prior to his death. We think he spent more than a few seconds with him. Clifford was obviously planning to kill himself, and we have reason to believe he wanted to tell someone where his client, Mr Muldanno, had disposed of the body of Senator Boyette.'

'What makes you think he wanted to tell?'

'It's a long story, but he had contacted an assistant in my office on two occasions and hinted that he might be willing to cut some deal and get out. He was scared. And he was drinking a lot. Very erratic behavior. He was sliding off the deep end, and wanted to talk.'

'Why do you think he talked to my client?'

127

'There's just a chance, okay. And we must look under every stone. Surely you understand.'

'I sense a bit of desperation.'

'A lot of desperation, Reggie. I'm levelling with you. We know who killed the Senator, but, frankly, I'm not ready for trial without a corpse.' He paused and smiled warmly at her. Despite his many obnoxious flaws, Roy had spent hours before juries and he knew how and when to act sincere.

And she'd spent many hours in therapy, and she could spot a fake. 'I'm not telling you that you cannot talk to Mark Sway. You cannot talk to him today, but maybe tomorrow. Maybe the next day. Things are moving fast. Mr Clifford's body is still warm. Let's slow down a bit, and take it one step at a time. Okay?'

'Okay.'

'Now, convince me Mark Sway was in the car with Jerome Clifford prior to the shooting.'

No problem. Foltrigg looked at a notepad, and reeled off the many places where fingerprints were matched. Rear taillights, trunk, front passenger door handle and lock switch, dash, gun, bottle of Jack Daniels. There was a tentative match on the hose, but it was not definite. They were working on it. Foltrigg was the prosecutor now, building a case with the indisputable evidence . . .

Reggie took pages of notes. She knew Mark had been in the car, but she had no idea he'd left such a wide trail.

'The whiskey bottle?' she asked.

Foltrigg flipped a page for the details. 'Yes, three definite prints. No question about it.'

Mark had told her about the gun, but not about the bottle. 'Seems a bit strange, doesn't it?'

'It's all strange at this point. The police officers who talked to him do not recall smelling alcohol, so I don't think he drank any of it. I'm sure he could explain it, you know, if only we could talk to him.'

'I'll ask him.'

'So he didn't tell you about the bottle?'

'No.'

'Did he explain the gun?'

'I cannot divulge what my client has explained to me.'

Foltrigg waited desperately for a hint, and this really angered him. Trumann likewise waited breathlessly. McThune stopped reading the report of a court-appointed psychiatrist.

'So he hasn't told you everything?' Foltrigg asked.

'He's told me a lot. It's possible he missed some of the details.'

'These details could be crucial.'

'I'll determine what's crucial and what's not. What else do you have?'

'Hand her the note,' Foltrigg instructed Trumann, who produced it from a file and handed it to her. She read it slowly, then read it again. Mark had not mentioned the note.

'Obviously two different pens,' Foltrigg explained. 'We found the blue one in the car, a cheap Bic, out of ink. Just speculating, it looks as though Clifford tried to add something after Mark left the car. The word 'where' seems to indicate the boy was gone. It's obvious they talked, exchanged names, and that the kid was in the car long enough to touch everything.'

'No prints on this?' she asked, waving the note.

'None. We've checked it thoroughly. The kid did not touch it.'

She calmly placed it next to her legal pad and folded her hands together. 'Well, Roy, I think the big question is, How did you guys match his fingerprints? How did you obtain one of his to match with the ones in the car?' She asked this with the same confident sneer Trumann and McThune had seen when she produced the tape less than four hours ago.

'Very simple. We lifted one off a soft drink can at the hospital last night.'

'Did you ask either Mark Sway or his mother before doing so?'

'No.'

'So you invaded the privacy of an eleven-year-old child.'

'No. We are trying to obtain evidence.'

'Evidence? Evidence for what? Not for a crime, I dare say. The crime has been committed and the body has been disposed of. You just can't find it. What other crime do we have here? Suicide? Watching a suicide?'

'Did he watch the suicide?'

'I can't tell you what he did or saw because he has confided in me as his lawyer. Our talks are privileged, you know that, Roy. What else have you taken from this child?'

'Nothing.'

She snorted as if she didn't believe this. 'What else do you have?'

'This is not enough?'

'I want it all.'

Foltrigg flipped pages back and forth and did a slow burn. 'You've seen the puffy left eye and the knot on his forehead. The police said there was a trace of blood on his lip when they found him at the scene. Clifford's autopsy revealed a spot of blood on the back of his right hand, and it's not his type.'

'Let me guess. It's Mark's.'

'Probably so. Same blood type.'

'How do you know his blood type?'

Foltrigg dropped the legal pad and rubbed his face. The most effective defense lawyers are those who keep the fighting away from the issues. They bitch and throw rocks over the tiny subplots of a case and hope the prosecution and the jury are diverted away from the obvious guilt of their clients. If there's something to hide, they scream at the other guy for violating technicalities. Right now they should be nailing down the facts of what, if anything, Clifford said to Mark. It should be so simple. But now the kid had a lawyer, and here they were trying to explain how they obtained certain crucial information. There was nothing wrong with lifting prints from a can without asking. Good police work. But from the mouth of a defense lawyer, it's suddenly a vicious invasion of privacy.

Next she would threaten a lawsuit. And now, the blood.

She was good. He found it difficult to believe she'd been practising only four years.

'From his brother's hospital admission records.'

'And how did you obtain the hospital records?'

'We have ways.'

Trumann braced for a reprimand. McThune hid behind the file. They had been burned by this temper. She'd made them stutter and stammer and sweat blood, and now it was time for old Roy to take a few punches. It was almost funny.

But she kept her cool. She slowly extended a skinny finger with white nail polish and pointed it at Roy. 'If you get near my client again and attempt to obtain anything from him without my permission, I'll sue you and the FBI. I'll file an ethics complaint with the state bar in Louisiana and Tennessee, and I'll haul your ass into Juvenile Court here and ask the judge to lock you up.' The words were spoken in an even voice, no emotion, but so matter-of-factly that everyone in the room, including Roy Foltrigg, knew that she would do exactly as she promised.

He smiled and nodded. 'Fine. Sorry if we've gotten a bit out of line. But we're anxious, and we must talk to your client.'

'Have you told me everything you know about Mark?'

Foltrigg and Trumann checked their notes. 'Yes, I think so.'

'What's that?' she insisted, pointing to the file McThune was lost in. He was reading about her suicide attempt, by pills, and it was alleged in the pleadings, sworn under oath, that she'd been in a coma for four days before pulling out. Evidently, her ex-husband, Dr Cardoni, a real piece of scum according to the pleadings, was a nasty sort with all the money and lawyers, and as soon as Regina/Reggie here took the pills he ran to court with a pile of motions to get the kids. Looking at the dates stamped on the papers, it was obvious the good doctor was filing requests and asking for hearings while she was lost in a coma and fighting for her life.

McThune didn't panic. He looked at her innocently and said, 'Just some of our internal stuff.' It was not a lie, because he was afraid to lie to her. She had the tape, and had sworn them to truthfulness.

'About my client?'

'Oh no.'

She studied her legal pad. 'Let's meet again tomorrow,' she said. It was not a suggestion, but a directive.

'We're really in a hurry, Reggie,' Foltrigg pleaded.

'Well I'm not. And I guess I'm calling the shots, aren't I?'

'I guess you are.'

'I need time to digest this and talk with my client.'

This was not what they wanted, but it was painfully clear this was all they would get. Foltrigg dramatically screwed the top on to his pen and slid his notes into his briefcase. Trumann and McThune followed his lead and for a minute the table shook as they shuffled paper and files and restuffed everything.

'What time tomorrow?' Foltrigg asked, slamming his briefcase and pushing away from the table.

'Ten. In this office.'

'Will Mark Sway be here?'

'I don't know.'

They stood and filed out of the room.

TWELVE

Wally Boxx called the office in New Orleans at least four times every hour. Foltrigg had forty-seven Assistant US Attorneys fighting all sorts of crime and protecting the interests of the government, and Wally was in charge of relaying orders from the boss in Memphis. In addition to Thomas Fink, three other attorneys were working on the Muldanno case, and Wally felt the need to call them every fifteen minutes with instructions, and the latest on Clifford. By noon, the entire office knew of Mark Sway and his little brother. The place buzzed with gossip and speculation. How much did the kid know? Would he lead them to the body? Initially, these questions were pondered in hushed whispers by the three Muldanno prosecutors, but by mid-afternoon the secretaries in the coffee room were exchanging wild theories about the suicide note and what was told to the kid before Clifford ate his bullet. All other work virtually stopped as Foltrigg's office waited for Wally's next call.

Foltrigg had been burned by leaks before. He'd fired people he suspected of talking too much. He'd required polygraphs for all lawyers, paralegals, investigators, and secretaries who worked for him. He kept sensitive information under lock and key for fear of leakage by his own people. He lectured and threatened.

But Roy Foltrigg was not the sort of person to inspire intense loyalty. He was not appreciated by many of the assistants. He played the political game. He used cases for his own raw ambition. He hogged the spotlight and took credit for all the good work, and blamed his subordinates for all the bad. He sought marginal indictments against elected officials for a few cheap headlines. He investigated his enemies and dragged their names through the press. He was a political whore whose only talent with the law was in the courtroom where he preached to juries and quoted scripture. He was a Reagan appointee with one year left, and most of the assistant attorneys were counting the days. They encouraged him to run for office. Any office.

The reporters in New Orleans began calling at 8 a.m. They wanted an official comment about Clifford from Foltrigg's office. They did not get one. Then Willis Upchurch performed at two o'clock, with Muldanno glowering at his side, and more reporters came snooping around the office. There were hundreds of phone calls to Memphis and back.

People talked.

They stood before the dirty window at the end of the hall on the ninth floor, and watched the rush-hour traffic of downtown. Dianne nervously lit a Virginia Slim, and blew a heavy cloud of smoke. 'Who is this lawyer?'

'Her name is Reggie Love.'

'How'd you find her?'

He pointed to the Sterick Building four blocks away. 'I went to her office in that building right there, and I talked to her.'

'Why, Mark?'

'These cops scare me, Mom. The police and FBI are crawling all over this place. And reporters. I had one catch me in the elevator this afternoon. I think we need some legal advice.'

'Lawyers don't work for free, Mark. You know we can't afford a lawyer.'

'I've already paid her,' he said like a tycoon.

'What? How can you pay a lawyer?'

'She wanted a small retainer, and she got one. I gave her

a dollar from that five that went for doughnuts this morning.'

'She's working for a dollar? She must be a great lawyer.'

'She's pretty good. I've been impressed so far.'

Dianne shook her head in amazement. During her nasty divorce, Mark, then age nine, had constantly criticized her lawyer. He watched hours of reruns of 'Perry Mason' and never missed 'LA Law.' It had been years since she'd won an argument with him.

'What has she done so far?' Dianne asked, as if she were emerging from a dark cave and seeing sunlight for the first time in a month.

'At noon, she met with some FBI agents, and ripped them up pretty good. And later, she met with them again in her office. I haven't talked with her since then.'

'What time is she coming here?'

'Around six. She wants to meet you and talk to Dr Greenway. You'll really like her, Mom.'

Dianne filled her lungs with smoke, and exhaled. 'But why do we need her, Mark? I don't understand why she's entered the picture. You've done nothing wrong. You and Ricky saw the car, you tried to help the man, but he shot himself anyway. And you guys saw it. Why do you need a lawyer?'

'Well, I did lie to the cops at first, and that scares me. And I was afraid we might get in trouble because we didn't stop the man from shooting himself. It's all pretty scary, Mom.'

She watched him intently as he explained this, and he avoided her eyes. There was a long pause. 'Have you told me everything?' She asked this very slowly, as if she knew.

At first he'd lied to her at the trailer while they waited on the ambulance, with Hardy lingering nearby, all ears. Then last night, in Ricky's room, under cross-examination by Greenway, he had told the first version of the truth. He remembered how sad she had been when she heard this revised story, and later how she'd said, 'You never lie to me, Mark.'

They'd been through so much together, and here he was

135

dancing around the truth, dodging questions, telling Reggie more than he'd told his mother. It made him sick.

'Mom, it all happened so fast yesterday. It was all a blur in my mind last night, but I've been thinking about it today. Thinking hard. I've gone through each step, minute by minute, and I'm remembering things now.'

'Such as?'

'Well, you know how this has affected Ricky. I think it shocked me sort of like that. Not as bad, but I'm remembering things now that I should have remembered last night when I talked to Dr Greenway. Does this make sense?'

Actually, it did make sense. Dianne was suddenly concerned. Two boys see the same event. One goes into shock. It's reasonable to believe the other would be affected. She hadn't thought of this. She leaned down next to him. 'Mark, are you all right?'

He knew he had her. 'I think so,' he said with a frown, as if a migraine were upon him.

'What have you remembered?' she asked cautiously.

He took a deep breath. 'Well, I remember –'

Greenway cleared his throat and appeared from nowhere. Mark whirled around. 'I need to be going,' Greenway said, almost as an apology. 'I'll check back in a couple of hours.'

Dianne nodded but said nothing.

Mark decided to get it over with. 'Look, Doctor, I was just telling Mom that I'm remembering things now for the first time.'

'About the suicide?'

'Yes sir. All day long I've been seeing flashes and recalling details. I think some of it might be important.'

Greenway looked at Dianne. 'Let's go back to the room and talk,' he said.

They walked to the room, closed the door behind them, and listened as Mark tried to fill in the gaps. It was a relief to unload this baggage, though he did most of the talking in the direction of the floor. It was an act, this painful pulling of scenes from a shocked and badly scarred mind and he

136

carried it off with finesse. He paused quite often, long pauses in which he searched for words to describe what was already firmly etched in his memory. He glanced at Greenway occasionally, and the doctor's expression never changed. He glanced at his mother from time to time, and she didn't appear to be disappointed. She maintained a look of motherly concern.

But when he got to the part about Clifford grabbing him, he could see them fidget. He kept his troubled eyes on the floor. Dianne sighed when he talked about the gun. Greenway shook his head when he told of the gunshot through the window. At times, he thought they were about to yell at him for lying last night, but he plowed ahead, obviously disturbed and deep in thought.

He carefully replayed every single event that Ricky could have seen and heard. The only details he kept to himself were Clifford's confessions. He vividly recalled the crazy stuff: La La Land and floating off to see the wizard.

When he finished, Dianne was sitting on the foldaway bed rubbing her head, talking about Valium. Greenway sat in a chair, hanging on every word. 'Is this all of it, Mark?'

'I don't know. It's all I can remember right now,' he mumbled, as if he had a toothache.

'You were actually in the car?' Dianne said without opening her eyes.

He pointed to his slightly swollen left eye. 'You see this. This is where he slapped me when I tried to get out of the car. I was dizzy for a long time. Maybe I was unconscious, I don't know.'

'You told me you were in a fight at school.'

'I don't remember telling you that, Mom, and if I did, well, maybe I was in shock or something.' Dammit. Trapped by another lie.

Greenway stroked his beard. 'Ricky saw you get grabbed, thrown in the car, the gunshot. Wow.'

'Yeah. It's coming back to me, real clear. I'm sorry I didn't remember it sooner, but my mind just went blank. Sort of like Ricky here.'

137

Another long pause.

'Frankly, Mark, I find it hard to believe you couldn't remember some of this last night,' Greenway said.

'Gimme a break, would you? Look at Ricky here. He saw what happened to me, and it drove him to the ozone. Did we talk last night?'

'Come on, Mark,' Dianne said.

'Of course we talked,' Greenway said with at least four new wrinkles across his forehead.

'Yeah, I guess we did. Don't remember much of it though.'

Greenway frowned at Dianne and their eyes locked. Mark walked into the bathroom and drank water out of a paper cup.

'It's okay,' Dianne said. 'Have you told the police this?'

'No. I just remembered it. Remember?'

Dianne nodded slowly and managed a very slight grin at Mark. Her eyes were narrow, and his suddenly found the floor. She believed all of his story about the suicide, but this sudden surge of clear memory did not fool her. She would deal with him later.

Greenway had his doubts too, but he was more concerned with treating his patient than reprimanding Mark. He gently stroked his beard and studied the wall. There was a long pause.

'I'm hungry,' Mark finally said.

Reggie arrived an hour late with apologies. Greenway had left for the day. Mark stumbled through the introductions. She smiled warmly at Dianne as they shook hands, then sat beside her on the bed. She asked her a dozen questions about Ricky. She was an immediate friend of the family, anxious and properly concerned about everything. What about her job? School? Money? Clothes?

Dianne was tired and vulnerable, and it was nice to talk to a woman. She opened up, and they went on for a while about Greenway saying this and that, about everything unrelated to Mark and his story and the FBI, the only reason for Reggie's being there.

138

Reggie had a sack of deli sandwiches and chips, and Mark spread them on a crowded table by Ricky's bed. He left the room to get drinks. They hardly noticed.

He bought two Dr Peppers in the waiting area and returned to the room without being stopped by cops, reporters, or Mafia gunmen. The women were deep into a conversation about McThune and Trumann trying to interrogate Mark. Reggie was telling the story in such a manner that Dianne had no choice but to mistrust the FBI. They were both shocked. Dianne was alive and animated for the first time in many hours.

Jack Nance and Associates was a quiet firm that advertised itself as security specialists, but was in fact nothing more than a couple of private investigators. Its ad in the yellow pages was one of the smallest in town. It did not want the run-of-the-mill divorce cases in which one spouse was sleeping around and the other wanted photos. It did not own a polygraph. It did not snatch children. It did not track down thieving employees.

Jack Nance himself was an ex-con with an impressive record who'd managed to avoid trouble for ten years. His associate was Cal Sisson, also a convicted felon who'd run a terrific scam with a bogus roofing company. Together they scratched out a nice living doing dirty work for rich people. They had once broken both hands of the teenaged boy-friend of a rich client's daughter after the kid slapped her. They had once deprogrammed a couple of Moonies, the children of another rich client. They were not afraid of violence. More than once, they had beaten a business rival who'd taken money from a client. They had once burned the downtown love nest of a client's wife and her lover.

There was a market for their brand of investigative work, and they were known in small circles as two very nasty and efficient men who would take your cash, do your dirty work, and leave no trail. They achieved amazing results. Every client came by referral.

Jack Nance was in his cluttered office after dark when

someone knocked on the door. The secretary had left for the day. Cal Sisson was stalking a crack dealer who'd hooked the son of a client. Nance was around forty, not a big man, but compact and extremely agile. He walked through the secretary's office and opened the front door. The face was a strange one.

'Looking for Jack Nance,' the man said.

'That's me.'

The man stretched out his hand, and they shook. 'My name's Paul Gronke. Can I come in?'

Nance opened the door wider and motioned for Gronke to enter. They stood in front of the secretary's desk. Gronke looked around the cramped and messy room.

'It's late,' Nance said. 'What do you want?'

'I need some fast work.'

'Who referred you?'

'I've heard of you. Word gets around.'

'Give me a name.'

'Okay. J. L. Grainger. I think you helped him on a business deal. He also mentioned a Mr Schwartz who was also quite pleased with your work.'

Nance thought about this for a second as he studied Gronke. He was a burly man with a thick chest, late thirties, badly dressed but didn't know it. Because of his clipped drawl, Nance immediately knew he was from New Orleans. 'I get a two-thousand-dollar retainer up front, nonrefundable, all in cash, before I lift a finger.' Gronke pulled a roll of bills from his left front pocket and peeled off twenty big ones. Nance relaxed. It was his fastest retainer in ten years. 'Sit down,' he said, taking the money and waving at a sofa. 'I'm listening.'

Gronke took a folded newspaper clipping from his jacket and handed it to Nance. 'Did you see this in today's paper?'

Nance looked at it. 'Yeah, I read it. How are you involved?'

'I'm from New Orleans. In fact, Mr. Muldanno is an old pal, and he's very disturbed to see his name suddenly show up here in the Memphis paper. It says he has Mafia ties and all. Can't believe a word in the newspapers. The press is going to ruin this country.'

'Was Clifford his lawyer?'

'Yeah. But now he has a new one. That's not important, though. Lemme tell you what's worrying him. He has a good source telling him these two boys know something.'

'Where are the boys?'

'One's in the hospital, a coma or something. He freaked out when Clifford shot himself. His brother was actually in the car with Clifford prior to the shooting, and we're afraid this kid might know something. He's already hired a lawyer, and is refusing to talk to the FBI. Looks real suspicious.'

'Where do I fit in?'

'We need someone with Memphis connections. We need to see the kid. We need to know where he is at all times.'

'What's his name?'

'Mark Sway. He's at the hospital, we think, with his mother. Last night they stayed in the room with the younger brother, a kid named Ricky Sway. Ninth floor at St Peter's. Room 943. We want you to find the kid, determine his location as of now, and then watch him.'

'Easy enough.'

'Maybe not. There are cops and probably FBI agents watching too. The kid's attracting a crowd.'

'I get a hundred bucks an hour, cash.'

'I know that.'

She called herself Amber, which along with Alexis happened to be the two most popular acquired names among strippers and whores in the French Quarter. She answered the phone, then carried it a few feet to the tiny bathroom where Barry Muldanno was brushing his teeth. 'It's Gronke,' she said, handing it to him. He took it, turned off the water, and admired her naked body as she crawled under the sheets. He stepped into the doorway. 'Yeah,' he said into the phone.

A minute later, he placed the phone on the table next to

141

the bed, and quickly dried himself off. He dressed in a hurry. Amber was somewhere under the covers.

'What time are you going to work?' he asked, tying his tie.

'Ten. What time is it?' Her head appeared between the pillows.

'Almost nine. I gotta run an errand. I'll be back.'

'Why? You got what you wanted.'

'I might want some more. I pay the rent here, sweetheart.'

'Some rent. Why don't you move me outta this dump? Get me a nice place?'

He tugged his sleeves from under his jacket, and admired himself in the mirror. Perfect, just perfect. He smiled at Amber. 'I like it here.'

'It's a dump. If you treated me right, you'd get me a nice place.'

'Yeah, yeah. See you later, sweetheart.' He slammed the door. Strippers. Get them a job, then an apartment, buy some clothes, feed them nice dinners, and then they get culture and start making demands. They were an expensive habit, but one he could not break.

He bounced down the steps in his alligator loafers, and opened the door onto Dumaine. He looked right and left, certain that someone was watching, and took off around the corner on to Bourbon. He moved in shadows, crossing and recrossing the street, then turned corners and retraced some of his steps. He zigzagged for eight blocks, then disappeared into Randy's Oysters on Decatur. If they stuck to him, they were supermen.

Randy's was a sanctuary. It was an old-fashioned New Orleans eatery, long and narrow, dark and crowded, off-limits for tourists, owned and operated by the family. He ran up the cramped staircase to the second floor where reserved seating was required and only a select few could get reservations. He nodded to a waiter, grinned at a beefy thug, and entered a private room with four tables. Three were empty, and at the fourth a solitary figure sat in virtual darkness reading by the light of a real candle. Barry approached, stopped, and waited to be invited. The man saw him and waved at a chair. Barry obediently took a seat.

Johnny Sulari was the brother of Barry's mother, and the undisputed head of the family. He owned Randy's, along with a hundred other assorted ventures. As usual, he was working tonight, reading financial statements by candle-light and waiting for dinner. This was Tuesday, just another night at the office. On Friday, Johnny would be here with an Amber or an Alexis or a Sabrina, and on Saturday he would be here with his wife.

He did not appreciate the interruption. 'What is it?' he asked.

Barry leaned forward, well aware that he was not wanted here at this moment. 'Just talked to Gronke in Memphis. Kid's hired a lawyer, and is refusing to talk to the FBI.'

'I can't believe you're so stupid, Barry, you know that?'

'We've had this conversation, okay?'

'I know. And we'll have it again. You're a dumbass, and I just want you to know that I think you're a real dumbass.'

'Okay. I'm a dumbass. But we need to make a move.'

'What?'

'We need to send Bono and someone else, maybe Pirini, maybe the Bull, I don't care, but we need a couple of men in Memphis. And we need them now.'

'You want to hit the kid?'

'Maybe. We'll see. We need to find out what he knows, okay? If he knows too much, then maybe we'll take him out.'

'I'm embarrassed we're related by blood, Barry. You're a complete fool, you know that?'

'Okay. But we need to move fast.'

Johnny picked up a stack of papers, and began reading. 'Send Bono and Pirini, but no more stupid moves. Okay? You're a idiot, Barry, an imbecile, and I don't want anything done up there until I say so. Understand?'

'Yes sir.'

'Leave now.' Johnny waved his hand, and Barry jumped to his feet.

143

THIRTEEN

By Tuesday evening, George Ord and his staff had managed to confine the activities of Foltrigg, Boxx, and Fink to the expansive library in the center of the offices. Here they'd set up camp. They had two phones. Ord loaned them a secretary and an intern. All other assistant attorneys were ordered to stay out of the library. Foltrigg kept the doors closed and spread his papers and mess over the sixteen-foot conference table in the middle of the room. Trumann was allowed to come and go. The secretary fetched coffee and sandwiches whenever the Reverend ordered.

Foltrigg had been a mediocre student of the law, and had managed to avoid the drudgery of legal research for the past fifteen years. He had learned to hate libraries in law school. Research was to be done by egghead scholars; that was his theory. Law could be practised only be real lawyers who could stand before juries and preach.

But out of sheer boredom, here he was in George Ord's library with Boxx and Fink, nothing to do but wait at the beck and call of one Reggie Love, and so he, the great Roy Foltrigg, lawyer extraordinaire, had his nose stuck in a thick law book with a dozen more stacked around him on the table. Fink, the egghead scholar, was on the floor between two shelves of books with his shoes off and research materials littered about. Boxx, also a lightweight legal intellect, went through the motions at the other end of Foltrigg's table. Boxx had not opened a law book in years, but for the moment there was simply nothing else to do. He

144

wore his only clean pair of boxer shorts and hoped like hell they left Memphis tomorrow.

At issue, at the heart of their research, was the question of how Mark Sway could be made to divulge information if he didn't want to. If someone possesses information crucial to a criminal prosecution, and that person chooses not to talk, then how can the information be obtained? For issue number two, Foltrigg wanted to know if Reggie Love could be made to divulge whatever Mark Sway had told her. The attorney-client privilege is almost sacred, but Roy wanted it researched anyway.

The debate over whether or not Mark Sway knew anything had ended hours ago with Foltrigg clearly victorious. The kid had been in the car. Clifford was crazy and wanted to talk. The kid had lied to the cops. And now the kid had a lawyer because the kid knew something and was afraid to talk. Why didn't Mark Sway simply come clean and tell all? Why? Because he was afraid of the killer of Boyd Boyette. Plain and simple.

Fink still had doubts, but was tired of arguing. His boss was not bright and was very stubborn, and when he closed his mind it remained closed forever. And there was a lot of merit to Foltrigg's arguments. The kid was making strange moves, especially for a kid.

Boxx, of course, stood firm behind his boss and believed everything he said. If Roy said the kid knew where the body was, then it was the gospel. Pursuant to one of his many phone calls, a half dozen Assistant US Attorneys were doing identical research in New Orleans.

Larry Trumann knocked and entered the library around ten Tuesday night. He'd been in McThune's office for most of the evening. Following Foltrigg's orders, they had begun the process of obtaining approval to offer Mark Sway safety under the Federal Witness Protection Program. They had made a dozen phone calls to Washington, twice speaking with the director of the FBI, F. Denton Voyles. If Mark Sway didn't give Foltrigg the answers he wanted in the morning, they would be ready with a most attractive offer.

145

Foltrigg said it would be an easy deal. The kid had nothing to lose. They would offer his mother a good job in a new city, one of her choosing. She would earn more than the six lousy bucks an hour she got at the lamp factory. The family would live in a house with a foundation, not a cheap trailer. There would be a cash incentive, maybe a new car.

Mark sat in the darkness on the thin mattress, and stared at his mother lying above him next to Ricky. He was sick of this room and this hospital. The foldaway bed was ruining his back. Tragically, Karen the beautiful was not at the nurses' station. The hallways were empty. No one waited for the elevators.

A solitary man occupied the waiting area. He flipped through a magazine and ignored the 'M*A*S*H' reruns on the television. He was on the sofa, which happened to be the spot Mark had planned to sleep. Mark stuck two quarters in the machine, and pulled out a Sprite. He sat in a chair and stared at the TV. The man was about forty, and looked tired and worried. Ten minutes passed, and 'M*A*S*H' went away. Suddenly, there was Gill Teal, the people's lawyer, standing calmly at the scene of a car wreck talking about defending rights and fighting insurance companies. Gill Teal, he's for real.

Jack Nance closed the magazine and picked up another. He glanced at Mark for the first time, and smiled. 'Hi there,' he said warmly, then looked at a *Redbook*.

Mark nodded. The last thing he needed in his life was another stranger. He sipped his drink, and prayed for silence.

'What're you doing here?' the man asked.

'Watching television,' Mark answered, barely audible.

The man stopped smiling and began reading an article. The midnight news came on, and there was a huge story about a typhoon in Pakistan. There were live pictures of dead people and dead animals piled along the shore like driftwood. It was the kind of footage one had to watch.

'That's awful, isn't it,' Jack Nance said to the TV as a helicopter hovered over a pile of human debris.

146

'It's gross,' Mark said, careful not to get friendly. Who knows – this guy could be just another hungry lawyer waiting to pounce on wounded prey.

'Really gross,' the man said, shaking his head at the suffering. 'I guess we have much to be thankful for. But it's hard to be thankful in a hospital, know what I mean?' He was suddenly sad again. He looked painfully at Mark.

'What's the matter?' Mark couldn't help but ask.

'It's my son. He's in real bad shape.' The man threw the magazine on the table and rubbed his eyes.

'What happened?' Mark asked. He felt sorry for this guy.

'Car wreck. Drunk driver. My boy was thrown out of the car.'

'Where is he?'

'ICU, first floor. I had to leave and get away. It's a zoo down there, people screaming and crying all the time.'

'I'm very sorry.'

'He's only eight years old.' He appeared to be crying, but Mark couldn't tell.

'My little brother's eight. He's in a room around the corner.'

'What's wrong with him?' the man asked without looking.

'He's in shock.'

'What happened?'

'It's a long story. And getting longer. He'll make it, though. I sure hope your kid pulls through.'

Jack Nance looked at his watch and suddenly stood. 'Me too. I need to go check on him. Good luck to you, uh, what's your name?'

'Mark Sway.'

'Good luck, Mark. I gotta run.' He walked to the elevators and disappeared.

Mark took his place on the couch, and within minutes was asleep.

FOURTEEN

The photos on the front page of Wednesday's edition of the *Memphis Press* had been lifted from the yearbook at Willow Road Elementary School. They were a year old – Mark was in fourth grade and Ricky the first. They were next to each other on the bottom third of the page, and under the cute, smiling faces were the names. Mark Sway. Ricky Sway. To the left was a story about Jerome Clifford's suicide and the bizarre aftermath in which the boys were involved. It was written by Slick Moeller, and he had pieced together a suspicious little story. The FBI was involved; Ricky was in shock; Mark had called 911 but hadn't given his name; the police had tried to interrogate Mark but he hadn't talked yet; the family had hired a lawyer, one Reggie Love (female); Mark's fingerprints were all over the inside of the car, including the gun. The story made Mark look like a cold-blooded killer.

Karen brought it to him around six as he sat in an empty semiprivate room directly across the hall from Ricky's. Mark was watching cartoons and trying to nap. Greenway wanted everyone out of the room except Ricky and Dianne. An hour earlier, Ricky had opened his eyes and asked to use the bathroom. He was back in the bed now, mumbling about nightmares and eating ice cream.

'You've hit the big time,' Karen said as she handed him the front section and put his orange juice on the table.

'What is it?' he asked, suddenly staring at his face in black and white. 'Damn!'

'Just a little story. I'd like your autograph when you have time.'

Very funny. She left the room and he read it slowly. Reggie had told him about the fingerprints and the note. He'd dreamed about the gun, but through a legitimate lapse in memory had forgotten about touching the whiskey bottle.

There was something unfair here. He was just a kid who'd been minding his own business, and now suddenly his picture was on the front page and fingers were pointed at him. How can a newspaper dig up old yearbook photos and run them whenever it chooses? Wasn't he entitled to a little privacy?

He threw the paper to the floor and walked to the window. It was dawn, drizzling outside, and downtown Memphis was slowly coming to life. Standing in the window of the empty room, looking at the blocks of tall buildings, he felt completely alone. Within an hour, a half million people would be awake, reading about Mark and Ricky Sway while sipping their coffee and eating their toast. The dark buildings would soon be filled with busy people gathering around desks and coffeepots, and they would gossip and speculate wildly about him and what happened with the dead lawyer. Surely the kid was in the car. There are fingerprints everywhere! How did the kid get in the car? How did he get out? They would read Slick Moeller's story as if every word were true, as if Slick had the inside dope.

It was not fair for a kid to read about himself on the front page and not have parents to hide behind. Any kid in this mess needed the protection of a father and the sole affection of a mother. He needed a shield against cops and FBI agents and reporters, and god forbid, the mob. Here he was, eleven years old, alone, lying, then telling the truth, then lying some more, never certain what to do next. The truth can get you killed – he'd seen that in a movie one time, and always remembered it when he felt the urge to lie to someone in authority. How could he get out of this mess?

He retrieved the paper from the floor and entered the

hall. Greenway had stuck a note on Ricky's door forbidding anyone from entering, including nurses. Dianne was having back pains from sitting in his bed and rocking, and Greenway had ordered another round of pills for her discomfort.

Mark stopped at the nurses' station, and handed the paper to Karen. 'Nice story, huh,' she said with a smile. The romance was gone. She was still beautiful but now playing hard to get, and he just didn't have the energy.

'I'm going to get a doughnut,' he said. 'You want one?'
'No thanks.'

He walked to the elevators, and pushed the Call button. The middle door opened and he stepped in.

At that precise second, Jack Nance turned in the darkness of the waiting room and whispered into his radio.

The elevator was empty. It was just a few minutes past six, a good half an hour before the rush hit. The elevator stopped at floor number eight. The door opened, and one man stepped in. He wore a white lab jacket, jeans, sneakers, and a baseball cap. Mark did not look at his face. He was tired of meeting new people.

The door closed, and suddenly the man grabbed Mark and pinned him in a corner. He clenched his fingers around Mark's throat. The man fell to one knee and pulled something from a pocket. His face was inches from Mark's, and it was a horrible face. He was breathing heavy. 'Listen to me, Mark Sway,' he growled. Something clicked in his right hand, and suddenly a shiny switchblade entered the picture. A very long switchblade. 'I don't know what Jerome Clifford told you,' he said urgently. The elevator was moving. 'But if you repeat a single word of it to anyone, including your lawyer, I'll kill you. And I'll kill your mother and your little brother. Okay? He's in Room 943. I've seen the trailer where you live. Okay? I've seen your school at Willow Road.' His breath was warm and had the smell of creamed coffee, and he aimed it directly at Mark's eyes. 'Do you understand me?' he sneered with a nasty smile.

The elevator stopped, and the man was on his feet by the door with the switchblade hidden by his leg. Although Mark was paralyzed, he was able to hope and pray that someone would get in the damned elevator with him. It was obvious he was not getting off at this point. They waited ten seconds at the sixth floor, and nobody entered. The doors closed, and they were moving again.

The man lunged at him again, this time with the switchblade an inch or two from Mark's nose. He pinned him in the corner with a heavy forearm, and suddenly jabbed the shiny blade at Mark's waist. Quickly and efficiently, he cut a belt loop. Then a second one. He'd already delivered his message, without interruption, and now it was time for a little reinforcement.

'I'll slice your guts out, do you understand me?' he demanded, and then released Mark.

Mark nodded. A lump the size of a golf ball clogged his dry throat, and suddenly his eyes were wet. He nodded yes, yes, yes.

'I'll kill you. Do you believe me?'

Mark stared at the knife, and nodded some more. 'And if you tell anyone about me, I'll get you. Understand?' Mark kept nodding, only faster now.

The man slid the knife into a pocket and pulled a folded eight by ten color photograph from under the lab jacket. He stuck it in Mark's face. 'You seen this before?' he asked, smiling now.

It was a department store portrait taken when Mark was in the second grade, and for years now it had hung in the den above the television. Mark stared at it.

'Recognize it?' the man barked at him.

Mark nodded. There was only one such photograph in the world.

The elevator stopped on the fifth floor, and the man moved quickly, again by the door. At last second, two nurses stepped in, and Mark finally breathed. He stayed in the corner, holding the railings, praying for a miracle. The switchblade had come closer with each assault, and he

151

simply could not take another one. On the third floor, three more people entered and stood between Mark and the man with the knife. In an instant, Mark's assailant was gone; through the door as it was closing.

'Are you okay?' A nurse was staring at him, frowning and very concerned. The elevator kicked and started down. She touched his forehead and felt a layer of sweat between her fingers. His eyes were wet. 'You look pale,' she said.

'I'm okay,' he mumbled weakly, holding the railings for support.

Another nurse looked down at him in the corner. They studied his face with much concern. 'Are you sure?'

He nodded, and the elevator door suddenly opened on the second floor. He darted through bodies and was in a narrow corridor dodging gurneys and wheelchairs. His well-worn Nike hightops squeaked on the clean linoleum as he ran to a door with an EXIT sign over it. He pushed through the door, and was in the stairwell. He grabbed the rails and started up, two steps at a time, churning and churning. The pain hit his thighs at the sixth floor, but he ran harder. He passed a doctor on the eighth floor, but never slowed. He ran, climbing the mountain at a record pace until the stairwell stopped on the fifteenth floor. He collapsed on a landing under a fire hose, and sat in the semidarkness until the sun filtered through a tiny painted window above him.

Pursuant to his agreement with Reggie, Clint opened the office at exactly eight, and after turning on the lights, made the coffee. It was Wednesday, southern pecan day. He looked through the countless one-pound bags of coffee beans in the refrigerator until he found southern pecan, and measured four perfect scoops into the grinder. She would know in an instant if he'd missed the measurement by half a teaspoon. She would take the first sip like a wine connoisseur, smack her lips like a rabbit, then pass judgment on the coffee. He added the precise quantity of water, flipped the switch, and waited for the first black drops to hit the canister. The aroma was delicious.

Clint enjoyed the coffee almost as much as his boss, and the meticulous routine of making it was only half-serious. They began each morning with a quiet cup as they planned the day and talked about the mail. They had met in a detox center eleven years ago when she was forty-one and he was seventeen. They had started law school at the same time, but he flunked out after a nasty round with coke. He'd been perfectly clean for five years, she for six. They had leaned on each other many times.

He sorted the mail and placed it carefully on her clean desk. He poured his first cup of coffee in the kitchen, and read with great interest the front page story about her newest client. As usual, Slick had his facts. And, as usual, the facts were stretched with a good dose of innuendo thrown in. The boys favored each other, but Ricky's hair was a shade lighter. He smiled with several teeth missing.

Clint placed the front page in the center of Reggie's desk.

Unless she was expected in court, Reggie seldom made it to the office before 9 a.m. She was a slow starter who usually hit her stride around four in the afternoon and preferred to work late.

Her mission as a lawyer was to protect abused and neglected children, and she did this with great skill and passion. The juvenile courts routinely called her for indigent work representing kids who needed lawyers but didn't know it. She was a zealous advocate for small clients who coüld not say thanks. She had sued fathers for molesting daughters. She had sued uncles for raping their nieces. She had sued mothers for abusing their babies. She had investigated parents for exposing their children to drugs. She served as legal guardian for more than twenty children. And she worked the Juvenile Court as appointed counsel for kids in trouble with the law. She performed pro bono work for children in need of commitment to mental facilities. The money was adequate, but not important. She had money once, lots of it, and it had brought nothing but misery.

She sipped the southern pecan, pronounced it good, and planned the day with Clint. It was a ritual adhered to whenever possible.

As she picked up the newspaper, the buzzer rang as the door opened. Clint jumped to answer it. He found Mark Sway standing in the reception room, wet from the drizzle and out of breath,

'Good morning, Mark. You're all wet.'

'I need to see Reggie.' His bangs stuck to his forehead and water dripped from his nose. He was in a daze.

'Sure.' Clint backed away from him, and returned with a hand towel from the rest room. He wiped Mark's face, and said, 'Follow me.'

Reggie was waiting in the center of her office. Clint closed the door and left them alone.

'What's the matter?' she asked.

'I think we need to talk.' She pointed, and he sat in a wingback chair and she sat on the sofa.

'What's going on, Mark?' His eyes were red and tired. He stared at the flowers on the coffee table.

'Ricky snapped out of it early this morning.'

'That's great. What time?'

'A couple of hours ago.'

'You look tired. Would you like some hot cocoa?'

'No. Did you see the paper this morning?'

'Yeah, I saw it. Does it scare you?'

'Of course it scares me.' Clint knocked on the door, then opened it and brought the hot cocoa anyway. Mark thanked him and held it with both hands. He was cold and the warm cup helped. Clint closed the door and was gone.

'When do we meet with the FBI?' he asked.

'In an hour. Why?'

He sipped the cocoa and it burned his tongue. 'I'm not sure I want to talk to them.'

'Okay. You don't have to, you know. I've explained all this.'

'I know. Can I ask you something?'

'Of course, Mark. You look scared.'

154

'It's been a rough morning.' He took another tiny sip, then another. 'What would happen to me if I never told anyone what I know?'

'You've told me.'

'Yeah, but you can't tell. And I haven't told you everything, right?'

'That's right.'

'I've told you that I know where the body is, but I haven't told – '

'I know, Mark. I don't know where it is. There's a big difference, and I certainly understand it.'

'Do you want to know?'

'Do you want to tell me?'

'Not really. Not now.'

She was relieved but didn't show it. 'Okay, then I don't want to know.'

'So what happens to me if I never tell?'

She'd thought about this for hours, and still had no answer. But she'd met Foltrigg, had watched him under pressure, and was convinced he would try all legal means to extract the information from her client. As much as she wanted to, she could not advise him to lie.

A lie would work just fine. One simple lie, and Mark Sway could live the rest of his life without regard to what happened in New Orleans. And why should he worry about Muldanno and Foltrigg and the late Boyd Boyette? He was just a kid, guilty of neither crime nor major sin.

'I think that an effort will be made to force you to talk.'

'How does it work?'

'I'm not sure. It's very rare, but I believe steps can be taken in court to force you to testify about what you know. Clint and I have been researching it.'

'I know what Clifford told me, but I don't know if it's the truth.'

'But you think it's the truth, don't you, Mark?'

'I think so, I guess. I don't know what to do.' He was mumbling softly, at times barely audible, unwilling to look at her. 'Can they make me talk?' he asked.

155

She answered carefully. 'It could happen. I mean, a lot of things could happen. But, yes, a judge in a courtroom one day soon could order you to talk.'

'And if I refused?'

'Good question, Mark. It's a gray area. If an adult refuses a court order, he's in contempt of court and runs the risk of being locked up. I don't know what they'd do with a child. I've never heard of it before.'

'What about a polygraph?'

'What do you mean?'

'Well, let's say they drag me into court, and the judge tells me to spill my guts, and I tell the story but leave out the most important part. And they think I'm lying. What then? Can they strap me in the chair and start asking questions? I saw it in a movie one time.'

'You saw a child take a polygraph?'

'No. It was some cop who got caught lying. But, I mean, can they do it to me?'

'I doubt it. I've never heard of it, and I'd be fighting like crazy to stop it.'

'But it could happen.'

'I'm not sure. I doubt it.' These were hard questions coming at her like gunfire, and she had to be careful. Clients often heard what they wanted to hear, and missed the rest. 'But I must warn you, Mark, if you lie in court you could be in big trouble.'

He thought about this for a second, and said, 'If I tell the truth I'm in bigger trouble.'

'Why?'

She waited a long time for a response. Every twenty seconds or so, he would take a sip of the cocoa, but he was not at all interested in answering this question. The silence did not bother him. He stared at the table, but his mind whirled away somewhere else.

'Mark, last night you indicated you were ready to talk to the FBI and tell them your story. Now, it's obvious you've changed your mind. Why? What's happened?'

Without a word, he gently placed the cup on the table and

covered his eyes with his fists. His chin dropped to his chest, and he started crying.

The door opened into the reception area and a Federal Express lady ran in with a box three inches thick. All smiles and perfect efficiency, she handed it to Clint and showed him where to sign. She thanked him, wished him a nice day, and vanished.

The package was expected. It was from Print Research, an amazing little outfit in D.C. that did nothing but scan two hundred daily newspapers nationwide and catalogue the stories. The news was clipped, copied, computerized, and readily available within twenty-four hours for those willing to pay. Reggie didn't want to pay, but she needed quick background on Boyette et al. Clint had placed the order yesterday, as soon as Mark left and Reggie had herself a new client. The search was limited to the New Orleans and Washington papers.

He removed the contents, a neat stack of eight and a half by eleven Xerox copies of newspaper stories, headlines, and photos, all arranged in perfect chronological order, all copied with the columns straight and the photos clean.

Boyette was an old Democrat from New Orleans, and he'd served several terms as an undistinguished rank and file member of the US House, when one day Senator Dauvin, an antebellum relic from the Civil War, suddenly died in office at the age of ninety-one. Boyette pulled strings and twisted arms, and in keeping with the great tradition of Louisiana politics rounded up some cash and found a home for it. He was appointed by the Governor to fill the unexpired portion of Dauvin's term. The theory was simple: If a man had enough sense to accumulate a bunch of cash, then he would certainly make a worthy US Senator.

Boyette became a member of the world's most exclusive club, and with time proved himself quite capable. Over the years he narrowly missed a few indictments, and evidently learned his lessons. He survived two close re-elections, and finally reached a point attained by most southern senators

157

where he was simply left alone. When this happened, Boyette slowly mellowed, and changed from a hell-raising segregationist to a rather liberal and open-minded statesman. He lost favor with three straight governors in Louisiana, and in doing so became an outcast with the petroleum and chemical companies that had ruined the ecology of the state.

So Boyd Boyette became a radical environmentalist, something unheard of among southern politicians. He railed against the oil and gas industry, and it vowed to defeat him. He held hearings in small bayou towns devastated by the oil boom and bust, and made enemies in the tall buildings in New Orleans. Senator Boyette embraced the crumbling ecology of his beloved state, and studied it with a passion.

Six years ago, someone in New Orleans had floated out a proposal to build a toxic waste dump in Lafourche Parish, about eighty miles southwest of New Orleans. It was quickly killed for the first time by local authorities. As is true with most ideas created by rich, corporate minds, it didn't go away, but rather came back a year later with a different name, a different set of consultants, new promises of local jobs, and a new mouthpiece doing the presenting. It was voted down by the locals for the second time, but the vote was much closer. A year passed, some money changed hands, cosmetic changes were made to the plans, and it was suddenly back on the agenda. The folks who lived around the site were hysterical. Rumors were rampant, especially a persistent one that the New Orleans mob was behind the dump and would not stop until it was a reality. Of course, millions were at stake.

The New Orleans papers did a credible job of linking the mob to the toxic waste site. A dozen corporations were involved, and names and addresses led to several known and undisputed crime figures.

The stage was set, the deal was done, the dump was to be approved, then Senator Boyd Boyette came crashing in with an army of federal regulators. He threatened investigations by a dozen agencies. He held weekly press conferences. He made speeches all over southern Louisiana. The advocates of the waste site ran for cover. The corporations issued terse statements of no comment. Boyette had them on the ropes, and he was enjoying himself immensely.

On the night of his disappearance, the Senator had attended an angry meeting of local citizens at a packed high school gymnasium in Houma. He left late, and alone, as was his custom, for the hour drive to his home near New Orleans. Years earlier, Boyette had grown weary of the constant small talk and incessant ass kissing of aides, and he preferred to drive by himself whenever possible. He was studying Russian, his fourth language, and he cherished the solitude of his Cadillac and the language tapes.

By noon the next day, it was determined the Senator was missing. The splashy headlines from New Orleans told the story. Bold headlines in the *Washington Post* suspected foul play. Days went by and the news was scarce. No body was found. A hundred old photos of the Senator were dug up and used by the newspapers. The story was becoming old when, suddenly, the name of Barry Muldanno was linked to the disappearance and this set off a frenzy of Mafia dirt and trash. A rather frightening mug shot of a young Muldanno ran on page one in New Orleans. The paper rehashed its earlier stories about the waste site and the mob. The Blade was a known hit man with a criminal record. And on and on.

Roy Foltrigg made a grand entrance into the story when he stepped in front of the cameras to announce the indictment of Barry Muldanno for the murder of Senator Boyd Boyette. He, too, got the front page in both New Orleans and Washington, and Clint remembered a similar photo in the Memphis paper. Big news, but no body. This, however, did not throttle Mr Foltrigg. He ranted against organized crime. He predicted certain victory. He preached his carefully prepared remarks with the flair of a veteran stage actor, shouting at all the right moments, pointing his

159

finger, waving the indictment. He had no comment about the absence of a corpse, but hinted that he knew something he couldn't tell and said he had no doubt the remains of the late Senator would be found.

There were pictures and stories when Barry Muldanno was arrested, or rather, turned himself in to the FBI. He spent three days in jail before bail was arranged, and there were photos of him leaving just as he had arrived. He wore a dark suit and smiled at the cameras. He was innocent, he proclaimed. It was a vendetta.

There were photos of bulldozers, taken from a distance, as the FBI trenched its way through the soggy soil of New Orleans searching for the body. More of Foltrigg performing for the press. More investigative reports of New Orleans's rich history of organized crime. The story seemed to lose steam as the search continued.

The Governor, a Democrat, appointed a crony to serve the remaining year and a half of Boyette's term. The New Orleans paper ran an analysis of the many politicians waiting anxiously to run for the Senate. Foltrigg was one of two Republicans rumored to be interested.

He sat next to her on the sofa, and wiped his eyes. He hated himself for crying, but it could not be helped. Her arm was around his shoulder, and she patted him gently.

'You don't have to say a word,' she repeated quietly.

'I really don't want to. Maybe later, if I have to, but not now. Okay?'

'Okay, Mark.'

There was a knock at the door. 'Come in,' Reggie said just loud enough to be heard. Clint appeared holding a stack of papers and looking at his watch.

'Sorry to interrupt. But it's almost ten, and Mr Foltrigg will be here in a minute.' He placed the papers on the coffee table in front of her. 'You wanted to see these before the meeting.'

'Tell Mr Foltrigg we have nothing to discuss,' Reggie said.

Clint frowned at her and looked at Mark. He sat close to

her as if he needed protecting. 'You're not going to see him?'

'No. Tell him the meeting's been cancelled because we have nothing to say,' she said, and nodded at Mark.

Clint glanced at his watch again and backed awkwardly to the door. 'Sure,' he said with a smile as if he suddenly enjoyed the idea of telling Foltrigg to take a hike. He closed the door behind him.

'Are you okay?' she asked.

'Not really.'

She leaned forward and began flipping through the copies of the clippings. Mark sat in a daze, tired and drained, still frightened after talking things over with his lawyer. She scanned the pages, reading the headlines and captions and pulling the photographs closer to her. About a third of the way through, she suddenly stopped and leaned back on the sofa. She handed Mark a close-up of Barry Muldanno as he smiled at the camera. It was from the New Orleans paper. 'Is this the man?'

Mark looked without touching it. 'No. Who is it?'

'It's Barry Muldanno.'

'That's not the man who grabbed me. I guess he's got a lot of friends.'

She placed the copy in the stack on the coffee table, and patted him on the leg.

'What're you gonna do?' he asked.

'Make a few calls. I'll talk to the administrator of the hospital and arrange security around Ricky's room.'

'You can't tell him about this guy, Reggie. They'll kill us. We can't tell anybody.'

'I won't. I'll explain to the hospital that there have been some threats. It's routine in criminal cases. They'll place a few guards on the ninth floor around the room.'

'I don't want to tell Mom either. She's stressed out with Ricky, and she's taking pills to sleep and pills to do this and that, and I just don't think she can handle this right now.'

'You're right.' He was a tough little kid, raised on the streets and wise beyond his years. She admired his courage.

161

'Do you think Mom and Ricky are safe?'

'Of course. These men are professionals, Mark. They won't do anything stupid. They'll lay low and listen. They may be bluffing.' She did not sound sincere.

'No, they're not bluffing. I saw the knife, Reggie. They're here in Memphis for one reason, and that's to scare the hell out of me. And it's working. I ain't talking.'

FIFTEEN

Foltrigg yelled only once, then stormed from the office making threats and slamming the door. McThune and Trumann were frustrated, but also embarrassed at his antics. As they left, McThune rolled his eyes at Clint as if he wanted to apologize for this pompous loudmouth. Clint relished the moment, and when the dust settled he walked to Reggie's office.

Mark had pulled a chair to the window, and sat watching it rain on the street and sidewalk below. Reggie was on the phone with the hospital administrator discussing security on the ninth floor. She covered the phone, and Clint whispered that they were gone. He left to get more cocoa for Mark, who never moved.

Within minutes, Clint took a call from George Ord, and he buzzed Reggie on the intercom. She'd never met the US Attorney from Memphis, but was not surprised that he was now on the phone. She allowed him to hold for one full minute, then picked up the phone. 'Hello.'

'Ms Love, this is –'

'It's Reggie, okay. Just Reggie. And you're George, right?' She called everyone by their first name, even stuffy judges in their proper little courtrooms.

'Right, Reggie. This is George Ord. Roy Foltrigg is in my office, and –'

'What a coincidence. He just left mine.'

'Yeah, and that's why I'm calling. He didn't get a chance to talk to you and your client.'

163

'Give him my apologies. My client has nothing to say to him.' She was talking and looking at the back of Mark's head. If he were listening, she couldn't tell. He was frozen in the chair at the window.

'Reggie, I think it would be wise if you at least meet with Mr Foltrigg again.'

'I have no desire to meet with Roy, nor does my client.' She could picture Ord speaking gravely into the phone with Foltrigg pacing around the office waving his arms.

'Well, this will not be the end of it, you know?'

'Is that a threat, George?'

'It's more of a promise.'

'Fine. You tell Roy and his boys that if anyone attempts to contact my client or his family I'll have their asses. Okay, George?'

'I'll relay the message.'

It was really sort of funny – it was not, after all, his case –but Ord could not laugh. He returned the receiver to its place, smiled to himself, and said, 'She says she ain't talking, the kid ain't talking, and if you or anyone else contacts the kid or his family she'll, uh, have your asses, as she put it.'

Foltrigg bit his lip and nodded at every word as if this was fine because he could play hardball with the best of them. He had regained his composure and was already implementing Plan B. He paced around the office as if in deep thought. McThune and Trumann stood by the door like sentries. Bored sentries.

'I want the kid followed, okay,' Foltrigg finally snapped at McThune. 'We're leaving for New Orleans, and I want you guys to tail him twenty-four hours a day. I want to know what he does, and, more importantly, he needs to be protected from Muldanno and his henchmen.'

McThune did not take orders from any US Attorney, and at this moment he was sick of Roy Foltrigg. And the idea of using three or four overworked agents to follow an eleven-year-old kid was quite stupid. But, it was not worth the fight. Foltrigg had a hot line to Director Voyles in

Washington, and Director Voyles wanted the body and he wanted a conviction almost as bad as Foltrigg.

'Okay,' he said. 'We'll get it done.'

'Paul Gronke's already here somewhere,' Foltrigg said as though he'd just heard fresh gossip. They knew the flight number and his time of arrival eleven hours ago. They had, however, managed to lose his trail once he left the Memphis airport. They had discussed it with Ord and Foltrigg and a dozen other FBI agents for two hours this morning. At this very moment, no less than eight agents were trying to find Gronke in Memphis.

'We'll find him,' McThune said. 'And we'll watch the kid. Why don't you get your ass back to New Orleans?'

'I'll get the van ready,' Trumann said officially as if the van was in fact *Air Force One*.

Foltrigg stopped pacing in front of Ord's desk. 'We're leaving, George. Sorry for the intrusion. I'll probably be back in a couple of days.'

What wonderful news, Ord thought. He stood, and they shook hands. 'Anytime,' he said. 'If we can help, just call.'

'I'll meet with Judge Lamond first thing in the morning. I'll let you know.'

Ord offered his hand again for one final shake. Foltrigg took it and headed for the door. 'Watch out for these thugs,' he advised McThune. 'I don't think he's dumb enough to touch the kid, but who knows.' McThune opened the door and waved him through. Ord followed.

'Muldanno's heard something,' Foltrigg continued, 'and they're just snooping around here.' He was in the outer office where Wally Boxx and Thomas Fink waited. 'But keep an eye on them, okay, George? These guys are really dangerous. And follow the kid, too, and watch his lawyer. And thanks a million. I'll call you tomorrow. Where's the van, Wally?'

After an hour of watching the sidewalks, sipping hot cocoa, and listening to his lawyer practice law, Mark was ready for a move. Reggie had called Dianne and explained that Mark was in her office killing time and helping with the paperwork. Ricky was much better, sleeping again. He'd consumed half a gallon of ice cream while Greenway asked him a hundred questions.

At eleven, Mark parked himself at Clint's desk and inspected the dictating equipment. Reggie had a client, a woman who desperately wanted a divorce, and they needed to plot strategy for an hour. Clint typed away on long paper and grabbed the phone every five minutes.

'How'd you become a secretary?' Mark asked, very bored with this candid view of the practice of law.

Clint turned and smiled at him. 'It was an accident.'

'Did you want to be a secretary when you were a kid?'

'No. I wanted to build swimming pools.'

'What happened?'

'I don't know. I got messed up on drugs, almost flunked out of high school, then went to college, then went to law school.'

'You have to go to law school to be a secretary in a law office?'

'No. I flunked out of law school, and Reggie gave me a job. It's fun, most of the time.'

'Where'd you meet Reggie?'

'It's a long story. We were friends in law school. We've been friends for a long time. She'll probably tell you about it when you meet Momma Love.'

'Momma who?'

'Momma Love. She hasn't told you about Momma Love?'

'No.'

'Momma Love is Reggie's mother. They live together, and she loves to cook for the kids Reggie represents. She fixes inside-out ravioli and spinach lasagne and all sorts of delicious Italian food. Everyone loves it.'

After two days of doughnuts and green Jell-O, the mention of thick, cheesy dishes cooked at someone's home was terribly inviting. 'When do you think I might meet Momma Love?'

166

'I don't know. Reggie takes most of her clients home, especially the younger ones.'

'Does she have any kids?'

'Two, but they're grown and live away.'

'Where does Momma Love live?'

'In midtown, not far from here. It's an old house she's owned for years. In fact, it's the house Reggie grew up in.'

The phone rang. Clint took the message and returned to his typewriter. Mark watched intently.

'How'd you learn to type so fast?'

The typing stopped, and he slowly turned and looked at Mark. He smiled, and said, 'In high school. I had this teacher who was like a drill sergeant. We hated her, but she made us learn. Can you type?'

'A little. I've had three years of computer at school.'

Clint pointed to his Apple next to the typewriter. 'We've got all sorts of computers around here.'

Mark glanced at it, but was not impressed. Everybody had computers. 'So how'd you get to be a secretary?'

'It wasn't planned. When Reggie finished law school, she didn't want to work for anybody, so she opened this office. It was about four years ago. She needed a secretary, and I volunteered. Have you seen a male secretary before?'

'No. Didn't know men could be secretaries. How's the money?'

Clint chuckled at this. 'It's okay. If Reggie has a good month, then I have a good month. We're sort of like partners.'

'Does she make a lot of money?'

'Not really. She doesn't want a lot of money. A few years ago she was married to a doctor, and they had a big house and lots of money. Everything went to hell, and she blames the money for most of it. She'll probably tell you about it. She's very honest about her life.'

'She's a lawyer and she doesn't want money?'

'Unusual, isn't it?'

'I'll say. I mean, I've seen a lot of lawyer shows on television, and all they do is talk about money. Sex and money.'

The phone rang. It was a judge, and Clint got real nice and chatted with him for five minutes. He hung up and returned to his typing. As he reached full speed, Mark asked, 'Who's that woman in there?'

Clint stopped, stared at the keys, and slowly turned around. His chair squeaked. He forced a quick smile. 'In there with Reggie?'

'Yeah.'

'Norma Thrash.'

'What's her problem?'

'She's got a bunch of them, really. She's in the middle of a nasty divorce. Husband's a real jerk.'

Mark was curious about how much Clint knew. 'Does he beat her up?'

'I don't think so,' he answered slowly.

'Do they have kids at all?'

'Two. I really can't say much about it. It's confidential, you know?'

'Yeah, I know. But you probably know everything, don't you? I mean, after all, you type it up.'

'I know most of what goes on. Sure. But Reggie doesn't tell me everything. For example, I have no idea what you've told her. I assume it's pretty serious, but she'll keep it to herself. I've read the newspaper. I've seen the FBI and Mr Foltrigg, but I don't know the details.'

This was exactly what Mark wanted to hear. 'Do you know Robert Hackstraw? They call him Hack.'

'He's a lawyer, isn't he?'

'Yeah. He represented my mother in her divorce a couple of years ago. A real moron.'

'You weren't impressed with her lawyer?'

'I hated Hack. He treated us like dirt. We'd go to his office and wait for two hours. Then he'd talk to us for ten minutes, and tell us he was in a big hurry, had to get to court because he was so important. I tried to convince Mom to get another lawyer, but she was too stressed out.'

'Did it go to trial?'

'Yeah. My ex-father thought he should get one kid,

didn't really care which one but he preferred Ricky 'cause he knew I hated him, so he hired a lawyer, and for two days my mother and my father trashed each other in court. They tried to prove each other was unfit. Hack was a complete fool in the courtroom, but my ex-father's lawyer was even worse. The judge hated both lawyers, and said he wasn't about to separate me and Ricky. I asked him if I could testify. He thought about it during lunch on the second day, and decided he wanted to hear what I had to say. I had asked Hack the same question, and he said something smart, like I was too young and dumb to testify.'

'But you testified.'

'Yeah, for three hours.'

'How'd it go?'

'I was pretty good, really. I just told about the beatings, the bruises, the stitches. I told him how much I hated my father. The judge almost cried.'

'And it worked?'

'Yeah. My father wanted some visitation rights, and I spent a lot of time explaining to the judge that I had no desire to ever see the man again once the trial was over. And, that Ricky was terrified of him. So the judge not only cut off all visitation, but also told my father to stay away from us.'

'Have you seen him since?'

'No. But I will one day. When I grow up, we'll catch him somewhere, me and Ricky, and we'll beat the living hell out of him. Bruise for bruise. Stitch for stitch. We talk about it all the time.'

Clint was no longer bored with this little conversation. He listened to every word. The kid was so casual about his plans for beating his father. 'You might go to jail.'

'He didn't go to jail when he beat us. He didn't go to jail when he stripped my mother naked and threw her in the street with blood all over her. That's when I hit him with the baseball bat.'

'You what?'

'He was drinking one night at home, and we could tell he

169

was about to get out of hand. We could always tell. Then he left to buy more beer. I ran down the street and borrowed an aluminum tee ball bat from Michael Moss. I hid it under my bed, and I remember praying for a good car wreck so he wouldn't come home. But he did. Mom was in their bedroom, hoping he would just pass out, which he did all the time. Ricky and I stayed in our room, waiting for the explosion.'

The phone rang again, and Clint quickly took the message and returned to the story.

'About an hour later there was all this yelling and cussing. The trailer was shaking. We locked the door. Ricky was under the bed, crying. Then Mom started yelling for me. I was seven years old, and Mom wanted me to rescue her. He was just beating the hell out of her, throwing her around, kicking her, ripping her shirt off, calling her a whore and a slut. I didn't even know what those words meant. I walked to the kitchen. I guess I was too scared to move. He saw me and threw a beer can at me. She tried to run outside, but he caught her and tore her pants off. God, he was hitting her so hard. Then he ripped off her underwear. Her lip was busted and there was blood everywhere. He threw her outside, completely naked, and dragged her into the street where, of course, the neighbors were watching. Then he laughed at her, and left her lying there. It was horrible.'

Clint leaned forward and hung on every word. Mark was speaking in a monotone, showing absolutely no emotion.

'When he came back to the trailer, the door was of course open, and I was waiting. I had pulled a kitchen chair beside the door, and I damned near took his head off with the baseball bat. A perfect shot to his nose. I was crying and scared to death, but I'll always remember the sound of the bat crunching his face. He fell on the sofa, and I hit him once in the stomach. I was trying to land a good one in the crotch, because I figured that would hurt the most. Know what I mean? I was swinging like crazy. I hit him once more on the ear, and that was all she wrote.'

170

'What happened?' Clint snapped.

'He got up, slapped me in the face, knocked me down, cussed me, then started kicking me. I remember being so scared I couldn't fight. His face was a bloody mess. He smelled awful. He was growling and slapping and tearing my clothes off. I started kicking like crazy when he pulled at my underwear, but he got them off and threw me outside. Not a bit of clothing. I guess he wanted me in the street with my mother, but about that time she made it to the door and fell on me.'

He told it all so calmly, as if he'd done it a hundred times and the script was memorized. No emotion, just the facts in short clipped sentences. He would look at the desk, then stare at the door without missing a word.

'What happened?' Clint asked, almost out of breath.

'One of the neighbors had called the cops. I mean, you can hear everything in the next trailer, so our neighbors had suffered through this with us. And that was not the first fight, not by a long shot. I remember seeing blue lights in the street, and he disappeared somewhere inside the trailer. Me and Mom got up real quick and ran inside and got dressed. Some of the neighbors saw me naked, though. We tried to wash the blood off before the cops came in. My father had settled down quite a bit, and was suddenly real friendly with the cops. Me and Mom waited in the kitchen. His nose was the size of a football, and the cops were more concerned with his face than with me and Mom. He called one of the cops Frankie as if they were buddies. There were two cops, and they got everybody separated. Frankie took him to the bedroom to cool him off. The other cop sat with Mom at the kitchen table. This is what they always did. I went to our room, and got Ricky out from under the bed. Mom told me later that he got real chummy with the cops, said it was just a family fight, nothing serious, and that most of it was my fault because I, for no reason, had attacked him with a baseball bat. The cops referred to it as just another domestic disturbance, same thing they always said. No charges were filed. They took him to the hospital where he

171

spent the night. Had to wear this ugly white mask for a while.'

'What'd he do to you?'

'He didn't drink for a long time after that. He apologized to us, promised it would never happen again. Sometimes he was okay when he wasn't drinking. But then he got worse. More beatings and all. Mom finally filed for divorce.'

'And he tried to get custody –'

'Yeah. He lied in court, and he was doing a pretty good job of it. He didn't know I was going to testify, so he denied a bunch of it and said Mom was lying about the rest. He was real cocky and cool in court, and our dumbass lawyer couldn't do anything with him. But, when I testified and told about the baseball bat and getting my clothes ripped off, that's when the judge had tears in his eyes. He got real mad at my ex-father, accused him of lying. Said he ought to throw his sorry ass in jail for lying. I told him I thought that's exactly what he should do.' He paused for a second.

The sentences were a bit slower, and Mark was losing steam. Clint was still mesmerized.

'Of course, Hack took full credit for another brilliant courtroom victory. Then he threatened to sue Mom if she didn't pay him. She had a bunch of bills, and he was calling twice a week wanting the rest of his fee, so she had to file for bankruptcy. Then she lost her job.'

'So you've been through a divorce, and then a bankruptcy?'

'Yeah. The bankruptcy lawyer was a real bozo too.'

'But you like Reggie?'

'Yeah. Reggie's cool.'

'That's good to hear.'

The phone rang, and Clint picked it up. A lawyer from Juvenile Court wanted some information on a client, and the conversation dragged on. Mark left to find the hot cocoa. He passed the conference room with pretty books covering the walls. He found the tiny kitchen next to the rest room.

There was a Sprite in the refrigerator, and he unscrewed

172

the top. Clint was amazed by his story, he could tell. He had left out many of the details, but it was all true. He was proud of it, in a way, proud of defending his mother, and the story always amazed people.

Then the tough little kid with the baseball bat remembered the knife attack in the elevator, and the folded photograph of the poor, fatherless family. He thought of his mother at the hospital, all alone and unprotected. He was suddenly scared again.

He tried to open a package of saltines, but his hands shook and the plastic wouldn't open. The shaking got worse and he couldn't stop it. He slumped to the floor and spilled the Sprite.

SIXTEEN

The light rain had stopped in time for the rush of secretaries who moved in hurried groups of three and four along the damp sidewalks in pursuit of lunch. The sky was gray and the streets were wet. Clouds of mist boiled and hissed behind each passing car along Third Street. Reggie and her client turned on Madison. Her briefcase was in her left hand, and with her right she held his hand and guided him through the crowd. She had places to go and walked quickly.

From a generic white Ford van parked almost directly in front of the Sterick Building, Jack Nance watched and radioed ahead. When they turned on Madison and were lost from sight, he listened. Within minutes, Cal Sisson, his partner, had them and was watching as they headed for the hospital, as expected. Five minutes later, they were in the hospital.

Nance locked the van and jaywalked across Third. He entered the Sterick Building, rode the elevator to the second floor, and gently turned the knob of the door with REGGIE LOVE – LAWYER on it. It was unlocked, which was a pleasant surprise. Eleven minutes had passed since noon. Virtually every lawyer with a nickel and dime solo practice in this city broke for lunch and locked the office. He opened the door and stepped inside as a hideous buzzer went off above his head and announced his arrival. Dammit! He'd hoped to enter through a locked door, something he was very proficient at, and dig through files without being

174

interrupted. It was easy work. Most of these small outfits thought nothing of security. The big firms were a different story, although in the off-hours Nance could enter any one of a thousand law offices in Memphis and find whatever he wanted. He'd done it at least a dozen times. There were two things ham and egg lawyers did not have at their offices – cash and security devices. They locked their doors, and that was it.

A young man appeared from the back, and said, 'Yes. Can I help you?'

'Yeah,' Nance said without a smile. All business. Rough day. 'I'm with the *Times-Picayune*, you know the paper in New Orleans. Looking for Reggie Love.'

Clint stopped ten feet away. 'She's not here.'

'When might she return?'

'Don't know. You have any identification?'

Nance was headed for the door. 'You mean, like little white cards you lawyers throw on the sidewalks. No, pal, I don't carry business cards. I'm a reporter.'

'Fine. What's your name?'

'Arnie Carpentier. Tell her I'll catch her later.' He opened the door, the buzzer worked again, and he was gone. Not a productive visit, but he'd met Clint and seen the front room and reception area. The next visit would take longer.

The ride to the ninth floor was uneventful. Reggie held his hand, which normally would have irritated him but was rather comforting under the circumstances. He studied his feet as they ascended. He was afraid to look up, afraid of more strangers. He squeezed her hand.

They spilled into the lobby on the ninth floor and had taken no more than ten steps before three people rushed them from the direction of the waiting area. 'Ms. Love! Ms. Love,' one of them yelled. Reggie at first was startled, but gripped Mark's hand tighter and kept walking. One had a microphone, one a notepad, and one a camera. The one with the notepad said, 'Ms. Love, just a few quick questions.'

They walked faster toward the nurses' station. 'No comment.'

'Is it true your client is refusing to cooperate with the FBI and the police?'

'No comment,' she said, looking ahead. They followed like bloodhounds. She leaned quickly to Mark, and said, 'Don't look at them and don't say a word.'

'It is true the US Attorney from New Orleans was in your office this morning?'

'No comment.'

Doctors, nurses, patients, everybody vacated the center of the hallway as Reggie and her famous client raced along followed by the yelping dogs.

'Did your client talk to Jerome Clifford before he died?'

She squeezed his hand harder and walked faster. 'No comment.'

As they neared the end of the hall, the clown with the camera suddenly dashed in front of them, knelt low as he backpedalled, and managed to get a shot before he landed on his ass. The nurses laughed. A security guard stepped forward at the nurses' station and raised his hands at the yelpers. They had met him before.

As Reggie and Mark rounded a bend in the hall, one called out, 'Is it true your client knows where Boyette is buried?'

There was a slight hesitation in her step. The shoulders jumped and the back arched, then she was over it and she and her client were gone.

Two overweight security guards in uniform sat in folding chairs by Ricky's door. They had pistols on their hips, and Mark noticed the pistols before anything else. One had a newspaper, which he promptly lowered as they approached. The other stood to greet them. 'Can I help you?' he asked Reggie.

'Yes. I'm the attorney for the family, and this is Mark Sway, the patient's brother.' She spoke in a professional whisper as if she had a right to be there and they didn't, so be quick with the questions because she had things to do.

'Dr. Greenway is expecting us,' she said as she walked to the door and knocked. Mark stood behind her, staring at the pistol, which was remarkably similar to the one poor Romey had used.

The security guard returned to his seat and his partner returned to his paper. Greenway opened the door and stepped outside, followed by Dianne, who had been crying. She hugged Mark and placed her arm on his shoulder.

'He's asleep,' Greenway said quietly to Reggie and Mark. 'Doing much better, but very tired.'

'He was asking about you,' Dianne whispered to Mark.

He looked at the moist eyes and asked, 'What's the matter, Mom?'

'Nothing. We'll talk about it later.'

'What's happened?'

Dianne looked at Greenway, then at Reggie, then at Mark. 'It's nothing,' she said.

'Your mother was fired this morning, Mark,' Greenway said. He looked at Reggie. 'These people sent a letter by courier informing her she'd been fired. Can you believe it? Had it delivered to the nurses here on the ninth floor, and one of them delivered it about an hour ago.'

'Let me see the letter,' Reggie said. Dianne pulled it from a pocket. Reggie unfolded it and read slowly. Dianne hugged Mark, and said, 'It'll be all right, Mark. We've managed before. I'll find another job.'

Mark bit his lip and wanted to cry.

'Can I keep this?' Reggie said as she stuffed it in her briefcase. Dianne nodded yes.

Greenway studied his watch as if he couldn't determine the correct time. 'I'm gonna grab a quick sandwich, and I'll be back here in twenty minutes. I want to spend a couple of hours with Ricky and Mark, alone.'

Reggie glanced at her watch. 'I'll be back around four. There are reporters here, and I want you to ignore them.' She was talking to all three of them.

'Yeah, just say no comment, no comment,' Mark added helpfully. 'It's really fun.'

177

Dianne missed the fun. 'What do they want?'

'Everything. They've seen the newspaper. The rumors are rampant. They smell a story, and they'll do anything to get information. I saw a television van on the street, and I suspect they're somewhere close by. I think it's best if you stay here with Mark.'

'Okay,' Dianne said.

'Where's a telephone?' Reggie said.

Greenway pointed in the direction of the nurses' station. 'Come on: I'll show you.'

'I'll see you guys at four, okay?' she said to Dianne and Mark. 'Remember, not a word to anyone. And stay close to this room.'

She and Greenway disappeared around the bend. The security guards were half-asleep. Mark and his mother entered the dark room and sat on the bed. A stale doughnut caught his attention, and he devoured it in four bites.

Reggie called her office, and Clint answered. 'You remember that lawsuit we filed last year on behalf of Penny Patoula?' she asked softly, looking around for the blood-hounds. 'It was sex discrimination, wrongful discharge, harassment, the works. I think we threw in everything. Circuit Court. Yeah, that's it. Pull the file. Change the name from Penny Patoula to Dianne Sway. The defendant will be Ark-Lon Fixtures. I want you to name the president individually. His name is Chester Tanfill. Yeah, make him a defendant too, and sue for wrongful discharge, labor violations, sexual harassment, throw in an equal rights charge, and ask for a million or two in damages. Do it now, and quickly. Prepare a summons, and a check for the filing fee. Run over to the courthouse and file it. I'll be there in about thirty minutes to pick it up, so hurry. I'll personally deliver it to Mr Tanfill.'

She hung up and thanked the nearest nurse. The reporters were loitering near the soft drink machine, but she was through the door to the stairwell before they saw her.

*

Ark-Lon Fixtures was a series of metal connected buildings on a street of such structures in a minimum wage industrial park near the airport. The front building was a faded orange in color, and expansion had taken place in every direction except toward the street. The newer additions were of the same general architecture but with different shades of orange. Trucks waited near a loading dock in the rear. An enclosed chain-link fence protected rolls of steel and aluminum.

Reggie parked near the front in a space reserved for visitors. She held her briefcase, and opened the door. A chesty woman with black hair and a long cigarette ignored her and listened to the phone stuck in her ear. Reggie stood before her, waiting impatiently. The room was dusty, dirty, and clouded with blue cigarette smoke. Matted pictures of beagles adorned the walls. Half the fluorescent lights were out.

'May I help you?' the receptionist asked as she lowered the phone.

'I need to see Chester Tanfill.'

'He's in a meeting.'

'I know. He's a very busy man, but I have something for him.'

The receptionist placed the phone on the desk. 'I see. And what might that be?'

'It's really none of your business. I need to see Chester Tanfill. It's urgent.'

This really pissed her off. The nameplate declared her to be Louise Chenault. 'I don't care how urgent it is, ma'am. You can't just barge in here and demand to see the president of this company.'

'This company is a sweatshop, and I've just sued it for two million bucks. And I've also sued Chester boy for a couple of million, and I'm telling you to find his sorry ass and get him out here immediately.'

Louise jumped to her feet, and backed away from the desk. 'Are you some kind of lawyer?'

Reggie pulled the lawsuit and the summons from the

179

briefcase. She looked at it, ignored Louise, and said, 'I am indeed a lawyer. And I need to serve these papers on Chester. Now find him. If he's not here in five minutes, I'll amend it and ask for five million in damages.'

Louise bolted from the room and ran through a set of double doors. Reggie waited a second, then followed. She walked through a room filled with tacky, cramped cubicles. Cigarette smoke seemed to ooze from every opening. The carpet was ancient shag and badly worn. She caught a glimpse of Louise's round rump darting into a door on the right, and she followed.

Chester Tanfill was in the process of standing behind his desk when Reggie barged in. Louise was speechless. 'You can leave now,' Reggie said rudely. 'I'm Reggie Love, Attorney-at-Law,' she said, glaring at Chester.

'Chester Tanfill,' he said without offering a hand. She wouldn't have taken it. 'This is a bit rude, Ms Love.'

'The name is Reggie, okay, Chester? Tell Louise to leave.'

He nodded and Louise gladly left, closing the door behind her.

'What do you want?' he snapped. He was wiry and gaunt, around fifty, with a spotted face and puffy eyes partially hidden behind wire-rimmed glasses. A drinking problem, she thought. The clothes were Sears or Penney's. His neck was turning dark red.

She threw the lawsuit and the summons on his desk. 'I'm serving you with this lawsuit.'

He smirked at it, a man unafraid of lawyers and their games. 'For what?'

'I represent Dianne Sway. You fired her this morning, and we're suing you this afternoon. How's that for swift justice?'

Chester's eyes narrowed and he looked at the lawsuit again. 'You're kidding.'

'You're a fool if you think I'm kidding. It's all right there, Chester. Wrongful discharge, sexual harassment, the works. A couple of million in damages. I file these things all the time. I must say, however, that this is one of the best I've seen. This poor woman has been at the hospital for two days with her son. Her doctor says she cannot leave his bedside. In fact, he's called here and explained her situation, but no, you assholes fire her for missing work. I can't wait to explain this to a jury.'

It sometimes took Chester's lawyer two days to return a phone call, and this woman, Dianne Sway, files a full-blown lawsuit within hours of being terminated. He slowly picked up the papers and studied the front page. 'I'm named personally?' he asked as if his feelings were hurt.

'You fired her, Chester. Don't worry though, when the jury returns a verdict against you individually, you can simply file for bankruptcy.'

Chester pulled his chair under him and carefully sat down. 'Please, sit,' he said, waving at a chair.

'No thanks. Who's your attorney?'

'Uh, geez, uh, Findley and Baker. But just wait a minute. Let me think about this.' He flipped the page and scanned the pleadings. 'Sexual harassment?'

'Yeah, that's a fertile field these days. Seems as though one of your supervisors has put the move on my client. Always suggesting things they might do in the rest room during lunch. Always telling dirty jokes. Lots of crude talk. It'll all come out at trial. Who should I call at Findley and Baker?'

'Just wait a minute.' He flipped the pages, then laid them on the desk. She stood next to his desk, glaring down. He rubbed his temples. 'I don't need this.'

'Neither did my client.'

'What does she want?'

'A little dignity. You run a sweatshop here. You prey on single working mothers who can barely feed their children on what you pay. They cannot afford to complain.'

He was rubbing his eyes now. 'Skip the lecture, okay. I just don't need this. There could, well, there might be some trouble at the top.'

'I couldn't care less about you and your troubles,

Chester. A copy of this lawsuit will be hand delivered to the *Memphis Press* this afternoon, and I'm sure it'll run tomorrow. The Sways are getting more than their share of ink these days.'

'What does she want?' he asked again.

'Are you trying to bargain?'

'Maybe. I don't think you can win this case, Ms Love, but I don't need the headache.'

'It'll be more than a headache, I promise. She makes nine hundred dollars a month, and takes home around six-fifty. That's eleven thousand bucks a year, and I promise your legal costs on this lawsuit will run five times that much. I'll obtain access to your personnel records. I'll take the depositions of other female employees. I'll open up your financial books. I'll subpoena all your records. And if I see anything the least bit improper, I'll notify the Equal Employment Opportunity Commission, the National Labor Relations Board, the IRS, OSHA, and anybody else who might be interested. I'll make you lose sleep, Chester. You'll wish a thousand times you hadn't fired my client.'

He slapped the table with both palms. 'What does she want, dammit!'

Reggie picked up her briefcase, and walked to the door. 'She wants her job. A raise would be nice, say from six bucks an hour to nine, if you can spare it. And if you can't, then do it anyway. Transfer her to another section, away from the dirty supervisor.'

Chester listened carefully. This was not too bad.

'She'll be in the hospital for a few weeks. She has bills, so I want the payroll checks to keep coming. In fact, Chester, I want the payroll checks delivered to the hospital, just like you clowns delivered her termination letter this morning. Every Friday, I want the check delivered. Okay?'

He slowly nodded yes.

'You have thirty days to answer the lawsuit. If you behave and do as I say, I'll dismiss it on the thirtieth day. You have my word. You don't have to tell your lawyers about it. Is it a deal?'

182

'Deal.'

Reggie opened the door. 'Oh, and send some flowers. Room 943. A card would be nice. In fact, send some fresh flowers every week. Okay, Chester?'

He was still nodding.

She slammed the door and left the grungy corporate offices of Ark-Lon Fixtures.

Mark and Ricky sat on the end of the foldaway bed and looked up into the bearded and intense face of Dr Greenway less than two feet away. Ricky wore a pair of Mark's hand-me-down pajamas with a blanket draped over his shoulders. He was cold, as usual, and scared, and uncertain about this first venture out of his bed, even though it was inches away. And he preferred his mother to be present, but the doctor had gently insisted on talking to the boys by themselves. Greenway had spent almost twelve hours now trying to win Ricky's confidence. He sat close to his big brother, who was bored with this little chat before it started.

The shades were pulled, the lights were dim, the room was dark except for a small lamp on a table by the bathroom. Greenway leaned forward with his elbows on his knees.

'Now, Ricky, I would like to talk about the other day when you and Mark went to the woods for a smoke. Okay?'

This frightened Ricky. How did Greenway know they were smoking? Mark leaned over an inch or two and said, 'It's okay, Ricky. I've already told them about it. Mom's not mad at us.'

'Do you remember going for a smoke?' Greenway asked.

Slowly, he nodded his head yes. 'Yes sir.'

'Why don't you tell me what you remember about you and Mark in the woods smoking a cigarette.'

He pulled the blanket tighter around him and knotted it with his hands at his stomach. 'I'm really cold,' he muttered, his teeth chattering.

'Ricky, the temperature is almost seventy-eight degrees

183

in here. And you've got the blanket and wool pajamas. Try and think about being warm, okay?'

He tried but it didn't help. Mark gently placed his arm around Ricky's shoulder, and this seemed to help.

'Do you remember smoking a cigarette?'

'I think so. Uh-huh.'

Mark glanced up at Greenway, then at Ricky.

'Okay. Do you remember seeing the big black car when it pulled up in the grass?'

Ricky suddenly stopped shaking and stared at the floor. He mumbled the word 'Yes,' and that would be his last word for twenty-four hours.

'And what did the big black car do when you first saw it?'

The mention of the cigarette had scared him, but the image of the black car and the fear it brought were simply too much. He bent over at the waist and placed his head on Mark's knee. His eyes were shut tightly, and he began sobbing, but with no tears.

Mark rubbed his hair, and repeated, 'It's okay, Ricky. It's okay. We need to talk about it.'

Greenway was unmoved. He crossed his bony legs and scratched his beard. He had expected this, and had warned Mark and Dianne that this first little session would not be productive. But it was very important.

'Ricky, listen to me,' he said in a childlike voice. 'Ricky, it's okay. I just want to talk to you. Okay, Ricky.'

But Ricky had had enough therapy for one day. He began to curl under the blanket, and Mark knew the thumb could not be far behind. Greenway nodded at him as if all was well. He stood, carefully lifted Ricky, and placed him in the bed.

SEVENTEEN

Wally Boxx stopped the van in heavy traffic on Camp Street, and ignored the horns and fingers as his boss and Fink and the FBI agents made a quick exit on to the sidewalk in front of the Federal Building. Foltrigg walked importantly up the steps with his entourage behind. In the lobby, a couple of bored reporters recognized him and began asking questions, but he was all business and had nothing but smiles and no comments.

He entered the offices of the United States Attorney for the Southern District of Louisiana, and the secretaries sprang to life. His assigned space in the building was a vast suite of small offices connected by hallways, and large open areas where the clerical staff performed, and smaller rooms where cubicles allowed some privacy for law clerks and paralegals. In all, forty-seven Assistant US Attorneys labored here under the commands of Reverend Roy. Another thirty-eight underlings plowed through the drudgery and paperwork and boring research and tedious attention to mindless details, all in an effort to protect the legal interests of Roy's client, the United States of America.

The largest office of course belonged to Foltrigg, and it was richly decorated with heavy wood and deep leather. Whereas most lawyers allow themselves only one Ego Wall with pictures and plaques and awards and certificates for Rotary Club memberships, Roy had covered no less than three of his with framed photographs and yellow fill-in-the-blank attendance diplomas from a hundred judicial conferences. He threw his jacket on the burgundy leather sofa, and headed directly for the main library where a meeting awaited him.

He had called six times during the five-hour trip from Memphis. There had been three faxes. Six assistants were waiting around a thirty-foot oak conference table covered with open law books and countless legal pads. All jackets were off and all sleeves rolled up.

He said hello to the group and took a chair at the center of the table. They each had a copy of a summarization of the FBI's findings in Memphis. The note, the fingerprints, the gun, everything. There was nothing new Foltrigg or Fink could tell them except that Gronke was in Memphis, and this was irrelevant to this group.

'What do you have, Bobby?' Foltrigg asked dramatically, as if the future of the American legal system rested upon Bobby and whatever he had uncovered in his research. Bobby was the dean of the assistants, a thirty-two-year veteran who hated courtrooms but loved libraries. In times of crisis when answers were needed for complex questions, they all turned to Bobby.

He rubbed his thick, gray hair and adjusted his black-rimmed glasses. Six months until retirement when he would be through with the likes of Roy Foltrigg. He'd seen a dozen of them come and go, most never heard from again. 'Well, I think we've narrowed it down,' he said, and most of them smiled. He began every report with the same line. To Bobby, legal research was a game of clearing away the piles of debris heaped upon even the simplest of issues, and narrowing the focus to that which is quickly grasped by judges and juries. Everything got narrowed down when Bobby handled the research.

'There are two avenues, neither very attractive but one or both might work. First, I suggest the Juvenile Court approach in Memphis. Under the Tennessee Youth Code, a petition can be filed with the Juvenile Court alleging certain misconduct by the child. There are various categories of wrongdoing, and the petition must classify the child as

186

either a delinquent or a child in need of supervision. A hearing is held, the Juvenile Court judge hears the proof and makes a determination as to what happens to the child. The same can be done for abused or neglected children. Same procedure, same court.'

'Who can file the petition?' Foltrigg asked.

'Well, the statute is very broad, and I think it's a terrible flaw in the law. But it plainly says that a petition can be filed by, and I quote, "any interested party." End of quote.'

'Can that be us?'

'Maybe. It depends on what we allege in our petition. And here's the sticky part – we must allege the kid has done, or is doing, something wrong, violating the law in some way. And the only violation even remotely touching this kid's behavior is, of course, obstruction of justice. So we must allege things we're not sure of, such as the kid's knowledge of where the body is. This could be tricky, since we're not certain.'

'The kid knows where the body is,' Foltrigg said flatly. Fink studied some notes and pretended not to hear, but the other six repeated the words to themselves. Did Foltrigg know things he hadn't yet told them? There was a pause as this apparent statement of fact settled in around the table.

'Have you told us everything?' Bobby asked, glancing at his cohorts.

'Yes,' Foltrigg replied. 'But I'm telling you the kid knows. It's my gut feeling.'

Typical Foltrigg. Creating facts with his guts, and expecting those under him to follow on faith.

Bobby continued. 'A Juvenile Court summons is served on the child's mother, and a hearing is held within seven days. The child must have a lawyer, and I understand one has already been obtained. The child has a right to be at the hearing and may testify if he so chooses.' Bobby wrote something on his legal pad. 'Frankly, this is the quickest way to get the kid to talk.'

'What if he refuses to talk on the witness stand?'

'Very good question,' Bobby said like a professor

pandering a first-year law student. 'It is completely discretionary with the judge. If we put on a good case and convince the judge the kid knows something, he has the authority to order the kid to talk. If the kid refuses, he may be in contempt of court.'

'Let's say he's in contempt. What happens then?'

'Difficult to say at this point. He's only eleven years old, but the judge could, as a last resort, incarcerate the child in a youth court facility until he purges himself of contempt.'

'In other words, until he talks.'

It was so easy to spoon-feed Foltrigg. 'That is correct. Mind you, this would be the most drastic course the judge could take. We have yet to find any precedent for the incarceration of an eleven-year-old child for contempt of court. We haven't checked all fifty states, but we've covered most of them.'

'It won't go that far,' Foltrigg predicted calmly. 'If we file a petition as an interested party, serve the kid's mother with papers, drag his little butt into court with his lawyer in tow, then I think he'll be so scared he'll tell what he knows. What about you, Thomas?'

'Yeah, I think it'll work. And what if it doesn't? What's the downside?'

'There's little risk,' Bobby explained. 'All Juvenile Court proceedings are closed. We can even ask that the petition be kept under lock and key. If it's dismissed initially for lack of standing or whatever, no one will know it. If we proceed to the hearing and A, the kid talks but doesn't know anything, or B, the judge refuses to make him talk, then we haven't lost anything. And C, if the kid talks out of fear or under threat of contempt, then we've gotten what we wanted. Assuming the kid knows about Boyette.'

'He knows,' Foltrigg said.

'The plan would not be so attractive if the proceedings were made public. We would look weak and desperate if we lost. It could, in my opinion, seriously undermine our chances at trial here in New Orleans if we try this and fail, and if it's in some way publicized.'

The door opened and Wally Boxx, fresh from having successfully parked the van, entered and seemed irritated that they had proceeded without him. He sat next to Foltrigg.

'But you're certain it can be done in private?' Fink asked.

'That's what the law says. I don't know how they apply it in Memphis, but the confidentiality is explicit in the code sections. There are even penalties for disclosure.'

'We'll need local counsel, someone in Ord's office,' Foltrigg said to Fink as if the decision had already been made. Then he turned to the group. 'I like the sound of this. Right now the kid and his lawyer are probably thinking it's all over. This will be a wake-up call. They'll know we're serious. They'll know they're headed for court. We'll make it plain to his lawyer that we'll not rest until we have the truth from the kid. I like this. Little downside risk. It'll take place three hundred miles from here, away from these morons with cameras we have around here. If we try it and fail, no big deal. No one will know. I like the idea of no cameras and no reporters.' He paused as if deep in thought, the field marshal surveying the plains, deciding where to send his tanks.

To everyone except Boxx and Foltrigg, the humour in this was delicious. The idea of the Reverend plotting strategies that did not include cameras was unheard of. He, of course, did not realize it. He bit his lip and nodded his head. Yes, yes, this was the best course. This would work.

Bobby cleared his throat. 'There is one other possible approach, and I don't like it but it's worth mentioning. A real longshot. If you assume the kid knows –'

'He knows.'

'Thank you. Assuming this, and assuming he has confided in his lawyer, there is the possibility of a federal indictment against her for obstruction of justice. I don't have to tell you the difficulty in piercing the attorney-client privilege; it's virtually impossible. The indictment would, of course, be used to sort of scare her into cutting some deal. I don't know. As I said, a real longshot.'

Foltrigg chewed on this for a second, but his mind was still churning over the first plan and it simply couldn't digest the second.

'A conviction might be difficult,' Fink said.

'Yep,' Bobby agreed. 'But a conviction would not be the goal. She would be indicted here, a long way from home, and I think it would be quite intimidating. Lots of bad press. Couldn't keep this one quiet, you know. She'd be forced to hire a lawyer. We could string it out for months, you know, the works. You might even consider obtaining the indictment, keeping it sealed, breaking the news to her, and offering some deal in return for its dismissal. Just a thought.'

'I like it,' Foltrigg said to no one's surprise. It had the stench of the government's jackboot, and these strategies always appealed to him. 'And we can always dismiss the indictment anytime we want.'

Ah yes! The Roy Foltrigg Special. Get the indictment, hold the press conference, beat the defendant to the ground with all sorts of threats, cut the deal, then quietly dismiss the indictment a year later. He'd done it a hundred times in seven years. He'd also eaten a few of his Specials when the defendant and/or his lawyer refused to deal and insisted on a trial. When this happened Foltrigg was always too busy with more important prosecutions, and the file was thrown at one of the younger assistants who invariably got his ass kicked. Invariably, Foltrigg placed the blame squarely on the assistant. He'd even fire one for losing the trial brought about by a Roy Foltrigg Special.

'That's Plan B, okay, on hold for right now,' he said, very much in control. 'Plan A is to file a petition in Juvenile Court first thing tomorrow morning. How long will it take to prepare it?'

'An hour,' answered Tank Mozingo, a burly assistant with the ponderous name of Thurston Alomar Mozingo, thus known simply as Tank. 'The petition is set out in the code. We simply add the allegations and fill in the blanks.'

'Get it done.' He turned to Fink. 'Thomas, you'll handle

this. Get on the phone to Ord and ask him to help us. Fly to Memphis tonight. I want the petition filed first thing in the morning, after you talk to the judge. Tell him how urgent this is.' Paper shuffled around the table as the research group began cleaning its mess. Their work was over. Fink took notes as Boxx darted for a legal pad. Foltrigg spewed forth instructions like King Solomon dictating to his scribes. 'Ask the judge for an expedited hearing. Explain how much pressure is behind this. Ask for complete confidentiality, including the closing of the petition and all other pleadings. Stress this, you understand. I'll be sitting by the phone in case I'm needed.'

Bobby was buttoning his cuffs. 'Look, Roy, there's something else we need to mention.'

'What is it?'

'We're playing hardball with this kid. Let's not forget the danger he's in. Muldanno is desperate. There are reporters everywhere. A leak here and a leak there, and the mob could silence the kid before he talks. There's a lot at stake.'

Roy flashed a confident smile. 'I know that, Bobby. In fact, Muldanno's already sent his boys to Memphis. The FBI up there is tracking them, and they're also watching the boy. Personally, I don't think Muldanno's stupid enough to try something, but we're not taking chances.' Roy stood and smiled around the room. 'Good work, men. I appreciate it.'

They mumbled their thankyous and left the library.

On the fourth floor of the Radisson Hotel in downtown Memphis, two blocks from the Sterick Building and five blocks from St Peter's, Paul Gronke played a monotonous game of gin rummy with Mack Bono, a Muldanno grunt from New Orleans. A heavily marked score sheet was on the floor under the table, abandoned. They had been playing for a dollar a game, but now no one cared. Gronke's shoes were on the bed. His shirt was unbuttoned. Heavy cigarette smoke clung to the ceiling. They were drinking bottled water because it was not yet five, but almost, and when the magic hour hit they'd call room service. Gronke checked his watch. He looked through the window at the buildings across Union Avenue. He played a card.

Gronke was a childhood friend of Muldanno's, a most trusted partner in many of his dealings. He owned a few bars and a tourist tee shirt shop in the Quarter. He'd broken his share of legs and had helped The Blade do the same. He did not know where Boyd Boyette was buried, and he wasn't about to ask, but if he pressed hard his friend would probably tell him. They were very close.

Gronke was in Memphis because The Blade had called him. And he was bored as hell sitting in this hotel room playing cards with his shoes off, drinking water and eating sandwiches, smoking Camels and waiting on the next move by an eleven-year-old kid.

Across the double beds, an open door led to the next room. It too had two beds and a cloud of smoke whirling around the ceiling vents. Jack Nance stood in the window watching the rush-hour traffic leave downtown. A radio and a cellular phone stood ready on a nearby table. Any minute Cal Sisson would call from the hospital with the latest about Mark Sway. A thick briefcase was open on one bed, and Nance in his boredom had spent most of the afternoon playing with his bugging devices.

He had a plan to drop a bug in Room 943. He had seen the lawyer's office, absent of special locks on the door, absent of cameras overhead, absent of any security devices. Typical lawyer. Wiring it would be easy. Cal Sisson had visited the doctor's office and found pretty much the same. A receptionist at a front desk. Sofas and chairs for the patients to wait for their shrink. A couple of drab offices down a hall. No special security. The client, this clown who liked to be called The Blade, had approved the wiring of the telephones in both the doctor's and lawyer's office. He also wanted files copied. Easy work. He also wanted a bug planted in Ricky's room. Easy work too, but the difficult part was receiving the transmission once the bug was in place. Nance was working on this.

As far as Nance was concerned, it was simply a surveillance job, nothing more or less. The client was paying top dollar in cash. If he wanted a child followed, it was easy. If he wanted to eavesdrop, no problem as long as he was paying.

But Nance had read the newspapers. And he had heard the whispers in the room next door. There was more here than simple surveillance. Broken legs and arms were not being discussed over gin rummy. These guys were deadly, and Gronke had already mentioned calling New Orleans for more help.

Cal Sisson was ready to bolt. He was fresh off probation, and another conviction would send him back for decades. A conviction for conspiracy to commit murder would send him away for life. Nance had convinced him to hold tight for one more day.

The cellular phone rang. It was Sisson. The lawyer just arrived at the hospital. Mark Sway's in Room 943 with his mother and lawyer.

Nance placed the phone on the table, and walked into the other room.

'Who was it?' Gronke asked with a Camel in his mouth.

'Cal. Kid's still at the hospital, now with his mother and his lawyer.'

'Where's the doctor?'

'He left an hour ago.' Nance walked to the dresser and poured a glass of water.

'Any sign of the Feds?' Gronke grunted.

'Yeah. Same two are hanging around the hospital. Doing the same thing we are, I guess. The hospital's keeping two security guards by the door, and another one close by.'

'You think the kid told them about meeting me this morning?' Gronke asked for the hundredth time of the day.

'He told someone. Why else would they suddenly surround his room with security guards?'

'Yeah, but the security guards are not Fibbies, are they? If he'd told the Fibbies, then they'd be sitting in the hall, don't you think?'

'Yeah.' This conversation had been repeated throughout the day. Who did the kid tell? Why were there suddenly guards by the door? And on and on. Gronke couldn't get enough of it.

Despite his arrogance and street punk posture, he seemed to be a man of patience. Nance figured it went with the territory. Killers had to be cold-blooded and patient.

EIGHTEEN

They left the hospital in her Mazda RX-7, his first ride in a sports car. The seats were leather but the floor was dirty. The car was not new, but it was cool, with a stick shift that she worked like a veteran race car driver. She said she liked to drive fast, which was fine with Mark. They darted through traffic as they left downtown and headed east. It was almost dark. The radio was on but barely audible, some FM station specializing in easy listening.

Ricky was awake when they left. He was staring at cartoons but saying little. A sad little tray of hospital food sat on the table, untouched by either Ricky or Dianne. Mark had not seen his mother eat three bites in two days. He felt sorry for her sitting there on the bed, staring at Ricky, worrying herself to death. The news from Reggie about the job and the raise had made her smile. Then it made her cry.

Mark was sick of the crying and the cold peas and the dark, cramped room, and he felt guilty for leaving but was delighted to be here in this sports car headed, he hoped, for a place of hot, heavy food with warm bread. Clint had mentioned inside-out ravioli and spinach lasagne, and for some reason visions of these rich, meaty dishes had stuck in his mind. Maybe there would be a cake and some cookies. But if Momma Love served green Jell-O, he might throw it at her.

He thought of these things as Reggie thought of being trailed. Her eyes went from the traffic to the mirror, and

195

back again. She drove much too fast, zipping between cars and changing lanes, which didn't bother Mark one bit.

'You think Mom and Ricky are safe?' he asked, watching the cars in front.

'Yes. Don't worry about them. The hospital promised to keep guards at the door.' She had talked to George Ord, her new pal, and explained her concern about the safety of the Sway family. She did not mention any specific threats, though Ord had asked. The family was getting unwanted attention, she had explained. Lots of rumors and gossip, most of it generated by a frustrated media. Ord had talked to McThune, then called her back and said the FBI would stay close to the room, but out of sight. She thanked him.

Ord and McThune were amused by it. The FBI already had people in the hospital. Now they had been invited.

She suddenly turned to the right at an intersection, and the tires squealed. Mark chuckled, and she laughed as though it was all fun but her stomach was flipping. They were on a smaller street with old homes and large oaks.

'This is my neighborhood,' she said. It was certainly nicer than his. They turned again, to another narrower street where the houses were smaller but still two and three stories tall with deep lawns and manicured hedgerows.

'Why do you take your clients home?' he asked.

'I don't know. Most of my clients are children who come from awful homes. I feel sorry for them, I guess. I get attached to them.'

'Do you feel sorry for me?'

'A little. But you're lucky, Mark, very lucky. You have a mother who's a good woman and who loves you very much.'

'Yeah, I guess so. What time is it?'

'Almost six. Why?'

Mark thought a second and counted the hours. 'Forty-nine hours ago Jerome Clifford shot himself. I wish we'd simply run away when we saw his car.'

'Why didn't you?'

'I don't know. It was like I just had to do something once I realized what was going on. I couldn't run away. He was

196

about to die, and I just couldn't ignore it. Something kept pulling me to his car. Ricky was crying and begging me to stop, but I just couldn't. This is all my fault.'

'Maybe, but you can't change it, Mark. It's done.' She glanced at her mirror and saw nothing.

'Do you think we're gonna be okay? I mean, Ricky and me and Mom? When this is all over, will things be like they were?'

She slowed and turned into a narrow driveway lined with thick, untrimmed hedges. 'Ricky will be fine. It might take time, but he'll be all right. Kids are tough, Mark. I see it every day.'

'What about me?'

'Everything will work out, Mark. Just trust me.' The Mazda stopped beside a large two-story house with a porch around the front of it. Shrubs and flowers grew to the windows. Ivy covered one end of the porch.

'Is this your house?' he asked, almost in awe.

'My parents bought it fifty-three years ago, the year before I was born. This is where I grew up. My daddy died when I was fifteen, but Momma Love, bless her heart, is still here.'

'You call her Momma Love?'

'Everyone calls her Momma Love. She's almost eighty, and in better shape than me.' She pointed to a garage straight ahead, behind the house. 'You see those three windows above the garage? That's where I live.'

Like the house, the garage needed a good coat of paint on the trim. Both were old and handsome, but there were weeds in the flower beds and grass growing in the cracks of the driveway.

They entered through a side door, and the aroma from the kitchen hit Mark hard. He was suddenly starving. A small woman with gray hair in a tight ponytail and dark eyes met them and hugged Reggie.

'Momma Love, meet Mark Sway,' Reggie said, waving at him. He and Momma Love were exactly the same height, and she gently hugged him and pecked him on the cheek.

He stood stiff, uncertain how to greet a strange eighty-year-old woman.

'Nice to meet you, Mark,' she said in his face. Her voice was strong and sounded much like Reggie's. She took his arm and led him to the kitchen table. 'Have a seat right here, and I'll get you something to drink.'

Reggie grinned at him as if to say 'Just do as she says because you have no choice.' She hung her umbrella on a rack behind the door and laid her briefcase on the floor.

The kitchen was small and cluttered with cabinets and shelves along three walls. Steam rose from the gas stove. A wooden table with four chairs sat squarely in the center of the room with pots and pans hanging from a beam above it. The kitchen was warm and created instant hunger.

Mark took the nearest chair and watched Momma Love scoot around, grabbing a glass from the cabinet, opening the refrigerator, filling the glass with ice, pouring tea from a pitcher.

Reggie kicked off her shoes and was stirring something in a pot on the stove. She and Momma Love chatted back and forth, the usual routine of how the day went and who'd called. A cat stopped at Mark's chair and examined him.

'That's Axle,' Momma Love said as she served the ice tea with a cloth napkin. 'She's seventeen years old, and very gentle.'

Mark drank the tea and left Axle alone. He was not fond of cats.

'How's your little brother' Momma Love asked.

'He's doing much better,' he said, and suddenly wondered how much Reggie had told her mother. Then he relaxed. If Clint knew very little, Momma Love probably knew even less. He took another sip. She waited for a longer answer. 'He started talking today.'

'That's wonderful!' she exclaimed with a huge smile and patted him on the shoulder.

Reggie poured her tea from a different pitcher, and doctored it with sweetener and lemon. She sat across from Mark at the table, and Axle jumped into her lap. She sipped tea, rubbed the cat, and began slowly removing her jewelry. She was tired.

'Are you hungry?' Momma Love asked, suddenly darting around the kitchen, opening the oven, stirring the pot, closing a drawer.

'Yes ma'am.'

'It's so nice to hear a young man with manners,' she said as she stopped for a second and smiled at him. 'Most of Reggie's kids have no manners. I haven't heard a "yes ma'am" in this house in years.' Then she was off again, wiping out a pan and placing it in the sink.

Reggie winked at him. 'Mark's been eating hospital food for three days, Momma Love, so he wants to know what you're cooking.'

'It's a surprise,' she said, opening the oven and releasing a thick aroma of meat and cheese and tomatoes. 'But I think you'll like it, Mark.'

He was certain he would like it. Reggie winked at him again as she twisted her head and removed a set of small diamond earrings. The pile of jewelry in front of her now included half a dozen bracelets, two rings, a necklace, a watch, and the earrings. Axle was watching it too. Momma Love was suddenly hacking away with a large knife on a cutting board. She whirled around and laid a basket of bread, hot and buttery, in front of him. 'I bake bread every Wednesday,' she said, patting his shoulder again, then off to the stove.

Mark grabbed the biggest slice and took a bite. It was soft and warm, unlike any bread he'd eaten. The butter and garlic melted instantly on his tongue.

'Momma Love is full-blooded Italian,' Reggie said, stroking Axle. 'Both her parents were born in Italy and immigrated to this country in 1902. I'm half Italian.'

'Who was Mr Love?' Mark asked, chomping away, butter on his lips and fingers.

'A Memphis boy. They were married when she was sixteen –'

'Seventeen,' Momma Love corrected without turning around.

199

Momma Love was now setting the table with plates and flatware. Reggie and her jewelry were in the way, so she gathered it all up and kicked and nudged Axle to the floor. 'When do we eat, Momma Love?' she asked.

'In a minute.'

'I'm going to run and change clothes,' she said. Axle sat on Mark's foot and rubbed the back of her head on his shin.

'I'm very sorry about your little brother,' Momma Love said, glancing at the door to make sure Reggie was indeed gone.

Mark swallowed a mouthful of bread, and wiped his mouth with the napkin. 'He'll be okay. We've got good doctors.'

'And you've got the best lawyer in the world,' she said sternly with no smile. She waited for verification.

'We sure do,' Mark said slowly.

She nodded her approval and started for the sink. 'What on earth did you boys see out there?'

Mark sipped his tea and stared at the gray ponytail. This could be a long night with plenty of questions. It would be best to stop it now. 'Reggie told me not to talk about it.' He bit into another piece of bread.

'Oh, Reggie always says that. But you can talk to me. All her kids do.'

In the last forty-nine hours, he'd learned much about interrogation. Keep the other guy on his heels. When the questions get old, dish out a few of your own. 'How often does she bring a kid home?'

She slid the pot off the burner, and thought a second. 'Maybe twice a month. She wants them to eat good food, so she brings them to Momma Love's. Sometimes they spend the night. One little girl stayed a month. She was so pitiful. Name was Andrea. The court took her away from her parents because they were Satan worshippers, doing animal sacrifices and all that mess. She was so sad. She lived upstairs here in Reggie's old bedroom, and she cried when she had to leave. Broke my heart too. I told Reggie "No

200

more kids," after that. But Reggie does what Reggie wants. She really likes you, you know.'

'What happened to Andrea?'

'Her parents got her back. I pray for her every day. Do you go to church?'

'Sometimes.'

'Are you a good Catholic?'

'No. It's a little, well, I'm not sure what kind of church it is. But it's not Catholic. Baptist, I think. We go every now and then.'

Momma Love listened to this with deep concern, terribly puzzled by the fact that he wasn't sure what kind of church he attended.

'Maybe I should take you to my church. St Luke's. It's a beautiful church. Catholics know how to build beautiful churches, you know.'

He nodded but could think of nothing to say. In a flash, she'd forgotten about churches and was back to the stove, opening the oven door and studying the dish with the concentration of Dr Greenway. She mumbled to herself and it was obvious she was pleased.

'Go wash your hands, Mark, right down the hall there. Kids nowadays don't wash their hands enough. Go along.' Mark crammed the last bite of bread into his mouth and followed Axle to the bathroom.

When he returned, Reggie was seated at the table, flipping through a stack of mail. The bread basket had been replenished. Momma Love opened the oven and pulled out a deep dish covered with aluminum foil. 'It's lasagne,' Reggie said to him with a trace of anticipation.

Momma Love launched into a brief history of the dish while she cut it into sections and dug out great hunks with a large spoon. Steam boiled from the pan. 'The recipe has been in my family for centuries,' she said, staring at Mark as if he cared about the lasagne's pedigree. He wanted it on his plate. 'Came over from the old country. I could bake it for my daddy when I was ten years old.' Reggie rolled her eyes a bit and winked at Mark. 'It has four layers, each with a different cheese.' She covered their plates with perfect squares of it. The four different cheeses ran together and oozed from the thick pasta.

The phone on the countertop rang, and Reggie answered. 'Go on and eat, Mark, if you want,' Momma Love said as she majestically set his plate in front of him. She nodded at Reggie's back. 'She might talk forever.' Reggie was listening and talking softly into the phone. It was obvious they were not supposed to hear.

Mark cut a huge bite with his fork, blew on it just enough to knock off the steam, and carefully raised it to his mouth. He chewed slowly, savoring the rich meat sauce, the cheeses, and who knew what else. Even the spinach was divine.

Momma Love watched and waited. She'd poured herself a second glass of wine, and held it halfway between the table and her lips as she waited for a response to her great-grandmother's secret recipe.

'It's great,' he said going for the second bite. 'Just great.' His only experience with lasagna had been a year or so earlier when his mother had pulled a plastic tray from the microwave and served it for dinner. Swanson's frozen, or something like that. He remembered a rubbery taste, nothing like this.

'You like it,' Momma Love said, taking a sip of her wine.

He nodded with a mouthful, and this pleased her. She took a small bite.

Reggie hung up and turned to the table. 'Gotta run downtown. The cops just picked up Ross Scott for shoplifting again. He's in jail crying for his mother, but they can't find her.'

'How long will you be gone?' Mark asked, his fork still.

'Couple of hours. You finish eating and visit with Momma Love. I'll take you to the hospital later.' She patted his shoulder, and then she was out the door.

Momma Love was silent until she heard Reggie's car start, then she said, 'What on earth did you boys see out there?'

Mark took a bite, chewed forever as she waited, then took a long drink of tea. 'Nothing. How do you make this stuff? It's great.'

'Well, it's an old recipe.'

She sipped the wine, and rattled on for ten minutes about the sauce. Then the cheeses.

Mark didn't hear a word.

He finished the peach cobbler and ice cream while she cleared the table and loaded the dishwasher. He thanked her again, said it was delicious for the tenth time, and stood with an aching stomach. He'd been sitting for an hour. Dinner at the trailer was usually a ten-minute affair. Most of the time they ate microwave meals on trays in front of the television. Dianne was too tired to cook.

Momma Love admired his empty bowl, and sent him to the den while she finished cleaning. The TV was color, but without remote control. No cable. A large family portrait hung above the sofa. He noticed it, then walked closer. It was an old photograph of the Love family, matted and framed by thick, curly wood. Mr and Mrs Love were on a small sofa in some studio with two boys in tight collars standing beside them. Momma Love had dark hair and a beautiful smile. Mr Love was a foot taller, and sat rigid and unsmiling. The boys were stiff and awkward, obviously not happy to be dressed in starched shirts and ties. Reggie was between her parents, in the center of the portrait. She had a wonderful, smirky smile, and it was obvious she was the center of the family's attention and enjoyed this immensely. She was ten or eleven, about Mark's age, and the face of this pretty little girl caught his attention and took his breath. He stared at her face and she seemed to laugh at him. She was full of mischief.

'Beautiful children, huh?' It was Momma Love, easing beside him and admiring her family.

'When was this?' Mark asked, still staring.

'Forty years ago,' she said slowly, almost sadly. 'We were all so young and happy then.' She stood next to him, their arms touching, shoulder to shoulder.

'Where are the boys?'

'Joey, on the right there, is the oldest. He was a test pilot for the Air Force, and was killed in 1964 in a plane crash. He's a hero.'

'I'm very sorry,' Mark whispered.

'Bennie, on the left, is a year younger than Joey. He's a marine biologist in Vancouver. He never comes to see his mother. He was here about two years ago for Christmas, then off again. He's never married, but I think he's okay. No grandkids by him either. Reggie's got the only grandkids.' She was reaching for a framed five by seven next to a lamp on an end table. She handed it to Mark. Two graduation photos with blue caps and gowns. The girl was pretty. The boy had mangy hair, a teenager's beard, and a look of sheer hatred in his eyes.

'These are Reggie's kids,' Momma Love explained without the slightest trace of either love or pride. 'The boy was in prison last time we heard anything. Selling dope. He was a good boy when he was little, but then his father got him and just ruined him. This was after the divorce. The girl is out in California trying to be an actress or singer or something; or so she says, but she's had drug problems too and we don't hear much. She was a sweet child too. I haven't seen her in almost ten years. Can you believe it? My only granddaughter. It's so sad.'

Momma Love was now sipping her third glass of wine, and the tongue was loose. If she could talk about her family long enough, then maybe she'd get around to his. And once they'd covered the families, perhaps they might discuss exactly what on earth the boys saw out there.

'Why haven't you seen her in ten years?' Mark asked, but only because he needed to say something. It was really a dumb question because he knew the answer might take hours. His stomach ached from the feast and he wanted to simply lie on the couch and be left alone.

'Regina, I mean, Reggie, lost her when she was about thirteen. They were going through this nightmare of a divorce, he was chasing other women and had girlfriends all over town, they even caught him with a cute little nurse at the hospital, but the divorce was a horrible nightmare and Reggie got to where she couldn't handle it. Joe, her ex-husband, was a good boy when they got married, but then made a bunch of money and got the doctor's attitude, you know, and he changed. Money went to his head.' She paused and took a sip. 'Awful, just awful. I do miss them, though. They're my only grandbabies.'

They didn't look like grandbabies, especially the boy. He was nothing but a punk.

'What happened to him?' Mark asked after a few seconds of silence.

'Well.' She sighed as if she hated to tell, but would do it anyway. 'He was sixteen when his father got him, wild and rotten already, I mean, his father was an ob-gyn and never had time for the kids and a boy needs a father, don't you think; and the boy, Jeff is his name, and he was out of control early. Then his father, who had all the money and all the lawyers, got Regina sent away and took the kids, and when this happened Jeff was pretty much on his own. With his father's money, of course. He finished high school almost at gunpoint, and within six months got caught with a bunch of drugs.' She stopped suddenly, and Mark thought she was about to cry. She took a sip. 'The last time I hugged him was when he graduated from high school. I saw his picture in the newspaper when he got in trouble, but he never called or anything. It's been ten years, Mark. I know I'll die without ever seeing them again.' She quickly rubbed her eyes, and Mark looked for a hole to crawl in.

She took his arm. 'Come with me. Let's go sit on the porch.'

He followed through a narrow foyer, through the front door, and they sat in the swing on the front porch. It was dark and the air was cool. They rocked gently in silence. Momma Love sipped the wine.

She decided to continue the saga. 'You see, Mark, once Joe got the kids, he just ruined them. Gave them plenty of money. Kept his old sleazy girlfriends around the house.

Flaunted it in front of the kids. Bought them cars. Amanda got pregnant in high school, and he arranged the abortion.'

'Why'd Reggie change her name?' he asked politely. Maybe when she answered, this saga would be finished.

'She spent several years in and out of institutions. This was after the divorce, and bless her heart, she was in bad shape, Mark. I cried myself to sleep every night worrying about my daughter. She lived with me most of the time. It took years, but she finally came through. Lots of therapy. Lots of money. Lots of love. And then she decided one day that the nightmare was over, that she would pick up the pieces and move on, and that she would create a new life. That's why she changed her name. She went to court and had it done legally. She fixed up the apartment over the garage. She gave me all these pictures, because she refuses to look at them. She went to law school. She became a new person with a new identity and a new name.'

'Is she bitter?'

'She fights it. She lost her children, and no mother can ever recover from that. But she tries not to think about them. They were brainwashed by their father, so they have no use for her. She hates him, of course, and I think it's probably healthy.'

'She's a very good lawyer,' he said as if he'd personally hired and fired many.

Momma Love moved closer, too close to suit Mark. She patted his knee and this irritated the hell out of him, but she was a sweet old woman and meant nothing by it. She'd buried a son and lost her only grandson, so he gave her a break. There was no moon. A soft wind gently rustled the leaves of the huge black oaks between the porch and the street. He was not anxious to return to the hospital, and so he decided this was pleasant after all. He smiled at Momma Love, but she was staring blankly into the darkness, lost in some deep thought. A heavy, folded quilt padded the swing.

He assumed she would work her way back to the shooting of Jerome Clifford, and this he wanted to avoid. 'Why does Reggie have so many kids for clients?'

206

She kept patting his knee. 'Because some kids need lawyers, though most of them don't know it. And most lawyers are too busy making money to worry about kids. She wants to help. She'll always blame herself for losing her kids, and she just wants to help others. She's very protective of her little clients.'

'I didn't pay her very much money.'

'Don't worry, Mark. Every month, Reggie takes at least two cases for free. They're called pro bono, which means the lawyer does the work without a fee. If she didn't want your case, she wouldn't have taken it.'

He knew about pro bono. Half the lawyers on television were laboring away on cases they wouldn't get paid for. The other half were sleeping with beautiful women and eating in fancy restaurants.

'Reggie has a soul, Mark, a conscience,' she continued, still patting gently. The wineglass was empty, but the words were clear and the mind was sharp. 'She'll work for no fee if she believes in the client. And some of her poor clients will break your heart, Mark. I cry all the time over some of these little fellas.'

'You're very proud of her, aren't you?'

'I am. Reggie almost died, Mark, a few years ago when the divorce was going on. I almost lost her. Then I almost went broke trying to get her back on her feet. But look at her now.'

'Will she ever get married again?'

'Maybe. She's dated a couple of men, but nothing serious. Romance is not at the top of her list. Her work comes first. Like tonight. It's almost eight o'clock, and she's at the city jail talking to a little troublemaker they picked up for shoplifting. Wonder what'll be in the newspaper in the morning.'

Sports, obituaries, the usual. Mark shifted uncomfortably and waited. It was obvious he was supposed to speak. 'Who knows.'

'What was it like having your picture on the front page of the paper?'

'I didn't like it.'

'Where'd they get those pictures?'

'They're school pictures.'

There was a long pause. The chains above them squeaked as the swing moved slowly back and forth. 'What was it like walking up on that dead man who'd just shot himself?'

'Pretty scary, but to be honest, my doctor told me not to discuss it because it stresses me out. Look at my little brother, you know. So, I'd better not say anything.'

She patted harder. 'Of course. Of course.'

Mark pressed with his toes, and the swing moved a bit faster. His stomach was still packed and he was suddenly sleepy. Momma Love was humming now. The breeze picked up, and he shivered.

Reggie found them on the dark porch, in the swing, rocking quietly back and forth. Momma Love sipped black coffee and patted him on the shoulder. Mark was curled in a knot beside her, his head resting in her lap, a quilt over his legs.

'How long has he been asleep?' she whispered.

'An hour or so. He got cold, then he got sleepy. He's a sweet child.'

'He sure is. I'll call his mother at the hospital, and see if he can stay here tonight.'

'He ate until he was stuffed. I'll fix him a good breakfast in the morning.'

NINETEEN

The idea was Trumann's, and it was a wonderful idea, one that would work and thus would be snared immediately by Foltrigg and claimed as his own. Life with Reverend Roy was a series of stolen ideas and credits when things worked. And when things went to hell, Trumann and his office took the blame, along with Foltrigg's underlings, and the press, and the jurors, and the corrupt defense bar, everybody but the great man himself.

But Trumann had quietly massaged and manipulated the egos of prima donnas before, and he could certainly handle this idiot.

It was late, and as he picked at the lettuce in his shrimp rémoulade in the dark corner of a crowded oyster bar, the idea hit him. He called Foltrigg's private office number, no answer. He dialled the number in the library, and Wally Boxx answered. It was nine-thirty, and Wally explained he and his boss were still buried deep in the law books, just a couple of workaholics slaving over the details and enjoying it. All in a day's work. Trumann said he'd be there in ten minutes.

He left the noisy café and walked hurriedly through the crowds on Canal Street. September was just another hot, sticky summer month in New Orleans. After two blocks he removed his jacket and walked faster. Two more blocks and his shirt was wet and clinging to his back and chest.

He darted through the crowds of tourists lumbering along Canal with their cameras and gaudy tee shirts, and wondered for the thousandth time why these people came to this city to spend hard-earned money on cheap entertainment and overpriced food. The average tourist on Canal Street wore black socks and white sneakers, was forty pounds overweight, and Trumann figured these people would return home and brag to their less fortunate friends about the delightful cuisine they had uniquely discovered and gorged themselves on in New Orleans. He bumped into a hefty woman with a small black box stuck in her face. She was actually standing near the curb and filming the front of a cheap souvenir store with suggestive street signs displayed for sale in the window. What sort of person would watch a video of a tacky souvenir shop in the French Quarter? Americans no longer experience vacations. They simply Sony them so they can ignore them for the rest of the year.

Trumann was in for a transfer. He was sick of tourists, traffic, humidity, crime, and he was sick of Roy Foltrigg. He turned by Rubinstein Brothers and headed for Poydras.

Foltrigg was not afraid of hard work. It came natural to him. He'd realized in law school that he was not a genius, and that to succeed he'd need to put in more hours. He studied his ass off, and finished somewhere in the middle of the pack. But he'd been elected president of the student body, and there was a certificate declaring this achievement framed in oak somewhere on one of his walls. His career as a political animal started at the moment when his law school classmates chose him as their president, a position most did not know existed and couldn't have cared less about. Job offers had been scarce for young Roy, and at the last minute he jumped at the chance to be an assistant city prosecutor in New Orleans. Fifteen thousand bucks a year in 1975. In two years he handled more cases than all the other city prosecutors combined. He worked. He put in long hours in a dead end job because he was going places. He was a star but no one noticed.

He began dabbling in local Republican politics, a lonely hobby, and learned to play the game. He met people with

210

money and clout, and landed a job with a law firm. He put in incredible hours and became a partner. He married a woman he didn't love because she had the right credentials and a wife brought respectability. Roy was on the move. There was a game plan.

He was still married to her but they slept in different rooms. The kids were now twleve and ten. A pretty family portrait.

He preferred the office to his home, which suited his wife just fine because she didn't like him but did enjoy his salary.

Roy's conference table was once again covered with law books and legal pads. Wally had shed his tie and jacket. Empty coffee cups littered the room. They were both tired.

The law was quite simple: Every citizen owes to society the duty of giving testimony to aid in the enforcement of the law. And, a witness is not excused from testifying because of his fear of reprisal threatening his and/or his family's lives. It was black letter law, as they say, carved in stone over the years by hundreds of judges and justices. No exceptions. No exemptions. No loopholes for scared little boys. Roy and Wally had read dozens of cases. Many were copied and highlighted and thrown about on the table. The kid would have to talk. If the Juvenile Court approach in Memphis fell through, Foltrigg planned to issue a subpoena for Mark Sway to appear before the grand jury in New Orleans. It would scare the little punk to death, and loosen his tongue.

Trumann walked through the door and said, 'You guys are working late.'

Wally Boxx pushed away from the table and stretched his arms mightily above his head. 'Yeah, a lot of stuff to cover,' he said, exhausted, waving his hand proudly at the piles of books and notes.

'Have a seat,' Foltrigg said, pointing at a chair. 'We're finishing up.' He stretched too, then cracked his knuckles. He loved his reputation as a workaholic, a man of importance unafraid of painful hours, a family man whose calling went beyond wife and kids. The job meant everything. His client was the United States of America.

211

Trumann had heard this eighteen-hour-a-day crap for seven years now. It was Foltrigg's favorite subject – talking about himself and the hours at the office and the body that needed no sleep. Lawyers wear their loss of sleep like a badge of honor. Real macho machines grinding it out around the clock.

'I've got an idea,' Trumann said, sitting across the table. 'You told me earlier about the hearing in Memphis tomorrow. In Juvenile Court.'

'We're filing a petition,' Roy corrected. 'I don't know when the hearing will take place. But we'll ask for a quick one.'

'Yeah, well, what about this? Just before I left the office this afternoon, I talked to K. O. Lewis, Voyles's number-one deputy.'

'I know K.O.,' Foltrigg interrupted. Trumann knew this was coming. In fact, he paused just a split second so Foltrigg could interrupt and set him straight about how close he was to K.O., not Mr Lewis, but simply K.O.

'Right. Well, he's in St Louis attending a conference, and he asked about the Boyette case and Jerome Clifford and the kid. I told him what we knew. He said feel free to call if he could do anything. Said Mr Voyles wants daily reports.'

'I know all this.'

'Right. Well, I was just thinking. St Louis is an hour's flight from Memphis, right. What if Mr Lewis presented himself to the Juvenile Court judge in Memphis first thing in the morning when the petition is filed, and what if Mr Lewis has a little chat with the judge and leans on him? We're talking about the number-two man in the FBI. He tells the judge what we think this kid knows.'

Foltrigg began nodding his approval, and when Wally saw this he began nodding too, only faster.

Trumann continued. 'And there's something else. We know Gronke is in Memphis, and it's safe to assume he's not there to visit Elvis's grave. Right? He's been sent there by Muldanno. So I was thinking, what if we assume the kid is

212

in danger, and Mr Lewis explains to the Juvenile Court judge that it's in the best interests of the kid for us to take him into custody? You know, for his own protection?'

'I like this,' Foltrigg said softly. Wally liked it too.

'The kid'll crack under the pressure. First, he's taken into custody by order of the Juvenile Court, same as any other case, and that'll scare the hell out of him. Might also wake up his lawyer. Hopefully the judge orders the kid to talk. At that point, the kid'll crack, I believe. If not, he's in contempt, maybe. Don't you think?'

'Yeah, he's in contempt, but we can't predict what the judge will do at that point.'

'Right. So Mr Lewis tells the judge about Gronke and his connections with the mob, and that we believe he's in Memphis to harm the kid. Either way, we get the kid in custody, away from his lawyer. The bitch.'

Foltrigg was wired now. He scribbled something on a legal pad. Wally stood and began pacing thoughtfully around the library, deep in thought as if things were conspiring to force him to make a significant decision.

Trumann could call her a bitch here in the privacy of an office in New Orleans. But he remembered the tape. And he would be happy to remain in New Orleans, far away from her. Let McThune deal with Reggie in Memphis.

'Can you get K.O. on the phone?' Foltrigg asked.

'I think so.' Trumann pulled a scrap of paper from a pocket and began punching numbers on the phone.

Foltrigg met Wally in the corner, away from the agent. 'It's a great idea,' Wally said. 'I'm sure this Juvenile Court judge is just some local yokel who'll listen to K.O. and do whatever he wants, don't you think?'

Trumann had Mr Lewis on the phone. Foltrigg watched him while listening to Wally. 'Maybe, but regardless, we get the kid in court quickly and I think he'll fold. If not, he's in custody, under our control and away from his lawyer. I like it.'

They whispered for a while as Trumann talked to K. O. Lewis. Trumann nodded at them, gave the okay sign with a big smile, and hung up. 'He'll do it,' he said proudly. 'He'll catch an early morning flight to Memphis and meet with Fink. Then they'll get with George Ord and descend on the judge.' Trumann was walking toward them, very proud of himself. 'Think about it. The US Attorney on one side, K. O. Lewis on the other, and Fink in the middle, first thing in the morning when the judge gets to the office. They'll have the kid talking in no time.'

Foltrigg flashed a wicked smile. He loved those moments when the power of the federal government shifted into high gear and landed hard on small, unsuspecting people. Just like that, with one phone call, the second in command of the FBI had entered the picture. 'It just might work,' he said to his boys. 'It just might work.'

In one corner of the small den above the garage, Reggie flipped through a thick book under a lamp. It was midnight, but she couldn't sleep, so she curled under a quilt and sipped tea while reading a book Clint had found titled *Reluctant Witnesses*. As far as law books go, it was quite thin. But the law was quite clear: Every witness has a duty to come forth and assist those authorities investigating a crime. A witness cannot refuse to testify on the grounds that he or she feels threatened. The vast majority of the cases cited in the book dealt with organized crime. Seems the Mafia has historically frowned on its people schmoozing with the cops, and has often threatened wives and children. The Supreme Court has said more than once that wives and children be damned. A witness must talk.

At some point in the very near future, Mark would be forced to talk. Foltrigg could issue a subpoena and compel his attendance before a grand jury in New Orleans. She, of course, would be able to attend. If Mark refused to testify before the grand jury, a quick hearing would be held before the trial judge who would undoubtedly order him to answer Foltrigg's questions. If he refused, the wrath of the court would be severe. No judge tolerates being disobeyed, but

214

federal judges can be especially nasty when their orders fall on deaf ears.

There are places to put eleven-year-old kids who find themselves in disfavor with the system. At the moment, she had no less than twenty clients scattered about in various training schools in Tennessee. The oldest was sixteen. All were secured behind fences with guards pacing about. They were called reform schools not long ago. Now they're training schools.

When ordered to talk, Mark would undoubtedly look to her. And this was why she couldn't sleep. To advise him to disclose the location of the Senator's body would be to jeopardize his safety. His mother and brother would be at risk. These were not people who could become instantly mobile. Ricky might be hospitalized for weeks. Any type of witness protection program would be postponed until he was healthy again. Dianne would be a sitting duck, if Muldanno were so inclined.

It would be proper and ethical and moral to advise him to cooperate, and that would be the easy way out. But what if he got hurt? He would point a finger at her. What if something happened to Ricky or Dianne? She, the lawyer, would be blamed.

Children make lousy clients. The lawyer becomes much more than a lawyer. With adults, you simply lay the pros and cons of each option on the table. You advise this way and that. You predict a little, but not much. Then you tell the adult it's time for a decision and you leave the room for a bit. When you return, you are handed a decision and you run with it. Not so with kids. They don't understand lawyerly advice. They want a hug and someone to make decisions. They're scared and looking for friends.

She'd held many small hands in courtrooms. She'd wiped many tears.

She imagined this scene: A huge, empty federal court-room in New Orleans with the doors locked and two marshals guarding it; Mark on the witness stand; Foltrigg in all his glory strutting around on his home turf, prancing

215

back and forth for the benefit of his little assistants and perhaps an FBI agent or two; the judge in a black robe. He was handling it delicately, and he probably disliked Foltrigg immensely because he was forced to see him all the time. He, the judge, asks Mark if he in fact refused to answer certain questions before the grand jury that very morning in a room just a short distance down the hall. Mark, looking upward at His Honor, answers yes. What was the first question? the judge asks Foltrigg, who's on his feet with a legal pad, strutting and prancing as if the room were filled with cameras. I asked him, Your Honor, if Jerome Clifford, prior to the suicide, said anything about the body of Senator Boyd Boyette. And he refused to answer, Your Honor. Then I asked him if Jerome Clifford in fact told him where the body is buried. And he refused to answer this question as well, Your Honor. And the judge leans down even closer to Mark. There is no smile. Mark stares at his lawyer. Why didn't you answer these questions? the judge asks. Because I don't want to, Mark answers, and it's almost funny. But there are no smiles. Well, the judge says, I am ordering you to answer these questions before the grand jury, do you understand me, Mark? I'm ordering you to return to the grand jury room right now and answer all of Mr Foltrigg's questions, do you understand this? Mark says nothing and doesn't move a muscle. He stares at his trusted lawyer, thirty feet away. What if I don't answer the questions? he finally asks, and this irritates the judge. You have no choice, young man. You must answer because I'm ordering it. And if I don't? Mark asks, terrified. Well, then, I'll find you in contempt and I'll probably incarcerate you until you do as I say. For a very long time, the judge growls.

Axle rubbed against the chair and startled her. The courtroom scene was gone. She closed the book and walked to the window. The best advice to Mark would be simply to lie. Tell a big one. At the critical moment, just explain how the late Jerome Clifford said nothing about Boyd Boyette. He was crazy and drunk and stoned, and said nothing, really. Who in the world could ever know the difference?

216

Mark was a cool liar.

He awoke in a strange bed between a soft mattress and a heavy layer of blankets. A dim lamp from the hallway cast a narrow light through the slit in the doorway. His battered Nikes were in a chair by the door, but the rest of his clothing was still on. He slid the blankets to his knees and the bed squeaked. He stared at the ceiling and vaguely remembered being escorted to this room by Reggie and Momma Love. Then he remembered the swing on the porch and being very tired.

Slowly, he swung his feet from the bed and sat on the edge of it. He remembered being led and pushed up the stairs. Things were clearing up. He sat in the chair and laced his sneakers. The floor was wooden and creaked softly as he walked to the door and opened it. The hinges popped. The hallway was still. Three other doors opened into it, and they were all closed. He eased to the stairway, and tiptoed down, in no hurry.

A light from the kitchen caught his attention, and he walked faster. The clock on the wall gave the time as two-twenty. He now remembered that Reggie didn't live here; she was above the garage. Momma Love was probably sound asleep upstairs, so he stopped the creeping along and crossed the foyer, unlocked the front door, and found his spot in the swing. The air was cool and the front lawn was pitch black.

For a moment, he was frustrated with himself for falling asleep and being put to bed in this house. He belonged at the hospital with his mother, sleeping on the same crippling bed, waiting for Ricky to snap out of it so they could leave and go home. He assumed Reggie had called Dianne, so his mother probably wasn't worried. In fact, she was probably pleased that he was here at this moment, eating good food and sleeping well. Mothers are like that.

He'd missed two days of school, according to his calculations. Today would be Thursday. Yesterday, he'd been attacked by the man with the knife in the elevator. The man with the family portrait. And the day before that,

217

Tuesday, he had hired Reggie. That, too, seemed like a month ago. And the day before that, Monday, he had awakened like any normal kid and gone off to school with no idea all this was about to happen. There must be a million kids in Memphis, and he would never understand how and why he was selected to meet Jerome Clifford just seconds before he put the gun in his mouth.

Smoking. That was the answer. Hazardous to your health. You could say that again. He was being punished by God for smoking and harming his body. Damn! What if he'd been caught with a beer.

A silhouette of a man appeared on the sidewalk, and stopped for a second in front of Momma Love's house. The orange glow of a cigarette flared in front of his face, then he walked very slowly out of sight. A little late for an evening stroll, Mark thought.

A minute passed, and he was back. Same man. Same slow walk. Same hesitation between the trees as he looked at the house. Mark held his breath. He was sitting in darkness and he knew he could not be seen. But this man was more than a nosy neighbor.

At exactly 4 a.m., a plain white Ford van with the license plates temporarily removed eased into Tucker Wheel Estates and turned on to East Street. The trailers were dark and quiet. The streets were deserted. The little village was peacefully asleep and would be for two more hours until dawn.

The van stopped in front of Number 17. The lights and engine were turned off. No one noticed it. After a minute, a man in a uniform opened the driver's door and stood in the street. The uniform resembled that of a Memphis cop – navy trousers, navy shirt, wide black belt with black holster, some type of gun on the hip, black boots, but no cap or hat. A decent imitation, especially at four in the morning when no one was watching. He held a rectangular cardboard container about the size of two shoe boxes. He glanced around, then carefully watched and listened to the trailer next door to Number 17. Not a sound. Not even the bark of a dog. He smiled to himself, and walked casually to the door of Number 17.

If he detected movement in a nearby trailer, he would simply knock slightly on the door and go through the routine of being a frustrated messenger looking for Ms Sway. But it wasn't necessary. Not a peep from the neighbors. So he quickly sat the box against the door, got in the van, and drove away. He had come and gone without a trace, leaving behind his little warning.

Exactly thirty minutes later, the box exploded. It was a quiet explosion, carefully controlled. The ground didn't shake and the porch didn't shatter. The door was blown open, and the flames were directed at the interior of the trailer. Lots of red and yellow flames and black smoke rolling through the rooms. The matchbox construction of the walls and floors was nothing more than kindling for the fire.

By the time Rufus Bibbs next door could punch 911, the Sway trailer was engulfed and beyond help. Rufus hung up the phone, and ran to find his garden hose. His wife and kids were running wild, trying to dress and get out of the trailer. Screams and shouts echoed on the street as the neighbors ran to the fire in an amazing array of pajamas and robes. Dozens of them watched the fire as garden hoses came from all directions and water was applied to the trailers next door. The fire grew and the crowd grew, and windows popped in the Bibbs trailer. The domino effect. More screams as more windows popped. Then sirens and red lights.

The crowd moved back as the firemen laid lines and pumped water. The other trailers were saved, but the Sway home was nothing but rubble. The roof and most of the floor were gone. The rear wall stood with a solitary window still intact.

More people arrived as the firemen sprayed the ruins. Walter Deeble, a loudmouth from South Street, started babbling about how cheap these damned trailers were with aluminum wiring and all. Hell, we all live in firetraps, he said with the pitch of a street preacher, and what we ought to do is sue that sonofabitch Tucker and force him to provide safe housing. He just might see his lawyer about it. Personally, he had eight smoke and heat detectors in his trailer because of the cheap aluminum wiring and all, and he just might talk to his lawyer.

By the Bibbs trailer, a small crowd gathered and thanked God the fire didn't spread.

Those poor Sways. What else could happen to them?

TWENTY

After a breakfast of cinnamon rolls and chocolate milk, they left the house and headed for the hospital. It was seven-thirty, much too early for Reggie but Dianne was waiting. Ricky was doing much better.

'What do you think'll happen today?' Mark asked.

For some reason this struck her as being funny. 'You poor child,' she said when she finished chuckling. 'You've been through a lot this week.'

'Yeah. I hate school, but it'd be nice to go back. I had this wild dream last night.'

'What happened?'

'Nothing. I dreamed everything was normal again, and I made it through a whole day with nothing happening to me. It was wonderful.'

'Well, Mark, I'm afraid I have some bad news.'

'I knew it. What is it?'

'Clint called a few minutes ago. You've made the front page again. It's a picture of both of us, evidently taken by one of those clowns at the hospital yesterday when we got off the elevator.'

'Great.'

'There's a reporter at the *Memphis Press* by the name of Slick Moeller. Everyone calls him the Mole. Mole Moeller. He covers the crime beat, sort of a legend around town. He's hot on this case.'

'He wrote the story yesterday.'

'That's right. He has a lot of contacts within the police

department. It sounds as if the cops believe Mr Clifford told you everything before he killed himself, and now you're refusing to cooperate.'

'Pretty accurate, wouldn't you say?'

She glanced at the rearview mirror. 'Yeah. It's spooky.'

'How does he know this stuff?'

'The cops talk to him, off the record of course, and he digs and digs until he puts the pieces together. And if the pieces don't fit perfectly, then Slick just sort of fills in the gaps. According to Clint, the story is based on unnamed sources within the Memphis Police Department, and there's a great deal of suspicion about how much you know. The theory is that since you've hired me, you must be hiding something.'

'Let's stop and get a newspaper.'

'We'll get one at the hospital. We'll be there in a minute.'

'Do you think those reporters'll be waiting again?'

'Probably. I told Clint to find a back entrance somewhere, and to meet us in the parking lot.'

'I'm really sick of this. Just sick of it. All my buddies are in school today, having a good time, being normal, fighting with girls during recess, playing jokes on the teachers, you know, the usual stuff. And look at me. Running around town with my lawyer, reading about my adventures in the newspapers, looking at my face on the front page, hiding from reporters, dodging killers with switchblades. It's like something out of a movie. A bad movie. I'm just sick of it. I don't know if I can take anymore. It's just too much.'

She watched him between glances at the street and traffic. His jaws were tight. He stared straight ahead, but saw nothing.

'I'm sorry, Mark.'

'Yeah, me too. So much for pleasant dreams, huh.'

'This could be a very long day.'

'What else is new? They were watching the house last night, did you know that?'

'I beg your pardon.'

'Yeah, somebody was watching the house. I was on the

porch at two-thirty this morning, and I saw a guy walking along the sidewalk. He was real casual, you know, just smoking a cigarette and looking at the house.'

'Could be a neighbor.'

'Right. At two-thirty in the morning.'

'Maybe someone was out for a walk.'

'Then why did he walk by the house three times in fifteen minutes?'

She glanced at him again and hit her brakes to avoid a car in front of them.

'Do you trust me, Mark?' she asked.

He looked at her as if surprised by the question. 'Of course I trust you, Reggie.'

She smiled and patted his arm. 'Then stick with me.'

One advantage of an architectural horror like St Peter's was the existence of lots of doors and exits few people knew about. With additions stuck here, and wings added over there as an afterthought, there had been created over the course of time little nooks and alleys seldom used and rarely discovered by lost security guards.

When they arrived, Clint had been hustling around the hospital for thirty minutes with no success. He'd managed to become lost himself three different times. He was sweating and apologizing as they met at the parking lot.

'Just follow me,' Mark said, and they darted across the street and entered through the emergency gate. They wove through heavy, rush-hour hall traffic and found an ancient escalator going down.

'I hope you know where you're going,' Reggie said, obviously in doubt and half-jogging in an effort to keep up with him. Clint was sweating even harder. 'No problem,' Mark said, and opened a door leading to the kitchen.

'We're in the kitchen, Mark,' Reggie said, looking around.

'Just be cool. Act like you're supposed to be here.'

He punched a button by a service elevator and the door opened instantly. He punched another button on the inside panel, and they lurched upward, headed for floor number ten. 'There are eighteen floors in the main section, but this elevator stops at number ten. It will not stop at nine. Figure it out.' He watched the numbers above the door and explained this like a bored tour guide.

'What happens on ten?' Clint asked between breaths.

'Just wait.'

The door opened on ten, and they stepped into a huge closet with rows of shelves filled with towels and bedsheets. Mark was off, darting between the aisles. He opened a heavy metal door and they were suddenly in the hallway with patient rooms right and left. He pointed to his left, kept walking, and stopped before an emergency exit door with red and yellow alarm warnings all over it. He grabbed the bar handle across the front of it, and Reggie and Clint stopped cold.

He pushed the door open, and nothing happened. 'Alarms don't work,' he said nonchalantly and bounded down the steps to the ninth floor. He opened another door, and suddenly they were in a quiet hallway with thick industrial carpet and no traffic. He pointed again, and they were off, past patient rooms, around a bend, and by the nurses' station where they glanced down another hall and saw the loiterers by the elevators.

'Good morning, Mark,' Karen the beautiful called out as they hurried by. But she said this without a smile.

'Hi, Karen,' he answered without slowing.

Dianne was sitting in a folding chair in the hall with a Memphis cop kneeling before her. She was crying, and had been for some time. The two security guards were standing together twenty feet away. Mark saw the cop and the tears and ran for his mother. She grabbed him and they hugged.

'What's the matter, Mom?' he asked, and she cried harder.

'Mark, your trailer burned last night,' the cop said. 'Just a few hours ago.'

Mark glared at him in disbelief, then squeezed his mother around the neck. She was wiping tears and trying to compose herself.

'How bad?' Mark asked.

'Real bad,' the cop said sadly as he stood and held his cap with both hands. 'Everything's gone.'

'What started the fire?' Reggie asked.

'Don't know right now. The fire inspector will be on the scene this morning. Could be electrical.'

'I need to talk to the fire inspector, okay,' Reggie insisted, and the cop looked her over.

'And who are you?' he asked.

'Reggie Love, attorney for the family.'

'Ah, yes. I saw the paper this morning.'

She handed him a card. 'Please ask the fire inspector to call me.'

'Sure, lady.' The cop carefully placed the hat on his head and looked down again at Dianne. He was sad again. 'Ms Sway, I'm very sorry about this.'

'Thank you,' she said, wiping her face. He nodded at Reggie and Clint, backed away, and left in a hurry. A nurse appeared and stood by just in case.

Dianne suddenly had an audience. She stood and stopped crying, even managed a smile at Reggie.

'This is Clint Van Hooser. He works for me,' Reggie said.

Dianne smiled at Clint. 'I'm very sorry,' he said.

'Thank you,' Dianne said softly. A few seconds of awkward silence followed as she finished wiping her face. Her arm was around Mark, who was still dazed.

'Did he behave?' Dianne asked.

'He was wonderful. He ate enough for a small army.'

'That's good. Thanks for having him over.'

'How's Ricky?' Reggie asked.

'He had a good night. Dr Greenway stopped by this morning, and Ricky was awake and talking. Looks much better.'

'Does he know about the fire?' Mark asked.

'No. And we're not telling him, okay?'

'Okay, Mom. Could we go inside and talk, just me and you?'

Dianne smiled at Reggie and Clint, and led Mark into the room. The door was closed, and the tiny Sway family was all alone with all its worldly possessions.

The Honorable Harry Roosevelt had presided over the Shelby County Juvenile Court for twenty-two years now, and despite the dismal and depressing nature of the court's business he had conducted its affairs with a great deal of dignity. He was the first black Juvenile Court judge in Tennessee, and when he'd been appointed by the Governor in the early seventies, his future was brilliant and there were glowing predictions of higher courts for him to conquer.

The higher courts were still there, and Harry Roosevelt was still here, in the deteriorating building known simply as Juvenile Court. There were much nicer courthouses in Memphis. On Main Street the Federal Building, always the newest in town, housed the elegant and stately courtrooms. The federal boys always had the best – rich carpet, thick leather chairs, heavy oak tables, plenty of lights, dependable air conditioning, lots of well-paid clerks and assistants. A few blocks away, the Shelby County Courthouse was a beehive of judicial activity as thousands of lawyers roamed its tiled and marbled corridors and worked their way through well-preserved and well-scrubbed courtrooms. It was an older building, but a beautiful one with paintings on the walls and a few statues scattered about. Harry could have had a courtroom over there, but he said no. And not far away was the Shelby County Justice Center with a maze of fancy new modern courtrooms with bright fluorescent lights and sound systems and padded seats. Harry could have had one of those too, but he turned it down.

He remained here, in the Juvenile Court Building, a converted high school blocks away from downtown with little parking and few janitors and more cases per judge than any other docket in the world. His court was the unwanted stepchild of the judicial system. Most lawyers shunned it. Most law students dreamed of plush offices in tall buildings and wealthy clients with thick wallets. Never did they dream of slugging their way through the roach-infested corridors of Juvenile Court.

Harry had turned down four appointments, all to courts where the heating systems worked in the winter. He had been considered for these appointments because he was smart and black, and he turned them down because he was poor and black. They paid him sixty thousand a year, lowest of any court in town, so he could feed his wife and four teenagers and live in a nice home. But he'd known hunger as a child, and those memories were vivid. He would always think of himself as a poor black kid.

And that's exactly the reason the once promising Harry Roosevelt remained a simple Juvenile Court judge. To him, it was the most important job in the world. By statute, he had exclusive jurisdiction over delinquent, unruly, dependent, and neglected children. He determined paternity of children born out of wedlock and enforced his own orders for their support and education, and in a county where half the babies were born to single mothers, this accounted for most of his docket. He terminated parental rights and placed abused children in new homes. Harry carried heavy burdens.

He weighed somewhere between three and four hundred pounds, and wore the same outfit every day – black suit, white cotton shirt, and a bow tie which he tied himself and did so poorly. No one knew if Harry owned one black suit or fifty. He always looked the same. He was an imposing figure on the bench, glaring down over his reading glasses at deadbeat fathers who refused to support their children. Deadbeat fathers, black and white alike, lived in fear of Judge Roosevelt. He would track them down and throw them in jail. He found their employers and tapped their paychecks. If you messed with Harry's subjects, or Harry's Kids, as they were known, you could find yourself handcuffed and standing pitifully before him with a bailiff on each side.

Harry Roosevelt was a legend in Memphis. The county fathers had seen fit to give him two more judges to help with

227

the caseload, but he maintained a brutal work schedule. He usually arrived before seven and made his own coffee. He started court promptly at nine and God help the lawyer who was late for court. He'd thrown several of them in jail over the years.

At eight-thirty, his secretary hauled in a box of mail and informed Harry that there was a group of men waiting outside who desperately needed to speak with him.

'What else is new?' he asked, eating the last bite of an apple Danish.

'You might want to meet with these gentlemen.'

'Oh really. Who are they?'

'One is George Ord, our distinguished US Attorney.'

'I taught George in law school.'

'Right. That's what he said, twice. There's also an Assistant US Attorney from New Orleans, a Mr Thomas Fink. And a Mr K. O. Lewis, Deputy Director of the FBI. And a couple of FBI agents.'

Harry looked up from a file and thought about this. 'A rather distinguished group. What do they want?'

'They wouldn't say.'

'Well, show them in.'

She left, and seconds later Ord, Fink, Lewis, and McThune filed into the crowded and cluttered office and introduced themselves to His Honor. Harry and the secretary moved files from the chairs and everyone looked for a seat. They exchanged brief pleasantries, and after a few minutes of this Harry looked at his watch and said, 'Gentlemen, I am scheduled to hear seventeen cases today. What can I do for you?'

Ord cleared his throat first. 'Well, Judge, I'm sure you've seen the papers the last two mornings, especially the front page stories about a boy by the name of Mark Sway.'

'Very intriguing.'

'Mr Fink here is prosecuting the man accused of killing Senator Boyette, and the case is scheduled for trial in New Orleans in a few weeks.'

'I'm aware of this. I've read the stories.'

228

'We are almost certain that Mark Sway knows more than he is telling. He's lied to the Memphis Police on several occasions. We think he talked at length with Jerome Clifford before the suicide. We know without a doubt he was in the car. We've tried to talk to the kid, but he has been very uncooperative. Now he's hired a lawyer and she's stonewalling.'

'Reggie Love is a regular in my court. A very competent attorney. Sometimes a bit overprotective of her clients, but there's nothing wrong with that.'

'Yes sir. We're very suspicious of the boy, and we feel quite strongly that he is withholding valuable information.'

'Such as?'

'Such as the location of the Senator's body.'

'How can you assume this?'

'There's a lot to the story, Your Honor. And it would take a while to explain it.'

Harry played with his bow tie and gave Ord one of his patented scowls. He was thinking. 'So you want me to bring the kid in and ask him questions.'

'Sort of. Mr Fink has brought with him a petition alleging the child to be a delinquent.'

This did not sit well with Harry. His shiny forehead was suddenly wrinkled. 'A rather serious allegation. What type of offense has the child committed?'

'Obstruction of justice.'

'You got any law?'

Fink had a file open, and he was on his feet handing a thin brief across the desk. Harry took it, and began reading slowly. The room was silent. K. O. Lewis had yet to say anything, and this bothered him because he was, after all, the number-two man at the FBI. And this judge seemed not to care.

Harry flipped a page and glanced at his watch. 'I'm listening,' he said in Fink's direction.

'It's our position, Your Honor, that through his misrepresentations Mark Sway has obstructed the investigation into this matter.'

'Which matter? The murder or the suicide?'

Excellent point, and as soon as he heard the question Fink knew Harry Roosevelt would not be a pushover. They were investigating a murder, not a suicide. There was no law against suicide, nor was there a law against witnessing one. 'Well, Your Honor, the suicide has some very direct links to the murder of Boyette, we think, and it's important for the kid to cooperate.'

'What if the kid knows nothing?'

'We can't be certain until we ask him. Right now he's impeding the investigation, and, as you well know, every citizen has a duty to assist law enforcement officials.'

'I'm well aware of that. It just seems a bit severe to allege the kid is a delinquent without any proof.'

'The proof will come, Your Honor, if we can get the kid on the witness stand, under oath, in a closed hearing and ask some questions. That's all we're trying to do.'

Harry tossed the brief into a pile of papers and removed his reading glasses. He chewed on a stem.

Ord leaned forward and spoke solemnly. 'Look, Judge, if we can take the kid into custody, then have an expedited hearing, we think this matter will be resolved. If he states under oath that he knows nothing about Boyd Boyette, then the petition is dismissed, the kid goes home, and the matter is over. It's routine. No proof, no finding of delinquency, no harm. But if he knows something relevant to the location of the body, then we have a right to know and we think the kid will tell us during the hearing.'

'There are two ways to make him talk, Your Honor,' Fink added. 'We can file this petition in your court and have a hearing, or we can subpoena the kid to face the grand jury in New Orleans. Staying here seems to be the quickest and best route, especially for the kid.'

'I do not want this kid subpoenaed before a grand jury,' Harry said sternly. 'Is that understood?'

They all nodded quickly, and they all knew full well that a federal grand jury could subpoena Mark Sway anytime it chose, regardless of the feelings of a local judge. This was typical of Harry. Immediately throwing his protective blanket around any child within reach of his jurisdiction.

'I'd much rather deal with it in my court,' he said, almost to himself.

'We agree, Your Honor,' Fink said. They all agreed.

Harry picked up his daily calendar. As usual, it was filled with more misery than he could possibly handle in one day. He studied it. 'These allegations of obstruction are rather shaky, in my opinion. But I can't prevent you from filing the petition. I suggest we hear this matter at the earliest possible time. If the kid in fact knows nothing, and I suspect this to be the case, then I want it over and done with. Quickly.'

This suited everyone.

'Let's do it during lunch today. Where is the kid now?'

'At the hospital,' Ord said. 'His brother will be there for an unspecified period of time. The mother is confined to the room. Mark just sort of roams about. Last night he stayed with his lawyer.'

'That sounds like Reggie,' Harry said with affection. 'I see no need to take him into custody.'

Custody was very important to Fink and Foltrigg. They wanted the kid picked up, hauled away in a police car, placed in a cell of some sort, and in general frightened to the point of talking.

'Your Honor, if I may,' K.O. finally said. 'We think custody is urgent.'

'Oh you do? I'm listening.'

McThune handed Judge Roosevelt a glossy eight by ten. Lewis handled the narration. 'The man in the picture is Paul Gronke. He's a thug from New Orleans, and a close associate of Barry Muldanno. He's been in Memphis since Tuesday night. That photo was taken as he entered the airport in New Orleans. An hour later he was in Memphis, and unfortunately we lost him when he left the airport here.' McThune produced two smaller photos. 'The guy with the dark shades is Mack Bono, a convicted murderer with strong mob ties in New Orleans. The guy in the suit is

231

Gary Pirini, another Mafia thug who works for the Sulari family. Bono and Pirini arrived in Memphis last night. They didn't come here to eat barbecued ribs.' He paused for dramatic effect. 'The kid's in serious danger, Your Honor. The family home is a house trailer in north Memphis, in a place called Tucker Wheel Estates.'

'I'm very familiar with the place,' Harry said, rubbing his eyes.

'About four hours ago, the trailer burned to the ground. The fire looks suspicious. We think it's intimidation. The kid has been roaming at will since Monday night. There's no father, and the mother cannot leave the younger son. It's very sad, and it's very dangerous.'

'So you've been watching him.'

'Yes sir. His lawyer asked the hospital to provide security guards outside the brother's room.'

'And she called me,' Ord added. 'She is very concerned about the kid's safety, and asked me to request FBI protection at the hospital.'

'And we complied,' added McThune. 'We've had at least two agents near the room for the past forty-eight hours. These guys are killers, Your Honor, and they're taking orders from Muldanno. And the kid's just roaming around oblivious to the danger.'

Harry listened to them carefully. It was a well-rehearsed full court press. By nature, he was suspicious of police and their kind, but this was not a routine case. 'Our laws certainly provide for the child to be taken into custody after the petition is filed,' he said to no one in particular. 'What happens to the kid if the hearing does not produce what you want, if the kid is in fact not obstructing justice?'

Lewis answered. 'We've thought about this, Your Honor, and we would never do anything to violate the secrecy of your hearings. But, we have ways of getting word to these thugs that the kid knows nothing. Frankly, if he comes clean and knows nothing, the matter is closed and Muldanno's boys will lose interest in him. Why should they threaten him if he knows nothing?'

232

'That makes sense,' Harry said. 'But what do you do if the kid tells you what you want to hear. He's a marked little boy at that point, don't you think? If these guys are as dangerous as you say, then our little pal could be in serious trouble.'

'We're making preliminary arrangements to place him in the witness protection program. All of them, Mark, his mother, and brother.'

'Have you discussed this with his attorney?'

'No sir,' Fink answered. 'The last time we were in her office she refused to meet with us. She's been difficult too.'

'Let me see your petition.'

Fink whipped it out and handed it to him. He carefully put on his reading glasses and studied it. When he finished, he handed it back to Fink.

'I don't like this, gentlemen. I just don't like the smell of it. I've seen a million cases, and never one involving a minor and a charge of obstructing justice. I have an uneasy feeling.'

'We're desperate, Your Honor,' Lewis confessed with a great deal of sincerity. 'We have to know what the kid knows, and we fear for his safety. This is all on the table. We're not hiding anything, and we're damned sure not trying to mislead you.'

'I certainly hope not.' Harry glared at them. He scribbled something on scratch paper. They waited and watched his every move. He glanced at his watch.

'I'll sign the order. I want the kid taken directly to the Juvenile Wing and placed in a cell by himself. He'll be scared to death, and I want him handled with velvet gloves. I'll personally call his lawyer later in the morning.'

They stood in unison and thanked him. He pointed to the door, and they left quickly without handshakes or farewells.

TWENTY-ONE

Karen knocked lightly and entered the dark room with a basket of fruit. The card brought get-well messages from the congregation of Little Creek Baptist Church. The apples and bananas and grapes were wrapped in green cellophane, and looked pretty sitting next to a rather large and expensive arrangement of colorful flowers sent by the concerned friends at Ark-Lon Fixtures.

The shades were drawn, the television was off, and when Karen closed the door to leave none of the Sways had moved. Ricky had changed positions, and was now lying on his back with his feet on the pillows and his head on the blankets. He was awake, but for the last hour had been staring blankly at the ceiling without saying a word or moving an inch. This was something new. Mark and Dianne sat next to each other on the foldaway bed with their feet tucked under them and whispered about such things as clothing and toys and dishes. There was fire insurance, but Dianne didn't know the extent of the coverage.

They spoke in hushed voices. It would be days or weeks before Ricky knew of the fire.

At some point in the morning, about an hour after Reggie and Clint left, the shock of the news wore off and Mark started thinking. It was easy to think in this dark room because there was nothing else to do. The television could be used only when Ricky wanted it. The shades remained closed if there was a chance he was sleeping. The door was always shut.

Mark had been sitting in a chair under the television, eating a stale chocolate chip cookie, when it occurred to him that maybe the fire was not an accident. Earlier, the man with the knife had somehow entered the trailer and found the portrait. His intent had been to wave the knife and wave the portrait, and forever silence little Mark Sway. And he had been most successful. What if the fire was just another reminder from the man with the switchblade? Trailers were easy to burn. The neighborhood was usually quiet at four in the morning. He knew this from experience.

This thought had stuck like a thick knot in his throat, and his mouth was suddenly dry. Dianne didn't notice. She'd been sipping coffee and patting Ricky.

Mark had wrestled with it for a while, then had taken a short walk to the nurses' station where Karen showed him the morning paper.

The thought was so horrible it seared itself into his mind, and after two hours of thinking about it he was convinced the fire was intentional.

'What will the insurance cover?' he asked.

'I'll have to call the agent. There are two policies, if I remember correctly. One is paid by Mr Tucker on the trailer, because he owns it, and the other is paid by us for the contents of the trailer. The monthly rent is supposed to include the premium for the insurance on the contents. I think that's how it works.'

This worried Mark immensely. There were many awful memories from the divorce, and he remembered his mother's inability to testify about any of the financial affairs of the family. She knew nothing. His ex-father paid the bills and kept the checkbook and filed the tax returns. Twice in the past two years the telephone had been cut off because Dianne had forgotten to pay the bills. Or so she said. He suspected each time that there was no money to pay the bills.

'But what will the insurance pay for?' he asked.

'Furniture, clothes, kitchen utensils, I guess. That's what it usually covers.'

There was a knock on the door, but it did not open. They waited, then another knock. Mark opened it slightly, and saw two new faces peering through the crack.

'Yes,' he said, expecting trouble because the nurses and security guards allowed no one to get this far. He opened the door a bit wider.

'Looking for Dianne Sway,' said the nearest face. There was volume to this, and Dianne started for the door.

'Who are you?' Mark asked, opening the door and walking into the hall. The two security guards were standing together to the left, and all five appeared frozen as if witnessing a horrible event. Mark locked eyes with Karen, and knew instantly something was terribly wrong.

'Detective Nassar, Memphis PD. This is Detective Klickman.'

Nassar wore a coat and tie, and Klickman wore a black jogging suit with sparkling new Nike Air Jordans. They were both young, probably early thirties, and Mark immediately thought of the old 'Starsky and Hutch' reruns. Dianne opened the door and stood behind her son.

'Are you Dianne Sway?' Nassar asked.

'I am,' she answered quickly.

Nassar pulled papers from his coat pocket and handed them over Mark's head to his mother. 'These are from Juvenile Court, Ms Sway. It's a summons for a hearing at noon today.'

Her hands shook wildly and the papers rattled as she tried hopelessly to make sense of this.

'Could I see your badges?' Mark asked, rather coolly under the circumstances. They both grabbed and reached and presented their identification under Mark's nose. He studied them carefully, and sneered at Nassar. 'Nice shoes,' he said to Klickman.

Nassar tried to smile. 'Ms Sway, the summons requires us to take Mark Sway into custody at this time.'

There was a heavy pause of two or three seconds as the word 'custody' settled in.

'What!' Dianne yelled at Nassar. She dropped the

236

papers. The 'What!' echoed down the hallway. There was more anger in her voice than fear.

'It's right here on the front page,' Nassar said, picking up the summons. 'Judge's orders.'

'You what!' she yelled again, and it shot through the air like the crack of a bullwhip. 'You can't take my son!' Dianne's face was red and her body, all hundred and fifteen pounds, was tense and coiled.

Great, thought Mark. Another ride in a patrol car. Then his mother yelled, 'You son of a bitch!' and Mark tried to calm her.

'Mom, don't yell. Ricky can hear you.'

'Over my dead body!' she yelled at Nassar, just inches away. Klickman backed away one step, as if to say this wild woman belonged to Nassar.

But Nassar was a pro. He'd arrested thousands. 'Look, Ms Sway, I understand how you feel. But I have my orders.'

'Whose orders!'

'Mom, please don't yell,' Mark pleaded.

'Judge Harry Roosevelt signed the order about an hour ago. We're just doing our job, Ms Sway. Nothing's gonna happen to Mark. We'll take care of him.'

'What's he done? Just tell me what's he done?' Dianne turned to the nurses. 'Can somebody help me here?' she pleaded and sounded so pitiful. 'Karen, do something, would you? Call Dr Greenway. Don't just stand there.'

But Karen and the nurses just stood there. The cops had already warned them.

Nassar was still trying to smile. 'If you'll read these papers, Ms Sway, you'll see that a petition has been filed in Juvenile Court alleging Mark here to be a delinquent because he won't cooperate with the police and FBI. And Judge Roosevelt wants to have a hearing at noon today. That's all.'

'That's all! You asshole! You show up here with your little papers and take away my son and you say "That's all"!'

237

'Not so loud, Mom,' Mark said. He hadn't heard such language from her since the divorce.

Nassar stopped trying to smile and pulled at the corners of his mustache. Klickman for some reason was glaring at Mark as if he were a serial killer they'd been tracking for years. There was a long pause. Dianne kept both hands on Mark's shoulders. 'You can't have him!'

Finally, Klickman said his first words. 'Look, Ms Sway, we have no choice. We have to take your son.'

'Go to hell,' she snapped. 'If you take him, you whip me first.'

Klickman was a meathead with little finesse, and for a split second his shoulders flinched as if he would accept this challenge. Then he relaxed and smiled.

'It's okay, Mom. I'll go. Call Reggie and tell her to meet me at the jail. She'll probably sue these clowns by lunch and have them fired by tomorrow.'

The cops grinned at each other. Cute little kid.

Nassar then made the very sad mistake of reaching for Mark's arm. Dianne lunged and struck like a cobra. Whap! She slapped him on his left cheek and screamed, 'Don't touch him! Don't touch him!'

Nassar grabbed his face, and Klickman instantly grabbed her arm. She wanted to strike again, but was suddenly spun around, and somehow in the midst of this her feet and Mark's became tangled and they hit the floor. 'You son of a bitch!' she kept screaming. 'Don't touch him!'

Nassar reached down for some reason, and Dianne kicked him on the thigh. But she was barefoot and there was little damage. Klickman was reaching down, and Mark was scrambling to get up, and Dianne was kicking and swinging and yelling, 'Don't touch him!' The nurses rushed forward and the security guards joined in as Dianne got to her feet.

Mark was pulled from the fracas by Klickman. Dianne was held by the two security guards. She was twisting and crying. Nassar was rubbing his face. The nurses were soothing and consoling and trying to separate everyone.

The door opened, and Ricky stood in it holding a stuffed

rabbit. He stared at Mark, whose wrists were being held by Klickman. He stared at his mother, whose wrists were being held by the security guards. Everyone froze and stared at Ricky. His face was as white as the sheets. His hair stuck out in all directions. His mouth was open, but he said nothing.

Then he started the low, mournful groan that only Mark had heard before. Dianne yanked her wrists free and picked him up. The nurses followed her into the room and they tucked him in the bed. They patted his arms and legs, but the groaning continued. Then the thumb went in his mouth and he closed his eyes. Dianne lay beside him in the bed and began humming 'Winnie the Pooh' and patting his arm.

'Let's go, kid,' Klickman said.

'You gonna handcuff me?'

'No. This is not an arrest.'

'Then what the hell is it?'

'Watch your language, kid.'

'Kiss my ass, you big stupid jock.' Klickman stopped cold and glared down at Mark.

'Watch your mouth, kid,' Nassar warned.

'Look at your face, hotshot. I think it's turning blue. Mom coldclocked you. Ha, Ha. I hope she broke your teeth.'

Klickman bent over and put his hands on his knees. He stared Mark directly in the eyes. 'Are you going with us, or shall we drag you out of here?'

Mark snorted and glared at him. 'You think I'm scared of you, don't you? Let me tell you something, meathead, I've got a lawyer who'll have me out in ten minutes. My lawyer is so good that by this afternoon you'll be looking for another job.'

'I'm scared to death. Now let's go.'

They started walking, a cop on each side of the defendant.

'Where are we going?'

'Juvenile Detention Center.'

'Is it sort of a jail?'

239

'It could be if you don't watch your smart mouth.'

'You knocked my mother down, you know that. She'll have your job for that.'

'She can have my job,' Klickman said. 'It's a rotten job because I have to deal with little punks like you.'

'Yeah, but you can't find another one, can you? There's no demand for idiots these days.'

They passed a small crowd of orderlies and nurses, and suddenly Mark was a star. The center of attention. He was an innocent man being led away to the slaughter. He swaggered a bit. They turned the corner, and then he remembered the reporters.

And they remembered him. A flash went off as they got to the elevators, and two of the loiterers with pencils and pads were suddenly standing next to Klickman. They waited for the elevator.

'Are you a cop?' one of them asked, staring at the glow-in-the-dark Nikes.

'No comment.'

'Hey, Mark, where are you going?' another asked from just a few feet behind. There was another flash.

'To jail,' he said loudly without turning around.

'Shut up, kid,' Nassar scolded. Klickman put a heavy arm on his shoulder. The photographer was beside them, almost to the elevator door. Nassar held up an arm to block his view. 'Get away,' he growled.

'Are you under arrest, Mark?' one of them yelled.

'No,' Klickman snapped just as the door opened. Nassar shoved Mark inside while Klickman blocked the door until it started to close.

They were alone in the elevator. 'That was a stupid thing to say, kid. Really stupid.' Klickman was shaking his head.

'Then arrest me.'

'Really stupid.'

'Is it against the law to talk to the press?'

'Just keep your mouth shut, okay?'

'Why don't you just beat the hell out of me, okay, meathead?'

240

'I'd love to.'

'Yeah, but you can't, right? Because I'm just a little kid, and you're a big stupid cop and if you touch me you'll get fired and sued and all that. You knocked my mother down, meathead, and you haven't heard the last of it.'

'Your mother slapped me,' Nassar said.

'Good for her. You clowns have no idea what she's been through. You show up to get me and act like it's no big deal, like just because you're cops and you've got this piece of paper then my mother is supposed to get happy and send me off with a kiss. A couple of morons. Just big, dumb, meatheaded cops.'

The elevator stopped, opened, and the two doctors entered. They stopped talking and looked at Mark. The door closed behind them, and they continued down. 'Can you believe these clowns are arresting me?' he asked the doctors.

They frowned at Nassar and Klickman.

'Juvenile Court offender,' Nassar explained. Why couldn't the little punk just shut up?

Mark nodded at Klickman. 'This one here with the cute shoes knocked my mother down about five minutes ago. Can you believe it?'

Both doctors looked at the shoes.

'Just shut up, Mark,' Klickman said.

'Is your mother okay?' one of the doctors asked.

'Oh she's great. My little brother's in the psychiatric ward. Our trailer burned to the ground a few hours ago. And then these thugs show up and arrest me right in front of my mother. Bigfoot here knocks her to the floor. She's doing great.'

The doctors stared at the cops. Nassar watched his feet and Klickman closed his eyes. The elevator stopped and a small crowd boarded. Klickman stayed close to Mark.

When all was quiet and they were moving again, Mark said loudly, 'My lawyer'll sue you jerks, you know that, don't you? You'll be unemployed this time tomorrow.' Eight sets of eyes looked down in the corner, then up at the pained face of Detective Klickman. Silence.

241

'Just shut up, Mark.'

'And what if I don't? You gonna rough me up like you did my mother. Throw me down, kick me a few times. You're just another meathead cop, you know that, Klickman? Just another fat cop with a gun. Why don't you lose a few pounds?'

Neat rows of sweat broke out across Klickman's forehead. He caught the eyes darting at him from the crowd. The elevator was barely moving. He could have strangled Mark.

Nassar was pressed into the other rear corner, and his ears were now ringing from the slap to the head. He couldn't see Mark Sway, but he could certainly hear him.

'Is your mother all right?' a nurse asked. She was standing next to Mark, looking down and very concerned.

'Yeah, she's having a great day. She'd be a lot better, of course, if these cops would leave her alone. They're taking me to jail, you know that?'

'What for?'

'I don't know. They won't tell me. I was just minding my own business, trying to console my mother because our trailer burned to the ground this morning and we lost everything we own, when they showed up with no warning, and here I am on the way to jail.'

'How old are you?'

'Only eleven. But that's not important to these guys. They'd arrest a four-year-old.'

Nassar groaned softly. Klickman kept his eyes closed.

'This is awful,' the nurse said.

'You should've seen it when they had me and my mother on the floor. Happened just a few minutes ago on the Psychiatric Wing. It'll be on the news tonight. Watch the papers. These clowns will be fired tomorrow. Then the lawsuit.'

They stopped on the ground floor, and the elevator emptied.

He insisted on riding in the rear seat, like a real criminal.

242

The car was an unmarked Chrysler but he spotted it a hundred yards away in the parking lot. Nassar and Klickman were afraid to speak to him. They rode in the front seat in complete silence, hoping he might do the same. They were not so lucky.

'You forgot to read me my rights,' he said as Nassar drove as fast as possible.

No response from the front seat.

'Hey, you clowns up there. You forgot to read me my rights.'

No response. Nassar drove faster.

'Do you know *how* to read me my rights.'

No response.

'Hey, meathead. Yeah, you with the shoes. Do you know how to read me my rights?'

Klickman's breathing was labored, but he was determined to ignore him. Oddly, Nassar had a crooked smile barely noticeable under the mustache. He stopped at a red light, looked both ways, then gunned the engine.

'Listen to me, meathead, okay. I'll do it myself, okay. I have the right to remain silent. Did you catch that? And, if I say anything, you clowns can use it against me in court. Get that, meathead? Of course, if I said anything you dumbasses would forget it. Then there's something about the right to a lawyer. Can you help with this one, meathead? Yo! meathead. What's the bit about the lawyer? I've seen it on television a million times.'

Meathead Klickman cracked his window so he could breathe. Nassar glanced at the shoes and almost laughed. The criminal sat low in the rear seat with his legs crossed.

'Poor meathead. Can't even read me my rights. This car stinks, meathead. Why don't you clean this car? It smells like cigarette smoke.'

'I hear you like cigarette smoke,' Klickman said, and felt much better about himself. Nassar giggled to help his friend. They'd taken enough crap off this brat.

Mark saw a crowded parking lot next to a tall building. Patrol cars were parked in rows next to the building.

243

Nassar turned into the lot and parked in the driveway.

They rushed him through the entrance doors and down a long hallway. He had finally stopped talking. He was on their turf. Cops were everywhere. Signs directed traffic to the DUI Holding Tank, the Jail, the Visitor's Room, the Receiving Room. Plenty of signs and rooms. They stopped at a desk with a row of closed-circuit monitors behind it, and Nassar signed some papers. Mark studied the surroundings. Klickman almost felt sorry for him. He looked even smaller.

They were off again. The elevator took them to the fourth floor, and again they stopped at a desk. A sign on the wall pointed to the Juvenile Wing, and Mark figured he was getting close.

A uniformed lady with a clipboard and a plastic tag declaring her to be Doreen stopped them. She looked at some papers, then at the clipboard. 'Says here Judge Roosevelt wants Mark Sway in a private room,' she said.

'I don't care where you put him,' Nassar said. 'Just take him.'

She was frowning and looking at her clipboard. 'Of course, Roosevelt wants all juveniles in private rooms. Thinks this is the Hilton.'

'It's not?'

She ignored this, and pointed at a piece of paper for Nassar to sign. He scribbled his name hurriedly, and said, 'He's all yours. God help you.'

Klickman and Nassar left without a word.

'Empty your pockets, Mark,' the lady said as she handed him a large metal container. He pulled out a dollar bill, some change, and a pack of gum. She counted it and wrote something on a card, which she then inserted on the end of the metal box. In a corner above the desk, two cameras captured Mark, and he could see himself on one of the dozen screens on the wall. Another lady in a uniform was stamping papers.

'Is this the jail?' Mark asked, cutting his eyes in all directions.

'We call it a detention center,' she said.

'What's the difference?'

This seemed to irritate her. 'Listen, Mark, we get all kinds of smart mouths up here, okay. You'll get along much better if you keep your mouth shut.' She leaned into his face with these words of warning, and her breath was stale cigarettes and black coffee.

'I'm sorry,' he said, and his eyes watered. It suddenly hit him. He was about to be locked in a room far away from his mother, far away from Reggie.

'Follow me,' Doreen said, proud of herself for restoring a little authority to the relationship. She whisked away with a ring of keys dangling and rattling from her waist. They opened a heavy, wooden door and started through a hallway with gray metal doors spaced evenly apart on both sides of the corridor. Each little room had a number beside it. Doreen stopped at Number 16, and unlocked it with one of her keys. 'In here,' she said.

Mark walked in slowly. The room was about twelve feet wide and twenty feet long. The lights were bright and the carpet was clean. Two bunk beds were to his right. Doreen patted the top bunk. 'You can have either bed,' she said, ever the hostess. 'Walls are cinder block and windows are nonbreakable, so don't try anything.' There were two windows – one in the door and one above the lavatory, and neither was big enough to stick his head through. 'Toilet's over there, stainless steel. Can't use ceramic anymore. Had a kid break one and slice his wrists with a piece of it. But that was in the old building. This place is much nicer, don't you think?'

It's gorgeous, Mark almost said. But he was sinking fast. He sat on the bottom bunk and rested his elbows on his knees. The carpet was pale green, the same type of commercial blend he'd been studying at the hospital.

'You okay, Mark?' Doreen asked without the slightest trace of sympathy. This was her job.

'Can I call my mother?'

'Not yet. You can make a few calls in about an hour.'

'Well, can you call her and just tell her I'm okay? She's worried sick.'

Doreen smiled and the makeup cracked around her eyes. She patted his head. 'Can't do it, Mark. Regulations. But she knows you're fine. My goodness, you'll be in court in a couple of hours.'

'How long do kids stay in here?'

'Not long. A few weeks occasionally, but this is sort of a holding area until the kids are processed and either sent back home or to a training school.' She was rattling her keys. 'Listen, I have to go now. The door locks automatically when it's closed, and if it opens without my little key here, then an alarm goes off and there's big trouble. So don't get any ideas, okay, Mark?'

'Yes ma'am.'

'Can I get you anything?'

'A telephone.'

'In just a little while, okay.'

Doreen closed the door behind her. There was a loud click, then silence.

He stared at the doorknob for a long time. This didn't seem like jail. There were no bars on the windows. The beds and floor were clean. The cinder block walls were painted a pleasant shade of yellow. He'd seen worse, in the movies.

There was so much to worry about. Ricky groaning like that again, the fire, Dianne slowly unraveling, cops and reporters glued to him. He didn't know where to start.

He stretched on the top bunk and studied the ceiling. Where in the world was Reggie?

TWENTY-TWO

The chapel was cold and damp. It was a round building stuck to the side of a mausoleum like a cancerous growth. It was raining outside, and two television crews from New Orleans huddled beside their vans and hid under umbrellas.

The crowd was respectable, especially for a man with no family. His remains were packaged tastefully in a porcelain urn sitting on a mahogany table. Hidden speakers from above brought forth one dreary dirge after another as the lawyers and judges and a few clients ventured in and sat near the rear. Barry The Blade strutted down the aisle with two thugs in tow. He was properly dressed in a black double-breasted suit with a black shirt and a black tie. Black lizard shoes. His ponytail was immaculate. He arrived late, and enjoyed the stares from the mourners. After all, he'd known Jerome Clifford for a long time.

Four rows back, the Right Reverend Roy Foltrigg sat with Wally Boxx and scowled at the ponytail. The lawyers and judges looked at Muldanno, then at Foltrigg, then back at Muldanno. Strange, seeing them in the same room.

The music stopped, and a minister of some generic faith appeared in the small pulpit behind the urn. He started with a lengthy obituary of Walter Jerome Clifford, and threw in everything but the names of his childhood pets. This was not unexpected because when the obituary was over there would be little to say.

It was a brief service, just as Romey had asked for in his

note. The lawyers and judges glanced at their watches. Another mournful lamentation started from above, and the minister excused everyone.

Romey's last hurrah was over in fifteen minutes. There were no tears. Even his secretary kept her composure. His daughter was not present. Very sad. He lived forty-four years and no one cried at his funeral.

Foltrigg kept his seat and scowled at Muldanno as he strutted down the aisle and out the door. Foltrigg waited until the chapel was empty, then made an exit with Wally behind him. The cameras were there, and that's exactly what he wanted. Earlier, Wally had leaked a juicy tidbit about the great Roy Foltrigg attending the service, and also that there was a chance Barry The Blade Muldanno would be present. Neither Wally nor Roy had any idea whether Muldanno would attend, but it was only a leak so who cared if it was accurate. It was working.

A reporter asked for a couple of minutes, and Foltrigg did what he always did. He glanced at his watch, looked terribly frustrated by this intrusion, and sent Wally after the van. Then he said what he always said, 'Okay, but make it quick. I'm due in court in fifteen minutes.' He hadn't been to court in three weeks. He usually went about once a month, but to hear him talk he lived in courtrooms, battling the bad guys, protecting the interests of the American taxpayers. A hard-charging crimebuster.

He squeezed under an umbrella and looked at the mini-cam. The reporter waved a microphone in his face. 'Jerome Clifford was a rival. Why did you attend his memorial service?'

He was suddenly sad. 'Jerome was a fine lawyer, and a friend of mine. We faced each other many times, but always respected each other.' What a guy. Gracious even in death. He hated Jerome Clifford and Jerome Clifford hated him, but the camera saw only the heartbreak of a grieving pal.

'Mr. Muldanno has hired a new lawyer and filed a motion for a continuance. What is your response to this?'

'As you know, Judge Lamond has scheduled a hearing on

the continuance request for tomorrow morning at 10 a.m. The decision will be his. The United States will be ready for trial whenever he sets it.'

'Do you expect to find the body of Senator Boyette before trial?'

'Yes. I think we're getting close.'

'Is it true you were in Memphis just hours after Mr Clifford shot himself?'

'Yes.' He sort of shrugged as if it was no big deal.

'There are news reports in Memphis that the kid who was with Mr Clifford when he shot himself may know something about the Boyette case. Any truth to this?'

He smiled sheepishly, another trademark. When the answer was yes, but he couldn't say it, but he wanted to send the message anyway, he just grinned at the reporters and said, 'I can't comment on that.'

'I can't comment on that,' he said, glancing around as if time was up and his busy trial calendar was calling.

'Does the boy know where the body is?'

'No comment,' he said with irritation. The rain grew harder, and splashed on his socks and shoes. 'I have to be going.'

After an hour in jail, Mark was ready to escape. He inspected both windows. The one above the lavatory had some wire in it, but that did not matter. What was troubling, though, was the fact that any object exiting through this window, including a boy, would fall directly down at least fifty feet, and the fall would be stopped by a concrete sidewalk lined with chain-link fencing and barbed wire. Also, both windows were thick and too small for escape, he determined.

He would be forced to make his break when they transported him, maybe take a hostage or two. He'd seen some great movies about jailbreaks. His favorite was *Escape from Alcatraz* with Clint Eastwood. He'd figure it out.

Doreen knocked on the door, jangled her keys, and stepped inside. She held a directory and a black phone, which she plugged into the wall. 'It's yours for ten minutes. No long distance.' Then she was gone, the door clicking loudly behind her, the cheap perfume floating heavy in the air and burning his eyes.

He found the number for St Peter's, asked for Room 943, and was informed that no calls were being put through to that room. Ricky's asleep, he thought. Must be bad. He found Reggie's number, and listened to Clint's voice on the recorder. He called Greenway's office, and was informed the doctor was at the hospital. Mark explained exactly who he was, and the secretary said she believed the doctor was seeing Ricky. He called Reggie again. Same recording. He left an urgent message – 'Get me out of jail, Reggie!' He called her home number, and listened to another recording.

He stared at the phone. With about seven minutes left, he had to do something. He flipped through the directory, and found the listings for the Memphis Police Department. He picked the North Precinct and dialed the number.

'Detective Klickman,' he said.

'Just a minute,' said the voice on the other end. He held for a few seconds, then a voice said, 'Who're you holding for?'

He cleared his throat and tried to sound gruff. 'Detective Klickman.'

'He's on duty.'

'When will he be in?'

'Around lunch.'

'Thanks.' Mark hung up quickly, and wondered if the lines were bugged. Probably not. After all, these phones were used by criminals, and people like himself to call their lawyers and talk business. There had to be privacy.

He memorized the precinct phone number and address, then flipped to the yellow pages under Restaurants. He punched a number, and a friendly voice said, 'Domino's Pizza. May I take your order.'

He cleared his throat and tried to sound hoarse. 'Yes, I'd like to order four of your large supremes.'

'Is that all?'

'Yes. Need them delivered at noon.'

'Your name?'

'I'm ordering them for Detective Klickman, North Precinct.'

'Delivered where?'

'North Precinct – 3633 Allen Road. Just ask for Klickman.'

'We've been there before, believe me. Phone number?'

'It's 555–8989.'

There was a short pause as the adding machine rang it up. 'That'll be forty-eight dollars and ten cents.'

'Fine. Don't need it until noon.'

Mark hung up, his heart pounding. But he'd done it once, and he could do it again. He found the Pizza Hut numbers, there were seventeen in Memphis, and started placing orders. Three said they were too far away from downtown. He hung up on them. One young girl was suspicious, said he sounded too young, and he hung up on her too. But for the most part it was just routine business – call, place the order, give the address and phone number, and allow free enterprise to handle the rest.

When Doreen knocked on the door twenty minutes later, he was ordering Klickman some Chinese food from Wong Boys. He quickly hung up and walked to the bunks. She took great satisfaction in removing the phone, like taking toys away from bad little boys. But she was not quick enough. Detective Klickman had ordered about forty deep dish supreme deluxe large pizzas and a dozen Chinese lunches, all to be delivered around noon, at a cost of somewhere in the neighborhood of five hundred dollars.

For his hangover, Gronke sipped his fourth orange juice of the morning and washed down another headache powder. He stood at the window of his hotel room, shoes off, belt unbuckled, shirt unbuttoned, and listened painfully as Jack Nance reported the disturbing news.

'Happened less than thirty minutes ago,' Nance said, sitting on the dresser, staring at the wall, trying to ignore this goon standing at the window with his back to him.

'Why?' Gronke grunted.

'Has to be youth court. They took him straight to jail. I mean, hell, they can't just pick a kid, or anybody else for that matter, and take him straight to jail. They had to file something in youth court. Cal's there now, checking it out. Maybe we'll have it soon, I don't know. Youth court records are locked up, I think.'

'Get the damned records, okay.'

Nance seethed but bit his tongue. He hated Gronke and his little band of cutthroats, and even though he needed the hundred bucks an hour he was tired of hanging around this dirty, smoky room like a flunky waiting to be barked at. He had other clients. Cal was a nervous wreck.

'We're trying,' he said.

'Try harder,' Gronke said to the window. 'Now I gotta call Barry and tell him the kid's been taken away and there's no way to get to him. Got him locked up somewhere, probably with a cop sittin' outside his door.' He finished the orange juice and tossed the can in the general direction of the wastebasket. It missed and rattled along the wall. He glared at Nance. 'Barry'll wanna know if there's a way to get the kid. What would you suggest?'

'I suggest you leave the kid alone. This is not New Orleans, and this is not just some little punk you can rub out and make everything wonderful. This kid's got baggage, lots of it. People are watching him. If you do something stupid, you'll have a hundred Fibbies all over your ass. You won't be able to breathe, and you and Mr Muldanno will rot in jail. Here, not New Orleans.'

'Yeah, yeah.' Gronke waved both hands at him in disgust and walked back to the window. 'I want you boys to keep watching him. If they move him anywhere, I wanna know it immediately. If they take him to court, I wanna know it. Figure it out, Nance. This is your city. You know the streets and alleys. At least you're supposed to. You're gettin' paid good money.'

'Yes sir,' Nance said loudly, then left the room.

TWENTY-THREE

For two hours every Thursday morning, Reggie disappeared into the office of Dr Elliot Levin, her longtime psychiatrist. Levin had been holding her hand for ten years. He was the architect who'd figured out the pieces and helped her put the puzzle back together. Their sessions were never disturbed.

Clint paced nervously in Levin's reception area. Dianne had called twice already. She had read the summons and petition to him over the phone. He had called Judge Roosevelt, and the detention center, and Levin's office, and now he waited impatiently for eleven o'clock. The receptionist tried to ignore him.

Reggie was smiling when Dr Levin finished with her. She pecked him on the cheek, and they walked hand in hand into his plush reception area where Clint was waiting. She stopped smiling. 'What's the matter?' she asked, certain something terrible had happened.

'We need to go,' Clint said, taking her arm and ushering her through the door. She nodded goodbye to Levin, who was watching with interest and concern.

They were on a sidewalk next to a small parking lot. 'They've picked up Mark Sway. He's in custody.'

'What! Who!'

'Cops. A petition was filed this morning alleging Mark to be a delinquent, and Roosevelt issued an order to take him into custody.' Clint was pointing. 'Let's take your car. I'll drive.'

'Who filed the petition?'

'Foltrigg. Dianne called from the hospital, that's where they got him. She had a big fight with the cops, and scared Ricky again. I've talked to her and assured her you'll go get Mark.'

They opened and slammed doors to Reggie's car, and sped from the parking lot. 'Roosevelt's scheduled a hearing for noon,' Clint explained.

'Noon! You must be kidding. That's fifty-six minutes from now.'

'It's an expedited hearing. I talked to him about an hour ago, and he wouldn't comment on the petition. Had very little to say, really. Where are we going?'

She thought about this for a second. 'He's in the detention center, and I can't get him out. Let's go to Juvenile Court. I want to see the petition, and I want to see Harry Roosevelt. This is absurd, a hearing within hours of filing the petition. The law says between three and seven days, not three and seven hours.'

'But isn't there a provision for expedited hearings?'

'Yeah, but only in extreme matters. They've fed Harry a bunch of crap. Delinquent! What's the kid done? This is crazy. They're trying to force him to talk, Clint, that's all.'

'So you didn't expect this?'

'Of course not. Not here, not in Juvenile Court. I've thought about a grand jury summons for Mark from New Orleans, but not Juvenile Court. He's committed no delinquent act. He doesn't deserve to be taken in.'

'Well, they got him.'

Jason McThune zipped his pants, and hit the lever three times before the antique urinal flushed. The bowl was stained with streaks of brown and the floor was wet, and he thanked God he worked in the Federal Building where everything was polished and spiffy. He'd lay asphalt with a shovel before he'd work in Juvenile Court.

But he was here now, like it or not, wasting time on the Boyette case because K. O. Lewis wanted him here.

And K. O. took orders from Mr F. Denton Voyles, Director of the FBI for forty-two years now. And in his forty-two years, no member of Congress and certainly no US Senator had been murdered. And the fact that the late Boyd Boyette had been hidden so neatly was galling. Mr Voyles was quite upset, not about the killing itself but about the FBI's inability to solve it completely.

McThune had a strong hunch Ms Reggie Love would arrive shortly, since her client had been snatched away from right under her nose, and he figured she'd be fuming when he saw her. Maybe she'd understand that these legal strategies were being hatched in New Orleans, not Memphis, and certainly not in his office. Surely she would understand that he, McThune, was just a humble FBI agent taking orders from above and doing what the lawyers told him. Perhaps he could dodge her until they were all in the courtroom.

Perhaps not. As McThune opened the rest room door and stepped into the hallway, he was suddenly face to face with Reggie Love. Clint was a step behind her. She saw him immediately, and within seconds he was backed against the wall and she was in his face. She was agitated.

'Morning, Ms Love,' he said, forcing a calm smile.

'It's Reggie, McThune.'

'Morning, Reggie.'

'Who's here with you?' she asked, glaring.

'Beg your pardon.'

'Your gang, your little band, your little group of government conspirators. Who's here?'

This was not a secret. He could discuss this with her. 'George Ord, Thomas Fink from New Orleans, K. O. Lewis.'

'Who's K. O. Lewis?'

'Deputy Director, FBI. From D.C.'

'What's he doing here?' Her questions were clipped and rapid, and aimed like arrows at McThune's eyes. He was pinned to the wall, afraid to move, but gallantly trying to appear nonchalant. If Fink or Ord or heaven forbid K. O.

255

Lewis happened into the hallway and saw him huddled with her like this he'd never recover.

'Well, I, uh –'

'Don't make me mention the tape, Mc Thune,' she said, mentioning the damned thing anyway. 'Just tell me the truth.'

Clint was standing behind her, holding her briefcase and watching the traffic. He appeared a bit surprised by this confrontation and the speed with which it was occurring. McThune shrugged as if he'd forgotten about the tape, and now that she mentioned it, what the hell. 'I think Foltrigg's office called Mr Lewis and asked him to come down. That's all.'

'That's all? Did you guys have a little meeting with Judge Roosevelt this morning?'

'Yes, we did.'

'Didn't bother to call me, did you?'

'Uh, the judge said he'd call you.'

'I see. Are you planning to testify during this little hearing?' She took a step back when she asked this and McThune breathed easier.

'I'll testify if I'm called as a witness.'

She stuck a finger in his face. The nail on the end of it was long, curved, carefully manicured, and painted red, and McThune watched it fearfully. 'You stick with the facts, okay. One lie, however small, or one bit of unsolicited self-serving crap to the judge, or one cheap shot remark that hurts my client, and I'll slice your throat, McThune. You understand?'

He kept smiling, glancing up and down the hall as if she were a pal and they were just having a tiny disagreement. 'I understand,' he said, grinning.

Reggie turned and walked away with Clint by her side. McThune turned and darted back into the rest room, though he knew she wouldn't hesitate to follow him in if she wanted something.

'What was that all about?' Clint asked.

'Just keeping him honest.' They wove through crowds of

litigants – paternity defendants, delinquent fathers, kids in trouble – and their lawyers huddled in small packs along the hallway.'

'What's the bit about the tape?'

'I didn't tell you about it?'

'No.'

'I'll play it for you later. It's hysterical.' She opened the door with JUDGE HARRY M. ROOSEVELT painted on it, and they entered a small cramped room with four desks in the center and rows of file cabinets around the walls. Reggie went straight for the first desk on the left where a pretty black girl was typing. The plate on her desk gave the name as Marcia Riggle. She stopped typing and smiled. 'Hello, Reggie,' she said.

'Hi, Marcia. Where's His Honor?'

On her birthdays, Marcia received flowers from the law offices of Reggie Love, and chocolates at Christmas. She was the right arm of Harry Roosevelt, a man so overworked he had no time to remember such things as speaking commitments and appointments and anniversaries. But Marcia always remembered. Reggie had handled her divorce two years ago. Momma Love had cooked lasagne for her.

'He's on the bench. Should be off in a few minutes. You're on for noon, you know.'

'That's what I hear.'

'He's tried to call you all morning.'

'Well, he didn't find me. I'll wait in his office.'

'Sure. You want a sandwich? I'm ordering lunch for him now.'

'No, thanks.' Reggie took her briefcase and asked Clint to wait in the hall and watch for Mark. It was twenty minutes before twelve, and he'd be arriving soon.

Marcia handed her a copy of the petition, and Reggie entered the judge's office as if it were hers. She closed the door behind her.

Harry and Irene Roosevelt had also eaten at Momma Love's

257

table. Few, if any, lawyers in Memphis spent as much time in Juvenile Court as Reggie Love, and over the past four years their lawyer-judge relationship had developed from one of mutual respect to one of friendship. About the only asset Reggie had been awarded in the divorce from Joe Cardoni was four season tickets for Memphis State basketball. The threesome – Harry, Irene, and Reggie – had watched many games at the Pyramid, sometimes joined by Elliot Levin, or another male friend of Reggie's. The basketball was usually followed by cheesecake at Café Expresso in The Peabody, or, depending on Harry's mood, maybe a late dinner at Grisanti's in midtown. Harry was always hungry, always planning the next meal. Irene fussed at him about his weight, so he ate more. Reggie occasionally kidded him about it, and each time she mentioned pounds or calories, he immediately asked about Momma Love and her pastas and cheeses and cobblers.

Judges are human. They need friends. He could eat and socialize with Reggie Love or any other lawyer for that matter and maintain his unbiased judicial discretion.

She marvelled at the organized debris of his office. The floor was an ancient, pale carpet, most of it covered with neat stacks of briefs and other legal wisdoms all somehow cropped off at the height of twelve inches. Saggy bookshelves lined two walls, but the books could not be seen for the files and more stacks of briefs and memos tucked in front of books with inches hanging perilously in mid-air. Red and manila files were crammed everywhere. Three old wooden chairs sat pitifully before the desk. One had files on it. One had files under it. One was vacant for the moment, but would doubtless be used for some type of storage by the end of the day. She sat on this one and looked at the desk.

Though it was allegedly made of wood, none was visible except for the front and side panels. The top could be leather or chrome, no one would ever know. Harry himself could not remember what the top of his desk looked like. The upper level was another of Marcia's neat rows of legal papers, cropped at eight inches. Twelve inches for the floor, eight for the desk. Underneath and next in depth was a huge daily calendar for 1986, which Harry had once used to draw and doodle while listening to lawyers bore him with their arguments. Under the calendar was no-man's-land. Even Marcia was afraid to go deeper.

She'd stuck a dozen notes on yellow Post-it pads to the back of his chair. Evidently, these were the most urgent of the morning's emergencies.

Despite the chaos of his office, Harry Roosevelt was the most organized judge Reggie had encountered in her four-year career. He was not forced to spend time studying the law because he'd written most of it. He was known for the economy of his words, so his orders and decrees tended to be lean by judicial standards. He didn't tolerate lengthy briefs written by lawyers, and he was abrupt with those who loved to hear themselves talk. He managed his time wisely, and Marcia took care of the rest. His desk and office were somewhat famous in Memphis legal circles, and Reggie suspected he enjoyed this. She admired him immensely, not just for his wisdom and integrity, but also for his dedication to this office. He could've moved up many years ago to a stuffier place on the bench with a fancy desk, and clerks and paralegals, and clean carpet, and dependable air-conditioning.

She flipped through the petition. Foltrigg and Fink were the petitioners, their signatures at the bottom. Nothing detailed, just broad, sweeping allegations about the juvenile, Mark Sway, obstructing a federal investigation by refusing to cooperate with the FBI and the US Attorney's office for the Southern District of Louisiana. She despised Foltrigg every time she saw his name.

But it could be worse. Foltrigg's name could be at the bottom of a grand jury subpoena demanding the appearance of Mark Sway in New Orleans. It would be perfectly legal and proper for Foltrigg to do this, and she was a bit surprised he had chosen Memphis as his forum. New Orleans would be next if this didn't work.

The door opened, and a massive black robe lumbered in

259

with Marcia in pursuit, holding a list and clicking off things that had to be done immediately. He listened without looking at her, unzipped the robe and threw it at a chair, the one with the files under it.

'Good morning, Reggie,' he said with a smile. He patted her on the shoulder as he walked behind her. 'That'll be all,' he said calmly to Marcia, who closed the door and left. He picked the little yellow notes from his chair without reading them, then fell in it.

'How's Momma Love?' he asked.

'She's fine. And you?'

'Marvellous. Not surprised to see you here.'

'You didn't have to sign a custody order. I would've brought him here, Harry, you know that. He fell asleep last night in the swing on Momma Love's porch. He's in good hands.'

Harry smiled and rubbed his eyes. Very few lawyers called him Harry in his office. But he rather enjoyed it when it came from her. 'Reggie, Reggie. You never believe your clients should be taken into custody.'

'That's not true.'

'You think all's well if you can just take them home and feed them.'

'It helps.'

'Yes, it does. But according to Mr Ord and the FBI, little Mark Sway could be in a world of danger.'

'What'd they tell you?'

'It'll come out during the hearing.'

'They must've been pretty convincing, Harry. I get an hour's notice of the hearing. That has to be a record.'

'I thought you'd like that. We can do it tomorrow if you'd prefer. I don't mind making Mr Ord wait.'

'Not with Mark in custody. Release him to my custody, and we'll do the hearing tomorrow. I need some time to think.'

'I'm afraid to release him until I hear proof.'

'Why?'

'According to the FBI, there are some very dangerous

people now in the city who may want to shut him up. Do you know a Mr Gronke, and his pals Bono and Pirini? Ever hear of these guys?'

'No.'

'Neither had I, until this morning. It seems that these gentlemen have arrived in our fair city from New Orleans, and that they're close associates of Mr Barry Muldanno, or The Blade, as I believe he's known down there. Thank God organized crime never found Memphis. This scares me, Reggie, really scares me. These men do not play games.'

'Scares me too.'

'Has he been threatened?'

'Yes. It happened yesterday at the hospital. He told me about it, and he's been with me ever since.'

'So now you're a bodyguard.'

'No, I'm not. But I don't think the code gives you the authority to order custody of children who may be in danger.'

'Reggie, dear, I wrote the code. I can issue a custody order for any child alleged to be delinquent.'

True, he wrote the law. And the appellate courts had long since ceased second-guessing Harry Roosevelt.

'And according to Foltrigg and Fink, what are Mark's sins?'

Harry snatched two tissues from a drawer and blew his nose. He smiled at her again. 'He can't keep quiet, Reggie. If he knows something, he must tell them. You know that.'

'You're assuming he knows something.'

'I'm not assuming anything. The petition makes certain allegations, and these allegations are based partly on fact and partly on assumption. Same as all petitions, I guess. Wouldn't you say? We never know the truth until we have the hearing.'

'How much of Slick Moeller's crap do you believe?'

'I believe nothing, Reggie, until it is told to me, under oath, in my courtroom, and then I believe about ten percent of it.'

There was a long pause as the judge debated whether to ask the question. 'So, Reggie, what does the kid know?'

'You know it's privileged, Harry.'

He smiled. 'So, he knows more than he should.'

'You could say that.'

'If it's crucial to the investigation, Reggie, then he must tell.'

'What if he refuses?'

'I don't know. We'll deal with that when it happens. How smart is this kid?'

'Very. Broken home, no father, working mother, grew up on the streets. The usual. I talked to his fifth-grade teacher yesterday, and he makes all A's except for math. He's very bright, besides being street smart.'

'No prior trouble.'

'None. He's a great kid, Harry. Remarkable, really.'

'Most of your clients are remarkable, Reggie.'

'This one is special. He's here through no fault of his own.'

'I hope he'll be fully advised by his lawyer. The hearing could get rough.'

'Most of my clients are fully advised.'

'They certainly are.'

There was a brief knock at the door and Marcia appeared. 'Your client is here, Reggie. Witness Room C.'

'Thanks.' She stood and walked to the door. 'I'll see you in a few minutes, Harry.'

'Yes. Listen to me. I'm tough on kids who don't obey me.'

'I know.'

He sat in a chair leaning against the wall, with his arms folded across his chest and a frustrated look on his face. He'd been treated like a convict for three hours now, and he was getting used to it. He felt safe. He hadn't been beaten by the cops or by his fellow inmates.

The room was tiny with no windows and bad lighting. Reggie entered and moved a folding chair near him. She'd been in this room under these circumstances many times. He smiled at her, obviously relieved.

'So how's jail?' she asked.

'They haven't fed me yet. Can we sue them?'

'Maybe. How's Doreen, the lady with the keys?'

'A real snot. How do you know her?'

'I've been there many times, Mark. It's my job. Her husband is serving thirty years in prison for bank robbery.'

'Good. I'll ask her about him if I see her again. Am I going back there, Reggie? I'd like to know what's going on, you know.'

'Well, it's very simple. We'll have a hearing before Judge Harry Roosevelt in a few moments, in his courtroom, that may last a couple of hours. The US Attorney and the FBI are claiming you possess important information, and I think we can expect them to ask the judge to make you talk.'

'Can the judge make me talk?'

Reggie was speaking very slowly and carefully. He was an eleven-year-old child, a smart one with plenty of street sense, but she'd seen many like him and knew that, at this moment, he was nothing but a scared little boy. He might hear her words, and he might not. Or, he might hear what he wanted to hear, so she had to be careful.

'No one can make you talk.'

'Good.'

'But the judge can put you back in the same little room if you don't talk.'

'Back in jail!'

'That's right.'

'I don't understand. I haven't done a damned thing wrong, and I'm in jail. I just don't understand this.'

'It's very simple. If, and I emphasize the word *if*, Judge Roosevelt instructs you to answer certain questions, and *if* you refuse, then he can hold you in contempt of court for not answering, for disobeying him. Now, I've never known an eleven-year-old kid to be held in contempt, but if you were an adult, and you refused to answer the judge's questions, then you'd go to jail for contempt.'

'But I'm a kid.'

'Yes, but I don't think he'll allow you to go free if you refuse to answer the questions. You see, Mark, the law is very clear in this area. A person who has knowledge of information crucial to a criminal investigation cannot withhold this information because he feels threatened. In other words, you can't keep quiet because you're afraid of what might happen to you or your family.'

'That's a stupid law.'

'I don't really agree with it either, but that's not important. It is the law, and there are no exceptions, not even for kids.'

'So I get thrown in jail for contempt?'

'It's very possible.'

'Can we sue the judge, or do something else to get me out?'

'No. You can't sue the judge. And Judge Roosevelt is a very good and fair man.'

'I can't wait to meet him.'

'It won't be long now.'

Mark thought about all this. His chair rocked methodically against the wall. 'How long would I be in jail?'

'Assuming, of course, you're sent there, probably until you decide to comply with the judge's orders. Until you talk.'

'Okay. What if I decide not to talk. How long will I stay in jail? A month? A year? Ten years?'

'I can't answer that, Mark. No one knows.'

'The judge doesn't know?'

'No. If he sends you to jail for contempt, I doubt if he has any idea how long he'll make you stay.'

Another long pause. He'd spent three hours in Doreen's little room, and it wasn't such a bad place. He'd seen movies about prison in which gangs fought and rampaged and homemade weapons were used to kill snitches. Guards tortured inmates. Inmates attacked each other. Hollywood at its finest. But this place wasn't so bad.

And look at the alternative. With no place to call home, the Sway family now lived in Room 943 of St Peter's Charity Hospital. But the thought of Ricky and his mother all alone and struggling without him was unbearable. 'Have you talked to my mother?' he asked.

'No, not yet. I will after the hearing.'

'I'm worried about Ricky.'

'Do you want your mother present in the courtroom when we have this hearing? She needs to be here.'

'No. She's got enough stuff on her mind. You and I can handle this mess.'

She touched his knee, and wanted to cry. Someone knocked on the door, and she said loudly, 'Just a minute.'

'The judge is ready,' came the reply.

Mark breathed deeply and stared at her hand on his knee. 'Can I just take the Fifth Amendment?'

'No. It won't work, Mark. I've already thought about it. The questions will not be asked to incriminate you. They will be asked for the purpose of gathering information you may have.'

'I don't understand.'

'I don't blame you. Listen to me carefully, Mark. I'll try to explain it. They want to know what Jerome Clifford told you before he died. They will ask you some very specific questions about the events immediately before the suicide. They will ask you what, if anything, Clifford told you about Senator Boyette. Nothing you tell them with your answers will in any way incriminate you in the murder of Senator Boyette. Understand? You had nothing to do with it. And, you had nothing to do with the suicide of Jerome Clifford. You broke no laws, okay? You're not a suspect in any crime or wrongdoing. Your answers cannot incriminate you. So, you cannot hide under the protection of the Fifth Amendment.' She paused and watched him closely. 'Understand?'

'No. If I didn't do anything wrong, why was I picked up by the cops and taken to jail? Why am I sitting here waiting for a hearing?'

'You're here because they think you know something valuable, and because, as I stated, every person has a duty to assist law enforcement officials in the course of their investigation.'

'I still say it's a stupid law.'

'Maybe so. But we can't change it today.'

He rocked forward and sat the chair on all fours. 'I need

265

to know something, Reggie. Why can't I just tell them I know nothing? Why can't I say that me and old Romey talked about suicide and going to heaven and hell, you know, stuff like that.'

'Tell lies?'

'Yeah. It'll work, you know. Nobody knows the truth but Romey, me, and you. Right? And Romey, bless his heart, ain't talking.'

'You can't lie in court, Mark.' She said this with all the sincerity she could muster. Hours of sleep had been lost trying to formulate the answer to this inevitable question. She wanted so badly to say 'Yes! That's it! Lie, Mark, lie!'

Her stomach ached and her hands almost shook, but she held firm. 'I cannot allow you to lie to the court. You'll be under oath, so you must tell the truth.'

'Then it was a mistake to hire you, wasn't it?'

'I don't think so.'

'Sure it was. You're making me tell the truth, and in this case the truth might get me killed. If you weren't around, I'd march in there and lie my little butt off and me and Mom and Ricky would all be safe.'

'You can fire me if you like. The court will appoint another lawyer.'

He stood and walked to the darkest corner of the room, and began crying. She watched his head sink and his shoulders sag. He covered his eyes with the back of his right hand, and sobbed loudly.

Though she'd seen it many times, the sight of a child scared and suffering was unbearable. She couldn't keep from crying too.

TWENTY-FOUR

Two deputies escorted him into the courtroom from a side door, away from the main hallway where the curious were known to lurk, but Slick Moeller anticipated this little maneuver and watched it all from behind a newspaper just a few feet away.

Reggie followed her client and the deputies. Clint waited outside. It was almost a quarter after noon, and the jungle of Juvenile Court had quieted a bit for lunch.

The courtroom was of a shape and design Mark had never seen on television. It was so small! And empty. There were no benches or seats for spectators. The judge sat behind an elevated structure between two flags with the wall just behind him. Two tables were in the center of the room, facing the judge, and one was already occupied with men in dark suits. To the judge's right was a tiny table where an older woman was flipping through a stack of papers, very bored with it all, it seemed, until he entered the room. A gorgeous young lady sat ready with a stenographic machine directly in front of the judge's bench. She wore a short skirt and her legs were attracting a lot of attention. She couldn't be older than sixteen, he thought as he followed Reggie to their table. A bailiff with a gun on his hip was the final actor in the play.

Mark took his seat, very much aware that everyone was staring at him. His two deputies left the room, and when the door closed behind them the judge picked up the file again and flipped through it. They had been waiting on the

267

juvenile and his lawyer, and now it was time for everyone to wait for the judge again. Rules of courtroom etiquette must be followed.

Reggie pulled a single legal pad from her briefcase and began writing notes. She held a tissue in one hand, and dabbed her eyes with it. Mark stared at the table, eyes still wet but determined to suck it up and be tough through this ordeal. People were watching.

Fink and Ord stared at the court reporter's legs. The skirt was halfway between knee and hip. It was tight and seemed to slide upward just a fraction of an inch every minute or so. The tripod holding her recording machine sat firmly between her knees. In the coziness of Harry's courtroom, she was fewer than ten feet away, and the last thing they needed was a distraction. But they kept staring. There! It slipped upward another quarter of an inch.

Baxter L. McLemore, a young attorney fresh from law school, sat nervously at the table with Mr Fink and Mr Ord. He was a lowly assistant with the county Attorney General's office, and it had fallen to his lot to prosecute on this day in Juvenile Court. This was certainly not the glamorous end of prosecution, but sitting next to George Ord was quite a thrill. He knew nothing about the Sway case, and Mr Ord had explained in the hallway just minutes earlier that Mr Fink would handle the hearing. With the court's permission, of course. Baxter was expected to sit there and look nice, and keep his mouth shut.

'Is the door locked?' the judge finally asked in the general direction of the bailiff.

'Yes sir.'

'Very well. I have reviewed the petition, and I am ready to proceed. For the record, I note the child is present along with counsel, and that the child's mother, who is alleged to be his custodial parent, was served with a copy of the petition and summons this morning. However, the child's mother is not present in the courtoom, and this concerns me.' Harry paused for a moment and seemed to read from the file.

Fink decided this was the appropriate time to establish himself in this matter, and he stood slowly, buttoning his jacket, and addressed the court. 'Your Honor, if I may, for the record, I'm Thomas Fink, Assistant US Attorney for the Southern District of Louisiana.'

Harry's gaze slowly left the file and settled on Fink, who was standing stiff-backed, very formal, frowning intelligently as he spoke, still fiddling with the top button of his jacket.

Fink continued. 'I am one of the petitioners in this matter, and, if I may, I would like to address the issue of the presence of the child's mother.' Harry said nothing, just stared as if in disbelief. Reggie couldn't help but smile. She winked at Baxter McLemore.

Harry leaned forward, and rested his elbows as if intrigued by these great words of wisdom flowing from this gifted legal mind.

Fink had found an audience. 'Your Honor, it's our position, the position of the petitioners, that this matter is of a nature so urgent that this hearing must take place immediately. The child is represented by counsel, quite competent counsel I might add, and none of the child's legal rights will be prejudiced by the absence of his mother. From what we understand, the mother's presence is required by the bedside of her youngest son, and so, well, who knows when she might be able to attend a hearing. We just think it's important, Your Honor, to proceed immediately with this hearing.'

'You don't say?' Harry asked.

'Yes sir. This is our position.'

'Your position, Mr Fink,' Harry said very slowly and very loudly with a pointed finger, 'is in that chair right there. Please sit, and listen to me very carefully, because I will say this only once. And if I have to say it again, I will do so as they are putting the handcuffs on you and taking you away for a night in our splendid jail.'

Fink fell into his chair, mouth open, gaping in disbelief.

Harry scowled over his reading glasses and looked straight down at Thomas Fink. 'Listen to me, Mr Fink.

This is not some fancy courtroom in New Orleans, and I am not one of your federal judges. This is my little private courtroom, and I make the rules, Mr Fink. Rule number one is that you speak only in my courtroom when you are first spoken to by me. Rule number two is that you do not grace His Honor with unsolicited speeches, comments, or remarks. Rule number three is that His Honor does not like to hear the voices of lawyers. His Honor has been hearing these voices for twenty years, and His Honor knows that lawyers love to hear themselves talk. Rule number four is that you do not stand in my courtroom. You sit at that table and say as little as possible. Do you understand these rules, Mr Fink?'

Fink stared blankly at Harry and tried to nod.

Harry wasn't finished. 'This is a tiny courtroom, Mr Fink, designed by myself a long time ago for private hearings. We can all see and hear each other just fine, so just keep your mouth shut and your butt in your seat, and we'll get along fine.'

Fink was still trying to nod. He gripped the arms of the chair, determined never to rise again. Behind him, McThune, the lawyer hater, barely suppressed a smile.

'Mr McLemore, I understand Mr Fink wants to handle this case for the prosecution. Is this agreeable?'

'Okay with me, Your Honor.'

'I'll allow it. But try and keep him in his seat.'

Mark was terrified. He had hoped for a kind, gentle old man with lots of love and sympathy. Not this. He glanced at Mr Fink, whose neck was crimson and whose breathing was loud and heavy, and he almost felt sorry for him.

'Ms Love,' the judge said, suddenly very warm and compassionate, 'I understand you may have an objection on behalf of the child.'

'Yes, Your Honor.' She leaned forward and spoke deliberately in the direction of the court reporter. 'We have several objections we'd like to make at this time, and I want them in the record.'

'Certainly,' Harry said, as if Reggie Love could have

anything she wanted. Fink sank lower and felt even dumber. So much for impressing the court with an initial burst of eloquence.

Reggie glanced at her notes. 'Your Honor, I request the transcript of these proceedings be typed and prepared as soon as possible to facilitate an emergency appeal if necessary.'

'So ordered.'

'I object to this hearing on several grounds. First, inadequate notice has been given to the child, his mother, and to his lawyer. About three hours have passed since the petition was served upon the child's mother, and though I have represented the child for three days now, and everyone involved has known this, I was not notified of this hearing until seventy-five minutes ago. This is unfair, absurd, and an abuse of discretion by the court.'

'When would you like to have the hearing, Ms Love?' Harry asked.

'Today's Thursday,' she said. 'What about Tuesday or Wednesday of next week?'

'That's fine. Say Tuesday at nine.' Harry looked at Fink, who still hadn't moved and was afraid to respond to this. 'Of course, Ms Love, the child will remain in custody until then.'

'The child does not belong in custody, Your Honor.'

'But I've signed a custody order, and I will not rescind it while we wait on a hearing. Our laws, Ms Love, provide for the immediate taking of alleged delinquents, and your client is being treated no differently from others. Plus, there are other considerations for Mark Sway, and I'm sure these will be discussed shortly.'

'Then I cannot agree on a continuance if my client will remain in custody.'

'Very well,' His Honor said properly. 'Let the record reflect a continuance was offered by the court and declined by the child.'

'And let the record also reflect the child declined a continuance because the child does not wish to remain in the Juvenile Detention Center any longer than he has to.'

271

'So noted,' Harry said with a slight grin. 'Please proceed, Ms Love.'

'We also object to this hearing because the child's mother is not present. Due to extreme circumstances, her presence is not possible at this time, and keep in mind, Your Honor, the poor woman was first notified barely three hours ago. The child here is eleven years old and deserves the assistance of his mother. As you know, Your Honor, our laws strongly favor the presence of the parents in these hearings, and to proceed without Mark's mother is unfair.'

'When can Ms Sway be available?'

'No one knows, Your Honor. She is literally confined to the hospital room with her son who's suffering from post-traumatic stress. Her doctor allows her out of the room only for minutes at a time. It could be weeks before she's available.'

'So you want to postpone this hearing indefinitely?'

'Yes sir.'

'All right. You've got it. Of course, the child will remain in custody pending the hearing.'

'The child does not belong in custody. The child will make himself available any time the court wants. There's nothing to be gained by keeping the child locked up until a hearing.'

'There are complicating factors in this case, Ms Love, and I'm not inclined to release this child before we have this hearing and it's determined how much he knows. It's that simple. I'm afraid to release him at this time. If I did so, and if something happened to him, I'd carry the guilt to my grave. Do you understand this, Ms Love?'

She understood, though she wouldn't admit it. 'I'm afraid you're making this decision based on facts not in evidence.'

'Maybe so. But I have wide discretion in these matters, and until I hear the proof I'm not inclined to release him.'

'That'll look good on appeal,' she snapped, and Harry didn't like it.

272

'Let the record reflect a continuance was offered to the child until his mother could be present, and the continuance was declined by the child.'

To which Reggie quickly responded, 'And also let the record reflect the child declined the continuance because the child does not wish to remain in the Juvenile Detention Center any longer than he has to.'

'So noted, Ms Love. Please continue.'

'The child moves this court to dismiss the petition filed against him on the grounds that the allegations are without merit and the petition has been filed in an effort to explore things the child *might* know. The petitioners, Fink and Foltrigg, are using this hearing as a fishing expedition for their desperate criminal investigation. Their petition is a hopeless mishmash of maybes and what ifs, and filed under oath without the slightest hint of the real truth. They're desperate, Your Honor, and they're here shooting in the dark hoping they hit something. The petition should be dismissed, and we should all go home.'

Harry glared down at Fink, and said, 'I'm inclined to agree with her, Mr Fink. What about it?'

Fink had settled into his chair and watched with comfort as Reggie's first two objections had been shot down by His Honor. His breathing almost returned to normal and his face had gone from crimson to pink, when suddenly the judge was agreeing with her and staring at him.

Fink bolted to the edge of his chair, almost stood but caught himself, and started stuttering. 'Well, uh, Your Honor, we, uh, can prove our allegations if given the chance. We, uh, believe what we've said in the petition –'

'I certainly hope so,' Harry sneered.

'Yes sir, and we know that this child is impeding an investigation. Yes sir, we are confident we can prove what we've alleged.'

'And if you can't?'

'Well, I, uh, we, feel sure that –'

'You realize, Mr Fink, that if I hear the proof in this case and find you're playing games, I can hold you in contempt.

273

And, knowing Ms Love the way I do, I'm sure there will be retribution from the child.'

'We intend to file suit first thing in the morning, Your Honor,' Reggie added helpfully. 'Against both Mr Fink and Roy Foltrigg. They're abusing this court and the juvenile laws of the state of Tennessee. My staff is working on the lawsuit right now.'

Her staff was sitting outside in the hallway eating a Snickers bar and sipping a diet cola. But the threat sounded ominous in the courtroom.

Fink glanced at George Ord, his co-counsel, who was sitting next to him making a list of things to do that afternoon, and nothing on the list had anything to do with Mark Sway or Roy Foltrigg. Ord supervised twenty-eight lawyers working thousands of cases, and he just didn't care about Barry Muldanno and the body of Boyd Boyette. It wasn't in his jurisdiction. Ord was a busy man, too busy to waste valuable time playing gofer for Roy Foltrigg.

But Fink was no featherweight. He'd seen his share of nasty trials and hostile judges and sceptical juries. He was rallying quite nicely. 'Your Honor, the petition is much like an indictment. Its truth cannot be ascertained without a hearing, and if we can get on with it we can prove our allegations.'

Harry turned to Reggie. 'I'll take this motion to dismiss under advisement, and I'll hear the petitioner's proof. If it falls short, then I'll grant the motion and we'll go from there.'

Reggie shrugged as if she expected this.

'Anything else, Ms Love?'

'Not at this time.'

'Call your first witness, Mr Fink,' Harry said. 'And make it brief. Get right to the point. If you waste time, I'll jump in with both feet and speed things along.'

'Yes sir. Sergeant Milo Hardy of the Memphis Police is our first witness.'

Mark had not moved during these preliminary skirmishes. He wasn't sure if Reggie had won them all, or lost them all, and for some reason he didn't care. There was something unfair about a system in which a little kid was brought into a courtroom and surrounded by lawyers arguing and sniping at each other under the scornful eye of a judge, the referee, and somehow in the midst of this barrage of laws and code sections and motions and legal talk the kid was supposed to know what was happening to him. It was hopelessly unfair.

And so he just sat and stared at the floor near the court reporter. His eyes were still wet and he couldn't make them stay dry.

The courtroom was silent as Sergeant Hardy was fetched. His Honor relaxed in his chair and removed his reading glasses. 'I want this on the record,' he said. He glared at Fink again. 'This is a private and confidential matter. This hearing is closed for a reason. I defy anyone to repeat any word uttered in this room today, or to discuss any aspect of this proceeding. Now, Mr Fink, I realize you must report to the US Attorney in New Orleans, and I realize Mr Foltrigg is a petitioner and has a right to know what happens here. And when you talk to him, please explain that I am very upset by his absence. He signed the petition, and he should be here. You may explain these proceedings to him, and only to him. No one else. And you are to tell him to keep his big mouth shut, do you understand, Mr Fink?'

'Yes, Your Honor.'

'Will you explain to Mr Foltrigg that if I get wind of any breach in the confidentiality of these proceedings that I will issue a contempt order and attempt to have him jailed?'

'Yes, Your Honor.'

He was suddenly staring at McThune and K. O. Lewis. They were seated immediately behind Fink and Ord.

'Mr McThune and Mr Lewis, you may now leave the courtroom,' Harry said abruptly. They grabbed the armrests as their feet hit the floor. Fink turned and stared at them, then looked at the judge.

'Uh, Your Honor, would it be possible for these gentlemen to remain in the –'

'I told them to leave, Mr Fink,' Harry said loudly. 'If they're gonna be witnesses, we'll call them later. If they're not witnesses, they have no business here and they can wait in the hall with the rest of the herd. Now, move along, gentlemen.'

McThune was practically jogging for the door, without the slightest hint of wounded pride, but K. O. Lewis was pissed. He buttoned his jacket and stared at His Honor, but only for a second. No one had ever won a staring contest with Harry Roosevelt, and K. O. Lewis was not about to try. He strutted for the door, which was already open as McThune dashed through it.

Seconds later, Sergeant Hardy entered and sat in the witness chair. He was in full uniform. He shifted his wide ass in the padded seat, and waited. Fink was frozen, afraid to begin without being told to do so.

Judge Roosevelt rolled his chair to the end of the bench and peered down at Hardy. Something had caught his attention, and Hardy sat like a fat toad on a stool until he realized His Honor was just inches away.

'Why are you wearing the gun?' Harry asked.

Hardy looked up, startled, then jerked his head to his right hip as if the gun was a complete surprise to him also. He stared at it as if the damned thing had somehow stuck itself to his body.

'Well, I –'

'Are you on duty or off, Sergeant Hardy?'

'Well, off.'

'Then why are you wearing a uniform, and why in the world are you wearing a gun in my courtroom?'

Mark smiled for the first time in hours.

The bailiff had caught on and was rapidly approaching the witness stand as Hardy jerked at his belt and removed the holster. The bailiff carried it away as if it were a murder weapon.

'Have you ever testified in court?' Harry asked.

Hardy smiled like a child and said, 'Yes sir, many times.'

'You have?'

'Yes sir. Many times.'

'And how many times have you testified while wearing your gun?'

'Sorry, Your Honor.'

Harry relaxed, looked at Fink, and waved at Hardy as if it was now permissible to get on with it. Fink had spent many hours in courtrooms during the past twenty years, and took great pride in his trial skills. His record was impressive. He was glib and smooth, quick on his feet.

But he was slow on his ass, and this sitting while interrogating a witness was such a radical way of finding truth. He almost stood again, caught himself again, and grabbed his legal pad. His frustration was apparent.

'Would you state your name for the record?' he asked in a short, rapid burst.

'Sergeant Milo Hardy, Memphis Police Department.'

'And what is your address?'

Harry held up a hand to cut off Hardy. 'Mr Fink, why do you need to know where this man lives?'

Fink stared in disbelief. 'I guess, Your Honor, it's just a routine question?'

'Do you know how much I hate routine questions, Mr Fink?'

'I'm beginning to understand.'

'Routine questions lead us nowhere, Mr Fink. Routine questions waste hours and hours of valuable time. I do not want to hear another routine question. Please.'

'Yes, Your Honor. I'll try.'

'I know it's hard.'

Fink looked at Hardy and tried desperately to think of a brilliantly original question. 'Last Monday, Sergeant, were you dispatched to the scene of a shooting?'

Harry held up his hands again, and Fink slumped in his seat. 'Mr Fink, I don't know how you folks do things in New Orleans, but here in Memphis we make our witnesses swear to tell the truth before they start testifying. It's called, "Placing them under oath." Does that sound familiar?'

Fink rubbed his temples and said, 'Yes sir. Could the witness please be sworn?'

277

The elderly woman at the desk suddenly came to life. She sprang to her feet and yelled at Hardy, who was less than fifteen feet away. 'Raise your right hand!'

Hardy did this, and was sworn to tell the truth. She returned to her seat, and to her nap.

'Now, Mr Fink, you may proceed,' Harry said with a nasty little smile, very pleased that he'd caught Fink with his pants down. He relaxed in his massive seat, and listened intently to the rapid question and answer routine that followed.

Hardy spoke in a chatty voice, eager to help, full of little details. He described the scene of the suicide, the position of the body, the condition of the car. There were photographs, if His Honor would like to see them. His Honor declined. They were completely irrelevant. Hardy produced a typed transcript of the 911 call made by Mark, and offered to play the recording if His Honor would like to hear it. No, His Honor said.

Then Hardy explained with great joy the capture of young Mark in the woods near the scene, and of their ensuing conversations in his car, at the Sway trailer, en route to the hospital, and over dinner in the cafeteria. He described his gut feelings that young Mark was not telling the complete truth. The kid's story was flimsy, and through skillful interrogation with just the right touch of subtlety, he, Hardy, was able to poke all sorts of holes in it.

The lies were pathetic. The kid said he and his brother stumbled upon the car and the dead body; that they did not hear any gunshots; that they were just a couple of kids playing in the woods, minding their own business, and somehow they found this body. Of course, none of Mark's story was true, and Hardy was quick to catch on.

With great detail, Hardy described the condition of Mark's face, the swollen eye and puffy lip, the blood around the mouth. Kid said he'd been in a fight at school. Another sad little lie.

After thirty minutes, Harry grew restless and Fink took the hint. Reggie had no cross-examination, and when

278

Hardy stepped down and left the room there was no doubt that Mark Sway was a liar who'd tried to deceive the cops. Things would get worse.

When His Honor had asked Reggie if she had any questions for Sergeant Hardy, she simply said, 'I've had no time to prepare for this witness.'

McThune was called as the next witness. He gave his oath to tell the truth and sat in the witness chair. Reggie slowly reached into her briefcase and withdrew a cassette tape. She held it casually in her hand, and when McThune glanced at her she tapped it softly on her legal pad. He closed his eyes.

She carefully placed the tape on the pad, and began tracing its edges with her pen.

Fink was quick, to the point, and by now fairly adept at avoiding even vaguely routine questions. It was a new experience for him, this efficient use of words, and the more he did it the more he liked it.

McThune was as dry as cornmeal. He explained the fingerprints they found all over the car, and on the gun and the bottle, and on the rear bumper. He speculated about the kids and the garden hose, and showed Harry the Virginia Slims cigarette butts found under the tree. He also showed Harry the suicide note left behind by Clifford, and again gave his thoughts about the additional words added by a different pen. He showed Harry the Bic pen found in the car, and said there was no doubt that Mr Clifford had used this pen to scrawl these words. He talked about the speck of blood found on Clifford's hand. It wasn't Clifford's blood, but was of the same type as Mark Sway's, who just happened to have a busted lip and a couple of wounds from the affair.

'You think Mr Clifford struck the child at some point during all this?' Harry asked.

'I think so, Your Honor.'

McThune's thoughts and opinions and speculations were objectionable, but Reggie kept quiet. She'd been through many of these hearings with Harry, and she knew he would hear it all and decide what to believe. Objecting would do no good.

Harry asked how the FBI obtained the fingerprint from the child to match those found in the car. McThune took a deep breath, and told about the Sprite can at the hospital, but was quick to point out that they were not investigating the child as a suspect when this happened, just as a witness, and so therefore they felt it was okay to lift the print. Harry didn't like this at all, but said nothing. McThune emphasized that if the child had been an actual suspect, they would never have dreamed of stealing a print. Never.

'Of course you wouldn't,' Harry said with enough sarcasm to make McThune blush.

Fink talked him through the events of Tuesday, the day after the suicide, when young Mark hired a lawyer. They tried desperately to talk with him, then to his lawyer, and things just deteriorated.

McThune behaved himself and stuck to the facts. He left the room in a quick dash for the door, and he left behind the undeniable fact that young Mark was quite a liar.

From time to time, Harry watched Mark during the testimony of Hardy and McThune. The kid was impassive, hard to read, preoccupied with an invisible spot somewhere on the floor. He sat low in his seat and ignored Reggie for the most part. His eyes were wet, but he was not crying. He looked tired and sad, and occasionally glanced at the witness when his lies were emphasized.

Harry had watched Reggie many times under these circumstances, and she usually sat very close to her young clients and whispered to them as the hearings progressed. She would pat them, squeeze their arms, give reassurances, lecture them if necessary. Normally, she was in constant motion, protecting her clients from the harsh reality of a legal system run by adults. But not today. She glanced at her client occasionally as if waiting for a signal, but he ignored her.

'Call your next witness,' Harry said to Fink, who was resting on his elbows, trying not to stand. He looked at Ord for help, then at His Honor.

'Well, Your Honor, this may sound a bit strange, but I'd like to testify next.'

Harry ripped off his reading glasses and glared at Fink. 'You're confused, Mr Fink. You're the lawyer, not a witness.'

'I know that, sir, but I'm also the petitioner, and, I know this may be a bit out of order, but I think my testimony could be important.'

'Thomas Fink, petitioner, lawyer, witness. You wanna play bailiff, Mr Fink? Maybe take down a bit of stenography? Perhaps wear my robe for a while? This is not a courtroom, Mr Fink, it's a theater. Why don't you just choose any role you like?'

Fink stared blankly at the bench without making eye contact with His Honor. 'I can explain, sir,' he said meekly.

'You don't have to explain, Mr Fink. I'm not blind. You boys have rushed in here half-ass prepared. Mr Foltrigg should be here, but he's not, and now you need him. You figured you could throw together a petition, bring in some FBI brass, hook in Mr Ord here, and I'd be so impressed I'd just roll over and do anything you asked. Can I tell you something, Mr Fink?'

Fink nodded.

'I'm not impressed. I've seen better work at high school mock trial competitions. Half the first-year law students at Memphis State could kick your butt, and the other half could kick Mr Foltrigg's.'

Fink was not agreeing, but he kept nodding for some reason. Ord slid his chair a few inches away from Fink's.

'What about it, Ms Love?' Harry asked.

'Your Honor, our rules of procedure and ethics are quite clear. An attorney trying a case cannot participate in the same trial as a witness. It's simple.' She sounded bored and frustrated, as if everyone should know this.

'Mr Fink?'

Fink was regaining himself. 'Your Honor, I would like to tell the court, under oath, certain facts regarding Mr Clifford's actions prior to the suicide. I apologize for this request, but under the circumstances it cannot be helped.'

There was a knock on the door, and the bailiff opened it

slightly. Marcia entered carrying a plate covered with a thick roast beef sandwich and a tall plastic glass of ice tea. She sat it before His Honor, who thanked her, and she was gone.

It was almost one o'clock, and suddenly everyone was starving. The roast beef and horseradish and pickles, and the side order of onion rings, emitted an appetizing aroma that wafted around the room. All eyes were on the kaiser roll, and as Harry picked it up to take a huge bite, he saw young Mark Sway watching his every move. He stopped the sandwich in mid-air, and noticed that Fink and Ord, and Reggie, and even the bailiff were staring in helpless anticipation.

Harry placed the sandwich on to the plate, and slid it to one side. 'Mr Fink,' he said, jabbing a finger in Fink's direction, 'stay where you are. Do you swear to tell the truth?'

'I do.'

'You'd better. You're now under oath. You have five minutes to tell me what's bugging you.'

'Yes, thank you, Your Honor.'

'You're so welcome.'

'You see, Jerome Clifford and I were in law school together, and we knew each other for many years. We had many cases together, always on opposite sides, of course.'

'Of course.'

'After Barry Muldanno was indicted, the pressure began to mount and Jerome began acting strange. Looking back, I think he was slowly cracking up, but at the time I didn't think much about it. I mean, you see, Jerome was always a strange one.'

'I see.'

'I was working on the case every day, many hours a day, and I talked to Jerome Clifford several times a week. We had preliminary motions and such, so I saw him in court occasionally. He looked awful. He gained a lot of weight, and was drinking too much. He was always late for meetings. Rarely bathed. Often, he failed to return phone

282

calls, which was unusual for Jerome. About a week before he died he called me at home one night, really drunk, and rambled on for almost an hour. He was crazy. Then, he called me at the òffice first thing the next morning and apologized. But he wouldn't get off the phone. He kept fishing around as if he was afraid he'd said too much the night before. At least twice he mentioned the Boyette body, and I became convinced Jerome knew where it was.'

Fink paused to allow this to sink in, but Harry was waiting impatiently.

'Well, he called me several times after that, kept talking about the body. I led him on. I implied that he'd said too much when he was drunk. I told him that we were considering an indictment against him for obstruction of justice.'

'Seems to be one of your favorites,' Harry said dryly.

'Anyway, Jerome was drinking heavily and acting bizarre. I confessed to him that the FBI was trailing him around the clock, which was not altogether true, but he seemed to believe it. He grew very paranoid, and called me several times a day. He'd get drunk and call me late at night. He wanted to talk about the body, but was afraid to tell everything. During our last phone conversation, I suggested that maybe we could cut a deal. If he'd tell us where the body was, then we'd help him bail out with no record, no conviction, nothing. He was terrified of his client, and he never once denied knowing where the body was.'

'Your Honor,' Reggie interrupted, 'this, of course, is pure hearsay and quite self-serving. There's no way to verify any of this.'

'You don't believe me?' Fink snapped at her.

'No, I don't.'

'I'm not sure I do either, Mr Fink,' Harry said. 'Nor am I sure why any of this has any relevance to this hearing.'

'My point, Your Honor, is that Jerome Clifford knew about the body and he was talking about it. Plus, he was cracking up.'

'I'll say he cracked up, Mr Fink. He put a gun in his mouth. Sounds crazy to me.'

Fink sort of hung in the air with his mouth open, uncertain if he should say anything else.

'Any more witnesses, Mr Fink?' Harry asked.

'No sir. We do, however, Your Honor, feel that, due to the unusual circumstances of this case, the child should take the stand and testify.'

Harry ripped off the reading glasses again, and leaned toward Fink. If he could have reached him, he might have gone for his neck.

'You what!'

'We, uh, feel that –'

'Mr Fink, have you studied the juvenile laws for this jurisdiction?'

'I have.'

'Great. Will you please tell us, sir, under which code section the petitioner has the right to force the child to testify?'

'I was merely stating our request.'

'That's great. Under which code section is the petitioner allowed to make such a request?'

Fink dropped his head a few inches and found something on his legal pad to examine.

'This is not a kangaroo court, Mr Fink. We do not create new rules as we go. The child cannot be forced to testify, same as any other criminal or Juvenile Court proceeding. Surely you understand this.'

Fink studied the legal pad with great intensity.

'Ten-minute recess!' His Honor barked. 'Everyone out of the courtroom, except Ms Love. Bailiff, take Mark to a witness room.' Harry was standing as he growled these instructions.

Fink, afraid to stand but none the less trying, hesitated for a split second too long, and this upset the judge. 'Out of here, Mr Fink,' he said rudely, pointing to the door.

Fink and Ord stumbled over each other as they clawed for the door. The court reporter and clerk followed them.

The bailiff escorted Mark away, and when he closed the door Harry unzipped his robe and threw it on a table. He took his lunch and sat it on the table before Reggie.

'Shall we dine?' he said, tearing the sandwich in two and placing half of it on a napkin for her. He slid the onion rings next to her legal pad. She took one and nibbled around the edges.

'Are you going to allow the kid to testify?' he asked with a mouth full of roast beef.

'I don't know, Harry. What do you think?'

'I think Fink's a dumbass, that's what I think.'

Reggie took a small bite of the sandwich and wiped her mouth.

'If you put him on,' Harry said, crunching, 'Fink'll ask him some very pointed questions about what happened in the car with Clifford.'

'I know. That's what worries me.'

'How will the kid answer the questions?'

'I honestly don't know. I've advised him fully. We've talked about it at length. And I have no idea what he'll do.'

Harry took a deep breath, and realized the ice tea was still on the bench. He took two paper cups from Fink's table, and poured them full of tea.

'It's obvious, Reggie, that he knows something. Why did he tell so many lies?'

'He's a kid, Harry. He was scared to death. He heard more than he should have. He saw Clifford blow his brains out. It scared him to death. Look at his poor little brother. It was a terrible thing to witness, and I think Mark initially thought he might get in trouble. So he lied.'

'I don't really blame him,' Harry said, taking an onion ring. Reggie bit into a pickle.

'What are you thinking?' she asked.

He wiped his mouth, and thought about this for a long time. This child was now his, one of Harry's Kids, and each decision from now on would be based on what was best for Mark Sway.

'If I can assume the child knows something very relevant

to the investigation in New Orleans, then several things might happen. First, if you put him on the stand and he gives the information Fink wants, then this matter is closed as far as my jurisdiction is concerned. The kid walks out of here, but he's in great danger. Second, if you put him on the stand, and he refuses to answer Fink's questions, then I will be forced to make him answer. If he refuses, he'll be in contempt. He cannot remain silent if he has crucial information. Either way, if this hearing is concluded here today without satisfactory answers by the child, I strongly suspect Mr Foltrigg will move quickly. He'll get a grand jury subpoena for Mark, and away you go to New Orleans. If he refuses to talk to the grand jury, he'll certainly be held in contempt by the federal judge, and I suspect he'll be incarcerated.'

Reggie nodded. She was in complete agreement. 'So what do we do, Harry?'

'If the kid goes to New Orleans, I lose control of him. I'd rather keep him here. If I were you, I'd put him on the stand and advise him not to answer the crucial questions. At least not for now. He can always do it later. He can do it tomorrow, or the next day. I'd advise him to withstand the pressure from the judge, and keep his mouth shut, at least for now. He'll go back to our Juvenile Detention Center, which is probably much safer than anything in New Orleans. By doing this, you protect the child from the New Orleans thugs, who scare even me, until the Feds can arrange something better. And you buy yourself some time to see what Mr Foltrigg will do in New Orleans.'

'You think he's in great danger?'

'Yes, and even if I didn't, I wouldn't take chances. If he spills his guts now, he could get hurt. I'm not inclined to release him today, under any circumstances.'

'What if Mark refuses to talk, and Foltrigg presents him with a grand jury subpoena?'

'I won't allow him to go.'

Reggie's appetite was gone. She sipped her tea from the paper cup and closed her eyes. 'This is so unfair to this boy, Harry. He deserves more from the system.'

'I agree. I'm open to suggestions.'

'What if I don't put him on the stand?'

'I'm not going to release him, Reggie. At least not today. Maybe tomorrow. Maybe the next day. This is happening awfully fast, and I suggest we take the safest route and see what happens in New Orleans.'

'You didn't answer my question. What if I don't put him on the stand?'

'Well, based on the proof I've heard, I'll have no choice but to find him to be a delinquent, and I'll send him back to Doreen. Of course, I could reverse myself tomorrow. Or the next day.'

'He's not a delinquent.'

'Maybe not. But if he knows something, and he refuses to tell, then he's obstructing justice.' There was a long pause. 'How much does he know, Reggie? If you'll tell me, I'll be in a better position to help him.'

'I can't tell you, Harry. It's privileged.'

'Of course it is,' he said with a smile. 'But it's rather obvious he knows plenty.'

'Yes, I guess it is.'

He leaned forward, and touched her arm. 'Listen to me, dear. Our little pal is in a world of trouble. So let's get him out of it. I say we take it one day at a time, keep him in a safe place where we call the shots, and in the meantime start talking to the Feds about their witness protection program. If that falls into place for the kid and his family, then he can tell these awful secrets and be protected.'

'I'll talk to him.'

TWENTY-FIVE

Under the stern supervision of the bailiff, a man named Grinder, they were reassembled and directed to their positions. Fink glanced about fearfully, uncertain whether to sit, stand, speak, or crawl under the table. Ord picked at the cuticle on a thumb. Baxter McLemore had moved his chair as far away from Fink as possible.

His Honor sipped the remains of the tea and waited until all was still. 'On the record,' he said in the general direction of the court reporter. 'Ms Love, I need to know if young Mark will testify.'

She was sitting a foot behind her client, and she looked at the side of his face. His eyes were still wet.

'Under the circumstances,' she said, 'he doesn't have much of a choice.'

'Is that a yes or a no?'

'I will allow him to testify,' she said, 'but I will not tolerate abusive questioning by Mr Fink.'

'Your Honor, please,' Fink said.

'Quiet, Mr Fink. Remember rule number one? Don't speak until spoken to.'

Fink glared at Reggie. 'A cheap shot,' he snarled.

'Knock it off, Mr Fink,' Harry said. All was quiet.

His Honor was suddenly all warmth and smiles. 'Mark, I want you to remain in your seat, next to your lawyer, while I ask you some questions.'

Fink winked at Ord. Finally, the kid would talk. This could be the moment.

'Raise your right hand, Mark,' His Honor said, and Mark slowly obeyed. The right hand, as well as the left, was trembling.

The elderly lady stood in front of Mark and properly swore him. He did not stand, but inched closer to Reggie.

'Now, Mark, I'm going to ask you some questions. If you don't understand anything I ask, please feel free to talk to your lawyer. Okay?'

'Yes sir.'

'I'll try to keep the questions clear and simple. If you need a break to step outside and talk to Reggie, Ms Love, just let me know. Okay?'

'Yes sir.'

Fink turned in his chair to face Mark and sat like a hungry puppy awaiting his Alpo. Ord finished his nails, and was ready with his pen and legal pad.

Harry reviewed his notes for a second, then smiled down at the witness. 'Now, Mark, I want you to explain to me exactly how you and your brother discovered Mr Clifford on Monday.'

Mark gripped the arms of his chair and cleared his throat. This was not what he expected. He'd never seen a movie in which the judge asked questions.

'We sneaked off into the woods behind the trailer park, to smoke a cigarette,' he began, and slowly led to the point where Romey stuck the water hose in the tail pipe the first time and got in the car.

'What'd you do then?' His Honor asked anxiously.

'I took it out,' he said, and told the story about his trips through the weeds to remove Romey's suicide device. Although he'd told this before, once or twice to his mother and Dr Greenway, and once or twice to Reggie, it had never seemed amusing to him. But as he told it now, the judge's eyes began to sparkle and his smile widened. He chuckled softly. The bailiff thought it was funny. The court reporter, always noncommittal, was enjoying it. Even the old woman at the clerk's desk was listening with her first smile of the proceedings.

But the humor turned sour as Mr Clifford grabbed him, slapped him around, and threw him in the car. Mark relived this with a straight face, staring at the brown pumps of the court reporter.

'So you were in the car with Mr Clifford before he died?' His Honor asked cautiously, very serious now.

'Yes sir.'

'And what did he do once he got you in the car?'

'He slapped me some more, yelled at me a few times, threatened me.' And Mark told all that he remembered about the gun, the whiskey bottle, the pills.

The small courtroom was deathly still, and the smiles were long gone. Mark's words were deliberate. His eyes avoided all others. He spoke as if in a trance.

'Did he fire the gun?' Judge Roosevelt asked.

'Yes sir,' he answered, and told them all about it.

When he finished this part of the story, he waited for the next question. Harry thought about it for a long minute.

'Where was Ricky?'

'Hiding in the bushes. I saw him sneak through the weeds, and I sort of figured he'd removed the water hose again. He did, I found out later. Mr Clifford kept saying he could feel the gas, and he asked me over and over if I could feel it. I said yes, twice I think, but I knew Ricky had come through.'

'And he didn't know about Ricky?' It was a throwaway question, irrelevant, but asked because Harry couldn't think of a better one at the moment.

'No sir.'

Another long pause.

'So you talked with Mr Clifford while you were in the car?'

Mark knew what was coming, as did everyone in the courtroom, so he jumped in quickly in an attempt to divert it.

'Yes sir. He was out of his mind, kept talking about floating off to see the Wizard of Oz, off to La La Land, then he would yell at me for crying, then he would apologize for hitting me.'

There was a pause as Harry waited to see if he was finished. 'Is that all he said?'

Mark glanced at Reggie, who was watching him carefully. Fink inched closer. The court reporter was frozen.

'What do you mean?' Mark asked, stalling.

'Did Mr Clifford say anything else?'

Mark thought about this for a second, and decided he hated Reggie. He could simply say 'No,' and the ballgame was over. No sir, Mr Clifford did not say anything else. He just rambled on like an idiot for about five minutes, then fell asleep, and I ran like hell. If he'd never met Reggie, and had not heard her lecture about being under oath and telling the truth, then he would simply say 'No sir.' And go home, or back to the hospital, or wherever.

Or would he? One day in the fourth grade the cops put on a show about police work, and one of them demonstrated a polygraph. He wired up Joey McDermant, the biggest liar in the class, and they watched as the needle went berserk every time Joey opened his mouth. 'We catch criminals lying every time,' the cop had boasted.

With cops and FBI agents swarming around him, could the polygraph be far away? He'd lied so much since Romey killed himself, and he was really tired of it.

'Mark, I asked you if Mr Clifford said anything else.'

'Like what?'

'Like, did he mention anything about Senator Boyd Boyette?'

'Who?'

Harry flashed a sweet little smile, then it was gone. 'Mark, did Mr Clifford mention anything about a case of his in New Orleans involving a Mr Barry Muldanno or the late Senator Boyd Boyette?'

A tiny spider was crawling next to the court reporter's brown pumps, and Mark watched it until it disappeared under the tripod. He thought about that damned polygraph again. Reggie said she would fight to keep it away from him, but what if the judge ordered it?

The long pause before his response said it all. Fink's

291

heart was laboring and his pulse had tripled. Aha! The little bastard *does* know!

'I don't think I want to answer that question,' he said, staring at the floor, waiting for the spider to reappear.

Fink looked hopefully at the judge.

'Mark, look at me,' Harry said like a gentle grandfather. 'I want you to answer the question. Did Mr Clifford mention Barry Muldanno or Boyd Boyette?'

'Can I take the Fifth Amendment?'

'No.'

'Why not? It applies to kids, doesn't it?'

'Yes, but not in this situation. You're not implicated in the death of Senator Boyette. You're not implicated in any crime.'

'Then why did you put me in jail?'

'I'm going to send you back there if you don't answer my questions.'

'I take the Fifth Amendment anyway.'

They were glaring at each other, witness and judge, and the witness blinked first. His eyes watered and he sniffed twice. He bit his lip, fighting hard not to cry. He clenched the armrests and squeezed until his knuckles were white. Tears dropped on to his cheeks, but he kept staring up into the dark eyes of the Honorable Harry Roosevelt.

The tears of an innocent little boy. Harry turned to his side and pulled a tissue from a drawer under the bench. His eyes were wet too.

'Would you like to talk to your attorney, in private?' he asked.

'We've already talked,' he said in a fading voice. He wiped his cheeks with a sleeve.

Fink was near cardiac arrest. He had so much to say, so many questions for this brat, so many suggestions for the court on how to handle this matter. The kid knew, dammit! Let's make him talk!

'Mark, I don't like to do this, but you must answer my questions. If you refuse, then you're in contempt of court. Do you understand this?'

292

'Yes sir. Reggie's explained it to me.'

'And did she explain that if you're in contempt, then I can send you back to the Juvenile Detention Center?'

'Yes sir. You can call it a jail if you like, it doesn't bother me.'

'Thank you. Do you want to go back to jail?'

'Not really, but I have no place else to go.' His voice was stronger and the tears had stopped. The thought of jail was not as frightening now that he'd seen the inside of it. He could tough it out for a few days. In fact, he figured he could take the heat longer than the judge. He was certain his name would appear in the paper again in the very near future. And the reporters would undoubtedly learn he was locked up by Harry Roosevelt for not talking. And surely the judge would catch hell for locking up a little kid who'd done nothing wrong.

Reggie'd told him he could change his mind anytime he got tired of jail.

'Did Mr Clifford mention the name Barry Muldanno to you?'

'Take the Fifth.'

'Did Mr Clifford mention the name Boyd Boyette to you?'

'Take the Fifth.'

'Did Mr Clifford say anything about the murder of Boyd Boyette?'

'Take the Fifth.'

'Did Mr Clifford say anything about the present location of the body of Boyd Boyette?'

'Take the Fifth.'

Harry removed his reading glasses for the tenth time, and rubbed his face. 'You can't take the Fifth, Mark.'

'I just did.'

'I'm ordering you to answer these questions.'

'Yes sir. I'm sorry.'

Harry took a pen and began writing.

'Your Honor,' Mark said. 'I respect you and what you're trying to do. But I cannot answer these questions because I'm afraid of what might happen to me or my family.'

'I understand, Mark, but the law does not allow private citizens to withhold information that might be crucial to a

293

criminal investigation. I'm following the law, not picking on you. I'm holding you in contempt. I'm not angry with you, but you leave me no choice. I'm ordering you to return to the Juvenile Detention Center where you will remain as long as you're in contempt.'

'How long will that be?'

'It's up to you, Mark.'

'What if I decide never to answer the questions?'

'I don't know. Right now we'll take it one day at a time.' Harry flipped through his calendar, found a spot, and made a note. 'We'll meet again at noon tomorrow, if that's agreeable with everyone.'

Fink was crushed. He stood, and was about to speak when Ord grabbed his arm and pulled him down. 'Your Honor, I don't think I can be here tomorrow,' he said. 'As you know, my office is in New Orleans, and –'

'Oh, you'll be here tomorrow, Mr Fink. You and Mr Foltrigg together. You chose to file your petition here in Memphis, in my court, and now I have jurisdiction over you. As soon as you leave here, I suggest you call Mr Foltrigg and tell him to be here at noon tomorrow. I want both petitioners, Fink and Foltrigg, right here at twelve o'clock sharp tomorrow. And if you're not here, I'll hold you in contempt, and tomorrow it'll be you and your boss being hauled off to jail.'

Fink's mouth was open but nothing came out. Ord spoke for the first time. 'Your Honor, I believe Mr Foltrigg has a hearing in federal court in the morning. Mr Muldanno has a new lawyer who's asking for a continuance, and the judge down there has set the hearing for tomorrow morning.'

'Is that true, Mr Fink?'

'Yes sir.'

'Then tell Mr Foltrigg to fax me a copy of the judge's order setting the hearing for tomorrow. I'll excuse him. But as long as Mark is in jail for contempt, I intend to bring him back here every other day to see if he wants to talk. I'll expect both petitioners to be here.'

'That's quite a hardship on us, Your Honor.'

'Not as hard as it's gonna be if you don't show up. You picked this forum, Mr Fink. Now you gotta live with it.'

Fink had flown to Memphis six hours earlier without a toothbrush or change of underwear. Now it appeared as though he might be forced to lease an apartment with bedrooms for himself and Foltrigg.

The bailiff had eased his way to the wall behind Reggie and Mark, and was watching His Honor and waiting for a signal.

'Mark, I'm going to excuse you now,' Harry said, scribbling on a form, 'and I'll see you again tomorrow. If you have any problems in the detention center, you inform me tomorrow and I'll take care of it. Okay?'

Mark nodded. Reggie squeezed his arm, and said, 'I'll talk to your mother, and I'll come see you in the morning.'

'Tell Mom I'm fine,' he whispered in her ear. 'I'll try and call her tonight.' He stood and left with the bailiff.

'Send in those FBI people,' Harry said to the bailiff as he was closing the door.

'Are we excused, Your Honor?' Fink asked. There was sweat on his forehead. He was anxious to leave this room and call Foltrigg with the horrible news.

'What's the hurry, Mr Fink?'

'Uh, no hurry, Your Honor.'

'Then relax. I want to talk, off the record, with you boys and the FBI people. Just take a minute.' Harry excused the court reporter and the old woman. McThune and Lewis entered and took their seats behind the lawyers.

Harry unzipped his robe, but did not remove it. He wiped his face with a tissue and sipped the last of the tea. They watched and waited.

'I do not intend to keep this child in jail,' he said, looking at Reggie. 'Maybe for a few days, but not long. It's apparent to me that he has some critical information, and he's duty bound to divulge it.'

Fink started nodding.

'He's scared, and we can all certainly understand that. Perhaps we can convince him to talk if we can guarantee his

295

safety, and that of his mother and brother. I'd like for Mr Lewis to help us on this. I'm open to suggestions.'

K. O. Lewis was ready. 'Your Honor, we have taken preliminary steps to place him in our witness protection program.'

'I've heard of it, Mr Lewis, but I'm not familiar with the details.'

'It's quite simple. We move the family to another city. We provide new identities. We find a good job for the mother, and get them a nice place to live. Not a trailer or an apartment, but a house. We make sure the boys are in a good school. There's some cash up front. And we stay close by.'

'Sounds tempting, Ms Love,' Harry said.

It certainly did. At the moment, the Sways had no home. Dianne worked in a sweatshop. There were no relatives in Memphis.

'They're not mobile right now,' she said. 'Ricky is confined to the hospital.'

'We've already located a children's psychiatrist in Portland that can take him right away,' Lewis explained. 'It's a private one, not a charity outfit like St Peter's, and it's one of the best in the country. They'll take him whenever we ask, and, of course, we'll pay for it. After he's released, we'll move the family to another city.'

'How long will it take to place the entire family into the program?' Harry asked.

'Less than a week,' Lewis answered. 'Director Voyles has given it top priority. The paperwork takes a few days, new driver's license, Social Security numbers, birth certificates, credit cards, things like this. The family has to make the decision to do it, and the mother must tell us where she wants to go. We'll take over from there.'

'What do you think, Ms Love?' Harry asked. 'Will Ms Sway go for it?'

'I'll talk to her. She's under enormous stress right now. One kid in a coma, the other in jail, and she lost everything in the fire the last night. The idea of running away in the middle of the night could be a hard sell, at least for now.'

'But you'll try?'

'I'll see.'

'Do you think she could be in court tomorrow? I'd like to talk to her.'

'I'll ask the doctor.'

'Good. This meeting is adjourned. I'll see you folks at noon tomorrow.'

The bailiff handed Mark to two Memphis policemen in plain clothes, and they took him through a side door into the parking lot. When they were gone, the bailiff climbed the stairs to the second floor and darted into an empty rest room. Empty, except for Slick Moeller.

They stood before the urinals, side by side, and stared at the graffiti.

'Are we alone?' asked the bailiff.

'Yep. What happened?' Slick had unzipped his pants and had both hands on his waist. 'Be quick.'

'Kid wouldn't talk, so he's going back to jail. Contempt.'

'What does he know?'

'I'd say he knows everything. It's rather obvious. He said he was in the car with Clifford, they talked about this and that, and when Harry pressed him on the New Orleans stuff the kid took the Fifth Amendment. Tough little bastard.'

'But he knows?'

'Oh sure. But he's not telling. Judge wants him back tomorrow at noon to see if a night in the slammer changes his mind.'

Slick zipped his pants and stepped away from the urinal. He took a folded one-hundred-dollar bill from his pocket and handed it to the bailiff.

'You didn't hear it from me,' the bailiff said.

'You trust me, don't you?'

'Of course.' And he did. Mole Moeller never revealed a source.

Moeller had three photographers poised at various places around the Juvenile Court Building. He knew the routines better than the cops themselves, and he figured they'd use the side door near the loading dock for a quick getaway with the kid. That's exactly what they did, and they almost made it to their unmarked car before a heavy woman in fatigues jumped from a parked van and nailed them straight on with her Nikon. The cops yelled at her, and tried to hide the kid behind them, but it was too late. They rushed him to their car, and pushed him into the backseat.

Just great, thought Mark. It was not yet 2 p.m., and so far this day had brought the burning of their trailer, his arrest at the hospital, his new home at the jail, the hearing with Judge Roosevelt, and now, another damned photographer shooting at him for what would undoubtedly be another front page story.

As the car squealed tires and raced away, he sunk low in the backseat. His stomach ached, not from hunger, but from fear. He was alone again.

TWENTY-SIX

Foltrigg watched the traffic on Poydras Street and waited on the call from Memphis. He was tired of pacing and checking his watch. He had tried to return phone calls and dictate letters, but it was hopeless. His mind could not leave the wonderful image of Mark Sway sitting in a witness chair somewhere in Memphis telling all his splendid secrets. Two hours had passed since the hearing was scheduled to start, and surely they'd take a recess along the way so Fink could dash to a phone and call him.

Larry Trumann was on standby, waiting for the call so they could swing into action with a posse of corpse hunters. They had become quite proficient in digging for bodies during the past eight months. They just hadn't found any.

But today would be different. Roy would take the call, walk to Trumann's office, and off they'd go to find the late Boyd Boyette. Foltrigg talked to himself, not a whisper or a mumble, but a full-blown speech in which he addressed the media with the thrilling announcement that, yes, they had indeed found the Senator, and, yes, he died of six bullet wounds to the head. The gun was a .22, and the bullet fragments were definitely, without the slightest doubt, fired from the same handgun that had been so meticulously traced to the defendant, Mr Barry Muldanno.

It would be a wonderful moment, this press conference.

Someone knocked slightly and the door opened before Roy could turn around. It was Wally Boxx, the only person allowed such casual entries.

'Heard anything?' Wally asked, walking to the window and standing next to his boss.

'No. Not a word. I wish Fink would get to a phone. He has specific orders.'

They stood in silence and watched the street.

'What's the grand jury doing?' Roy asked.

'The usual. Routine indictments.'

'Who's in there?'

'Hoover. He's finishing up with the drug bust in Gretna. Should be through this afternoon.'

'Are they scheduled to work tomorrow?'

'No. They've had a hard week. We promised them yesterday they could take off tomorrow. What're you thinking?'

Foltrigg shifted weight slightly and scratched his chin. His eyes had a faraway look, and he watched the cars below but didn't see them. Heavy thinking was sometimes painful for him. 'Think about this. If, for some reason, the kid doesn't talk, and if Fink drills a dry hole with the hearing, what do we do then? I say we go to the grand jury, get subpoenas for both the kid and his lawyer, and drag them down here. The kid's gotta be scared right now, and he's still in Memphis. He'll be terrified when he has to come here.'

'Why would you subpoena his lawyer?'

'To scare her. Pure harassment. Shake 'em both up. We get the subpoenas today, keep them sealed, sit on them until late tomorrow afternoon when everything's closing for the weekend, then we serve the kid and his lawyer. The subpoenas will require their presence before our grand jury at 10 a.m. Monday morning. They won't have a chance to run to court and quash the subpoenas because it's the weekend and everything's shut down and all the judges are out of town. They'll be too scared not to show up here Monday morning, on our turf, Wally. Right down the hall here, in our building.'

'What if the kid doesn't know anything?'

Roy shook his head in frustration. They'd had this

300

conversation a dozen times in the last forty-eight hours. 'I thought that was established.'

'Maybe. And maybe the kid's talking right now.'

'He probably is.'

A secretary squeaked through on the intercom and announced that Mr Fink was holding on line one. Foltrigg walked to his desk and grabbed the phone. 'Yes!'

'The hearing's over, Roy,' Fink reported. He sounded relieved and tired.

Foltrigg hit the switch for the speakerphone, and fell into his chair. Wally perched his tiny butt on the corner of the desk. 'Wally's here with me, Tom. Tell us what happened.'

'Nothing much. The kid's back in jail. He wouldn't talk, so the judge found him in contempt.'

'What do you mean, he wouldn't talk?'

'He wouldn't talk. The judge handled both the direct and the cross-examinations, and the kid admitted being in the car and talking with Clifford. But when the judge asked questions about Boyette and Muldanno, the kid took the Fifth Amendment.'

'The Fifth Amendment!'

'That's right. He wouldn't budge. Said jail wasn't so bad after all, and that he had no other place to go.'

'But he knows, doesn't he, Tom? The little punk knows.'

'Oh, there's no question about it. Clifford told him everything.'

Foltrigg slapped his hands together. 'I knew it! I knew it! I knew it! I've been telling you boys this for three days now.' He jumped to his feet and squeezed his hands together. 'I knew it!'

Fink continued. 'The judge has scheduled another hearing for noon tomorrow. He wants the kid brought back in to see if he's changed his mind. I'm not too optimistic.'

'I want you at that hearing, Tom.'

'Yes, and the judge wants you too, Roy. I explained you had a hearing on the continuance motion in the morning, and he insisted that you fax him a copy of the hearing order. He said he'd excuse you under those circumstances.'

301

'Is he some kind of nut?'

'No. He's not a nut. He said he plans to hold these little hearings quite often next week, and he expects both of us, as petitioners, to be there.'

'Then he is a nut.'

Wally rolled his eyes and shook his head. These local judges could be such fools.

'After the hearing, the judge talked to us about placing the kid and his family in witness protection. He thinks he can convince the kid to talk if we can guarantee his safety.'

'That could take weeks.'

'I think so too, but K. O. told the judge it could be done in a matter of days. Frankly, Roy, I don't think the kid will talk until we can make some guarantees. He's a tough little guy.'

'What about his lawyer?'

'She played it cool, didn't say much, but she and the judge are pretty tight. I got the impression the kid's getting a lot of advice. She's no dummy.'

Wally just had to say something. 'Tom, it's me, Wally. What do you think will happen over the weekend?'

'Who knows? As I said, I don't think this kid'll change his mind overnight, and I don't think the judge plans to release him. The judge knows about Gronke and the Muldanno boys, and I get the impression he wants the kid locked up for his own protection. Tomorrow's Friday, so it looks like the kid will stay where he is over the weekend. And I'm sure the judge will call us back in on Monday for another chat.'

'Are you coming in, Tom?' Roy asked.

'Yeah, I'll catch a flight out in a couple of hours, and fly back here in the morning.' Fink's voice was now very tired.

'I'll be waiting for you here tonight, Tom. Good work.'

'Yeah.'

Fink faded away and Roy hit the switch.

'Get the grand jury ready,' he snapped at Wally, who bounced off the desk and headed for the door. 'Tell Hoover to take a break. This won't take but a minute. Get me the

Mark Sway file. Inform the clerk that the subpoenas will be sealed until they are served late tomorrow.'

Wally was through the door and gone. Foltrigg returned to the window, mumbling to himself, 'I knew it. I just knew it.'

The cop in the suit signed Doreen's clipboard, and left with his partner. 'Follow me,' she said to Mark as if he'd sinned again and her patience was wearing thin. He followed her, watching her wide rear end rock from side to side in a pair of tight, black polyester pants. A thick, shiny belt squeezed her narrow waist and held an assortment of key rings, two black boxes which he assumed to be pagers, and a pair of handcuffs. No gun. Her shirt was official white with markings up and down the sleeves and gold trim around the collar.

The hall was empty as she opened his door and motioned for him to return to his little room. She followed him in and eased around the walls like a dope dog sniffing at the airport. 'Sort of surprised to see you back here,' she said, inspecting the toilet.

He could think of nothing to say to this, and he was not in the mood for conversation. As he watched her stoop and bend, he thought about her husband serving thirty years for bank robbery, and if she insisted on chatting he might just bring this up. That would quiet her down and send her on her way.

'Must've upset Judge Roosevelt,' she said, looking through the windows.

'I guess so.'

'How long are you in for?'

'He didn't say. I have to go back tomorrow.'

She walked to the bunks and began patting the blanket. 'I've been reading about you and your little brother. Pretty strange case. How's he doing?'

Mark stood by the door, hoping she would just go away. 'He's probably gonna die,' he said sadly.

'No!'

'Yeah, it's awful. He's in a coma, you know, sucking his thumb, grunting and slobbering every now and then. His eyes have rolled back into his head. Won't eat.'

'I'm sorry I asked.' Her heavily decorated eyes were wide open, and she had stopped touching everything.

Yeah, I'll bet you're sorry you asked, Mark thought. 'I need to be there with him,' Mark said. 'My mom's there, but she's all stressed out. Taking a lot of pills, you know.'

'I'm so sorry.'

'It's awful. I've been feeling dizzy myself. Who knows, I could end up like my brother.'

'Can I get you anything?'

'No. I just need to lie down.' He walked to the bottom bunk and fell into it. Doreen knelt beside him, deeply troubled now.

'Anything you want, honey, you just let me know, okay?'

'Okay. Some pizza would be nice.'

She stood and thought about this for a second. He closed his eyes as if in deep pain.

'I'll see what I can do.'

'I haven't had lunch, you know.'

'I'll be right back,' she said, and she left. The door clicked loudly behind her. Mark bolted to his feet and listened to it.

TWENTY-SEVEN

The room was dark as usual; the lights off, the door shut, the blinds drawn, the only illumination the moving blue shadows of the muted television high on the wall. Dianne was mentally drained and physically beat from lying in bed with Ricky for eight hours, patting and hugging and cooing and trying to be strong in this damp, dark little cell.

Reggie had stopped by two hours ago, and they'd sat on the edge of the foldaway bed and talked for thirty minutes. She explained the hearing, assured her Mark was being fed and in no physical danger, described his room at the detention center because she'd seen one before, told her he was safer there than here, and talked about Judge Roosevelt and the FBI and their witness protection program. At first, and under the circumstances, the idea was attractive – they would simply move to a new city with new names and a new job and a decent place to live. They could run from this mess and start over. They could pick a large city with big schools and the boys would get lost in the crowd. But the more she lay there curled on one side and stared above Ricky's little head at the wall, the less she liked the idea. In fact, it was a horrible idea – living on the run forever, always afraid of an unexpected knock on the door, always in a panic when one of the boys was late getting home, always lying about their past.

This little plan was forever. What if, she began asking herself, one day, say five or ten years from now, long after the trial in New Orleans, some person she's never met lets something slip and it's heard by the wrong ears, and their trails are quickly traced? And when Mark is, say, a senior in high school, somebody waits on him after a ballgame and sticks a gun to his head? His name wouldn't be Mark, but he would be dead none the less.

She had almost decided to veto the idea of witness protection when Mark called her from the jail. He said he'd just finished a large pizza, was feeling great, nice place and all, was enjoying it more than the hospital, food was better, and he chatted so eagerly she knew he was lying. He said he was already plotting his escape, and would soon be out. They talked about Ricky, and the trailer, and the hearing today and the hearing tomorrow. He said he was trusting Reggie's advice, and Dianne agreed this was best. He apologized for not being there to help with Ricky, and she fought tears when he tried to sound so mature. He apologized again for all this mess.

Their conversation had been brief. She found it difficult to talk to him. She had little motherly advice, and felt like a failure because her eleven-year-old son was in jail and she couldn't get him out. She couldn't go see him. She couldn't go talk to the judge. She couldn't tell him to talk or to remain quiet because she was scared too. She couldn't do a damned thing but stay here in this narrow bed and stare at the walls and pray that she would wake up and the nightmare would be over.

It was 6 p.m., time for the local news. She watched the silent face of the anchorperson and hoped it wouldn't happen. But it didn't take long. After two dead bodies were carried from a landfill, a black-and-white still photo of Mark and the cop she'd slapped this morning was suddenly on the screen. She turned up the volume.

The anchorperson gave the basics about the taking of Mark Sway, careful not to call it an arrest, then went to a reporter standing in front of the Juvenile Court Building. He rattled on a few seconds about a hearing he knew nothing about, gushed breathlessly that the child, Mark Sway, had been taken back to the Juvenile Detention

Center, and that another hearing would be held tomorrow in Judge Roosevelt's courtroom. Back in the studio, the anchorperson brought 'em up to date on young Mark and the tragic suicide of Jerome Clifford. They ran a quick clip of the mourners leaving the chapel that morning in New Orleans, and had a second or two of Roy Foltrigg talking to a reporter under an umbrella. Back quickly to the anchorperson, who began quoting Slick Moeller's stories, and the suspicion mounted. No comments from the Memphis Police, the FBI, the US Attorney's office, or the Shelby County Juvenile Court. The ice got thinner as she skated into the vast, murky world of unnamed sources, all of whom were short on facts but long on speculation. When she mercifully finished and broke for a commercial, the uninformed could easily believe that young Mark Sway had shot not only Jerome Clifford but Boyd Boyette as well.

Dianne's stomach ached, and she hit the power button. The room was even darker. She had not taken a single bite of food in ten hours. Ricky twitched and grunted, and this irritated her. She eased from the bed, frustrated with him, frustrated with Greenway for the lack of progress, sick of this hospital with its dungeon-like decor and lighting, horrified at a system that allowed children to be jailed for being children, and, above all, scared of these lurking shadows who'd threatened Mark and burned the trailer and obviously were quite willing to do more. She closed the bathroom door behind her, sat on the edge of the bathtub, and smoked a Virginia Slim. Her hands trembled and her thoughts were a blur. A migraine was forming at the base of her skull, and by midnight she would be paralyzed. Maybe the pills would help.

She flushed the skinny cigarette butt, and sat on the edge of Ricky's bed. She had vowed to get through this ordeal one day at a time, but damned if the days weren't getting worse. She couldn't take much more.

Barry The Blade had picked this dumpy little bar because it was quiet, dark, and he remembered it from his teenage years as a young and aspiring hoodlum on the streets of New Orleans. It was not one he routinely frequented, but it was deep in the Quarter, which meant he could park off Canal and dart through the tourists on Bourbon and Royal, and there was no way the Feds could follow him.

He found a tiny table in the back, and sipped a vodka gimlet while waiting for Gronke.

He wanted to be in Memphis himself, but he was out on bond and his movements were restricted. Permission was required before he could leave the state, and he knew better than to ask. Communication with Gronke had been difficult. The paranoia was eating him alive. For eight months now, every curious stare was another cop watching his every move. A stranger behind him on the sidewalk was another Fibbie hiding in the darkness. His phones were tapped. His car and house were bugged. He was afraid to speak half the time because he could almost feel the sensors and hidden mikes.

He finished the gimlet and ordered another one. A double. Gronke arrived twenty minutes late, and crowded his bulky frame into a chair in the corner. The ceiling was seven feet above them.

'Nice place,' Gronke said. 'How you doin'?'

'Okay.' Barry snapped his fingers and the waiter walked over.

'Beer. Grolsch,' Gronke said.

'Did they follow you?' Barry asked.

'I don't think so. I've zigzagged through half the Quarter, you know.'

'What's happening up there?'

'Memphis?'

'No. Milwaukee, you dumbass,' Barry said with a smile. 'What's happening with the kid?'

'He's in jail, and he ain't talkin'. They took him in this morning, had some kinda hearing at lunch before the youth court, then took him back to jail.'

The bartender carried a heavy tray of dirty beer mugs through the swinging doors into the dirty, cramped

308

kitchen, and when he cleared the doors, two FBI agents in jeans stopped him. One flashed a badge while the other took the tray.

'What the hell?' the bartender asked, backing to the wall while staring at the badge just inches from the tip of his wide nose.

'FBI. Need a favor,' said Special Agent Scherff calmly, all business. The other agent pressed forward. The bartender owned two felony convictions, and had been enjoying his freedom for less than six months. He became eager.

'Sure. Anything.'

'What's your name?' asked Scherff.

'Uh, Dole. Link Dole.' He'd used so many names over the years it was difficult keeping them straight.

The agents inched forward even more and Link began to fear an attack. 'Okay, Link. Can you help us?'

Link nodded rapidly. The cook stirred a pot of rice, with a cigarette barely hanging from his lips. He glanced their way once but had other things on his mind.

'There are two men out there having a drink in the rear corner, on the right side where the ceiling is low.'

'Yeah, okay, sure. I'm not involved, am I?'

'No, Link. Just listen.' Scherff pulled a matching set of salt and pepper shakers from his pocket. 'Put these on a tray with a bottle of ketchup. Go to the table, just routine, you know, and switch these with the ones sitting there now. Ask these guys if they want something to eat, or another drink. You understand?'

Link was nodding but not understanding. 'Uh, what's in these?'

'Salt and pepper,' Scherff said. 'And a little bug that allows us to hear what these guys are saying. They're criminals, okay, Link, and we have them under surveillance.'

'I really don't want to get involved,' Link said, knowing full well that if they threatened even slightly he'd bust his ass to get involved.

'Don't make me angry,' Scherff said, waving the shakers.

'Okay, okay.'

A waiter kicked open the swinging doors and shuffled behind them with a stack of dirty dishes. Link took the shakers. 'Don't tell anyone,' he said, trembling.

'It's a deal, Link. This is our little secret. Now, is there an empty closet around here?' Scherff asked this while looking around the cramped and cluttered kitchen. The answer was obvious. There had not been an empty square foot in this dump in fifty years.

Link thought a second or two, very anxious to help his new friends. 'No, but there's a little office right above the bar.'

'Great, Link. Go exchange these, and we'll set up some equipment in the office.' Link held them gingerly as if they might explode, and returned to the bar.

A waiter placed a heavy green bottle of Grolsch in front of Gronke and disappeared.

'The little bastard knows something, doesn't he?' The Blade said.

'Of course. Otherwise, this wouldn't be happening. Why would he get himself a lawyer? Why would he clam up like this?' Gronke drained half his Grolsch with one, thirsty gulp.

Link approached them with a tray loaded with a dozen salt and pepper shakers and bottles of ketchup and mustard. 'You guys eating dinner?' he asked, all business, as he swapped the shakers and bottles on their table.

Barry waved him off. Gronke said, 'No.' And Link was gone. Fewer than thirty feet away, Scherff and three more agents crowded over a small desk and flipped open heavy briefcases. One of the agents grabbed earphones and stuck them to his head. He smiled.

'This kid scares me, man,' Barry said. 'He's told his lawyer, so that makes two more who know.'

'Yeah, but he ain't talkin', Barry. Think about it. We got to him. I showed him the picture. We took care of the trailer. The kid is scared to death.'

'I don't know. Is there any way to get him?'

310

'Not right now. I mean, hell, the cops have him. He's locked up.'

'There are ways, you know. I doubt if security is tight at a jail for kids.'

'Yeah, but the cops are scared too. They're all over the hospital. Got guards sittin' in the hallway. Fibbies dressed like doctors runnin' all over the place. These people are terrified of us.'

'But they can make him talk. They can put him in the mouse program, throw a buncha money at his mother. Hell, buy them a fancy new house trailer, maybe a double-wide or something. I'm just nervous as hell, Paul. If this kid was clean we would've never heard about him.'

'We can't hit the kid, Barry.'

'Why not?'

'Because he's a kid. Because everybody's watching him right now. Because if we do, a million cops'll hound us to our graves. It won't work.'

'What about his mother or his brother?'

Gronke took another shot of beer, and shook his head in frustration. He was a tough thug who could threaten with the best of them, but, unlike his friend, he was not a killer. This random search for victims scared him. He said nothing.

'What about his lawyer?' Barry asked.

'Why would you kill her?'

'Maybe I hate lawyers. Maybe it'll scare the kid so bad he'll go into a coma like his brother. I don't know.'

'And maybe killing innocent people in Memphis is not such a good idea. The kid'll just get another lawyer.'

'We'll kill the next one too. Think about it, Paul, this could do wonders for the legal profession,' Barry said with a loud laugh. Then he leaned forward as if a terribly private thought hit him. His chin was inches from the salt shaker. 'Think about it, Paul. If we knock off the kid's lawyer, then no lawyer in his right mind would represent him. Get it?'

'You're losin' it, Barry. You're crackin' up.'

'Yeah, I know. But it's a great thought, ain't it? Smoke

311

her, and the kid won't talk to his own mother. What's her name, Rollie or Ralphie?'

'Reggie. Reggie Love.'

'What the hell kinda name is that for a broad?'

'Don't ask me.'

Barry drained his glass and snapped again for the waiter. 'What's she sayin' on the phone?' he asked, in low again, just above the shaker.

'Don't know. We couldn't go in last night.'

The Blade was suddenly angry. 'You what!' The wicked eyes were fierce and glowing.

'Our man is doing it tonight, if all goes well.'

'What kinda place has she got?'

'Small office in a tall building downtown. It should be easy.'

Scherff pressed the earphone closer to his head. Two of his pals did likewise. The only sound in the room was a slight clicking noise from the recorder.

'Are these guys any good?'

'Nance is pretty smooth and cool under pressure. His partner, Cal Sisson, is a loose cannon. Afraid of his shadow.'

'I want the phones fixed tonight.'

'It'll be done.'

Barry lifted an unfiltered Camel and blew smoke at the ceiling. 'Are they protecting the lawyer?' He asked this as his eyes narrowed. Gronke looked away.

'I don't think so.'

'Where does she live? What kinda place?'

'She's got a cute little apartment behind her mother's house.'

'She live alone?'

'I think so.'

'She'd be easy, wouldn't she? Break in, take her out, steal a few things. Just another house burglary gone sour. What do you think?'

Gronke shook his head and studied a young blonde at the bar.

'What do you think?' Barry repeated.

'Yeah, it'd be easy.'

'Then let's do it. Are you listening to me, Paul?'

Paul was listening, but avoiding the evil eyes. 'I'm not in the mood to kill anyone,' he said, still staring at the blonde.

'That's fine. I'll get Pirini to do it.'

Several years earlier, a detainee, as they're called in the Juvenile Detention Center, a twelve-year-old, died in the room next to Mark's from an epileptic seizure. A ton of bad press and a nasty lawsuit followed, and though Doreen had not been on duty when it happened, she had none the less been shaken by it. An investigation followed. Two people were terminated. And a new set of regulations came down.

Doreen's shift ended at five, and the last thing she did was check on Mark. She'd stopped by on the hour throughout the afternoon, and watched with growing concern as his condition worsened. He was withdrawing before her very eyes, saying less with each visit, just lying there in bed staring at the ceiling. At five, she brought a county paramedic with her. Mark was given a quick physical, and pronounced alive and well. Vital signs were strong. When she left, she rubbed his temples like a sweet little grandmother and promised to return bright and early tomorrow, Friday. And she sent more pizza.

Mark told her he thought he could make it until then. He'd try to survive the night. Evidently she left instructions, because the next floor supervisor, a short plump little woman named Telda, immediately knocked on his door and introduced herself. For the next four hours, Telda knocked repeatedly and entered the room, staring wildly at his eyes as if he were crazy and something was about to snap.

Mark watched television, no cable, until the news started at ten, then brushed his teeth and turned off the lights. The bed was quite comfortable, and he thought of his mother trying to sleep on that rickety cot the nurses had rolled into Ricky's room.

The pizza was from Domino's, not some leathery slab of cheese someone threw in a microwave, but a real pizza Doreen had probably paid for. The bed was warm, the

313

pizza was real, and the door was locked. He felt safe, not only from the other inmates and the gangs and violence certain to be close by, but especially from the man with the switchblade who knew his name and had the picture. The man who'd burned the trailer. He'd thought about this guy every moment of every hour since he dashed from the elevator early yesterday morning. He'd thought about him on Momma Love's porch last night, and sitting in the courtroom this afternoon listening to Hardy and McThune. He'd worried about him hanging around the hospital where Dianne was unaware.

Sitting in a parked car on Third Street in downtown Memphis at Midnight was not Cal Sisson's idea of safe fun, but the doors were locked and there was a gun under the seat. His felony convictions forbade him from owning or possessing a firearm, but this was Jack Nance's car. It was parked behind a delivery van near Madison, a couple of blocks from the Sterick Building. There was nothing suspicious about the car. Traffic was light.

Two uniformed cops on foot strolled along the sidewalk and stopped fewer than five feet from Cal. They stared at him. He glanced in the mirror, and saw another pair. Four cops! One of them sat on the trunk, and the car shook. Had the parking meter run out on him? No, he'd paid for an hour and been here less than ten minutes. Nance said it was a thirty-minute job.

Two more cops joined the two on the sidewalk, and Cal started sweating. The gun worried him, but a good lawyer could convince his probation officer that the gun was not his. He was merely driving for Nance.

An unmarked police car parked behind him, and two cops in plain clothes joined the others. Eight cops!

One in jeans and a sweatshirt bent at the waist and stuck his badge to Cal's window. There was a radio on the seat next to his leg, and thirty seconds ago he should have punched the blue button and warned Nance. But now it was too late. The cops had materialized from nowhere.

314

He slowly rolled down his window. The cop leaned forward and their faces were inches apart. 'Evening, Cal. I'm Lieutenant Byrd, Memphis PD.'

The fact that he called him Cal made him shudder. He tried to remain calm. 'What can I do for you, Officer?'

'Where's Jack?'

Cal's heart stopped and sweat popped through his skin. 'Jack who?'

Jack who. Byrd glanced over his shoulder and smiled at his partner. The uniformed cops had surrounded the car. 'Jack Nance. Your good friend. Where is he?'

'I haven't seen him.'

'Well, what a coincidence. I haven't seen him either. At least not for the past fifteen minutes. In fact, the last time I saw Jack was at the corner of Union and Second, less than a half an hour ago, and he was getting out of this car here. And you drove away, and, surprise, here you are.'

Cal was breathing, but it was difficult. 'I don't know what you're talking about.'

Byrd unlocked the door and opened it. 'Get out, Cal,' he demanded, and Cal complied. Byrd slammed the door and shoved him against it. Four of the cops surrounded him. The other three were looking in the direction of the Sterick Building. Byrd was in his face.

'Listen to me, Cal. Accomplice to breaking and entering carries seven years. You have three prior convictions, so you'll be charged as a habitual offender, and guess how much time you're looking at.'

His teeth were chattering and his body was shaking. He shook his head no, as if he didn't understand and wanted Byrd to tell him.

'Thirty years, no parole.'

He closed his eyes and slumped. His breathing was heavy.

'Now,' Byrd continued, very cool, very cruel. 'We're not worried about Jack Nance. When he finishes with Ms Love's phones, we've got some boys waiting for him outside the building. He'll be arrested, booked, and in due course sent away. But we don't figure he'll talk much. You follow?'

315

Cal nodded quickly.

'But, Cal, we figure you might want to cut a deal. Help us a little, know what I mean?'

He was still nodding, only faster.

'We figure you'll tell us what we need to know, and in return, we'll let you walk.'

Cal stared at him desperately. His mouth was open, his chest pounding away.

Byrd pointed to the sidewalk on the other side of Madison. 'You see that sidewalk, Cal?'

Cal took a long, hopeful look at the empty sidewalk. 'Yeah,' he said eagerly.

'Well, it's all yours. Tell me what I want to hear, and you walk. Okay? I'm offering you thirty years of freedom, Cal. Don't be stupid.'

'Okay.'

'When does Gronke return from New Orleans?'

'In the morning, around ten.'

'Where's he staying?'

'Holiday Inn Crowne Plaza.'

'Room number?'

'It's 782.'

'Where are Bono and Pirini?'

'I don't know.'

'Please, Cal, we're not idiots. Where are they?'

'They're in 783 and 784.'

'Who else from New Orleans is here?'

'That's it. That's all I know.'

'Can we expect more people from New Orleans?'

'I swear I don't know.'

'Do they have any plans to hit the boy, his family, or his lawyer?'

'It's been discussed, but no definite plans. I wouldn't be a part of it, you know.'

'I know, Cal. Any plans to bug more phones?'

'No. I don't think so. Just the lawyer.'

'What about the lawyer's house?'

'No, not to my knowledge.'

316

'No other bugs or wires or phone taps?'

'Not to my knowledge.'

'No plans to kill anybody?'

'No.'

'If you're lying, I'll come get you, Cal, and it's thirty years.'

'I swear it.'

Suddenly, Byrd slapped him on the left side of his face, then grabbed his collar and squeezed it together. Cal's mouth was open and his eyes showed absolute terror. 'Who burned the trailer?' Byrd snarled at him as he pushed him harder against the car.

'Bono and Pirini,' he said without the slightest hesitation.

'Were you in on it, Cal?'

'No. I swear.'

'Any more fires planned?'

'Not to my knowledge.'

'Then what the hell are they doing here, Cal?'

'They're just waiting, listening, you know, just in case they're needed for something else. Depends on what the kid does.'

Byrd squeezed tighter. He showed him his teeth and twisted the collar. 'One lie, Cal, and I'm all over your ass, okay?'

'I'm not lying, I swear,' Cal said in a shrill voice.

Byrd turned him loose and nodded at the sidewalk. 'Go, and sin no more.' The wall of cops opened, and Cal walked through them and into the street. He hit the sidewalk at full stride, and was last seen jogging into the darkness.

TWENTY-EIGHT

Friday morning. Reggie sipped strong, black coffee in the darkness of predawn, and waited for another unpredictable day as counsel for Mark Sway. It was a cool, clear morning, the first of many in September; and the first hint that the hot, sticky days of the Memphis summer were coming to an end. She sat in a wicker rocker on the small balcony stuck to the rear of her apartment, and tried to unscramble the past five hours of her life.

The cops had called her at one-thirty, said there was an emergency at her office, and asked her to come down. She'd called Clint, and together they had gone to her office where a half dozen cops were waiting. They had allowed Jack Nance to finish his dirty work and leave the building before they nailed him. They showed Reggie and Clint the three phones and the tiny transmitters glued into the receivers, and they said Nance did pretty good work.

As she watched, they carefully removed the transmitters and kept them for evidence. They explained how Nance entered, and more than once they commented on her lack of security. She said she wasn't that concerned about security. There were no real assets in the office.

She'd checked her files, and everything appeared to be in order. The Mark Sway file was in her briefcase at home, and she kept it there when she slept. Clint examined his desk and said there was a chance Nance went through his files. But Clint's desk was not well organized to begin with, so he couldn't be certain.

The police had known Nance was coming, they had explained, but they wouldn't say how they knew. He was allowed easy access into the building – unlocked doors, absent security guards, etc. – and they had a dozen men watching him. He was in custody now, and so far had said nothing. One cop had taken her aside, and in hushed confidence explained about Nance's connection to Gronke, and to Bono and Pirini. They had been unable to find the latter two; their hotel rooms had been abandoned. Gronke was in New Orleans, and they had him under surveillance.

Nance would serve a couple of years, maybe more. For an instant, she'd wanted the death penalty.

The cops had gradually left. Around three, she and Clint were left alone with the empty offices and the startling knowledge that a professional had entered and laid his traps. A man hired by killers had been there, gathering information so there could be more killings, if necessary. The place made her nervous, and she and Clint had left shortly after the cops and found a coffee shop in midtown.

And so with three hours' sleep and a nerve-racking day about to begin, she sipped her coffee and watched the eastern sky turn orange. She thought about Mark, and how he'd arrived in her office on Wednesday, barely two days ago, wet from the rain and scared to death, and told her about being threatened by a man with a switchblade. This man was big and ugly, and waved the knife and produced a photo of the Sway family. She had listened with horror as this small, shivering child described the switchblade. It was a frightening event to hear about, but it had happened to someone else. She was not directly involved. The knife was not pointed at her.

But that was Wednesday, and this was Friday, and the same bunch of thugs had now violated her, and things were a helluva lot more dangerous. Her little client was safely tucked away in a nice jail with security guards at his beck and call, and here she was sitting alone in the darkness thinking about Bono and Pirini and who knew who else might be out there.

Though it couldn't be seen from Momma Love's house, an unmarked car was parked in the street not far away. Two FBI agents were on guard, just in case. Reggie had agreed to this.

She pictured a hotel room, clouds of cigarette smoke hanging along the ceiling, empty beer bottles littering the floor, curtains drawn, and a small group of badly dressed hoodlums hovering over a small table listening to a tape recorder. She was on the tape recorder, talking to clients, to Dr Levin, to Momma Love, just chatting away as if everything were private. The hoods were bored for the most part, but occasionally one would chuckle and grunt.

Mark didn't use her office phones, and the strategy of bugging them was ridiculous. These people obviously believed Mark knew about Boyette, and that he and his lawyer were stupid enough to discuss this knowledge over the phone.

The phone in the kitchen rang, and Reggie jumped. She checked her watch – six-twenty. It had to be more trouble because no one called at this hour. She walked inside and caught it after the fourth ring. 'Hello.'

It was Harry Roosevelt. 'Good morning, Reggie. Sorry to wake you.'

'I was awake.'

'Have you seen the paper?'

She swallowed hard. 'No. What is it?'

'It's a front page spread with two big pictures of Mark, one as he's leaving the hospital, under arrest as it says, and the other as he's leaving court yesterday, cops on both sides. Slick Moeller wrote it, and he knows all about the hearing. He's got his facts straight, for a change. He says Mark refused to answer my questions about his knowledge of Boyette and such, and that I found him in contempt and sent him to jail. Makes me sound like Hitler.'

'But how does he know this?'

'Cites unnamed sources.'

She was counting the people in the courtroom during the hearing. 'Was it Fink?'

'I doubt it. Fink would have nothing to gain by leaking this, and the risks are too great. It has to be someone who's not too bright.'

'That's why I said Fink.'

'Good point, but I doubt it was a lawyer. I plan to issue a subpoena for Mr Moeller to appear in my court at noon today. I'll demand he give me his source, or I'll throw him in jail for contempt.'

'Wonderful idea.'

'It shouldn't take long. We'll have Mark's little hearing afterward. Okay?'

'Sure, Harry. Listen, there's something you should know. It's been a long night.'

'I'm listening,' he said. Reggie gave him the quick version of the bugging of her office, with particular emphasis on Bono and Pirini and the fact they had not been found.

'Good Lord,' he said. 'These people are crazy.'

'And dangerous.'

'Are you scared?'

'Of course I'm scared. I've been violated, Harry, and it's frightening to know they've been watching.'

There was a long pause on the other end. 'Reggie, I'm not going to release Mark under any circumstances, not today anyway. Let's see what happens over the weekend. He's much safer where he is.'

'I agree.'

'Have you talked to his mother?'

'Yesterday. She was lukewarm on the idea of witness protection. It might take some time. Poor thing is nothing but ragged nerves.'

'Work on her. Can she be present in court today? I'd like to see her.'

'I'll try.'

'See you at noon.'

She poured another cup of coffee and returned to the balcony. Axle slept under the rocker. The first light of dawn crept through the trees. She held the warm mug with both hands and tucked her bare feet under the heavy bathrobe. She sniffed the aroma and thought about how much she despised the press. So now the world would know about the hearing. So much for confidentiality. Her little client was suddenly more vulnerable. It was obvious now, the fact that he knew something he shouldn't know. If not, why wouldn't he simply have talked when the judge instructed him to?

This game was growing more dangerous by the hour. And she, Reggie Love, Attorney and Counselor-at-Law, was supposed to have all the answers and dispense perfect advice. Mark would look at her with those scared blue eyes, and ask what to do next. How the hell was she supposed to know?

They were after her too.

Doreen woke Mark early. She'd fixed blueberry muffins for him, and she nibbled on one and watched him with great concern. Mark sat in a chair, holding a muffin but not eating it, just staring blankly at the floor. He slowly raised the muffin to his mouth, took a tiny bite, then lowered it to his lap. Doreen watched every move.

'Are you okay, sweetheart?' she asked him.

Mark nodded slowly. 'Oh, I'm fine,' he said in a hollow, hoarse voice.

Doreen patted his knee, then his shoulder. Her eyes were narrow and she was very troubled. 'Well, I'll be around all day,' she said as she stood and walked to the door. 'And I'll be checking on you.'

Mark ignored her, and took another small bite of his muffin. The door slammed and clicked, and suddenly he crammed the rest of it in his mouth and reached for another.

He turned on the television, but with no cable he was forced to watch Bryant Gumbel. No cartoons. No old movies. Just Willard in a hat eating corn on the cob and sweet potato sticks.

Doreen returned twenty minutes later. The keys jangled outside, the lock popped, and the door opened. 'Mark, come with me,' she said. 'You have a visitor.'

He was suddenly still again, detached, lost in another world. He moved slowly. 'Who?' he said in that voice.

'Your lawyer.'

He stood and followed her into the hallway. 'Are you sure you're okay?' she asked, squatting in front of him. He nodded slowly, and they walked to the stairs.

Reggie was waiting in a small conference room one floor below. She and Doreen exchanged pleasantries, old acquaintances, and the door was locked. They sat on opposite sides of a small, round table.

'Are we buddies?' she asked with a smile.

'Yeah. I'm sorry about yesterday.'

'You don't need to apologize, Mark. Believe me, I understand. Did you sleep well?'

'Yeah. Much better than at the hospital.'

'Doreen says she's worried about you.'

'I'm fine. I'm much better off than Doreen.'

'Good.' Reggie pulled a newspaper from her briefcase and placed the front page on the table. He read it very slowly.

'You've made the front page three days in a row,' she said, trying to coax a smile.

'It's getting old. I thought the hearing was private.'

'Supposed to be. Judge Roosevelt called me early this morning. He's very upset about the story. He plans to bring in the reporter and grill him about it.'

'It's too late for that, Reggie. The story is right here in print. Everybody sees it. It's pretty obvious I'm the kid who knows too much.'

'Right.' She waited as he read it again and studied the pictures of himself.

'Have you talked to your mother?' she asked.

'Yes ma'am. Yesterday afternoon around five. She sounded tired.'

'She is. I saw her before you called, and she's hanging in there. Ricky had a bad day.'

'Yeah. Thanks to those stupid cops. Let's sue them.'

'Maybe later. We need to talk about something. After

323

you left the courtroom yesterday, Judge Roosevelt talked to the lawyers and the FBI. He wants you, your mother, and Ricky placed in the Federal Witness Protection Program. He thinks it's the best way to protect you, and I tend to agree.'

'What is it?'

'The FBI moves you to a new location, a very secret one, far away from here, and you have new names, new schools, new everything. Your mother has a new job, one that pays a lot more than six dollars an hour. After a few years there, they might move you again, just to be safe. They'll place Ricky in a much better hospital until he's better. Government pays for everything, of course.'

'Do I get a new bike?'

'Sure.'

'Just kidding. I saw this once in a movie. A Mafia movie. This informant ratted on the Mafia, and the FBI helped him vanish. He had plastic surgery. They found him a new wife, you know, the works. Sent him off to Brazil or some place.'

'What happened?'

'It took them about a year to find him. They killed his wife too.'

'It was just a movie, Mark. You really have no choice. It's the safest thing to do.'

'Of course, I have to tell them everything before they do all these wonderful things for us.'

'That's part of the deal.'

'The Mafia never forgets, Reggie.'

'You've watched too many movies, Mark.'

'Maybe so. But has the FBI ever lost a witness in this program?'

The answer was yes, but she couldn't cite a specific example. 'I don't know, but we'll meet with them and you can ask all the questions you want.'

'What if I don't want to meet with them? What if I want to stay in my little cell here until I'm twenty years old and Judge Roosevelt finally dies? Then can I get out?'

'Fine. What about your mother and Ricky? What happens to them when he's released from the hospital and they have no place to go?'

'They can move in with me. Doreen'll take care of us.'

Damn, he was quick for an eleven-year-old. She paused for a moment and smiled at him. He glared at her.

'Listen, Mark, do you trust me?'

'Yes, Reggie. I do trust you. You're the only person in the world I trust right now. So please help me.'

'There's no easy way out, okay.'

'I know that.'

'Your safety is my only concern. The safety of you and your family. Judge Roosevelt feels the same way. Now, it'll take a few days to work out the details of the witness program. The judge instructed the FBI yesterday to start moving on it immediately, and I think it's the best thing to do.'

'Did you discuss it with my mother?'

'Yes. She wants to talk about it some more. I think she liked the idea.'

'But how do you know it'll work, Reggie? Is it totally safe?'

'Nothing is totally safe, Mark. There are no guarantees.'

'Wonderful. Maybe they'll find us, maybe they won't. That'll make life exciting, won't it.'

'Do you have a better idea?'

'Sure. It's very simple. We collect the insurance money from the trailer. We find another one, and we move into it. I keep my mouth shut and we live happily ever after. I don't really care if they ever find this body, Reggie. I just don't care.'

'I'm sorry, Mark, but that can't happen.'

'Why not?'

'Because you happen to be very unlucky. You have some important information, and you'll be in trouble until you give it up.'

'And then I could be dead.'

'I don't think so, Mark.'

He crossed his arms over his chest and closed his eyes. There was a slight bruise high on his left cheek, and it was turning brown. This was Friday. He'd been slapped by

Clifford on Monday, and though it seemed like weeks ago the bruise reminded her that things were happening much too fast. The poor kid still bore the wounds of the attack.

'Where would we go?' he asked softly, his eyes still closed.

'Far away. Mr Lewis with the FBI mentioned a children's psychiatric hospital in Portland that's supposed to be one of the best. They'll place Ricky in it with the best of everything.'

'Can't they follow us?'

'The FBI can handle it.'

He stared at her. 'Why do you suddenly trust the FBI?'

'Because there's no one else to trust.'

'How long will all this take?'

'There are two problems. The first is the paperwork and details. Mr Lewis said it could be done within a week. The second is Ricky. It might be a few days before Dr Greenway will allow him to be moved.'

'So I'm in jail for another week?'

'Looks like it. I'm sorry.'

'Don't be sorry, Reggie. I can handle this place. In fact, I could stay here for a long time if they'd leave me alone.'

'They're not going to leave you alone.'

'I need to talk to my mother.'

'She might be at the hearing today. Judge Roosevelt wants her there. I suspect he'll have a meeting, off the record, with the FBI people and discuss the witness protection program.'

'If I'm gonna stay in jail, why have the hearing?'

'In contempt matters, the judge is required to bring you back into court periodically to allow you to purge yourself of contempt, in other words, to do what he wants you to do.'

'The law stinks, Reggie. It's silly, isn't it?'

'Oftentimes, yes.'

'I had a wild thought last night as I was trying to go to sleep. I thought – what if the body is not where Clifford said it is. What if Clifford was just crazy and talking out of his head? Have you thought about that, Reggie?'

326

'Yes. Many times.'

'What if all this is a big joke?'

'We can't take that chance, Mark.'

He rubbed his eyes and slid his chair back. He began walking around the small room, suddenly very nervous. 'So we just pack up and leave our lives behind, right? That's easy for you to say, Reggie. You're not the one who'll have the nightmares. You'll go on like nothing ever happened. You and Clint. Momma Love. Nice little law office. Lots of clients. But not us. We'll live in fear for the rest of our lives.'

'I don't think so.'

'But you don't know, Reggie. It's easy to sit here and say everything'll be fine. Your neck's not on the line.'

'You have no choice, Mark.'

'Yes I do. I could lie.'

It was just a motion for a continuance, normally a rather boring and routine legal skirmish, but nothing was boring when Barry The Blade Muldanno was the defendant and Willis Upchurch was the mouthpiece. Throw in the enormous ego of the Reverend Roy Foltrigg and the press manipulation skills of Wally Boxx, and this innocuous little hearing for a continuance took on the air of an execution. The courtroom of the Honorable James Lamond was crowded with the curious, the press, and a small army of jealous lawyers who had more important things to do but just happened to be in the neighborhood. They milled about and spoke in grave tones while keeping anxious eyes on the media. Cameras and reporters attract lawyers like blood attracts sharks.

Beyond the railing that separated the players from the spectators, Foltrigg stood in the center of a tight circle of his assistants and whispered, frowning as if they were planning an invasion. He was decked out in his Sunday best – dark three-piece suit, white shirt, red-and-blue silk tie, hair perfect, shoes shined to a glow. He faced the audience, but of course was much too preoccupied to notice anyone. Across the way, Muldanno sat with his back to the gaggle of

327

onlookers and pretended to ignore everyone. He was dressed in black. The ponytail was perfect and arched down to the bottom of his collar. Willis Upchurch sat on the edge of the defense table, also facing the press while engaging himself in a highly animated conversation with a paralegal. If it was humanly possible, Upchurch loved the attention more than Foltrigg.

Muldanno did not yet know of the arrest of Jack Nance eight hours earlier in Memphis. He did not know Cal Sisson had spilled his guts. He had not heard from either Bono or Pirini, and he had sent Gronke back to Memphis this morning in complete ignorance of the night's events.

Foltrigg, on the other hand, was feeling quite smug. Based on the taped conversation gathered from the salt shaker, he would obtain on Monday indictments against Muldanno and Gronke for obstruction of justice. Convictions would be easy. He had them in the bag. He had Muldanno facing five years.

But Roy didn't have the body. And trying Barry The Blade on obstruction charges would not generate anywhere near the publicity of a nasty murder trial complete with color glossies of the decomposed corpse and pathologists' reports about bullet entries and trajectories and exits. Such a trial would last for weeks, and Roy would shine on the evening news every night. He could just see it.

He'd sent Fink back to Memphis early this morning with the grand jury subpoenas for the kid and his lawyer. That should liven things up a bit. He should have the kid talking by Monday afternoon, and maybe, with just a little luck, he'd have the remains of Boyette by Monday night. This thought had kept him at the office until three in the morning. He strutted to the clerk's desk for nothing in particular, then strutted back, glaring at Muldanno, who ignored him.

The courtroom deputy stopped in front of the bench and yelled instructions for all to sit. Court was now in session, the Honorable James Lamond presiding. Lamond appeared from a side door, and was escorted to the bench by an assistant carrying a stack of heavy files. In his early fifties, Lamond was a baby among federal judges. One of countless Reagan appointees, he was typical – all business, no smiles, cut the crap and let's get on with it. He had been the US Attorney for the Southern District of Louisiana immediately prior to Roy Foltrigg, and he hated his successor as much as anyone. Six months after taking the job, Foltrigg had embarked upon a speaking tour of the district in which he presented charts and graphs to Rotarians and Civitans and declared with statistical evidence that his office was now much more efficient than it had been in prior years. Indictments were up. Dope dealers were behind bars. Public officials were running scared. Crime was in trouble, and the public's interest was now being fiercely protected because he, Roy Foltrigg, was now the chief federal prosecutor in the district.

It was a stupid thing to do because it insulted Lamond and angered the other judges. They had little use for the Reverend.

Lamond gazed at the crowded courtroom. Everyone was seated. 'My goodness,' he started. 'I'm delighted at the interest shown here today, but honestly, it's just a hearing on a simple motion.' He glared at Foltrigg, who sat in the middle of six assistants. Upchurch had a local lawyer on each side, and two paralegals sitting behind him.

'The court is ready to proceed upon the motion of the defendant, Barry Muldanno, for a continuance. The court notes that this matter is set for trial three weeks from next Monday. Mr Upchurch, you filed the motion, so you may proceed. Please be brief.'

To the surprise of everyone, Upchurch was indeed brief. He simply stated what was common knowledge about the late Jerome Clifford, and explained to the court that he had a trial in federal court in St Louis beginning three weeks from Monday. He was glib, relaxed, and completely at home in this strange courtroom. A continuance was necessary, he explained, with remarkable efficiency, because he needed time to prepare a defense for what

329

would undoubtedly be a long trial. He finished in ten minutes.

'How much time do you need?' Lamond asked.

'Your Honor, I have a busy trial calendar, and I'll be happy to show it to you. In all fairness, six months would be a reasonable delay.'

'Thank you. Anything else?'

'No sir. Thank you, Your Honor.' Upchurch took his seat as Foltrigg was leaving his and heading for the podium directly in front of the bench. He glanced at his notes and was about to speak when Lamond beat him to it.

'Mr Foltrigg, surely you don't deny that the defense is entitled to more time, in light of the circumstances?'

'No, Your Honor, I don't deny this. But I think six months is entirely too much time.'

'So how much would you suggest?'

'A month or two. You see, Your Honor, I –'

'I'm not going to sit up here and listen to a haggle over two months or six or three or four, Mr Foltrigg. If you concede the defendant is entitled to a delay, then I'll take this matter under advisement and set this case for trial whenever my calendar will allow.'

Lamond knew Foltrigg needed a delay worse than Muldanno. He just couldn't ask for it. Justice must always be on the attack. Prosecutors are incapable of asking for more time.

'Well, yes, Your Honor,' Foltrigg said loudly. 'But it's our position that needless delays should be avoided. This matter has dragged on long enough.'

'Are you suggesting this court is dragging its feet, Mr Foltrigg?'

'No, Your Honor, but the defendant is. He's filed every frivolous motion known to American jurisprudence to stall this prosecution. He's tried every tactic, every –'

'Mr Foltrigg. Mr Clifford is dead. He can't file any more motions. And now the defendant has a new lawyer, who, as I see it, has only filed one motion.'

Foltrigg looked at his notes and started a slow burn. He

had not expected to prevail in this little matter, but he certainly hadn't expected to get kicked in the teeth.

'Do you have anything relevant to say?' His Honor asked, as if Foltrigg had yet to say anything of substance.

He grabbed his legal pad and stormed back to his seat. A rather pitiful performance. He should've sent an underling.

'Anything else, Mr Upchurch?' Lamond asked.

'No sir.'

'Very well. Thanks to all of you for your interest in this matter. Sorry it has been so brief. Maybe we'll do more next time. An order for a new trial setting will be forthcoming.'

Lamond stood just minutes after he'd sat, and was gone. The reporters filed out, and of course were followed by Foltrigg and Upchurch, who walked to opposite ends of the hallway and held impromptu press conferences.

TWENTY-NINE

Though Slick Moeller had reported jailhouse riots, rapes, and beatings, and though he'd stood on the safe side of the doors and bars, he'd never actually, physically, been inside a jail cell. And though this thought was heavy on his mind, he kept his cool and projected the aura of the surefooted reporter and confident believer in the First Amendment. He had a lawyer on each side, high-paid studs from a hundred-man firm that had represented the *Memphis Press* for decades, and they had assured him a dozen times in the past two hours that the Constitution of the United States of America was his friend and on this day would be his shield. Slick wore jeans, a safari jacket, and hiking boots, very much the weather-beaten reporter.

Harry was not impressed with the aura being projected by this weasel. Nor was he impressed with the silk-stocking, blue-blooded Republican mouthpieces who'd never before darkened the doors to his courtroom. Harry was upset. He sat on his bench and read for the tenth time Slick's morning story. He also reviewed applicable First Amendment cases dealing with reporters and their confidential sources. And he took his time so Slick would sweat.

The doors were locked. The bailiff, Slick's friend Grinder, stood quite nervously by the bench. Following the judge's order, two uniformed deputies sat directly behind Slick and his lawyers, and seemed poised and ready for action. This bothered Slick and his lawyers, but they tried not to show it.

The same court reporter with an even shorter skirt filed her nails and waited for the words to start flowing. The same grouchy old woman sat at her table and flipped through the *National Enquirer*. They waited and waited. It was almost twelve-thirty. As usual, the docket was packed and things were behind schedule. Marcia had a club sandwich waiting for Harry between hearings. The Sway hearing was next.

He leaned forward on his elbows and glared down at Slick, who at a hundred and thirty pounds weighed probably a third of what Harry did. 'On the record,' he barked at the stenographer, and she started pecking away.

Cool as he was, Slick jerked with these first words and sat upright.

'Mr Moeller, I've brought you here under summons because you've violated a section of the Tennessee Code regarding the confidentiality of my proceedings. This is a very grave matter because we're dealing with the safety and well-being of a small child. Unfortunately, the law does not provide criminal penalties, only contempt.'

He removed his reading glasses and began rubbing them with a handkerchief. 'Now, Mr Moeller,' he said like a frustrated grandfather, 'as upset as I am with you and your story, I am much more troubled by the fact that someone leaked this information to you. Someone who was in this courtroom during the hearing yesterday. Your source troubles me greatly.'

Grinder leaned against the wall and pressed his calves against it to keep his knees from shaking. He would not look at Slick. His first heart attack had been only six years ago, and if he didn't control himself this might be the big one.

'Please sit in the witness chair, Mr Moeller,' Harry instructed with a sweep of the hand. 'Be my guest.'

Slick was sworn by the old grouch. He placed one hiking boot on one knee, and looked at his attorneys for reassurance. They were not looking at him. Grinder studied the ceiling tiles.

333

'You are under oath, Mr Moeller,' Harry reminded him just seconds after he'd been sworn.

'Yes sir,' he uttered and feebly attempted to smile at this huge man who was sitting high above him and peering down over the railing of the bench.

'Did you in fact write the story in today's paper with your name on it?'

'Yes sir.'

'Did you write it by yourself, or did someone assist you?'

'Well, Your Honor, I wrote every word, if that's what you mean.'

'That's what I mean. Now, in the fourth paragraph of this story, you write, and I quote, "Mark Sway refused to answer questions about Barry Muldanno or Boyd Boyette." End quote. Did you write that, Mr Moeller?'

'Yes sir.'

'And were you present during the hearing yesterday when the child testified?'

'No sir.'

'Were you in this building?'

'Uh, yes sir, I was. Nothing wrong with that, is there?'

'Be quiet, Mr Moeller. I'll ask the questions, and you answer them. Do you understand the relationship here?'

'Yes sir.' Slick pleaded with his eyes to his lawyers, but both were deep into reading at this moment. He felt alone.

'So you weren't present. Now, Mr Moeller, how did you learn that the child refused to answer my questions about Barry Muldanno or Boyd Boyette?'

'I had a source.'

Grinder had never thought of himself as a source. He was just a low-paid courtroom bailiff with a uniform and a gun, and bills to pay. He was about to be sued by Sears for his wife's credit card. He wanted to wipe the sweat from his forehead but was afraid to move.

'A source,' Harry repeated, mocking Slick. 'Of course you had a source, Mr Moeller. I assumed this. You weren't here. Someone told you. This means you had a source. Now, who was your source?'

The lawyer with the grayest hair quickly stood to speak. He was dressed in standard big-firm attire – charcoal suit, white button-down, red tie but with a daring yellow stripe on it, and black shoes. His name was Alliphant. He was a partner who normally avoided courtrooms. 'Your Honor, if I may.'

Harry grimaced, and he slowly turned from the witness. His mouth was open as if he were shocked at this daring interruption. He scowled at Alliphant, who repeated himself. 'If I may, Your Honor.'

Harry let him hang there for an eternity, then said, 'You haven't been in my courtroom before, have you, Mr Alliphant?'

'No sir,' he answered, still standing.

'I didn't think so. Not one of your usual hangouts. How many lawyers are in your firm, Mr Alliphant?'

'A hundred and seven, at last count.'

Harry whistled and shook his head. 'That's a buncha lawyers. Do any of them practice in Juvenile Court?'

'Well, I'm sure some do, Your Honor.'

'Which ones?'

Alliphant stuck one hand in one pocket while running a loose finger along the edge of his legal pad. He did not belong here. His legal world was one of boardrooms and thick documents, of fat retainers and fancy lunches. He was rich because he billed three hundred dollars an hour and had thirty partners doing the same. His firm prospered because it paid seventy associates fifty thousand a year and expected them to bill five times that. He was here ostensibly because he was chief counsel for the paper, but actually because no one in the firm's litigation section could make the hearing on two hours' notice.

Harry despised him, his firm, and their ilk. He did not trust the corporate types who came down from the tall buildings to mingle with the lower class only when necessary. They were arrogant and afraid to get their hands dirty.

'Sit down, Mr Alliphant,' he said, pointing. 'You do not stand in my courtroom. Sit.'

Alliphant awkwardly backed into his chair.

'Now what are you trying to say, Mr Alliphant?'

'Well, Your Honor, we object to these questions, and we object to the court's interrogation of Mr Moeller on the grounds that his story is protected free speech under the First Amendment of the Constitution. Now –'

'Mr Alliphant, have you read the applicable code section dealing with closed hearings in juvenile matters? Surely you have.'

'Yes sir, I have. And, frankly, Your Honor, I have some real problems with this section.'

'Oh you do? Go on.'

'Yes sir. It's my opinion that this code section is unconstitutional, as written. I have some cases here from other –'

'Unconstitutional?' Harry asked with raised eyebrows.

'Yes sir,' Alliphant answered firmly.

'Do you know who wrote the code section, Mr Alliphant?'

Alliphant turned to his associate as if he knew every-thing. But he shook his head.

'I wrote it, Mr Alliphant,' Harry said loudly. 'Me. *Moi*. Yours truly. And if you knew anything about juvenile law in this state, you would know that I am the expert because I wrote the law. Now, what can you say about that?'

Slick slid down in his chair. He'd covered a thousand trials. He'd seen lawyers hammered by angry judges, and he knew their clients usually suffered.

'I contend it's unconstitutional, Your Honor,' Alliphant said gallantly.

'And the last thing I intend to do, Mr Alliphant, is to get into a long, hot-air debate with you about the First Amendment. If you don't like the law, then take it up on appeal and get it changed. I honestly don't care. But right now, while I'm missing lunch, I want your client to answer the question.' He turned back to Slick, who was waiting in terror. 'Now, Mr Moeller, who was your source?'

Grinder was about to vomit. He stuck his thumbs under

336

his belt and pressed against his stomach. By reputation, Slick was a man of his word. He always protected his sources.

'I cannot reveal my source,' Slick said in an effort at great drama, the martyr willing to face death. Grinder took a deep breath. Such sweet words.

Harry immediately motioned for the two deputies. 'I find you in contempt, Mr Moeller, and order you to jail.' The deputies stood beside Slick, who looked around wildly for help.

'Your Honor,' Alliphant said, standing without thinking. 'We object to this! You cannot –'

Harry ignored Alliphant. He spoke to the deputies. 'Take him to the city jail. No special treatment. No favors. I'll bring him back Monday for another try.'

They yanked Slick up and handcuffed him. 'Do something!' he yelled at Alliphant, who was saying, 'This is protected speech, Your Honor. You can't do this.'

'I'm doing it, Mr Alliphant,' Harry yelled. 'And if you don't sit down, you'll be in the same cell with your client.'

Alliphant dropped into his chair.

They dragged Slick to the door, and as they opened it, Harry had one final thing to say. 'Mr Moeller, if I read one word in your paper written by you while in jail, I'll let you sit there for a month before I bring you back. You understand.'

Slick couldn't speak. 'We'll appeal, Slick,' Alliphant promised as they shoved him through and closed the door. 'We'll appeal.'

Dianne Sway sat in a heavy wood chair, holding her oldest son and watching the sunlight filter through the dusty, broken blinds of Witness Room B. The tears were gone and words had failed them.

After five days and four nights of involuntary confinement in the psychiatric ward, she at first had been happy to leave it. But happiness these days came in tiny spurts, and she now longed to return to Ricky's bed. Now that she'd seen Mark, and held him and cried with him, she knew he was safe. Under the circumstances, that was all a mother could ask.

She didn't trust her instincts or judgment. Five days in a cave takes away any sense of reality. The endless series of shocks had left her drained and stunned. The drugs – pills to sleep and pills to wake up and pills to get through it – deadened the mind so that her life was a series of snapshots thrown on the table one at a time. The brain worked, but in slow motion.

'They want us to go to Portland,' she said, rubbing his arm.

'Reggie talked to you about it.'

'Yes, we had a long talk yesterday. There's a good place for Ricky out there, and we can start over.'

'Sounds good, but it scares me.'

'Scares me too, Mark. I don't want to live the next forty years looking over my shoulder. I read a story one time in some magazine about a Mafia informant who helped the FBI and they agreed to hide him. Just like they want us to do. I think it took two years before the Mafia found him and blew him up in his car.'

'I think I saw the movie.'

'I can't live like that, Mark.'

'Can we get another trailer?'

'I think so. I talked to Mr Tucker this morning, and he says he had the trailer covered with plenty of insurance. He said he had another one for us. And I still have my job. In fact, they delivered my paycheck to the hospital this morning.'

Mark smiled at the thought of returning to the trailer park and hanging out with the kids. He even missed school.

'These people are deadly, Mark.'

'I know. I've met them.'

She thought for a second, then asked, 'You what?'

'I guess it's something else I forgot to tell you.'

'I'd like to hear it.'

'It happened a couple of days ago at the hospital. I don't

338

know which day. They're all running together.' He took a deep breath. He told her about his encounter with the man and the switchblade and their family portrait. Normally, she, or any mother, would have been shocked. But for Dianne, it was just another event in this horrible week.

'Why didn't you tell me?' she asked.

'Because I didn't want to worry you.'

'You know, we might not be in this trouble if you'd told me everything up front.'

'Don't fuss at me, Mom. I can't take it.'

She couldn't take it either, so she dropped it. Reggie knocked on the door and it opened. 'We need to go,' she said. 'The judge is waiting.'

They followed her through the hall and around a corner. Two deputies trailed behind. 'Are you nervous?' Dianne whispered.

'No. It's no big deal, Mom.'

Harry was munching on the sandwich and flipping through the file when they entered the courtroom. Fink, Ord, and Baxter McLemore, the Juvenile Court prosecutor-of-the-day, were all seated together at their table, all quiet and subdued, all bored and waiting for what would undoubtedly be a quick appearance by the kid. Fink and Ord were captivated by the court reporter's legs and skirt. Her figure was obscene – tiny waist, healthy breasts, slender legs. She was the only redeeming element in this rinky-dink courtroom, and Fink had to admit to himself that he'd thought about her on the flight to New Orleans yesterday. And he'd thought about her all the way back to Memphis. She was not disappointing him. The skirt was at mid-thigh and inching upward.

Harry looked at Dianne and gave his best smile. His large teeth were perfect and his eyes were warm. 'Hello, Ms Sway,' he said sweetly. She nodded and tried to smile.

'It is a pleasure meeting you, and I'm sorry it has to be under these circumstances.'

'Thank you, Your Honor,' she said softly to the man who'd ordered her son to jail.

Harry looked at Fink with contempt. 'I trust everyone

has read this morning's *Memphis Press*. It has a fascinating story about our proceedings yesterday, and the man who wrote the story is now in jail. I intend to investigate this matter further, and I am confident I will find the leak.'

Grinder, by the door, was suddenly ill again.

'And when I find it, I intend to fix it with a contempt order. So, ladies and gentlemen, keep your mouths shut. Not a word to anyone.' He took the file. 'Now, Mr Fink, where's Mr Foltrigg?'

Sitting firmly in place, Fink answered, 'He's in New Orleans, Your Honor. I have a copy of the court order you requested.'

'Fine. I'll take your word for it. Madam Clerk, swear the witness.'

Madam Clerk threw her hand in the air, and barked at Mark, 'Raise your right hand.' Mark stood awkwardly, and was sworn.

'You can remain in your seat,' Harry said. Reggie was on his right, Dianne on the left.

'Mark, I'm going to ask you some questions, okay?'

'Yes sir.'

'Prior to his death, did Mr Clifford say anything to you about a Mr Barry Muldanno?'

'I'm not going to answer that.'

'Did Mr Clifford mention the name of Boyd Boyette?'

'I'm not going to answer that.'

'Did Mr Clifford say anything about the murder of Boyd Boyette?'

'I'm not going to answer that.'

'Did Mr Clifford say anything about the present location of the body of Boyd Boyette?'

'I'm not going to answer that.'

Harry paused and looked at his notes. Dianne had stopped breathing and was staring blankly at Mark. 'It's okay, Mom,' he whispered to her.

'Your Honor,' he said in a strong, confident voice. 'I want you to understand that I'm not answering for the same reasons I gave yesterday. I'm just scared, that's all.'

Harry nodded but gave no expression. He was neither angry nor pleased. 'Mr Bailiff, take Mark back to the witness room, and keep him there until we finish. He can talk to his mother before he's transported to the detention center.'

Grinder's knees were putty, but he managed to lead Mark from the courtroom.

Harry unzipped his robe. 'Let's go off the record. Madam Clerk, you and Ms Gregg can go to lunch.' It was not an offer, but a demand. Harry wanted fewer ears in the courtroom.

Ms Gregg swung her legs toward Fink, and his heart stopped. He and Ord watched with their mouths open as she stood, took her purse, and pranced from the courtroom.

'Get the FBI, Mr Fink,' Harry instructed.

McThune and a weary K. O. Lewis were fetched and took seats behind Ord. Lewis was a busy man with a thousand important items stacked on his desk in Washington, and he'd asked himself a hundred times in the past twenty-four hours why he'd come to Memphis. Of course, Director Voyles wanted him here, which clarified his priorities immensely.

'Mr Fink, you indicated before the hearing there is an urgent matter that I should know about.'

'Yes sir. Mr Lewis would like to address it.'

'Mr Lewis. Please be brief.'

'Yes, Your Honor. We've had Barry Muldanno under surveillance for several months, and yesterday we obtained by electronic means a conversation between Muldanno and Paul Gronke. It took place in a bar in the French Quarter, and I think you need to hear it.'

'You have the tape?'

'Yes sir.'

'Then let it roll.' Harry was suddenly unconcerned with time.

McThune quickly assembled a tape player and speaker on the desk in front of Fink, and Lewis inserted a micro-cassette. 'The first voice you'll hear is that of Muldanno,' he explained like a chemist preparing a demonstration. 'Then Gronke.'

The courtroom was still and quiet as the scratchy but very clear voices squawked from the speaker. The entire conversation was captured; the suggestion by Muldanno of hitting the kid, and Gronke's doubts about getting to him; the idea of hitting the kid's mother or brother, and Gronke's protests of killing innocent people; Muldanno's talk of killing his lawyer, and the laughter about it doing wonders for the legal profession; the boasting of Gronke about taking care of the trailer; and finally the plans to bug the lawyer's phones that night.

It was chilling. Fink and Ord had heard it ten times already, so they were noncommittal. Reggie closed her eyes when the taking of her life was so nonchalantly bantered about. Dianne was rigid with fear. Harry stared at the speaker as if he could see their faces, and when the tape was finished and Lewis punched the button, he simply said, 'Play it again.'

They listened to it the second time, and the shock began to wear off. Diane was trembling. Reggie held her arm and tried to be brave, but the easy talk of killing the kid's lawyer made her blood run cold. Dianne's skin broke out in goose pimples, and her eyes began to water. She thought of Ricky, who at this moment was being watched by Greenway and a nurse, and prayed he was safe.

'I've heard enough,' Harry said when the tape stopped. Lewis took his seat, and they waited for His Honor to give direction. He wiped his eyes with a handkerchief, then took a long drink of ice tea. He smiled at Dianne. 'Now, Ms Sway, do you understand why we've placed Mark in the detention center?'

'I think so.'

'Two reasons. The first is that he refused to answer my questions, but at the moment, that's not nearly as important as the second. He's in great danger, as you've just heard. What would you like for me to do next?'

It was an unfair question posed to a scared, deeply

troubled, and irrational person, and she didn't like him asking it. She just shook her head. 'I don't know,' she mumbled.

Harry spoke slowly, and there was no doubt he knew exactly what should be done next. 'Reggie has told me that she's discussed the witness protection program with you. Tell me what you think.'

Dianne raised her head and bit her lip. She thought for a few seconds and tried to focus on the tape recorder. 'I do not want those people,' she said deliberately, nodding at the recorder, 'following me and my children for the rest of our lives. And I'm afraid that will happen if Mark gives you what you want.'

'You'll have the protection of the FBI and every necessary agency of the US Government.'

'But no one can completely guarantee our safety. These are my children, Your Honor, and I'm a single parent. There's no one else. If I make a mistake, I could lose, well, I can't even imagine it.'

'I think you'll be safe, Ms Sway. There are thousands of government witnesses now being protected.'

'But some have been found, haven't they?'

It was a quiet question that hit hard. Neither McThune nor Lewis could deny the fact that witnesses had been lost. There was a long silence.

'Well, Ms Sway,' Harry finally said with a great deal of compassion, 'what's the alternative?'

'Why can't you arrest these people? Lock them up somewhere. I mean, it looks as if they're just roaming free terrorizing me and my family, and also Reggie here. What're the damned cops doing?'

'It's my understanding, Ms Sway, that one arrest was made last night. The police here are looking for the two men who burned your trailer, two thugs from New Orleans named Bono and Pirini, but they haven't found them. Is that correct, Mr Lewis?'

'Yes sir. We think they're still in the city. And I might add, Your Honor, that the US Attorney in New Orleans

343

intends to indict Muldanno and Gronke early next week on charges of obstruction of justice. So they'll be in custody very soon.'

'But this is the Mafia, isn't it?' Dianne asked.

Every idiot who could read the newspapers knew it was the Mafia. It was a Mafia killing by a Mafia gunman whose family had been Mafia hoods in New Orleans for four decades. Her question was so simple, yet it implied the obvious: The Mafia is an invisible army with plenty of soldiers.

Lewis did not wish to answer the question, so he waited for His Honor, who likewise hoped it would simply go away. There was a long, awkward silence.

Dianne cleared her throat and spoke in a much stronger voice. 'Your Honor, when you guys can show me a way to completely protect my children, then I'll help you. But not until then.'

'So you want him to stay in jail,' Fink blurted.

She turned and glared at Fink, less than ten feet away. 'Sir, I'd rather have him in a detention center than in a grave.'

Fink slumped in his chair and stared at the floor. Seconds ticked away. Harry looked at his watch, and zipped his robe. 'I suggest we meet again Monday at noon. Let's take things one day at a time.'

THIRTY

Paul Gronke finished his unexpected trip to Minneapolis as the Northwest 727 lifted off the runway and started for Atlanta. From Atlanta, he hoped to catch a direct flight to New Orleans, and once home he had no plans to leave for a long time. Maybe years. Regardless of his friendship with Muldanno, Gronke was tired of this mess. He could break a thumb or a leg when necessary, and he could huff and puff and scare almost anybody. But he did not particularly enjoy stalking little kids and waving switchblades at them. He made a nice living off his clubs and beer joints, and if The Blade needed help, he'd just have to lean on his family. Gronke was not family. He was not Mafia. And he was not going to kill anyone for Barry Muldanno.

He'd made two phone calls this morning as soon as his flight arrived at the Memphis airport. The first call spooked him because no one answered. He then dialled a backup number for a recorded message, and again there was no answer. He walked quickly to the Northwest ticket counter and paid cash for a one-way ticket to Minneapolis. Then he found the Delta counter and paid cash for a one-way ticket to Dallas-Fort Worth. Then he bought a ticket to Chicago, on United. He roamed the concourses for an hour, watching his back and seeing nothing, and at the last second hopped on Northwest.

Bono and Pirini had strict instructions. The two phone calls meant one of two things: either the cops had them, or they were forced to pull up stakes and haul ass. Neither thought was comforting.

The flight attendant brought two beers. It was a few minutes after one, too early to start drinking, but he was edgy, and what the hell. It was 5 p.m. somewhere.

Muldanno would flip out and start throwing things. He'd run to his uncle and borrow some more thugs. They'd descend upon Memphis and start hurting people. Finesse was not Barry's long suit.

Their friendship had started in high school, in the tenth grade, their last year of formal education before they dropped out and began hustling on the streets of New Orleans. Barry's route to crime was preordained by family. Gronke's was a bit more complicated. Their first venture had been a fencing operation that had been wildly successful. The profits, however, were siphoned off by Barry and sent to the family. They peddled some drugs, ran some numbers, managed a whorehouse, all cash-rich ventures. But Gronke saw little of the cash. After ten years of this lopsided partnership, he told Barry he wanted a place of his own. Barry helped him buy a topless bar, then a porno house. Gronke made money and was able to keep it. At about this point in their careers, Barry started his killing, and Gronke established more distance between them.

But they remained friends. A month or so after Boyette disappeared, the two of them spent a long weekend at Johnny Sulari's house in Acapulco with a couple of strippers. After the girls had passed out one night, they went for a long walk on the beach. Barry was drinking tequila and talking more than usual. His name had just surfaced as a suspect. He bragged to his friend about the killing.

The landfill in Lafourche Parish was worth millions to the Sulari family. Johnny's scheme was to eventually route most of the garbage from New Orleans to it. Senator Boyette had been an unexpected enemy. His antics had attracted lots of negative publicity for the dump, and the more ink Boyette received the crazier he'd become. He'd launched federal investigations. He'd called in dozens of EPA bureaucrats who'd prepared massive volumes of studies, most of which condemned the landfill. In Washington, he'd hounded the Justice Department until it initiated its own investigation into the allegations of mob involvement. Senator Boyette became the biggest obstacle to Johnny's gold mine.

The decision had been made to hit Boyette.

Sipping from a bottle of Cuervo Gold, Barry laughed about the killing. He stalked Boyette for six months, and was pleasantly surprised to learn that the Senator, who was divorced, had an affinity for young women. Cheap young women, the kind he could find in a bordello and buy for fifty bucks. His favorite place was a seedy roadhouse halfway between New Orleans and Houma, the site of the landfill. It was in oil country, and frequented by offshore roustabouts and the cute little whores they attracted. Evidently, the Senator knew the owner and had a special arrangement. He always parked behind a garbage dumpster, away from the gravel lot crowded with monster pickups and Harleys. He always used the rear entrance by the kitchen.

The Senator's trips to Houma became more frequent. He was raising hell in town meetings and holding press conferences every week. And he enjoyed the drives back to New Orleans with his little quickies at the roadhouse.

The hit was easy, Barry said as they sat on the beach with foamy saltwater rushing around them. He trailed Boyette for twenty miles after a rowdy landfill meeting in Houma, and waited patiently in the darkness behind the roadhouse. When Boyette emerged after his little liaison, he hit him in the head with a nightstick and quickly threw him in the backseat. He stopped a few miles down the road and pumped four bullets in his head. The body was wrapped in garbage bags and placed in the trunk.

Imagine that, Barry had marveled, a US Senator snatched from the darkness of a run-down bordello. He'd served for twenty-one years, chaired powerful committees, eaten at the White House, trotted around the globe searching for ways to spend taxpayers' money, had eighteen assistants and gofers working for him, and, bam! Just like that, got caught with his pants down. Barry thought it was hilarious. One of his easiest jobs, he said, as if there'd been hundreds.

A state trooper had stopped Barry for speeding ten miles outside of New Orleans. Imagine that, he said, chatting with a cop with a warm body in the trunk. He talked football and avoided a ticket. But then he panicked, and decided to hide the body in a different place. Gronke was tempted to ask where, but thought better of it.

The case against him was shaky. The trooper's records placed Barry in the vicinity at the time of the disappearance. But with no body, there was no proof of the time of death. One of the prostitutes saw a man who resembled Barry in the shadows of the parking lot while the Senator was being entertained. She was now under government protection, but not expected to make a good witness. Barry's car had been cleaned and sanitized. No blood samples, no fibers or hair. The star of the government's case was a Mafia informant, a man who'd spent twenty of his forty-two years in jail, and who was not expected to live to testify. A .22 caliber Ruger had been seized from the apartment of one of Barry's girlfriends, but, again, with no corpse it was impossible to determine the cause of death. Barry's fingerprints were on the gun. It was a gift, said the girlfriend.

Juries are hesitant to convict without first knowing for certain that the victim is indeed dead. And Boyette was such an eccentric character that rumors and gossip had produced all sorts of wild speculation about his disappearance. One published report detailed his recent history of psychiatric problems, and thus had given rise to a popular theory that he'd gone nuts and run off with a teenage hooker. He had gambling debts. He drank too much. His ex-wife had sued him for fraud in the divorce. And on and on.

Boyette had plenty of reasons to disappear.

And now, an eleven-year-old kid in Memphis knew where he was buried. Gronke opened the second beer.

★

348

Doreen held Mark's arm and walked him to his room. His steps were measured and he stared at the floor in front of them as if he'd just witnessed a car bomb in a crowded marketplace.

'Are you okay, baby?' she asked, the wrinkles around her eyes bunched together with terrible concern.

He nodded and plodded along. She quickly unlocked the door, and placed him on the bottom bunk.

'Lie right here, sweetheart,' she said, pulling back the covers and swinging his legs on to the bed. She knelt beside him and searched his eyes for answers. 'Are you sure you're okay?'

He nodded but could say nothing.

'Do you want me to call a doctor?'

'No,' he managed to say in a hollow voice. 'I'm fine.'

'I think I'll get a doctor,' she said. He grabbed her arm and squeezed tightly.

'I just need some rest,' he mumbled. 'That's all.'

She unlocked the door with the key and slowly eased out, her eyes never leaving Mark. When the door closed and clicked, he swung his feet to the floor.

At three Friday afternoon, Harry Roosevelt's legendary patience was gone. His weekend would be spent in the Ozarks, fishing with his two sons, and as he sat on the bench and looked at the courtroom still crowded with deadbeat dads awaiting sentencing for nonpayment, his mind kept wandering to thoughts of long sleepy mornings and cool mountain streams. At least two dozen men filled the pews of the main courtroom, and most had either current wives or current girlfriends sitting anxiously at their elbows. A few had brought their lawyers, though there was no legal relief available at this moment. All of them would soon be serving weekend sentences at the Shelby Country Penal Farm for failing to pay child support.

Harry wanted to adjourn by four, but it looked doubtful. His two sons waited in the back row. Outside, the Jeep was packed, and when the gavel finally rapped for the last time, they would rush His Honor from the building and whisk him away to the Buffalo River. That was the plan anyway. They were bored, but they had been here before many times.

In spite of the chaos in the front of the courtroom – clerks hauling bundles of files in and out, lawyers whispering as they waited, deputies standing by, defenders being shuffled to the bench then out the door – Harry's assembly line moved with determined efficiency. He glared at each deadbeat, scolded a bit, sometimes a quick lecture, then he signed an order and moved on to the next one.

Reggie eased into the courtroom and made her way to the clerk seated next to the bench. They whispered for a minute with Reggie pointing to a document she'd brought with her. She laughed at something that was probably not that funny, but Harry heard her and motioned her to the bench.

'Something wrong?' he asked with his hand over the microphone.

'No. Mark's fine, I guess. I need a quick favor. It's another case.'

Harry smiled and turned off the mike. Typical Reggie. Her cases were always the most important and needed immediate attention. 'What is it?' he asked.

The clerk handed Harry the file while Reggie handed him an order. 'It's another snatch and run by the Welfare Department,' she said in a low voice. No one was listening. No one cared.

'Who's the kid?' he asked, flipping through the file.

'Ronald Allan Thomas the Third. Also known as Trip Thomas. He was taken into custody last night by Welfare and placed in a foster home. His mother hired me an hour ago.'

'Says here he's been abandoned and neglected.'

'Not true, Harry. It's a long story, but I assure you this kid has good parents and a clean home.'

'And you want the kid released?'

'Immediately. I'll pick him up myself, and take him home to Momma Love if I have to.'

350

'And feed him lasagne.'

'Of course.'

Harry scanned the order and signed his name at the bottom. 'I'll have to trust you, Reggie.'

'You always do. I saw Damon and Al back there. They look rather bored.'

Harry handed the order to the clerk who stamped it. 'So am I. When I get this riffraff cleared from my courtroom, we're going fishing.'

'Good luck. I'll see you Monday.'

'Have a nice weekend, Reggie. You'll check on Mark, won't you?'

'Of course.'

'Try and talk some sense into his mother. The more I think about it, the more I'm convinced these people must cooperate with the Feds and enter the witness program. Hell, they have nothing to lose by starting over. Convince her they'll be protected.'

'I'll try. I'll spend some time with her this weekend. Maybe we can wrap it up Monday.'

'I'll see you then.'

Reggie winked at him, and backed away from the bench. The clerk handed her a copy of the order, and she left the courtroom.

THIRTY-ONE

Thomas Fink, fresh from another exciting flight from Memphis, entered Foltrigg's office at four-thirty Friday afternoon. Wally Boxx sat like a faithful lapdog on the sofa, writing what Fink presumed to be another speech for their boss, or perhaps a press release for upcoming indictments. Roy's shoeless feet were on his desk and the phone was cradled on his shoulder. He was listening with his eyes closed. The day had been a disaster. Lamond had embarrassed him in a crowded courtroom. Roosevelt had failed to make the kid talk. He'd had it with judges.

Fink removed his jacket and sat down. Foltrigg ended his phone chat and hung up. 'Where are the grand jury subpoenas?' he asked.

'I hand-delivered them to the US marshal in Memphis, and gave him strict instructions not to serve them until he heard from you.'

Boxx left the sofa and sat next to Fink. It would be a shame if he were excluded from a conversation.

Roy rubbed his eyes and ran his fingers through his hair. Frustrating, very frustrating. 'So what's the kid gonna do, Thomas? You were there. You saw the kid's mother. You heard her voice. What's gonna happen?'

'I don't know. It's obvious the kid has no plans to talk anytime soon. He and his mother are terrified. They've watched too much television, seen too many Mafia informants blown to bits. She's convinced they won't be safe in witness protection. She's really scared. The woman's been through hell this week.'

'That's real touching,' Boxx mumbled.

'I have no choice but to use the subpoenas,' Foltrigg said gravely, pretending to be troubled by this thought. 'They leave me no choice. We were fair and reasonable. We asked the youth court in Memphis to help us with the kid, and it simply has not worked. It's time we got these people down here, on our turf, in our courtroom, in front of our people, and made them talk. Don't you agree, Thomas?'

Fink was not in full agreemnt. 'Jurisdiction worries me. The kid is under the jurisdiction of the Juvenile Court up there, and I'm not sure what'll happen when he gets the subpoena.'

Roy was smiling. 'That's right, but the court is closed for the weekend. We've done some research, and I think federal law supersedes state law on this one, don't you, Wally?'

'I think so. Yes,' said Wally.

'And I've talked to the marshal's office here. I've told them I want the boys in Memphis to pick the kid up tomorrow and bring him here so he can face the grand jury Monday. I don't think the locals in Memphis will interfere with the US marshal's office. We've made arrangements to house him here in the Juvenile Wing at city jail. Should be a piece of cake.'

'What about the lawyer?' asked Fink. 'You can't make her testify. If she knows anything, she learned it in the course of her representation of the kid. It's privileged.'

'Pure harassment,' Foltrigg admitted with a smile. 'She and the kid will be scared to death on Monday. We'll be calling the shots, Thomas.'

'Speaking of Monday. Judge Roosevelt wants us in his courtroom at noon.'

Roy and Wally had a good laugh at this. 'He'll be a lonely judge, won't he,' Foltrigg said with a chuckle. 'You, me, the kid, and the kid's lawyer will all be down here. What a fool.'

Fink did not join their laughter.

*

At five, Doreen knocked on the door, and rattled keys until it opened. Mark was on the floor playing checkers against himself, and immediately became a zombie. He sat on his feet, and stared at the checkerboard as if in a trance.

'Are you okay, Mark?'

Mark didn't answer.

'Mark, honey, I'm really worried about you. I think I'll call the doctor. You might be going into shock, just like your little brother.'

He shook his head slowly, and looked at her with mournful eyes. 'No, I'm okay. I just need some rest.'

. 'Could you eat something?'

'Maybe some pizza.'

'Sure, baby. I'll get one ordered. Look, honey, I get off duty in five minutes, but I'll tell Telda to watch you real close, okay. Will you be all right till I get back in the morning?'

'Maybe,' he moaned.

'Poor child. You got no business in here.'

'I'll make it.'

Telda was much less concerned than Doreen. She checked on Mark twice. On her third visit to his room, around eight o'clock, she brought visitors. She knocked and opened the door slowly, and Mark was about to do his trance routine when he saw the two large men in suits.

'Mark, these men are US marshals,' Telda said nervously. Mark stood near the toilet. The room was suddenly tiny.

'Hi, Mark,' said the first one. 'I'm Vern Duboski, deputy US marshal.' His words were crisp and precise. A Yankee. But that was all Mark noticed. He was holding some papers.

'You are Mark Sway?'

He nodded, unable to speak.

'Don't be afraid, Mark. We just have to give you these papers.'

354

He looked at Telda for help, but she was clueless. 'What are they?' he asked nervously.

'It's a grand jury subpoena, and it means that you have to appear before a federal grand jury on Monday in New Orleans. Now, don't worry, we're gonna come get you tomorrow afternoon and drive you down.'

A nervous pain shot through his stomach and he was weak. His mouth was dry. 'Why?' he asked.

'We can't answer that, Mark. It's none of our business, really. We're just following orders.'

Mark stared at the papers Vern was waving. New Orleans! 'Have you told my mother?'

'Well, you see, Mark, we're required to give her a copy of these same papers. We'll explain everything to her, and we'll tell her you'll be fine. In fact, she can go with you if she wants.'

'She can't go with me. She can't leave Ricky.'

The marshals looked at each other. 'Well, anyway, we'll explain everything to her.'

'I have a lawyer, you know. Have you told her?'

'No. We're not required to notify the attorneys, but you're welcome to call her if you like.'

'Does he have access to a telephone?' the second one asked Telda.

'Only if I bring him one,' she said.

'You can wait thirty minutes, can't you?'

'If you say so,' Telda said.

'So, Mark, in about thirty minutes you can call your lawyer.' Duboski paused and looked at his sidekick. 'Well, good luck to you, Mark. Sorry if we scared you.'

They left him standing near the toilet, leaning on the wall for support, more confused than ever, scared to death. And angry. The system was rotten. He was sick of laws and lawyers and courts, of cops and agents and marshals, of reporters and judges and jailers. Dammit!

He yanked a paper towel from the wall and wiped his eyes, then sat on the toilet.

He swore to the walls that he would not go to New Orleans.

Two other deputy marshals would serve Dianne, and two
more would serve Ms Reggie Love at home, and all this
serving of subpoenas was carefully coordinated to happen at
roughly the same time. In reality, one deputy marshal, or
one unemployed concrete worker for that matter, could
have served all three subpoenas at a leisurely pace and
completed the job in an hour. But it was more fun to use six
men in three cars with radios and telephones and guns, and
to strike quickly under cover of darkness like a Special
Forces assault unit.

They knocked on Momma Love's kitchen door, and
waited until the porch light came on and she appeared
behind the screen. She instantly knew they were trouble.
During the nightmare of Reggie's divorce and commitments and legal warfare with Joe Cardoni, there had been
several deputies and men in dark suits standing at her
doorway at odd hours. These guys always brought trouble.

'Can I help you?' she asked with a forced smile.

'Yes ma'am. We're looking for one Reggie Love.'

They even talked like cops. 'And who are you?' she asked.

'I'm Mike Hedley, and this is Terry Flagg. We're US
marshals.'

'US marshals, or deputy US marshals? Let me see
some ID.'

This shocked them, and in perfect synchronization they
reached into their pockets for their badges. 'We're deputy
US marshals, ma'am.'

'That's not what you said,' she said, examining the
badges held up to the screen door.

Reggie was sipping coffee on the tiny balcony of her
apartment when she heard the car doors slam. She was now
peeking around the corner and looking down at the two
men standing under the light. She could hear the voices,
but could not understand what they were saying.

'Sorry, ma'am,' Hedley said.

'Why do you want one Reggie Love?' Momma Love
asked with a suspicious frown.

'Does she live here?'

'Maybe, maybe not. What do you want?'

Hedley and Flagg looked at each other. 'We're supposed to serve her with a subpoena.'

'A subpoena for what?'

'May I ask who you are?' Flagg said.

'I'm her mother. Now what's the subpoena for?'

'It's a grand jury subpoena. She's supposed to appear before a grand jury in New Orleans on Monday. We can just leave it with you, if you like.'

'I'm not accepting service of it,' she said, as if she fought with process servers every week. 'You have to actually serve her, if I'm not mistaken.'

'Where is she?'

'She doesn't live here.'

This irritated them. 'That's her car,' Hedley said, nodding at Reggie's Mazda.

'She doesn't live here,' Momma Love repeated.

'Okay, but is she here now?'

'No.'

'Do you know where she is?'

'Have you tried her office? She works all the time.'

'But why is her car here?'

'Sometimes she rides with Clint, her secretary. They may be having dinner, or something.'

They gave each other frustrated stares. 'I think she's here,' Hedley said, suddenly aggressive.

'You're not paid to think, son. You're paid to serve those damned papers, and I'm telling you she's not here.' Momma Love raised her voice when she said this, and Reggie heard it.

'Can we search the house?' Flagg asked.

'If you have a warrant, you can search the house. If you don't have a warrant, it's time to get off my property.'

They both took a step back, and stopped. 'I hope you're not obstructing the service of a federal subpoena,' Hedley said gravely. It was supposed to have an ominous, dire ring to it, but Hedley failed miserably.

'And I hope you're not trying to threaten an old woman.' Her hands were on her hips and she was ready for combat.

They surrendered and backed away. 'We'll be back,' Hedley promised as he opened his car door.

'I'll be here,' she shouted angrily, opening the front door. She stood on the small porch and watched as they backed into the street. She waited for five minutes, and when she was certain they were gone, she went to Reggie's apartment over the garage.

Dianne took the subpoena from the polite and apologetic gentleman without comment. She read it by the light of the dim lamp next to Ricky's bed. It contained no instructions, just a command for Mark to appear before the grand jury at 10 a.m at the address below. There was no hint of how he was to get there; no clue as to when he might return; no warning of what could happen if he failed to comply or failed to talk.

She called Reggie, but there was no answer.

Though Clint's apartment was only fifteen minutes away, the drive took almost an hour. She zigzagged through midtown, then raced around the interstate going nowhere in particular, and when she was certain she was not being followed, she parked on a street crowded with empty cars. She walked four blocks to his apartment.

His nine o'clock date had been abruptly cancelled, and it was a date with a lot of promise. 'I'm sorry,' Reggie said as he opened the door and she eased through it.

'That's okay. Are you all right?' He took her bag and waved at the sofa. 'Sit down.'

Reggie was no stranger to the apartment. She found a diet Coke in the refrigerator and sat on a bar stool. 'It was the US marshal's office with a grand jury subpoena. Ten o'clock Monday morning in New Orleans.'

'But they didn't serve you?'

'No. Momma Love ran them off.'

'Then you're off the hook.'

358

'Yeah, unless they find me. There's no law against dodging subpoenas. I need to call Dianne.'

Clint handed her a phone, and she punched the numbers from memory. 'Relax, Reggie,' he said, and kissed her gently on the cheek. He picked up stray magazines and turned on the stereo. Dianne was on the phone, and Reggie managed three words before she was forced to listen. Subpoenas were everywhere. One for Reggie, one for Dianne, and one for Mark. Reggie tried to calm her. Dianne had called the detention center, but couldn't get through to Mark. Phones were unavailable at this hour, she'd been told. They talked for five minutes. Reggie, badly shaken herself, tried to convince Dianne everything was fine. She, Reggie, was in control. She promised to call her in the morning, then hung up.

'They can't take Mark,' Clint said. 'He's under the jurisdiction of our Juvenile Court.'

'I need to talk to Harry. But he's out of town.'

'Where is he?'

'Fishing somewhere with his sons.'

'This is more important than fishing, Reggie. Let's find him. He can stop it, can't he?'

She was thinking of a hundred things at once. 'This is pretty slick, Clint. Think about it. Foltrigg waits until late Friday to serve subpoenas for Monday morning.'

'How can he do this?'

'It's easy. He just did it. In a criminal case like this, a federal grand jury can subpoena any witness from anywhere, regardless of time and distance. And the witness must appear unless he or she can first quash the subpoena.'

'How do you quash one?'

'You file a motion in federal court to void the subpoena.'

'Lemme guess, federal court in New Orleans?'

'That's right. We're forced to find the trial judge early Monday morning in New Orleans and beg him to allow an emergency hearing to quash the subpoena.'

'It won't work, Reggie.'

'Of course it won't work. That's the way Foltrigg

359

planned it.' She gulped the diet Coke. 'Do you have any coffee?'

'Sure.' He began opening drawers.

Reggie was thinking out loud. 'If I can dodge the subpoena until Monday, Foltrigg will be forced to issue another one. Then maybe I'll have time to quash. The problem is Mark. They're not after me, because they know they can't force me to talk.'

'Do you know where the damned body is, Reggie?'

'No.'

'Does Mark?'

'Yes.'

He froze for a moment, then ran water in the pot.

'We have to figure out a way to keep Mark here, Clint. We can't allow him to go to New Orleans.'

'Call Harry.'

'Harry's fishing in the mountains.'

'Then call Harry's wife. Find out where he's fishing in the mountains. I'll go get him if necessary.'

'You're right.' She grabbed the phone and started calling.

THIRTY-TWO

Final room check at the Juvenile Detention Center was 10 p.m., when they made sure all lights and televisions were off. Mark heard Telda rattling keys and giving commands across the hall. His shirt was soaked, unbuttoned, and sweat ran to his navel and puddled around the zipper of his jeans. The television was off. His breathing was heavy. His thick hair was watery and rows of sweat ran to his eyebrows and dripped from the tip of his nose. She was next door. His face was crimson and hot.

Telda knocked, then unlocked Mark's door. The light was on and this immediately irritated her. She took a step inside, glanced at the bunks, but he wasn't there.

Then she saw his feet beside the toilet. He was curled tightly with his knees on his chest, motionless except for rapid, heavy breathing.

His eyes were closed, and his left thumb was in his mouth.

'Mark!' she shouted, suddenly terrified. 'Mark! Oh my god!' She ran from the room to get help, and was back within seconds with Denny, her partner, who took a quick look.

'Doreen was worried about this,' Denny said, touching the sweat on Mark's stomach. 'Damn, he's soaking wet.'

Telda was pinching his wrist. 'His pulse is crazy. Look at him breathe. Call an ambulance!'

'The poor kid's in shock, isn't he?'

'Go call an ambulance!'

Denny lumbered from the room and the floor shook. Telda picked Mark up and carefully placed him on the bottom bunk, where he curled again and brought his knees to his chest. The thumb never left his mouth. Denny was back with a clipboard. 'This must be Doreen's handwriting. Says here to check on him every half hour, and if there's any doubt, to rush him to St Peter's and call Dr Greenway.'

'This is all my fault,' Telda said. 'I shouldn't have allowed those damned marshals in here. Scared the poor boy to death.'

Denny knelt beside her, and with a thick thumb peeled back the right eyelid. 'Damn! His eyes have rolled back. This kid's in trouble,' he said with all the gravity of a brain surgeon.

'Get a washcloth over here,' Telda said, and Denny did as told. 'Doreen was telling me this is what happened to his little brother. They saw that shooting on Monday, both of them, and the little one's been in shock ever since.' Denny handed her the cloth and she wiped Mark's forehead.

'Damn, his heart's gonna explode,' Denny said, on his knees again next to Telda. 'He's breathing like crazy.'

'Poor kid. I should've run those marshals off,' Telda said.

'I would have. They got no right coming on this floor.' He jabbed another thumb into the left eye, and Mark groaned and twitched. Then he started the moaning, just like Ricky, and this scared them even more. A low, dull, pitchless sound from deep in the throat. He sucked hard on the thumb.

A paramedic from the main jail three floors down ran into the room, followed by another jailer. 'What's up?' he asked as Telda and Denny moved.

'I think it's called traumatic shock or stress or something,' Telda said. 'He's been acting strange all day, then about an hour ago two US marshals were here to give him a subpoena.' The paramedic was not listening. He gripped a wrist and found the pulse. Telda rattled on. 'They scared

362

him to death, and I think it sent him into shock. I should've watched him after that, but I got busy.'

'I would've run those damned marshals off,' Denny said. They stood side by side behind the paramedic.

'This is what happened to his little brother, you know, the one who's been in the newspaper all week. The shooting and all.'

'He's gotta go,' the paramedic said, standing, frowning, and talking into his radio. 'Hurry up with the stretcher to the fourth floor,' he barked into it. 'Got a kid in bad shape.'

Denny stuck the clipboard in front of the paramedic. 'Says here to take him to St Peter's. Dr Greenway.'

'That's where his brother is,' Telda added. 'Doreen told me all about it. She was worried this might happen. Said she almost sent for an ambulance this afternoon. Said he's been slipping away all day. I should've been more careful.'

The stretcher arrived with two more paramedics. Mark was quickly laid on it and covered with a blanket. A strap was placed across his thighs and another on his chest. His eyes never opened, but he managed to keep the thumb in his mouth.

And he managed to emit the painful, monotonous groan that frightened the paramedics and sped the stretcher along. It rolled quickly past the front station, and into an elevator.

'You ever seen this before?' one paramedic mumbled under his breath to the other.

'Not that I recall.'

'He's burning up.'

'The skin is normally cool and clammy with shock. I've never seen this.'

'Yeah. Maybe traumatic shock is different. Check out that thumb.'

'Is this the kid the mob's after?'

'Yeah. Front page today and yesterday.'

'I guess he's gone over the edge.'

The elevator stopped, and they pushed the stretcher hurriedly through a series of short hallways, all busy and filled with the usual Friday night madness of city jail. A set of double doors flew open, and they were at the ambulance.

The ride to St Peter's took less than ten minutes, half as long as the wait once they arrived. Three other ambulances were in the process of depositing their occupants. St Peter's received the vast majority of Memphis knife wounds, gunshot victims, beaten wives, and mangled bodies from weekend car wrecks. The pace was hectic twenty-four hours a day, but from sunset Friday until late Sunday, the place was in chaos.

They rolled him through the bay and on to the white-tiled floors where the stretcher stopped and the paramedics waited and filled out forms. A small army of nurses and doctors scrambled around a new patient and all yelled at the same time. People ran in every direction. A half dozen cops milled about. Three more stretchers were parked haphazardly in the wide hallway.

A nurse ventured by, stopped for a second, and asked the paramedics, 'What is it?' One of them handed her a form.

'So he's not bleeding,' she said, as if nothing mattered except flowing blood.

'No. Looks like stress or shock or something. Runs in the family.'

'He can wait. Roll him to Intake. I'll be back in a minute.' And she was off.

They wove the stretcher through heavy traffic, and stopped in a small room off the main hallway. The forms were presented to another nurse, who scribbled something without looking at Mark. 'Where's Dr Greenway?' she asked the paramedics.

They looked at each other, and shrugged at the nurse.

'You haven't called him?' she asked.

'Well, no.'

'Well, no,' she repeated to herself and rolled her eyes. What a couple of dumbasses. 'Look, this is a war zone, okay. We're talking blood and guts. We've lost two people in that hallway right there in the past thirty minutes. Psychiatric emergencies do not get top priority around here.'

364

'You want us to shoot him?' one of them said, nodding at Mark, and this really pissed her off.

'No. I want you to leave. I'll take care of him, but you guys just get the hell out of here.'

'You signed the forms, lady. He's all yours.' They smiled at her, and headed for the door.

'Is there a policeman with him?' she asked.

'Nope. He's just a juvenile.' They were gone.

Mark managed to roll on to his left side and bring his knees to his chest. The straps were not tight. His eyes opened slightly. A black man was lying across three chairs in one corner of the room. An empty stretcher with blood on the sheets was by a green door next to a water fountain. The nurse answered the phone, said a few words, and left the room. Mark quickly unhooked the straps and jumped to the floor. There was no crime in walking around. He was a nut case now, so what if she caught him on his feet.

The forms she'd been holding were on the counter. He grabbed them, and pushed the stretcher through the green door, which led to a cramped corridor with small rooms on both sides. He abandoned the stretcher and threw the forms in a garbage can. The exit signs led to a door with a window in it. It opened into the madhouse of Admissions.

Mark smiled to himself. He'd been here before. He watched the chaos through the window and picked the spot where he and Hardy had stood after Greenway and Dianne disappeared with Ricky. He eased through the door, and casually made his way through the snarled throng of sick and wounded trying anxiously to get admitted. Running and darting might attract attention, so he played it cool. He rode his favorite escalator to the basement, and found an empty wheelchair by the stairs. It was adult-size, but he worked the wheels and rolled himself past the cafeteria to the morgue.

Clint had fallen asleep on the sofa. Letterman was almost over when the phone rang. Reggie grabbed it. 'Hello.'

'Hi, Reggie. It's me, Mark.'

365

'Mark! How are you, dear?'

'Doing great, Reggie. Just wonderful.'

'How'd you find me?' she asked, turning off the TV.

'I called Momma Love and woke her. She gave me this number. It's Clint's place, right?'

'Right. How'd you get to a phone? It's awful late.'

'Well, I'm not in jail anymore.'

She stood and walked to the snack bar. 'Where are you, dear?'

'At the hospital. St Peter's.'

'I see. And how'd you get there?'

'They brought me in an ambulance.'

'Are you okay?'

'Great.'

'Why'd they take you in an ambulance?'

'I had an attack of post-traumatic stress syndrome, and they rushed me over.'

'Should I come see you?'

'Maybe. What's this grand jury stuff?'

'Nothing but an attempt to scare you into talking.'

'Well, it worked. I'm more scared than ever.'

'You sound fine.'

'Nervous energy, Reggie. I'm scared to death.'

'I mean, you don't sound like you're in shock or anything.'

'I recovered real quick. I faked them out, Reggie, okay? I jogged in my little cell for half an hour, and when they found me I was soaking wet and in bad shape, as they say.'

Clint sat up on the sofa and listened intently.

'Have you seen a doctor?' she asked, frowning at Clint.

'Not exactly.'

'What does that mean?'

'It means I walked out of the emergency room. It means I've escaped, Reggie. It was so easy.'

'Oh my god!'

'Relax. I'm fine. I'm not going back to jail, Reggie. And I'm not going to see the grand jury in New Orleans. They'll just lock me up down there, won't they?'

366

'Listen, Mark, you can't do this. You can't escape. You must –'

'I've already escaped, Reggie. And you know something?'

'What?'

'I doubt if anyone knows it yet. This place is so crazy, I doubt if they've missed me yet.'

'What about the cops?'

'What cops?'

'Didn't a cop go with you to the hospital?'

'No. I'm just a kid, Reggie. I had two huge paramedics, but I'm just a little kid and at the same time I was in a coma, sucking my thumb, moaning and groaning, just like Ricky. You'd have been proud. It was like something out of a movie. Once I got here, they turned their backs, and just like that, I walked away.'

'You can't do this, Mark.'

'It's done, okay? And I'm not going back.'

'What about your mother?'

'Oh, I talked to her about an hour ago, by phone of course. She freaked out, but I convinced her I was fine. She didn't like it, told me to come to Ricky's room. We had a big fight over the phone, but she settled down. I think she's on pills again.'

'But you're at the hospital?'

'That's right.'

'Where? In which room?'

'Are you still my lawyer?'

'Of course I'm your lawyer.'

'Good. So if I tell you something, you can't repeat it, right?'

'Right.'

'Are you my friend, Reggie?'

'Of course I'm your friend.'

'That's good, because right now you're the only friend I have. Will you help me, Reggie? I'm really scared.'

'I'll do anything, Mark. Where are you?'

'In the morgue. There's a little office in the corner, and

367

I'm hiding under the desk. The lights are off. If I hang up real quick, you'll know somebody walked in. They've brought in two bodies while I've been here, but so far no one's come to the office.'

'The morgue?'

Clint bolted to his feet and stood beside her.

'Yeah. I've been here before. I know this place pretty well, remember.'

'Sure.'

'Who's in the morgue?' Clint whispered. She frowned at him and shook her head.

'Mom said they have a subpoena for you too, Reggie. Is this true?'

'Yes, but they haven't served me. That's why I'm here at Clint's. If they don't hand me the subpoena, then I don't have to go.'

'So you're hiding too?'

'I guess.'

Suddenly his end clicked and the dial tone followed. She stared at the receiver, then quickly placed it on the phone. 'He hung up,' she said.

'What the hell's going on!' Clint asked.

'It's Mark. He's escaped from jail.'

'He what!'

'He's hiding in the morgue at St Peter's.' She said this as if she didn't believe it. The phone rang, and she snatched it. 'Hello.'

'Sorry about that. The door to the morgue opened, then closed. I thought they were bringing in another body.'

'Are you safe, Mark?'

'Hell no, I'm not safe. But I'm a kid, okay. And now I'm a psychiatric case. So if they catch me, I'll just go into shock again and they'll put me in a room. Then I'll figure out another way to escape, maybe.'

'You can't hide forever.'

'Neither can you.'

She marvelled once again at his quick tongue. 'You're right, Mark. So what do we do?'

'I don't know. I really would like to leave Memphis. I'm sick of cops and jails.'

'Where do you want to go?'

'Well, let me ask you something. If you come and get me, and we leave town together, then you could get in trouble for helping me escape. Right?'

'Yes. I'd be an accomplice.'

'What would they do to you?'

'We'll worry about that later. I've done worse things.'

'So you'll help me?'

'Yes, Mark. I'll help you.'

'And you won't tell anybody?'

'We may need Clint.'

'Okay, you can tell Clint. But nobody else, okay?'

'You have my word.'

'And you won't try to talk me into going back to jail?'

'I promise.'

There was a long pause. Clint was near panic.

'Okay, Reggie. You know the main parking lot, the one next to that big green building?'

'Yes.'

'Drive into it, just like you're looking for a place to park. Go real slow. I'll be hiding between some cars.'

'That place is dark and dangerous, Mark.'

'It's Friday night, Reggie. Everything around here is dark and dangerous.'

'But there's a guard in the exit booth.'

'That guard sleeps half the time. It's a guard, not a cop. I know what I'm doing, Okay?'

'Are you sure?'

'No. But you said you'd help me.'

'I will. When should I be there?'

'As fast as you can.'

'I'll be in Clint's car. It's a black Honda Accord.'

'Good. Hurry.'

'I'm on my way. Be careful, Mark.'

'Relax, Reggie. This is just like the movies.'

She hung up, and took a deep breath.

'My car?' Clint asked.

'They're looking for me too.'

'You're crazy, Reggie. This is insane. You can't run away with an escaped, I don't know, whatever the hell he is. They'll arrest you for contributing. You'll be indicted. You'll lose your license.'

'Where's my bag?'

'In the bedroom.'

'I need your keys, and your credit cards.'

'My credit cards! Look, Reggie, I love you, sweetheart, but my car and my plastic?'

'How much cash do you have?'

'Forty bucks.'

'Give it here. I'll pay you back.' She headed for the bedroom.

'You've lost your mind.'

'I've lost it before, remember.'

'Come on, Reggie.'

'Get a grip, Clint. We're not blowing anything. I've got to help Mark. He's sitting in a dark office in the morgue at St Peter's begging for help. What am I supposed to do?'

'Well, hell! I think you should attack the place with a shotgun and blow people away. Anything for Mark Sway.'

She threw her toothbrush in a canvas bag. 'Give me the credit cards and the cash, Clint. I'm in a hurry.'

He reached in his pockets. 'You're nuts. This is ridiculous.'

'Stay by the phone. Do not leave this place, okay. I'll call you later.' She grabbed his keys, cash, and two credit cards – Visa and Texaco.

He followed her to the door. 'Take it easy with the Visa. It's almost to the limit.'

'Why am I not surprised?' She kissed him on the cheek. 'Thanks, Clint. Take care of Momma Love.'

'Call me,' he said, thoroughly defeated.

She eased through the door and disappeared in the darkness.

THIRTY-THREE

From the moment Mark jumped into the car and hid on the floor, Reggie became an accomplice to his escape. But, unless he murdered someone before they were caught, it was doubtful her crime would be punishable by incarceration. She was thinking more along the lines of community service, perhaps a bit of restitution, and forty years of probation. Hell, she'd give them all the probation they wanted. It would be her first offense. She, and her lawyer, could make a strong argument that the kid was being hunted by the Mafia, and he was all alone, and, well, dammit, somebody had to do something! She couldn't worry about legal niceties when her client was out there begging for help. Maybe she could pull strings and keep her license to practice.

She paid the parking guard fifty cents, and refused eye contact. She had circled through the lot one time. The guard was in another world. Mark was rolled into a tight coil somewhere in the darkness under the dashboard, and he remained there until she turned on Union and headed for the river.

'Is it safe now?' he asked nervously.

'I think so.'

He sprang into the seat, and surveyed the landscape. The digital clock gave the time as twelve-fifty. The six lanes of Union Avenue were deserted. She drove three blocks, catching red lights at each one, while waiting for Mark to speak.

371

'So where are we going?' she finally asked.

'The Alamo.'

'The Alamo?' she repeated without a trace of a smile.

He shook his head. Adults could be so dumb at times. 'It's a joke, Reggie.'

'Sorry.'

'I take it you haven't seen *Pee-Wee's Big Adventure*.'

'Is that a movie?'

'Forget it. Just forget it.' They waited for another red light.

'I like your car better,' he said, rubbing his hand along the Accord's console and taking a sudden interest in the radio.

'That's good, Mark. This street is about to stop at the river, and I think we should discuss exactly where it is you want to go.'

'Well, right now, I just want to leave Memphis, okay? I really don't care where we go, I just want to get out of Dodge.'

'And once we leave Memphis, where might we be going? A destination would be nice.'

'Let's cross the bridge by the Pyramid, okay?'

'Fair enough. You want to go to Arkansas?'

'Why not? Yeah, sure, let's go to Arkansas.'

'Fair enough.'

With that decision out of the way, he leaned forward and carefully inspected the radio. He pushed a button, turned a knob, and Reggie braced for a loud burst of rap or heavy metal. He made adjustments with both hands. Just a kid with a new toy. He should be home in a warm bed, and he should sleep late since it's Saturday. And fresh from bed he should watch cartoons, then, still in pajamas, play Nintendo with all its buttons and gadgets, much like he was doing right then with the radio. The Four Tops finished a song.

'You listen to oldies?' she asked, genuinely surprised.

'Sometimes. I thought you'd like it. It's almost one o'clock in the morning, not the best time for the loud stuff, you know.'

372

'Why do you think I like oldies?'

'Well, Reggie, to be perfectly honest, I can't see you at a rap concert. And besides, the radio in your car was on this station last time I rode in it.'

Union Avenue stopped at the river, and they sat at another red light. A police car stopped next to them, and the cop behind the wheel frowned at Mark.

'Don't look at him,' Reggie scolded.

The light changed, and she turned right on to Riverside Drive. The cop followed. 'Don't turn around,' she said under her breath. 'Just act normal.'

'Damn, Reggie, why is he following us?'

'I have no idea. Just be cool.'

'He recognized me. My face has been plastered all over the newspapers this week, and the cop recognized me. This is just great, Reggie. We make our big escape, and ten minutes later the cops nail us.'

'Be quiet, Mark. I'm trying to drive and watch him at the same time.'

He eased downward, sliding slowly until his butt was on the edge of the seat and his head was just above the door handle. 'What's he doing?' he whispered.

Her eyes darted back and forth from the mirror to the street. 'Just following. No, wait. Here he comes.'

The police car eased by them, then sped away. 'He's gone,' she said, and Mark breathed again.

They entered I-40 at the downtown ramp, and were on the bridge over the Mississippi River. He gazed at the brightly lit Pyramid to the right, then spun around to admire the Memphis skyline fading in the distance. He stared in awe, as if he'd never seen it before. Reggie wondered if the poor child had ever left Memphis.

An Elvis song started. 'You like Elvis?' he asked.

'Mark, believe it or not, when I was a teenager growing up in Memphis, a bunch of us girls would ride over to Elvis's house on Sundays and watch him play touch football. This was before he was really famous, and he still lived at home with his parents in a nice little house. He went to Humes High School, which is now Northside.'

'I live in north Memphis. At least I did. I don't know where I live now.'

'We'd go to his concerts, and we'd see him hanging out around town. He was just an average guy, at first, then things changed. He got so famous he couldn't live a normal life.'

'Just like me, Reggie,' he said with a sudden smile. 'Think of it. Me and Elvis. Pictures on the front page. Photographers everywhere. All sorts of people looking for us. It's tough being famous.'

'Yeah, and wait till tomorrow, in the Sunday paper. I can see the headlines now, big, bold letters – SWAY ESCAPES.'

'It's great! And they'll have my smiling face on the front page again with cops all around me like I'm some kind of serial killer. And those same cops will sound so stupid trying to explain how an eleven-year-old kid escaped from jail. I wonder if I'm the youngest kid to ever escape from jail.'

'Probably.'

'I do feel sorry for Doreen, though. Do you think she'll get in trouble?'

'Was she on duty?'

'No. It was Telda and Denny. Wouldn't bother me if they got fired.'

'Doreen's probably okay. She's been there a long time.'

'I faked her out, you know. I started acting like I was going into shock, just fading away to La La Land as Romey called it. Every time she checked on me, I acted weirder and weirder; quit talking to her, just stared at the ceiling and groaned. She knows all about Ricky, and she became convinced it was happening to me too. Yesterday, she brought in a medic from the jail, and he examined me. Said I was fine. But Doreen was worried. I guess I used her.'

'How'd you get out?'

'Played like I was in shock, you know. I worked up a good sweat running around my little cell, then curled up in

374

a ball and sucked my thumb. It scared them so bad, they called the ambulance. I knew if I could make it to St Peter's, I was home free. That place is a zoo.'

'And you just disappeared?'

'They had me on this stretcher, and when they turned their backs I got up and, yeah, just disappeared. Look, Reggie, there were people dying right and left, so no one was concerned with me. It was easy.'

They were over the bridge and into Arkansas. The highway was flat and lined on both sides by truck stops and motels. He turned to admire the Memphis skyline once more, but it was gone.

'What are you looking for?' she asked.

'Memphis. I like to look at the tall buildings downtown. A teacher told me once that people actually live in those tall buildings. It's hard to believe.'

'Why is it hard to believe?'

'I saw a movie once about this little rich kid who lived in a tall building in a city, and he roamed around the streets just having a great time. He knew the cops by their first names. He stopped taxis when he wanted to go somewhere. And at night, he'd sit on the balcony and watch the streets below. I've always thought that would be a wonderful way to live. No cheap house trailers. No trashy neighbors. No pickups parked in the street in front of your house.'

'You can have it, Mark. It's yours, if you want it.'

He gave her a long look. 'How?'

'Right now the FBI will give you whatever you want. You can live in a tall building in a big city, or you can live in a cabin in the mountains. You pick the place.'

'I've been thinking about that.'

'You can live on a beach and play in the ocean, or you can live in Orlando and go to Disney World every day.'

'That'd be okay for Ricky. I'm too old. I've heard the tickets are too expensive.'

'You'd probably get a lifetime pass, if you asked for it. Right now, Mark, you and your mom can get anything you want.'

375

'Yeah, but, Reggie, who wants it if you're afraid of your shadow. For three nights now, I've had nightmares about these people, Reggie. I don't want to be scared for the rest of my life. They'll get me one day, I know they will.'

'So what do you do, Mark?'

'I don't know, but I've been thinking real hard about something.'

'I'm listening.'

'One good thing about jail is that it allows you to think a lot.' He placed one foot on one knee and wrapped his fingers around it. 'Think about this, Reggie. What if Romey told me a lie? He was drunk, taking pills, out of his mind. Maybe he was just talking to hear himself talk. I was there, remember. The man was crazy. Said all sorts of weird things, and at first I believed all of it. I was scared to death, and I wasn't thinking clearly. My head was hurting where he'd slapped me. But now, well, I'm not so sure. All week I've been remembering crazy stuff he said and did, and maybe I was too eager to believe everything.'

She was driving exactly fifty-five miles per hour and hanging on every word. She had no idea where he was going with this, and she had no idea where the car was going either.

'But I couldn't take a chance, right? I mean, what if I'd told the cops everything and they found the body right where Romey said? Everybody's happy but the Mafia, and who knows what would happen to me. And what if I'd told the cops everything, but Romey was lying and they found no body. I'm off the hook, right, because in reality I didn't know anything at all. What a joker, that Romey. But it was too big a risk.' He paused for a half a mile. The Beach Boys sang 'California Girls.' 'So I've had a brainstorm.'

By now, she could almost feel this brainstorm. Her heart stopped and she managed to keep the wheels between the white lines of the right lane. 'And what might that be?' she asked nervously.

'I think we should see if Romey was lying or not.'

She cleared her dry throat. 'You mean, go find the body.'

376

'That's right.'

She wanted to laugh at this innocent humor of a hyperactive mind, but at the moment she didn't have the strength. 'You must be kidding.'

'Well, let's talk about it. You and I are both expected to be in New Orleans Monday morning, right?'

'I guess. I haven't seen a subpoena.'

'But I'm your client, and I've got a subpoena. So even if they didn't give you one, you'd still have to go with me, right?'

'That's true.'

'And now we're on the run, right? Just you and me, Bonnie and Clyde, running from the cops.'

'I guess you could say that.'

'Where's the last place they'd look for us? Think about it, Reggie. Where's the last place in the world they'd expect us to run to?'

'New Orleans.'

'Right. Now, I don't know anything about hiding out, but since you're dodging a subpoena and you're a lawyer and all, and you deal with criminals all the time, I figure you could get us to New Orleans and no one would know it. Right?'

'I suppose so.' She was beginning to agree with him, and she was shocked by her own words.

'And if you can get us to New Orleans, then we'll find Romey's house.'

'Why Romey's house?'

'That's where the body's supposed to be.'

This was the last thing in the world she wanted to know. She slowly removed her glasses and rubbed her eyes. A slight headache was forming between her temples, and it would only get worse.

Romey's house? The home of Jerome Clifford, deceased? He had said this very slowly, and she had heard it very slowly. She glared at taillights in front of them but there was nothing but a red blur. Romey's house? The victim of the murder was buried at the home of the accused's lawyer.

This was beyond bizarre. Her mind raced wildly in circles asking itself a hundred questions and answering none of them. She glanced in the mirror, and was suddenly aware that he was staring at her with a curious smile.

'Now you know, Reggie,' he said.

'But how, why –'

'Don't ask because I don't know. It's crazy, isn't it? That's why I think Romey could've made it up. A crazy mind created this weird story about the body being at his house.'

'So, you don't think it's really there?' she asked, seeking reassurance.

'We won't know until we look. If it's not there, I'm off the hook and life returns to normal.'

'But what if it's there?'

'We'll worry about that when we find it.'

'I don't like your brainstorm.'

'Why not?'

'Look, Mark, son, client, friend, if you think I'm going to New Orleans to dig up a dead body, then you're crazy.'

'Of course I'm crazy. Me and Ricky, just a couple of nut cases.'

'I won't do it.'

'Why not, Reggie?'

'It's much too dangerous, Mark. It's insane, and it could get us killed. I won't go, and I can't let you do it.'

'Why is it dangerous?'

'Well, it's just dangerous. I don't know.'

'Think about it, Reggie. We check on the body, okay. Then if it's not where Romey said, I'm home free. We'll tell the cops to drop everything against us, and in return I'll tell them what I know. And since I don't know where the body really is, the Mafia couldn't care less about me. We walk.'

We walk. Too much television. 'And if we find the body?'

'Good question. Think about this slowly, Reggie. Try and think like a kid. If we find the body, and then you call the FBI and tell them you know exactly where it is because

378

you've seen it with your own eyes, then they'll give us
anything we want.'

'And what exactly do you want?'

'Probably Australia. A nice house, plenty of money for
my mother. New car. Maybe some plastic surgery. I saw
that once in a movie. They rearranged this guy's entire face.
He was dog ugly to start with, and he snitched on some drug
dealers just so he could get a new face. Looked like a movie
star when it was over. About two years later, the drug
dealers gave him another new face.'

'You're serious?'

'About the movie?'

'No, about Australia.'

'Maybe.' He paused and looked out the window.
'Maybe.'

They listened to the radio and didn't speak for several
miles. Traffic was light. Memphis was farther away.

'Let's make a deal,' he said, looking out his window.

'Maybe.'

'Let's go to New Orleans.'

'I'm not digging for a body.'

'Okay, okay. But let's go there. No one will expect us.
We'll talk about the body when we get there.'

'We've already talked about it.'

'Just go to New Orleans, okay?'

The highway intersected another one, and they were on
top of an overpass. She pointed to her right. Ten miles
away, the Memphis skyline glowed and flickered under a
half-moon. 'Wow,' he said in awe. 'It's beautiful.'

Neither of them could know that it would be his last look
at Memphis.

They stopped in Forrest City, Arkansas, for gas and snacks.
Reggie paid for cupcakes, a large coffee, and a Sprite, while
Mark hid on the floor. Minutes later, they were back on the
interstate headed for Little Rock.

Steam poured from the Styrofoam cup as she drove and
watched him inhale four cupcakes. He ate like a kid –

crumbs on his pants and in the seat, cream filling on his fingers, which he licked as if he hadn't seen food in a month. It was almost two-thirty. The road was empty except for convoys of tractor-trailer rigs. She set the cruise control on sixty-five.

'Do you think they're chasing us yet?' he asked, finishing the last cupcake and opening the Sprite. There was a certain excitement in his voice.

'I doubt it. I'm sure the police are searching the hospital, but why would they suspect we're together?'

'I'm worried about Mom. I called her, you know, before I called you. Told her about the escape, and that I was hiding in the hospital. She got real mad. But I think I convinced her I'm safe. I hope they don't give her a hard time.'

'They won't. But she'll worry herself sick.'

'I know. I don't mean to be cruel, but I think she can handle it. Look at what she's already been through. My mom's pretty tough.'

'I'll tell Clint to call her later today.'

'Are you going to tell Clint where we're going?'

'I'm not sure where we're going.'

He thought about this as two trucks roared by and the Honda veered to the right.

'What would you do, Reggie?'

'For starters, I don't think I would have escaped.'

'That's a lie.'

'I beg your pardon.'

'Sure it is. You're dodging a subpoena, aren't you? I'm doing the same thing. So what's the difference? You don't want to face the grand jury. I don't want to face the grand jury, so here we are on the run. We're in the same boat, Reggie.'

'There's only one difference. You were in jail, and you escaped. That's a crime.'

'I was in a jail for juveniles, and juveniles do not commit crimes. Isn't that what you told me? Juveniles are rowdy, or delinquent, or in need of supervision, but juveniles do not commit crimes. Right?'

380

'If you say so. But it was wrong to escape.'

'It's done. I can't undo it. It's wrong for you to dodge the law too, isn't it?'

'Absolutely not. There's no crime in avoiding a subpoena. I was doing fine until I picked you up.'

'Then stop the car and let me out.'

'Oh sure. Please be serious, Mark.'

'I am serious.'

'Right. And what'll you do when you get out?'

'Oh, I don't know. I'll go as far as I can, and if I get caught then I'll just go into shock and they'll send me back to Memphis. I'll claim I was crazy, and they'll never know you were involved. Just stop anytime you feel like it, and I'll get out.' He leaned forward and punched the Seek button on the radio. For five miles they listened to Conway Twitty and Tammy Wynette.

'I hate country music,' she said, and he turned it off.

'Can I ask you something?' she said.

'Sure.'

'Suppose we go to New Orleans and find the body. And, according to your plan, we then cut a deal with the FBI and you go into their witness protection plan. You, Dianne, and Ricky then fly off into the sunset to Australia or wherever, right?'

'I guess.'

'Then, why not cut a deal and tell them now?'

'Now you're thinking, Reggie,' he said, patronizingly, as if she'd finally awakened and was beginning to see the light.

'Thank you so much,' she said.

'It took me a while to figure it out. The answer is easy. I don't completely trust the FBI. Do you?'

'Not completely.'

'And I'm not willing to give them what they want until me, my mother, and my brother are already far away. You're a good lawyer, Reggie, and you wouldn't allow your client to take any chances, would you?'

'Go on.'

'Before I tell these clowns anything, I want to make sure

381

we are safely put away somewhere. It'll take some time to move Ricky. If I told them now, the bad guys might find out before we can disappear. It's too risky.'

'But what if you told them now, and they didn't find the body? What if Clifford was, as you say, joking?'

'I would never know, would I? I'd be undercover somewhere, getting a nose job, changing my name to Tommy or something, and all of it would be for nothing. It makes more sense to know now, Reggie, if Romey told me the truth.'

She shook her bewildered head. 'I'm not sure I follow you.'

'I'm not sure I follow me, either. But one thing is for certain: I'm not going to New Orleans with the US marshals. I'm not going to face the grand jury on Monday and refuse to answer questions so they can throw my little butt in jail down there.'

'Good point. So how do we spend our weekend?'

'How far is it to New Orleans?'

'Five or six hours.'

'Let's go. We can always chicken out once we get there.'

'How much trouble will it be to find the body?'

'Probably not much.'

'Can I ask where it is at Clifford's house?'

'Well, it's not hanging in a tree or lying in the bushes. It'll take a little work.'

'This is completely crazy, Mark.'

'I know. It's been a bad week.'

THIRTY-FOUR

So much for a quiet Saturday morning with the kids. Jason McThune studied his feet on the rug next to his bed, and tried to focus on the clock on the wall by the bathroom door. It was almost six, still dark outside, and the cobwebs from a late night bottle of wine blurred his eyes. His wife rolled over and grunted something he could not understand.

Twenty minutes later, he found her deep under the covers and kissed her goodbye. He might not be home for a week, he said, but doubted if she heard. Saturdays at work and days out of town were the norm. Nothing unusual.

But today would be unusual. He opened the door and the dog ran into the backyard. How could an eleven-year-old kid simply disappear? The Memphis Police had no idea. He just vanished, the lieutenant said.

Not surprisingly, traffic was light in the predawn hours as he headed for the Federal Building downtown. He punched numbers on his car phone. Agents Brenner, Latchee, and Durston were roused from sleep and instructed to meet him immediately. He flipped through his black book and found the Alexandria number for K. O. Lewis.

K. O. was not asleep, but neither was he in the mood to be disturbed. He was eating his oatmeal, enjoying his coffee, chatting with his wife, and just how in the hell could an eleven-year-old kid disappear while in police custody? he demanded. McThune told him what he knew, which was nothing, and asked him to be ready to come to Memphis. It

383

could be a long weekend. K. O. said he would make a couple of calls, find the jet, and call him back at the office.

At the office McThune called Larry Trumann in New Orleans, and was delighted when Trumann answered the phone disoriented and obviously trying to sleep. This was Trumann's case, though McThune had worked on it all week. And just for fun, he called George Ord and asked him to come on down with the rest of the gang. McThune explained he was hungry, and could George please bring some Egg McMuffins.

By seven, Brenner, Latchee, and Durston were in his office gulping coffee and speculating wildly. Ord arrived next without the food, then two uniformed Memphis policemen knocked on the door to the outer office. Ray Trimble, Deputy Chief of Police and a legend in Memphis law enforcement, was with them.

They assembled in McThune's office, and Trimble, in fluent coptalk, got right to the point. 'Subject was transported from the detention center by ambulance to St Peter's around ten-thirty last night. Subject was signed in by the paramedics at St Peter's ER, at which time the paramedics left. Subject was not accompanied by Memphis Police or jail personnel. Paramedics are certain a nurse, one Gloria Watts, female white, signed subject in, but no paperwork can be found. Ms Watts has stated she had subject in ER Intake Room, and was called out of room for an undetermined reason. She was absent for no more than ten minutes, and upon her return, subject was gone. The paperwork was gone too, and Ms Watts assumed subject had been taken to ER for examination and treatment.' Trimble slowed a bit and cleared his throat as if this was somehow unpleasant. 'At approximately five this morning, Ms Watts was evidently preparing to leave her shift, and she checked the Intake records. She thought of the subject, and began asking questions. Subject could not be found in ER, and Admissions had no record of his arrival. Hospital Security was called, then Memphis PD. At this time, a thorough search of the hospital is under way.'

384

'Six hours,' McThune said in disbelief.

'I beg your pardon,' Trimble said.

'It took six hours to realize the kid was missing.'

'Yes sir, but we don't run the hospital, you see.'

'Why was the kid transported to the hospital without security?'

'I can't answer that. An investigation will be undertaken. It looks like an oversight.'

'Why was the kid taken to the hospital?'

Trimble took a file from a briefcase, and handed McThune a copy of Telda's report. He read it carefully. 'Says he went into shock after the US marshals left. What the hell were the marshals doing there?'

Trimble opened the file again, and handed McThune the subpoena. He read it carefully, then handed it to George Ord.

'Anything else, Chief?' he said to Trimble, who had never taken a seat and had never stopped pacing slightly. He was anxious to leave.

'No sir. We'll complete the search, and call you immediately if we find anything. We've got about four dozen men there right now, and we've been checking for a little over an hour.'

'Have you talked to the kid's mother?'

'No sir. Not yet. She's still asleep. We're watching the room in case he tries to get to her.'

'I'll talk to her first, Chief. I'll be over in about an hour. Make sure no one sees her before I do.'

'No problem.'

'Thank you, Chief.' Trimble clicked his heels together, and for an instant looked as though he wanted to salute. He was gone, along with his officers.

McThune looked at Brenner and Latchee. 'You guys call every available agent. Get them here right now. Immediately.' They bolted from the room.

'What about the subpoena?' he asked Ord, who was still holding it.

'I can't believe it. Foltrigg's lost his mind.'

385

'You knew nothing about it?'

'Of course not. This kid is under the jurisdiction of the Juvenile Court. I wouldn't think of trying to reach him. Would you want to piss off Harry Roosevelt?'

'I don't think so. We need to call him. I'll do it, and you call Reggie Love. I'd rather not talk to her.'

Ord left the room to find a phone. 'Call the US marshal,' McThune snapped at Durston. 'Get the scoop on this subpoena. I want to know everything about it.'

Durston left, and suddenly McThune was alone. He raced through a phone book until he found the Roosevelts. But there was no Harry. If he had a number, it was unlisted, and that was perfectly understandable with no less than fifty thousand single mothers trying to collect unpaid child support. McThune made three quick calls to lawyers he knew, and the third one said that Harry lived on Kensington Street. He would send an agent when he could spare one.

Ord returned shaking his head. 'I talked to Reggie Love's mother, but she asked more questions than I did. I don't think she's there.'

'I'll send two men as soon as possible. I guess you'd better call Foltrigg, the dumbass.'

'Yeah, I guess you're right.' Ord turned and left the office again.

At eight, McThune left the elevator on the ninth floor of St Peter's with Brenner and Durston following close behind. Three more agents, decked out in a splendid variety of hospital garb, met him at the elevator and walked with him to Room 943. Three massive security guards stood near the door. McThune knocked gently, and motioned for his small squadron to back away. He didn't want to scare the poor woman.

The door opened slightly. 'Yes,' came a weak voice from the darkness.

'Ms Sway, I'm Jason McThune, Special Agent, FBI. I saw you in court yesterday.'

386

The door opened wider, and Dianne stepped into the crack. She said nothing, just waited for his next words.

'Can I talk to you in private?'

She glanced to her left – three security guards, two agents, and three men in scrubs and lab jackets. 'In private?' she said.

'We can walk this way,' he said, nodding toward the end of the hall.

'Is something the matter?' she asked, as if nothing else could possibly go wrong.

'Yes ma'am.'

She took a deep breath, and disappeared. Seconds later, she eased through the door with her cigarettes, and closed it gently behind her. They walked slowly in the center of the empty hall.

'I don't suppose you've talked to Mark,' McThune said.

'He called me yesterday afternoon from the jail,' she said, sticking a cigarette between her lips. It was not a lie; Mark had indeed called her from the jail.

'Since then?'

'No,' she lied. 'Why?'

'He's missing.'

She hesitated for a step, then continued. 'What do you mean, he's missing?' She was surprisingly calm. She's probably just numb to all this, McThune thought. He gave her a quick version of Mark's disappearance. They stopped at the window and looked at downtown.

'My god, do you think the Mafia's got him?' she asked, and her eyes watered immediately. She held the cigarette with a trembling hand, unable to light it.

McThune shook his head confidently. 'No. They don't even know. We're keeping a lid on it. I think he just walked away. Right here, in the hospital. We figured he might have tried to contact you.'

'Have you searched this place? He knows it really well, you know.'

'They've been searching for three hours, but it looks doubtful. Where would he go?'

387

She finally lit the cigarette and took a long drag, then exhaled a small cloud. 'I have no idea.'

'Well, let me ask you something. What do you know about Reggie Love? Is she in town this weekend? Was she planning a trip?'

'Why?'

'We can't find her either. She's not at home. Her mother ain't saying much. You received a subpoena last night, right?'

'That's right.'

'Well, Mark got one, and they tried to serve one on Reggie Love, but they haven't found her yet. Is it possible Mark's with her?'

I hope so, Dianne thought. She hadn't thought about this. In spite of the pills she hadn't slept fifteen minutes since he'd called. But Mark on the loose with Reggie was a new idea. A much more pleasant idea.

'I don't know. It's possible, I guess.'

'Where would they be, you know, the two of them together?'

'How the hell am I supposed to know? You're the FBI. I hadn't thought about that until five seconds ago, and now you're asking me where they are. Give me a break.'

McThune felt stupid. It was not a bright question, and she was not as frail as he thought.

Dianne puffed her cigarette, and watched the cars crawl along the streets below. Knowing Mark, he was probably changing diapers in the nursery or assisting with surgery in orthopedics, or maybe scrambling eggs in the kitchen. St Peter's was the largest hospital in the state. There were thousands of people under its varied roofs. He'd roamed the halls and made dozens of friends, and it would take them days to find him. She expected him to call any minute.

'I need to get back,' she said, sticking the filter in an ashtray.

'If he contacts you, I need to know it.'

'Sure.'

'And if you hear from Reggie Love, I'd appreciate a

call. I'll leave two men here on this floor, in case you need them.'

She walked away.

By eight-thirty, Foltrigg had assembled in his office the usual crew of Wally Boxx, Thomas Fink, and Larry Trumann, who arrived last with his hair still wet from a quick shower.

Foltrigg was dressed like a fraternity pledge in his pressed chinos, starched cotton button-down, and shiny loafers. Trumann wore a jogging suit. 'The lawyer's missing too,' he announced as he poured coffee from a thermos.

'When did you hear this?' Foltrigg asked.

'Five minutes ago, on my car phone. McThune called me. They went to her house to serve her around eight, but couldn't find her. She's disappeared.'

'What else did McThune say?'

'They're still searching the hospital. The kid spent three days there and knows it very well.'

'I doubt if he's there,' Foltrigg said with his customary quick command of unknown facts.

'Does McThune think the kid's with the lawyer?' Boxx asked.

'Who in hell knows? She'd be kind of stupid to help the kid escape, wouldn't she?'

'She's not that bright,' Foltrigg said scornfully.

Neither are you, thought Trumann. You're the idiot who issued the subpoenas that started this latest episode. 'McThune's spoken twice this morning with K. O. Lewis. He's on standby. They plan to search the hospital until noon, then give up. If the kid's not found by then, Lewis will zip to Memphis.'

'You think Muldanno's involved?' Fink asked.

'I doubt it. Looks like the kid strung them along until he got to the hospital, and at that point he was on home turf. I'll bet he called the lawyer, and now they're hiding somewhere in Memphis.'

389

'I wonder if Muldanno knows,' Fink said, looking at Foltrigg.

'His people are still in Memphis,' Trumann said. 'Gronke's here, but we haven't seen Bono or Pirini. Hell, they might have a dozen boys up there by now.'

'Has McThune called in the dogs?' Foltrigg asked.

'Yeah. He's got everyone in his office working on it. They're watching her house, her secretary's apartment, they've even sent two men to find Judge Roosevelt, who's fishing somewhere in the mountains. Memphis PD has the hospital choked off.'

'What about the phones?'

'Which phones?'

'The phones in the hospital room. He's a kid, Larry, you know he'll try to call his mother.'

'It takes approval from the hospital. McThune said they're working on it. But it's Saturday, and the necessary people are not in.'

Foltrigg stood behind his desk, and walked to the window. 'The kid had six hours before anyone realized he was missing, right?'

'That's what they said.'

'Have they found the lawyer's car?'

'No. They're still looking.'

'I'll bet they don't find it in Memphis. I'll bet the kid and Ms Love are in the car.'

'Oh really.'

'Yeah. Haulin' ass.'

'And where might they be haulin' ass to?'

'Somewhere far away.'

At nine-thirty, a Memphis policeman called in the tag number of an illegally parked Mazda. It belonged to one Reggie Love. The message was quickly sent to Jason McThune at his office in the Federal Building.

Ten minutes later, two FBI agents knocked on the door to apartment Number 28 at Bellevue Gardens. They waited, and knocked again. Clint hid in the bedroom. If they kicked the door down, then he would simply be sleeping on this lovely and peaceful Saturday morning. They knocked the third time, and the phone started to ring. It startled him, and he almost lunged for it. But his answering machine was on. If the cops would come to his apartment, then they would certainly not hesitate to call. After the tone, he heard Reggie's voice. He lifted the receiver, and quickly whispered, 'Reggie, call me right back.' He hung up.

They knocked the fourth time, and left. The lights were off and the curtains covered every window. He stared at the phone for five minutes, and it finally rang. The answering machine gave its message, then the tone. Again, it was Reggie.

'Hello,' he said quickly.

'Good morning, Clint,' she said cheerfully. 'How are things in Memphis?'

'Oh, the usual, you know, cops watching my apartment, banging on the door. Typical Saturday.'

'Cops?'

'Yeah. For the past hour, I've been sitting in my closet watching my little television. The news is all over the place. They haven't mentioned you, yet, but Mark's on every channel. Right now, it's simply a disappearance, not an escape.'

'Have you talked to Dianne?'

'I called her about an hour ago. The FBI had just told her he was missing. I explained he was with you, and this calmed her a bit. Frankly, Reggie, she's been shocked so much I don't think it registered. Where are you?'

'We've checked into a motel in Metairie.'

'I'm sorry. Did you say Metairie? As in Louisiana? Right outside of New Orleans?'

'That's the place. We drove all night.'

'Why the hell are you down there, Reggie? Of all the places to hide, why did you pick a suburb of New Orleans? Why not Alaska?'

'Because it's the last place we'd be expected. We're safe,

391

Clint. I paid cash and registered under another name. We'll sleep a bit, then see the city.'

'See the city? Come on, Reggie, what's going on?'

'I'll explain it later. Have you talked to Momma Love?'

'No. I'll call her right now.'

'Do that. I'll call back this afternoon.'

'You're crazy, Reggie. Do you know that? You've lost your mind.'

'I know. But I've been crazy before. Goodbye now.'

Clint placed the phone on the table, and stretched on the unmade bed. She had indeed been crazy before.

THIRTY-FIVE

Barry the Blade entered the warehouse alone. Gone was the swaggering strut of the quickest gun in town. Gone was the smirking scowl of the cocky street hood. Gone were the flashy suit and Italian loafers. The earrings were in a pocket. The ponytail was tucked under his collar. He'd shaved just an hour ago.

He climbed the rusted steps to the second level, and thought about playing on these same stairs as a child. His father was alive then, and after school he'd hang around here until dark, watching containers come and go, listening to the stevedores, learning their language, smoking their cigarettes, looking at their magazines. It was a wonderful place to grow up, especially for a boy who wanted to be nothing but a gangster.

Now, the warehouse was not as busy. He walked along the runway next to the dirty, painted windows overlooking the river. His steps echoed through the vast emptiness below. A few dusty containers were scattered about, and hadn't been moved in years. His uncle's black Cadillacs were parked together near the docks. Tito, the faithful chauffeur, polished a fender. He glanced up at the sound of footsteps, and waved at Barry.

Though he was quite anxious, he walked deliberately, trying not to strut. Both hands were stuck deep in his pockets. He watched the river through the ancient windows. An imitation paddle wheeler hauled tourists downriver for a breathtaking tour of more warehouses and

393

perhaps a barge or two. The runway stopped at a metal door. He pushed a button and looked directly into the camera above his head. A loud click, and the door opened. Mo, a former stevedore who'd given him his first beer when he was twelve, stood there, wearing a dreadful suit. Mo had at least four guns either on him or within reach. He nodded at Barry, and waved him on. Mo had been a friendly guy until he'd started wearing suits, which happened about the same time he saw *The Godfather*, and he hadn't smiled since.

Barry walked through a room with two empty desks, and knocked on a door. He took a deep breath. 'Come in,' a voice said gently, and he entered his uncle's office.

Johnny Sulari was ageing nicely. A big man, in his seventies, he stood straight and moved quickly. His hair was brilliantly gray, and not a fraction of the hairline had receded. His forehead was small, and the hair started two inches above the eyebrows and was slicked back in shiny waves. As usual, he wore a dark suit, with the jacket hanging on a rack by the window. The tie was navy and terribly boring. The red suspenders were his trademark. He smiled at Barry and waved to a worn leather chair, the same one Barry had sat in as a child.

Johnny was a gentleman, one of the last in a declining business being quickly overrun by younger men who were greedier and nastier. Men like his nephew here.

But it was a forced smile. This was not a social call. They'd talked more in the past three days than in the past three years.

'Bad news, Barry?' Johnny asked, knowing the answer.

'You might say so. The kid's disappeared in Memphis.'

Johnny stared icily at Barry, who, for one of the few times in his life, did not stare back. The eyes failed him. The lethal, legendary eyes of Barry The Blade Muldanno were blinking and watching the floor.

'How could you be so stupid?' Johnny asked calmly. 'Stupid to leave the body around here. Stupid to tell your lawyer. Stupid. Stupid. Stupid.'

The eyes blinked faster and he shifted his weight. He nodded in agreement, now penitent. 'I need help, okay.'

'Of course you need help. You've done a very stupid thing, and now you need someone to rescue you.'

'It concerns all of us, I think.'

Johnny's eyes flashed pure anger, but he controlled himself. He was always under control. 'Oh, really. Is that a threat, Barry? You're coming into my office to ask for help and you're threatening me? Are you planning to do some talkin'? Come on, boy. If you're convicted, you'll take it to your grave.'

'That's true, but I'd rather not be convicted, you know. There's still time.'

'You're a dumbass, Barry. Have I ever told you that?'

'I think so.'

'You stalked the man for weeks. You caught him sneaking out of a dirty little whorehouse. All you had to do was hit him over the head, coupla bullets, clean out his pockets, leave the body for the whores to trip over, and the cops would say it's just another cheap murder. They woulda never suspected anybody. But, no, Barry, you're too dumb to keep it simple.'

Barry shifted again and watched the floor.

Johnny glared at him and unwrapped a cigar. 'Answer my questions slowly, okay? I don't wanna know too much, you understand?'

'Yeah.'

'Is the body here in the city?'

'Yeah.'

Johnny clipped the end of the cigar and licked it slowly. He shook his head in disgust. 'How stupid. Is it easy to get to?'

'Yeah.'

'Have the Feds been close to it?'

'I don't think so.'

'Is it underground?'

'Yeah.'

'How long will it take to dig it up or whatever you have to do?'

'An hour, maybe two.'

'So it's not in dirt?'

'Concrete.'

Johnny lit the cigar with a match, and relaxed the wrinkles above his eyes. 'Concrete,' he repeated. Maybe the boy wasn't quite as stupid as he thought. Forget it. He was plenty stupid. 'How many men?'

'Two or three. I can't do it. They're watching every move I make. If I go near the place, I'll just lead them to it.'

Plenty stupid, all right. He blew a smoke ring. 'A parking lot? A sidewalk?'

'Under a garage.' Barry shifted again, and kept his eyes on the floor.

Johnny blew another smoke ring. 'A garage. A parking garage?'

'A garage behind a house.'

He studied the thin layer of ashes at the end of the cigar, then slowly placed it between his teeth. He wasn't stupid, he was dumb. He puffed it twice. 'When you say house, do you mean a house on a street with other houses near it?'

'Yeah.' At the time of the burial, Boyd Boyette had been in his trunk for twenty-five hours. Options were limited. He was near panic, and was afraid to leave the city. It wasn't such a bad idea, at the time.

'And these other houses have people living in them, right? People with ears and eyes?'

'I haven't met them, you know, but I would assume so.'

'Don't get cute with me.'

Barry slid an inch in his chair. 'Sorry,' he said.

Johnny stood and walked slowly to the tinted windows directly above the river. He shook his head in disbelief, and puffed his cigar in frustration. Then he turned and walked back to his seat. He placed the cigar in the ashtray and leaned forward on his elbows. 'Whose house?' he asked, stonefaced and ready to explode.

Barry swallowed hard and recrossed his legs. 'Jerome Clifford's.'

There was no eruption. Johnny was known to have ice

water in his veins, and took great pride in staying cool. He was a rarity in this profession, but his level head had made him lots of money. And kept him alive. He placed his left hand completely over his mouth as if there was no way he could believe this. 'Jerome Clifford's house,' he repeated.

Barry nodded. At the time, Clifford had been skiing in Colorado, and Barry knew this because Clifford had invited him to go. He lived alone in a big house with dozens of shady trees. The garage was a separate structure sitting by itself in the backyard. It was a perfect place, he had thought, because no one would ever suspect it.

And he'd been right – it was a perfect place. The Feds hadn't been near it. It was not a mistake. He'd planned to move it later. The mistake had been to tell Clifford.

'And you want me to send in three men to dig it up, without making a sound, and dispose of it properly?'

'Yes sir. It could save my ass.'

'Why do you say this?'

'Because I'm afraid this kid knows where it is, and he's disappeared. Who knows what he's doing? It's just too risky. We gotta move the body, Johnny. I'm begging you.'

'I hate beggars, Barry. What if we get caught? What if a neighbour hears something and calls the cops, and they show up, just checkin' on a prowler, you know, and, son of a bitch, there's three boys diggin' up a corpse.'

'They won't get caught.'

'How do you know! How'd you do it? How'd you bury him in concrete without getting caught?'

'I've done it before, okay.'

'I wanna know!'

Barry straightened himself a bit, and recrossed his legs. 'The day after I hit him, I unloaded six bags of ready-mix at the garage. I was in a truck with bogus tags, dressed like a yard boy, you know. No one seemed to notice. The nearest house is a good thirty yards away, and there's trees everywhere. I went back at midnight in the same truck and unloaded the body in the garage. Then I left. There's a ditch behind the garage, and a park on the other side of the

397

ditch. I just walked through the trees, climbed across the ditch, and sneaked into the garage. Took about thirty minutes to dig a shallow grave, put the body in it, and mix the concrete. The floor of the garage is gravel, white rock, you know. I went back the next night, after the stuff had dried, and covered it with the gravel. He's got this old boat, and so I rolled the boat back over it. When I left, everything was perfect. Clifford never had a clue.'

'Until you told him, of course.'

'Yeah, until I told him. It was a mistake, I admit.'

'Sounds like a lot of hard work.'

'I've done it before, okay. It's easy. I was gonna move it later, but then the Feds got involved and they've followed me for eight months.'

Johnny was nervous now. He relit the cigar and returned to the window. 'You know, Barry,' he said, looking at the water, 'you've got some talent, boy, but you're an idiot when it comes to removing the evidence. We've always used the Gulf out there. Whatever happened to barrels and chains and weights?'

'I promise it won't happen again. Just help me now, and I'll never make this mistake again.'

'There won't be a next time, Barry. If you somehow survive this, I'm gonna let you drive a truck for a while, then maybe run a fence for a year or so. I don't know. Maybe you can go to Vegas and spend a little time with Rock.'

Barry stared at the back of the silver head. He'd lie for the moment, but he would not drive a truck or fence or kiss Rock's ass. 'Whatever you say, Johnny. Just help me.'

Johnny returned to his seat behind the desk. He pinched the bridge of his nose. 'I guess it's urgent.'

'Tonight. This kid's on the loose. He's scared, and it's just a matter of time before he tells someone.'

Johnny closed his eyes and shook his head.

Barry continued. 'Give me three men. I'll tell them exactly how to do it, and I promise they won't get caught. It'll be easy.'

Johnny nodded slowly, painfully. Okay, Okay. He stared at Barry. 'Now get the hell outta here.'

After seven hours of searching, Chief Trimble declared St Peter's to be free of Mark Sway. He huddled in the lobby near Admissions with his officers, and pronounced the search over. They would continue to patrol the tunnels and walkways and corridors, and stand guard at the elevators and stairwells, but they were all now convinced the kid had eluded them. Trimble called McThune at his office with the news.

McThune was not surprised. He had been briefed periodically throughout the morning as the search fizzled. And there was no sign of Reggie. Momma Love had been bothered twice, and now she refused to answer the door. She'd told them to either produce a search warrant, or get the hell off her property. There was no probable cause for a search warrant, and he suspected Momma Love knew this. The hospital had consented to the wiring of the phone in Room 943. Less than thirty minutes earlier, two agents, posing as orderlies, had entered the room while Dianne was down the hall talking to the Memphis Police. Instead of inserting the device, they simply switched phones. They were in the room less than a minute. The child, they reported, was asleep and never moved. The line was direct to the outside, and tapping in through the hospital switchboard would've taken at least two hours and involved other people.

Clint had not been found, but there was no valid reason to obtain a search warrant for his apartment, so they simply watched it.

Harry Roosevelt had been located in a rented boat somewhere along the Buffalo River in Arkansas. McThune had talked to him around eleven. Harry was livid, to say the least, and was now en route back to the city.

Ord had called Foltrigg twice during the morning, but, uncharacteristically, the great man had little to say. The brilliant strategy of ambush by subpoena had blown up in his face, and he was plotting some serious damage control.

K. O. Lewis was already on board Director Voyles's jet, and two agents had been dispatched to meet him at the airport. He would arrive around two.

An All-Points-Bulletin for Mark Sway had been on the national wire since early morning. McThune was reluctant to add the name of Reggie Love to it. Though he hated lawyers, he found it difficult to believe one would actually help a child escape. But as the morning dragged on and there was no sign of her, he became convinced that their disappearances were more than coincidental. At eleven, he added her name to the APB, along with a physical description and a comment that she was probably travelling with Mark Sway. If they were in fact together, and if they had crossed a state line, the offense would be federal and he'd have the pleasure of nailing her.

There was little to do but wait. He and George Ord feasted on cold sandwiches and coffee for lunch. Another phone call, another reporter asking questions. No comment.

Another phone call, and Agent Durston walked into the office and held up three fingers. 'Line three,' he said. 'It's Brenner at the hospital.' McThune hit the button. 'Yeah,' he barked at the phone.

Brenner was in Room 945, next door to Ricky. He spoke in a guarded voice. 'Jason, listen, we just heard a phone call from Clint Van Hooser to Dianne Sway. He told her he had just talked to Reggie, that she and Mark were in New Orleans, and everything was fine.'

'New Orleans!'

'That's what he said. No indication of exactly where, just New Orleans. Dianne said almost nothing, and the entire conversation lasted under two minutes. He said he was calling from his girlfriend's apartment in East Memphis, and he promised to call back later.'

'Where in East Memphis?'

'We can't determine that, and he didn't say. We'll try and trace it next time. He hung up too quick. I'll send the tape over.'

'Do that.' McThune punched another button, and Brenner was gone. He immediately called Larry Trumann in New Orleans.

THIRTY-SIX

The house was in the bend of an old, shady street, and as they approached it Mark instinctively slid downward in the seat until only his eyes and the top of his head were visible in the window. He was wearing a black-and-gold Saints cap Reggie had bought him at a Wal-Mart along with a pair of jeans and two sweatshirts. A street map was folded badly and stuffed beside the hand brake.

'It's a big house,' he said from under the cap as they drove through the bend without the slightest decrease in speed. Reggie saw as much as she could, but she was driving on a strange street and trying desperately not to appear suspicious. It was 3 p.m., hours before dark, and they could drive and look for the rest of the afternoon if they wished. She, too, wore a Saints cap, solid black, and it covered her short gray hair. Her eyes hid behind large sunglasses.

She held her breath as they passed the mailbox with the name Clifford on the side in small, gold, stick-on lettering. It certainly was a big house, but nothing spectacular for this neighborhood. It was of English Tudor design, with dark wood and dark brick, and ivy covering all of one side and most of the front. It was not particularly pretty, she thought as she remembered the newspaper article in which Clifford was described as a divorced father of one. It was obvious, to her at least, that the house did not have the advantage of a woman living in it. Though she could glance at it only as she made the bend and cut her eyes in all directions, looking at once for neighbors, cops, thugs, the garage, and the house, she noticed there were no flowers in the beds and the hedges needed trimming. The windows were covered with dark, drab curtains.

It was not pretty, but it was certainly peaceful. It sat in the center of a large lot with dozens of heavy oaks around it. The driveway ran along a thick hedge and disappeared somewhere around back. Though Clifford had been dead for five days, the grass was neatly trimmed. There was no clue that the house was now uninhabited. There was no hint of any suspicion. Perhaps it was the perfect place to hide a body.

'There's the garage,' Mark said, peeking now. It was a separate structure, fifty or so feet from the house, obviously built much later. A small sidewalk led to the house. A red Triumph Spitfire was on blocks next to the garage.

Mark jerked and stared at the house through the rear window as they eased down the street. 'What do you think, Reggie?'

'Looks awfully quiet, doesn't it?'

'Yeah.'

'Is it what you expected?' she asked.

'I don't know. I watch all those cops shows, you know, and for some reason I could just see Romey's house with yellow police line tape strung all over the place.'

'Why? No crime was committed there. It's just the home of a man who committed suicide. Why would the cops be interested?'

The house was out of sight, and Mark turned around and sat straight in the seat. 'Do you think they've searched it?' he asked.

'Probably. I'm sure they got a search warrant for his house and office, but what could they find? He carried his little secret with him.'

They stopped at an intersection, then continued their tour of the neighborhood.

'What happens to his house?' Mark asked.

'I'm sure he had a will. His heirs will get the house and his assets.'

402

'Yeah. You know, Reggie, I guess I need a will. With everybody after me and all. What do you think?'

'What, exactly, do you own?'

'Well, now that I'm famous and all, I figure the Hollywood people will be knocking on my door. I realize we don't have a door at the present time, but something's gotta happen about that, Reggie, don't you think? I mean, we gotta have a door, of some sort? Anyway, they'll want to do this big movie about the kid who knew too much, and, I hate to say this for obvious reasons, but if these goons put me away, then the movie will be huge and Mom and Ricky will be on easy street. Follow me?'

'I think so. You want a will so Dianne and Ricky will get the movie rights to your life story?'

'Exactly.'

'You don't need one.'

'Why not?'

'They'll get all your assets anyway.'

'Just as well. Saves me attorney's fees.'

'Could we talk about something other than wills and death?'

He shut up and watched the houses on his side of the street. He'd slept most of the night in the backseat, then napped for five hours in the motel room. She, on the other hand, had driven all night and napped less than two hours. She was tired, scared, and beginning to snap at him.

They zigzagged at a leisurely pace through the tree-lined streets. The weather was warm and clear. At every house, people were either mowing grass or pulling weeds or painting shutters. Spanish moss hung from stately oaks. It was Reggie's first tour of New Orleans, and she wished the circumstances were better.

'Are you getting tired of me, Reggie?' he asked without looking at her.

'Of course not. Are you tired of me?'

'No, Reggie. Right now, you're my only friend in the entire world. I just hope I'm not bugging you.'

'I promise.'

Reggie had studied the street map for two hours. She completed a wide loop, and now they were on Romey's street again. They eased by the house without slowing, both gawking at the double garage with a pitched gable above the retractable doors. It needed painting. The concrete drive stopped twenty feet from the doors and turned to the rear of the house. A ragged hedgerow over six feet high ran along one side of the garage and blocked the view of the nearest house, which was at least a hundred feet away. Behind the garage, the small rear lawn stopped at a chain-link fence, and beyond the fence was a heavily wooded area.

They said nothing during the second viewing of Romey's house. The black Accord wandered aimlessly through the neighborhood and stopped near a tennis court in an open area called West Park. Reggie unfolded the street map, and twisted and flipped it until it covered most of the front seat. Mark watched two heavy housewives engage in truly horrible tennis. But they were cute, with their pink and green socks and matching sun visors. A biker approached on a narrow asphalt trail, then disappeared deep into the woods.

Once again, Reggie attempted to fold the map. 'This is the place,' she said.

'Do you want to chicken out?' he asked.

'Sort of. What about you?'

'I don't know. We've come this far. Seems kinda silly to run away now. The garage looked harmless to me.'

She was still folding the map. 'I guess we can try, and if we get spooked, we'll just run back here.'

'Where are we now?'

She opened the door. 'Let's go for a walk.'

The bike trail ran beside a soccer field, then cut through a dense section of woods. The branches of the trees met above it, giving a tunnel-like darkness. The bright sunlight flickered through intermittently. An occasional biker forced them from the asphalt for a few seconds.

The walk was refreshing. After three days in the hospital, two days in jail, seven hours in the car, and six hours in the motel, Mark could barely restrain himself as they rambled through the woods. He missed his bike, and he thought how nice it would be if he and Ricky were here on this trail, racing through the trees without a worry in the world. Just kids again. He missed the crowded streets of the trailer park with kids running everywhere and games of all sorts materializing without a moment's notice. He missed the private little trails of his own woods around Tucker Wheel Estates and the long, solitary walks he had enjoyed all his life. And, strange as it seemed, he missed his hiding places under his own personal trees and beside creeks that belonged to him where he could sit and think, and, yes, sneak a cigarette or two. He hadn't touched one since Monday.

'What am I doing here?' he asked, barely audible.

'It was your idea,' she said, hands stuck deep in her new jeans, also from Wal-Mart.

'It's been my favorite question this week – "What am I doing, here?" I've asked it everywhere, the hospital, the jail, the courtroom. Everywhere.'

'You want to go home, Mark?'

'What's home?'

'Memphis. I'll take you back to your mother.'

'Yeah, but I won't stay with her, will I? In fact, we probably wouldn't even make it to Ricky's room before they grabbed me, and off I'd go, back to jail, back to court, back to see Harry, who'd really be ticked, wouldn't he?'

'Yeah, but I can work on Harry.'

Nobody worked on Harry, Mark had decided. He could see himself sitting in court trying to explain why he'd escaped. Harry would send him back to the detention center where his sweetheart Doreen would be a different person. No pizza. No television. They'd probably put leg chains on him and throw him in solitary.

'I can't go back, Reggie. Not now.'

They had discussed their various options until both were tired of the subject. Nothing had been settled. Each new idea immediately raised a dozen problems. Each course of

405

action ran in all directions and eventually led to disaster. They had both reached, through different routes, the unmistakable conclusion that there was no simple solution. There was no reasonable thing to do. There was no plan even remotely attractive.

But neither believed they would actually dig for the body of Boyd Boyette. Something would happen along the way to spook them, and they'd run back to Memphis. This was yet to be admitted by either.

Reggie stopped at the half-mile marker. To the left was an open, grassy area with a pavilion in the center for picnics. To the right, a small foot trail ventured deeper into the trees. 'Let's try this,' she said, and they left the bike route.

He followed close behind. 'Do you know where you're going?'

'No. But follow me anyway.'

The trail widened a bit, then suddenly gave out and disappeared. Empty beer bottles and chip bags littered the ground. They wove through trees and brush until they found a small clearing. The sun was suddenly bright. Reggie shielded her eyes with her hand and looked at a straight row of trees stretching before them.

'I think that's the creek,' she said.

'What creek?'

'According to the map, Clifford's street borders West Park, and there's a little green line that appears to be a creek or bayou or something running behind his house.'

'It's nothing but trees.'

She shuffled sideways for a few feet, then stopped and pointed. 'Look, there are roofs on the other side of those trees. I think it's Clifford's street.'

Mark stood beside her and strained on tiptoes. 'I see them.'

'Follow me,' she said, and they headed for the row of trees,

It was a beautiful day. They were out for a stroll in the park. This was public property. Nothing to be afraid of.

The creek was nothing but a dry bed of sand and litter.

They picked their way down through the vines and brush, and stood where the water once ran many years before. Even the mud had dried. They climbed the opposite bank, a much steeper one but with more vines and saplings to grab on to.

Reggie was breathing hard when they stopped on the other side of the creek bed. 'Are you scared?' she asked.

'No. Are you?'

'Of course, and you are too. Do you want to keep going?'

'Sure, and I'm not afraid. We're just out for a hike, that's all.' He was terrified and wanted to run, but they had made it this far without incident. And there was a certain thrill in sneaking through the jungle like this. He'd done it a thousand times around the trailer park. He knew to watch for snakes and poison ivy. He'd learned how to line up three trees ahead of him to keep from getting lost. He'd played hide-and-seek in rougher terrain than this. He suddenly crouched low and darted ahead. 'Follow me.'

'This is not a game,' she said.

'Just follow me, unless, of course, you're scared.'

'I'm terrified. I'm fifty-two years old, Mark. Now slow down.'

The first fence they saw was made of cedar, and they stayed in the trees and moved behind the houses. A dog barked in their general direction, but they could not be seen from the house. Then a chain-link fence, but it was not Clifford's. The woods and underbrush thickened, but from nowhere came a small trail that ran parallel to the fence row.

Then, they saw it. On the other side of a chain-link fence, the red Triumph Spitfire sat alone and abandoned next to Romey's garage. The edge of the woods stopped less than twenty feet from the fence, and between it and the rear wall of the garage a dozen or so oaks and elms with Spanish moss shaded the backyard.

Not surprisingly, Romey was a slob. He had piled boards and bricks, buckets and rakes, all sorts of debris behind the garage and out of sight of the street.

There was a small gate in the chain-link fence. The

garage had a window and a door in the rear wall. Sacks of unused and ruined fertilizer were stacked against it. An old lawn mower with the handles off was parked by the door. On the whole, the yard was overgrown and had been for some time. Weeds along the fence were knee-high.

They squatted in the trees and stared at the garage. They would get no closer. The neighbor's patio and charcoal grill were a stone's throw away.

Reggie tried to catch her breath, but it was not possible. She clutched Mark's hand, and found it impossible to believe that the body of a United States Senator was buried less than a hundred feet from where she was now hiding.

'Are we gonna go in there?' Mark asked. It was almost a challenge, though she detected a trace of fear. Good, she thought, he is scared.

She caught her breath long enough to whisper. 'No. We've come far enough.'

He hesitated for a long time, then said, 'It'll be easy.'

'It's a big garage,' she said.

'I know exactly where it is.'

'Well, I haven't pressed you on this, but don't you think it's time to share it with me?'

'It's under the boat.'

'He told you this?'

'Yes. He was very specific. It's buried under the boat.'

'What if there's no boat?'

'Then we haul ass.'

He was finally sweating and breathing hard. She'd seen enough. She stayed low and began backing away. 'I'm leaving now,' she said.

K. O. Lewis never left the plane. McThune and company were waiting when it landed, and they rushed aboard as it refuelled. Thirty minutes later, they left for New Orleans where Larry Trumann now waited anxiously.

Lewis didn't like it. What the hell was he supposed to do in New Orleans? It was a big city. They had no idea what she was driving. In fact, they didn't know if Reggie and

408

Mark had driven, flown, or taken a bus or a train. It was a tourist and convention city with thousands of hotel rooms and crowded streets. Until they made a mistake, it would be impossible to find them.

But Director Voyles wanted him on the scene, and so off he went to New Orleans. Find the kid and make him talk – those were his instructions. Promise him anything.

THIRTY-SEVEN

Two of the three, Leo and Ionucci, were veteran leg-breakers for the Sulari family, and were actually related by blood to Barry The Blade, though they often denied it. The third, a huge kid with massive biceps, a wide neck, and thick waist, was known simply as the Bull, for obvious reasons. He'd been sent on this unusual errand to perform most of the grunt work. Barry assured them it would not be difficult. The concrete was thin. The body was small. Chip a little here, and chip a little there, and before they knew it they'd see a black garbage bag.

Barry had diagrammed the floor of the garage, and marked with exact confidence the position of the grave. He had drawn a map with a line starting at the parking lot of West Park and running between the tennis courts, across the soccer field, through a patch of trees, then across another field with a picnic pavilion, then along the bike route for a ways until a footpath led to the ditch. It would be easy, he had assured them all afternoon.

The bike trail was deserted, and with good reason. It was ten minutes after eleven, Saturday night. The air was muggy, and by the time they reached the footpath they were breathing heavily and sweating. The Bull, much younger and fitter, followed the other two and smiled to himself as they bitched quietly in the blackness about the humidity. They were in their late thirties, he guessed, chain-smokers of course, abusive drinkers, sloppy eaters. They were griping about sweating, and they hadn't walked a mile yet.

410

Leo was in charge of this expedition, and he carried the flashlight. They were dressed in solid black. Ionucci followed like a bloodhound with heartworms, head down, breathing hard, lethargic, mad at the world for being here. 'Careful,' Leo said as they eased down the ditch bank in heavy weeds. They were not exactly woodsy types. This place had been frightening enough at 6 p.m. when they first walked it off. Now it was terrifying. The Bull expected at any moment to step on a thick, squirming snake. Of course, if he was bitten, he could turn around with justification, and, he hoped, find the car. His two buddies would then be forced to go it alone. He tripped on a log, but kept his balance. He almost wished for a snake.

'Careful,' Leo said for the tenth time, as if saying it made things safer. They eased along the dark and weedy creek bed for two hundred yards, then climbed the other bank. The flashlight was turned off, and they crouched low through the brush until they were behind Clifford's chain-link fence. They rested on their knees.

'This is stupid, you know,' Ionucci said between loud breaths. 'Since when do we dig up bodies?'

Leo was surveying the darkness of Clifford's backyard. Not a single light. They had driven by only minutes earlier, and noticed a small gas light burning in a globe near the front door, but the rear was complete darkness. 'Shut up,' he said without moving his head.

'Yeah, yeah,' Ionucci mumbled. 'It's stupid.' His screaming lungs were almost audible. Sweat dripped from his chin. The Bull knelt behind them, shaking his head at their unfitness. They were used primarily as bodyguards and drivers, occupations that required little exertion. Legend held that Leo did his first killing when he was seventeen, but was forced to quit a few years later when he served time. The Bull had heard that Ionucci had been shot twice over the years, but this was unconfirmed. The people who generated these stories were not known for telling the truth.

'Let's go,' Leo said like a field marshal. They scooted

411

across the grass to the gate in Clifford's fence, then through it. They darted between the trees until they landed against the rear wall of the garage. Ionucci was in pain. He fell to all fours and heaved mightily. Leo crawled to a corner and looked for movement next door. Nothing. Nothing but the sounds of Ionucci's impending cardiac arrest. The Bull peeked around the other corner and watched the rear of Clifford's house.

The neighborhood was asleep. Even the dogs had called it a night.

Leo stood and tried to open the rear door. It was locked. 'Stay here,' he said, and slid low around the garage until he came to the front door. It was locked also. Back to the rear, he said, 'We gotta break some glass. It's locked too.'

Ionucci produced a hammer from a pouch on his waist, and Leo began tapping lightly on the dirty pane just above the doorknob. 'Watch that corner,' he said to the Bull, who crawled behind him and looked in the direction of the Ballantine home next door.

Leo pecked and pecked until the pane was broken. He carefully removed broken pieces and tossed them aside. When the jagged edges were clear, he slid his left arm through and unlocked the door. He turned on the flashlight, and the three eased inside.

Barry said he remembered the place being a mess, and Clifford obviously had been too busy to tidy things up before he passed on. The first thing they noticed was that the floor was gravel, not concrete. Leo kicked at the white rocks beneath his feet. If Barry had told them about the gravel flooring, he didn't remember it.

The boat was in the center of the garage. It was a sixteen-foot outboard ski rig with a heavy layer of dust over it. Three of the four trailer tires were flat. This boat had not touched water in years. Layers of junk were piled against it. Garden tools, sacks of aluminum cans, stacks of newspapers, rusted patio furniture. Romey didn't need a garbage service. Hell, he had a garage. Thick spiderwebs were strung in every corner. Unused tools hung from the walls.

412

Clifford, for some reason, had been a prodigious collector of wire clothes hangers. Thousands of them hung on strands of wire above the boat. Rows and rows of clothes hangers. At some point, he'd grown weary of running the wire, so he'd simply driven long nails into the wall studs and packed hundreds of hangers on them. Romey, the environmentalist, had also collected cans and plastic containers, obviously with the lofty goal of recycling. But he'd been a busy man, and so a small mountain of green garbage bags stuffed with cans and bottles filled half of the garage. He'd been such a slob, he'd even thrown some of the bags into the boat.

Leo aimed the small light at a point directly under the main beam of the trailer. He motioned for the Bull, who eased on to all fours and began brushing away the white rock gravel. From the waist pouch, Ionucci produced a small trowel. The Bull took it and scraped away more gravel. His two partners stood over his shoulders.

Two inches down, the scraping sound changed when he struck concrete. The boat was in the way. The Bull stood, slowly lifted the hitch, and with a mighty strain rolled the front of the trailer five feet to the side. The side of the trailer brushed against the mountain of aluminum cans, and there was a prolonged racket. The men froze, and listened.

'You gotta be careful.' Leo whispered the obvious. 'Stay here, and don't move.' He left them standing in the dark beside the boat, and eased through the rear door. He stood beside a tree behind the garage and watched the Ballantine house next door. It was dark and quiet. A patio light cast a dim glow around the grill and flower beds, but nothing moved. Leo watched and waited. He doubted the neighbors could hear a jackhammer. He crept back inside the garage and aimed the flashlight at the spot of concrete under the gravel. 'Let's clear it off,' he said, and the Bull returned to his knees.

Barry had explained that he'd first dug a shallow grave, approximately six feet by two feet, and no more than eighteen inches deep. Then he'd stuffed the body into it.

413

Then he'd packed the pre-mix concrete around the body, which was wrapped in black plastic garbage bags. Then he'd added water to his little recipe. He'd returned the next day to cover it all with gravel and put the boat in place.

He'd done a fine job. Given Clifford's talent for organization, it would be another five years before the boat was moved. Barry had explained that this was just a temporary grave. He'd planned to move it, but the Feds started trailing him. Leo and Ionucci had disposed of a few bodies, usually in weighted barrels over water, but they were impressed with Barry's temporary hiding place.

The Bull scraped and brushed, and soon the entire concrete surface was clear. Ionucci knelt on the other side of it, and he and the Bull began chipping away with chisels and hammers. Leo placed the flashlight on the gravel beside them, and eased again through the rear door. He crouched low and moved to the front of the garage. All was quiet. The chiselling could be heard, all right. He walked quickly to the rear of Clifford's house, maybe fifty feet away, and the sounds were barely audible. He smiled to himself. Had the Ballantines been awake, they could not have heard it.

He darted back to the garage, and sat in the darkness between a corner and the Spitfire. He could see the empty street. A small, black car eased around the bend in front of the house, and was gone. No other traffic. Through the hedge, he could see the outline of the Ballantine house. Nothing moved. The only sounds were the muffled chippings of concrete from the grave of Boyd Boyette.

Clint's Accord stopped near the tennis courts. A red Cadillac was parked near the street. Reggie turned off the lights and the engine.

They sat in silence and stared through the windshield at the dark soccer field. This is a wonderful place to get mugged, she thought to herself, but didn't mention it. There was plenty to fear without thinking of muggers.

Mark hadn't said much since dark. They had napped, together on one bed, for an hour after the pizza had been

414

delivered to their motel room. They had watched television. He had asked her repeatedly about the time, as if he had an appointment with a firing squad. At ten, she was convinced he would chicken out. At eleven, he was pacing around the room, and going back and forth to the bathroom.

But here they were at eleven-forty, sitting in a hot car on a dark night, planning an impossible mission that neither really wanted.

'Do you think anybody knows we're here?' he asked softly.

She looked at him. His gaze was lost somewhere beyond the soccer field. 'You mean, here in New Orleans?'

'Yeah. Do you think anyone knows we're in New Orleans?'

'No. I don't think so.'

This seemed to satisfy him. She'd talked to Clint around seven. A Memphis TV station had reported that she was missing as well, but things appeared to be quiet. Clint hadn't left his bedroom in twelve hours, he said, so would they please hurry up and do whatever the hell they were planning. He'd called Momma Love. She was worried, but doing okay under the circumstances.

They left the car and walked along the bike trail.

'Are you sure you want to do this?' she asked, looking around nervously. The trail was pitch black, and in places only the asphalt beneath their feet kept them from wandering into the trees. They walked slowly, side by side, and held hands.

As she took one uncertain step after another, Reggie asked herself what she was doing here on this trail, in these woods of this city, at this moment, with this kid whom she loved dearly but was not willing to die for. She clutched his hand and tried to be brave. Surely, she prayed, something would happen very soon and they would dash back to the car and leave New Orleans.

'I've been thinking,' Mark said.

'Why am I not surprised?'

'It might be too hard to actually find the body, you know.

415

So, this is what I've decided. You'll stay in the trees close to the ditch, you see, and I'll sneak through the backyard and into the garage. I'll look under the boat, you know, just to make sure it's there, then we'll get out of here.'

'You think you can just look under the boat and see the body?'

'Maybe I can see where it is, you know?'

She squeezed his hand tighter. 'Listen to me, Mark. We're sticking together, okay. If you go to the garage, then I'm going too.' Her voice was remarkably firm. Surely, they wouldn't make it to the garage.

There was a break in the trees. A light on a pole revealed the picnic pavilion to their left. The footpath started to the right. Mark pressed a switch, and the beam from a small flashlight hit the ground in front of them. 'Follow me,' he said. 'Nobody can see us out here.'

He moved deftly through the woods without a sound. Back in the motel room, he had recounted many stories of his late night walks through the woods around the trailer park, and of the games the boys played in the darkness. Jungle games, he called them. With the light in his hand, he moved faster now, brushing past limbs and dodging saplings.

'Slow down, Mark,' she said more than once.

He held her hand and helped her down the ditch bank. They climbed to the other side, and crept through the woods and underbrush until they found the mysterious trail that had surprised them hours earlier. The fences started. They moved slowly, quietly, and Mark turned off the flashlight.

They were in the dense trees directly behind Clifford's house. They knelt and caught their breath. Through the brush and weeds they could see the outline of the rear of the garage.

'What if we don't see the body?' she asked. 'What then?'

'We'll worry about that when it happens.'

This was not the moment for another long discussion about his options. On all fours, he crawled to the edge of the

416

thick underbrush. She followed. They stopped twenty feet from the gate in thick, wet weeds. The backyard was dark and still. Not a light or sound or movement. The entire street was sound asleep.

'Reggie, I want you to stay here. Keep your head down. I'll be back in a minute.'

'No sir!' she whispered loudly. 'You can't do this, Mark!'

He was already moving. This was a game to him, just another jungle game with his little buddies giving chase and shooting guns with colored water. He slid through the grass like a lizard, and opened the gate just wide enough to slide through.

Reggie followed on all fours through the weeds, then stopped. He was already out of sight. He stopped behind the first tree, and listened. He crawled to the next one, and heard something. Chink! Chink! He froze on his hands and knees. The sounds were coming from the garage. Chink! Chink! Very slowly, he peeked around the tree and stared at the rear door. Chink! Chink! He glanced back at Reggie, but the woods and underbrush were black. She was nowhere in sight. He looked at the door again. Something was different. He crawled to the next tree, ten feet closer. The sounds were louder. The door was open slightly, and a windowpane was missing.

Somebody was in there! Chink! Chink! Chink! Somebody was hiding in there with the lights off, and he was digging! Mark breathed deeply, and crawled behind a pile of debris less than ten feet from the rear door. He hadn't made a sound, and he knew it. The grass was taller around the debris, and he crawled through it like a chameleon, very slowly. Chink! Chink!

He crouched low, and started for the rear door. The ragged end of a rotted two-by-four caught his ankle and he tripped. The pile of debris rattled and an empty paint bucket fell to the ground.

Leo bounced to his feet and darted to the rear of garage. He yanked a .38 with a silencer from his waist, and scooted in the darkness until he was at the corner where he squatted

417

and listened. The chiselling had stopped inside. Ionucci peeked through the rear door.

Reggie heard the racket behind the garage, and fell to her stomach in the wet grass. She closed her eyes and said a prayer. What the hell was she doing here?

Leo sneaked to the pile of debris, then cut around it with the gun drawn and ready to fire. He squatted again, and patiently studied the darkness. The fence was barely visible. Nothing moved. He slid next to a tree fifteen feet behind the garage, and waited. Ionucci watched him closely. Long seconds passed without a sound. Leo stood upright and crept slowly toward the gate. A twig snapped under his foot, freezing him in place for a second.

He moved around the backyard, bolder now but with the gun still ready, and leaned against a tree, a thick oak with limbs hanging low near the Ballantine property line. In the unkempt hedgerow less than twelve feet away, Mark crouched on all fours and held his breath. He watched the dark figure move between the trees in the darkness, and he knew if he kept still he would not be found. He exhaled slowly, his eyes glued to the silhouette of the man by the tree.

'What is it?' a deep voice asked from the garage. Leo slid the gun into the waist of his pants and eased backward. Ionucci was standing outside the door. 'What is it?' he repeated.

'I don't know,' Leo said in a half-whisper. 'Maybe just a cat or something. Get back to work.'

The door closed softly, and Leo paced silently back and forth behind the garage for five minutes. Five minutes, but it seemed like an hour to Mark.

Then the dark figure eased around the corner and was gone. Mark watched every move. He slowly counted to one hundred, then crawled along the hedgerow until it stopped at the fence. He paused at the gate and counted to thirty. All was quiet except for the distant, muffled chiselling. Then he darted to the edge of the brush where Reggie was crouching in terror. She grabbed him as they ducked into the heavier undergrowth.

418

'They're in there!' he said, out of breath.

'Who?!'

'I don't know! They're digging up the body!'

'What happened?!'

He was breathing rapidly. His head bobbed up and down as he swallowed and tried to speak. 'I tripped on something, and this one guy, I think he had a gun, almost found me. God I was scared!'

'You're still scared. And so am I! Let's get outta here!'

'Listen, Reggie. Wait a minute. Listen! Can you hear it?'

'No! Hear what?'

'That chinking noise. I can't hear it either. We're too far away.'

'And I say we get farther away. Let's go.'

'Just wait a minute, Reggie. Dammit!'

'They're killers, Mark. They're Mafia people. Let's get the hell out of here!'

He breathed through his teeth, and glared at her. 'Settle down, Reggie. Just settle down, okay. Look, no one can see us here. You can't even see these trees from the garage. I tried, okay. Now settle down.'

She fell to her knees, and they stared at the garage. He placed his finger to his lips. 'We're safe here, okay,' he whispered. 'Listen.'

They listened, but the sounds could not be heard.

'Mark, these are Muldanno's people. They know you've escaped. They're panicking. They've got guns and knives and who knows what else. Let's go. They beat us. It's all over. They win.'

'We can't let them take the body, Reggie. Think about it. If they get away with it, it'll never be found.'

'Good. You're off the hook, and the Mafia forgets about you. Now let's go.'

'No, Reggie. We gotta do something.'

'What! You want to pick a fight with Mafia thugs? Come on, Mark. This is crazy.'

'Just wait a minute.'

'Okay. I'll wait exactly one minute, then I'm gone.'

He turned and smiled at her. 'You won't leave me, Reggie. I know you better than that.'

'Don't push me, Mark. Now I know how Ricky felt when you were playing around with Clifford and his little water hose.'

'Just be quiet, okay. I'm thinking.'

'That's what scares me.'

She sat on her butt with her legs crossed in front of her. Leaves and vines rubbed her face and neck. He rocked gently on all fours like a lion ready to kill, and finally said, 'I've got an idea.'

'Of course you do.'

'Stay here.'

She suddenly grabbed the back of his neck and pulled his face to hers. 'Listen, buster, this is not one of your little jungle games where you shoot rubber darts and throw dirt clods. Those are not your little buddies in there playing hide-and-seek, or GI Joe, or whatever the hell you play. This is life and death, Mark. You just made one mistake, and you got lucky. One more, and you'll be dead. Now let's get the hell outta here! Now!'

He was still for a few seconds as she scolded him, then he jerked viciously away. 'Stay here, and don't move,' he said with stiff jaws. He crept from the brush, through the grass to the fence.

Just inside the gate was an abandoned flower bed outlined with sunken timbers and covered with weeds. He crawled to it, and picked out three rocks with all the fussiness of a chef selecting tomatoes at the market. He watched both corners of the garage, then made a silent retreat into the darkness.

Reggie was waiting, and she had not moved a muscle. He knew she could not find her way to the car. He knew she needed him. They huddled again in the brush.

'Mark, this is insane, son,' she pleaded. 'Please. These people are not playing games.'

'They're too busy to worry about us, okay. We're safe here, Reggie. Look, if they came tearing out of that door right now, they could never find us. We're safe here, Reggie. Trust me.'

'Trust you! You'll get yourself killed.'

'Stay here.'

'What! Please, Mark! No more games!'

He ignored her and pointed to a spot near three trees, about thirty feet away. 'I'll be right back,' he said, and he disappeared.

He crawled through the brush until he was behind the Ballantine house. He could barely see the edge of Romey's garage. Reggie was lost in the dark undergrowth.

The patio was small and dimly lit. There were three white wicker chairs and a charcoal grill. A large plate-glass window overlooked it, and it was this window that attracted his attention. He stood behind a tree, and measured the distance, which he estimated to be the length of two house trailers. The rock would have to be low enough to miss the branches, yet high enough to clear a row of hedges. He took a deep breath, and threw it as hard as he could.

Leo jumped at the sound from next door. He crept in front of the garage and peeked through the hedge. The patio was quiet and still. It sounded like a rock landing on wooden decking and rattling around next to the brick. Maybe it was just a dog. He watched for a long time, and nothing happened. They were safe. Another false alarm.

Mr Ballantine rolled over and stared at the ceiling. He was in his early sixties, and sleep had been difficult since the removal of the disc a year and a half ago. He had just dozed off, and was awakened by a sound. Or was it a sound? No place was safe in New Orleans anymore, and he'd paid two thousand dollars for an alarm system six months earlier. Crime was everywhere. They were thinking about moving.

He rolled to one side, and had just closed his eyes when the window crashed. He bolted to the door, turned on the bedroom light, and yelled, 'Get up, Wanda! Get up!' Wanda was reaching for her robe, and Mr Ballantine was grabbing the shotgun from the closet. The alarm was wailing. They raced down the hall, yelling at each other and flipping on light switches. The glass had scattered throughout the den, and Mr. Ballantine aimed the shotgun at the window as if to prevent another attack. 'Call the police!' he barked at her. '911!'

'I know the number!'

'Hurry up!' He tiptoed in his house shoes around the glass, crouching low with the gun as if a burglar had chosen to enter the house through the window. He fought his way to the kitchen where he punched numbers on a control panel, and the sirens stopped.

Leo had just resettled into his guard post next to the Spitfire when the crash shattered the stillness. He bit a hole in his tongue as he scrambled to his feet and darted once again to the hedge. A siren screamed briefly, then stopped. A man in a red nightshirt down to his knees was running on to the patio with a shotgun.

Leo crept quickly to the rear door of the garage. Ionucci and the Bull were crouched in terror beside the boat. Leo stepped on a rake, and the handle landed on a bag full of aluminum cans. The three stopped breathing. Voices could be heard next door.

'What the hell is it?' Ionucci demanded through clenched teeth. He and the Bull were shiny with sweat. Their shirts were stuck to their bodies. Their heads were soaking wet.

'I don't know,' Leo bristled, spitting blood, inching toward the window facing the hedge that separated the Ballantine property. 'Something went through a window, I think. I don't know. Crazy bastard's got a shotgun!'

'A what!' Ionucci almost shrieked. He and the Bull slowly raised their heads to the window and joined Leo there. The crazy man with the shotgun was stomping around his backyard, yelling at the trees.

Mr Ballantine was sick of New Orleans and sick of drugs and sick of punks trying to rob and pillage, and he was sick of crime and living in fear like this, and he was just so damned sick of it all he raised his shotgun and fired once at

422

the trees for good measure. That'll teach the slimy little bastards that he meant business. Come back to his house, and you'll leave in a hearse. BOOM!

Mrs Ballantine stood in the doorway in her pink robe, and screamed when he fired and wounded the trees.

The three heads in the garage next door hit the dirt when the shooting started. 'Sumbitch is crazy!' Leo screeched. Slowly, they raised their heads again in perfect unison, and at precisely that instant, the first police car pulled into the Ballantine driveway with blue and red lights flashing wildly.

Ionucci was the first one out the door, followed by the Bull, then Leo. They were in a huge hurry, but at the same time careful not to attract attention from the idiots next door. They scooted along, close to the ground, dashing from tree to tree, trying desperately to make it to the woods before there was more gunfire. The retreat was orderly.

Mark and Reggie huddled deep in the brush. 'You're crazy,' she kept muttering, and it was not idle talk. She honestly believed that her client was mentally unbalanced. But she hugged him anyway, and they squeezed close together. They didn't see the three silhouettes scampering along until they crossed through the fence.

'There they are,' Mark whispered, pointing. Not thirty seconds earlier, he had told her to watch the gate.

'Three of them,' he whispered. The three leaped into the underbrush, less than twenty feet from where they were hiding, and disappeared into the woods.

They squeezed closer together. 'You're crazy,' she said again.

'Maybe so. But it's working.'

The shotgun blast had almost sent Reggie over the edge. She'd been trembling when they arrived here. She'd been mortified when he returned with news that someone was in the garage. She'd damned near screamed when he threw the rock through the window. But the shotgun was the final straw. Her heart was pounding and her hands were trembling.

423

And oddly, at this moment, she knew they couldn't run. The three grave robbers were now between them and their car. There was no escape.

The shotgun blast brought the neighborhood to life. Floodlights filled backyards as men and women in bathrobes walked on to patios and looked in the direction of the Ballantines'. Voices shouted inquiries across fences. Dogs came to life. Mark and Reggie withdrew deeper into the brush.

Mr Ballantine and one of the cops walked along the rear fence, searching perhaps for more felonious rocks. It was hopeless. Reggie and Mark could hear voices, but they could not understand what was being said. Mr Ballantine yelled a lot.

The cops settled him down, then helped him tape clear plastic over the window. The red and blue lights were turned off, and after twenty minutes, the cops left.

Reggie and Mark waited, trembling and holding hands. Bugs crawled over their skin. The mosquitoes were brutal. The weeds and burrs stuck to their dark sweatshirts. The lights in the Ballantine house finally went off, and they waited some more.

THIRTY-EIGHT

A few minutes after one, the clouds broke and the half-moon lightened Romey's backyard and garage for a moment. Reggie glanced at her watch. Her legs were numb from squatting. Her back ached from sitting on her tail. Oddly, though, she had become accustomed to her little spot in the jungle, and after surviving the thugs, the cops, and the idiot with the shotgun, she was feeling remarkably safe. Her breathing and pulse were normal. She was not sweating, though her jeans and shirt were still wet from exertion and humidity. Mark swatted and slapped mosquitoes, and said little. He was eerily calm. He chewed on a weed, watched the fence row, and acted as if he and he alone knew precisely when to make the next move.

'Let's go for a little walk,' he said, rising from his knees.

'Where to? The car?'

'No. Just down the trail. My leg is about to cramp.'

Her right leg was numb below the knee. Her left leg was dead below the hip, and she stood with great difficulty. She followed him through the brush until they were on the small trail parallel to the creek. He moved deftly through the darkness without the benefit of the flashlight, swatting mosquitoes and stretching his legs.

They stopped deep in the woods, out of sight of the fence rows of Romey's neighbors.

'I really think we should leave now,' she said, a bit louder since the houses were no longer in view. 'I have this fear of snakes, you see, and I don't want to step on one.'

He did not look at her, but stared in the direction of the ditch. 'I don't think it's a good idea to leave now,' he whispered.

She knew he had a reason for saying this. She'd not won an argument in the past six hours. 'Why?'

'Because those men could still be around here. In fact, they could be close by waiting for things to settle down so they can return. If we head for the car, we might meet them.'

'Mark, I can't take any more of this, okay? This may be fun and games for you, but I'm fifty-two years old and I've had it. I can't believe I'm hiding in this jungle at one o'clock in the morning.'

He put his forefinger over his lips. 'Shhhhhh. You're talking too loud. And this isn't a game.'

'Dammit, I know it's not a game! Don't lecture me.'

'Keep your cool, Reggie. We're safe now.'

'Safe my ass! I won't feel safe until I lock the door at the motel.'

'Then leave. Go on. Find your way back to the car, and leave.'

'Sure, and let me guess. You'll stay here, right?'

The moonlight disappeared, and suddenly the woods were darker. He turned his back to her and began walking toward their hiding place. She instinctively followed him, and this irritated her because at this moment she was depending on an eleven-year-old. But she followed him anyway, along a trail invisible to her, through the dense woods to the undergrowth, to about the same point where they'd waited before. The garage was barely visible.

The blood had returned to her legs, though they were very stiff. Her lower back throbbed. She could rub her hand across her forearm and feel the bumps from the mosquito bites. There was a thin sliver of blood on the back of her left hand, probably from a sticker in the brush or perhaps a weed. If she ever made it back to Memphis, she vowed to join a health club and get in shape. Not that she planned any more ventures like this, but she was tired of aching and gasping for breath.

Mark lowered on to one knee, stuck another weed in his mouth to chew on, and watched the garage.

They waited, almost in silence, for an hour. When she'd reached the point of leaving him and running wildly through the woods, Reggie said, 'Okay, Mark, I'm leaving. Do what you've got to do, because I'm leaving now.' But she didn't move.

They crouched together, and he pointed at the garage as if she didn't know where it was. 'I'm crawling up there, okay, with the flashlight, and I'm looking at the body, or the grave, or whatever they were digging at, okay?'

'No.'

'It won't take but a second, maybe. If I'm lucky, I'll be right back.'

'I'm going with you,' she said.

'No. I want you to stay here. I'm worried that those guys are watching too, somewhere along the tree line. If they come after me, I want you to start yelling and run like crazy.'

'No. No way, sweetheart. If you're looking at the body, then I'm looking at the body, and I'm not arguing about it. That's final.'

He looked at her eyes, four or five inches away, and decided not to argue. Her head was shaking and her jaw was tight. She looked cute under the cap.

'Then follow me, Reggie. Stay low, and listen. Always listen, okay.'

'All right, all right. I'm not totally helpless. In fact, I'm getting pretty good at crawling.'

They attacked from the brush on all fours again, two figures sliding in the still darkness. The grass was wet and cool. The gate, still open from the hasty retreat of the grave robbers, squeaked slightly when Reggie hooked it with a foot. Mark glared at her. They stopped behind the first tree, then eased to the next. Not a sound from anywhere. It was 2 a.m., and the neighborhood was silent. Mark, however, was worried about the nut next door with the gun. He doubted the man would sleep well with a thin sheet of

427

plastic over the window, and he could envision him sitting in the kitchen watching the patio and waiting for the snap of a twig before he began blasting away again. They stopped at the next tree, then crawled to the junk pile.

She nodded once, taking small, quick breaths. They crouched and darted to the rear door of the garage, which was slightly open. Mark stuck his head inside. He turned on the flashlight and aimed it at the floor. Reggie eased in behind him.

The odor was thick and pungent, like a dead animal rotting in the sun. Reggie instinctively covered her nose and mouth. Mark breathed deeply, then held his breath.

The only open space in the cluttered room was in the center, where the boat had been parked. They crouched over the concrete slab. 'I'm getting sick,' Reggie said, barely opening her mouth.

Another ten minutes, and the body would have been out. They had started in the center, somewhere around the torso, and chipped away at each side. The black garbage bags, partially decomposed by the cement, had been ripped away. A ragged little trench had been cut away toward the feet and knees.

Mark had seen enough. He picked up a chisel, one that had been left behind, and jabbed it into black plastic.

'Don't!' Reggie whispered loudly, backing away but still seeing it all.

He ripped through the garbage bag with the chisel, and followed it closely with the light. He made a slow turn, then pulled the plastic with his hand. He bolted upright in horror, then slowly placed the light squarely into the decaying face of the late Senator Boyd Boyette.

Reggie took another step backward, and fell on to a pile of bags filled with aluminum cans. The racket was deafening in the still air. She scrambled and fought to get up in the darkness, but the thrashing and kicking created more noise. Mark grabbed a hand, and pulled her toward the boat. 'I'm sorry!' she whispered, standing two feet from the corpse without thinking about it.

428

'Shhhhh,' Mark said as he stepped on to a box and peeked through the window. A light came on next door. The shotgun could not be far behind.

'Let's go,' he said. 'Stay low.'

They eased through the rear door, and Mark closed it behind them. A door slammed at the neighbor's. He hit his hands and knees and slid around the debris pile, past the trees, and through the gate. Reggie was on his heels. They stopped crawling when they reached the brush. They crouched low and scampered like squirrels until they found the trail. Mark turned on the flashlight, and they didn't slow until they were at the creek. He ducked into some weeds, and turned off the light.

'What's the matter?' she asked, breathing hard, terrified, and damned sure not willing to pause in this getaway.

'Did you see his face?' Mark asked, in awe of what they'd just done.

'Of course I saw his face. Now let's go.'

'I want to see it again.'

She almost slapped him. Then she stood upright, hands on hips, and started walking toward the creek.

Mark ran beside her with the flashlight. 'I was just kidding.' She stopped and glared at him, then he took her hand and led her down the bank to the creek bed.

They entered the expressway by the Superdome and headed for Metairie. Traffic was light, though heavier than in most cities at two-thirty on a Sunday morning. Not a word had been spoken since they'd jumped in the car at West Park and left the area. And the silence bothered neither.

Reggie contemplated how close she'd been to death. Mafia hoods, snakes, crazy neighbors, police, guns, shock, heart attack – it would've made no difference. She was indeed fortunate to be here, racing along the expressway, soaked with perspiration, covered with insect bites, bloody from the wounds of nature, and dirty from a night in the jungle. It could've been so much worse. She'd take a hot shower at the motel, maybe sleep a little, then worry about the next move. She was exhausted from the fear and sudden shocks. She was in pain from the crawling and stooping. She was too old for this nonsense. The things lawyers do.

Mark gently scratched the bites on his left forearm, and watched the lights of New Orleans thin as they left downtown. 'Did you see that brown stuff on his face?' he asked without looking at her.

Though the face was now forever seared into her memory, she could not, at the moment, recall any brown stuff on it. It was a small, shriveled, partially decayed face, and one that she wished she could forget.

'I saw only the worms,' she said.

'The brown stuff was blood,' he said with the authority of a medical examiner.

She did not wish to pursue this conversation. There were more important things to discuss now that the silence was broken.

'I think we need to talk about your plans, now that this little escapade is behind us,' she said, glancing at him.

'We need to move fast, Reggie. Those guys will be back to get the body, don't you think?'

'Yes. For once I agree. They might be back now, for all we know.'

He scratched the other forearm, and placed an ankle on a knee. 'I've been thinking.'

'I'm sure you have.'

'There are two things I don't like about Memphis. The heat, and the flat land. There are no hills or mountains, you know what I mean? I've always thought it would be so nice to live in the mountains where the air is cool and the snow is deep in the wintertime. Wouldn't that be fun, Reggie?'

She smiled to herself and changed lanes. 'Sounds wonderful. Any particular mountain?'

'Out west somewhere. I love to watch those old "Bonanza" reruns with Hoss and Little Joe. Adam was okay, but it really ticked me off when he left. I've watched them since I was a little kid, and I've always thought it would be neat to live out there.'

'What happened to the tall buildings and the crowded city?'

'That was yesterday. Today, I'm thinking about mountains.'

'Is that where you want to go, Mark?'

'I think so. Can I?'

'It can be arranged. Right now, they'll agree to almost anything.'

He stopped scratching and locked his fingers around his knee. His voice was tired. 'I can't go back to Memphis, can I, Reggie?'

'No,' she said softly.

'I didn't think so.' He thought about this for a few seconds. 'It's just as well, I guess. There's not much left there.'

'Think of it as yet another adventure, Mark. A new home, new school, new job for your mother. You'll have a much nicer place to live, new friends, mountains all around you if that's what you want.'

'Be honest with me, Reggie. Do you think they'll ever find me?'

She had to say no. At this moment, he had no choice. She would run and hide with him no more. They had to either call the FBI and strike a deal, or call the FBI and turn themselves in. This little trip was about to be over.

'No, Mark. They'll never find you. You have to trust the FBI.'

'I don't trust the FBI, and you don't either.'

'I don't completely distrust them. But right now, they've got the only game in town.'

'And I have to play along with them?'

'Unless you have a better idea.'

Mark was in the shower. Reggie dialled Clint's number, and listened as the phone rang a dozen times before he answerd. It was almost 3 a.m.

431

'Clint, it's me.'

His voice was thick and slow. 'Reggie?'

'Yes, me, Reggie. Listen to me, Clint. Turn on the light, put your feet on the floor, and listen to me.'

'I'm listening.'

'Jason McThune's phone number is listed in the Memphis directory. I want you to call him, and tell him you need Larry Trumann's home phone number in New Orleans. Got that?'

'Why don't you look in the New Orleans phone book?'

'Don't ask questions, Clint. Just do as I say. Trumann's not listed down here.'

'What's going on, Reggie?' His words were much quicker.

'I'll call you back in fifteen minutes. Make some coffee. This could be a long day.' She hung up and unlaced her muddy sneakers.

Mark finished a quick shower, and ripped open a new package of underwear. He'd been embarrassed when Reggie bought them, but now it seemed so unimportant. He slipped into a new, yellow tee shirt, and pulled on his new but dirty Wal-Mart jeans. No socks. He wasn't going anywhere for a while, according to his attorney.

He left the tiny bathroom. Reggie was lying on the bed, shoes off, weeds and grass on the cuffs of her jeans. He sat on the edge of her bed, and stared at the wall.

'Feel better?' she asked.

He nodded, said nothing, then lay beside her. She pulled him close to her body, and placed an arm under his wet head. 'I'm all messed up, Reggie,' he said softly. 'I don't know what happens next anymore.'

The tough little boy who threw rocks through windows and outsmarted killers and cops and raced fearlessly through dark woods began to cry. He bit his lip and squinted his eyes, but couldn't stop the tears. She held him closer. Then he broke, finally, and sobbed loudly with no attempt to hold it back, no effort at being tough now. He cried without shame or embarrassment. His body shook and he squeezed her arm.

432

'It's okay, Mark,' she whispered in his ear. 'Everything's okay.' With her free hand, she wiped tears from her cheeks, and squeezed him even closer. Now it was up to her. She had to be the lawyer again, the counselor who moved daringly and called the shots. His life was once again in her hands.

The television was on but the sound was off. Its gray and blue shadows cast a dim light over the small room with its double beds and cheap furniture.

Jo Trumann grabbed the phone and searched the darkness for the clock. Ten minutes before four. She handed it to her husband, who took it and sat in the center of the bed. 'Hello,' he grunted.

'Hi, Larry. It's me, Reggie Love, remember?'

'Yeah. Where are you?'

'Here in New Orleans. We need to talk, and the sooner the better.'

He almost said something smart about the hour of the day, but thought better of it. It was important, or she wouldn't be calling. 'Sure. What's going on, Reggie?'

'Well, we've found the body, for starters.'

Trumann was suddenly on his feet and sliding into his house shoes. 'I'm listening.'

'I've seen the body, Larry. About two hours ago. I saw it with my own eyes. Smelled it too.'

'Where are you?' Trumann pressed a button on the recorder by the phone.

'I'm at a pay phone, so no cute stuff, okay?'

'Okay.'

'The people who buried the body tried to retrieve it last night, but they were unable to do so. Long story, Larry. I'll explain it later. I'm willing to bet they'll try again very soon.'

'Is the kid with you?'

'Yes. He knew where it was, and we came, we saw, and we conquered. You'll have it by noon today if you do as I say.'

'Anything.'

'That's the spirit, Larry. The kid wants to cut a deal. So we need to talk.'

'When and where?'

'Meet me in the Raintree Inn on Veterans Boulevard in Metairie. There's a grill that's open all night. How long will it take?'

'Give me forty-five minutes.'

'The sooner you get here, the sooner you'll get the body.'

'Can I bring someone with me?'

'Who?'

'K. O. Lewis.'

'He's in town?'

'Yeah. We knew you were here, so Mr Lewis flew in a few hours ago.'

There was hesitation on her end. 'How'd you know I was here?'

'We have ways.'

'Who have you wired, Trumann? Talk to me. I want a straight answer.' Her voice was firm, yet with a trace of panic.

'Can I explain it when we meet?' he asked, kicking himself in the ass for opening this can of worms.

'Explain it now,' she commanded.

'I'll be happy to explain when –'

'Listen, asshole. I'm cancelling the meeting unless you tell me right now who's been wired. Talk, Trumann.'

'Okay. We bugged the kid's mother's room at the hospital. It was a mistake. I didn't do it, okay. Memphis did it.'

'What'd they hear?'

'Not much. Your man Clint called yesterday afternoon and told her you guys were in New Orleans. That's all, I swear.'

'Would you lie to me, Trumann?' she asked, thinking of the tape from their first encounter.

'I'm not lying, Reggie,' Trumann insisted, thinking of the same damned tape.

434

There was a long pause in which he heard nothing but her breathing. 'Just you and K. O. Lewis,' she said. 'No one else. If Foltrigg shows up, all deals are off.'

'I swear.'

She hung up. Trumann immediately called K. O. Lewis at the Hilton. Then he called McThune in Memphis.

THIRTY-NINE

Exactly forty-five minutes later, Trumann and Lewis walked nervously into the near empty grill at the Raintree Inn. Reggie waited at a table in the corner, far away from anyone. Her hair was wet and she wore no makeup. A bulky tee shirt with LSU TIGERS in purple letters was tucked into a pair of faded jeans. She sipped black coffee, and neither stood nor smiled as they approached and sat opposite her.

'Good morning, Ms Love,' Lewis said in an attempt to be nice.

'It's Reggie, okay, and it's too early for pleasantries. Are we alone?'

'Of course,' Lewis said. At that moment eight FBI agents were guarding the parking lot, and more were on the way.

'No bugs, wire, body mikes, salt shakers, or ketchup bottles?'

'None.'

A waiter appeared, and they ordered coffee.

'Where's the kid?' Trumann asked.

'He's around. You'll see him soon enough.'

'Is he safe?'

'Of course he's safe. You boys couldn't catch him if he was on the streets begging for food.'

She handed Lewis a piece of paper. 'These are the names of three psychiatric hospitals that specialize in children. Battenwood in Rockford, Illinois. Ridgewood in Tallahassee. And Grant's Clinic in Phoenix. Any one of the three will do.'

Their eyes went slowly from her face to the list. They focused and studied it. 'But we've already checked with the clinic in Portland,' Lewis said, puzzled.

'I don't care where you've checked, Mr Lewis. Take this list, and check again. I suggest you do it quickly. Call Washington, get them out of bed, and get it done.'

He folded the list and placed it under his elbow. 'You, uh, you say you've seen the body,' he asked, trying to sound authoritative but failing miserably.

She smiled. 'I have. Less than three hours ago. Muldanno's men were trying to get it, but we scared them off.'

'We?'

'Mark and I.'

They both studied her intently, and waited for precious details of this wild, impossible little story. The coffee arrived, and they ignored both it and the waiter.

'We're not eating,' Reggie said rudely, and the waiter left.

'Here's the deal,' she said. 'There are a few provisions, none of which are in the least bit negotiable. Do it my way, do it now, and you might get the body before Muldanno carries it away and drops it in the ocean. If you blow it, gentlemen, I doubt you'll ever get this close again.'

They nodded furiously.

'Did you fly here on a private jet?' she asked Lewis.

'Yes. It's the Director's.'

'How many does it seat?'

'Twenty or so.'

'Good. Send it back to Memphis right now. I want you to pick up Dianne and Ricky Sway, along with his doctor and Clint. Fly them here immediately. McThune is welcome to come. We'll meet them at the airport, and when Mark is safely on board and the plane is gone, I'll tell you where the body is. How about it so far?'

'No problem,' Lewis said. Trumann was speechless.

'The entire family enters the witness protection plan. First, they pick the hospital, and when Ricky is able to move, they'll pick the city.'

437

'No problem.'

'Complete change of identification, nice little house, the works. This woman needs to stay home and raise her kids for a while, so I'd suggest a monthly allowance in the sum of four thousand dollars, guaranteed for three years. Plus an initial cash outlay of twenty-five thousand. They lost everything in the fire, remember?'

'Of course. These things are easy.' Lewis was so eager, she wished she'd asked for more.

'If, at some point, she wants to return to work, then I'd suggest a nice, cushy government job with no responsibilities, short hours, and a fat salary.'

'We have plenty of those.'

'Should they desire to move at any time, and to any place, they'll be allowed to do so, at your expense, of course.'

'We do it all the time.'

Trumann was smiling now, though he was trying not to.

'She'll need a car.'

'No problem.'

'Ricky may need extended treatment.'

'We'll cover it.'

'I want Mark examined by a psychiatrist, though I suspect he's in better shape than we are.'

'Done.'

'There are a couple of other minor matters, and they'll be covered in the agreement.'

'What agreement?'

'The agreement I'm having typed as we speak. It'll be signed by myself, Dianne Sway, Judge Harry Roosevelt, and you, Mr Lewis, on behalf of Director Voyles.'

'What else is in the agreement?' Lewis asked.

'I want your assurance that you'll do everything in your power to compel the attendance of Roy Foltrigg before the Juvenile Court of Shelby County, Tennessee. Judge Roosevelt will want to discuss a few matters with him, and I'm sure Foltrigg will resist. If a subpoena is issued for him, I want it served by you, Mr Trumann.'

'Gladly,' Trumann said with a nasty smile.

'We'll do what we can,' Lewis added, a bit confused.

'Good. Go make your phone calls. Get the plane in the air. Call McThune and tell him to pick up Clint Van Hooser and take him to the hospital. Get that damned bug off her phone, because I need to talk to her.'

'No problem.' They jumped to their feet.

'We'll meet right here in thirty minutes.'

Clint hammered away on his ancient Royal portable. His third cup of coffee shook each time he slapped the return and rattled the kitchen table. He studied his hurried chicken-scratch handwriting on the back of an *Esquire*, and tried to remember each provision as she'd spouted it over the phone. If he finished it, it would be, without a doubt, the sloppiest legal document ever prepared. He cursed and grabbed the Liquid Paper.

A knock on the door startled him. He ran his fingers through his unkempt and unwashed hair, and walked to the door. 'Who is it?'

'FBI.'

Not so loud, he almost said. He could hear the neighbors now, gossiping about him and his predawn arrest. Probably drugs, they would say.

He cracked the door and peeked under the safety chain. Two agents with puffy eyes stood in the darkness. 'We were told to come get you,' one said apologetically.

'I need some ID.'

They stuck their badges near the door. 'FBI,' the first one said.

Clint opened the door wider, and waved them in. 'I'll be a few more minutes. Have a seat.'

They stood awkwardly in the center of the den as he returned to the table and the typewriter. He pecked slowly. The chicken scratch failed him, and he ad-libbed the rest. The important points were there, he hoped. She always found something to change in his typing at the office, but this would have to do. He pulled it carefully from the Royal, and placed it in a small briefcase.

439

'Let's go,' he said.

At five-forty, Trumann returned alone to the table where Reggie waited. He brought two cellular phones. 'Thought we might need these,' he said.

'Where'd you get them?' Reggie asked.

'They were delivered to us here.'

'By some of your men?'

'That's right.'

'Just for fun, how many men do you have right now within a quarter of a mile of this place?'

'I don't know. Twelve or thirteen. It's routine, Reggie. They might be needed. We'll send a few to protect the kid, if you'll tell me where he is. I assume he's alone.'

'He's alone, and he's fine. Did you talk to McThune?'

'Yes. They've already picked up Clint.'

'That was fast.'

'Well, to be honest, we've had men watching his apartment for twenty-four hours now. We simply woke them up, and told them to knock on his door. We found your car, Reggie, but we couldn't find Clint's.'

'I'm driving it.'

'That's what I figured. Pretty slick, but we would've found you within twenty-four hours.'

'Don't be so cocky, Trumann. You've been looking for Boyette for eight months.'

'True. How'd the kid escape?'

'It's a long story. I'll save it for later.'

'You could be implicated, you know.'

'Not if you guys sign our little agreement.'

'We'll sign it, don't worry.' One of the phones rang, and Trumann grabbed it. As he listened, K. O. Lewis hurried to the table and brought his own cellular phone. He jumped into his chair, and leaned across the table, his eyes glowing with excitement. 'Talked to Washington. We're checking the hospitals right now. Everything looks fine. Director Voyles will call here in a minute. He'll probably want to talk to you.'

'How about the plane?'

Lewis checked his watch. 'It's leaving now, should be in Memphis by six-thirty.'

Trumann placed a hand over his phone. 'This is McThune. He's at the hospital waiting for Dr Greenway and the administrator. They've made contact with Judge Roosevelt, and he's on his way down there.'

'Have you de-bugged her phone?' Reggie asked.

'Yes.'

'Removed the salt shakers?'

'No salt shakers. Everything's clean.'

'Good. Tell him to call back in twenty minutes,' she said.

Trumann mumbled into the phone and flipped a switch. Within seconds, K. O.'s phone beeped. He stuck it to his head, and broke into a large smile. 'Yes sir,' he said, most respectfully. 'Just a second.'

He jabbed the phone at Reggie. 'It's Director Voyles. He'd like to speak with you.'

Reggie took it slowly, and said, 'This is Reggie Love.' Lewis and Trumann watched like two kids waiting for ice cream.

A deep and very clear voice came from the other end. Though Denton Voyles had never been fond of the press during his forty-two years as Director of the FBI, they occasionally captured a brief word or two. The voice was familiar. 'Ms Love, this is Denton Voyles. How are you?'

'Just fine. The name's Reggie, okay.'

'Sure, Reggie. Listen, K. O. just brought me up to date, and I want to assure you the FBI will do anything you want to protect this kid and his family. K. O. has full authority to act for me. We'll also protect you if you wish.'

'I'm more concerned about the child, Denton.'

Trumann and Lewis glanced at each other. She had just called him Denton, a feat no one had dared to attempt before. And she was not the least disrespectful.

'If you want, you can fax me the agreement here and I'll sign it myself,' he said.

'That won't be necessary, but thanks.'

'And my plane is at your disposal.'

'Thank you.'

'And I promise that we'll see to it that Mr Foltrigg has to face the music in Memphis. We had nothing to do with the grand jury subpoenas, you understand?'

'Yes, I know.'

'Good luck to you, Reggie. You guys work out the details. Lewis can move mountains. Call me if you need me. I'll be at the office all day.'

'Thank you,' she said, and handed the phone back to K. O. Lewis, the mountain mover.

The assistant night manager of the grill, a young man of no more than nineteen with a peach fuzz mustache and an attitude, walked to the table. These people had been here for an hour, and from all indications they had set up camp. There were three phones in the center of the table. Some papers were lying about. The woman wore a sweatshirt and jeans. One of the men wore a cap and no socks. 'Excuse me,' he said curtly, 'can I be of assistance?'

Trumann glanced over his shoulder, and snapped. 'No.'

He hesitated, and took a step closer. 'I'm the assistant night manager, and I demand to know what you're doing here.'

Trumann snapped his fingers loudly, and two gentlemen reading the Sunday paper at a table not far away jumped to their feet and whipped badges from their pockets. They stuck them into the face of the assistant night manager. 'FBI,' they said together as they each took an arm and led him away. He did not return. The grill was still deserted.

A phone rang, and Lewis took it. He listened carefully. Reggie opened the Sunday New Orleans paper. At the bottom of the front page was her face. The picture was taken from the bar registry, and it was next to Mark's fourth-grade class photo. Side by side. Escaped. Disappeared. On the run. Boyette and all that. She turned to the comics.

'That was Washington,' Lewis reported as he placed the phone on the table. 'The clinic in Rockford is full. They're checking on the other two.'

442

Reggie nodded and sipped her coffee. The sun was making its first efforts of the day. Her eyes were red and her head was hurting, but the adrenaline was pumping. With a little luck, she would be home by dark.

'Look, Reggie, could you give us an idea how long it'll take to get to the body?' Trumann asked with great caution. He didn't want to press; didn't want to upset her. But he needed to start planning. 'Muldanno's still out there, and if he gets it first, we're all up a creek.' He paused and waited for her to say something. 'It's in the city, right?'

'If you don't get lost, you should be able to find it in fifteen minutes.'

'Fifteen minutes,' he repeated slowly, as if this was too good to be true. Fifteen minutes.

FORTY

Clint hadn't smoked a cigarette in four years, but he found himself puffing nervously on a Virginia Slim. Dianne had one too, and they stood at the end of the hall and watched as the day broke over downtown Memphis. Greenway was in the room with Ricky. Next door, Jason McThune, the hospital administrator, and a small collection of FBI agents waited. Both Clint and Dianne had talked to Reggie in the past thirty minutes.

'The Director has given his word,' Clint said, sucking hard on the narrow cigarette, trying to extract a little smoke. 'There's no other choice, Dianne.'

She stared through the window with one arm across her chest and the other hand holding the cigarette near her mouth. 'We just leave, right? We just get on the plane and fly off into the sunset, and everybody lives happily ever after?'

'Something like that.'

'What if I don't want to, Clint?'

'You can't say no.'

'Why not?'

'It's very simple. Your son has made the decision to talk. He's also made the decision to enter the witness protection program, so like it or not, you have to go too. You and Ricky.'

'I'd like to talk to my son.'

'You can talk to him in New Orleans. If you can change his mind, then the deal's off. Reggie's not dropping the big news until you guys are on the plane and in the air.'

Clint was trying to be firm, yet compassionate. She was

444

scared, weak, and vulnerable. Her hands trembled as she placed the filter between her lips.

'Ms Sway,' a heavy voice said from behind. They turned to find the Honorable Harry M. Roosevelt standing behind them in a massive, bright blue jogging suit with Memphis State Tigers emblazoned across the front. It had to be a triple extra-large, and it stopped six inches above his ankles. A pair of ancient but seldom used running shoes covered his long feet. He was holding the two-page agreement Clint had typed.

She acknowledged his presence but said nothing.

'Hello, Your Honor,' Clint said quietly.

'I just talked to Reggie,' he said to Dianne. 'I'd say they've had a rather eventful trip.' He stepped between them and ignored Clint. 'I've read this agreement, and I'm inclined to sign it. I think it's in the best interests of Mark for you to do the same.'

'Is that an order?' she asked.

'No. I do not have the power to bind you to this agreement,' he said, then flashed a huge, warm smile. 'But, I would if I could.'

She placed the cigarette in an ashtray on the windowsill, and stuck both hands deep into the pockets of her jeans. 'And if I don't?'

'Then Mark will be returned here, placed back in detention, and beyond that, who knows. He will eventually be forced to talk. The situation is much more urgent now.'

'Why?'

'Because we now know for a fact that Mark knows where the body is. So does Reggie. They could be in great danger. You're at the point, Ms Sway, where you have to trust people.'

'That's easy for you to say.'

'Indeed it is. But if I were you, I'd sign this and get on the plane.'

Dianne slowly took the agreement from His Honor. 'Let's go talk to Dr Greenway.'

They followed her down the hall to the room next to Ricky's.

Twenty minutes later, the ninth floor of St Peter's was
sealed off by a dozen FBI agents. The waiting room was
evacuated. The nurses were told to remain at their station.
Three of the elevators were stopped on the ground floor.
The other was held in place on the ninth by an agent.

The door to Room 943 opened, and little Ricky Sway,
drugged and sound asleep, was wheeled into the hallway on
a stretcher pushed by Jason McThune and Clint Van
Hooser. On this, his sixth day of confinement, he was no
better than when he first arrived. Greenway walked along
one side, Dianne the other. Harry followed along for a few
steps, then stopped.

The stretcher was pushed into the waiting elevator,
which descended to the fourth floor, also secured by FBI
agents. It was rushed a short distance to a service elevator,
where Agent Durston held the door, then taken to the
second floor, also secured. Ricky never moved. Dianne
held his arm and jogged beside the stretcher.

They maneuvered through a series of short corridors and
metal doors, and were suddenly on a flat roof. A helicopter
was waiting. Ricky was loaded quickly, and Dianne, Clint,
and McThune climbed aboard.

Minutes later, the helicopter landed near a hangar at
Memphis International Airport. A half dozen FBI agents
guarded the pad as Ricky was rolled to a nearby jet.

At ten minutes before seven, a cellular phone rang at the
corner table of the Raintree Grill, and Trumann grabbed it.
He listened and checked his watch. 'They're in the air,' he
announced and set the phone down. Lewis was talking to
Washington again.

Reggie breathed deeply and smiled at Trumann. 'The
body's in concrete. You'll need a few hammers and chisels.'

Trumann choked on his orange juice. 'Okay. Anything
else?'

'Yeah. Place a couple of your boys near the intersection of
St Joseph and Carondelet.'

'Close by?'

'Just do it, okay.'

'Done. Anything else?'

'I'll be back in a minute.' Reggie walked to the registra-
tion desk, and asked the clerk to check the fax machine.
The clerk returned with a copy of the two-page agreement,
which Reggie read closely. The typing was horrible, but the
words were perfect. She returned to the table. 'Let's get
Mark,' she said.

Mark finished brushing his teeth for the third time, and sat
on the edge of the bed. His black-and-gold Saints canvas
bag was packed with dirty clothes and new underwear.
Cartoons were on, but he was not interested.

He heard a car door, then footsteps, then a knock. 'Mark,
it's me,' Reggie said.

He opened the door, but she did not step inside. 'Are you
ready to go?'

'I guess.' The sun was up and the parking lot was visible.
A familiar face was behind her. It was one of the FBI agents
from the first meeting at the hospital. Mark grabbed his
bag, and stepped out into the parking lot. Three cars were
waiting. A man opened the rear door of the middle car, and
Mark and his attorney got in.

The little motorcade sped away.

'Everything's fine,' Reggie said, taking his hand. The
two men in the front seat stared straight ahead. 'Ricky and
your mother are on the plane. They'll be here in about an
hour. Are you okay?'

'I guess. Have you told them?' he whispered.

'Not yet,' she answered. 'Not until you're on the plane
and in the air.'

'Are all these guys FBI agents?'

She nodded and patted his hand. He suddenly felt
important, sitting in the rear of his own black car, being
rushed to the airport to board a private jet, cops all around just
to protect him. He crossed his legs and sat a bit straighter.

He'd never flown before.

447

FORTY-ONE

Barry paced nervously before the tinted windows in Johnny's office, and watched the tugs and barges on the river. His nasty eyes were red, but not from booze or partying. He hadn't slept. He'd waited here at the warehouse for the body to be delivered to him, and when Leo and company arrived around one without it, he had called his uncle.

Johnny, on this fine Sunday morning, was wearing neither tie nor suspenders. He paced slowly behind his desk, puffing blue smoke from his third cigar of the day. A thick cloud hung not far above his head.

The screaming and ass chewing had ended hours ago. Barry had cursed Leo and Ionucci and the Bull, and Leo had cursed back. But with time, the panic subsided. Throughout the night, Leo had periodically driven by Clifford's house, always in a different vehicle, and seeing nothing unusual. The body was still there.

Johnny decided to wait twenty-four hours and try again. They would watch the place during the day, and attack with full force after dark. The Bull assured him he could have the body out of the concrete in ten minutes.

Just be cool, Johnny had told everyone. Just be cool.

Roy Foltrigg finished the Sunday paper on the patio of his suburban split-level, and walked barefooted across the wet grass with a cup of cold coffee. He had slept little. He had waited in the darkness on his front porch for the paper to arrive, then ran to fetch it in his pajamas and bathrobe. He had called Trumann, but, strangely, Mrs Trumann wasn't sure where her husband had gone.

He inspected his wife's rosebushes along the back fence, and asked himself for the hundredth time where Mark Sway would run to. There was no doubt, at least in his mind, that Reggie had helped him escape. She'd obviously gone crazy again, and run off with the kid. He smiled to himself. He'd have the pleasure of busting her ass.

The hangar was a quarter of a mile from the main terminal, in a row of identical buildings all drab gray and sitting quietly together. The words Gulf Air were painted in orange letters above the tall double doors, which were opening as the three cars stopped in front of the hangar. The floor was sparkling concrete, painted green without a speck of dirt and covered with nothing but two private jets side by side in a far corner. A few lights were on, and their reflections glowed on the green floor. The building was big enough for a stock car race, Mark thought as he stretched his neck for a glimpse of the two jets.

With the doors out of the way, the entire front of the hangar was now open. Three men walked hurriedly along the back wall as if searching for something. Two more stood by one door. Outside, another half dozen moved slowly about, keeping their distance from the cars that had just parked.

'Who are these people?' Mark asked, in the general direction of the front seat.

'They're with us,' Trumann said.

'They're FBI agents,' Reggie clarified.

'Why so many?'

'They're just being careful,' she said. 'How much longer, do you think?' she asked Trumann.

He glanced at his watch. 'Probably thirty minutes.'

'Let's walk around,' she said, opening her door. As if on cue, the other eleven doors in the little parade opened and the cars emptied. Mark looked around at the other hangars, and the terminal, and a plane landing on the runway in front of them. This had become terribly exciting. Not three weeks ago, he'd beaten the crap out of a subdivision kid at school after the kid taunted him because he'd never flown. If they could only see him now. Rushed to the airport by private car, waiting for his private jet to take him anywhere he wanted to go. No more trailers. No more fights with subdivision kids. No more notes to Mom, because now she would be at home. He'd decided, sitting alone in the motel room, that this was a wonderful idea. He'd come to New Orleans and outsmarted the Mafia in its own backyard, and he could do it again.

He caught a few stares from the agents by the door. They cut their eyes quickly at him, then looked away. Just checking him out. Maybe he'd sign some autographs later.

He followed Reggie into the vast hangar, and the two private jets caught his attention. They were like small, shiny toys sitting under the Christmas tree waiting to be played with. One was black, the other silver, and Mark stared at them.

A man in an orange shirt with Gulf Air on a patch above the pocket closed the door to a small office inside the hangar and walked in their direction. K. O. Lewis met him, and they talked quietly. The man waved at the office, and said something about coffee.

Larry Trumann knelt beside Mark, still staring at the jets. 'Mark, do you remember me?' he asked with a smile.

'Yes sir. I met you at the hospital.'

'That's right. My name's Larry Trumann.' He offered his hand, and Mark shook it slowly. Children are not supposed to shake hands with adults. 'I'm an FBI agent here in New Orleans.'

Mark nodded and kept staring at the jets.

'Would you like to look at them?' Trumann asked.

'Can I?' he asked, suddenly friendly to Trumann.

'Sure.' Trumann stood and placed a hand on Mark's shoulder. They walked slowly across the gleaming concrete, the sounds of Trumann's steps echoing upward.

They stopped in front of the black jet. 'Now this is a Lear Jet,' Trumann began.

Reggie and K. O. Lewis left the small office with tall cups of steaming coffee. The agents who'd escorted them here had slipped into the shadows of the hangar. They sipped what must've been their tenth cups of this long morning, and watched as Trumann and the kid inspected the jets.

'He's a brave kid,' Lewis said.

'He's remarkable,' Reggie said. 'At times he thinks like a terrorist, then he cries like a little child.'

'He is a child.'

'I know. But don't tell him. It may upset him, and, hell, who knows what he might do.' She took a long sip. 'Truly remarkable.'

K. O. blew into his cup, then took a tiny sip. 'We've pulled some strings. There's a room waiting for Ricky at Grant's Clinic in Phoenix. We need to know if that's the destination. The pilot called five minutes ago. He has to get clearance, file a flight plan, you know.'

'Phoenix it is. Complete confidentiality, okay? Register the kid under another name. Same for the mother and Mark. Keep some of your boys nearby. I want you to pay for his doctor's trip out there and for a few days of work.'

'No problem. The people in Phoenix have no idea what's coming. Have you guys talked about a permanent home?'

'A little, not much. Mark says he wants to live in the mountains.'

'Vancouver's nice. We vacationed there last summer. Absolutely gorgeous.'

'Out of the country?'

'No problem. Director Voyles said they can go any-where. We've placed a few witnesses outside the States, and I think the Sways are perfect candidates. These people will be taken care of, Reggie. You have my word.'

The man in the orange shirt joined Mark and Trumann, and was now in charge of the tour. He lowered the steps to the black Lear, and the three disappeared inside.

'I must confess,' Lewis said after he swallowed another

451

scalding dose of coffee, 'I was never convinced the kid knew.'

'Clifford told him everything. He knew exactly where it was.'

'Did you?'

'No. Not until yesterday. When he first came to my office, he told me that he knew, but he didn't tell me where it was. Thank God for that. He kept it to himself until we were near the body yesterday afternoon.'

'Why'd you come here? Seems awfully risky.'

Reggie nodded at the jets. 'You'll have to ask him. He insisted we find the body. If Clifford lied to him, then he figured he was off the hook.'

'And so you just drove down here and looked for the body? Just like that?'

'It was a bit more involved. It's a long story, K. O., and I'll give you all the details over a long dinner.'

'I can't wait.'

Mark's small head was now in the cockpit, and Reggie half expected the engines to start, the plane to taxi slowly from the hangar, out onto the runway, and Mark to dazzle them with a perfect takeoff. She knew he could do it.

'Are you concerned about your own safety?' Lewis asked.

'Not really. I'm just a humble lawyer. What would they gain by coming after me?'

'Retribution. You don't understand the way they think.'

'Indeed I don't.'

'Director Voyles would like for us to stick close for a few months, at least until the trial is over.'

'I don't care what you do, I just don't want to see anyone who's watching me, okay?'

'Fine. We have ways.'

The tour moved to the second jet, a silver Citation, and for the moment Mark Sway had forgotten about dead bodies and bad guys lurking in shadows. The steps came down, and he climbed aboard with Trumann in tow.

An agent with a radio walked to Reggie and Lewis, and

said, 'They're on final approach.' They followed him to the opening of the hangar near the cars. A minute later Mark and Trumann joined them, and as they watched the sky to the north a tiny plane appeared.

'That's them,' Lewis said. Mark inched his way next to Reggie and took her hand. The plane grew larger as it approached the runway. It, too, was black, but much larger than the jets in the hangar. Agents, some in suits and some in jeans, began moving around as the plane taxied to them. It stopped a hundred feet away, and the engines died. A full minute passed before the door opened and the stairs hit the ground.

Jason McThune trotted down first, and when he stepped on to the tarmac a dozen FBI agents had the plane surrounded. Dianne and Clint were next. They joined McThune, and together the three walked briskly toward the hangar.

Mark released Reggie's hand and ran to meet his mother. Dianne grabbed and hugged him, and for an awkward second or two everyone else either watched or looked at the terminal in the distance.

They said nothing as they embraced. He squeezed her tightly around the neck, and finally said, through tears, 'I'm sorry, Mom. I'm so sorry.' She clutched his head and pressed it to her shoulder, and at the same time thought of strangling him and of never letting go.

Reggie led them into the small but clean office, and offered Dianne coffee. She declined. Trumann, McThune, Lewis, and the gang waited nervously outside the door. Trumann, especially, was anxious. What if they changed their minds? What if Muldanno got the body? What if? He paced and fidgeted, glanced at the locked door, asked Lewis a hundred questions. Lewis sipped coffee and tried to remain calm. It was now twenty minutes before eight. The sun was bright, the air humid.

Mark sat in his mother's lap, and Reggie, the lawyer, sat behind the desk. Clint stood by the door.

'I'm glad you came,' Reggie said to Dianne.

'I didn't have much of a choice.'

'You do now. You can change your mind, if you want. You can ask me anything.'

'Do you realize how fast all this is happening, Reggie? Six days ago, I came home and found Ricky curled in his bed sucking his thumb. Then Mark and the cop showed up. Now I'm being asked to become someone else and run away to another world. My god.'

'I understand,' Reggie said. 'But we can't stop things.'

'Are you mad at me, Mom?' he asked.

'Yeah. No cookies for a week.' She stroked his hair. There was a long pause.

'How's Ricky?' Reggie asked.

'About the same. Dr Greenway is trying to bring him around so he can enjoy the plane ride. But they had to drug him slightly when we left the hospital.'

'I'm not going back to Memphis, Mom,' Mark said.

'The FBI has contacted a children's psychiatric hospital in Phoenix, and they're waiting for you now,' Reggie explained. 'It's a good one. Clint checked it out Friday. It's been highly recommended.'

'So we're going to live in Phoenix?' Dianne asked.

'Only until Ricky is released. Then you go wherever you want. Canada. Australia. New Zealand. It's up to you. Or you can stay in Phoenix.'

'Let's go to Australia, Mom. They still have real cowboys down there. Saw it in a movie once.'

'No more movies for you, Mark,' Dianne said, still rubbing his head. 'We wouldn't be here if you hadn't watched so many movies.'

'What about TV?'

'No. From now on, you'll do nothing but read books.'

The office was silent for a long time. Reggie had nothing else to say. Clint was dead tired and about to fall asleep on his feet. Dianne's mind was moving clearly now, for the first time in a week. Frightened as she was, she had escaped the dungeon at St Peter's. She had seen sunlight and smelled real air. She was holding her lost son, and the other one would improve. All these people were trying to help. The lamp factory was history. Employment was now a thing of the past. No more cheap trailers. No more worries about past due child support and unpaid bills. She could watch the boys grow up. She could join the PTA. She could buy some clothes and do her nails. Good gosh, she was only thirty years old. With a little effort and a little money, she could be attractive again. There were men out there.

As dark and treacherous as the future seemed, it could not be as horrible as the past six days. Something had to give. She was due a break. Have a little faith, baby.

'I guess we'd better get to Phoenix,' she said.

Reggie grinned with relief. She pulled the agreement from a briefcase Clint brought with him. It had been signed by Harry and McThune. Reggie added her signature, and handed the pen to Dianne. Mark, now bored with hugs and tears, walked to the wall and admired a series of framed color photos of jets. 'On second thought, I might be a pilot,' he said to Clint.

Reggie took the agreement. 'I'll be back in a minute,' she said, opening the door and closing it behind her.

Trumann jumped when it opened. Hot coffee splashed from his trembling cup and burned his right hand. He cursed, and slung at the floor, then wiped it on his pants.

'Relax, Larry,' Reggie said. 'Everything's fine. Sign here.' She stuck the agreement in his face, and Trumann scrawled his name. K. O. did the same.

'Get the plane ready,' Reggie said. 'They're going to Phoenix.'

K. O. turned and flashed a hand signal at the agents by the hangar entry. McThune jogged toward them with more instructions. Reggie returned to the office and closed the door.

K. O. and Trumann shook hands and smiled goofily. They stared at the door to the office.

'What now?' Trumann mumbled.

455

'She's a lawyer,' K. O. said. 'Nothing's ever easy with lawyers.'

McThune walked to Trumann and handed him an envelope. 'It's a subpoena for the Reverend Roy Foltrigg,' he said with a smile. 'Judge Roosevelt issued it this morning.'

'On Sunday morning?' Trumann asked, taking the envelope.

'Yeah. He called his clerk, and they met at his office. He's very excited about seeing Foltrigg back in Memphis.'

The three chuckled at this. 'It'll be served upon the Reverend this morning,' Trumann said.

After a minute, the door opened. Clint, Dianne, Mark, then Reggie filed out and headed for the tarmac. The engines were started. Agents scurried about. Trumann and Lewis escorted them to the hangar doors, and stopped.

K. O., ever the diplomat, offered his hand to Dianne, and said, 'Good luck, Ms Sway. Jason McThune will escort you to Phoenix, and handle things once you get there. You are completely safe. And if we can do anything to help, please let us know.'

Dianne gave a sweet smile and shook his hand. Mark offered his, and said, 'Thanks, K. O. You've been a real pain in the ass.' But he was smiling, and it struck everyone as being funny.

K. O. laughed. 'Good luck to you, Mark, and I assure you, son, you've been a bigger pain.'

'Yeah, I know. Sorry about all this.' He shook hands with Trumann, and walked away with his mother and McThune. Reggie and Clint remained by the hangar door.

At some point, about halfway to the jet, Mark stopped. As if suddenly scared, he froze in place and watched as Dianne climbed the steps to the plane. At no time during the past twenty-four hours had it occurred to him that Reggie would be left behind. He had simply assumed, for whatever reason, that she would stay with them until this ordeal was over. She would fly off with them, and hang around the new hospital until they were safe. And as he

456

stood there, a tiny figure on the vast tarmac, motionless and stunned, he realized she was not beside him. She was back there with Clint and the FBI.

He turned slowly, and stared at her in terror as this reality sunk in. He took two steps toward her, then stopped. Reggie left her small group and walked to him. She knelt on the tarmac, and looked into his panicked eyes.

He bit his lip. 'You can't come with us, can you?' he asked slowly in a frightened voice. Though they had talked for hours, this subject was never touched.

She shook her head as her eyes watered.

He wiped his eyes with the back of his hand. The FBI agents were close by, but not watching. For once in his life, he was not ashamed to cry in public. 'But I want you to go,' he said.

'I can't, Mark.' She leaned forward, took both of his shoulders, and hugged him gently. 'I can't go.'

Tears flooded his cheeks. 'I'm sorry about all this. You didn't deserve it.'

'But if it hadn't happened, Mark, I never would've met you.' She kissed him on the cheek, and held his shoulders tight. 'I love you, Mark. I'll miss you.'

'I'll never see you again, will I?' His lip quivered and tears dripped off his chin. His voice was frail.

She gritted her teeth and shook her head. 'No, Mark.'

Reggie took a deep breath, and stood. She wanted to grab him, and take him home to Momma Love. He could have the bedroom upstairs, and all the spaghetti and ice cream he could eat.

Instead, she nodded at the plane where Dianne was standing in the door, waiting patiently. He wiped his cheeks again. 'I'll never see you again,' he said, almost to himself. He turned, and made a feeble attempt to straighten his shoulders, but he couldn't. He walked slowly to the steps, and glanced back for one last look.

457

FORTY-TWO

Minutes later, as the plane taxied to the end of the runway, Clint eased to her side and took her hand. They watched silently as it took off and finally disappeared in the clouds.

She wiped tears from both cheeks. 'I think I'll become a real estate lawyer,' she said. 'I can't take any more of this.'

'He's quite a kid,' Clint said.

'It hurts, Clint.'

He squeezed her hand harder. 'I know.'

Trumann appeared quietly beside her, and the three of them looked at the sky. She noticed him, and pulled the micro-cassette tape from her pocket. 'It's yours,' she said. He took it.

'The body is in the garage behind Jerome Clifford's house,' she said, still wiping tears, '886 East Brookline.'

Trumann turned to his left and stuck a radio to his mouth. The agents bolted for their cars. Reggie and Clint did not move.

'Thanks, Reggie,' Trumann said, now suddenly anxious to leave.

She nodded at the distant clouds. 'Don't thank me,' she said. 'Thank Mark.'

THE
STREET
LAWYER

ONE

The man with the rubber boots stepped into the elevator behind me, but I didn't see him at first. I smelled him though – the pungent odor of smoke and cheap wine and life on the street without soap. We were alone as we moved upward, and when I finally glanced over I saw the boots, black and dirty and much too large. A frayed and tattered trench coat fell to his knees. Under it, layers of foul clothing bunched around his midsection, so that he appeared stocky, almost fat. But it wasn't from being well fed; in the wintertime in D.C., the street people wear everything they own, or so it seems.

He was black and aging – his beard and hair were half-gray and hadn't been washed or cut in years. He looked straight ahead through thick sunglasses, thoroughly ignoring me, and making me wonder for a second why, exactly, I was inspecting him.

He didn't belong. It was not his building, not his elevator, not a place he could afford. The lawyers on all eight floors worked for my firm at hourly rates that still seemed obscene to me, even after seven years.

Just another street bum in from the cold. Happened all the time in downtown Washington. But we had security guards to deal with the riffraff.

We stopped at six, and I noticed for the first time that he had not pushed a button, had not selected a

1

floor. He was following me. I made a quick exit, and as I stepped into the splendid marble foyer of Drake & Sweeney I glanced over my shoulder just long enough to see him standing in the elevator, looking at nothing, still ignoring me.

Madam Devier, one of our very resilient receptionists, greeted me with her typical look of disdain. 'Watch the elevator,' I said.

'Why?'

'Street bum. You may want to call security.'

'Those people,' she said in her affected French accent.

'Get some disinfectant too.'

I walked away, wrestling my overcoat off my shoulders, forgetting the man with the rubber boots. I had nonstop meetings throughout the afternoon, important conferences with important people. I turned the corner and was about to say something to Polly, my secretary, when I heard the first shot.

Madam Devier was standing behind her desk, petrified, staring into the barrel of an awfully long handgun held by our pal the street bum. Since I was the first one to come to her aid, he politely aimed it at me, and I too became rigid.

'Don't shoot,' I said, hands in the air. I'd seen enough movies to know precisely what to do.

'Shut up,' he mumbled, with a great deal of composure.

There were voices in the hallway behind me. Someone yelled, 'He's got a gun!' And then the voices disappeared into the background, growing fainter and fainter as my colleagues hit the back door. I could almost see them jumping out the windows.

To my immediate left was a heavy wooden door that led to a large conference room, which at that moment happened to be filled with eight lawyers from our

2

litigation section. Eight hard-nosed and fearless litigators who spent their hours chewing up people. The toughest was a scrappy little torpedo named Rafter, and as he yanked open the door saying 'What the hell?' the barrel swung from me to him, and the man with the rubber boots had exactly what he wanted.

'Put that gun down,' Rafter ordered from the doorway, and a split second later another shot rang through the reception area, a shot that went into the ceiling somewhere well above Rafter's head and reduced him to a mere mortal. Turning the gun back to me, he nodded, and I complied, entering the conference room behind Rafter. The last thing I saw on the outside was Madam Devier shaking at her desk, terror-stricken, headset around her neck, high heels parked neatly next to her wastebasket.

The man with the rubber boots slammed the door behind me, and slowly waved the gun through the air so that all eight litigators could admire it. It seemed to be working fine; the smell of its discharge was more noticeable than the odor of its owner.

The room was dominated by a long table, covered with documents and papers that only seconds ago seemed terribly important. A row of windows overlooked a parking lot. Two doors led to the hallway.

'Up against the wall,' he said, using the gun as a very effective prop. Then he placed it very near my head, and said, 'Lock the doors.'

Which I did.

Not a word from the eight litigators as they scrambled backward. Not a word from me as I quickly locked the doors, then looked at him for approval.

For some reason, I kept thinking of the post office and all those horrible shootings – a disgruntled employee returns after lunch with an arsenal and wipes out fifteen of his co-workers. I thought of the

3

playground massacres – and the slaughters at fast-food restaurants.

And those victims were innocent children and otherwise decent citizens. We were a bunch of lawyers!

Using a series of grunts and gun thrusts, he lined the eight litigators up against the wall, and when their positions suited him he turned his attention to me. What did he want? Could he ask questions? If so, he could get anything he damned well pleased. I couldn't see his eyes because of the sunglasses, but he could see mine. The gun was pointed at them.

He removed his filthy trench coat, folded it as if it were new, and placed it in the center of the table. The smell that had bothered me in the elevator was back, but not important now. He stood at the end of the table and slowly removed the next layer – a bulky gray cardigan.

Bulky for a reason. Under it, strapped to his waist, was a row of red sticks, which appeared to my untrained eye to be dynamite. Wires ran like colored spaghetti from the tops and bottoms of the sticks, and silver duct tape kept things attached.

My first instinct was to bolt, to lunge with arms and legs flapping and flailing for the door, and hope for luck, hope for a bad shot as I scrambled for the lock, then another bad shot as I fell through the doorway into the hallway. But my knees shook and my blood ran cold. There were gasps and slight moans from the eight against the wall, and this perturbed our captor. 'Please be quiet,' he said in the tone of a patient professor. His calmness unnerved me. He adjusted some of the spaghetti around his waist, then from a pocket in his large trousers produced a neat bundle of yellow nylon rope and a switchblade.

For good measure, he waved the gun at the horrified faces in front of him, and said, 'I don't want to hurt anybody.'

4

That was nice to hear but hard to take seriously. I counted twelve red sticks – enough, I was certain, to make it instantaneous and painless.

Then the gun was back on me. 'You,' he said, 'tie them up.'

Rafter had had enough. He took one very small step forward and said, 'Look, pal, just exactly what do you want?'

The third shot sailed over his head into the ceiling, where it lodged harmlessly. It sounded like a cannon, and Madam Devier or some female shrieked in the foyer. Rafter ducked, and as he attempted to stand upright the beefy elbow of Umstead caught him squarely in the chest and returned him to his position against the wall.

'Shut up,' Umstead said with clenched jaws.

'Do not call me Pal,' the man said, and Pal was instantly discarded as a reference.

'What would you like us to call you?' I asked, sensing that I was about to become the leader of the hostages. I said this very delicately, with great deference, and he appreciated my respect.

'Mister,' he said. Mister was perfectly fine with everyone in the room.

The phone rang, and I thought for a split second he was going to shoot it. Instead he waved it over, and I placed it squarely before him on the table. He lifted the receiver with his left hand; his right still held the gun, and the gun was still pointed at Rafter.

If the nine of us had a vote, Rafter would be the first sacrificial lamb. Eight to one.

'Hello,' Mister said. He listened briefly, then hung up. He carefully backed himself into the seat at the end of the table and sat down.

'Take the rope,' he said to me.

He wanted all eight of them attached at the wrists. I cut rope and tied knots and tried my best not to look

5

at the faces of my colleagues as I hastened their deaths. I could feel the gun at my back. He wanted them bound tightly, and I made a show of practically drawing blood while leaving as much slack as possible.

Rafter mumbled something under his breath and I wanted to slap him. Umstead was able to flex his wrists so that the ropes almost fell loose when I finished with him. Malamud was sweating and breathing rapidly. He was the oldest, the only partner, and two years past his first heart attack.

I couldn't help but look at Barry Nuzzo, my one friend in the bunch. We were the same age, thirty-two, and had joined the firm the same year. He went to Princeton, I went to Yale. Both of our wives were from Providence. His marriage was working – three kids in four years. Mine was in the final stage of a long deterioration.

Our eyes met and we both were thinking about his kids. I felt lucky to be childless.

The first of many sirens came into range, and Mister instructed me to close the blinds over the five large windows. I went about this methodically, scanning the parking lot below as if being seen might somehow save me. A lone police car sat empty with its lights on; the cops were already in the building.

And there we were, nine white boys and Mister.

At last count, Drake & Sweeney had eight hundred lawyers in offices around the world. Half of them were in D.C., in the building Mister was terrorizing. He instructed me to call 'the boss' and inform him that he was armed and wired with twelve sticks of dynamite. I called Rudolph, managing partner of my division, antitrust, and relayed the message.

'You okay, Mike?' he asked me. We were on Mister's new speakerphone, at full volume.

'Wonderful,' I said. 'Please do whatever he wants.'

6

'What does he want?'

'I don't know yet.'

Mister waved the gun and the conversation was over.

Taking my cue from the pistol, I assumed a standing position next to the conference table, a few feet from Mister, who had developed the irritating habit of playing absent-mindedly with the wires coiled against his chest.

He glanced down and gave a slight tug at a red wire. 'This red one here, I give it a yank and it's all over.' The sunglasses were looking at me when he finished this little warning. I felt compelled to say something.

'Why would you do that?' I asked, desperate to open a dialogue.

'I don't want to, but why not?'

I was struck by his diction – a slow, methodical rhythm with no hurry and each syllable getting equal treatment. He was a street bum at the moment, but there had been better days.

'Why would you want to kill us?' I asked.

'I'm not going to argue with you,' he announced. No further questions, Your Honor.

Because I'm a lawyer and live by the clock, I checked my watch so that whatever happened could be duly recorded, if we somehow managed to survive. It was one-twenty. Mister wanted things quiet, and so we endured a nerve-racking period of silence that lasted fourteen minutes.

I could not believe that we were going to die. There appeared to be no motive, no reason to kill us. I was certain that none of us had ever met him before. I remembered the ride on the elevator, and the fact that he seemed to have no particular destination. He was just a nut in search of hostages, which unfortunately would have made the killings seem almost normal by today's standards.

7

It was precisely the kind of senseless slaughter that would grab the headlines for twenty-four hours and make people shake their heads. Then the dead lawyer jokes would start.

I could see the headlines and hear the reporters, but I refused to believe it would happen.

I heard voices in the foyer, sirens outside; a police radio squawked somewhere down the hallway.

'What did you eat for lunch?' Mister asked me, his voice breaking the silence. Too surprised to consider lying, I hesitated for a second, then said, 'A grilled chicken Caesar.'

'Alone?'

'No, I met a friend.' He was a law school buddy from Philly.

'How much did it cost, for both of you?'

'Thirty bucks.'

He didn't like this. 'Thirty bucks,' he repeated. 'For two people.' He shook his head, then looked at the eight litigators. If he polled them, I hoped they planned to lie. There were some serious stomachs among the group, and thirty bucks wouldn't cover their appetizers.

'You know what I had?' he asked me.

'No.'

'I had soup. Soup and crackers at a shelter. Free soup, and I was glad to get it. You could feed a hundred of my friends for thirty bucks, you know that?'

I nodded gravely, as if I suddenly realized the weight of my sin.

'Collect all the wallets, money, watches, jewelry,' he said, waving the gun again.

'May I ask why?' I asked.

'No.'

I placed my wallet, watch, and cash on the table,

8

and began rummaging through the pockets of my fellow hostages.

'It's for the next of kin,' Mister said, and we all exhaled.

He instructed me to place the loot in a briefcase, lock it, and call 'the boss' again. Rudolph answered on the first ring. I could envision the SWAT leader camped in his office.

'Rudolph, it's me, Mike, again. I'm on the speaker-phone.'

'Yes, Mike. Are you okay?'

'Just fine. Look, this gentleman wants me to open the door nearest the reception area and place a black briefcase in the hallway. I will then close the door and lock it. Understand?'

'Yes.'

With the gun touching the back of my head, I slowly cracked the door and tossed the briefcase into the hallway. I did not see a person anywhere.

Few things can keep a big-firm lawyer from the joys of hourly billing. Sleep is one, though most of us slept little. Eating actually encouraged billing, especially lunch when the client was picking up the check. As the minutes dragged on, I caught myself wondering how in the world the other four hundred lawyers in the building would manage to bill while waiting for the hostage crisis to end. I could just see them out there in the parking lot, most of them sitting in their cars to keep warm, chatting away on cell phones, billing somebody. The firm, I decided, wouldn't miss a beat.

Some of the cutthroats down there didn't care *how* it ended. Just hurry up and get it over with.

Mister seemed to doze for a second. His chin dipped, and his breathing was heavier. Rafter grunted to get my attention, then jerked his head to one side as if to suggest I make a move. Problem was, Mister held

9

the gun with his right hand, and if he was indeed napping, then he was doing so with the dreaded red wire held firmly in his left hand.

And Rafter wanted me to be the hero. Though Rafter was the meanest and most effective litigator in the firm, he was not yet a partner. He was not in my division, and we weren't in the Army. I didn't take orders.

'How much money did you make last year?' Mister, very much awake, asked me, his voice clear.

Again, I was startled. 'I, uh, gosh, let me see –'

'Don't lie.'

'A hundred and twenty thousand.'

He didn't like this either. 'How much did you give away?'

'Give away?'

'Yes. To charities.'

'Oh. Well, I really don't remember. My wife takes care of the bills and things like that.'

All eight litigators seemed to shift at once.

Mister didn't like my answer, and he was not about to be denied. 'Who, like, fills in your tax forms?'

'You mean for the IRS?'

'Yeah, that's it.'

'It's handled by our tax division, down on the second floor.'

'Here in this building?'

'Yes.'

'Then get it for me. Get me the tax records for everybody here.'

I looked at their faces, and a couple wanted to say, 'Just go ahead and shoot me.' I must've hesitated too long, because Mister shouted, 'Do it now!' And he used the gun when he shouted.

I called Rudolph, who also hesitated, and so I shouted at him. 'Just fax them in here,' I demanded. 'Last year's only.'

10

We stared at the fax machine in the corner for fifteen minutes, afraid Mister might start executing us if our 1040's didn't hurry along.

TWO

Freshly anointed as scribe for the group, I sat where Mister pointed with the gun and clutched the faxes. My buddies had been standing for almost two hours, backs to the wall, still joined together, barely able to move, and they were beginning to slouch and slump and look miserable.

But their level of discomfort was about to rise significantly.

'You first,' he said to me. 'What's your name?'

'Michael Brock,' I answered politely. Nice to meet you.

'How much money did you make last year?'

'I've already told you. A hundred and twenty thousand. Before taxes.'

'How much did you give away?'

I was certain I could lie. I was not a tax lawyer, but I was confident I could dance around his questions. I found my 1040 and took my time flipping through the pages. Claire had earned thirty-one thousand dollars as a second-year surgical resident, so our gross income looked quite handsome. But we paid fifty-three thousand in taxes – federal income and an amazing variety of others – and after repayment of student loans, Claire's educational expenses, twenty-four hundred a month for a very nice apartment in Georgetown, two late-model cars with the obligatory mortgages, and a host of other costs naturally related to a comfortable lifestyle, we had invested only twenty-two thousand in mutual funds.

Mister was waiting patiently. In fact, his patience was beginning to unnerve me. I assumed that the SWAT boys were crawling in the air vents, climbing nearby trees, scampering across the roofs of buildings next door, looking at blueprints of our offices, doing all the things you see on TV with the goal of somehow placing a bullet through his skull, and he seemed oblivious to it. He had accepted his fate and was ready to die. Not true for the rest of us.

He continually toyed with the red wire, and that kept my heart rate over a hundred.

'I gave a thousand dollars to Yale,' I said. 'And two thousand to the local United Way.'

'How much did you give to poor people?'

I doubted if the Yale money went to feed needy students. 'Well, the United Way spreads the money around the city, and I'm sure some of it went to help the poor.'

'How much did you give to the hungry?'

'I paid fifty-three thousand dollars in taxes, and a nice chunk of it went for welfare, Medicaid, aid to dependent children, stuff like that.'

'And you did this voluntarily, with a giving spirit?'

'I didn't complain,' I said, lying like most of my countrymen.

'Have you ever been hungry?'

He liked simple answers, and my wit and sarcasm would not be productive. 'No,' I said. 'I have not.'

'Have you ever slept in the snow?'

'No.'

'You make a lot of money, yet you're too greedy to hand me some change on the sidewalk.' He waved the gun at the rest of them. 'All of you. You walk right by me as I sit and beg. You spend more on fancy coffee

13

than I do on meals. Why can't you help the poor, the sick, the homeless? You have so much.'

I caught myself looking at those greedy bastards along with Mister, and it was not a pretty sight. Most were staring at their feet. Only Rafter glared down the table, thinking the thoughts all of us had when we stepped over the Misters of D.C.: If I give you some change you'll (1) run to the liquor store, (2) only beg more, (3) never leave the sidewalk.

Silence again. A helicopter hovered nearby, and I could only imagine what they were planning in the parking lot. Pursuant to Mister's instructions, the phone lines were on hold, so there was no communication. He had no desire to talk to or negotiate with anyone. He had his audience in the conference room.

'Which of these guys makes the most money?' he asked me.

Malamud was the only partner, and I shuffled the papers until I found his.

'That would be me,' Malamud offered.

'What is your name?'

'Nate Malamud.'

I flipped through Nate's return. It was a rare moment to see the intimate details of a partner's success, but I got no pleasure from it.

'How much?' Mister asked me.

Oh, the joys of the IRS code. What would you like, sir? Gross? Adjusted gross? Net? Taxable? Income from salaries and wages? Or income from business and investments?

Malamud's salary from the firm was fifty thousand dollars a month, and his annual bonus, the one we all dreamed about, was five hundred and ten thousand. It had been a very good year, and we all knew it. He was one of many partners who had earned over a million dollars.

I decided to play it safe. There was lots of other

14

income tucked away near the back of the return – rental properties, dividends, a small business – but I guessed that if Mister somehow grabbed the return he would struggle with the numbers.

'One point one million,' I said, leaving another two hundred thousand on the table.

He contemplated this for a moment. 'You made a million dollars,' he said to Malamud, who wasn't the least bit ashamed of it.

'Yes, I did.'

'How much did you give to the hungry, and the homeless?'

I was already scouring his itemized deductions for the truth.

'I don't recall exactly. My wife and I give to a lot of charities. I know there was a donation, I think for five thousand, to the Greater D.C. Fund, which, as I'm sure you know, distributes money to the needy. We give a lot. And we're happy to do it.'

'I'm sure you're very happy,' Mister replied, with the first hint of sarcasm.

He wasn't about to allow us to explain how generous we *really* were. He simply wanted the hard facts. He instructed me to list all nine names, and beside each write last year's income, then last year's gifts to charities.

It took some time, and I didn't know whether to hurry or be deliberate. Would he slaughter us if he didn't like the math? Perhaps I shouldn't hurry. It was immediately obvious that we rich folks had made lots of money while handing over precious little of it. At the same time, I knew the longer the situation dragged on, the crazier the rescue scenarios would become.

He hadn't mentioned executing a hostage every hour. He didn't want his buddies freed from jail. He didn't seem to want anything, really.

I took my time. Malamud set the pace. The rear was

brought up by Colburn, a third-year associate who grossed a mere eighty-six thousand. I was dismayed to learn my pal Barry Nuzzo earned eleven thousand more than I did. We would discuss it later.

'If you round it off, it comes to three million dollars,' I reported to Mister, who appeared to be napping again, with his fingers still on the red wire.

He slowly shook his head. 'And how much for the poor people?'

'Total contributions of one hundred eighty thousand.'

'I don't want total contributions. Don't put me and my people in the same class with the symphony and the synagogue, and all your pretty white folks clubs where you auction wine and autographs and give a few bucks to the Boy Scouts. I'm talking about food. Food for hungry people who live here in the same city you live in. Food for little babies. Right here. Right in this city, with all you people making millions, we got little babies starving at night, crying 'cause they're hungry. How much for food?'

He was looking at me. I was looking at the papers in front of me. I couldn't lie.

He continued. 'We got soup kitchens all over town, places where the poor and homeless can get something to eat. How much money did you folks give to the soup kitchens? Any?'

'Not directly,' I said. 'But some of these charities –'

'Shut up!'

He waved the damned gun again.

'How about homeless shelters? Places we sleep when it's ten degrees outside. How many shelters are listed there in those papers?'

Invention failed me. 'None,' I said softly.

He jumped to his feet, startling us, the red sticks fully visible under the silver duct tape. He kicked his chair back. 'How 'bout clinics? We got these little

16

clinics where doctors – good decent people who used to make lots of money – come and donate their time to help the sick. They don't charge nothing. Government used to help pay the rent, help buy the medicine and supplies. Now the government's run by Newt and all the money's gone. How much do you give to the clinics?'

Rafter looked at me as if I should do something, perhaps suddenly see something in the papers and say, 'Damn! Look here! We gave half a million bucks to the clinics and soup kitchens.'

That's exactly what Rafter would do. But not me. I didn't want to get shot. Mister was a lot smarter than he looked.

I flipped through the papers as Mister walked to the windows and peeked around the mini-blinds. 'Cops everywhere,' he said, just loud enough for us to hear. 'And lots of ambulances.'

He then forgot about the scene below and shuffled along the edge of the table until he stopped near his hostages. They watched every move, with particular attention paid to the explosives. He slowly raised the gun, and aimed it directly at Colburn's nose, less than three feet away.

'How much did you give to the clinics?'

'None,' Colburn said, closing his eyes tightly, ready to cry. My heart froze and I held my breath.

'How much to the soup kitchens?'

'None.'

'How much to the homeless shelters?'

'None.'

Instead of shooting Colburn, he aimed at Nuzzo and repeated the three questions. Nuzzo had identical responses, and Mister moved down the line, pointing, asking the same questions, getting the same answers. He didn't shoot Rafter, much to our dismay.

'Three million dollars,' he said in disgust, 'and not a

dime for the sick and hungry. You are miserable people.'

We felt miserable. And I realized he was not going to kill us.

How could an average street bum acquire dynamite? And who would teach him how to wire it?

At dusk he said he was hungry, and he told me to call the boss and order soup from the Methodist Mission at L Street and Seventeenth, Northwest. They put more vegetables in the broth, Mister said. And the bread was not as stale as in most kitchens.

'The soup kitchen does carryout?' Rudolph asked, his voice incredulous. It echoed around the room from the speakerphone.

'Just do it, Rudolph!' I barked back at him. 'And get enough for ten people.' Mister told me to hang up, and again put the lines on hold.

I could see our friends and a squadron of cops flying across the city, through rush-hour traffic, and descending upon the quiet little mission where the ragged street people hunched over their bowls of broth and wondered what the hell was going on. Ten orders to go, extra bread.

Mister made another trip to the window when we heard the helicopter again. He peeked out, stepped back, tugged at his beard, and pondered the situation. What type of invasion could they possibly be planning that would involve a helicopter? Maybe it was to evacuate the wounded.

Umstead had been fidgeting for an hour, much to the dismay of Rafter and Malamud, who were joined to him at the wrists. He finally couldn't stand it any longer.

'Uh, sir, excuse me, but I really have to, uh, go to the boys' room.'

18

Mister kept tugging. 'Boys' room. What's a boys' room?'

'I need to pee, sir,' Umstead said, very much like a third-grader. 'I can't hold it any longer.'

Mister looked around the room, and noticed a porcelain vase sitting innocently on a coffee table. With another wave of the gun, he ordered me to untie Umstead.

'The boys' room is over there,' Mister said.

Umstead removed the fresh flowers from the vase, and with his back to us urinated for a long time while we studied the floor. When he finally finished, Mister told us to move the conference table next to the windows. It was twenty feet long, solid walnut like most of the furniture at Drake & Sweeney, and with me on one end and Umstead grunting on the other, we managed to inch it over about six feet until Mister said stop. He made me latch Malamud and Rafter together, leaving Umstead a free man. I would never understand why he did this.

Next, he forced the remaining seven bound hostages to sit on the table with their backs to the wall. No one dared ask why, but I figured he wanted a shield from sharpshooters. I later learned that the police had snipers perched on a building next door. Perhaps Mister had seen them.

After standing for five hours, Rafter and company were relieved to be off their feet. Umstead and I were told to sit in chairs, and Mister took a seat at the end of the table. We waited.

Life in the streets must teach one patience. He seemed content to sit in silence for long periods of time, his eyes hiding behind the glasses, his head perfectly still.

'Who are the evictors?' he mumbled, to no one in particular, and he waited a couple of minutes before saying it again.

19

We looked at each other, confused, with no clue what he was talking about. He appeared to be staring at a spot on the table, not far from Colburn's right foot.

'Not only do you ignore the homeless, you help put them in the streets.'

We, of course, nodded along, all singing from the same sheet. If he wanted to heap verbal abuse on us, we were perfectly willing to accept it.

Our carryout arrived at a few minutes before seven. There was a sharp knock on the door. Mister told me to place a call and warn the police that he would kill one of us if he saw or heard anyone outside. I explained this carefully to Rudolph, and I stressed that no rescue should be attempted. We were negotiating.

Rudolph said he understood.

Umstead walked to the door, unlocked it, and looked at Mister for instructions. Mister was behind him, with the gun less than a foot from Umstead's head.

'Open the door very slowly,' Mister said.

I was standing a few feet behind Mister when the door opened. The food was on a small cart, one of our paralegals used to haul around the enormous amounts of paper we generated. I could see four large plastic containers of soup, and a brown paper bag filled with bread. I don't know if there was anything to drink. We never found out.

Umstead took one step into the hallway, grabbed the cart, and was about to pull it back into the conference room when the shot cracked through the air. A lone police sniper was hiding behind a credenza next to Madam Devier's desk, forty feet away, and he got the clear look he needed. When Umstead bent over to grab the cart, Mister's head was exposed for a split second, and the sniper blew it off.

Mister lurched backward without uttering a sound,

20

and my face was instantly covered with blood and fluids. I thought I'd been hit too, and I remember screaming in pain. Umstead was yelling somewhere in the hall. The other seven scrambled off the table like scalded dogs, all yelling and digging toward the door, half of them dragging the other half. I was on my knees, clutching my eyes, waiting for the dynamite to explode, then I bolted for the other door, away from the mayhem. I unlocked it, yanked it open, and the last time I saw Mister he was twitching on one of our expensive Oriental rugs. His hands were loose at his sides, nowhere near the red wire.

The hallway was suddenly filled with SWAT guys, all clad in fierce-looking helmets and thick vests, dozens of them crouching and reaching. They were a blur. They grabbed us and carried us through the reception area to the elevators.

'Are you hurt?' they asked me.

I didn't know. There was blood on my face and shirt, and a sticky liquid that a doctor later described as cerebrospinal fluid.

THREE

On the first floor, as far away from Mister as they could get, the families and friends were waiting. Dozens of our associates and colleagues were packed in the offices and hallways, waiting for our rescue. A loud cheer went up when they saw us.

Because I was covered with blood, they took me to a small gym in the basement. It was owned by our firm and virtually ignored by the lawyers. We were too busy to exercise, and anyone caught working out would almost certainly be assigned more work.

I was instantly surrounded by doctors, none of whom happened to be my wife. Once I convinced them the blood was not mine, they relaxed and conducted a routine exam. Blood pressure was up, pulse was crazy. They gave me a pill.

What I really wanted was a shower. They made me lie on a table for ten minutes while they watched my blood pressure. 'Am I in shock?' I asked.

'Probably not.'

I certainly felt like it. Where was Claire? For six hours I was held at gunpoint, life hanging by a thread, and she couldn't be bothered to come wait with the rest of the families.

The shower was long and hot. I washed my hair three times with heavy shampoo, then I stood and dripped for an eternity. Time was frozen. Nothing mattered. I was alive, breathing and steaming.

I changed into someone else's clean gym clothes, which were much too big, and went back to the table for another check of my blood pressure. My secretary, Polly, came in and gave me a long hug. I needed it desperately. She had tears in her eyes.

'Where's Claire?' I asked her.

'On call. I've tried calling the hospital.'

Polly knew there wasn't much left of the marriage.

'Are you okay?' she asked.

'I think so.'

I thanked the doctors and left the gym. Rudolph met me in the hall and gave me a clumsy embrace. He used the word 'congratulations,' as if I had accomplished something.

'No one expects you to work tomorrow,' he said. Did he think a day off would cure all my problems?

'I haven't thought about tomorrow,' I said.

'You need some rest,' he added, as if the doctors hadn't thought of this.

I wanted to speak to Barry Nuzzo, but my fellow hostages had already left. No one was injured, just a few rope burns on the wrists.

With the carnage held to a minimum, and the good guys up and smiling, the excitement at Drake & Sweeney waned quickly. Most of the lawyers and staff had waited nervously on the first floor, far away from Mister and his explosives. Polly had my overcoat, and I put it on over the large sweat suit. My tasseled loafers looked odd, but I didn't care.

'There are some reporters outside,' Polly said.

Ah, yes, the media. What a story! Not just your garden-variety on-the-job shooting, but a bunch of lawyers held hostage by a street crazy.

But they didn't get their story, did they? The lawyers escaped, the bad guy took a bullet, the

23

explosives fizzled when their owner hit the floor. Oh, what could've been! A shot, then a bomb, a flash of white light as the windows shattered, arms and legs landing in the street, all duly recorded live by Channel Nine for the evening's lead story.

'I'll drive you home,' Polly said. 'Follow me.' I was very thankful someone was telling me what to do. My thoughts were slow and cumbersome, one still-frame after another, with no concept of plot or setting.

We left the ground floor through a service door. The night air was sharp and cold, and I breathed its sweetness until my lungs ached. As Polly ran to get her car, I hid at the corner of the building and watched the circus out front. There were police cars, ambulances, television vans, even a fire truck. They were packing and leaving. One of the ambulances was parked with its rear to the building, no doubt waiting to carry Mister to the morgue.

I'm alive! I am alive! I said this over and over, smiling for the first time. I'm alive!

I closed my eyes tightly and offered a short but sincere prayer of thanks.

The sounds began coming back. As we sat in silence, Polly behind the wheel, driving slowly and waiting for me to say something, I heard the piercing clap of the sniper's rifle. Then the thud as it found its mark, and the stampede as the other hostages scrambled off the table and through the door.

What had I seen? I had glanced at the table where the seven were staring intently at the door, then back to Mister as he raised the gun and pointed it at Umstead's head. I was directly behind him when he was hit. What stopped the bullet from leaving him and getting me? Bullets go through walls and doors and people.

'He was not going to kill us,' I said, barely loud enough to be heard.

Polly was relieved to hear my voice. 'What was he doing then?'

'I don't know.'

'What did he want?'

'He never said. It's amazing how little was actually said. We sat for hours just looking at each other.'

'Why wouldn't he talk to the police?'

'Who knows? That was his biggest mistake. If he'd kept the phones open, I could've convinced the cops that he was not going to kill us.'

'You don't blame the cops, do you?'

'No. Remind me to write them letters.'

'Are you working tomorrow?'

'What else would I do tomorrow?'

'Just thought you might need a day off.'

'I need a year off. One day won't help.'

Our apartment was the third floor of a rowhouse on P Street in Georgetown. Polly stopped at the curb. I thanked her and got out, and I could tell from the dark windows that Claire was not home.

I met Claire the week after I moved to D.C. I was just out of Yale with a great job in a rich firm, a brilliant future like the other fifty rookies in my class. She was finishing her degree in political science at American University. Her grandfather was once the governor of Rhode Island, and her family has been well connected for centuries.

Drake & Sweeney, like most large firms, treats the first year as a boot camp. I worked fifteen hours a day, six days a week, and on Sundays Claire and I would have our weekly date. Sunday nights I was in the office. We thought that if we got married, we would have more time together. At least we could share a bed, but sleep was about all we did.

25

The wedding was large, the honeymoon brief, and when the luster wore off I was back at the office ninety hours a week. During the third month of our union, we actually went eighteen days without sex. She counted.

She was a sport for the first few months, but she grew weary of being neglected. I did not blame her, but young associates don't complain in the hallowed offices of Drake & Sweeney. Less than ten percent of each class will make partner, so the competition is ruthless. The rewards are great, at least a million bucks a year. Billing lots of hours is more important than a happy wife. Divorce is common. I didn't dream of asking Rudolph to lighten my load.

By the end of our first year together, Claire was very unhappy and we had started to quarrel.

She decided to go to med school. Tired of sitting at home watching TV, she figured she could become as self-absorbed as I was. I thought it was a wonderful idea. It took away most of my guilt.

After four years with the firm, they started dropping hints about our chances of making partner. The hints were collected and compared among many of the associates. It was generally felt that I was on the fast track to a partnership. But I had to work even harder.

Claire became determined to spend more time away from the apartment than I did, and so both of us slid into the silliness of extreme workaholism. We stopped fighting and simply drifted apart. She had her friends and interests, I had mine. Fortunately, we did not make the mistake of reproducing.

I wish I had done things differently. We were in love once, and we let it get away.

As I entered the dark apartment, I needed Claire for the first time in years. You come face to face with death and you need to talk about it. You need to be needed, to be stroked, to be told that someone cares.

26

I fixed a vodka with ice and sat on the sofa in the den. I fumed and pouted because I was alone, then my thoughts switched to the six hours I'd spent with Mister.

Two vodkas later, I heard her at the door. She unlocked it, and called, 'Michael.'

I didn't say a word because I was still pouting and fuming. She walked into the den, and stopped when she saw me. 'Are you all right?' she asked with genuine concern.

'I'm fine,' I said softly.

She dropped her bag and overcoat, and walked to the sofa, where she hovered over me.

'Where have you been?' I asked.

'At the hospital.'

'Of course.' I took a long drink. 'Look, I've had a bad day.'

'I know all about it, Michael.'

'You do?'

'Of course I do.'

'Then where the hell were you?'

'At the hospital.'

'Nine of us held hostage for six hours by a crazy man. Eight families show up because they're somewhat concerned. We get lucky and escape, and I have to catch a ride home with my secretary.'

'I couldn't be there.'

'Of course you couldn't. How thoughtless of me.'

She sat down in a chair next to the sofa. We glared at each other. 'They made us stay at the hospital,' she began, very icy. 'We knew about the hostage situation, and there was a chance there could've been casualties. It's standard procedure in that situation – they notify the hospitals, and everyone is placed on standby.'

Another long drink as I tried to think of something sharp to say.

27

'I couldn't help you at your office,' she continued. 'I was waiting at the hospital.'

'Did you call?'

'I tried. The phone lines were jammed. I finally got a cop, and he hung up on me.'

'It was over two hours ago. Where have you been?'

'In OR. We lost a little boy in surgery; he was hit by a car.'

'I'm sorry,' I said. I could never comprehend how doctors faced so much death and pain. Mister was only the second corpse I had ever laid eyes on.

'I'm sorry too,' she said, and with that she went to the kitchen and returned with a glass of wine. We sat in the semi-darkness for a while. Because we did not practice communication, it did not come easy.

'Do you want to talk about it?' she asked.

'No. Not now.' And I really didn't. The alcohol mixed with the pills, and my breathing became heavy. I thought of Mister, how calm and peaceful he was, even though he waved a gun and had dynamite strapped to his stomach. He was thoroughly unmoved by long stretches of silence.

Silence was what I wanted. Tomorrow I would talk.

FOUR

The chemicals worked until four the next morning, when I awoke to the harsh smell of Mister's sticky brain fluid weaving through my nostrils. I was frantic for a moment in the darkness. I rubbed my nose and eyes, and thrashed around the sofa until I heard someone move. Claire was sleeping in a chair next to me.

'It's okay,' she said softly, touching my shoulder. 'Just a bad dream.'

'Would you get me some water?' I said, and she went to the kitchen.

We talked for an hour. I told her everything I could remember about the event. She sat close to me, rubbing my knee, holding the glass of water, listening carefully. We had talked so little in the past few years.

She had to make her rounds at seven, so we cooked breakfast together, waffles and bacon. We ate at the kitchen counter with a small television in front of us. The six o'clock news began with the hostage drama. There were shots of the building during the crisis, the mob outside, some of my fellow captives hurriedly leaving when it was over. At least one of the helicopters we had heard belonged to the news station, and its camera had zoomed down for a tight shot of the window. Through it, Mister could be seen for a few seconds as he peeked out.

His name was DeVon Hardy, age forty-five, a Vietnam vet with a short criminal record. A mug shot from an arrest for burglary was put on the screen behind the early morning newsperson. It looked nothing like Mister – no beard, no glasses, much younger. He was described as homeless with a history of drug use. No motive was known. No family had come forward.

There were No comments from our side, and the story fizzled.

The weather was next. Heavy snow was expected to hit by late afternoon. It was the twelfth day of February, and already a record had been set for snowfall.

Claire drove me to the office, where at six-forty I was not surprised to see my Lexus parked among several other imports. The lot was never empty. We had people who slept at the office.

I promised to call her later in the morning, and we would try to have lunch at the hospital. She wanted me to take it easy, at least for a day or two.

What was I supposed to do? Lie on the sofa and take pills? The consensus seemed to be that I needed a day off, after which I guessed I would be expected to return to my duties at full throttle.

I said good morning to the two very alert security guards in the lobby. Three of the four elevators were open, waiting, and I had a choice. I stepped onto the one Mister and I had taken, and things slowed to a crawl.

A hundred questions at once: Why had he picked our building? Our firm? Where had he been in the moments before he entered the lobby? Where were the security guards who usually loitered near the front? Why me? Hundreds of lawyers came and went all day long. Why the sixth floor?

And what was he after? I did not believe DeVon

30

Hardy went to the trouble of wrapping himself with explosives and risking his life, humble as it was, to chastise a bunch of wealthy lawyers over their lack of generosity. He could've found richer people. And perhaps greedier ones.

His question, 'Who are the evictors?,' was never answered. But it wouldn't take long.

The elevator stopped, and I stepped off, this time without anyone behind me. Madam Devier was still asleep at that hour, somewhere, and the sixth floor was quiet. In front of her desk I paused and stared at the two doors to the conference room. I slowly opened the nearest one, the one where Umstead stood when the bullet shot over his head and into Mister's. I took a long breath and flipped a light switch.

Nothing had happened. The conference table and chairs were in perfect order. The Oriental rug upon which Mister died had been replaced with an even prettier one. A fresh coat of paint covered the walls. Even the bullet hole in the ceiling above Rafter's spot was gone.

The powers that be at Drake & Sweeney had spent some dough the previous night to make sure the incident never occurred. The room might attract a few of the curious throughout the day, and there certainly could be nothing to gawk at. It might make folks neglect their work for a minute or two. There simply couldn't be any trace of street trash in our pristine offices.

It was a cold-blooded cover-up, and, sadly, I understood the rationale behind it. I was one of the rich white guys. What did I expect, a memorial? A pile of flowers brought in by Mister's fellow street people?

I didn't know what I expected. But the smell of fresh paint made me nauseous.

On my desk every morning, in precisely the same spot, were *The Wall Street Journal* and *The Washington*

31

Post. I used to know the name of the person who put them there, but it was long forgotten. On the front page of the *Post*'s Metro section, below the fold, was the same mug shot of DeVon Hardy, and a large story about yesterday's little crisis.

I read it quickly because I figured I knew more details than any reporter. But I learned a few things. The red sticks were not dynamite. Mister had taken a couple of broom handles, sawed them into little pieces, wrapped the ominous silver tape around them, and scared the living hell out of us. The gun was a .44 automatic, stolen.

Because it was the *Post*, the story dealt more with DeVon Hardy than with his victims, though, in all fairness, and much to my satisfaction, not a single word had been uttered by anyone at Drake & Sweeney.

According to one Mordecai Green, Director of the 14th Street Legal Clinic, DeVon Hardy had worked for many years as a janitor at the National Arboretum. He'd lost his job as a result of budget cutting. He had served a few months in jail for burglary, then landed in the streets. He'd struggled with alcohol and drugs, and was routinely picked up for shoplifting. Green's clinic had represented him several times. If there was family, his lawyer knew nothing about it.

As to motive, Green had little to offer. He did say that DeVon Hardy had been evicted recently from an old warehouse in which he had been squatting.

An eviction is a legal procedure, carried out by lawyers. I had a pretty good idea which one of the thousands of D.C. firms had tossed Mister into the streets.

The 14th Street Legal Clinic was funded by a charity and worked only with the homeless, according to Green. 'Back when we got federal money, we had seven lawyers. Now we're down to two,' he said.

Not surprisingly, the *Journal* didn't mention the story. Had any of the nine corporate lawyers in the nation's fifth-largest silk-stocking firm been killed or even slightly wounded, it would've been on the front page.

Thank God it wasn't a bigger story. I was at my desk, reading my papers, in one piece with lots of work to do. I could've been at the morgue alongside Mister.

Polly arrived a few minutes before eight with a big smile and a plate of homemade cookies. She was not surprised to see me at work.

In fact, all nine of the hostages punched in, most ahead of schedule. It would've been a glaring sign of weakness to stay home with the wife and get pampered.

'Arthur's on the phone,' Polly announced. Our firm had at least ten Arthurs, but only one prowled the halls without the need of a last name. Arthur Jacobs was the senior partner, the CEO, the driving force, a man we admired and respected greatly. If the firm had a heart and soul, it was Arthur. In seven years, I had spoken to him three times.

I told him I was fine. He complimented me on my courage and grace under pressure, and I almost felt like a hero. I wondered how he knew. He had probably talked to Malamud first, and was working his way down the ladder. So the stories would begin, then the jokes. Umstead and his porcelain vase would no doubt cause much hilarity.

Arthur wanted to meet with the ex-hostages at ten, in the conference room, to record our statements on video.

'Why?' I asked.

'The boys in litigation think it's a good idea,' he said, his voice razor-sharp in spite of his eighty years. 'His family will probably sue the cops.'

'Of course,' I said.

'And they'll probably name us as defendants. People will sue for anything, you know.'

Thank goodness, I almost said. Where would we be without lawsuits?

I thanked him for his concern, and he was gone, off to call the next hostage.

The parade started before nine, a steady stream of well-wishers and gossipers lingering by my office, deeply concerned about me but also desperate for the details. I had a pile of work to do, but I couldn't get to it. In the quiet moments between guests, I sat and stared at the row of files awaiting my attention, and I was numb. My hands wouldn't reach.

It was not the same. The work was not important. My desk was not life and death. I had seen death, almost felt it, and I was naive to think I could simply shrug it off and bounce back as if nothing had happened.

I thought about DeVon Hardy and his red sticks with the multicolored wires running in all directions. He'd spent hours building his toys and planning his assault. He'd stolen a gun, found our firm, made a crucial mistake that cost him his life, and no one, not one single person I worked with, gave a damn about him.

I finally left. The traffic was getting worse, and I was getting chatted up by people I couldn't stand. Two reporters called. I told Polly I had some errands to run, and she reminded me of the meeting with Arthur. I went to my car, started it and turned on the heater, and sat for a long time debating whether to participate in the reenactment. If I missed it, Arthur would be upset. No one misses a meeting with Arthur.

I drove away. It was a rare opportunity to do something stupid. I'd been traumatized. I had to leave.

34

Arthur and the rest of the firm would just have to give me a break.

I drove in the general direction of Georgetown, but to no place in particular. The clouds were dark; people scurried along the sidewalks; snow crews were getting ready. I passed a beggar on M Street, and wondered if he knew DeVon Hardy. Where do the street people go in a snowstorm?

I called the hospital and was informed that my wife would be in emergency surgery for several hours. So much for our romantic lunch in the hospital cafeteria.

I turned and went northeast, past Logan Circle, into the rougher sections of the city until I found the 14th Street Legal Clinic. Fourteenth at Q, NW. I parked at the curb, certain I would never again see my Lexus.

The clinic occupied half of a three-story red-brick Victorian mansion that had seen better days. The windows on the top floor were boarded with aging plywood. Next door was a grungy Laundromat. The crack houses couldn't be far away.

The entrance was covered by a bright yellow canopy, and I didn't know whether to knock or to just barge in. The door wasn't locked, and I slowly turned the knob and stepped into another world.

It was a law office of sorts, but a very different one from the marble and mahogany of Drake & Sweeney. In the large room before me there were four metal desks, each covered with a suffocating collection of files stacked a foot high. More files were placed haphazardly on the worn carpet around the desks. The wastebaskets were filled, and wadded sheets of legal paper had rolled off and onto the floor. One wall was covered with file cabinets in a variety of colors. The word processors and phones were ten years old. The wooden bookshelves were sagging. A large fading photograph of Martin Luther King hung crookedly on the back wall. Several smaller offices branched off the front room.

It was busy and dusty and I was fascinated with the place.

A fierce Hispanic woman stopped typing after watching me for a moment. 'You looking for somebody?' she asked. It was more of a challenge than a request. A receptionist at Drake & Sweeney would be fired on the spot for such a greeting.

She was Sofia Mendoza, according to a nameplate tacked to the side of her desk, and I would soon learn that she was more than a receptionist. A loud roar came from one of the side rooms, and startled me without fazing Sofia.

'I'm looking for Mordecai Green,' I said politely, and at that moment he followed his roar and stomped out of his side office and into the main room. The floor shook with each step. He was yelling across the room for someone named Abraham.

Sofia nodded at him, then dismissed me and returned to her typing. Green was a huge black man, at least six five with a wide frame that carried a lot of weight. He was in his early fifties, with a gray beard and round eyeglasses that were framed in red. He took a look at me, said nothing, yelled again for Abraham while sauntering across the creaking floor. He disappeared into an office, then emerged seconds later without Abraham.

Another look at me, then, 'Can I help you?'

I walked forward and introduced myself.

'Nice to meet you,' he said, but only because he had to. 'What's on your mind?'

'DeVon Hardy,' I said.

He looked at me for a few seconds, then glanced at Sofia, who was lost in her work. He nodded toward his office, and I followed him into a twelve-by-twelve room with no windows and every square inch of

36

available floor space covered with manila files and battered law books.

I handed him my gold-embossed Drake & Sweeney card, which he studied with a deep frown. Then he gave it back to me, and said, 'Slumming, aren't you?'

'No,' I said, taking the card.

'What do you want?'

'I come in peace. Mr. Hardy's bullet almost got me.'

'You were in the room with him?'

'Yep.'

He took a deep breath and lost the frown. He pointed to the only chair on my side. 'Have a seat. But you might get dirty.'

We both sat, my knees touching his desk, my hands thrust deep into the pockets of my overcoat. A radiator rattled behind him. We looked at each other, then looked away. It was my visit, I had to say something. But he spoke first.

'Guess you had a bad day, huh?' he said, his raspy voice lower and almost compassionate.

'Not as bad as Hardy's. I saw your name in the paper, that's why I came.'

'I'm not sure what I'm supposed to do.'

'Do you think the family will sue? If so, then maybe I should leave.'

'There's no family, not much of a lawsuit. I could make some noise with it. I figure the cop who shot him is white, so I could squeeze a few bucks out of the city, probably get a nuisance settlement. But that's not my idea of fun.' He waved his hand over the desk. 'God knows I got enough to do.'

'I never saw the cop,' I said, realizing it for the first time.

'Forget about a lawsuit. Is that why you're here?'

'I don't know why I'm here. I went back to my desk this morning like nothing happened, but I couldn't think straight. I took a drive. Here I am.'

He shook his head slowly, as if he was trying to understand this. 'You want some coffee?'

'No thanks. You knew Mr. Hardy pretty well.'

'Yeah, DeVon was a regular.'

'Where is he now?'

'Probably in the city morgue at D.C. General.'

'If there's no family, what happens to him?'

'The city buries the unclaimed. On the books it's called a pauper's funeral. There's a cemetery near RFK Stadium where they pack 'em in. You'd be amazed at the number of people who die unclaimed.'

'I'm sure I would.'

'In fact, you'd be amazed at every aspect of homeless life.'

It was a soft jab, and I was not in the mood to spar. 'Do you know if he had AIDS?'

He cocked his head back, looked at the ceiling, and rattled that around for a few seconds. 'Why?'

'I was standing behind him. The back of his head was blown off. I got a face full of blood. That's all.'

With that, I crossed the line from a bad guy to just an average white guy.

'I don't think he had AIDS.'

'Do they check them when they die?'

'The homeless?'

'Yes.'

'Most of the time, yes. DeVon, though, died by other means.'

'Can you find out?'

He shrugged and thawed some more. 'Sure,' he said reluctantly, and took his pen from his pocket. 'Is that why you're here? Worried about AIDS?'

'I guess it's one reason. Wouldn't you be?'

'Sure.'

Abraham stepped in, a small hyper man of about forty who had public interest lawyer stamped all over him. Jewish, dark beard, horn-rimmed glasses, rumpled blazer, wrinkled khakis, dirty sneakers, and the weighty aura of one trying to save the world.

He did not acknowledge me, and Green was not one for social graces. 'They're predicting a ton of snow,' Green said to him. 'We need to make sure every possible shelter is open.'

'I'm working on it,' Abraham snapped, then abruptly left.

'I know you're busy,' I said.

'Is that all you wanted? A blood check.'

'Yeah, I guess. Any idea why he did it?'

He removed his red glasses, wiped them with a tissue, then rubbed his eyes. 'He was mentally ill, like a lot of these people. You spend years on the streets, soaked with booze, stoned on crack, sleeping in the cold, getting kicked around by cops and punks, it makes you crazy. Plus, he had a bone to pick.'

'The eviction.'

'Yep. A few months ago, he moved into an abandoned warehouse at the corner of New York and Florida. Somebody threw up some plywood, chopped up the place, and made little apartments. Wasn't a bad place as far as homeless folk go – a roof, some toilets, water. A hundred bucks a month, payable to an ex-pimp who fixed it up and claimed he owned it.'

'Did he?'

'I think so.' He pulled a thin file from one of the stacks on his desk, and, miraculously, it happened to be the one he wanted. He studied its contents for a moment. 'This is where it gets complicated. The property was purchased last month by a company called RiverOaks, some big real estate outfit.'

'And RiverOaks evicted everyone?'

'Yep.'

'Odds are, then, that RiverOaks would be represented by my firm.'

'Good odds, yes.'

39

'Why is it complicated?'

'I've heard it secondhand that they got no notice before the eviction. The people claim they were paying rent to the pimp, and if so, then they were more than squatters. They were tenants, thus entitled to due process.'

'Squatters get no notice?'

'None. And it happens all the time. Street folk will move into an abandoned building, and most of the time nothing happens. So they think they own it. The owner, if he's inclined to show up, can toss 'em without notice. They have no rights at all.'

'How did DeVon Hardy track down our firm?'

'Who knows? He wasn't stupid, though. Crazy, but not stupid.'

'Do you know the pimp?'

'Yeah. Completely unreliable.'

'Where did you say the warehouse was?'

'It's gone now. They leveled it last week.'

I had taken enough of his time. He glanced at his watch, I glanced at mine. We swapped phone numbers and promised to keep in touch.

Mordecai Green was a warm, caring man who labored on the streets protecting hordes of nameless clients. His view of the law required more soul than I could ever muster.

On my way out, I ignored Sofia because she certainly ignored me. My Lexus was still parked at the curb, already covered with an inch of snow.

FIVE

I drifted through the city as the snow fell. I couldn't
recall the last time I had driven the streets of D.C.
without being late for a meeting. I was warm and dry
in my heavy luxury car, and I simply moved with the
traffic. There was no place to go.

The office would be off-limits for a while, what with
Arthur mad at me; and I'd have to suffer through a
hundred random drop-ins, all of which would start
with the phony 'How you doin'?'

My car phone rang. It was Polly, panicky. 'Where
are you?' she asked.

'Who wants to know?'

'A lot of people. Arthur for one. Rudolph. Another
reporter called. There are some clients in need of
advice. And Claire called from the hospital.'

'What does she want?'

'She's worried, like everybody else.'

'I'm fine, Polly. Tell everybody I'm at the doctor's
office.'

'Are you?'

'No, but I could be. What did Arthur say?'

'He didn't call. Rudolph did. They were waiting for
you.'

'Let 'em wait.'

A pause, then a very slow 'Okay. When might you
be dropping by?'

41

'Don't know. I guess whenever the doctor releases me. Why don't you go home; we're in the middle of a storm. I'll call you tomorrow.' I hung up on her.

The apartment was a place I had rarely seen in the light of day, and I couldn't stand the thought of sitting by the fire and watching it snow. If I went to a bar, I'd probably never leave.

So I drove. I flowed with the traffic as the commuters began a hasty retreat into the Maryland and Virginia suburbs, and I breezed along near-empty streets coming back into the city. I found the cemetery near RFK where they buried the unclaimed, and I passed the Methodist Mission on Seventeenth where last night's uneaten dinner originated. I drove through sections of the city I had never been near and probably would never see again.

By four, the city was empty. The skies were darkening, the snow was quite heavy. Several inches already covered the ground, and they were predicting a lot more.

Of course, not even a snowstorm could shut down Drake & Sweeney. I knew lawyers there who loved midnights and Sundays because the phones didn't ring. A heavy snow was a delightful respite from the grueling drudgery of nonstop meetings and conference calls.

I was informed by a security guard in the lobby that the secretaries and most of the staff had been sent home at three. I took Mister's elevator again.

In a neat row in the center of my desk were a dozen pink phone messages, none of which interested me. I went to my computer and began searching our client index.

RiverOaks was a Delaware corporation, organized in 1977, headquartered in Hagerstown, Maryland. It was privately held, thus little financial information was

42

available. The attorney was N. Braden Chance, a name unknown to me.

I looked him up in our vast database. Chance was a partner in our real estate division, somewhere down on the fourth floor. Age forty-four, married, law school at Duke, undergrad at Gettysburg, an impressive but thoroughly predictable résumé.

With eight hundred lawyers threatening and suing daily, our firm had over thirty-six thousand active files. To make sure our office in New York didn't sue one of our clients in Chicago, each new file was entered immediately into our data system. Every lawyer, secretary, and paralegal at Drake & Sweeney had a PC, and thus instant access to general information about all files. If one of our probate attorneys in Palm Beach handled the estate of a rich client, I could, if I were so inclined, punch a few keys and learn the basics of our representation.

There were forty-two files for RiverOaks, almost all of them real estate transactions in which the company had purchased property. Chance was the attorney of record on every file. Four were eviction actions, three of which took place last year. The first phase of the search was easy.

On January 31, RiverOaks purchased property on Florida Avenue. The seller was TAG, Inc. On February 4, our client evicted a number of squatters from an abandoned warehouse on the property – one of whom, I now knew, was Mister DeVon Hardy, who took the eviction personally and somehow tracked down the lawyers.

I copied the file name and number, and strolled to the fourth floor.

No one joined a large firm with the goal of becoming a real estate lawyer. There were far more glamorous arenas in which to establish reputations. Litigation was the all-time favorite, and the litigators

43

were still the most revered of all God's lawyers, at least within the firm. A few of the corporate fields attracted top talent – mergers and acquisitions was still hot, securities was an old favorite. My field, antitrust, was highly regarded. Tax law was horribly complex, but its practitioners were greatly admired. Governmental relations (lobbying) was repulsive but paid so well that every D.C. firm had entire wings of lawyers greasing the skids.

But no one set out to be a real estate lawyer. I didn't know how it happened. They kept to themselves, no doubt reading fine print in mortgage documents, and were treated as slightly inferior lawyers by the rest of the firm.

At Drake & Sweeney, each lawyer kept his current files in his office, often under lock and key. Only the retired files were accessible by the rest of the firm. No lawyer could be compelled to show a file to another lawyer, unless requested by a senior partner or a member of the firm's executive committee.

The eviction file I wanted was still listed as current, and after the Mister episode I was certain it was well protected.

I saw a paralegal scanning blueprints at a desk next to a secretarial pool, and I asked him where I might find the office of Braden Chance. He nodded to an open door across the hall.

To my surprise, Chance was at his desk, projecting the appearance of a very busy lawyer. He was perturbed by my intrusion, and rightfully so. Proper protocol would have been for me to call ahead and set up a meeting. I wasn't worried about protocol.

He didn't ask me to sit. I did so anyway, and that didn't help his mood.

'You were one of the hostages,' he said irritably when he made the connection.

44

'Yes, I was.'

'Must've been awful.'

'It's over. The guy with the gun, the late Mr. Hardy, was evicted from a warehouse on February 4. Was it one of our evictions?'

'It was,' he snapped. Because of his defensiveness, I guessed the file had been picked through during the day. He'd probably reviewed it thoroughly with Arthur and the brass. 'What about it?'

'Was he a squatter?'

'Damned sure was. They're all squatters. Our client is trying to clean up some of that mess.'

'Are you sure he was a squatter?'

His chin dropped and his eyes turned red. Then he took a breath. 'What are you after?'

'Could I see the file?'

'No. It's none of your business.'

'Maybe it is.'

'Who is your supervising partner?' He yanked out his pen as if to take down the name of the person who would reprimand me.

'Rudolph Mayes.'

He wrote in large strokes. 'I'm very busy,' he said. 'Would you please leave?'

'Why can't I see the file?'

'Because it's mine, and I said no. How's that?'

'Maybe that's not good enough.'

'It's good enough for you. Why don't you leave?' He stood, his hand shaking as he pointed to the door. I smiled at him and left.

The paralegal heard everything, and we exchanged puzzled looks as I passed his desk. 'What an ass,' he said very quietly, almost mouthing the words.

I smiled again and nodded my agreement. An ass and a fool. If Chance had been pleasant and explained that Arthur or some other honcho from above had ordered the file sealed, then I wouldn't have been as

45

suspicious. But it was obvious there was something in the file.

Getting it would be the challenge.

With all the cell phones Claire and I owned – pocket, purse, and car, not to mention a couple of pagers – communication should've been a simple matter. But nothing was simple with our marriage. We hooked up around nine. She was exhausted from another one of her days, which were inevitably more fatiguing than anything I could possibly have done. It was a game we shamelessly played – my job is more important because I'm a doctor/lawyer.

I was tiring of the games. I could tell she was pleased that my brush with death had produced aftershocks, that I'd left the office to wander the streets. No doubt her day had been far more productive than mine.

Her goal was to become the greatest female neurosurgeon in the country, a brain surgeon even males would turn to when all hope was lost. She was a brilliant student, fiercely determined, blessed with enormous stamina. She would bury the men, just as she was slowly burying me, a well-seasoned marathon man from the halls of Drake & Sweeney. The race was getting old.

She drove a Miata sports car, no four-wheel drive, and I was worried about her in the bad weather. She would be through in an hour, and it would take that long for me to drive to Georgetown Hospital. I would pick her up there, and we would try to find a restaurant. If not, it would be Chinese carryout, our standard fare.

I began arranging papers and objects on my desk, careful to ignore the neat row of my ten most current files. I kept only ten on my desk, a method I'd learned from Rudolph, and I spent time with each file every

46

day. Billing was a factor. My top ten invariably included the wealthiest clients, regardless of how pressing their legal problems. Another trick from Rudolph.

I was expected to bill twenty-five hundred hours a year. That's fifty hours a week, fifty weeks a year. My average billing rate was three hundred dollars an hour, so I would gross for my beloved firm a total of seven hundred and fifty thousand dollars. They paid me a hundred and twenty thousand of this, plus another thirty for benefits, and assigned two hundred thousand to overhead. The partners kept the rest, divided annually by some horrendously complex formula that usually caused fistfights.

It was rare for one of our partners to earn less than a million a year, and some earned over two. And once I became a partner, I would be a partner for life. So if I made it when I was thirty-five, which happened to be the fast track I was on, then I could expect thirty years of glorious earnings and immense wealth.

That was the dream that kept us at our desks at all hours of the day and night.

I was scribbling these numbers, something I did all the time and something I suspect every lawyer in our firm did, when the phone rang. It was Mordecai Green.

'Mr. Brock,' he said politely, his voice clearly audible but competing with a din in the background.

'Yes. Please call me Michael.'

'Very well. Look, I made some calls, and you have nothing to worry about. The blood test was negative.'

'Thank you.'

'Don't mention it.'

'Just thought you'd want to know as soon as possible.'

'Thanks,' I said again, as the racket rose behind him. 'Where are you?'

'At a homeless shelter. A big snow brings 'em in faster than we can feed them, so it takes all of us to keep up. Gotta run.'

The desk was old mahogany, the rug was Persian, the chairs were a rich crimson leather, the technology was state-of-the-art, and as I studied my finely appointed office, I wondered, for the first time in many years there, how much all of it cost. Weren't we just chasing money? Why did we work so hard; to buy a richer rug, an older desk?

There in the warmth and coziness of my beautiful room, I thought of Mordecai Green, who at that moment was volunteering his time in a busy shelter, serving food to the cold and hungry, no doubt with a warm smile and a pleasant word.

Both of us had law degrees, both of us had passed the same bar exam, both of us were fluent in the tongue of legalese. We were kindred to some degree. I helped my clients swallow up competitors so they could add more zeros to the bottom line, and for this I would become rich. He helped his clients eat and find a warm bed.

I looked at the scratchings on my legal pad – the earnings and the years and the path to wealth – and I was saddened by them. Such blatant and unashamed greed.

The phone startled me.

'Why are you at the office?' Claire asked, each word spoken slowly because each word was covered with ice.

I looked in disbelief at my watch. 'I, uh, well, a client called from the West Coast. It's not snowing out there.'

I think it was a lie I'd used before. It didn't matter.

'I am waiting, Michael. Should I walk?'

'No. I'll be there as fast as I can.'

48

I'd kept her waiting before. It was part of the game –
we were much too busy to be prompt.

I ran from the building, into the storm, not really
too concerned that another night had been ruined.

SIX

The snow had finally stopped. Claire and I sipped our coffee by the kitchen window. I was reading the paper by the light of a brilliant morning sun. They had managed to keep National Airport open.

'Let's go to Florida,' I said. 'Now.'

She gave me a withering look. 'Florida?'

'Okay, the Bahamas. We can be there by early afternoon.'

'There's no way.'

'Sure there is. I'm not going to work for a few days, and –'

'Why not?'

'Because I'm cracking up, and around the firm if you crack up, then you get a few days off.'

'You are cracking up.'

'I know. It's kinda fun, really. People give you space, treat you with velvet gloves, kiss your ass. Might as well make the most of it.'

The tight face returned, and she said, 'I can't.'

And that was the end of that. It was a whim, and I knew she had too many obligations. It was a cruel thing to do, I decided as I returned to the paper, but I didn't feel bad about it. She wouldn't have gone with me under any circumstances.

She was suddenly in a hurry – appointments, classes, rounds, the life of an ambitious young surgical resident. She showered and changed and was ready to go. I drove her to the hospital.

We didn't talk as we inched through the snow-filled streets.

'I'm going to Memphis for a couple of days,' I said matter-of-factly when we arrived at the hospital entrance on Reservoir Street.

'Oh really,' she said, with no discernible reaction.

'I need to see my parents. It's been almost a year. I figure this is a good time. I don't do well in snow, and I'm not in the mood for work. Cracking up, you know.'

'Well, call me,' she said, opening her door. Then she shut it – no kiss, no good-bye, no concern. I watched her hurry down the sidewalk and disappear into the building.

It was over. And I hated to tell my mother.

My parents were in their early sixties, both healthy and trying gamely to enjoy forced retirement. Dad was an airline pilot for thirty years. Mom had been a bank manager. They worked hard, saved well, and provided a comfortable upper-middle-class home for us. My two brothers and I had the best private schools we could get into.

They were solid people, conservative, patriotic, free of bad habits, fiercely devoted to each other. They went to church on Sundays, the parade on July the Fourth, Rotary Club once a week, and they traveled whenever they wanted.

They were still grieving over my brother Warner's divorce three years earlier. He was an attorney in Atlanta who married his college sweetheart, a Memphis girl from a family we knew. After two kids, the marriage went south. His wife got custody and moved to Portland. My parents got to see the grandkids once a year, if all went well. It was a subject I never brought up.

I rented a car at the Memphis airport and drove east into the sprawling suburbs where the white people lived. The blacks had the city; the whites, the suburbs. Sometimes the blacks would move into a subdivision, and the whites would move to another one, farther away. Memphis crept eastward, the races running from each other.

My parents lived on a golf course, in a new glass house designed so that every window overlooked a fairway. I hated the house because the fairway was always busy. I didn't express my opinions, though.

I had called from the airport, so Mother was waiting with great anticipation when I arrived. Dad was on the back nine somewhere.

'You look tired,' she said after the hug and kiss. It was her standard greeting.

'Thanks, Mom. You look great.' And she did. Slender and bronze from her daily tennis and tanning regimen at the country club.

She fixed iced tea and we drank it on the patio, where we watched other retirees fly down the fairway in their golf carts.

'What's wrong?' she said before a minute passed, before I took the first sip.

'Nothing. I'm fine.'

'Where's Claire? You guys never call us, you know. I haven't heard her voice in two months.'

'Claire's fine, Mom. We're both alive and healthy and working very hard.'

'Are you spending enough time together?'

'No.'

'Are you spending any time together?'

'Not much.'

She frowned and rolled her eyes with motherly

concern. 'Are you having trouble?' she asked, on the attack.

'Yes.'

'I knew it. I knew it. I could tell by your voice on the phone that something was wrong. Surely you're not headed for a divorce too. Have you tried counseling?'

'No. Slow down.'

'Then why not? She's a wonderful person, Michael. Give the marriage everything you have.'

'We're trying, Mother. But it's difficult.'

'Affairs? Drugs? Alcohol? Gambling? Any of the bad things?'

'No. Just two people going their separate ways. I work eighty hours a week. She works the other eighty.'

'Then slow down. Money isn't everything.' Her voice broke just a little, and I saw wetness in her eyes.

'I'm sorry, Mom. At least we don't have kids.'

She bit her lip and tried to be strong, but she was dying inside. And I knew exactly what she was thinking: two down, one to go. She would take my divorce as a personal failure, the same way she broke down with my brother's. She would find some way to blame herself.

I didn't want the pity. To move things along to more interesting matters, I told her the story of Mister, and, for her benefit, downplayed the danger I'd been in. If the story made the Memphis paper, my parents had missed it.

'Are you all right?' she asked, horrified.

'Of course. The bullet missed me. I'm here.'

'Oh, thank God. I mean, well, emotionally are you all right?'

'Yes, Mother, I'm all together. No broken pieces. The firm wanted me to take a couple of days off, so I came home.'

'You poor thing. Claire, and now this.'

'I'm fine. We had a lot of snow last night, and it was a good time to leave.'

'Is Claire safe?'

'As safe as anybody in Washington. She lives at the hospital, probably the smartest place to be in that city.'

'I worry about you so much. I see the crime statistics, you know. It's a very dangerous city.'

'Almost as dangerous as Memphis.'

We watched a ball land near the patio, and waited for its owner to appear. A stout lady rolled out of a golf cart, hovered over the ball for a second, then shanked it badly.

Mother left to get more tea, and to wipe her eyes.

I don't know which of my parents got the worst end of my visit. My mother wanted strong families with lots of grandchildren. My father wanted his boys to move quickly up the ladder and enjoy the rewards of our hard-earned success.

Late that afternoon my dad and I did nine holes. He played; I drank beer and drove the cart. Golf had yet to work its magic on me. Two cold ones and I was ready to talk. I had repeated the Mister tale over lunch, so he figured I was just loafing for a couple of days, collecting myself before I roared back into the arena.

'I'm getting kind of sick of the big firm, Dad,' I said as we sat by the third tee, waiting for the foursome ahead to clear. I was nervous, and my nervousness irritated me greatly. It was my life, not his.

'What's that supposed to mean?'

'Means I'm tired of what I'm doing.'

'Welcome to the real world. You think the guy working a drill press in a factory doesn't get tired of what he's doing? At least you're getting rich.'

So he took round one, almost by a knockout. Two

holes later, as we stomped through the rough looking for his ball, he said, 'Are you changing jobs?'

'Thinking about it.'

'Where are you going?'

'I don't know. It's too early. I haven't been looking for another position.'

'Then how do you know the grass is greener if you haven't been looking?' He picked up his ball and walked off.

I drove alone on the narrow paved trail while he stalked down the fairway chasing his shot, and I wondered why that gray-haired man out there scared me so much. He had pushed all of his sons to set goals, work hard, strive to be Big Men, with everything aimed at making lots of money and living the American dream. He had certainly paid for anything we needed.

Like my brothers, I was not born with a social conscience. We gave offerings to the church because the Bible strongly suggests it. We paid taxes to the government because the law requires it. Surely, somewhere in the midst of all this giving some good would be done, and we had a hand in it. Politics belonged to those willing to play that game, and besides, there was no money to be made by honest people. We were taught to be productive, and the more success we attained, the more society would benefit, in some way. Set goals, work hard, play fair, achieve prosperity.

He double-bogeyed the fifth hole, and was blaming it on his putter when he climbed into the cart.

'Maybe I'm not looking for greener pastures,' I said.

'Why don't you just go ahead and say what you're trying to say?' he said. As usual, I felt weak for not facing the issue boldly.

'I'm thinking about public interest law.'

'What the hell is that?'

55

'It's when you work for the good of society without making a lot of money.'

'What are you, a Democrat now? You've been in Washington too long.'

'There are lots of Republicans in Washington. In fact, they've taken over.'

We rode to the next tee in silence. He was a good golfer, but his shots were getting worse. I'd broken his concentration.

Stomping through the rough again, he said, 'So some wino gets his head blown off and you gotta change society. Is that it?'

'He wasn't a wino. He fought in Vietnam.'

Dad flew B-52's in the early years of Vietnam, and this stopped him cold. But only for a second. He wasn't about to yield an inch. 'One of those, huh?'

I didn't respond. The ball was hopelessly lost, and he wasn't really looking. He flipped another onto the fairway, hooked it badly, and away we went.

'I hate to see you blow a good career, son,' he said. 'You've worked too hard. You'll be a partner in a few years.'

'Maybe.'

'You need some time off, that's all.'

That seemed to be everybody's remedy.

I took them to dinner at a nice restaurant. We worked hard to avoid the topics of Claire, my career, and the grandkids they seldom saw. We talked about old friends and old neighborhoods. I caught up on the gossip, none of which interested me in the least.

I left them at noon on Friday, four hours before my flight, and I headed back to my muddled life in D.C.

SEVEN

Of course, the apartment was empty when I returned Friday night, but with a new twist. There was a note on the kitchen counter. Following my cue, Claire had gone home to Providence for a couple of days. No reason was given. She asked me to phone when I got home.

I called her parents' and interrupted dinner. We labored through a five-minute chat in which it was determined that both of us were indeed fine, Memphis was fine and so was Providence, the families were fine, and she would return sometime Sunday afternoon.

I hung up, fixed coffee, and drank a cup staring out the bedroom window, watching the traffic crawl along P Street, still covered with snow. If any of the snow had melted, it wasn't obvious.

I suspected Claire was telling her parents the same dismal story I had burdened mine with. It was sad and odd and yet somehow not surprising that we were being honest with our families before we faced the truth ourselves. I was tired of it and determined that one day very soon, perhaps as early as Sunday, we would sit somewhere, probably at the kitchen table, and confront reality. We would lay bare our feelings and fears and, I was quite sure, start planning our separate futures. I knew she wanted out, I just didn't know how badly.

I practiced the words I would say to her out loud until they sounded convincing, then I went for a long walk. It was ten degrees with a sharp wind, and the chill cut through my trench coat. I passed the handsome homes and cozy rowhouses, where I saw real families eating and laughing and enjoying the warmth, and moved onto M Street, where throngs of those suffering from cabin fever filled the sidewalks. Even a freezing Friday night on M was never dull; the bars were packed, the restaurants had waiting lines, the coffee shops were filled.

I stood at the window of a music club, listening to the blues with snow packed around my ankles, watching the young couples drink and dance. For the first time in my life, I felt like something other than a young person. I was thirty-two, but in the last seven years I had worked more than most people do in twenty. I was tired, not old but bearing down hard on middle age, and I admitted that I was no longer fresh from college. Those pretty girls in there would never look twice at me now.

I was frozen, and it was snowing again. I bought a sandwich, stuffed it into a pocket, and slogged my way back to the apartment. I fixed a strong drink, and a small fire, and I ate in the semi-darkness, very much alone.

In the old days, Claire's absence for the weekend would have given me guilt-free grounds to live at the office. Sitting by the fire, I was repulsed by that thought. Drake & Sweeney would be standing proudly long after I was gone, and the clients and their problems, which had seemed so crucial, would be tended to by other squads of young lawyers. My departure would be a slight bump in the road for the firm, scarcely noticeable. My office would be taken minutes after I walked out.

At some time after nine, the phone rang, jolting me

58

from a long, somber daydream. It was Mordecai Green, speaking loudly into a cell phone. 'Are you busy?' he asked.

'Uh, not exactly. What's going on?'

'It's cold as hell, snowing again, and we're short on manpower Do you have a few hours to spare?'

'To do what?'

'To work. We really need able bodies down here. The shelters and soup kitchens are packed, and we don't have enough volunteers.'

'I'm not sure I'm qualified.'

'Can you spread peanut butter on bread?'

'I think so.'

'Then you're qualified.'

'Okay, where do I go?'

'We're ten blocks or so from the office. At the intersection of Thirteenth and Euclid, you'll see a yellow church on your right. Ebenezer Christian Fellowship. We're in the basement.'

I scribbled this down, each word getting shakier because Mordecai was calling me into a combat zone. I wanted to ask if I should pack a gun. I wondered if he carried one. But he was black, and I wasn't. What about my car, my prized Lexus?

'Got that?' he growled after a pause.

'Yeah. Be there in twenty minutes,' I said bravely, my heart already pounding.

I changed into jeans, a sweatshirt, and designer hiking boots. I took the credit cards and most of the cash out of my wallet. In the top of a closet, I found an old wool-lined denim jacket, stained with coffee and paint, a relic from law school, and as I modeled it in the mirror I hoped it made me look non-affluent. It did not. If a young actor wore it on the cover of *Vanity Fair*, a trend would start immediately.

I desperately wanted a bulletproof vest. I was

59

scared, but as I locked the door and stepped into the snow, I was also strangely excited.

The drive-by shootings and gang attacks I had expected did not materialize. The weather kept the streets empty and safe, for the moment. I found the church and parked in a lot across the street. It looked like a small cathedral, at least a hundred years old and no doubt abandoned by its original congregation.

Around a corner I saw some men huddled together, waiting by a door. I brushed past them as if I knew exactly where I was going, and I entered the world of the homeless.

As badly as I wanted to barge ahead, to pretend I had seen this before and had work to do, I couldn't move. I gawked in amazement at the sheer number of poor people stuffed into the basement. Some were lying on the floor, trying to sleep. Some were sitting in groups, talking in low tones. Some were eating at long tables and others in their folding chairs. Every square inch along the walls was covered with people sitting with their backs to the cinder blocks. Small children cried and played as their mothers tried to keep them close. Winos lay rigid, snoring through it all. Volunteers passed out blankets and walked among the throng, handing out apples.

The kitchen was at one end, bustling with action as food was prepared and served. I could see Mordecai in the background, pouring fruit juice into paper cups, talking incessantly. A line waited patiently at the serving tables.

The room was warm, and the odors and aromas and the gas heat mixed to create a thick smell that was not unpleasant. A homeless man, bundled up much like Mister, bumped into me and it was time to move.

I went straight to Mordecai, who was delighted to see me. We shook hands like old friends, and he

60

introduced me to two volunteers whose names I never heard.

'It's crazy,' he said. 'A big snow, a cold snap, and we work all night. Grab that bread over there.' He pointed to a tray of sliced white bread. I took it and followed him to a table.

'It's real complicated. You got bologna here, mustard and mayo there. Half the sandwiches get mustard, half get mayo, one slice of bologna, two slices of bread. Do a dozen with peanut butter every now and then. Got it?'

'Yeah.'

'You catch on quick.' He slapped me on the shoulder and disappeared.

I hurriedly made ten sandwiches, and declared myself to be proficient. Then I slowed, and began to watch the people as they waited in line, their eyes downcast but always glancing at the food ahead. They were handed a paper plate, a plastic bowl and spoon, and a napkin. As they shuffled along, the bowl was filled with soup, half a sandwich was placed on the plate, then an apple and a small cookie were added. A cup of apple juice was waiting at the end.

Most of them said a quiet 'Thanks' to the volunteer handing out the juice, then they moved away, gingerly holding the plate and bowl. Even the children were still and careful with their food.

Most seemed to eat slowly, savoring the warmth and feel of food in their mouths, the aroma in their faces. Others ate as fast as possible.

Next to me was a gas stove with four burners, each with a large pot of soup cooking away. On the other side of it, a table was covered with celery, carrots, onions, tomatoes, and whole chickens. A volunteer with a large knife was chopping and dicing with a vengeance. Two more volunteers manned the stove.

61

Several hauled the food to the serving tables. For the moment, I was the only sandwich man.

'We need more peanut butter sandwiches,' Mordecai announced as he returned to the kitchen. He reached under the table and grabbed a two-gallon jug of generic peanut butter. 'Can you handle it?'

'I'm an expert,' I said.

He watched me work. The line was momentarily short; he wanted to talk.

'I thought you were a lawyer,' I said, spreading peanut butter.

'I'm a human first, then a lawyer. It's possible to be both – not quite so much on the spread there. We have to be efficient.'

'Where does the food come from?'

'Food bank. It's all donated. Tonight we're lucky because we have chicken. That's a delicacy. Usually it's just vegetables.'

'This bread is not too fresh.'

'Yes, but it's free. Comes from a large bakery, their day-old stuff. You can have a sandwich if you like.'

'Thanks. I just had one. Do you eat here?'

'Rarely.' From the looks of his girth, Mordecai had not maintained a diet of vegetable soup and apples. He sat on the edge of the table and studied the crowd. 'Is this your first trip to a shelter?'

'Yep.'

'What's the first word that comes to mind?'

'Hopeless.'

'That's predictable. But you'll get over it.'

'How many people live here?'

'None. This is just an emergency shelter. The kitchen is open every day for lunch and dinner, but it's not technically a shelter. The church is kind enough to open its doors when the weather is bad.'

I tried to understand this. 'Then where do these people live?'

'Some are squatters. They live in abandoned buildings, and they're the lucky ones. Some live on the streets; some in parks; some in bus stations; some under bridges. They can survive there as long as the weather is tolerable. Tonight they would freeze.'

'Then where are the shelters?'

'Scattered about. There are about twenty – half privately funded, the other half run by the city, which, thanks to the new budget, will soon close two of them.'

'How many beds?'

'Five thousand, give or take.'

'How many homeless?'

'That's always a good question because they're not the easiest group to count. Ten thousand is a good guess.'

'Ten thousand?'

'Yep, and that's just the people on the street. There are probably another twenty thousand living with families and friends, a month or two away from homelessness.'

'So there are at least five thousand people on the streets?' I said, my disbelief obvious.

'At least.'

A volunteer asked for sandwiches. Mordecai helped me, and we made another dozen. Then we stopped and watched the crowd again. The door opened, and a young mother entered slowly, holding a baby and followed by three small children, one of whom wore a pair of shorts and mismatched socks, no shoes. A towel was draped over its shoulders. The other two at least had shoes, but little clothing. The baby appeared to be asleep.

The mother seemed dazed, and once inside the basement was uncertain where to go next. There was not a spot at a table. She led her family toward the food, and two smiling volunteers stepped forward to help. One parked them in a corner near the kitchen and began serving them food, while the other covered them with blankets.

Mordecai and I watched the scene develop. I tried not to stare, but who cared?

'What happens to her when the storm is over?' I asked.

'Who knows? Why don't you ask her?'

That put me on the spot. I was not ready to get my hands dirty.

'Are you active in the D.C. bar association?' he asked.

'Somewhat. Why?'

'Just curious. The bar does a lot of pro bono work with the homeless.'

He was fishing, and I wasn't about to get caught. 'I work on death penalty cases,' I said proudly, and somewhat truthfully. Four years earlier, I had helped one of our partners write a brief for an inmate in Texas. My firm preached pro bono to all its associates, but the free work had damned well better not interfere with the billings.

We kept watching the mother and her four children. The two toddlers ate their cookies first while the soup was cooling. The mother was either stoned or in shock.

'Is there a place she can go to right now and live?' I asked.

'Probably not,' Mordecai answered nonchalantly, his large feet swinging from the edge of the table. 'As of yesterday, the waiting list for emergency shelter had five hundred names on it.'

'For emergency shelter?'

'Yep. There's one hypothermia shelter the city graciously opens when the temperature drops below freezing. That might be her only chance, but I'm sure it's packed tonight. The city is then kind enough to close the shelter when things thaw.'

The sous-chef had to leave, and since I was the nearest volunteer who wasn't busy at the moment, I was pressed into duty. While Mordecai made sandwiches, I chopped celery, carrots, and onions for an hour, all under the careful eye of Miss Dolly, one of the founding members of the church, who'd been in charge of feeding the homeless for eleven years now. It was her kitchen. I was honored to be in it, and I was told at one point that my chunks of celery were too large. They quickly became smaller. Her apron was white and spotless, and she took enormous pride in her work.

'Do you ever get used to seeing these people?' I asked her at one point. We were standing in front of the stove, distracted by an argument in the back somewhere. Mordecai and the minister intervened and peace prevailed.

'Never, honey,' she said, wiping her hands on a towel. 'It still breaks my heart. But in Proverbs it says, "Happy is the man who feeds the poor." That keeps me going.'

She turned and gently stirred the soup. 'Chicken's ready,' she said in my direction.

'What does that mean?'

'Means you take the chicken off the stove, pour the broth into that pot, let the chicken cool, then bone it.'

There was an art to boning, especially using Miss Dolly's method. My fingers were hot and practically blistered when I finished.

EIGHT

Mordecai led me up a dark stairway to the foyer. 'Watch your step,' he said, almost in a whisper, as we pushed through a set of swinging doors into the sanctuary. It was dim, because people were trying to sleep everywhere. They were sprawled on the pews, snoring. They were squirming under the pews, mothers trying to make children be still. They were huddled in the aisles, leaving a narrow path for us as we worked our way toward the pulpit. The choir loft was filled with them too.

'Not many churches will do this,' he whispered as we stood near the altar table and surveyed the rows of pews.

I could understand their reluctance. 'What happens Sunday?' I whispered back.

'Depends on the weather. The Reverend is one of us. He has, on occasion, canceled worship instead of running them out.'

I was not sure what 'one of us' meant, but I didn't feel like a member of the club. I heard the ceiling creak, and realized that there was a U-shaped balcony above us. I squinted and slowly focused on another mass of humanity layered in the rows of seats up there. Mordecai was looking too.

'How many people . . .' I mumbled, unable to finish the thought.

'We don't count. We just feed and shelter.'

A gust of wind hit the side of the building and rattled the windows. It was considerably colder in the sanctuary than in the basement. We tiptoed over bodies and left through a door by the organ.

It was almost eleven. The basement was still crowded, but the soup line was gone. 'Follow me,' Mordecai said.

He took a plastic bowl and held it forth for a volunteer to fill. 'Let's see how well you cook,' he said with a smile.

We sat in the middle of the pack, at a folding table with street people at our elbows. He was able to eat and chat as if everything was fine; I wasn't. I played with my soup, which, thanks to Miss Dolly, was really quite good, but I couldn't get beyond the fact that I, Michael Brock, an affluent white boy from Memphis and Yale and Drake & Sweeney, was sitting among the homeless in the basement of a church in the middle of Northwest D.C. I had seen one other white face, that of a middle-aged wino who had eaten and disappeared.

I was sure my Lexus was gone, certain I could not survive five minutes outside the building. I vowed to stick to Mordecai, whenever and however he decided to leave.

'This is good soup,' he pronounced. 'It varies,' he explained. 'Depends on what's available. And the recipe is different from place to place.'

'I got noodles the other day at Martha's Table,' said the man sitting to my right, a man whose elbow was closer to my bowl than my own.

'Noodles?' Mordecai asked, in mock disbelief. 'In your soup?'

'Yep. 'Bout once a month you get noodles. Course everybody knows it now, so it's hard to get a table.'

I couldn't tell if he was joking or not, but there was a

twinkle in his eye. The idea of a homeless man lamenting the lack of tables in his favorite soup kitchen struck me as humorous. Hard to get a table; how many times had I heard that from friends in Georgetown?

Mordecai smiled. 'What's your name?' he asked the man. I would learn that Mordecai always wanted a name to go with a face. The homeless he loved were more than victims; they were his people.

It was a natural curiosity for me too. I wanted to know how the homeless became homeless. What broke in our vast system of public assistance to allow Americans to become so poor they lived under bridges?

'Drano,' he said, chomping on one of my larger celery chunks.

'Drano?' Mordecai said.

'Drano,' the man repeated.

'What's your last name?'

'Don't have one. Too poor.'

'Who gave you the name Drano?'

'My momma.'

'How old were you when she gave you the name Drano?'

''Bout five.'

'Why Drano?'

'She had this baby who wouldn't shut up, cried all the time, nobody could sleep. I fed it some Drano.' He told the story while stirring his soup. It was well rehearsed, well delivered, and I didn't believe a word of it. But others were listening, and Drano was enjoying himself.

'What happened to the baby?' Mordecai asked, playing the straight guy.

'Died.'

'That would be your brother,' Mordecai said.

'Nope. Sister.'

68

'I see. So you killed your sister.'

'Yeah, but we got plenty of sleep after that.'

Mordecai winked at me, as if he'd heard similar tales.

'Where do you live, Drano?' I asked.

'Here, in D.C.'

'Where do you stay?' Mordecai asked, correcting my vernacular.

'Stay here and there. I got a lot of rich women who pay me to keep them company.'

Two men on the other side of Drano found this amusing. One snickered, the other laughed.

'Where do you get your mail?' Mordecai asked.

'Post office,' he replied. Drano would have a quick answer for every question, so we left him alone.

Miss Dolly made coffee for the volunteers after she had turned off her stove. The homeless were bedding down for the night.

Mordecai and I sat on the edge of a table in the darkened kitchen, sipping coffee and looking through the large serving window at the huddled masses. 'How late will you stay?' I asked.

He shrugged. 'Depends. You get a coupla hundred people like this in one room, something usually happens. The Reverend would feel better if I stay.'

'All night?'

'I've done it many times.'

I hadn't planned on sleeping with these people. Nor had I planned on leaving the building without Mordecai to guard me.

'Feel free to leave whenever you want,' he said. Leaving was the worst of my limited options. Midnight, Friday night, on the streets of D.C. White boy, beautiful car. Snow or not, I didn't like my odds out there.

'You have a family?' I asked.

'Yes. My wife is a secretary in the Department of

69

Labor. Three sons. One's in college, one's in the Army.' His voice trailed away before he got to son number three. I wasn't about to ask.

'And one we lost on the streets ten years ago. Gangs.'

'I'm sorry.'

'What about you?'

'Married, no kids.'

I thought about Claire for the first time in several hours. How would she react if she knew where I was? Neither of us had found time for anything remotely related to charity work.

She would mumble to herself, 'He's really cracking up,' or something to that effect.

I didn't care.

'What does your wife do?' he asked, making light conversation.

'She's a surgical resident at Georgetown.'

'You guys'll have it made, won't you? You'll be a partner in a big firm, she'll be a surgeon. Another American dream.'

'I guess.'

The Reverend appeared from nowhere and pulled Mordecai deep into the kitchen for a hushed conversation. I took four cookies from a bowl and walked to the corner where the young mother sat sleeping with her head propped on a pillow and the baby tucked under her arm. The toddlers were motionless under the blankets. But the oldest child was awake.

I squatted close to him, and held out a cookie. His eyes glowed and he grabbed it. I watched him eat every bite, then he wanted another. He was small and bony, no more than four years old.

The mother's head fell forward, jolting her. She looked at me with sad, tired eyes, then realized I was playing cookie man. She offered a faint smile, then rearranged the pillow.

'What's your name?' I whispered to the little boy. After two cookies, he was my friend for life.

'Ontario,' he said, slowly and plainly.

'How old are you?'

He held up four fingers, then folded one down, then raised it again.

'Four?' I asked.

He nodded, and extended his hand for another cookie, which I gladly gave him. I would have given him anything.

'Where do you stay?' I whispered.

'In a car,' he whispered back.

It took a second for this to sink in. I wasn't sure what to ask next. He was too busy eating to worry about conversation. I had asked three questions; he'd given three honest answers. They lived in a car.

I wanted to run and ask Mordecai what you do when you find people who live in a car, but I kept smiling at Ontario. He smiled back. He finally said, 'You got more apple juice?'

'Sure,' I said, and walked to the kitchen, where I filled two cups.

He gulped one down, and I handed him the second cup.

'Say thanks,' I said.

'Thanks,' he said, and stuck out his hand for another cookie.

I found a folding chair and took a position next to Ontario, with my back to the wall. The basement was quiet at times, but never still. Those who live without beds do not sleep calmly. Occasionally, Mordecai would pick his way around the bodies to settle some flare-up. He was so large and intimidating that no one dared challenge his authority.

With his stomach filled again, Ontario dozed off, his little head resting on his mother's feet. I slipped into the kitchen, poured another cup of coffee, and went back to my chair in the corner.

Then the baby erupted. Its pitiful voice wailed forth with amazing volume, and the entire room seemed to ripple with the noise. The mother was dazed, tired, frustrated at having been aroused from sleep. She told it to shut up, then placed it on her shoulder, and rocked back and forth. It cried louder, and there were rumblings from the other campers.

With a complete lack of sense or thought, I reached over and took the child, smiling at the mother as I did so in an attempt to win her confidence. She didn't care. She was relieved to get rid of it.

The child weighed nothing, and the damned thing was soaking wet. I realized this as I gently placed its head on my shoulder and began patting its rear. I moved to the kitchen, desperately searching for Mordecai or another volunteer to rescue me. Miss Dolly had left an hour earlier.

To my relief and surprise, the child grew quiet as I walked around the stove, patting and cooing and looking for a towel or something. My hand was soaked.

Where was I? What the hell was I doing? What would my friends think if they could see me in the dark kitchen, humming to a little street baby, praying that the diaper was only wet?

I didn't smell anything foul, though I was certain I could feel lice jumping from its head to mine. My best friend Mordecai appeared and turned on a switch. 'How cute,' he said.

'Do we have any diapers?' I hissed at him.

'Big job or little job?' he asked happily, walking toward the cabinets.

'I don't know. Just hurry.'

He pulled out a pack of Pampers, and I thrust the child at him. My denim jacket had a large wet spot on the left shoulder. With incredible deftness he placed the baby on the cutting board, removed the wet diaper, revealing a baby girl, cleaned her with a wipe of some sort, rediapered her with a fresh Pamper, then thrust her back at me. 'There she is,' he said proudly. 'Good as new.'

'The things they don't teach you in law school,' I said, taking the child.

I paced the floor with her for an hour, until she fell asleep. I wrapped her in my jacket, and gently placed her between her mother and Ontario.

It was almost 3 A.M., Saturday, and I had to go. My freshly pricked conscience could take only so much in one day. Mordecai walked me to the street, thanked me for coming, and sent me away coatless into the night. My car was sitting where I left it, covered with new snow.

He was standing in front of the church, watching me as I drove away.

NINE

Since my run-in with Mister on Tuesday, I had not billed a single hour for dear old Drake & Sweeney. I'd been averaging two hundred a month for five years, which meant eight per day for six days, with a couple left over. No day could be wasted and precious few hours left unaccounted for. When I fell behind, which rarely happened, I would work twelve hours on a Saturday and perhaps do the same on a Sunday. And if I wasn't behind, I would do only seven or eight hours on Saturday and maybe a few on Sunday. No wonder Claire went to med school.

As I stared at the bedroom ceiling late Saturday morning, I was almost paralyzed with inaction. I did not want to go to the office. I hated the thought. I dreaded the neat little rows of pink phone messages Polly had on my desk, the memos from higher-ups arranging meetings to inquire about my well-being, the nosy chitchat from the gossipers, and the inevitable 'How you doin'?' from friends and those genuinely concerned and those who couldn't care less. What I dreaded most, though, was the work. Antitrust cases are long and arduous, with files so thick they require boxes, and what was the point anyway? One billion-dollar corporation fighting another. A hundred lawyers involved, all cranking out paper.

I admitted to myself that I'd never loved the work. It

was a means to an end. If I practiced it with a fury, became a whiz and perfected a specialty, then one day soon I would be in demand. It could've been tax or labor or litigation. Who could love antitrust law?

By sheer will, I forced myself out of bed and into the shower.

Breakfast was a croissant from a bakery on M, with strong coffee, all taken with one hand on the wheel. I wondered what Ontario was having for breakfast, then told myself to stop the torture. I had the right to eat without feeling guilty, but food was losing its importance for me.

The radio said the day's high would be twenty degrees, the low near zero, with no more snow for a week.

I made it as far as the building's lobby before being accosted by one of my brethren. Bruce somebody from communications stepped onto the elevator when I did, and said gravely, 'How you doin', pal?'

'Fine. You?' I shot back.

'Okay. Look, we're pulling for you, you know. Hang in there.'

I nodded as if his support was crucial. Mercifully, he left on the second floor, but not before favoring me with a locker-room pat on the shoulder. Give 'em hell, Bruce.

I was damaged goods. My steps were slower as I passed Madam Devier's desk and the conference room. I went down the marble hallway until I found my office and slumped into the leather swivel, exhausted.

Polly had several ways of leaving behind the phone litter. If I had been diligent in returning calls, and if she happened to be pleased with my efforts, she would leave one or two message slips near my phone. If, however, I had not, and if this happened to displease her, then she liked nothing better than to line them up in the center of my desk, a sea of pink, all perfectly arranged in chronological order.

I counted thirty-nine messages, several urgent, several from the brass. Rudolph especially seemed to be irritated, judging by Polly's trail. I read them slowly as I collected them, then set them aside. I was determined to finish my coffee, in peace and without pressure, and so I was sitting at my desk, holding the cup with both hands, staring into the unknown, looking very much like someone teetering on the edge of a cliff, when Rudolph walked in.

The spies must have called him; a paralegal on the lookout, or maybe Bruce from the elevator. Perhaps the entire firm was on alert. No. They were too busy.

'Hello, Mike,' he said crisply, taking a seat, crossing his legs, settling in for serious business.

'Hi, Rudy,' I said. I had never called him Rudy to his face. It was always Rudolph. His current wife and the partners called him Rudy, but no one else.

'Where have you been?' he asked, without the slightest hint of compassion.

'Memphis.'

'Memphis?'

'Yeah, I needed to see my parents. Plus the family shrink is there.'

'A shrink?'

'Yes, he observed me for a couple of days.'

'Observed you?'

'Yeah, in one of those swanky little units with Persian rugs and salmon for dinner. A thousand bucks a day.'

'For two days? You were in for two days?'

'Yeah.' The lying didn't bother me, nor did I feel bad because the lying didn't bother me. The firm can be harsh, even ruthless, when it decides to be, and I was in no mood for an ass-chewing from Rudolph. He had marching orders from the executive committee, and he would make a report minutes after leaving my office. If I could thaw him, the report would go soft, the brass would relax. Life would be easier, for the short term.

'You should've called somebody,' he said, still hard, but the crack was coming.

'Come on, Rudolph. I was locked down. No phones.' There was just enough agony in my voice to soften him.

After a long pause, he said, 'Are you okay?'

'I'm fine.'

'You're fine?'

'The shrink said I'm fine.'

'One hundred percent?'

'A hundred and ten. No problems, Rudolph. I needed a little break, that's all. I'm fine. Back at full throttle.'

That was all Rudolph wanted. He smiled and relaxed and said, 'We have lots of work to do.'

'I know. I can't wait.'

He practically ran from my office. He would go straight to the phone and report that one of the firm's many producers was back in the saddle.

I locked the door and turned off the lights, then spent a painful hour covering my desk with papers and scribblings. Nothing was accomplished, but at least I was on the clock.

When I couldn't stand it any longer, I stuffed the phone messages in my pocket and walked out. I escaped without getting caught.

I stopped at a large discount pharmacy on Massachusetts, and had a delightful shopping spree. Candy and small toys for the kids, soap and toiletries for them all, socks and sweatpants in a variety of children's sizes. A large carton of Pampers. I had never had so much fun spending two hundred dollars.

77

And I would spend whatever was necessary to get them into a warm place. If it was a motel for a month, no problem. They would soon become my clients, and I would threaten and litigate with a vengeance until they had adequate housing. I couldn't wait to sue somebody.

I parked across from the church, much less afraid than I had been the night before, but still sufficiently scared. Wisely, I left the care packages in the car. If I walked in like Santa Claus it would start a riot. My intentions were to leave there with the family, take them to a motel, check them in, make sure they were bathed and cleaned and disinfected, then feed them until they were stuffed, see if they needed medical attention, maybe take them to get shoes and warm clothes, then feed them again. I didn't care what it would cost or how long it might take.

Nor did I care if people thought I was just another rich white guy working off a little guilt.

Miss Dolly was pleased to see me. She said hello and pointed to a pile of vegetables with skins in need of removal. First, though, I checked on Ontario and family, and couldn't find them. They were not in their spot, so I roamed through the basement, stepping over and around dozens of street people. They were not in the sanctuary, nor in the balcony.

I chatted with Miss Dolly as I peeled potatoes. She remembered the family from last night, but they had already left when she arrived around nine.

'Where would they go?' I wondered.

'Honey, these people move. They go from kitchen to kitchen, shelter to shelter. Maybe she heard they're giving out cheese over in Brightwood, or blankets somewhere. She might even have a job at McDonald's and she leaves the kids with her sister. You never know. But they don't stay in one place.'

I seriously doubted if Ontario's mother had a job,

78

but I wasn't about to debate this with Miss Dolly in her kitchen.

Mordecai arrived as the line was forming for lunch. I saw him before he saw me, and when our eyes made contact his entire face smiled.

A new volunteer had sandwich duty; Mordecai and I worked the serving tables, dipping ladles into the pots and pouring the soup into the plastic bowls. There was an art to it. Too much broth and the recipient might glare at you. Too many vegetables and there would be nothing left but broth. Mordecai had perfected his technique years ago; I suffered a number of glaring looks before I caught on. Mordecai had a pleasant word for everyone we served – hello, good morning, how are you, nice to see you again. Some of them smiled back, others never looked up.

As noon approached, the doors grew busier and the lines longer. More volunteers appeared from nowhere, and the kitchen hummed with the pleasant clutter and bang of happy people busy with their work. I kept looking for Ontario. Santa Claus was waiting, and the little fella didn't have a clue.

We waited until the lines were gone, then filled a bowl each. The tables were packed, so we ate in the kitchen, leaning against the sink.

'You remember that diaper you changed last night?' I asked between bites.

'As if I could forget.'

'I haven't seen them today.'

He chewed and thought about it for a second. 'They were here when I left this morning.'

'What time was that?'

'Six. They were in the corner over there, sound asleep.'

'Where would they go?'

'You never know.'

'The little boy told me they stayed in a car.'
'You talked to him?'
'Yeah.'
'And now you want to find him, don't you?'
'Yeah.'
'Don't count on it.'

After lunch, the sun popped through and the movement began. One by one they walked by the serving table, took an apple or an orange, and left the basement.

'The homeless are also restless,' Mordecai explained as we watched. 'They like to roam around. They have rituals and routines, favorite places, friends on the streets, things to do. They'll go back to their parks and alleys and dig out from the snow.'

'It's twenty degrees outside. Near zero tonight,' I said.

'They'll be back. Wait till dark, and this place will be hopping again. Let's take a ride.'

We checked in with Miss Dolly, who excused us for a while. Mordecai's well-used Ford Taurus was parked next to my Lexus. 'That won't last long around here,' he said, pointing at my car. 'If you plan to spend time in this part of town, I'd suggest you trade down.'

I hadn't dreamed of parting with my fabulous car. I was almost offended.

We got into his Taurus and slid out of the parking lot. Within seconds I realized Mordecai Green was a horrible driver, and I attempted to fasten my seat belt. It was broken. He seemed not to notice.

We drove the well-plowed streets of Northwest Washington, blocks and sections of boarded-up rowhouses, past projects so tough ambulance drivers refused to enter, past schools with razor wire glistening on top of the chain link, into neighborhoods permanently scarred by riots. He was an amazing tour guide.

80

Every inch was his turf, every corner had a story, every street had a history. We passed other shelters and kitchens. He knew the cooks and the Reverends. Churches were good or bad, with no blurring of the lines. They either opened their doors to the homeless or kept them locked. He pointed out the law school at Howard, a place of immense pride for him. His legal education had taken five years, at night, while he worked a full-time job and a part-time one. He showed me a burned-out rowhouse where crack dealers once operated. His third son, Cassius, had died on the sidewalk in front of it.

When we were near his office, he asked if it would be all right to stop in for a minute. He wanted to check his mail. I certainly didn't mind. I was just along for the ride.

It was dim, cold, and empty. He flipped on light switches and began talking. 'There are three of us. Me, Sofia Mendoza, and Abraham Lebow. Sofia's a social worker, but she knows more street law than me and Abraham combined.' I followed him around the cluttered desks. 'Used to have seven lawyers crammed in here, can you believe it? That was when we got federal money for legal services. Now we don't get a dime, thanks to the Republicans. There are three offices over there, three here on my side.' He was pointing in all directions. 'Lots of empty space.'

Maybe empty from a lack of personnel, but it was hard to walk without tripping over a basket of old files or a stack of dusty law books.

'Who owns the building?' I asked.

'The Cohen Trust. Leonard Cohen was the founder of a big New York law firm. He died in eighty-six; must've been a hundred years old. He made a ton of money, and late in life he decided he didn't want to die with any of it. So he spread it around, and one of his many creations was a trust to help poverty lawyers

81

assist the homeless. That's how this place came to be. The trust operates three clinics – here, New York, and Newark. I was hired in eighty-three, became the director in eighty-four.'

'All your funding comes from one source?'

'Practically all. Last year the trust gave us a hundred and ten thousand dollars. Year before, it was a hundred fifty, so we lost a lawyer. It gets smaller every year. The trust has not been well managed, and it's now eating the principal. I doubt if we'll be here in five years. Maybe three.'

'Can't you raise money?'

'Oh, sure. Last year we raised nine thousand bucks. But it takes time. We can practice law, or we can raise funds. Sofia is not good with people. Abraham is an abrasive ass from New York. That leaves just me and my magnetic personality.'

'What's the overhead?' I asked, prying but not too worried. Almost every nonprofit group published an annual report with all the figures.

'Two thousand a month. After expenses and a small reserve, the three of us split eighty-nine thousand dollars. Equally. Sofia considers herself a full partner. Frankly, we're afraid to argue with her. I took home almost thirty, which, from what I hear, is about average for a poverty lawyer. Welcome to the street.'

We finally made it to his office, and I sat across from him.

'Did you forget to pay your heating bill?' I asked, almost shivering.

'Probably. We don't work much on weekends. Saves money. This place is impossible to heat or cool.'

That thought had never occurred to anyone at Drake & Sweeney. Close on weekends, save money. And marriages.

'And if we keep it too comfortable, our clients won't

leave. So it's cold in the winter, hot in the summer, cuts down on the street traffic. You want coffee?'

'No thanks.'

'I'm joking, you know. We wouldn't do anything to discourage the homeless from being here. The climate doesn't bother us. We figure our clients are cold and hungry, so why should we worry about those matters. Did you feel guilty when you ate breakfast this morning?'

'Yes.'

He gave me the smile of a wise old man who'd seen it all. 'That's very common. We used to work with a lot of young lawyers from the big firms, pro bono rookies I call them, and they would tell me all the time that they lost interest in food at first.' He patted his ample midsection. 'But you'll get over it.'

'What did the pro bono rookies do?' I asked. I knew I was moving toward the bait, and Mordecai knew I knew.

'We sent them into the shelters. They met the clients, and we supervised the cases for them. Most of the work is easy, it just takes a lawyer on the phone barking at some bureaucrat who won't move. Food stamps, veterans' pensions, housing subsidies, Medicaid, aid to children – about twenty-five percent of our work deals with benefits.'

I listened intently, and he could read my mind. Mordecai began to reel me in.

'You see, Michael, the homeless have no voice. No one listens, no one cares, and they expect no one to help them. So when they try to use the phone to get benefits due them, they get nowhere. They are put on hold, permanently. Their calls are never returned. They have no addresses. The bureaucrats don't care, and so they screw the very people they're supposed to help. A seasoned social worker can at least get the bureaucrats to listen, and maybe look at the file and maybe return a phone call. But you get a lawyer on the phone, barking and raising hell, and things happen. Bureaucrats get motivated. Papers get processed. No address? No problem. Send the check to me, I'll get it to the client.'

His voice was rising, both hands waving through the air. On top of everything else, Mordecai was the consummate storyteller. I suspected he was very effective in front of a jury.

'A funny story,' he said. 'About a month ago, one of my clients went down to the Social Security office to pick up an application for benefits, should've been a routine matter. He's sixty years old and in constant pain from a crooked back. Sleep on rocks and park benches for ten years, you got back problems. He waited in line outside the office for two hours, finally got in the door, waited another hour, made it up to the first desk, tried to explain what he wanted, and proceeded to get a tongue lashing from a hard-ass secretary who was having a bad day. She even commented on his odor. He was humiliated, of course, and left without his paperwork. He called me. I made my calls, and last Wednesday we had a little ceremony down at the Social Security office. I was there, along with my client. The secretary was there too, along with her supervisor, her supervisor's supervisor, the D.C. office director, and a Big Man from the Social Security Administration. The secretary stood in front of my client, and read a one-page apology. It was real nice, touching. She then handed me his application for benefits, and I got assurances from everybody present that it would receive immediate attention. That's justice, Michael, that's what street law is all about. Dignity.'

The stories rolled on, one after the other, all ending with the street lawyers as the good guys, the homeless as the victors. I knew he had tucked away in his repertoire just as many heartbreaking tales, probably more, but he was laying the groundwork.

I lost track of time. He never mentioned his mail. We finally left and drove back to the shelter.

It was an hour before dark, a good time, I thought, to get tucked away in the cozy little basement, before the hoodlums began roaming the streets. I caught myself walking slowly and confidently when Mordecai was at my side. Otherwise, I would've been slashing through the snow, bent at the waist, my nervous feet barely touching the ground.

Miss Dolly had somehow procured a pile of whole chickens, and she was laying for me. She boiled the birds; I picked their steaming flesh.

Mordecai's wife, JoAnne, joined us for the rush hour. She was as pleasant as her husband, and almost as tall. Both sons were six six. Cassius had been six nine, a heavily recruited basketball star when he was shot at the age of seventeen.

I left at midnight. No sign of Ontario and his family.

TEN

Sunday began with a late morning call from Claire, another stilted chat she initiated only to tell me what time she would be home. I suggested we have dinner at our favorite restaurant, but she was not in the mood. I didn't ask her if anything was wrong. We were beyond that.

Since our apartment was on the third floor, I had been unable to make satisfactory arrangements to have the Sunday *Post* home-delivered. We had tried various methods, but I never found the paper half the time.

I showered and dressed in layers. The weatherman predicted a high of twenty-five, and as I was getting ready to leave the apartment the newsperson rattled off the morning's top story. It stopped me cold; I heard the words, but they didn't register immediately. I walked closer to the TV on the kitchen counter, my feet heavy, my heart frozen, my mouth open in shock and disbelief.

Sometime around 11 P.M., D.C. police found a small car near Fort Totten Park, in Northeast, in a war zone. It was parked on the street, its bald tires stuck in the frozen slush. Inside were a young mother and her four children, all dead from asphyxiation. The police suspected the family lived in the car, and was trying to stay warm. The automobile's tailpipe was buried in a pile of snow plowed from the street. A few details, but no names.

I raced to the sidewalk, sliding in the snow but staying on my feet, then down P Street to Wisconsin, over to Thirty-fourth to a news-stand. Out of breath and horrified, I grabbed a paper. On the bottom corner of the front page was the story, obviously thrown in at the last minute. No names.

I yanked open Section A, dropping the rest of the paper onto the wet sidewalk. The story continued on page fourteen with a few standard comments from the police and the predictable warnings about the dangers of clogged tailpipes. Then the heartbreaking details: The mother was twenty-two. Her name was Lontae Burton. The baby was Temeko. The toddlers, Alonzo and Dante, were twins, age two. The big brother was Ontario, age four.

I must have made a strange sound, because a jogger gave me an odd look, as if I might be dangerous. I began walking away, holding the paper open, stepping on the other twenty sections.

'Excuse me!' a nasty voice called from behind. 'Would you like to pay for that?' I kept walking.

He approached from the rear and yelled, 'Hey, pal!' I stopped long enough to pull a five-dollar bill from my pocket and throw it at his feet, hardly looking at him.

On P, near the apartment, I leaned on a brick retaining wall in front of someone's splendid row-house. The sidewalk had been meticulously shoveled. I read the story again, slowly, hoping that somehow the ending would be different. Thoughts and questions came in torrents, and I couldn't keep up with them. But two repeated themselves: Why didn't they return to the shelter? And, did the baby die wrapped in my denim jacket?

Thinking was burden enough. Walking was almost impossible. After the shock, the guilt hit hard. Why

87

didn't I do something Friday night when I first saw them? I could have taken them to a warm motel and fed them.

The phone was ringing when I entered my apartment. It was Mordecai. He asked if I'd seen the story. I asked if he remembered the wet diaper. Same family, I said. He'd never heard their names. I told him more about my encounter with Ontario.

'I'm very sorry, Michael,' he said, much sadder now.

'So am I.'

I couldn't say much, the words wouldn't form, so we agreed to meet later. I went to the sofa, where I remained for an hour without moving.

Then I went to my car and removed the bags of food and toys and clothing I'd bought for them.

Only because he was curious, Mordecai came to my office at noon. He'd been in plenty of big firms in his time, but he wanted to see the spot where Mister fell. I gave him a brief tour with a quick narration of the hostage affair.

We left in his car. I was thankful for the light Sunday traffic because Mordecai had no interest in what the other cars were doing.

'Lontae Burton's mother is thirty-eight years old, serving a ten-year sentence for selling crack,' he informed me. He'd been on the phone. 'Two brothers, both in jail. Lontae had a history of prostitution and drugs. No idea of who the father, or fathers, might be.'

'Who's your source?'

'I found her grandmother in a housing project. The last time she saw Lontae she had only three kids, and she was selling drugs with her mother. According to the grandmother, she cut her ties with her daughter and granddaughter because of the drug business.'

'Who buries them?'

'Same people who buried DeVon Hardy.'

'How much would a decent funeral cost?'

'It's negotiable. Are you interested?'

'I'd like to see them taken care of.'

We were on Pennsylvania Avenue, moving past the mammoth office buildings of Congress, the Capitol in the background, and I couldn't help but offer a silent curse or two at the fools who wasted billions each month while people were homeless. How could four innocent children die in the streets, practically in the shadow of the Capitol, because they had no place to live?

They shouldn't have been born, some people from my side of town would say.

The bodies had been taken to the Office of the Chief Medical Examiner, which also housed the morgue. It was a two-story brown aggregate building at D.C. General Hospital. They would be held there until claimed. If no one came forward within forty-eight hours, they would receive a mandatory embalming, be placed in wooden caskets, and quickly buried in the cemetery near RFK.

Mordecai parked in a handicapped space, paused for a second, and said, 'Are you sure you want to go in?'

'I think so.'

He'd been there before, and he had called ahead. A security guard in an ill-fitting uniform dared to stop us, and Mordecai snapped so loud it scared me. My stomach was in knots anyway.

The guard retreated, happy to get away from us. A set of plate-glass doors had the word MORGUE painted in black. Mordecai entered as if he owned the place.

'I'm Mordecai Green, attorney for the Burton family,' he growled at the young man behind the desk. It was more of a challenge than an announcement.

89

The young man checked a clipboard, then fumbled with some more papers.

'What the hell are you doing?' Mordecai snapped again.

The young man looked up with an attitude, and then realized how large his adversary really was. 'Just a minute,' he said, and went to his computer.

Mordecai turned to me and said loudly, 'You'd think they have a thousand dead bodies in there.'

I realized that he had no patience whatsoever with bureaucrats and government workers, and I remembered his story about the apology from the Social Security secretary. For Mordecai, half of the practice of law was bullying and barking.

A pale gentleman with badly dyed black hair and a clammy handshake appeared and introduced himself as Bill. He wore a blue lab jacket and shoes with thick rubber soles. Where do they find people to work in a morgue?

We followed him through a door, down a sterile hallway where the temperature began dropping, and, finally, to the main holding room.

'How many you got today?' Mordecai asked, as if he stopped by all the time to count bodies.

Bill turned the doorknob and said, 'Twelve.'

'You okay?' Mordecai asked me.

'I don't know.'

Bill pushed the metal door, and we stepped in. The air was frigid, the smell antiseptic. The floor was white tile, the lighting blue fluorescent. I followed Mordecai, my head down, trying not to look around, but it was impossible. The bodies were covered from head to ankle with white sheets, just like you see on television. We passed a set of white feet, a tag around a toe. Then some brown ones.

We turned and stopped in a corner, a gurney to the left, a table to the right.

Bill said, 'Lontae Burton,' and dramatically pulled the sheet down to her waist. It was Ontario's mother all right, in a plain white gown. Death had left no marks on her face. She could've been sleeping. I couldn't stop staring at her.

'That's her,' Mordecai said, as if he'd known her for years. He looked at me for verification, and I managed a nod. Bill wheeled around, and I held my breath. Only one sheet covered the children.

They were lying in a perfect row, tucked closely together, hands folded over their matching gowns, cherubs sleeping, little street soldiers finally at peace.

I wanted to touch Ontario, to pat him on the arm and tell him I was sorry. I wanted to wake him up, take him home, feed him, and give him everything he could ever want.

I took a step forward for a closer look. 'Don't touch,' Bill said.

When I nodded, Mordecai said, 'That's them.'

As Bill covered them, I closed my eyes and said a short prayer, one of mercy and forgiveness. Don't let it happen again, the Lord said to me.

In a room down the hall, Bill pulled out two large wire baskets containing the personal effects of the family. He dumped them on a table, and we helped him inventory the contents. The clothing they wore was dirty and threadbare. My denim jacket was the nicest item they owned. There were three blankets, a purse, some cheap toys, baby formula, a towel, more dirty clothes, a box of vanilla wafers, an unopened can of beer, some cigarettes, two condoms, and about twenty dollars in bills and change.

'The car is at the city lot,' Bill said. 'They say it's full of junk.'

'We'll take care of it,' Mordecai said.

We signed the inventory sheets, and left with the

91

personal assets of the Lontae Burton family. 'What do we do with this stuff?' I asked.

'Take it to the grandmother. Do you want your coat back?'

'No.'

The funeral parlor was owned by a minister Mordecai knew. He didn't like him because the Reverend's church was not friendly enough to the homeless, but he could deal with him.

We parked in front of the church, on Georgia Avenue near Howard University, a cleaner part of town without as many boards over windows.

'It's best if you stay here,' he said. 'I can talk to him a lot plainer if we're alone.'

I didn't want to sit in the car by myself, but by then I trusted him with my life anyway. 'Sure,' I said, sinking a few inches and glancing around.

'You'll be all right.'

He left, and I locked the doors. After a few minutes, I relaxed, and began to think. Mordecai wanted to be alone with the minister for business reasons. My presence would've complicated matters. Who was I and what was my interest in the family? The price would rise immediately.

The sidewalk was busy. I watched the people scurry by, the wind cutting them sharply. A mother with two children passed me, bundled in nice clothing, all holding hands. Where were they last night when Ontario and family were huddled in the frigid car, breathing the odorless carbon monoxide until they floated away? Where were the rest of us?

The world was shutting down. Nothing made sense. In less than a week, I had seen six dead street people, and I was ill-equipped to handle the shock. I was an educated white lawyer, well fed and affluent, on the fast track to serious wealth and all the wonderful things it would buy. Sure the marriage was over, but I would bounce back. There were plenty of fine women out there. I had no serious worries.

I cursed Mister for derailing my life. I cursed Mordecai for making me feel guilty. And Ontario for breaking my heart.

A knock on the window jolted me. My nerves were shot to hell anyway. It was Mordecai, standing in the snow next to the curb. I cracked the window.

'He says he'll do it for two thousand bucks, all five.'

'Whatever,' I said, and he disappeared.

Moments later he was back, behind the wheel and speeding away. 'The funeral will be Tuesday, here at the church. Wooden caskets, but nice ones. He'll get some flowers, you know, make it look nice. He wanted three thousand, but I convinced him that there would be some press, so he might get himself on television. He liked that. Two thousand isn't bad.'

'Thanks, Mordecai.'

'Are you okay?'

'No.'

We said little as we drove back to my office.

Claire's younger brother James had been diagnosed with Hodgkin's disease – thus the family summit in Providence. It had nothing to do with me. I listened to her talk about the weekend, the shock of the news, the tears and prayers as they leaned on each other and comforted James and his wife. Hers is a family of huggers and criers, and I was thrilled she had not called me to come up. The treatment would start immediately; the prognosis was good.

She was happy to be home, and relieved to have someone to unload on. We sipped wine in the den, by the fire, a quilt over our feet. It was almost romantic, though I was too scarred to even think of being sentimental. I made a valiant effort at hearing her

93

words, grieving appropriately for poor James, interjecting fitting little phrases.

This was not what I had expected, and I wasn't sure if it was what I wanted. I thought we might shadowbox, perhaps even skirmish. Soon it had to get ugly, then hopefully turn civil as we handled our separation like real adults. But after Ontario, I was not prepared to deal with any issue involving emotion. I was drained. She kept telling me how tired I looked. I almost thanked her.

I listened hard until she finished, then the conversation slowly drifted to me and my weekend. I told her everything – my new life as a volunteer in the shelters, then Ontario and his family. I showed her the story in the paper.

She was genuinely moved, but also puzzled. I was not the same person I'd been a week earlier, and she was not sure she liked the latest version any better than the old. I was not sure either.

ELEVEN

As young workaholics, Claire and I did not need alarm clocks, especially for Monday mornings, when we faced an entire week of challenges. We were up at five, eating cereal at five-thirty, then off in separate directions, practically racing to see who could leave first.

Because of the wine, I had managed to sleep without being haunted by the nightmare of the weekend. And as I drove to the office, I was determined to place some distance between myself and the street people. I would endure the funeral. I would somehow find the time to do pro bono work for the homeless. I would pursue my friendship with Mordecai, probably even become a regular in his office. I would drop in occasionally on Miss Dolly and help her feed the hungry. I would give money and help raise more of it for the poor. Certainly I could be more valuable as a source of funds than as another poverty lawyer.

Driving in the dark to the office, I decided that I needed a string of eighteen-hour days to readjust my priorities. My career had suffered a minor derailment; an orgy of work would straighten things out. Only a fool would jump away from the gravy train I was riding.

I chose a different elevator from Mister's. He was history; I shut him out of my mind. I did not look at the conference room where he died. I threw my briefcase and coat on a chair in my office and went for coffee. Bouncing down the hallway before six in the morning, speaking to a colleague here, a clerk there, removing my jacket, rolling up my sleeves – it was great to be back.

I scanned *The Wall Street Journal* first, partly because I knew it would have nothing to do with dying street people in D.C. Then, the *Post*. On the front page of the Metro section, there was a small story about Lontae Burton's family, with a photo of her grandmother weeping outside an apartment building. I read it, then put it aside. I knew more than the reporter, and I was determined not to be distracted.

Under the *Post* was a plain manila legal-sized file, the kind our firm used by the millions. It was unmarked, and that made it suspicious. It was just lying there, exposed, on the center of my desk, placed there by some anonymous person. I opened it slowly.

There were only two sheets of paper inside. The first was a copy of yesterday's story in the *Post*, the same one I'd read ten times and shown to Claire last night. Under it was a copy of something lifted from an official Drake & Sweeney file. The heading read: EVICTEES – RIVEROAKS/TAG, INC.

The left-hand column contained the numbers one through seventeen. Number four was DeVon Hardy. Number fifteen read: Lontae Burton, and three or four children.

I slowly laid the file on the desk, stood and walked to the door, locked it, then leaned on it. The first couple of minutes passed in absolute silence. I stared at the file in the center of the desk. I had to assume it was true and accurate. Why would anyone fabricate such a thing? Then I picked it up again, carefully. Under the second sheet of paper, on the inside of the

96

file itself, my anonymous informant had scribbled with a pencil: The eviction was legally and ethically wrong.

It was printed in block letters, in an effort to avoid detection should I have it analyzed. The markings were faint, the lead hardly touching the file.

I kept the door locked for an hour, during which time I took turns standing at the window watching the sunrise and sitting at my desk staring at the file. The traffic increased in the hallway, and then I heard Polly's voice. I unlocked the door, greeted her as if everything was swell, and proceeded to go through the motions.

The morning was packed with meetings and conferences, two of them with Rudolph and clients. I performed adequately, though I couldn't remember anything we said or did. Rudolph was so proud to have his star back at full throttle.

I was almost rude to those who wanted to chat about the hostage crisis and its aftershocks. I appeared to be the same, and I was my usual hard-charging self, so the concerns about my stability vanished. Late in the morning, my father called. I could not remember the last time he'd called me at the office. He said it was raining in Memphis; he was sitting around the house, bored, and, well, he and my mother were worried about me. Claire was fine, I explained; then to find safe ground, I told him about her brother James, a person he had met once, at the wedding. I sounded properly concerned about Claire's family, and that pleased him.

Dad was just happy to reach me at the office. I was still there, making the big money, going after more. He asked me to keep in touch.

Half an hour later, my brother Warner called from his office, high above downtown Atlanta. He was six years older, a partner in another megafirm, a no-holds-barred litigator. Because of the age difference, Warner and I had never been close as kids, but we enjoyed each other's company. During his divorce three years earlier, he had confided in me weekly.

He was on the clock, same as I, so I knew the conversation would be brief. 'Talked to Dad,' he said. 'He told me everything.'

'I'm sure he did.'

'I understand how you feel. We all go through it. You work hard, make the big money, never stop to help the little people. Then something happens, and you think back to law school, back to the first year, when we were full of ideals and wanted to use our law degrees to save humanity. Remember that?'

'Yes. A long time ago.'

'Right. During my first year of law school, they took a survey. Over half my class wanted to do public interest law. When we graduated three years later, everybody went for the money. I don't know what happened.'

'Law school makes you greedy.'

'I suppose. Our firm has a program where you can take a year off, sort of a sabbatical, and do public interest law. After twelve months, you return as if you never left. You guys do anything like that?'

Vintage Warner. I had a problem, he already had the solution. Nice and neat. Twelve months, I'm a new man. A quick detour, but my future is secure.

'Not for associates,' I said. 'I've heard of a partner or two leaving to work for this administration or that one, then returning after a couple of years. But never an associate.'

'But your circumstances are different. You've been traumatized, damned near killed simply because you were a member of the firm. I'd throw my weight around some, tell 'em you need time off. Take a year, then get your ass back to the office.'

'It might work,' I said, trying to placate him. He was a type A personality, pushy as hell, always one word away from an argument, especially with the family. 'I gotta run,' I said. So did he. We promised to talk more later.

Lunch was with Rudolph and a client at a splendid restaurant. It was called a working lunch, which meant we abstained from alcohol, which also meant we would bill the client for the time. Rudolph went for four hundred an hour, me for three hundred. We worked and ate for two hours, so the lunch cost the client fourteen hundred dollars. Our firm had an account with the restaurant, so it would be billed to Drake & Sweeney, and somewhere along the way our bean counters in the basement would find a way to bill the client for the cost of the food as well.

The afternoon was nonstop calls and conferences. Through sheer willpower, I kept my game face and got through it, billing heavily as I went. Antitrust law had never seemed so hopelessly dense and boring.

It was almost five before I found a few minutes alone. I said good-bye to Polly, and locked the door again. I opened the mysterious file and began making random notes on a legal pad, scribblings and flowcharts with arrows striking RiverOaks and Drake & Sweeney from all directions. Braden Chance, the real estate partner I'd confronted about the file, took most of the shots for the firm.

My principal suspect was his paralegal, the young man who had heard our sharp words, and who, seconds later, had referred to Chance as an 'ass' when I was leaving their suite. He would know the details of the eviction, and he would have access to the file.

With a pocket phone to avoid any D&S records, I called a paralegal in antitrust. His office was around the corner from mine. He referred me to another, and with little effort I learned that the guy I wanted was

Hector Palma. He'd been with the firm about three years, all in real estate. I planned to track him down, but outside the office.

Mordecai called. He inquired about my dinner plans for the evening. 'I'll treat,' he said.

'Soup?'

He laughed. 'Of course not. I know an excellent place.'

We agreed to meet at seven. Claire was back in her surgeon's mode, oblivious to time, meals, or husband. She had checked in mid-afternoon, just a quick word on the run. Had no idea when she might be home, but very late. For dinner, every man for himself. I didn't hold it against her. She had learned the fast-track lifestyle from me.

We met at a restaurant near Dupont Circle. The bar at the front was packed with well-paid government types having a drink before fleeing the city. We had a drink in the back, in a tight booth.

'The Burton story is big and getting bigger,' he said, sipping a draft beer.

'I'm sorry, I've been in a cave for the past twelve hours. What's happened?'

'Lots of press. Four dead kids and their momma, living in a car. They find them a mile from Capitol Hill, where they're in the process of reforming welfare to send more mothers into the streets. It's beautiful.'

'So the funeral should be quite a show.'

'No doubt. I've talked to a dozen homeless activists today. They'll be there, and they're planning to bring their people with them. The place will be packed with street people. Again, lots of press. Four little coffins next to their mother's, cameras catching it all for the six o'clock news. We're having a rally before and a march afterward.'

'Maybe something good will come from their deaths.'

'Maybe.'

As a seasoned big-city lawyer, I knew there was a purpose behind every lunch and dinner invitation. Mordecai had something on his mind. I could tell by the way his eyes followed mine.

'Any idea why they were homeless?' I asked, fishing.

'No. Probably the usual. I haven't had time to ask questions.'

Driving over, I had decided that I could not tell him about the mysterious file and its contents. It was confidential, known to me only because of my position at Drake & Sweeney. To reveal what I had learned about the activities of a client would be an egregious breach of professional responsibility. The thought of divulging it scared me. Plus, I had not verified anything.

The waiter brought salads, and we began eating. 'We had a firm meeting this afternoon,' Mordecai said between bites. 'Me, Abraham, Sofia. We need some help.'

I was not surprised to hear that. 'What kind of help?'

'Another lawyer.'

'I thought you were broke.'

'We keep a little reserve. And we've adopted a new marketing strategy.'

The idea of the 14th Street Legal Clinic worried about a marketing strategy was humorous, and that was what he intended. We both smiled.

'If we could get the new lawyer to spend ten hours a week raising money, then he could afford himself.'

Another series of smiles.

He continued. 'As much as we hate to admit it, our survival will depend on our ability to raise money. The

101

Cohen Trust is declining. We've had the luxury of not begging, but now it's gotta change.'

'What's the rest of the job?'

'Street law. You've had a good dose of it. You've seen our place. It's a dump. Sofia's a shrew. Abraham's an ass. The clients smell bad, and the money is a joke.'

'How much money?'

'We can offer you thirty thousand a year, but we can only promise you half of it for the first six months.'

'Why?'

'The trust closes its books June thirtieth, at which time they'll tell us how much we get for the next fiscal year, beginning July first. We have enough in reserve to pay you for the next six months. After that, the four of us will split what's left after expenses.'

'Abraham and Sofia agreed to this?'

'Yep, after a little speech by me. We figure you have good contacts within the established bar, and since you're well educated, nice-looking, bright, and all that crap, you should be a natural at raising money.'

'What if I don't want to raise money?'

'Then the four of us could lower our salaries even more, perhaps go to twenty thousand a year. Then to fifteen. And when the trust dries up, we could hit the streets, just like our clients. Homeless lawyers.'

'So I'm the future of the 14th Street Legal Clinic?'

'That's what we decided. We'll take you in as a full partner. Let's see Drake & Sweeney top that.'

'I'm touched,' I said. I was also a bit frightened. The job offer was not unexpected, but its arrival opened a door I was hesitant to walk through.

Black bean soup arrived, and we ordered more beer.

'What's Abraham's story?' I asked.

'Jewish kid from Brooklyn. Came to Washington to work on Senator Moynihan's staff. Spent a few years on the Hill, landed on the street. Extremely bright. He spends most of his time coordinating litigation with pro bono lawyers from big firms. Right now he's suing the Census Bureau to be certain the homeless get counted. And he's suing the D.C. school system to make sure homeless kids get an education. His people skills leave a lot to be desired, but he's great in the back room plotting litigation.'

'And Sofia?'

'A career social worker who's been taking night classes in law school for eleven years. She acts and thinks like a lawyer, especially when she's abusing government workers. You'll hear her say, "This is Sofia Mendoza, Attorney-at-Law," ten times a day.'

'She's also the secretary?'

'Nope. We don't have secretaries. You do your own typing, filing, coffee making.' He leaned forward a few inches, and lowered his voice. 'The three of us have been together for a long time, Michael, and we've carved out little niches. To be honest, we need a fresh face with some new ideas.'

'The money is certainly appealing,' I said, a weak effort at humor.

He grinned anyway. 'You don't do it for the money. You do it for your soul.'

My soul kept me awake most of the night. Did I have the guts to walk away? Was I seriously considering taking a job which paid so little? I was literally saying good-bye to millions.

The things and possessions I longed for would become fading memories.

The timing wasn't bad. With the marriage over, it somehow seemed fitting that I make drastic changes on all fronts.

103

TWELVE

I called in sick Tuesday. 'Probably the flu,' I told
Polly, who, as she was trained to do, wanted specifics.
Fever, sore throat, headaches? All of the above. Any
and all, I didn't care. One had better be completely
sick to miss work at the firm. She would do a form and
send it to Rudolph. Anticipating his call, I left the
apartment and wandered around Georgetown during
the early morning. The snow was melting fast; the
high would be in the fifties. I killed an hour loitering
along Washington Harbor, sampling cappuccino from
a number of vendors, watching the rowers freeze on
the Potomac.

At ten, I left for the funeral.

The sidewalk in front of the church was barricaded.
Cops were standing around, their motorcycles parked
on the street. Farther down were the television vans.

A large crowd was listening to a speaker yell into a
microphone as I drove by. There were a few hastily
painted placards held above heads, for the benefit of
the cameras. I parked on a side street three blocks
away, and hurried toward the church. I avoided the
front by heading for a side door, which was being
guarded by an elderly usher. I asked if there was a
balcony. He asked if I was a reporter.

He took me inside, and pointed to a door. I thanked

him and went through it, then up a flight of shaky stairs until I emerged on the balcony overlooking a beautiful sanctuary below. The carpet was burgundy, the pews dark wood, the windows stained and clean. It was a very handsome church, and for a second I could understand why the Reverend was reluctant to open it to the homeless.

I was alone, with my choice of seating. I walked quietly to a spot above the rear door, with a direct view down the center aisle to the pulpit. A choir began singing outside on the front steps, and I sat in the tranquillity of the empty church, the music drifting in. The music stopped, the doors opened, the stampede began. The balcony floor shook as the mourners poured into the sanctuary. The choir took its place behind the pulpit. The Reverend directed traffic – the TV crews in one corner, the small family in the front pew, the activists and their homeless down the center section. Mordecai ambled in with two people I didn't know. A door to one side opened, and the prisoners marched out – Lontae's mother and two brothers, clad in blue prison garb, cuffed at the wrists and ankles, chained together and escorted by four armed guards. They were placed in the second pew, center aisle, behind the grandmother and some other relatives.

When things were still, the organ began, low and sad. There was a racket under me, and all heads turned around. The Reverend assumed the pulpit and instructed us to stand.

Ushers with white gloves rolled the wooden coffins down the aisle, and lined them end to end across the front of the church with Lontae's in the center. The baby's was tiny, less than three feet long. Ontario's, Alonzo's, and Dante's were midsized. It was an appalling sight, and the wailing began. The choir started to hum and sway.

The ushers arranged flowers around the caskets,

and I thought for one horrifying second they were going to open them. I had never been to a black funeral before. I had no idea what to expect, but I had seen news clips from other funerals in which the casket was sometimes opened, the family kissing the corpse. The vultures with the cameras were ever ready.

But the caskets remained closed, and so the world didn't learn what I knew – that Ontario and family looked very much at peace.

We sat down, and the Reverend served up a lengthy prayer. Then a solo from sister somebody, then moments of silence. The Reverend read Scripture, and preached for a bit. He was followed by a homeless activist who delivered a scathing attack on a society and its leaders who allowed such a thing to happen. She blamed Congress, especially the Republicans, and she blamed the city for its lack of leadership, and the courts, and the bureaucracy. But she saved her harshest diatribe for the upper classes, those with money and power who didn't care for the poor and the sick. She was articulate and angry, very effective, I thought, but not exactly at home at a funeral.

They clapped for her when she finished. The Reverend then spent a very long time blasting everyone who wasn't of color and had money.

A solo, some more Scripture, then the choir launched into a soulful hymn that made me want to cry. A procession formed to lay hands upon the dead, but it quickly broke down as the mourners began wailing and rubbing the caskets. 'Open them up,' someone screamed, but the Reverend shook his head no. They bunched toward the pulpit, crowding around the caskets, yelling and sobbing as the choir cranked it up several notches. The grandmother was the loudest, and she was stroked and soothed by the others.

I couldn't believe it. Where were these people during the last months of Lontae's life? Those little bodies lying up there in boxes had never known so much love.

The cameras inched closer as more and more mourners broke down. It was more of a show than anything else.

The Reverend finally stepped in and restored order. He prayed again with organ music in the background. When he finished, a long dismissal began as the people paraded by the caskets one last time.

The service lasted an hour and a half. For two thousand bucks, it wasn't a bad production. I was proud of it.

They rallied again outside, and began a march in the general direction of Capitol Hill. Mordecai was in the middle of it, and as they disappeared around a corner, I wondered how many marches and demonstrations he had been in. Not enough, he would probably answer.

Rudolph Mayes had become a partner at Drake & Sweeney at the age of thirty, still a record. And if life continued as he planned, he would one day be the oldest working partner. The law was his life, as his three former wives could attest. Everything else he touched was disastrous, but Rudolph was the consummate big-firm team player.

He was waiting for me at 6 P.M. in his office behind a pile of work. Polly and the secretaries were gone, as were most of the paralegals and clerks. The hall traffic slowed considerably after five-thirty.

I closed the door, sat down. 'Thought you were sick,' he said.

'I'm leaving, Rudolph,' I said as boldly as I could, but my stomach was in knots.

He shoved books out of the way, and put the cap on his expensive pen. 'I'm listening.'

107

'I'm leaving the firm. I have an offer to work for a public interest firm.'

'Don't be stupid, Michael.'

'I'm not being stupid. I've made up my mind. And I want out of here with as little trouble as possible.'

'You'll be a partner in three years.'

'I've found a better deal than that.'

He couldn't think of a response, so he rolled his eyes in frustration. 'Come on, Mike. You can't crack up over one incident.'

'I'm not cracking up, Rudolph. I'm simply moving into another field.'

'None of the other eight hostages are doing this.'

'Good for them. If they're happy, then I'm happy for them. Besides, they're in litigation, a strange breed.'

'Where are you going?'

'A legal clinic near Logan Circle. It specializes in homeless law.'

'Homeless law?'

'Yep.'

'How much are they paying you?'

'A bloody fortune. Wanna make a donation to the clinic?'

'You're losing your mind.'

'Just a little crisis, Rudolph. I'm only thirty-two, too young for the midlife crazies. I figure I'll get mine over with early.'

'Take a month off. Go work with the homeless, get it out of your system, then come back. This is a terrible time to leave, Mike. You know how far behind we are.'

'Won't work, Rudolph. It's no fun if there's a safety net.'

'Fun? You're doing this for fun?'

'Absolutely. Think how much fun it would be to work without looking at a time clock.'

'What about Claire?' he asked, revealing the depths of his desperation. He hardly knew her, and he was the least qualified person in the firm to dispense marital advice.

'She's okay,' I said. 'I'd like to leave Friday.'

He grunted in defeat. He closed his eyes, slowly shook his head. 'I don't believe this.'

'I'm sorry, Rudolph.'

We shook hands and promised to meet for an early breakfast to discuss my unfinished work.

I didn't want Polly to hear it secondhand, so I went to my office and called her. She was at home in Arlington, cooking dinner. It ruined her week.

I picked up Thai food and took it home. I chilled some wine, fixed the table, and began rehearsing my lines.

If Claire suspected an ambush, it wasn't evident. Over the years we had developed the habit of simply ignoring each other, as opposed to fighting. Therefore, our tactics were unrefined.

But I liked the idea of a blindside, of being thoroughly prepared with the shock, then ready with the quips. I thought it would be nice and unfair, completely acceptable within the confines of a crumbling marriage.

It was almost ten; she had eaten on the run hours earlier, so we went straight to the den with glasses of wine. I stoked the fire and we settled into our favorite chairs. After a few minutes I said, 'We need to talk.'

'What is it?' she asked, completely unworried.

'I'm thinking of leaving Drake & Sweeney.'

'Oh really.' She took a drink. I admired her coolness. She either expected this or wanted to seem unconcerned.

'Yes. I can't go back there.'

'Why not?'

'I'm ready for a change. The corporate work is suddenly boring and unimportant, and I want to do something to help people.'

'That's nice.' She was already thinking about the money, and I was anxious to see how long it would take to get around to it. 'In fact, that's very admirable, Michael.'

'I told you about Mordecai Green. His clinic has offered me a job. I'm starting Monday.'

'Monday?'

'Yes.'

'So you've made your decision already.'

'Yes.'

'Without any discussion with me. I have no say in the matter, is that right?'

'I can't go back to the firm, Claire. I told Rudolph today.'

Another sip, a slight grinding of the teeth, a flash of anger but she let it pass. Her self-control was amazing.

We watched the fire, hypnotized by the orange flames. She spoke next. 'Can I ask what this does for us financially?'

'It changes things.'

'How much is the new salary?'

'Thirty thousand a year.'

'Thirty thousand a year,' she repeated. Then she said it again, somehow making it sound even lower. 'That's less than what I make.'

Her salary was thirty-one thousand, a figure that would increase dramatically in the years to come – serious money was not far away. For purposes of the discussion, I planned to have no sympathy for any whining about money.

'You don't do public interest law for the money,' I said, trying not to sound pious. 'As I recall, you didn't go to med school for the money.'

Like every med student in the country, she had

begun her studies vowing that money was not the attraction. She wanted to help humanity. Same for law students. We all lied.

She watched the fire and did the math. I guessed she was probably thinking about the rent. It was a very nice apartment; at twenty-four hundred a month it should've been even nicer. The furnishings were adequate. We were proud of where we lived – right address, beautiful rowhouse, swanky neighborhood – but we spent so little time there. And we seldom entertained. Moving would be an adjustment, but we could endure it.

We had always been open about our finances; nothing was hidden. She knew we had around fifty-one thousand dollars in mutual funds, and twelve thousand in the checking account. I was amazed at how little we'd saved in six years of marriage. When you're on the fast track at a big firm, the money seems endless.

'I guess we'll have to make adjustments, won't we?' she said, staring coldly at me. The word 'adjustments' was dripping with connotations.

'I suppose so.'

'I'm tired,' she said. She drained her glass, and went to the bedroom.

How pathetic, I thought. We couldn't even muster enough rancor to have a decent fight.

Of course, I fully realized my new status in life. I was a wonderful story – ambitious young lawyer transformed into an advocate for the poor; turns back on blue-chip firm to work for nothing. Even though she thought I was losing my mind, Claire had found it hard to criticize a saint.

I put a log on the fire, fixed another drink, and slept on the sofa.

THIRTEEN

The partners had a private dining room on the eighth floor, and it was supposed to be an honor for an associate to eat there. Rudolph was the sort of klutz who would think that a bowl of Irish oatmeal at 7 A.M. in their special room would help return me to my senses. How could I turn my back on a future filled with power breakfasts?

He had exciting news. He'd spoken with Arthur late the night before and there was in the works a proposal to grant me a twelve-month sabbatical. The firm would supplement whatever salary the clinic paid. It was a worthy cause, they should do more to protect the rights of the poor. I would be treated as the firm's designated pro bono boy for an entire year, and they could all feel good about themselves. I would return with my batteries recharged, my other interests quelled, my talents once again directed to the glory of Drake & Sweeney.

I was impressed and touched by the idea, and I could not simply dismiss it. I promised him I would think about it, and quickly. He cautioned that it would have to be approved by the executive committee since I was not a partner. The firm had never considered such a leave for an associate.

Rudolph was desperate for me to stay, and it had little to do with friendship. Our antitrust division was logjammed with work, and we needed at least two more senior associates with my experience. It was a terrible time for me to leave, but I didn't care. The firm had eight hundred lawyers. They would find the bodies they needed.

The year before I had billed just under seven hundred fifty thousand dollars. That was why I was eating breakfast in their fancy little room, and listening to their urgent plans to keep me. It also made sense to take my annual salary, throw it at the homeless or any charity I wished, for that matter, then entice me back after one year.

Once he finished with the idea of the sabbatical, we proceeded to review the most pressing matters in my office. We were listing things to do when Braden Chance sat at a table not far from ours. He didn't see me at first. There were a dozen or so partners eating, most alone, most deep in the morning papers. I tried to ignore him, but I finally looked over and caught him glaring at me.

'Good morning, Braden,' I said loudly, startling him and causing Rudolph to jerk around to see who it was.

Chance nodded, said nothing, and suddenly became involved with some toast.

'You know him?' Rudolph asked, under his breath.

'We've met,' I said. During our brief encounter in his office, Chance had demanded the name of my supervising partner. I'd given him Rudolph's name. It was obvious he had not lodged any complaints.

'An ass,' Rudolph said, barely audible. It was unanimous. He flipped a page, immediately forgot about Chance, and plowed ahead. There was a lot of unfinished work in my office.

I found myself thinking of Chance and the eviction file. He had a soft look, with pale skin, delicate features, a fragile manner. I could not imagine him in the streets, examining abandoned warehouses filled

113

with squatters, actually getting his hands dirty to make sure his work was thorough. Of course he never did that; he had paralegals. Chance sat at his desk and supervised the paperwork, billing several hundred an hour while the Hector Palmas of the firm took care of the nasty details. Chance had lunch and played golf with the executives of RiverOaks; that was his role as a partner.

He probably didn't know the names of the people evicted from the RiverOaks/TAG warehouse, and why should he? They were just squatters, nameless, faceless, homeless. He wasn't there with the cops when they were dragged from their little dwellings and thrown into the streets. But Hector Palma probably saw it happen.

And if Chance didn't know the names of Lontae Burton and family, then he couldn't make the connection between the eviction and their deaths. Or maybe he did know now. Maybe someone had told him.

These questions would have to be answered by Hector Palma, and soon. It was Wednesday. I was leaving on Friday.

Rudolph wrapped up our breakfast at eight, just in time for another meeting in his office with some very important people. I went to my desk and read the *Post*. There was a gut-wrenching photo of the five unopened caskets in the sanctuary, and a thorough review of the service and the march afterward.

There was also an editorial, a well-written challenge to all of us with food and roofs to stop and think about the Lontae Burtons of our city. They were not going away. They could not be swept from the streets and deposited in some hidden place so we didn't have to see them. They were living in cars, squatting in shacks, freezing in makeshift tents, sleeping on park benches, waiting for beds in crowded and sometimes dangerous shelters. We shared the same city; they were a part of

114

our society. If we didn't help them, they would multiply in numbers. And they would continue to die in our streets.

I cut the editorial from the paper, folded it, and placed it in my wallet.

Through the paralegal network, I made contact with Hector Palma. It would not be wise to approach him directly; Chance was probably lurking nearby.

We met in the main library on the third floor, between stacks of books, away from security cameras and anybody else. He was extremely nervous.

'Did you put that file on my desk?' I asked him point-blank. There was little time for games.

'What file?' he asked, cutting his eyes around as if gunmen were tracking us.

'The RiverOaks/TAG eviction. You handled it, right?'

He didn't know how much I knew, or how little. 'Yeah,' he said.

'Where's the file?'

He pulled a book off the shelf and acted as though he were deep in research. 'Chance keeps all the files.'

'In his office?'

'Yes. Locked in a file cabinet.' We were practically whispering. I had not been nervous about the meeting, but I caught myself glancing around. Anybody watching would have immediately known that we were up to something.

'What's in the file?' I asked.

'Bad stuff.'

'Tell me.'

'I have a wife and four kids. I'm not about to get fired.'

'You have my word.'

'You're leaving. What do you care?'

Word traveled fast, but I was not surprised. I often

wondered who gossiped more, the lawyers or their secretaries. Probably the paralegals.

'Why did you put that file on my desk?' I asked.

He reached for another book, his right hand literally shaking. 'I don't know what you're talking about.'

He flipped a few pages, then walked to the end of the row. I followed along, certain no one was anywhere near us. He stopped and found another book; he still wanted to talk.

'I need that file,' I said.

'I don't have it.'

'Then how can I get it?'

'You'll have to steal it.'

'Fine. Where do I get a key?'

He studied my face for a moment, trying to decide how serious I was. 'I don't have a key,' he said.

'How'd you get the list of evictees?'

'I don't know what you're talking about.'

'Yes you do. You put it on my desk.'

'You're as crazy as hell,' he said, and walked away. I waited for him to stop, but he kept going, past the rows of shelves, past the stacked tiers, past the front desk, and out of the library.

I had no intention of busting my ass my last three days at the firm, regardless of what I'd led Rudolph to believe. Instead, I covered my desk with antitrust litter, shut the door, stared at the walls, and smiled at all the things I was leaving behind. The pressure was lifting with every breath. No more labor with a time clock wrapped around my throat. No more eighty-hour weeks because my ambitious colleagues might be doing eighty-five. No more brown-nosing those above me. No more nightmares about getting the partnership door slammed in my face.

I called Mordecai and formally accepted the job. He laughed, and joked about finding a way to pay me. I

116

would start Monday, but he wanted me to stop by earlier for a brief orientation. I pictured the interior of the 14th Street Legal Clinic, and wondered which of the empty, cluttered offices I would be assigned. As if it mattered.

By late afternoon, I was spending most of my time accepting grave farewells from friends and colleagues convinced I had truly lost my mind.

I took it well. After all, I was approaching sainthood.

Meanwhile, my wife was visiting a divorce lawyer, a female one with the reputation of being a merciless ball-squeezer.

Claire was waiting for me when I arrived home at six, rather early. The kitchen table was covered with notes and computer spreadsheets. A calculator sat ready. She was icy, and well prepared. This time, I walked into the ambush.

'I suggest we get a divorce, on the grounds of irreconcilable differences,' she began pleasantly. 'We don't fight. We don't point fingers. We admit what we have been unable to say – the marriage is over.'

She stopped and waited for me to say something. I couldn't act surprised. Her mind was made up; what good would it do to object? I had to seem as cold-blooded as she. 'Sure,' I said, trying to be as nonchalant as possible. There was an element of relief in finally being honest. But it did bother me that she wanted the divorce more than I did.

To keep the upper hand, she then mentioned her meeting with Jacqueline Hume, her new divorce lawyer, dropping the name as if it were a mortar round, then relaying for my benefit the self-serving opinions her mouthpiece had delivered.

'Why did you hire a lawyer?' I asked, interrupting.

'I want to make sure I'm protected.'

'And you think I would take advantage of you?'

117

'You're a lawyer. I want a lawyer. It's that simple.'

'You could've saved a lot of money by not hiring her,' I said, trying to be a little contentious. After all, this was a divorce.

'But I feel much better now that I have.'

She handed me Exhibit A, a worksheet of our assets and liabilities. Exhibit B was a proposed split of these. Not surprisingly, she intended to get the majority. We had cash of twelve thousand dollars, and she wanted to use half of it to pay off the bank lien on her car. I would get twenty-five hundred of the remainder. No mention of paying off the sixteen thousand owed on my Lexus. She wanted forty thousand of the fifty-one thousand dollars we had in mutual funds. I got to keep my 401K.

'Not exactly an even split,' I said.

'It's not going to be equal,' she said with all the confidence of one who had just hired a pit bull.

'Why not?'

'Because I'm not the one going through a midlife crisis.'

'So it's my fault?'

'We're not assigning fault. We're dividing the assets. For reasons known only to you, you've decided to take a cut in pay of ninety thousand dollars a year. Why should I suffer the consequences? My lawyer is confident she can convince a judge that your actions have wrecked us financially. You want to go crazy, fine. But don't expect me to starve.'

'Small chance of that.'

'I'm not going to bicker.'

'I wouldn't either if I were getting everything.' I felt compelled to cause some measure of trouble. We couldn't scream and throw things. We damned sure weren't going to cry. We couldn't make nasty accusations about affairs or chemical addictions. What kind of divorce was this?

118

A very sterile one. She ignored me and continued down her list of notes, one no doubt prepared by the mouthpiece. 'The apartment lease is up June thirtieth, and I'll stay here until then. That's ten thousand in rent.'

'When would you like me to leave?'

'As soon as you'd like.'

'Fine.' If she wanted me out, I wasn't about to beg to stay. It was an exercise in one-upsmanship. Which side of the table could show more disdain than the other?

I almost said something stupid, like, 'You got someone else moving in?' I wanted to rattle her, to watch her do an instant thaw.

Instead, I kept my cool. 'I'll be gone by the weekend,' I said. She had no response, but she didn't frown.

'Why do you think you're entitled to eighty percent of the mutual funds?' I asked.

'I'm not getting eighty percent. I'll spend ten thousand in rent, another three thousand in utilities, two thousand to pay off our joint credit cards, and we'll owe about six thousand in taxes incurred together. That's a total of twenty-one thousand.'

Exhibit C was a thorough list of the personal property, beginning with the den and ending in the empty bedroom. Neither of us would dare fall into a squabble over pots and pans, so the division was quite amicable. 'Take what you want,' I said several times, especially when addressing items such as towels and bed linens. We traded a few things, doing it with finesse. My position on several assets was driven more by a reluctance to physically move them than by any pride of ownership.

I wanted a television and some dishes. Bachelorhood had been sprung suddenly upon me, and I had trouble contemplating the furnishing of a new place.

119

She, on the other hand, had spent hours living in the future.

But she was fair. We finished the drudgery of Exhibit C, and declared ourselves to be equitably divided. We would sign a separation agreement, wait six months, then go to court together and legally dissolve our union.

Neither of us wanted any postgame chat. I found my overcoat, and went for a long walk through the streets of Georgetown, wondering how life had changed so dramatically.

The erosion of the marriage had been slow, but certain. The change in careers had hit like a bullet. Things were moving much too fast, but I was unable to stop them.

FOURTEEN

The sabbatical concept was killed in the executive committee. While no one was supposed to know what that group did in its private meetings, it was reported to me by a very somber Rudolph that a bad precedent could be set. With a firm so large, granting a year's leave to one associate might trigger all sorts of requests from other malcontents.

There would be no safety net. The door would slam when I walked through it.

'Are you sure you know what you're doing?' he asked, standing before my desk. There were two large storage boxes on the floor next to him. Polly was already packing my junk.

'I'm sure,' I said with a smile. 'Don't worry about me.'

'I tried.'

'Thanks, Rudolph.' He left, shaking his head.

After Claire's blindside the night before, I had not been able to think about the sabbatical. More urgent thoughts cluttered my brain. I was about to be divorced, and single, and homeless myself.

Suddenly I was concerned with a new apartment, not to mention a new job and office and career. I closed the door, and scanned the real estate section of the classifieds.

I would sell the car and get rid of the four-hundred-eighty-dollar-a-month payment. I'd buy a clunker, insure it heavily, and wait for it to disappear into the darkness of my new neighborhoods. If I wanted a decent apartment in the District, it became apparent that most of my new salary would go for rent.

I left early for lunch, and spent two hours racing around Central Washington looking at lofts. The cheapest was a dump for eleven hundred a month, much too much for a street lawyer.

Another file awaited me upon my return from lunch; another plain manila legal-sized one, with no writing on the outside of it. Same spot on my desk. Inside, two keys were taped to the left side, a typed note was stapled to the right. It read:

> Top key is to Chance's door. Bottom key is to file drawer under window. Copy and return. Careful, Chance is very suspicious. Lose the keys.

Polly appeared instantly, as she so often did; no knock, not a sound, just a sudden ghostlike presence in the room. She was pouting and ignoring me. We'd been together for four years, and she claimed to be devastated by my departure. We weren't really that close. She'd be reassigned in days. She was a very nice person, but the least of my worries.

I quickly closed the file, not knowing if she had seen it. I waited for a moment as she busied herself with my storage boxes. She didn't mention it – strong evidence that she was unaware of it. But since she saw everything in the hallway around my office, I couldn't imagine how Hector or anyone else could enter and leave without being seen.

Barry Nuzzo, fellow hostage and friend, dropped by to have a serious talk. He shut the door and stepped around the boxes. I didn't want to discuss my leaving, so I told him about Claire. His wife and Claire were both from Providence, a fact that seemed oddly significant in Washington. We had socialized with them a few times over the years, but the group friendship had gone the way of the marriage.

He was surprised, then saddened, then seemed to shake it off quite well. 'You're having a bad month,' he said. 'I'm sorry.'

'It's been a long slide,' I said.

We talked about the old days, the guys who had come and gone. We had not bothered to replay the Mister affair over a beer, and that struck me as strange. Two friends face death together, walk away from it, then get too busy to help each other with the aftermath.

We eventually got around to it; it was difficult to avoid with the storage boxes in the middle of the floor. I realized that the incident was the reason for our conversation.

'I'm sorry I let you down,' he said.

'Come on, Barry.'

'No, really. I should've been here.'

'Why?'

'Because it's obvious you've lost your mind,' he said with a laugh.

I tried to enjoy his humor. 'Yeah, I'm a little crazy now, I guess, but I'll get over it.'

'No, seriously, I heard you were having trouble. I tried to find you last week but you were gone. I was worried about you, but I've been in trial, you know, the usual.'

'I know.'

'I really feel bad for not being here, Mike. I'm sorry.'

'Come on. Stop it.'

'We all got the hell scared out of us, but you could've been hit.'

123

'He could've killed all of us, Barry. Real dynamite, a missed shot, boom. Let's not replay it.'

'The last thing I saw as we were scrambling out the door was you, covered with blood, screaming. I thought you were hit. We got outside, in a pile, with people grabbing us, yelling, and I was waiting for the blast. I thought, Mike's still in there, and he's hurt. We stopped by the elevators. Somebody cut the ropes from our wrists, and I glanced back just in time to see you as the cops grabbed you. I remember the blood. All that damned blood.'

I didn't say anything. He needed this. Somehow it would ease his mind. He could report to Rudolph and the others that he had at least tried to talk me out of it.

'All the way down, I kept asking, "Did Mike get hit? Did Mike get hit?" No one could answer. It seemed like an hour passed before they said you were okay. I was going to call you when I got home, but the kids wouldn't leave me alone. I should have.'

'Forget it.'

'I'm sorry, Mike.'

'Please don't say that again. It's over, done with. We could've talked about it for days, and nothing would've changed.'

'When did you realize you were leaving?'

I had to think about this for a moment. The truthful answer was at the point Sunday when Bill yanked the sheets back and I saw my little pal Ontario finally at peace. It was then and there, at that moment, in the city morgue, that I became someone else.

'Over the weekend,' I said, with no further explanation. He didn't need one.

He shook his head, as if the storage boxes were primarily his fault. I decided to help him through it. 'You couldn't have stopped me, Barry. No one could.'

Then he began nodding, in agreement because he understood somehow. A gun in your face, the clock stops, priorities emerge at once – God, family, friends. Money falls to the bottom. The Firm and the Career vanish as each awful second ticks by and you realize this could be the last day of your life.

'How about you?' I asked. 'How are you doing?'

The Firm and the Career stay on the bottom for a few short hours.

'We started a trial on Thursday. In fact, we were preparing for it when Mister interrupted us. We couldn't ask the Judge for a continuance because the client had been waiting four years for a trial date. And we weren't injured, you know. Not physically, anyway. So we kicked into high gear, started the trial, and never slowed down. The trial saved us.'

Of course it did. Work is therapy, even salvation at Drake & Sweeney. I wanted to scream at him, because two weeks ago I would have said the same thing.

'Good,' I said. How nice. 'So you're okay?'

'Sure.' He was a litigator, a macho player with Teflon skin. He also had three kids, so the luxury of a thirtysomething detour was out of the question.

The clock suddenly called him. We shook hands, embraced, and made all the usual promises to keep in touch.

I kept the door closed so I could stare at the file and decide what to do. Before long I'd made a few assumptions. One, the keys worked. Two, it was not a setup; I had no known enemies and I was leaving anyway. Three, the file was really in the office, in the drawer under the window. Four, it was possible to get it without being caught. Five, it could be copied in a short period of time. Six, it could then be returned as if nothing had happened. Seven, and the biggest of all, it actually contained damning evidence.

I wrote these down on a legal pad. Taking the file would be grounds for instant dismissal, but I didn't care about that. Same for getting caught in Chance's office with an unauthorized key.

Copying it would be the challenge. Since no file at the firm was less than an inch thick, there would probably be a hundred pages to Xerox, assuming I copied everything. I would have to stand in front of a machine for several minutes, exposed. That would be too dangerous. Secretaries and clerks did the copying, not lawyers. The machines were high-tech, complicated, and no doubt just waiting to jam the instant I pushed a button. They were also coded – buttons had to be pushed so that every copy could be billed to a client. And they were in open areas. I couldn't think of a single copier in a corner. Perhaps I could find one in another section of the firm, but my presence there would be suspicious.

I would have to leave the building with it, and that would border on being a criminal act. I wouldn't steal the file, though, just borrow it.

At four, I walked through the real estate section with my sleeves rolled up, holding a stack of files as if I had serious business there. Hector was not at his desk. Braden Chance was in his office, with his door cracked, his bitchy voice on the phone. A secretary smiled at me as I strolled by. I saw no security cameras peeking down from above. Some floors had them; others didn't. Who'd want to breach security in real estate?

I left at five. I bought sandwiches at a deli and drove to my new office.

My partners were still there, waiting for me. Sofia actually smiled as we shook hands, but only for an instant.

'Welcome aboard,' Abraham said gravely, as if I were climbing onto a sinking ship. Mordecai waved his arms at a small room next to his.

'How about this?' he said. 'Suite E.'

'Beautiful,' I said, stepping into my new office. It was about half the size of the one I'd just left. My desk at the firm wouldn't fit in it. There were four file cabinets on one wall, each a different color. The light was a bare bulb hanging from the ceiling. I didn't see a phone.

'I like it,' I said, and I wasn't lying.

'We'll get you a phone tomorrow,' he said, pulling the shades down over a window AC unit. 'This was last used by a young lawyer named Banebridge.'

'What happened to him?'

'Couldn't handle the money.'

It was getting dark, and Sofia seemed anxious to leave. Abraham retreated to his office. Mordecai and I ate dinner at his desk – the sandwiches I'd brought with the bad coffee he'd brewed.

The copier was a bulky one of eighties' vintage, free of code panels and the other bells and whistles favored by my former firm. It sat in a corner of the main room, near one of the four desks covered with old files.

'What time are you leaving tonight?' I asked Mordecai between bites.

'I don't know. In an hour I guess. Why?'

'Just curious. I'm going back to Drake & Sweeney for a couple of hours, last-minute stuff they want me to finish. Then I'd like to bring a load of my office junk here, tonight. Would that be possible?'

He was chewing his food. He reached into a drawer, pulled out a ring with three keys on it, and tossed it to me. 'Come and go as you please,' he said.

'Will it be safe?'

'No. So be careful. Park right out there, as close to the door as you can. Walk fast. Then lock yourself in.'

He must have seen the fear in my eyes, because he said, 'Get used to it. Be smart.'

I walked fast and smart to my car at six-thirty. The

sidewalk was empty; no hoodlums, no gunfire, not a scratch on my Lexus. I felt proud as I unlocked it and drove away. Maybe I could survive on the streets.

The drive back to Drake & Sweeney took eleven minutes. If it took thirty minutes to copy Chance's file, then it would be out of his office for about an hour. Assuming all went well. And he would never know. I waited until eight, then walked casually down to real estate, my sleeves rolled up again as if I were hard at work.

The hallways were deserted. I knocked on Chance's door, no answer. It was locked. I then checked every office, knocking softly at first, then harder, then turning the knob. About half were locked. Around each corner, I checked for security cameras. I looked in conference rooms and typing pools. Not a soul.

The key to his door was just like mine, same color and size. It worked perfectly, and I was suddenly inside a dark office and faced with the decision of whether or not to turn on the lights. A person driving by couldn't tell which office was suddenly lit, and I doubted if anyone in the hallway could see a ray of light at the bottom of the door. Plus, it was very dark, and I didn't have a flashlight. I locked the door, turned on the lights, went straight to the file drawer under the window, and unlocked it with the second key. On my knees, I quietly pulled the drawer out.

There were dozens of files, all relating to RiverOaks, all arranged neatly according to some method. Chance and his secretary were well organized, a trait our firm cherished. A thick one was labeled RiverOaks/TAG, Inc. I gently removed it, and began to flip through it. I wanted to make sure it was the right file.

A male voice yelled 'Hey!' in the hallway, and I jumped out of my skin.

Another male voice answered from a few doors

128

down, and the two struck up a conversation somewhere very near Chance's door. Basketball talk. Bullets and Knicks.

With rubbery knees, I walked to the door. I turned off the lights, listening to their talk. Then I sat on Braden's fine leather sofa for ten minutes. If I was seen leaving the office empty-handed, nothing would be done. Tomorrow was my last day anyway. Of course I wouldn't have the file either.

What if someone spotted me leaving with the file? If they confronted me, I would be dead.

I pondered the situation furiously, getting caught in every scenario. Be patient, I kept telling myself. They'll go away. Basketball was followed by girls, neither sounded married, probably a couple of clerks from Georgetown's law school, working nights. Their voices soon faded.

I locked the drawer in the dark and took the file. Five minutes, six, seven, eight. I quietly opened the door, slowly placed my head in the crack, and looked up and down the hall. No one. I scooted out, past Hector's desk, and headed for the reception area, walking briskly while trying to appear casual.

'Hey!' someone yelled from behind. I turned a corner, and glanced back just quickly enough to see a guy coming after me. The nearest door was to a small library. I ducked inside; luckily it was dark. I moved between tiers of books until I found another door on the other side. I opened it, and at the end of a short hallway I saw an exit sign above a door. I ran through it. Figuring I could run faster down the stairs than up them, I bounded down, even though my office was two floors above. If by chance he recognized me, he might go there looking for me.

I emerged on the ground floor, out of breath, without a coat, not wanting to be seen by anyone, especially the security person guarding the elevators to

129

keep out any more street people. I went to a side exit, the same one Polly and I had used to avoid the reporters the night Mister got shot. It was freezing and a light rain was falling as I ran to my car.

The thoughts of a bungling first-time thief. It was a stupid thing to do. Very stupid. Did I get caught? No one saw me leave Chance's office. No one knew I had a file that wasn't mine.

I shouldn't have run. When he yelled, I should've stopped, chatted him up, acted as if everything were fine, and if he wanted to see the file, I'd rebuke him and send him away. He was probably just one of the lowly clerks I had heard earlier.

But why had he yelled like that? If he didn't know me, why was he trying to stop me from the other end of the hallway? I drove onto Massachusetts, in a hurry to get the copying done and somehow get the file back where it belonged. I had pulled all-nighters before, and if I had to wait until 3 A.M. to sneak back to Chance's office, then I would do so.

I relaxed a little. The heater was blowing at full speed.

There was no way to know that a drug bust had gone bad, a cop had been shot, a Jaguar owned by a dealer was speeding down Eighteenth Street. I had the green light on New Hampshire, but the boys who shot the cop weren't concerned with the rules of the road. The Jaguar was a blur to my left, then the air bag exploded in my face.

When I came to, the driver's door was pinching my left shoulder. Black faces were staring in at me through the shattered window. I heard sirens, then drifted away again.

One of the paramedics unlatched my seat belt, and they pulled me over the console and through the passenger door. 'I don't see any blood,' someone said.

'Can you walk?' a paramedic asked. My shoulder and ribs were hurting. I tried to stand, but my legs wouldn't work.

'I'm okay,' I said, sitting on the edge of a stretcher. There was a racket behind me, but I couldn't turn around. They strapped me down, and as I entered the ambulance I saw the Jaguar, upside down and surrounded by cops and medics.

I kept saying, 'I'm okay, I'm okay,' as they checked my blood pressure. We were moving; the siren faded.

They took me to the emergency room at George Washington University Medical Center. X-rays revealed no breaks of any type. I was bruised and in terrible pain. They filled me with pain-killers and rolled me up to a private room.

I awoke sometime in the night. Claire was sleeping in a chair next to my bed.

FIFTEEN

She left before dawn. A sweet note on the table told me that she had to make her rounds, and that she would return mid-morning. She had talked to my doctors, and it was likely that I would not die.

We seemed perfectly normal and happy, a cute couple devoted to each other. I drifted off wondering why, exactly, we were going through the process of a divorce.

A nurse woke me at seven and handed me the note. I read it again as she rattled on about the weather – sleet and snow – and took my blood pressure. I asked her for a newspaper. She brought it thirty minutes later with my cereal. The story was front page, Metro. The narc was shot several times in a gun battle; his condition was critical. He'd killed one dealer. The second dealer was the Jaguar driver, who died at the scene of the crash under circumstances still to be investigated. I was not mentioned, which was fine.

Had I not been involved, the story would have been an everyday shootout between cops and crack dealers, ignored and unread by me. Welcome to the streets. I tried to convince myself it could've happened to any D.C. professional, but it was a hard sell. To be in that part of town after dark was to ask for trouble.

My upper left arm was swollen and already turning blue – the left shoulder and collarbone stiff and tender to the touch. My ribs were sore to the point of keeping me perfectly still. They hurt only when I breathed. I made it to the bathroom where I relieved myself and looked at my face. An air bag is a small bomb. The impact stuns the face and chest. But the damage was minimal: slightly swollen nose and eyes, an upper lip that had a new shape. Nothing that wouldn't disappear over the weekend.

The nurse was back with more pills. I made her identify each one, then I said no to the entire collection. They were for pain and stiffness, and I wanted a clear head. The doc popped in at seven-thirty for a quick going-over. With nothing broken or ripped, my hours as a patient were numbered. He suggested another round of X-rays, to be safe. I tried to say no, but he had already discussed the matter with my wife.

So I limped around my room for an eternity, testing my wounded body parts, watching the morning news-babble, hoping no one I knew would suddenly enter and see me in my yellow paisley gown.

Finding a wrecked car in the District is a baffling chore, especially when initiated so soon after the accident. I started with the phone book, my only source, and half the numbers in Traffic went unanswered. The other half were answered with great indifference. It was early, the weather was bad. It was Friday, why get involved?

Most wrecked cars were taken to a city lot on Rasco Road, up in Northeast. I learned this from a secretary at the Central Precinct. She worked in Animal Control; I was dialing police extensions at random. Other cars were sometimes taken to other lots, and there was a good chance mine could still be attached to the wrecker. The wreckers were privately owned, she explained, and this had always caused trouble. She once worked in Traffic, but hated it over there.

I thought of Mordecai, my new source for all information related to the street. I waited until nine to call him. I told him the story, assured him I was in great shape in spite of being in a hospital, and asked him if he knew how to find a wrecked car. He had some ideas.

I called Polly with the same story.

'You're not coming in?' she asked, her voice faltering.

'I'm in the hospital, Polly. Are you listening to me?'

There was hesitation on her end, confirming what I feared. I could envision a cake with a punch bowl next to it, probably in a conference room, on the table, with fifty people standing around it proposing toasts and making short speeches about how wonderful I was. I had been to a couple of those parties myself. They were awful. I was determined to avoid my own send-off.

'When are you getting out?' she asked.

'Don't know. Maybe tomorrow.' It was a lie; I was leaving before noon, with or without my medical team's approval.

More hesitation. The cake, the punch, the important speeches from busy people, maybe even a gift or two. How would she handle it?

'I'm sorry,' she said.

'Me too. Is anybody looking for me?'

'No. Not yet.'

'Good. Please tell Rudolph about the accident, and I'll call him later. Gotta go. They want more tests.'

And so my once promising career at Drake & Sweeney sputtered to an end. I skipped my own retirement party. At the age of thirty-two I was freed from the shackles of corporate servitude, and the money. I was left to follow my conscience. I would've felt great if not for the knife sticking through my ribs every time I moved.

Claire arrived after eleven. She huddled with my doctor in the hall. I could hear them out there, speaking their language. They stepped into my room, jointly announced my release, and I changed into clean clothes she had brought from home. She drove me there, a short trip during which little was said. There was no chance at reconciliation. Why should a simple car wreck change anything? She was there as a friend and a doctor, not a wife.

She fixed tomato soup and tucked me into the sofa. She lined up my pills on the kitchen counter, gave me my instructions, and left.

I was still for ten minutes, long enough to eat half the soup and a few of the saltines, then I was on the phone. Mordecai had found nothing.

Working from the classifieds, I began calling Realtors and apartment locating services. Then I called for a sedan from a car service. I took a long, hot shower to loosen my bruised body.

My driver was Leon. I sat in the front with him, trying not to grimace and groan with each pothole he hit.

I couldn't afford a nice apartment, but at the least I wanted one that was safe. Leon had some ideas. We stopped at a news-stand and I picked up two free brochures on District real estate.

In Leon's opinion, a good place to live right now, but this could change in six months, he warned me, was Adams-Morgan, north of Dupont Circle. It was a well-known district, one I had been through many times, never with any desire to stop and browse. The streets were lined with turn-of-the-century rowhouses, all of which were still inhabited, which, in D.C., meant a vibrant neighborhood. The bars and clubs were hot at the moment, according to Leon, and the best new restaurants were there. The seedy sections were just around the corner, and of course one had to be extremely careful. If important people like senators got themselves mugged on Capitol Hill, then no one was safe.

Driving toward Adams-Morgan, Leon was suddenly confronted with a pothole larger than his car. We bounced through it, getting airborne for what seemed to be ten seconds, then landing very hard. I couldn't help but scream as the entire left side of my torso collapsed in pain.

Leon was horrified. I had to tell him the truth, where I'd slept last night. He slowed down considerably, and became my Realtor. He helped me up the stairs at my first prospect, a run-down flat with the unmistakable smell of cat urine emanating from the carpet. In no uncertain terms, Leon told the landlord she should be ashamed showing the place in such condition.

The second stop was a loft five floors above the street, and I almost didn't make it up the stairs. No elevator. And not much heating. Leon politely thanked the manager.

The next loft was four floors up, but with a nice, clean elevator. The rowhouse was on Wyoming, a pretty shaded street just off Connecticut. The rent was five hundred and fifty a month, and I had already said yes before I saw the place. I was sinking fast, thinking more and more about the pain pills I'd left on the counter, and ready to rent anything.

Three tiny rooms in an attic with sloping ceilings, a bathroom with plumbing that seemed to be working, clean floors, and something of a view over the street.

'We'll take it,' Leon said to the landlord. I was leaning on a door frame, ready to collapse. In a small office in the basement, I hurriedly read the lease, signed it, and wrote a check for the deposit and first month's rent.

I'd told Claire I'd be out by the weekend. I was determined to make it happen.

If Leon was curious about my move from the swankiness of Georgetown to a three-room pigeonhole in Adams-Morgan, he didn't ask. He was too much of a professional. He returned me to our apartment, and he waited in the car while I swallowed my pills and took a quick nap.

A phone was ringing somewhere in the midst of my chemical-induced fog. I stumbled forth, found it, managed to say, 'Hello.'

Rudolph said, 'Thought you were in the hospital.'

I heard his voice, and recognized it, but the fog was still clearing. 'I was,' I said, thick-tongued. 'Now I'm not. What do you want?'

'We missed you this afternoon.'

Ah yes. The punch and cake show. 'I didn't plan to be in a car wreck, Rudolph. Please forgive me.'

'A lot of people wanted to say good-bye.'

'They can drop me a line. Tell them to just fax it over.'

'You feel lousy, don't you?'

'Yes, Rudolph. I feel like I've just been hit by a car.'

'Are you on medication?'

'Why do you care?'

'Sorry. Look, Braden Chance was in my office an hour ago. He's quite anxious to see you. Odd, don't you think?'

The fog lifted and my head was much clearer. 'See me about what?'

'He wouldn't say. But he's looking for you.'

'Tell him I've left.'

'I did. Sorry to bother you. Stop by if you get a minute. You still have friends here.'

'Thanks, Rudolph.'

I stuffed the pills in my pockets. Leon was napping in the car. As we sped away, I called Mordecai. He'd found the accident report; it listed a Hundley Towing as the wrecker service. Hundley Towing used an answering machine for most of its calls. The streets were slick, lots of accidents, a busy time for people who owned tow trucks. A mechanic had finally answered the phone around three, but proved to be completely useless.

Leon found the Hundley place on Rhode Island near Seventh. In better days it had been a full-service gas station, now it was a garage, towing service, used-car lot, and U-Haul trailer rental. Every window was adorned with black bars. Leon maneuvered as close as possible to the front door. 'Cover me,' I said, as I got out and dashed inside. The door kicked back when I walked through, hitting me on my left arm. I doubled over in pain. A mechanic wearing overalls and grease rounded a corner and glared at me.

I explained why I was there. He found a clipboard and studied papers stuck to it. In the rear, I could hear men talking and cursing – no doubt they were back there shooting dice, drinking whiskey, probably selling crack.

'The police have it,' he said, still looking at the papers.

'Any idea why?'

'Not really. Was there a crime or something?'

'Yeah, but my car wasn't involved with the crime.'

He gave me a blank look. He had his own problems.

'Any idea where it might be?' I asked, trying to be pleasant.

'When they impound them, they usually take them to a lot up on Georgia, north of Howard.'

'How many lots does the city have?'

He shrugged and began walking away. 'More than one,' he said, and disappeared.

I managed the door with care, then bolted for Leon's car.

It was dark when we found the lot, half a city block lined with chain link and razor wire. Inside were hundreds of wrecked cars, arranged haphazardly, some stacked on top of others.

Leon stood with me on the sidewalk, peering through the chain link. 'Over there,' I said, pointing. The Lexus was parked near a shed, facing us. The impact had demolished the left front. The fender was gone; the engine exposed and crushed.

'You're a very lucky man,' Leon said.

Next to it was the Jaguar, its roof flattened, all windows missing.

There was an office of some type in the shed, but it was closed and dark. The gates were locked with heavy chains. The razor wire glistened in the rain. There were tough guys hanging around a corner, not far away. I could feel them watching us.

'Let's get out of here,' I said.

Leon drove me to National Airport, the only place I knew to rent a car.

The table was set; carryout Chinese was on the stove. Claire was waiting, and worried to some degree, though it was impossible to tell how much. I told her I had to go rent a car, pursuant to instructions from my insurance company. She examined me like a good doctor, and made me take a pill.

'I thought you were going to rest,' she said.

'I tried. It didn't work. I'm starving.'

It would be our last meal together as husband and wife, ending the same way we'd begun, with something fast and prepared elsewhere.

'Do you know someone named Hector Palma?' she asked, halfway through dinner.

I swallowed hard. 'Yes.'

'He called an hour ago. Said it was important that he talk to you. Who is he?'

'A paralegal with the firm. I was supposed to spend the morning with him going over one of my cases. He's in a tight spot.'

'Must be. He wants to meet with you at nine tonight, at Nathan's on M.'

'Why a bar?' I mused.

'He didn't say. Sounded suspicious.'

My appetite vanished, but I kept eating to appear unmoved. Not that it was necessary. She couldn't have cared less.

I walked to M Street, in a light rain that was turning to sleet, and in significant pain. Parking would've been impossible on Friday night. And I hoped to stretch my muscles some, and clear my head.

The meeting could be nothing but trouble, and I prepped for it as I walked. I thought of lies to cover my trail, and more lies to cover the first set. Now that I had stolen, the lying didn't seem like such a big deal. Hector might be working for the firm; there was a chance he could be wired. I would listen carefully, and say little.

Nathan's was only half-full. I was ten minutes early, but he was there, waiting for me in a small booth. As I approached he suddenly jumped from his seat and thrust a hand at me. 'You must be Michael. I'm Hector Palma, from real estate. Nice to meet you.'

It was an assault, a burst of personality that put me on my heels. I shook hands, reeling, and said something like, 'Nice to meet you.'

He pointed to the booth. 'Here, have a seat,' he

said, all warmth and smiles. I delicately bent and squeezed my way into the booth.

'What happened to your face?' he asked.

'I kissed an air bag.'

'Yeah, I heard about the accident,' he said quickly. Very quickly. 'Are you okay? Any broken bones?'

'No,' I said slowly, trying to read him.

'Heard the other guy got killed,' he said, a split second after I'd spoken. He was in charge of this conversation. I was supposed to follow along.

'Yeah, some drug dealer.'

'This city,' he said, as the waiter appeared. 'What'll you have?' Hector asked me.

'Black coffee,' I said. At that moment, as he pondered his choice of drinks, one of his feet began tapping me on the leg.

'What kind of beer do you have?' he asked the waiter, a question they hated. The waiter looked straight ahead and began rattling off brands.

The tapping brought our eyes together. His hands were together on the table. Using the waiter as a shield, he barely curled his right index finger and pointed to his chest.

'Molson,' he announced suddenly, and the waiter left.

He was wired, and they were watching. Wherever they were, they couldn't see through the waiter. Instinctively, I wanted to turn and examine the other people in the bar. But I withstood the temptation, thanks in no small part to a neck as pliable as a board.

That explained the hearty hello, as if we'd never met. Hector had been grilled all day, and he was denying everything.

'I'm a paralegal in real estate,' he explained. 'You've met Braden Chance, one of our partners.'

'Yes.' Since my words were being recorded, I would offer little.

141

'I work primarily for him. You and I spoke briefly one day last week when you visited his office.'

'If you say so. I don't remember seeing you.'

I caught a very faint smile, a relaxing around the eyes, nothing a surveillance camera could catch. Under the table, I tapped his leg with my foot. Hopefully we were dancing to the same tune.

'Look, the reason I asked you to meet me is because a file is missing from Braden's office.'

'Am I the accused?'

'Well, no, but you're a possible suspect. It was the file you asked for when you sort of barged into his office last week.'

'Then I *am* being accused,' I said hotly.

'Not yet. Relax. The firm is doing a thorough investigation of the matter, and we're simply talking to everyone we can think of. Since I heard you ask Braden for the file, the firm instructed me to talk to you. It's that simple.'

'I don't know what you're talking about. It's that simple.'

'You know nothing about the file?'

'Of course not. Why would I take a file from a partner's office?'

'Would you take a polygraph?'

'Certainly,' I said firmly, even indignantly. There was no way in hell I would take a polygraph.

'Good. They're asking all of us to do it. Everybody remotely near the file.'

The beer and coffee arrived, giving us a brief pause to evaluate and reposition. Hector had just told me he was in deep trouble. A polygraph would kill him. Did you meet Michael Brock before he left the firm? Did you discuss the missing file? Did you give him copies of anything taken from the file? Did you assist him in obtaining the missing file? Yes or no. Hard questions

142

with simple answers. There was no way he could lie and survive the test.

'They're fingerprinting too,' he said. He said this in a lower voice, not in an effort to avoid the hidden mike, but rather to soften the blow.

It didn't work. The thought of leaving prints had never occurred to me, neither before the theft, nor since. 'Good for them,' I said.

'In fact, they lifted prints all afternoon. From the door, the light switch, the file cabinet. Lots of prints.'

'Hope they find their man.'

'It's really coincidental, you know. Braden had a hundred active files in his office, and the only one missing is the one you were quite anxious to see.'

'Are you trying to say something?'

'I just said it. A real coincidence.' He was doing this for the benefit of our listeners.

I thought perhaps I should perform too. 'I don't like the way you said it,' I practically yelled at him. 'If you want to accuse me of something, then go to the cops, get a warrant, and get me picked up. Otherwise, keep your stupid opinions to yourself.'

'The cops are already involved,' he said, very coolly, and my contrived temper melted. 'It's a theft.'

'Of course it's a theft. Go catch your thief and stop wasting your time with me.'

He took a long drink. 'Did someone give you a set of keys to Braden's office?'

'Of course not.'

'Well, they found this empty file on your desk, with a note about the two keys. One to the door, the other to a file cabinet.'

'I know nothing about it,' I said, as arrogantly as possible while trying to remember the last place I'd put the empty file. My trail was widening. I'd been trained to think like a lawyer, not a criminal.

Another long drink by Hector, another sip of coffee by me.

Enough had been said. The messages had been delivered, one by the firm, the other by Hector himself. The firm wanted the file back, with its contents uncompromised. Hector wanted me to know that his involvement could cost him his job.

It was up to me to save him. I could return the file, confess, promise to keep it sealed, and the firm would probably forgive me. There would be no harm. Protecting Hector's job could be a condition of the return.

'Anything else?' I asked, suddenly ready to leave.

'Nothing. When can you do the polygraph?'

'I'll give you a call.'

I picked up my coat and left.

SIXTEEN

For reasons that I would soon understand, Mordecai had an intense dislike for District cops, even though most were black. In his opinion, they were rough on the homeless, and that was the standard he invariably used to measure good and bad.

But he knew a few. One was Sergeant Peeler, a man described by Mordecai as 'from the streets.' Peeler worked with troubled kids in a community center near the legal clinic, and he and Mordecai belonged to the same church. Peeler had contacts, and could pull enough strings to get me to my car.

He walked into the clinic shortly after nine Saturday morning. Mordecai and I were drinking coffee and trying to stay warm. Peeler didn't work Saturdays. I got the impression he would have rather stayed in bed.

With Mordecai doing the driving and talking, and with me in the back, we rode through the slick streets into Northeast. The snow they had forecast was instead a cold rain. Traffic was light. It was another raw February morning; only the hearty ventured onto the sidewalks.

We parked at the curb near the padlocked gates to the city lot just off Georgia Avenue. Peeler said, 'Wait here.' I could see the remains of my Lexus.

He walked to the gates, pushed a button on a pole, and the door to the office shed opened. A small, thin uniformed policeman with an umbrella came over, and he and Peeler exchanged a few words.

Peeler returned to the car, slamming the door and shaking the water off his shoulders. 'He's waiting for you,' he said.

I stepped into the rain, raised my umbrella, and walked quickly to the gates where Officer Winkle was waiting without the slightest trace of humor or goodwill. He produced keys by the dozens, somehow found the three that fit the heavy padlocks, and said to me, 'Over here,' as he opened the gates. I followed him through the gravel lot, avoiding when possible the potholes filled with brown water and mud. My entire body ached with every move, so my hopping and dodging were restricted. He went straight to my car.

I went right to the front seat. No file. After a moment of panic, I found it behind the driver's seat, on the floor, intact. I grabbed it, and was ready to go. I was in no mood to survey the damage I'd walked away from. I had survived in one piece, and that was all that mattered. I'd haggle with the insurance company next week.

'Is that it?' Winkle asked.

'Yes,' I said, ready to bolt.

'Follow me.'

We entered the shed where a butane heater roared in a corner, blasting us with hot air. He selected one of ten clipboards from the wall, and began staring at the file I was holding. 'Brown manila file,' he said as he wrote. 'About two inches thick.' I stood there clutching it as if it were gold. 'Is there a name on it?'

I was in no position to protest. One smart-ass remark, and they would never find me. 'Why do you need it?' I asked.

'Put it on the table,' he said.

On the table it went. 'RiverOaks slash TAG, Inc.,'

146

he said, still writing. 'File number TBC-96–3381.' My trail widened even more.

'Do you own this?' he asked, pointing, with no small amount of suspicion.

'Yes.'

'Okay. You can go now.'

I thanked him, and got no response. I wanted to jog across the lot, but walking was enough of a challenge. He locked the gates behind me.

Mordecai and Peeler both turned around and looked at the file once I was inside. Neither had a clue. I had told Mordecai only that the file was very important. I needed to retrieve it before it was destroyed.

All that effort for one plain manila file?

I was tempted to flip through it as we drove back to the clinic. But I didn't.

I thanked Peeler, said good-bye to Mordecai, and drove, cautiously, to my new loft.

The source of the money was the federal government, no surprise in D.C. The Postal Service planned to construct a twenty-million-dollar bulk-mail facility in the city, and RiverOaks was one of several aggressive real estate companies hoping to build, lease, and manage it. Several sites had been considered, all in rough and decaying sections of the city. A short list of three had been announced the previous December. RiverOaks had begun snapping up all the cheap real estate it might need.

TAG was a duly registered corporation whose sole stock-holder was Tillman Gantry, described in a file memo as a former pimp, small-time hustler, and twice-convicted felon. One of many such characters in the city. After crime, Gantry had discovered used cars and real estate. He purchased abandoned buildings, sometimes doing quickie renovations and reselling,

147

sometimes offering space for rent. Fourteen TAG properties were listed in a file summary. Gantry's path crossed that of RiverOaks' when the U.S. Postal Service needed more space.

On January 6, the Postal Service informed River-Oaks by registered mail that the company had been chosen to be the contractor/owner/landlord of the new bulk facility. A memorandum of agreement provided for annual rental payments of $1.5 million, for a guaranteed period of twenty years. The letter also said, with nongovernmental-like haste, that a final agreement between RiverOaks and the Postal Service would have to be signed no later than March 1, or the deal was off. After seven years of contemplating and planning, the Feds wanted it built overnight.

RiverOaks, and its lawyers and Realtors, went to work. In January, the company purchased four properties on Florida near the warehouse where the eviction took place. The file had two maps of the area, with shaded colors indicating lots purchased and lots under negotiation.

March 1 was only seven days away. Small wonder Chance missed the file so quickly. He was working with it every day.

The warehouse on Florida Avenue had been purchased by TAG the previous July for a sum not revealed in the file. RiverOaks bought it for two hundred thousand dollars on January 31, four days before the eviction that sent DeVon Hardy and the Burton family into the streets.

On the bare wooden floor of what would become my living room, I carefully removed each sheet of paper from the file, examined it, then described it in detail on a legal pad so that I could put it back together in perfect order. There was the usual collection of papers I assumed to be in every real estate file: tax records for prior years, a chain of title, previous

148

deeds, an agreement for the purchase and sale of the property, correspondence with the Realtor, closing papers. It was a cash deal, so no bank was involved.

On the left inside flap of the file was the journal, a preprinted form used to log each entry by date and brief description. You could judge the organizational capacity of a Drake & Sweeney secretary by the level of detail in a file's journal. Every piece of paper, map, photo, or chart – anything and everything that was punched into a file was supposed to be recorded in the journal. This had been drilled into our heads during boot camp. Most of us had learned the hard way – there was nothing more frustrating than flipping through a thick file in search of something that had not been logged in with sufficient detail. If you can't find it in thirty seconds, the axiom said, it's useless.

Chance's file was meticulous; his secretary was a woman of details. But there had been tampering.

On January 22, Hector Palma went to the warehouse, alone, for a routine, prepurchase inspection. As he was entering a designated door, he was mugged by two street punks who hit him over the head with a stick of some sort, and took his wallet and cash at knifepoint. He stayed at home on January 23, and prepared a memo to the file describing the assault. The last sentence read: 'Will return on Monday, January 27, with guard, to inspect.' The memo was properly logged into the file.

But there was no memo from his second visit. A January 27 entry into the journal said: HP memo – site visit, inspection of premises.

Hector went to the warehouse on the twenty-seventh, with a guard, inspected the place, no doubt found that serious squatting was under way, and prepared a memo, which, judging by his other paper-work, was probably quite thorough.

149

The memo had been removed from the file. Certainly no crime, and I had taken things from files all the time without making a note in the journal. But I damned sure put them back. If an item was logged in, it was supposed to be in the file.

The closing took place on January 31, a Friday. The following Tuesday, Hector returned to the warehouse to remove the squatters. He was assisted by a guard from a private security firm, a District cop, and four roughnecks from an eviction company. It took three hours, according to his memo, which ran for two pages. Though he tried to mask his emotions, Hector didn't have the stomach for evictions.

My heart stopped when I read the following: 'The mother had four children, one an infant. She lived in a two-room apartment with no plumbing. They slept on two mattresses on the floor. She fought with the policeman while her children watched. She was eventually removed.'

So Ontario watched while his mother fought.

There was a list of those evicted, seventeen in all, with children excluded, the same list someone had placed on my desk Monday morning with a copy of the *Post* story.

In the back of the file, lying loose without the benefit of a journal entry, were eviction notices for the seventeen. They had not been used. Squatters have no rights, including the right to be notified. The notices had been prepared as an afterthought, an effort to cover the trail. They had probably been stuck in after the Mister episode by Chance himself, just in case he might need them.

The tampering was obvious, and foolish. But then Chance was a partner. It was virtually unheard of for a partner to surrender a file.

It hadn't been surrendered; it had been stolen. An

act of larceny, a crime for which evidence was now being gathered. The thief was an idiot.

As part of my preemployment ritual seven years earlier, I had been fingerprinted by private investigators. It would be a simple matter to match those prints with the ones lifted from Chance's file cabinet. It would take only minutes. I was certain it had already been done. Could there be a warrant for my arrest? It was inevitable.

Most of the floor was covered when I finished, three hours after I started. I carefully reassembled the file, then drove to the clinic and copied it.

She was shopping, her note said. We had nice luggage, an item we failed to mention when we split the assets. She would be traveling more than I in the near future, so I took the cheap stuff – duffel and gym bags. I didn't want to get caught, so I threw the basics into a pile on the bed – socks, underwear, tee shirts, toiletries, shoes, but only the ones I had worn in the past year. She could discard the others. I hurriedly cleaned out my drawers and my side of the medicine cabinet. Wounded and aching, physically and otherwise, I hauled the bags down two flights of stairs to my rental car, then went back up for a load of suits and dress clothes. I found my old sleeping bag, unused for at least the last five years, and carried it down, along with a quilt and a pillow. I was entitled to my alarm clock, radio, portable CD player with a few CD's, thirteen-inch color TV on the kitchen counter, one coffeepot, hair dryer, and the set of blue towels.

When the car was full, I left a note telling her I was gone. I placed it next to the one she'd left, and refused to stare at it. My emotions were mixed and just under the skin, and I was not equipped to deal with them. I'd never moved out before; I wasn't sure how it was done.

151

I locked the door and walked down the stairs. I knew I would be back in a couple of days to get the rest of my things, but the trip down felt like the last time.

She would read the note, check the drawers and closets to see what I had taken, and when she realized I had indeed moved out, she would sit in the den for a quick tear. Maybe a good cry. But it would be over before long. She would easily move to the next phase.

As I drove away, there was no feeling of liberation. It wasn't a thrill to be single again. Claire and I had both lost.

SEVENTEEN

I locked myself inside the office. The clinic was colder Sunday than it had been on Saturday. I wore a heavy sweater, corduroy pants, thermal socks, and I read the paper at my desk with two steaming cups of coffee in front of me. The building had a heating system, but I wasn't about to meddle with it.

I missed my chair, my leather executive swivel that rocked and reclined and rolled at my command. My new one was a small step above a folding job you'd rent for a wedding. It promised to be uncomfortable on good days; in my pummeled condition at that moment, it was a torture device.

The desk was a battered hand-me-down, probably from an abandoned school; square and boxlike, with three drawers down each side, all of which actually opened, but not without a struggle. The two clients' chairs on the other side were indeed folding types – one black, the other a greenish color I'd never seen before.

The walls were plaster, painted decades ago and allowed to fade into a shade of pale lemon. The plaster was cracked; the spiders had taken over the corners at the ceiling. The only decoration was a framed placard advertising a March for Justice on the Mall in July of 1988.

The floor was ancient oak, the planks rounded at

153

the edges, evidence of heavy use in prior years. It had been swept recently, the broom still standing in a corner with a dustpan, a gentle cue that if I wanted the dirt cleared again, then it was up to me.

Oh how the mighty had fallen! If my dear brother Warner could've seen me sitting there on Sunday, shivering at my sad little desk, staring at the cracks in the plaster, locked in so that my potential clients couldn't mug me, he would've hurled insults so rich and colorful that I would've been compelled to write them down.

I couldn't comprehend my parents' reaction. I would be forced to call them soon, and deliver the double shock of my changes of address.

A loud bang at the door scared the hell out of me. I bolted upright, unsure of what to do. Were the street punks coming after me? Another knock as I moved toward the front, and I could see a figure trying to look through the bars and thick glass of the front door.

It was Barry Nuzzo, shivering and anxious to get to safety. I got things unlocked, and let him in.

'What a slumhole!' he began pleasantly, looking around the front room as I relocked the door.

'Quaint, isn't it?' I said, reeling from his presence and trying to figure out what it meant.

'What a dump!' He was amused by the place. He walked around Sofia's desk, slowly taking off his gloves, afraid to touch anything for fear of starting an avalanche of files.

'We keep the overhead low, so we can take all the money home,' I said. It was an old joke around Drake & Sweeney. The partners were constantly bitching about the overhead, while at the same time most were concerned about redecorating their offices.

'So you're here for the money?' he asked, still amused.

'Of course.'

154

'You've lost your mind.'

'I've found a calling.'

'Yeah, you're hearing voices.'

'Is that why you're here? To tell me I'm crazy?'

'I called Claire.'

'And what did she say?'

'Said you had moved out.'

'That's true. We're getting a divorce.'

'What's wrong with your face?'

'Air bag.'

'Oh, yeah. I forgot. I heard it was just a fender bender.'

'It was. The fenders got bent.'

He draped his coat over a chair, then hurriedly put it back on. 'Does low overhead mean you don't pay your heating bill?'

'Now and then we skip a month.'

He walked around some more, peeking into the small offices to the side. 'Who pays for this operation?' he asked.

'A trust.'

'A declining trust?'

'Yes, a rapidly declining trust.'

'How'd you find it?'

'Mister hung out here. These were his lawyers.'

'Good old Mister,' he said. He stopped his examination for a moment, and stared at a wall. 'Do you think he would've killed us?'

'No. Nobody was listening to him. He was just another homeless guy. He wanted to be heard.'

'Did you ever consider jumping him?'

'No, but I thought about grabbing his gun and shooting Rafter.'

'I wish you had.'

'Maybe next time.'

'Got any coffee?'

'Sure. Have a seat.'

I didn't want Barry to follow me into the kitchen, because it left much to be desired. I found a cup, washed it quickly, and filled it with coffee. I invited him into my office.

'Nice,' he said, looking around.

'This is where all the long balls are hit,' I said proudly. We took positions across the desk, both chairs squeaking and on the verge of collapse.

'Is this what you dreamed about in law school?' he asked.

'I don't remember law school. I've billed too many hours since then.'

He finally looked at me, without a smirk or a smile, and the kidding was set aside. As bad as the thought was, I couldn't help but wonder if Barry was wired. They had sent Hector into the fray with a bug under his shirt; they would do the same with Barry. He wouldn't volunteer, but they could apply the pressure. I was the enemy.

'So you came here searching for Mister?' he said.

'I guess.'

'What did you find?'

'Are you playing dumb, Barry? What's happening at the firm? Have you guys circled the wagons? Are you coming after me?'

He weighed this carefully, while taking quick sips from his mug. 'This coffee is awful,' he said, ready to spit.

'At least it's hot.'

'I'm sorry about Claire.'

'Thanks, but I'd rather not talk about it.'

'There's a file missing, Michael. Everyone's pointing at you.'

'Who knows you're here?'

'My wife.'

'The firm send you?'

'Absolutely not.'

I believed him. He'd been a friend for seven years, close at times. More often than not, though, we'd been too busy for friendship.

'Why are they pointing at me?'

'The file has something to do with Mister. You went to Braden Chance and demanded to see it. You were seen near his office the night it disappeared. There is evidence someone gave you some keys that perhaps you shouldn't have had.'

'Is that all?'

'That, and the fingerprints.'

'Fingerprints?' I asked, trying to appear surprised.

'All over the place. The door, the light switch, the file cabinet itself. Perfect matches. You were there, Michael. You took the file. Now what will you do with it?'

'How much do you know about the file?'

'Mister got evicted by one of our real estate clients. He was a squatter. He went nuts, scared the hell out of us, you almost got hit. You cracked up.'

'Is that all?'

'That's all they've told us.'

'They being?'

'They being the big dogs. We got memos late Friday – the entire firm, lawyers, secretaries, paralegals, everybody – informing us that a file had been taken, you were the suspect, and that no member of the firm should have any contact with you. I am forbidden to be here right now.'

'I won't tell.'

'Thanks.'

If Braden Chance had made the connection between the eviction and Lontae Burton, he was not the type who would admit this to anyone. Not even his fellow partners. Barry was being truthful. He probably thought my only interest in the file was DeVon Hardy.

'Then why are you here?'

'I'm your friend. Things are crazy right now. My God we had cops in the office on Friday, can you believe that? Last week it was the SWAT team, and we were hostages. Now you've jumped off a cliff. And the thing with Claire. Why don't we take a break? Let's go somewhere for a couple of weeks. Take our wives.'

'Where?'

'I don't know. Who cares. The islands.'

'What would that accomplish?'

'We could thaw out for one thing. Play some tennis. Sleep. Get recharged.'

'Paid for by the firm?'

'Paid for by me.'

'Forget about Claire. It's over, Barry. It took a long time, but it's over.'

'Okay. The two of us will go.'

'But you're not supposed to have any contact with me.'

'I have an idea. I think I can go to Arthur and have a long chat. We can unwind this thing. You bring back the file, forget whatever is in it, the firm forgives and forgets too, you and I go play tennis for two weeks on Maui, then when we return you go back to your plush office where you belong.'

'They sent you, didn't they?'

'No. I swear.'

'It won't work, Barry.'

'Give me a good reason. Please.'

'There's more to being a lawyer than billing hours and making money. Why do we want to become corporate whores? I'm tired of it, Barry. I want to make a difference.'

'You sound like a first-year law student.'

'Exactly. We got into this business because we thought the law was a higher calling. We could fight injustice and social ills, and do all sorts of great things

158

because we were lawyers. We were idealistic once. Why can't we do it again?'

'Mortgages.'

'I'm not trying to recruit. You have three kids; luckily Claire and I have none. I can afford to go a little nuts.'

A radiator in a corner, one I had not yet noticed, began to rattle and hiss. We watched it and waited hopefully for a little heat. A minute passed. Then two.

'They're gonna come after you, Michael,' he said, still looking at the radiator, but not seeing.

'They? You mean we?'

'Right. The firm. You can't steal a file. Think about the client. The client has a right to expect confidentiality. If a file walks out, the firm has no choice but to go after it.'

'Criminal charges?'

'Probably. They're mad as hell, Michael. You can't blame them. There's also talk of a disciplinary action with the bar association. An injunction is likely. Rafter is already working on it.'

'Why couldn't Mister have aimed a little lower?'

'They're coming hard.'

. 'The firm has more to lose than I do.'

He studied me. He did not know what was in the file. 'There's more than Mister?' he asked.

'A lot more. The firm has tremendous exposure. If they come after me, I go after the firm.'

'You can't use a stolen file. No court in the country will allow it into evidence. You don't understand litigation.'

'I'm learning. Tell them to back off. Remember, I've got the file, and the file's got the dirt.'

'They were just a bunch of squatters, Michael.'

'It's much more complicated than that. Someone needs to sit down with Braden Chance and get the truth. Tell Rafter to do his homework before he pulls

159

some harebrained stunt. Believe me, Barry, this is front-page stuff. You guys will be afraid to leave your homes.'

'So you're proposing a truce? You keep the file, we leave you alone.'

'For now anyway. I don't know about next week or the week after.'

'Why can't you talk to Arthur? I'll referee. The three of us will get in a room, lock the door, work this thing out. What do you say?'

'It's too late. People are dead.'

'Mister got himself killed.'

'There are others.' And with that, I had said enough. Though he was my friend, he would repeat most of our conversation to his bosses.

'Would you like to explain?' he said.

'I can't. It's confidential.'

'That has a phony sound to it, coming from a lawyer who steals files.'

The radiator gurgled and burped, and it was easier to watch it than to talk for a while. Neither of us wanted to say things we would later regret.

He asked about the other employees of the clinic. I gave him a quick tour. 'Unbelievable,' he mumbled, more than once.

'Can we keep in touch?' he said at the door.

'Sure.'

EIGHTEEN

My orientation lasted about thirty minutes, the time it took us to drive from the clinic to the Samaritan House in Petworth, in Northeast. Mordecai handled the driving and the talking; I sat quietly, holding my briefcase, as nervous as any rookie about to be fed to the wolves. I wore jeans, a white shirt and tie, an old navy blazer, and on my feet I had well-worn Nike tennis shoes and white socks. I had stopped shaving. I was a street lawyer, and I could dress any way I wanted.

Mordecai, of course, had instantly noted the change in style when I walked into his office and announced I was ready for work. He didn't say anything, but his glance lingered on the Nikes. He had seen it all before – big-firm types coming down from the towers to spend a few hours with the poor. For some reason, they felt compelled to grow whiskers and wear denim.

'Your clientele will be a mixture of thirds,' he said, driving badly with one hand, holding coffee with another, oblivious to any of the other vehicles crowded around us. 'About a third are employed, a third are families with children, a third are mentally disabled, a third are veterans. And about a third of those eligible for low-income housing receive it. In the past fifteen years, two and a half million low-cost housing units

161

have been eliminated, and the federal housing programs have been cut seventy percent. Small wonder people are living on the streets. Governments are balancing budgets on the backs of the poor.'

The statistics flowed forth with no effort whatsoever. This was his life and his profession. As a lawyer trained to keep meticulous notes, I fought the compulsion to rip open my briefcase and begin scribbling. I just listened.

'These people have minimum-wage jobs, so private housing is not even considered. They don't even dream about it. And their earned income has not kept pace with housing costs. So they fall farther and farther behind, and at the same time assistance programs take more and more hits. Get this: Only fourteen percent of disabled homeless people receive disability benefits. Fourteen percent! You'll see a lot of these cases.'

We squealed to a stop at a red light, his car partially blocking the intersection. Horns erupted all around us. I slid lower in the seat, waiting for another collision. Mordecai hadn't the slightest clue that his car was impeding rush-hour traffic. He stared blankly ahead, in another world.

'The frightening part of homelessness is what you don't see on the street. About half of all poor people spend seventy percent of their income trying to keep the housing they have. HUD says they should spend a third. There are tens of thousands of people in this city who are clinging to their roofs; one missed paycheck, one unexpected hospital visit, one unseen emergency, and they lose their housing.'

'Where do they go?'

'They rarely go straight to the shelters. At first, they'll go to their families, then friends. The strain is enormous because their families and friends also have

162

subsidized housing, and their leases restrict the number of people who can live in one unit. They're forced to violate their leases, which can lead to eviction. They move around, sometimes they leave a kid with this sister and a kid with that friend. Things go from bad to worse. A lot of homeless people are afraid of the shelters, and they are desperate to avoid them.'

He paused long enough to drink his coffee. 'Why?' I asked.

'Not all shelters are good. There have been assaults, robberies, even rapes.'

And this was where I was expected to spend the rest of my legal career. 'I forgot my gun,' I said.

'You'll be okay. There are hundreds of pro bono volunteers in this city. I've never heard of one getting hurt.'

'That's good to hear.' We were moving again, somewhat safer.

'About half of the people have some type of substance abuse problem, like your pal DeVon Hardy. It's very common.'

'What can you do for them?'

'Not much, I'm afraid. There are a few programs left, but it's hard to find a bed. We were successful in placing Hardy in a recovery unit for veterans, but he walked away. The addict decides when he wants to get sober.'

'What's the drug of choice?'

'Alcohol. It's the most affordable. A lot of crack because it's cheap too. You'll see everything, but the designer drugs are too expensive.'

'What will my first five cases be?'

'Anxious, aren't you?'

'Yeah, and I don't have a clue.'

'Relax. The work is not complicated; it takes patience. You'll see a person who's not getting benefits, probably food stamps. A divorce. Someone

163

with a complaint against a landlord. An employment dispute. You're guaranteed a criminal case.'

'What type of criminal case?'

'Small stuff. The trend in urban America is to criminalize homelessness. The big cities have passed all sorts of laws designed to persecute those who live on the streets. Can't beg, can't sleep on a bench, can't camp under a bridge, can't store personal items in a public park, can't sit on a sidewalk, can't eat in public. Many of these have been struck down by the courts. Abraham has done some beautiful work convincing federal judges that these bad laws infringe on First Amendment rights. So the cities selectively enforce general laws, such as loitering, vagrancy, public drunkenness. They target the homeless. Some guy with a nice suit gets drunk in a bar and pees in an alley, no big deal. A homeless guy pees in the same alley, and he's arrested for urinating in public. Sweeps are common.'

'Sweeps?'

'Yes. They'll target one area of the city, shovel up all the homeless, dump them somewhere else. Atlanta did it before the Olympics – couldn't have all those poor people begging and sleeping on park benches with the world watching – so they sent in the S.S. troops and eliminated the problem. Then the city bragged about how pretty everything looked.'

'Where did they put them?'

'They damned sure didn't take them to shelters because they don't have any. They simply moved them around; dumped them in other parts of the city like manure.' A quick sip of coffee as he adjusted the heater – no hands on the wheel for five seconds. 'Remember, Michael, everybody has to be somewhere. These people have no alternatives. If you're hungry, you beg for food. If you're tired, then you sleep wherever you can find a spot. If you're homeless, you have to live somewhere.'

'Do they arrest them?'

'Every day, and it's stupid public policy. Take a guy living on the streets, in and out of shelters, working somewhere for minimum wage, trying his best to step up and become self-sufficient. Then he gets arrested for sleeping under a bridge. He doesn't want to be sleeping under a bridge, but everybody's got to sleep somewhere. He's guilty because the city council, in its brilliance, has made it a crime to be homeless. He has to pay thirty bucks just to get out of jail, and another thirty for his fine. Sixty bucks out of a very shallow pocket. So the guy gets kicked down another notch. He's been arrested, humiliated, fined, punished, and he's supposed to see the error of his ways and go find a home. Get off the damned streets. It's happening in most of our cities.'

'Wouldn't he be better off in jail?'

'Have you been to jail lately?'

'No.'

'Don't go. Cops are not trained to deal with the homeless, especially the mentally ill and the addicts. The jails are overcrowded. The criminal justice system is a nightmare to begin with, and persecuting the homeless only clogs it more. And here's the asinine part: It costs twenty-five percent more per day to keep a person in jail than to provide shelter, food, transportation, and counseling services. These, of course, would have a long-term benefit. These, of course, would make more sense. Twenty-five percent. And that doesn't include the costs of arrests and processing. Most of the cities are broke anyway, especially D.C. – that's why they're closing shelters, remember – yet they waste money by making criminals out of the homeless.'

165

'Seems ripe for litigation,' I said, though he needed no prompting.

'We're suing like crazy. Advocates all over the country are attacking these laws. Damned cities are spending more on legal fees than on building shelters for the homeless. You gotta love this country. New York, richest city in the world, can't house its people, so they sleep on the streets and panhandle on Fifth Avenue, and this upsets the sensitive New Yorkers, so they elect Rudy WhatsHisFace who promises to clean up the streets, and he gets his blue ribbon city council to outlaw homelessness, just like that – can't beg, can't sit on the sidewalk, can't be homeless – and they cut budgets like hell, close shelters and cut assistance, and at the same time they spend a bloody fortune paying New York lawyers to defend them for trying to eliminate poor people.'

'How bad is Washington?'

'Not as bad as New York, but not much better, I'm afraid.' We were in a part of town I would not have driven through in broad daylight in an armored vehicle two weeks ago. The storefronts were laden with black iron bars; the apartment buildings were tall, lifeless structures with laundry hanging over the railings. Each was gray-bricked, each stamped with the architectural blandness of hurried federal money.

'Washington is a black city,' he continued, 'with a large welfare class. It attracts a lot of people who want change, a lot of activists and radicals. People like you.'

'I'm hardly an activist or a radical.'

'It's Monday morning. Think of where you've been every Monday morning for the past seven years.'

'At my desk.'

'A very nice desk.'

'Yes.'

'In your elegantly appointed office.'

'Yes.'

166

He offered me a large grin, and said, 'You are now a radical.'

And with that, orientation ended.

Ahead on the right was a group of heavily clad men, huddled over a portable butane burner on a street corner. We turned beside them, and parked at the curb. The building was once a department store, many years in the past. A hand-painted sign read: Samaritan House.

'It's a private shelter,' Mordecai said. 'Ninety beds, decent food, funded by a coalition of churches in Arlington. We've been coming here for six years.'

A van from a food bank was parked by the door; volunteers unloaded boxes of vegetables and fruit. Mordecai spoke to an elderly gentleman who worked the door, and we were allowed inside.

'I'll give you a quick tour,' Mordecai said. I stayed close to him as we walked through the main floor. It was a maze of short hallways, each lined with small square rooms made of unpainted Sheetrock. Each room had a door, with a lock. One was open. Mordecai looked inside and said, 'Good morning.'

A tiny man with wild eyes sat on the edge of a cot, looking at us but saying nothing. 'This is a good room,' Mordecai said to me. 'It has privacy, a nice bed, room to store things, and electricity.' He flipped a switch by the door and the bulb of a small lamp went out. The room was darker for a second, then he flipped the switch again. The wild eyes never moved.

There was no ceiling for the room; the aging panels of the old store were thirty feet above.

'What about a bathroom?' I asked.

'They're in the back. Few shelters provide individual baths. Have a nice day,' he said to the resident, who nodded.

Radios were on, some with music, some with news

167

talk. People were moving about. It was Monday morning; they had jobs and places to be.

'Is it hard to get a room here?' I asked, certain of the answer.

'Nearly impossible. There's a waiting list a mile long, and the shelter can screen who gets in.'

'How long do they stay here?'

'It varies. Three months is probably a good average. This is one of the nicer shelters, so they're safe here. As soon as they get stable, the shelter starts trying to relocate them into affordable housing.'

He introduced me to a young woman in black combat boots who ran the place. 'Our new lawyer,' was my description. She welcomed me to the shelter. They talked about a client who'd disappeared, and I drifted along the hallway until I found the family section. I heard a baby cry and walked to an open door. The room was slightly larger, and divided into cubicles. A stout woman of no more than twenty-five was sitting in a chair, naked from the waist up, breast-feeding an infant, thoroughly unfazed by my gawking ten feet away. Two small children were tumbling over a bed. Rap came from a radio.

With her right hand, the woman cupped her unused breast and offered it to me. I bolted down the hall and found Mordecai.

Clients awaited us. Our office was in a corner of the dining hall, near the kitchen. Our desk was a folding table we borrowed from the cook. Mordecai unlocked a file cabinet in the corner, and we were in business. Six people sat in a row of chairs along the wall.

'Who's first?' he announced, and a woman came forward with her chair. She sat across from her lawyers, both ready with pen and legal pad, one a seasoned veteran of street law, the other clueless.

Her name was Waylene, age twenty-seven, two children, no husband.

'Half will come from the shelter,' Mordecai said to me as we took notes. 'The other half come from the streets.'

'We take anybody?'

'Anybody who's homeless.'

Waylene's problem was not complicated. She had worked in a fast-food restaurant before quitting for some reason Mordecai deemed irrelevant, and she was owed her last two paychecks. Because she had no permanent address, the employer had sent the checks to the wrong place. The checks had disappeared; the employer was unconcerned.

'Where will you be staying next week?' Mordecai asked her.

She wasn't sure. Maybe here, maybe there. She was looking for a job, and if she found one, then other events might occur, and she could possibly move in with so and so. Or get a place of her own.

'I'll get your money, and I'll have the checks sent to my office.' He handed her a business card. 'Phone me at this number in a week.'

She took the card, thanked us, and hurried away.

'Call the taco place, identify yourself as her attorney, be nice at first, then raise hell if they don't cooperate. If necessary, stop by and pick up the checks yourself.'

I wrote down these instructions as if they were complicated. Waylene was owed two hundred ten dollars. The last case I worked on at Drake & Sweeney was an antitrust dispute with nine hundred million dollars at stake.

The second client was unable to articulate a specific legal problem. He just wanted to talk to someone. He was drunk or mentally ill, probably both, and Mordecai walked him to the kitchen and poured him coffee.

'Some of these poor folks can't resist getting in a line,' he said.

169

Number three was a resident of the shelter, had been for two months, so the address challenge was simpler. She was fifty-eight, clean and neat, and the widow of a veteran. According to the stack of paperwork I rummaged through while my co-counsel talked to her, she was entitled to veteran's benefits. But the checks were being sent to a bank account in Maryland, one she could not access. She explained this. Her paperwork verified it. Mordecai said, 'VA is a good agency. We'll get the checks sent here.'

The line grew as we efficiently worked the clients. Mordecai had seen it all before: food stamps disrupted for lack of a permanent address; a landlord's refusal to refund a security deposit; unpaid child support; an arrest warrant for writing bad checks; a claim for Social Security disability benefits. After two hours and ten clients, I moved to the end of the table and began interviewing them myself. During my first full day as a poverty lawyer, I was on my own, taking notes and acting just as important as my co-counsel.

Marvis was my first solo client. He needed a divorce. So did I. After listening to his tale of sorrow, I felt like racing home to Claire and kissing her feet. Marvis' wife was a prostitute, who at one time had been a decent sort until she discovered crack. The crack led her to a pusher, then to a pimp, then to life on the streets. Along the way, she stole and sold everything they owned and racked up debts he got stuck with. He filed for bankruptcy. She took both kids and moved in with her pimp.

He had a few general questions about the mechanics of divorce, and since I knew only the basics I winged it as best I could. In the midst of my note-taking, I was struck by a vision of Claire sitting in her lawyer's fine office, at that very moment, finalizing plans to dissolve our union.

'How long will it take?' he asked, bringing me out of my brief daydream.

'Six months,' I answered. 'Do you think she will contest it?'

'What do you mean?'

'Will she agree to the divorce?'

'We ain't talked about it.'

The woman had moved out a year earlier, and that sounded like a good case of abandonment to me. Throw in the adultery, and I figured the case was a cinch.

Marvis had been at the shelter for a week. He was clean, sober, and looking for work. I enjoyed the half hour I spent with him, and I vowed to get his divorce.

The morning passed quickly; my nervousness vanished. I was reaching out to help real people with real problems, little people with no other place to go for legal representation. They were intimidated not only by me but also by the vast world of laws and regulations and courts and bureaucracies. I learned to smile, and make them feel welcome. Some apologized for not being able to pay me. Money was not important, I told them. Money was not important.

At twelve, we surrendered our table so lunch could be served. The dining area was crowded; the soup was ready.

Since we were in the neighborhood, we stopped for soul food at the Florida Avenue Grill. Mine was the only white face in the crowded restaurant, but I was coming to terms with my whiteness. No one had tried to murder me yet. No one seemed to care.

Sofia found a phone that happened to be working. It was under a stack of files on the desk nearest the door. I thanked her, and retreated to the privacy of my office. I counted eight people sitting quietly and waiting for Sofia, the nonlawyer, to dispense advice.

171

Mordecai suggested that I spend the afternoon working on the cases we had taken in during the morning at Samaritan. There was a total of nineteen. He also implied that I should work diligently so that I could help Sofia with the traffic.

If I thought the pace would be slower on the street, I was wrong. I was suddenly up to my ears with other people's problems. Fortunately, with my background as a self-absorbed workaholic, I was up to the task.

My first phone call, however, went to Drake & Sweeney. I asked for Hector Palma in real estate, and was put on hold. I hung up after five minutes, then called again. A secretary finally answered, then put me on hold again. The abrasive voice of Braden Chance was suddenly barking in my ear, 'Can I help you?'

I swallowed hard, and said, 'Yes, I was holding for Hector Palma.' I tried to raise my voice and clip my words.

'Who is this?' he demanded.

'Rick Hamilton, an old friend from school.'

'He doesn't work here anymore. Sorry.' He hung up, and I stared at the phone. I thought about calling Polly, and asking her to check around, see what had happened to Hector. It wouldn't take her long. Or maybe Rudolph, or Barry Nuzzo, or my own favorite paralegal. Then I realized that they were no longer my friends. I was gone. I was off-limits. I was the enemy. I was trouble and the powers above had forbidden them to talk to me.

There were three Hector Palmas in the phone book. I was going to call them, but the phone lines were taken. The clinic had two lines, and four advocates.

NINETEEN

I was in no hurry to leave the clinic at the end of my first day. Home was an empty attic, not much larger than any three of the cubbyholes at the Samaritan House. Home was a bedroom with no bed, a living room with cableless TV, a kitchen with a card table and no fridge. I had vague, distant plans to furnish and decorate.

Sofia left promptly at five, her standard hour. Her neighborhood was rough, and she preferred to be home with the doors locked at dark. Mordecai left around six, after spending thirty minutes with me discussing the day. Don't stay too late, he warned, and try to leave in pairs. He had checked with Abraham Lebow, who planned to work until nine, and suggested we leave together. Park close. Walk fast. Watch everything.

'So what do you think?' he asked, pausing by the door on the way out.

'I think it's fascinating work. The human contact is inspiring.'

'It'll break your heart at times.'

'It already has.'

'That's good. If you reach the point where it doesn't hurt, then it's time to quit.'

'I just started.'

'I know, and it's good to have you. We've needed a WASP around here.'

'Then I'm just happy to be a token.'

He left, and I closed the door again. I had detected an unspoken, open-door policy; Sofia worked out in the open, and I had been amused throughout the afternoon as I heard her berate one bureaucrat after another over the phone while the entire clinic listened. Mordecai was an animal on the phone, his deep gravel voice roaring through the air, making all sorts of demands and vile threats. Abraham was much quieter, but his door was always open.

Since I didn't yet know what I was doing, I preferred to keep mine closed. I was sure they would be patient.

I called the three Hector Palmas in the phone book. The first was not the Hector I wanted. The second number was not answered. The third was voice mail for the real Hector Palma; the message was brusque: We're not home. Leave message. We'll return your call.

It was his voice.

With infinite resources, the firm had many ways and places to hide Hector Palma. Eight hundred lawyers, 170 paralegals, offices in Washington, New York, Chicago, L.A., Portland, Palm Beach, London, and Hong Kong. They were too smart to fire him because he knew too much. So they would double his pay, promote him, move him to a different office in a new city with a larger apartment.

I wrote down his address from the phone book. If the voice mail was still working, perhaps he hadn't yet moved. With my newly acquired street savvy, I was sure I could track him down.

There was a slight knock on the door, which opened as it was being tapped. The bolt and knob were worn and wobbly, and the door would shut but it wouldn't

174

catch. It was Abraham. 'Got a minute?' he said, sitting down.

It was his courtesy call, his hello. He was a quiet, distant man with an intense, brainy aura that would have been intimidating except for the fact that I had spent the past seven years in a building with four hundred lawyers of all stripes and sorts. I had met and known a dozen Abrahams, aloof and earnest types with little regard for social skills.

'I wanted to welcome you,' he said, then immediately launched into a passionate justification for public interest law. He was a middle-class kid from Brooklyn, law school at Columbia, three horrible years with a Wall Street firm, four years in Atlanta with an anti-death-penalty group, two frustrating years on Capitol Hill, then an ad in a lawyer's magazine for an advocate's position with the 14th Street Legal Clinic had caught his attention.

'The law is a higher calling,' he said. 'It's more than making money.' Then he delivered another speech, a tirade against big firms and lawyers who rake in millions in fees. A friend of his from Brooklyn was making ten million a year suing breast implant companies from coast to coast. 'Ten million dollars a year! You could house and feed every homeless person in the District!'

Anyway, he was delighted I had seen the light, and sorry about the episode with Mister.

'What, specifically, do you do?' I asked. I was enjoying our talk. He was fiery and bright, with a vast vocabulary that kept me reeling.

'Two things. Policy. I work with other advocates to shape legislation. And I direct litigation, usually class actions. We've sued the Commerce Department because the homeless were grossly underrepresented in the ninety census. We've sued the District school system for refusing to admit homeless children. We've

175

sued as a class because the District wrongfully terminated several thousand housing grants without due
process. We've attacked many of the statutes designed
to criminalize homelessness. We'll sue for almost
anything if the homeless are getting screwed.'

'That's complicated litigation.'

'It is, but, fortunately, here in D.C. we have lots of
very good lawyers willing to donate their time. I'm the
coach. I devise the game plan, put the team together,
then call the plays.'

'You don't see clients?'

'Occasionally. But I work best when I'm in my little
room over there, alone. That's the reason I'm glad
you're here. We need help with the traffic.'

He jumped to his feet; the conversation was over.
We planned our getaway at precisely nine, and he was
gone. In the midst of one of his speeches, I had
noticed he did not have a wedding band.

The law was his life. The old adage that the law was
a jealous mistress had been taken to a new level by
people like Abraham and myself.

The law was all we had.

The district police waited until almost 1 A.M., then
struck like commandos. They rang the doorbell, then
immediately started hitting the door with their fists. By
the time Claire could collect her wits, get out of bed,
and pull something on over her pajamas, they were
kicking the door, ready to smash it in. 'Police!' they
announced after her terrified inquiry. She slowly
opened the door, then stepped back in horror as four
men – two in uniforms and two in suits – rushed in as
if lives were in danger.

'Stand back!' one demanded. She was unable to
speak.

'Stand back!' he screamed at her.

They slammed the door behind them. The leader,

176

Lieutenant Gasko, in a cheap tight suit, stepped forward and jerked from his pocket some folded papers. 'Are you Claire Brock?' he asked, in his worst Columbo impersonation.

She nodded, mouth open.

'I'm Lieutenant Gasko. Where's Michael Brock?'

'He doesn't live here anymore,' she managed to utter. The other three hovered nearby, ready to pounce on something.

There was no way Gasko could believe this. But he didn't have a warrant for arrest, just one authorizing a search. 'I have a search warrant for this apartment, signed by Judge Kisner at five P.M. this afternoon.' He unfolded the papers and held them open for her to see, as if the fine print could be read and appreciated at that moment.

'Please stand aside,' he said. Claire backed up even farther.

'What are you looking for?' she asked.

'It's in the papers,' Gasko said, tossing them onto the kitchen counter. The four fanned out through the apartment.

The cell phone was next to my head, which was resting on a pillow on the floor at the opening of my sleeping bag. It was the third night I'd slept on the floor, part of my effort to identify with my new clients. I was eating little, sleeping even less, trying to acquire an appreciation for park benches and sidewalks. The left side of my body was purple down to the knee, extremely sore and painful, and so I slept on my right side.

It was a small price to pay. I had a roof, heat, a locked door, a job, the security of food tomorrow, the future.

I found the cell phone and said, 'Hello.'

'Michael!' Claire hissed in a low voice. 'The cops are searching the apartment.'

'What?'

'They're here now. Four of them, with a search warrant.'

'What do they want?'

'They're looking for a file.'

'I'll be there in ten minutes.'

'Please hurry.'

I roared into the apartment like a man possessed. Gasko happened to be the first cop I encountered. 'I'm Michael Brock. Who the hell are you?'

'Lieutenant Gasko,' he said with a sneer.

'Let me see some identification.' I turned to Claire, who was leaning on the refrigerator holding a cup of coffee. 'Get me a piece of paper,' I said.

Gasko pulled his badge from his coat pocket, and held it high for me to see.

'Larry Gasko,' I said. 'You'll be the first person I sue, at nine o'clock this morning. Now, who's with you?'

'There are three others,' Claire said, handing me a sheet of paper. 'I think they're in the bedrooms.'

I walked to the rear of the apartment, Gasko behind me, Claire somewhere behind him. I saw a plain-clothes cop in the guest bedroom on all fours peeking under the bed. 'Let me see some identification,' I yelled at him. He scrambled to his feet, ready to fight. I took a step closer, gritted my teeth, and said, 'ID, asshole.'

'Who are you?' he asked, taking a step back, looking at Gasko.

'Michael Brock. Who are you?'

He flipped out a badge. 'Darrell Clark,' I announced loudly as I scribbled it down. 'Defendant number two.'

'You can't sue me,' he said.

'Watch me, big boy. In eight hours, in federal court,

178

I will sue you for a million bucks for an illegal search. And I'll win, and get a judgment, then I'll hound your ass until you file for bankruptcy.'

The other two cops appeared from my old bedroom, and I was surrounded by them.

'Claire,' I said. 'Get the video camera please. I want this recorded.' She disappeared into the living room.

'We have a warrant signed by a judge,' Gasko said, somewhat defensively. The other three took a step forward to tighten the circle.

'The search is illegal,' I said bitterly. 'The people who signed the warrant will be sued. Each of you will be sued. You will be placed on leave, probably without pay, and you will face a civil lawsuit.'

'We have immunity,' Gasko said, glancing at his buddies.

'Like hell you do.'

Claire was back with the camera. 'Did you tell them I didn't live here?' I asked her.

'I did,' she said, and raised the camera to her eye.

'Yet you boys continued the search. At that point it became illegal. You should've known to stop, but of course that wouldn't be any fun, would it? It's much more fun to pilfer through the private things of others. You had a chance, boys, and you blew it. Now you'll have to pay the consequences.'

'You're nuts,' Gasko said. They tried not to show fear – but they knew I was a lawyer. They had not found me in the apartment, so maybe I knew what I was talking about. I did not. But at that moment, it sounded good.

The legal ice upon which I was skating was very thin.

I ignored him. 'Your names please,' I said to the two uniformed cops. They produced badges. Ralph Lilly and Robert Blower. 'Thanks,' I said like a real smart-

179

ass. 'You will be defendants number three and four. Now, why don't you leave.'

'Where's the file?' Gasko asked.

'The file is not here because I don't live here. That's why you're going to get sued, Officer Gasko.'

'Get sued all the time, no big deal.'

'Great. Who's your attorney?'

He couldn't pull forth the name of one in the crucial split-second that followed. I walked to the den, and they reluctantly followed.

'Leave,' I said. 'The file is not here.'

Claire was nailing them with the video, and that kept their bitching to a minimum. Blower mumbled something about lawyers as they shuffled toward the door.

I read the warrant after they were gone. Claire watched me, sipping coffee at the kitchen table. The shock of the search had worn off; she was once again subdued, even icy. She would not admit to being frightened, would not dare seem the least bit vulnerable, and she certainly wasn't about to give the impression that she needed me in any way.

'What's in the file?' she asked.

She didn't really want to know. What Claire wanted was some assurance that it wouldn't happen again.

'It's a long story.' In other words, don't ask. She understood that.

'Are you really going to sue them?'

'No. There are no grounds for a suit. I just wanted to get rid of them.'

'It worked. Can they come back?'

'No.'

'That's good to hear.'

I folded the search warrant and stuck it in a pocket. It covered only one item – the RiverOaks/TAG file, which at the moment was well hidden in the walls of my new apartment along with a copy of it.

'Did you tell them where I live?' I asked.

'I don't know where you live,' she answered. Then there was a space of time during which it would have been appropriate for her to ask where, in fact, I did live. She did not.

'I'm very sorry this happened, Claire.'

'It's okay. Just promise it won't happen again.'

'I promise.'

I left without a hug, a kiss, a touching of any kind. I simply said good night and walked through the door. That was precisely what she wanted.

TWENTY

Tuesday was an intake day at the Community for Creative Non-Violence, or CCNV, by far the largest shelter in the District. Once again Mordecai handled the driving. His plan was to accompany me for the first week, then turn me loose on the city.

My threats and warnings to Barry Nuzzo had fallen on deaf ears. Drake & Sweeney would play hardball, and I wasn't surprised. The predawn raid of my former apartment was a rude warning of what was to come. I had to tell Mordecai the truth about what I'd done.

As soon as we were in the car and moving, I said, 'My wife and I have separated. I've moved out.'

The poor guy was not prepared for such dour news at eight in the morning. 'I'm sorry,' he said, looking at me and almost hitting a jaywalker.

'Don't be. Early this morning, the cops raided the apartment where I used to live, looking for me, and, specifically, a file I took when I left the firm.'

'What kind of file?'

'The DeVon Hardy and Lontae Burton file.'

'I'm listening.'

'As we now know, DeVon Hardy took hostages and got himself killed because Drake & Sweeney evicted him from his home. Evicted with him were sixteen others, and some children. Lontae and her little family were in the group.'

He mulled this over, then said, 'This is a very small city.'

'The abandoned warehouse happened to be on land RiverOaks planned to use for a postal facility. It's a twenty-million-dollar project.'

'I know the building. It's always been used by squatters.'

'Except they weren't squatters, at least I don't think so.'

'Are you guessing? Or do you know for sure?'

'For now, I'm guessing. The file has been tampered with; papers taken, papers added. A paralegal named Hector Palma handled the dirty work, the site visits, and the actual eviction, and he's become my deep throat. He sent an anonymous note informing me that the evictions were wrongful. He provided me with a set of keys to get the file. As of yesterday, he no longer works at the office here in the District.'

'Where is he?'

'I'd love to know.'

'He gave you keys?'

'He didn't hand them to me. He left them on my desk, with instructions.'

'And you used them?'

'Yes.'

'To steal a file?'

'I didn't plan to steal it. I was on my way to the clinic to copy it when some fool ran a red light and sent me to the hospital.'

'That's the file we retrieved from your car?'

'That's it. I was going to copy it, take it back to its little spot at Drake & Sweeney, and no one would have ever known.'

'I question the wisdom of that.' He wanted to call me a dumb-ass, but our relationship was still new.

183

'What's missing from it?' he asked.

I summarized the history of RiverOaks and its race to build the mail facility. 'The pressure was on to grab the land fast. Palma went to the warehouse the first time, and got mugged. Memo to the file. He went again, the second time with a guard, and that memo is missing. It was properly logged into the file, then removed, probably by Braden Chance.'

'So what's in the memo?'

'Don't know. But I have a hunch that Hector inspected the warehouse, found the squatters in their makeshift apartments, talked to them, and learned that they were in fact paying rent to Tillman Gantry. They were not squatters, but tenants, entitled to all the protections under landlord-tenant law. By then, the wrecking ball was on its way, the closing had to take place, Gantry was about to make a killing on the deal, so the memo was ignored and the eviction took place.'

'There were seventeen people.'

'Yes, and some children.'

'Do you know the names of the others?'

'Yes. Someone, Palma I suspect, gave me a list. Placed it on my desk. If we can find those people, then we have witnesses.'

'Maybe. It's more likely, though, that Gantry has put the fear of hell in them. He's a big man with a big gun, fancies himself as a godfather type. When he tells people to shut up, they do so or you find them in a river.'

'But you're not afraid of him, are you, Mordecai? Let's go find him, push him around some; he'll break down and tell all.'

'Spent a lot of time on the streets, have you? I've hired a dumb-ass.'

'He'll run when he sees us.'

The humor wasn't working at that hour. Neither

was his heater, though the fan was blowing at full speed. The car was freezing.

'How much did Gantry get for the building?' he asked.

'Two hundred thousand. He'd bought it six months earlier; there's no record in the file indicating how much he paid for it.'

'Who'd he buy it from?'

'The city. It was abandoned.'

'He probably paid five thousand for it. Ten at the most.'

'Not a bad return.'

'Not bad. It's a step up for Gantry. He's been a nickel and dimer – duplexes and car washes and quick-shop groceries, small ventures.'

'Why would he buy the warehouse and rent space for cheap apartments?'

'Cash. Let's say he pays five thousand for it, then spends another thousand throwing up a few walls and installing a couple of toilets. He gets the lights turned on, and he's in business. Word gets out; renters show up; he charges them a hundred bucks a month, payable only in cash. His clients are not concerned with paperwork anyway. He keeps the place looking like a dump, so if the city comes in he says they're just a bunch of squatters. He promises to kick them out, but he has no plans to. It happens all the time around here. Unregulated housing.'

I almost asked why the city didn't intervene and enforce its laws, but fortunately I caught myself. The answer was in the potholes too numerous to count or avoid; and the fleet of police cars, a third of which were too dangerous to drive; and the schools with roofs caving in; and the hospitals with patients stuffed in closets; and the five hundred homeless mothers and children unable to find a shelter. The city simply didn't work.

And a renegade landlord, one actually getting people off the streets, did not seem like a priority.

'How do you find Hector Palma?' he asked.

'I'm assuming the firm would be smart enough not to fire him. They have seven other offices, so I figure they've got him tucked away somewhere. I'll find him.'

We were downtown. He pointed, and said, 'See those trailers stacked on top of each other. That's Mount Vernon Square.'

It was half a city block, fenced high to hinder a view from the outside. The trailers were different shapes and lengths, some dilapidated, all grungy.

'It's the worst shelter in the city. Those are old postal trailers the government gave to the District, which in turn had the brilliant idea of filling them with homeless. They're packed in those trailers like sardines in a can.'

At Second and D, he pointed to a long, three-story building – home to thirteen hundred people.

The CCNV was founded in the early seventies by a group of war protestors who had assembled in Washington to torment the government. They lived together in a house in Northwest. During their protests around the Capitol, they met homeless veterans of Vietnam, and began taking them in. They moved to larger quarters, various places around the city, and their number grew. After the war, they turned their attention to the plight of the D.C. homeless. In the early eighties, an activist named Mitch Snyder appeared on the scene, and quickly became a passionate and noisy voice for street people.

CCNV found an abandoned junior college, one built with federal money and still owned by the government, and invaded it with six hundred squatters. It became their headquarters, and their home. Various efforts were made to displace them, all to no

186

avail. In 1984, Snyder endured a fifty-one-day hunger strike to call attention to the neglect of the homeless. With his reelection a month away, President Reagan boldly announced his plans to turn the building into a model shelter for the homeless. Snyder ended his strike. Everyone was happy. After the election, Reagan reneged on his promise, and all sorts of nasty litigation ensued.

In 1989, the city built a shelter in Southeast, far away from downtown, and began planning the removal of the homeless from the CCNV. But the city found the homeless to be an ornery lot. They had no desire to leave. Snyder announced that they were boarding up windows and preparing for a siege. Rumors were rampant – eight hundred street people were in there; weapons were stockpiled; it would be a war.

The city backed away from its deadlines, and managed to make peace. The CCNV grew to thirteen hundred beds. Mitch Snyder committed suicide in 1990, and the city named a street after him.

It was almost eight-thirty when we arrived, time for the residents to leave. Many had jobs, most wanted to leave for the day. A hundred men loitered around the front entrance, smoking cigarettes and talking the happy talk of a cold morning after a warm night's rest.

Inside the door on the first level, Mordecai spoke to a supervisor in the 'bubble.' He signed his name and we walked across the lobby, weaving through and around a swarm of men leaving in a hurry. I tried hard not to notice my whiteness, but it was impossible. I was reasonably well dressed, with a jacket and tie. I had known affluence for my entire life, and I was adrift in a sea of black – young tough street men, most of whom had criminal records, few of whom had three dollars in their pockets. Surely one of them would break my neck and take my wallet. I avoided eye

187

contact and frowned at the floor. We waited by the intake room.

'Weapons and drugs are automatic lifetime bans,' Mordecai said, as we watched the men stream down the stairway. I felt somewhat safer.

'Do you ever get nervous in here?' I asked.

'You get used to it.' Easy for him to say. He spoke the language.

On a clipboard next to the door was a sign-up sheet for the legal clinic. Mordecai took it and we studied the names of our clients. Thirteen so far. 'A little below average,' he said. While we waited for the key, he filled me in. 'That's the post office over there. One of the frustrating parts of this work is keeping up with our clients. Addresses are slippery. The good shelters allow their people to send and receive mail.' He pointed to another nearby door. 'That's the clothes room. They take in between thirty and forty new people a week. The first step is a medical exam; tuberculosis is the current scare. Second step is a visit there for three sets of clothes – underwear, socks, everything. Once a month, a client can come back for another suit, so by the end of the year he has a decent wardrobe. This is not junk. They get more clothing donated than they can ever use.'

'One year?'

'That's it. They boot them after one year, which at first may seem harsh. But it isn't. The goal is self-sufficiency. When a guy checks in, he knows he has twelve months to clean up, get sober, acquire some skills, and find a job. Most are gone in less than a year. A few would like to stay forever.'

A man named Ernie arrived with an impressive ring of keys. He unlocked the door to the intake room, and disappeared. We set up our clinic, and were ready to dispense advice. Mordecai walked to the door with the

188

clipboard, and called out the first name: 'Luther Williams.'

Luther barely fit through the door, and the chair popped as he fell into it across from us. He wore a green work uniform, white socks, and orange rubber shower sandals. He worked nights at a boiler room under the Pentagon. A girlfriend had moved out and taken everything, then run up bills. He lost his apartment, and was ashamed to be in the shelter. 'I just need a break,' he said, and I felt sorry for him.

He had a lot of bills. Credit agencies were hounding him. For the moment, he was hiding at CCNV.

'Let's do a bankruptcy,' Mordecai said to me. I had no idea how to do a bankruptcy. I nodded with a frown. Luther seemed pleased. We filled out forms for twenty minutes, and he left a happy man.

The next client was Tommy, who slid gracefully into the room and extended a hand upon which the fingernails had been painted bright red. I shook it; Mordecai did not. Tommy was in drug rehab full-time – crack and heroin – and he owed back taxes. He had not filed a tax return for three years, and the IRS had suddenly discovered his oversights. He also hadn't paid a couple of thousand in back child support. I was somewhat relieved to learn he was a father, of some sort. The rehab was intense – seven days a week – and prevented full-time employment.

'You can't bankrupt the child support, nor the taxes,' Mordecai said.

'Well, I can't work because of the rehab, and if I drop out of rehab then I'll get on drugs again. So if I can't work and can't go bankrupt, then what can I do?'

'Nothing. Don't worry about it until you finish rehab and get a job. Then call Michael Brock here.'

Tommy smiled and winked at me, then floated out of the room.

'I think he likes you,' Mordecai said.

Ernie brought another sign-up sheet with eleven names on it. There was a line outside the door. We embraced the strategy of separation; I went to the far end of the room, Mordecai stayed where he was, and we began interviewing clients two at a time.

The first one for me was a young man facing a drug charge. I wrote down everything so I could replay it to Mordecai at the clinic.

Next was a sight that shocked me: a white man, about forty, with no tattoos, facial scars, chipped teeth, earrings, bloodshot eyes, or red nose. His beard was a week old and his head had been shaved about a month earlier. When we shook hands I noticed his were soft and moist. Paul Pelham was his name, a three-month resident of the shelter. He had once been a doctor.

Drugs, divorce, bankruptcy, and the revocation of his license were all water under his bridge, recent memories but fading fast. He just wanted someone to talk to, preferably someone with a white face. Occasionally, he glanced fearfully down the table at Mordecai.

Pelham had been a prominent gynecologist in Scranton, Pennsylvania – big house, Mercedes, pretty wife, couple of kids. First he abused Valium, then got addicted to harder stuff. He also began sampling the delights of cocaine and the flesh of various nurses in his clinic. On the side, he was a real estate swinger with developments and lots of bank financing. Then he dropped a baby during a routine delivery. It died. Its father, a well-respected minister, witnessed the accident. The humiliation of a lawsuit, more drugs, more nurses, and everything collapsed. He caught herpes from a patient, gave it to his wife, she got everything and moved to Florida.

I was spellbound by his story. With every client I had met so far during my brief career as a homeless lawyer, I had wanted to hear the sad details of how each ended up on the streets. I wanted reassurance that it couldn't happen to me; that folks in my class needn't worry about such misfortune.

Pelham was fascinating because for the first time I could look at a client and say, yes, perhaps that could be me. Life could conspire to knock down just about anyone. And he was quite willing to talk about it.

He hinted that perhaps his trail was not cold. I had listened long enough and was about to ask why, exactly, did he need a lawyer when he said, 'I hid some things in my bankruptcy.'

Mordecai was shuffling clients in and out while the two white boys chatted, so I began taking notes again. 'What kind of things?'

His bankruptcy lawyer had been crooked, he said, then he launched into a windy narrative about how the banks had foreclosed too early and ruined him. His words were soft and low, and each time Mordecai glanced down at us Pelham stopped.

'And there's more,' he said.

'What?' I asked.

'This is confidential, isn't it? I mean, I've used lots of lawyers, but I've always paid them. God knows how I've paid them.'

'It's extremely confidential,' I said earnestly. I may have been working for free, but the payment or nonpayment of fees did not affect the attorney-client privilege.

'You can't tell a soul.'

'Not a word.' It dawned on me that living in a homeless shelter in downtown D.C. with thirteen hundred others would be a wonderful way to hide.

This seemed to satisfy him. 'When I was rolling,' he said, even quieter, 'I found out that my wife was seeing another man. One of my patients told me. When you examine naked women, they'll tell you

191

everything. I was devastated. I hired a private detective, and sure enough, it was true. The other man, well, let's say that he just disappeared one day.' He stopped, and waited for me to respond.

'Disappeared?'

'Yep. Has never been seen since.'

'Is he dead?' I asked, stunned.

He nodded slightly.

'Do you know where he is?'

Another nod.

'How long ago was this?'

'Four years.'

My hand shook as I tried to write down everything. He leaned forward, and whispered, 'He was an FBI agent. An old boyfriend from college – Penn State.'

'Come on,' I said, completely uncertain if he were telling the truth.

'They're after me.'

'Who?'

'The FBI. They've been chasing me for four years.'

'What do you want me to do?'

'I don't know. Maybe cut a deal. I'm tired of being stalked.' I analyzed this for a moment as Mordecai finished with a client and called for another. Pelham watched every move he made.

'I'll need some information,' I said. 'Do you know the agent's name?'

'Yep. I know when and where he was born.'

'And when and where he died.'

'Yep.'

He had no notes or papers with him.

'Why don't you come to my office? Bring the information. We can talk there.'

'Let me think about it,' he said, looking at his watch. He explained that he worked part-time as a janitor in a church, and he was late. We shook hands, and he left.

I was rapidly learning that one of the challenges of being a street lawyer was to be able to listen. Many of my clients just wanted to talk to someone. All had been kicked and beaten down in some manner, and since free legal advice was available, why not unload on the lawyers? Mordecai was a master at gently poking through the narratives and determining if there was an issue for him to pursue. I was still awed by the fact that people could be so poor.

I was also learning that the best case was one that could be handled on the spot, with no follow-up. I had a notebook filled with applications for food stamps, housing assistance, Medicare, Social Security cards, even driver's licenses. When in doubt, we filled out a form.

Twenty-six clients passed through our session before noon. We left exhausted.

'Let's take a walk,' Mordecai said when we were outside the building. The sky was clear, the air cold and windy and refreshing after three hours in a stuffy room with no windows. Across the street was the U.S. Tax Court, a handsome modern building. In fact, the CCNV was surrounded by much nicer structures of more recent construction. We stopped at the corner of Second and D, and looked at the shelter.

'Their lease expires in four years,' Mordecai said. 'The real estate vultures are already circling. A new convention center is planned two blocks over.'

'That'll be a nasty fight.'

'It'll be a war.'

We crossed the street and strolled toward the Capitol.

'That white guy. What's his story?' Mordecai asked.

Pelham had been the only white guy. 'Amazing,' I said, not sure where to start. 'He was once a doctor, up in Pennsylvania.'

'Who's chasing him now?'

'What?'

'Who's chasing him now?'

'FBI.'

'That's nice. Last time it was the CIA.'

My feet stopped moving; his did not. 'You've seen him before?'

'Yeah, he makes the rounds. Peter something or other.'

'Paul Pelham.'

'That changes too,' he said, over his shoulder. 'Tells a great story, doesn't he?'

I couldn't speak. I stood there, watching Mordecai walk away, hands deep in his trench coat, his shoulders shaking because he was laughing so hard.

TWENTY-ONE

When I mustered the courage to explain to Mordecai that I needed the afternoon off, he very brusquely informed me that my standing was equal to the rest, that no one monitored my hours, and that if I needed time off, then I should damned well take it. I left the office in a hurry. Only Sofia seemed to notice.

I spent an hour with the claims adjuster. The Lexus was a total wreck; my company was offering $21,480, with a release so it could then go after the insurer of the Jaguar. I owed the bank $16,000, so I left with a check for $5,000 and change, certainly enough to buy a suitable vehicle, one appropriate to my new position as a poverty lawyer, and one that wouldn't tempt car thieves.

Another hour was wasted in the reception area of my doctor. As a busy attorney with a cell phone and many clients, I stewed as I sat among the magazines and listened to the clock tick.

A nurse made me strip to my boxers, and I sat for twenty minutes on a cold table. The bruises were turning dark brown. The doctor poked and made things worse, then pronounced me good for another two weeks.

I arrived at Claire's lawyer's office promptly at four, and was met by an unsmiling receptionist dressed like a man. Bitchiness resonated from every corner of the place. Every sound was anti-male: the abrupt, husky voice of the gal answering the phone; the sounds of some female country crooner wafting through the speakers; the occasional shrill voice from down the hall. The colors were soft pastel: lavender and pink and beige. The magazines on the coffee table were there to make a statement: hard-hitting female issues, nothing glamorous or gossipy. They were to be admired by the visitors, not read.

Jacqueline Hume had first made a ton of money cleaning out wayward doctors, then had created a fierce reputation by destroying a couple of philandering senators. Her name struck fear into every unhappily married D.C. male with a nice income. I was anxious to sign the papers and leave.

Instead, I was allowed to wait for thirty minutes, and was on the verge of creating a nasty scene when an associate fetched me and led me to an office down the hall. She handed me the separation agreement, and for the first time I saw the reality. The heading was: Claire Addison Brock versus Michael Nelson Brock.

The law required us to be separated for six months before we could be divorced. I read the agreement carefully, signed it, and left. By Thanksgiving I would be officially single again.

My fourth stop of the afternoon was the parking lot of Drake & Sweeney, where Polly met me at precisely five with two storage boxes filled with the remaining souvenirs from my office. She was polite and efficient, but tight-lipped and of course in a hurry. They probably had her wired.

I walked several blocks and stopped at a busy corner. Leaning on a building, I dialed Barry Nuzzo's number. He was in a meeting, as usual. I gave my name, said it was an emergency, and within thirty seconds Barry was on the phone.

196

'Can we talk?' I asked. I assumed the call was being recorded.

'Sure.'

'I'm just down the street, at the corner of K and Connecticut. Let's have coffee.'

'I can be there in an hour.'

'No. It's right now, or forget it.' I didn't want the boys to be able to plot and scheme. No time for wires either.

'Okay, let's see. Yeah, all right. I can do it.'

'I'm at a Bingler's Coffee.'

'I know it.'

'I'm waiting. And come alone.'

'You've been watching too many movies, Mike.'

Ten minutes later, we were sitting in front of the window of a crowded little shop, holding hot coffee and watching the foot traffic on Connecticut.

'Why the search warrant?' I asked.

'It's our file. You have it, we want it back. Very simple.'

'You're not going to find it, okay. So stop the damned searches.'

'Where do you live now?'

I grunted and gave him my best smart-ass laugh. 'The arrest warrant usually follows the search warrant,' I said. 'Is that the way it's going to happen?'

'I'm not at liberty to say.'

'Thanks, pal.'

'Look, Michael, let's start with the premise that you're wrong. You've taken something that's not yours. That's stealing, plain and simple. And in doing so, you've become an adversary of the firm's. I, your friend, still work for the firm. You can't expect me to help you when your actions may be damaging to the firm. You created this mess, not me.'

'Braden Chance is not telling everything. The guy's

197

a worm, an arrogant little jerk who committed mal-practice, and now he's trying to cover his ass. He wants you to think it's a simple matter of a stolen file and that it's safe to come after me. But the file can humiliate the firm.'

'So what's your point?'

'Lay off. Don't do anything stupid.'

'Like get you arrested?'

'Yeah, for starters. I've been looking over my shoulder all day, and it's no fun.'

'You shouldn't steal.'

'I didn't plan to steal, okay? I borrowed the file. I planned to copy and return it, but I never made it.'

'So you finally admit you have it.'

'Yeah. But I can deny it too.'

'You're playing, Michael, and this is not a game. You're gonna get yourself hurt.'

'Not if you guys lay off. Just for now. Let's have a truce for a week. No more search warrants. No arrests.'

'Okay, and what are you offering?'

'I won't embarrass the firm with the file.'

Barry shook his head and gulped hot coffee. 'I'm not in a position to make deals. I'm just a lowly associate.'

'Is Arthur calling the shots?'

'Of course.'

'Then tell Arthur I'm talking only to you.'

'You're assuming too much, Michael. You're assuming the firm wants to talk to you. Frankly, they don't. They are highly agitated by the theft of the file, and by your refusal to return it. You can't blame them.'

'Get their attention, Barry. This file is front-page news; big bold headlines with noisy journalists follow-ing up with a dozen stories. If I get arrested, I'll go straight to the *Post*.'

'You've lost your mind.'

'Probably so. Chance had a paralegal named Hector Palma. Have you heard of him?'

'No.'

'You're out of the loop.'

'I never claimed to be in.'

'Palma knows too much about the file. As of yesterday, he no longer works where he worked last week. I don't know where he is, but it would be interesting to find out. Ask Arthur.'

'Just give the file back, Michael. I don't know what you're planning to do with it, but you can't use it in court.'

I took my coffee and stepped off the stool. 'A truce for one week,' I said, walking away. 'And tell Arthur to put you in the loop.'

'Arthur doesn't take orders from you,' he snapped at me.

I left quickly, darting through people on the sidewalk, practically running toward Dupont Circle, anxious to leave Barry behind and anyone else they'd sent along to spy.

The Palmas' address, according to the phone book, was an apartment building in Bethesda. Since I was in no hurry and needed to think, I circled the city on the Beltway, bumper to bumper with a million others.

I gave myself fifty-fifty odds of being arrested within the week. The firm had no choice but to come after me, and if Braden Chance was in fact hiding the truth from Arthur and the executive committee, then why not play hardball? There was enough circumstantial evidence of my theft to convince a magistrate to issue an arrest warrant.

The Mister episode had rattled the firm. Chance had been called onto the carpet, grilled at length by the brass, and it was inconceivable that he admitted any deliberate wrongdoing. He lied, and he did so with

199

the hope that he could doctor the file and somehow survive. His victims, after all, were only a bunch of homeless squatters.

How, then, was he able to dispose of Hector so quickly? Money was no object – Chance was a partner. If I had been Chance, I would've offered cash to Hector, cash on one hand with the threat of immediate termination on the other. And I would've called a partner buddy in, say, Denver, and asked for a favor – a quick transfer for a paralegal. It would not have been difficult.

Hector was away, hiding from me and anyone else who came with questions. He was still employed, probably at a higher salary.

Then what about the polygraph? Had it been simply a threat used by the firm against both Hector and myself? Could he have taken the test and passed? I doubted it.

Chance needed Hector to keep the truth hidden. Hector needed Chance to protect his job. At some point, the partner blocked any notion of a polygraph, if in fact it had been seriously considered.

The apartment complex was long and rambling, new sections added as the sprawl moved northward away from the city. The streets around it were packed with fast food, fast gas, video rentals, everything hurried commuters needed to save time.

I parked next to some tennis courts, and began a tour of the various units. I took my time; there was no place to go after this adventure. District cops could be lurking anywhere with a warrant and handcuffs. I tried not to think of the horror stories I'd heard about the city jail.

But one stuck like a cattle brand seared into my memory. Several years earlier, a young Drake & Sweeney associate spent several hours after work on Friday drinking in a bar in Georgetown. As he was trying to get to Virginia, he was arrested on suspicion of driving under the influence. At the police station, he refused a breath test, and was immediately thrown into the drunk tank. The cell was overcrowded; he was the only guy with a suit, the only guy with a nice watch, fine loafers, white face. He accidentally stepped on the foot of a fellow inmate, and he was then beaten to a bloody mess. He spent three months in a hospital getting his face rebuilt, then went home to Wilmington, where his family took care of him. The brain damage was slight, but enough to disqualify him for the rigors of a big firm.

The first office was closed. I trudged along a sidewalk in search of another. The phone address did not list an apartment number. It was a safe complex. There were bikes and plastic toys on the small patios. Through the windows I could see families eating and watching television. The windows were not defended by rows of bars. The cars crammed into the parking lots were of the midsized commuter variety, mostly clean and with all four hubcaps.

A security guard stopped me. Once he determined that I posed no threat, he pointed in the direction of the main office, at least a quarter of a mile away.

'How many units are in this place?' I asked.

'A lot,' he answered. Why should he know the number?

The night manager was a student eating a sandwich, a physics textbook opened before him. But he was watching the Bullets-Knicks game on a small TV. I asked about Hector Palma, and he pecked away on a keyboard. G-134 was the number.

'But they've moved,' he said with a mouthful of food.

'Yeah, I know,' I said. 'I worked with Hector. Friday was his last day. I'm looking for an apartment, and I was wondering if I could see his.'

201

He was shaking his head no before I finished. 'Only on Saturdays, man. We have nine hundred units. And there's a waiting list.'

'I'm gone on Saturday.'

'Sorry,' he said, taking another bite and glancing at the game.

I removed my wallet. 'How many bedrooms?' I asked.

He glanced at the monitor. 'Two.'

Hector had four children. I was sure his new digs were more spacious.

'How much a month?'

'Seven-fifty.'

I took out a one-hundred-dollar bill, which he immediately saw. 'Here's the deal. Give me the key. I'll take a look at the place and be back in ten minutes. No one will ever know.'

'We have a waiting list,' he said again, dropping the sandwich onto a paper plate.

'Is it there in that computer?' I asked, pointing.

'Yeah,' he said, wiping his mouth.

'Then it would be easy to shuffle.'

He found the key in a locked drawer, and grabbed the money. 'Ten minutes,' he said.

The apartment was nearby, on the ground floor of a three-story building. The key worked. The smell of fresh paint escaped through the door before I went inside. In fact, the painting was still in progress; in the living room there was a ladder, drop-cloths, white buckets.

A team of fingerprinters could not have found a trace of the Palma clan. All drawers, cabinets, and closets were bare; all carpets and padding ripped up and gone. Even the tub and toilet bowl stains had been removed. No dust, cobwebs, dirt under the kitchen sink. The place was sterile. Every room had a fresh coat of dull white, except the living room, which was half-finished.

I returned to the office and tossed the key on the counter.

'How about it?' he asked.

'Too small,' I said. 'But thanks anyway.'

'You want your money back?'

'Are you in school?'

'Yes.'

'Then keep it.'

'Thanks.'

I stopped at the door, and asked, 'Did Palma leave a forwarding address?'

'I thought you worked with him,' he said.

'Right,' I said, and quickly closed the door behind me.

TWENTY-TWO

The little woman was sitting against our door when I arrived for work Wednesday morning. It was almost eight; the office was locked; the temperature was below freezing. At first I thought she had parked herself there for the night, using our doorway to battle the wind. But when she saw me approach, she immediately jumped to her feet and said, 'Good morning.'

I smiled, said hello, and started fumbling keys.

'Are you a lawyer?' she asked.

'Yes I am.'

'For people like me?'

I assumed she was homeless, and that was all we asked of our clients. 'Sure. Be my guest,' I said as I opened the door. It was colder inside than out. I adjusted a thermostat, one that, as far as I had been able to determine, was connected to nothing. I made coffee and found some stale doughnuts in the kitchen. I offered them to her, and she quickly ate one.

'What's your name?' I asked. We were sitting in the front, next to Sofia's desk, waiting for the coffee and praying for the radiators.

'Ruby.'

'I'm Michael. Where do you live, Ruby?'

'Here and there.' She was dressed in a gray Georgetown Hoya sweat suit, thick brown socks, dirty white sneakers with no brand name. She was between thirty and forty, rail-thin, and slightly cockeyed.

'Come on,' I said with a smile. 'I need to know where you live. Is it a shelter?'

'Used to live in a shelter, but had to leave. Almost got raped. I got a car.'

I had seen no vehicles parked near the office when I arrived. 'You have a car?'

'Yes.'

'Do you drive it?'

'It don't drive. I sleep in the back.'

I was asking questions without a legal pad, something I was not trained to do. I poured two large paper cups of coffee, and we retreated to my office, where, mercifully, the radiator was alive and gurgling. I closed the door. Mordecai would arrive shortly, and he had never learned the art of a quiet entry.

Ruby sat on the edge of my brown folding client's chair, her shoulders slumped, her entire upper body wrapped around the cup of coffee, as if it might be the last warm thing in life.

'What can I do for you?' I asked, armed with a full assortment of legal pads.

'It's my son, Terrence. He's sixteen, and they've taken him away.'

'Who took him?'

'The city, the foster people.'

'Where is he now?'

'They got him.'

Her answers were short, nervous bursts, quick on the heels of each question. 'Why don't you relax and tell me about Terrence?' I said.

And she did. With no effort at eye contact, and with both hands on the coffee cup, she zipped through her narrative. Several years earlier, she couldn't remember how long, but Terrence was around ten, they were living alone in a small apartment. She was arrested for

205

selling drugs. She went to jail for four months. Terrence went to live with her sister. Upon her release, she collected Terrence, and they began a nightmare existence living on the streets. They slept in cars, squatted in empty buildings, slept under bridges in warm weather, and retreated to the shelters when it was cold. Somehow, she kept him in school. She begged on the sidewalks; she sold her body – 'tricking' as she called it; she peddled a little crack. She did whatever it took to keep Terrence fed, in decent clothes, and in school.

But she was an addict, and couldn't kick the crack. She became pregnant, and when the child was born the city took it immediately. It was a crack baby.

She seemed to have no affection for the baby; only for Terrence. The city began asking questions about him, and mother and child slid deeper into the shadows of the homeless. Out of desperation, she went to a family she had once worked for as a maid, the Rowlands, a couple whose children were grown and away from home. They had a warm little house near Howard University. She offered to pay them fifty dollars a month if Terrence could live with them. There was a small bedroom above the back porch, one she'd cleaned many times, and it would be perfect for Terrence. The Rowlands hesitated at first, but finally agreed. They were good people, back then. Ruby was allowed to visit Terrence for an hour each night. His grades improved; he was clean and safe, and Ruby was pleased with herself.

She rearranged her life around his: new soup kitchens and dinner programs closer to the Rowlands; different shelters for emergencies; different alleys and parks and abandoned cars. She scraped together the money each month, and never missed a nightly visit with her son.

Until she was arrested again. The first arrest was for

prostitution; the second was for sleeping on a park bench in Farragut Square. Maybe there was a third one, but she couldn't remember.

She was rushed to D.C. General once when someone found her lying in a street, unconscious. She was placed in a dry-out tank for addicts, but walked out after three days because she missed Terrence.

She was with him one night in his room when he stared at her stomach and asked if she was pregnant again. She said she thought so. Who was the father? he demanded. She had no idea. He cursed her and yelled so much that the Rowlands asked her to leave.

While she was pregnant, Terrence had little to do with her. It was heartbreaking – sleeping in cars, begging for coins, counting the hours until she could see him, then being ignored for an hour while she sat in a corner of his room watching him do his homework.

Ruby began crying at that point in her story. I made some notes, and listened as Mordecai stomped around the front room, trying to pick a fight with Sofia.

Her third delivery, only a year before, produced another crack baby, one immediately taken by the city. She didn't see Terrence for four days while she was in the hospital recovering from the birth. When she was released, she returned to the only life she knew.

Terrence was an A student, excellent in math and Spanish, a trombone player and an actor in school dramas. He was dreaming of the Naval Academy. Mr. Rowland had served in the military.

Ruby arrived one night for a visit in bad shape. A fight started in the kitchen when Mrs. Rowland confronted her. Harsh words were exchanged; ultimatums thrown down. Terrence was in the middle of it; three against one. Either she got help, or she would be banned from the house. Ruby declared that she would simply take her boy and leave. Terrence said he wasn't going anywhere.

The next night, a social worker from the city was waiting for her with paperwork. Someone had already been to court. Terrence was being taken into foster care. The Rowlands would be his new parents. He had already lived with them for three years. Visitation would be terminated until she underwent rehab and was clean for a period of sixty days.

Three weeks had passed.

'I want to see my son,' she said. 'I miss him so bad.'

'Are you in rehab?' I asked.

She shook her head quickly and closed her eyes.

'Why not?' I asked.

'Can't get in.'

I had no idea how a crack addict off the street got admitted to a recovery unit, but it was time to find out. I pictured Terrence in his warm room, well fed, well dressed, safe, clean, sober, doing his homework under the strict supervision of Mr. and Mrs. Rowland, who had grown to love him almost as much as Ruby did. I could see him eating breakfast at the family table, reciting vocabulary lists over hot cereal as Mr. Rowland ignored the morning paper and grilled him on his Spanish. Terrence was stable and normal, unlike my poor little client, who lived in hell.

And she wanted me to handle their reunion.

'This will take some time, okay,' I said, thoroughly clueless about how long anything would take. In a city where five hundred families waited for a small space in an emergency shelter, there couldn't be many beds available for drug addicts.

'You won't see Terrence until you're drug-free,' I said, trying not to sound pious.

Her eyes watered and she said nothing.

I realized just how little I knew about addiction. Where did she get her drugs? How much did they cost? How many hits and highs each day? How long would it take to dry her out? Then to cure her? What were her chances of kicking a habit she'd had for over a decade?

And what did the city do with all those crack babies?

She had no paperwork, no address, no identification, nothing but a heartbreaking story. She seemed perfectly content sitting in my chair, and I began to wonder how I might ask her to leave. The coffee was gone.

Sofia's shrill voice brought back reality. There were sharp voices around her. As I raced for the door, my first thought was that another nut like Mister had walked in with a gun.

But there were other guns. Lieutenant Gasko was back, again with plenty of help. Three uniformed cops were approaching Sofia, who was bitching unmercifully but to no avail. Two in jeans and sweatshirts were waiting for action. As I walked out of my office, Mordecai walked out of his.

'Hello, Mikey,' Gasko said to me.

'What the hell is this!' Mordecai growled and the walls shook. One of the uniformed cops actually reached for his service revolver.

Gasko went straight for Mordecai. 'It's a search,' he said, pulling out the required papers and flinging them at Mordecai. 'Are you Mr. Green?'

'I am,' he answered, snatching the papers.

'What are you looking for?' I yelled at Gasko.

'Same thing,' he yelled back. 'Give it to us, and we'll be happy to stop.'

'It's not here.'

'What file?' Mordecai asked, looking at the search warrant.

'The eviction file,' I replied.

'Haven't seen your lawsuit,' Gasko said to me. I

209

recognized two of the uniformed cops as Lilly and Blower. 'A lotta big talk,' Gasko said.

'Get the hell outta here!' Sofia barked at Blower as he inched toward her desk.

Gasko was very much in charge. 'Listen, lady,' he said, with his usual sneer. 'We can do this two ways. First, you put your ass in that chair and shut up. Second, we put the cuffs on you and you sit in the back of a car for the next two hours.'

One cop was poking his head into each of the side offices. I felt Ruby ease behind me.

'Relax,' Mordecai said to Sofia. 'Just relax.'

'What's upstairs?' Gasko asked me.

'Storage,' Mordecai replied.

'Your storage?'

'Yes.'

'It's not there,' I said. 'You're wasting your time.'

'Then we'll have to waste it, won't we?'

A prospective client opened the front door, startling those of us inside. His eyes darted quickly around the room, then settled on the three men in uniform. He made a hasty retreat into the safety of the streets.

I asked Ruby to leave too. Then I stepped into Mordecai's office and closed the door.

'Where's the file?' he asked in a low voice.

'It's not here, I swear. This is just harassment.'

'The warrant looks valid. There's been a theft; it's reasonable to assume the file would be with the attorney who stole it.'

I tried to say something lawyerly and bright, some piercing legal nugget that would stop the search cold and send the cops running. But words failed me. Instead, I was embarrassed at having brought the police to nose through the clinic.

'Do you have a copy of the file?' he asked.

'Yes.'

'Have you thought about giving them their original?'

'I can't. That would be an admission of guilt. They don't know for a fact that I have the file. And even if I gave it back, they would know that I had copied it.'

He rubbed his beard and agreed with me. We stepped out of his office just as Lilly missed a step near the unused desk next to Sofia's. An avalanche of files slid onto the floor. Sofia yelled at him; Gasko yelled at her. The tension was quickly moving away from words and in the direction of physical conflict.

I locked the front door so our clients wouldn't see the search. 'Here's the way we'll do it,' Mordecai announced. The cops glared, but they were anxious for some direction. Searching a law office was quite unlike raiding a bar filled with minors.

'The file isn't here, okay. We'll start with that promise. You can look at all the files you want, but you can't open them. That would violate client confidentiality. Agreed?'

The other cops looked at Gasko, who shrugged as if that was acceptable.

We started in my office; all six cops, me, and Mordecai crammed into the tiny room, working hard at avoiding contact. I opened each drawer of my desk, none of which would open unless yanked viciously. At one point I heard Gasko whisper to himself, 'Nice office.'

I removed each file from my cabinets, waved them under Gasko's nose, and returned them to their place. I'd only been there since Monday, so there wasn't much to search.

Mordecai slipped from the room and went to Sofia's desk, where he used the phone. When Gasko declared my office to be officially searched, we left it, just in time to hear Mordecai say into the receiver, 'Yes, Judge, thank you. He's right here.'

His smile showed every tooth as he thrust the phone at Gasko. 'This is Judge Kisner, the gentleman who

211

signed the search warrant. He would like to speak to you.'

Gasko took the phone as if it were owned by a leper. 'This is Gasko,' he said, holding it inches from his head.

Mordecai turned to the other cops. 'Gentlemen, you may search this room, and that's it. You cannot go into the private offices to the sides. Judge's orders.'

Gasko mumbled, 'Yes sir,' and hung up.

We monitored their movements for an hour, as they went from desk to desk – four of them in all, including Sofia's. After a few minutes, they realized the search was futile, and so they prolonged it by moving as slowly as possible. Each desk was covered with files long since closed. The books and legal publications had last been looked at years earlier. Some stacks were covered with dust. A few cobwebs had to be dealt with.

Each file was tabbed, with the case name either typed or hand-printed. Two of the cops wrote down the names of the files as they were called out by Gasko and the others. It was tedious, and utterly hopeless.

They saved Sofia's desk for last. She handled things herself, calling off the name of each file, spelling the simpler ones like Jones, Smith, Williams. The cops kept their distance. She opened drawers just wide enough for a quick peek. She had a personal drawer, which no one wanted to see. I was sure there were weapons in there.

They left without saying good-bye. I apologized to Sofia and Mordecai for the intrusion, and retreated to the safety of my office.

TWENTY-THREE

Number five on the list of evictees was Kelvin Lam, a name vaguely familiar to Mordecai. He once estimated the number of homeless in the District to be around ten thousand. There were at least that many files scattered throughout the 14th Street Legal Clinic. Every name rang a bell with Mordecai.

He worked the circuits, the kitchens and shelters and service providers, the preachers and cops and other street lawyers. After dark we drove downtown to a church wedged between high-priced office buildings and ritzy hotels. In a large basement two levels below, the Five Loaves dinner program was in full swing. The room was lined with folding tables, all surrounded by hungry folks eating and talking. It was not a soup kitchen; the plates were filled with corn, potatoes, a slice of something that was either turkey or chicken, fruit salad, bread. I had not eaten dinner, and the aroma made me hungry.

'I haven't been here in years,' Mordecai said as we stood by the entrance looking down at the dining area. 'They feed three hundred a day. Isn't it wonderful?'

'Where does the food come from?'

'D.C. Central Kitchen, an outfit in the basement of the CCNV. They've developed this amazing system of collecting excess food from local restaurants, not leftovers, but uncooked food that will simply go bad if

213

not used immediately. They have a fleet of refrigerated trucks, and they run all over the city collecting food which they take to the kitchen and prepare, frozen dinners. Over two thousand a day.'

'It looks tasty.'

'It's really quite good.'

A young lady named Liza found us. She was new at Five Loaves. Mordecai had known her predecessor, whom they talked about briefly as I watched the people eat.

I noticed something I should have seen before. There were different levels of homelessness, distinct rungs on the socioeconomic ladder. At one table, six men ate and talked happily about a basketball game they had seen on television. They were reasonably well dressed. One wore gloves while he ate, and except for that, the group could've been sitting in any working-class bar in the city without being immediately branded as homeless. Behind them, a hulking figure with thick sunglasses ate alone, handling the chicken with his fingers. He had rubber boots similar to the ones Mister wore at the time of his death. His coat was dirty and frayed. He was oblivious to his surroundings. His life was noticeably harder than the lives of the men laughing at the next table. They had access to warm water and soap; he couldn't have cared less. They slept in shelters. He slept in parks with the pigeons. But they were all homeless.

Liza did not know Kelvin Lam, but she would ask around. We watched her as she moved through the crowd, speaking to the people, pointing to the wastebaskets in one corner, fussing over an elderly lady. She sat between two men, neither of whom looked at her as they talked. She went to another table, then another.

Most surprisingly, a lawyer appeared, a young associate from a large firm, a pro bono volunteer with

214

the Washington Legal Clinic for the Homeless. He recognized Mordecai from a fund-raiser the year before. We did law talk for a few minutes, then he disappeared into a back room to begin three hours of intake.

'The Washington Legal Clinic has a hundred and fifty volunteers,' Mordecai said.

'Is that enough?' I asked.

'It's never enough. I think we should revive our pro bono volunteer program. Maybe you'd like to take charge and supervise it. Abraham likes the idea.'

It was nice to know that Mordecai and Abraham, and no doubt Sofia too, had been discussing a program for me to run.

'It will expand our base, make us more visible in the legal community, and help with raising money.'

'Sure,' I said, without conviction.

Liza was back. 'Kelvin Lam is in the rear,' she said, nodding. 'Second table from the back. Wearing the Redskins cap.'

'Did you talk to him?' Mordecai asked.

'Yes. He's sober, pretty sharp, said he's been staying at CCNV, works part-time on a garbage truck.'

'Is there a small room we can use?'

'Sure.'

'Tell Lam a homeless lawyer needs to talk to him.'

Lam didn't say hello or offer to shake hands. Mordecai sat at a table. I stood in a corner. Lam took the only available chair, and gave me a look that made my skin crawl.

'Nothing's wrong,' Mordecai said in his best soothing tone. 'We need to ask you a few questions, that's all.'

Not a peep out of Lam. He was dressed like a resident of a shelter – jeans, sweatshirt, sneakers, wool jacket – as opposed to the pungent multilayered garb of one sleeping under a bridge.

'Do you know a woman named Lontae Burton?' Mordecai asked. He would do the talking for us lawyers.

Lam shook his head no.

'DeVon Hardy?'

Another no.

'Last month, were you living in an abandoned warehouse?'

'Yep.'

'At the corner of New York and Florida?'

'Uh-huh.'

'Were you paying rent?'

'Yep.'

'A hundred dollars a month?'

'Yep.'

'To Tillman Gantry?'

Lam froze, and closed his eyes to ponder the question. 'Who?' he asked.

'Who owned the warehouse?'

'I paid rent to some dude named Johnny.'

'Who did Johnny work for?'

'Don't know. Don't care. Didn't ask.'

'How long did you live there?'

"Bout four months.'

'Why did you leave?'

'Got evicted.'

'Who evicted you?'

'I don't know. The cops showed up one day with some other dudes. They yanked us and threw us on the sidewalk. Couple of days later, they bulldozed the warehouse.'

'Did you explain to the cops that you were paying rent to live there?'

'A lot of people were saying that. This one woman with little kids tried to fight with the police, but didn't

216

do no good. Me, I don't fight with cops. It was a bad scene, man.'

'Were you given any paperwork before the eviction?'

'No.'

'Any notice to get out?'

'No. Nothing. They just showed up.'

'Nothing in writing?'

'Nothing. Cops said we were just squatters; had to get out right then.'

'So you moved in last fall, sometime around October.'

'Something like that.'

'How did you find the place?'

'I don't know. Somebody said they were renting little apartments in the warehouse. Cheap rent, you know. So I went over to check it out. They were putting up some boards and walls and things. There was a roof up there, a toilet not far away, running water. It wasn't a bad deal.'

'So you moved in?'

'Right.'

'Did you sign a lease?'

'No. Dude told me that the apartment was illegal, so nothing was in writing. Told me to say I was squatting in case anybody asked.'

'And he wanted cash?'

'Only cash.'

'Did you pay every month?'

'Tried to. He came around on the fifteenth to collect.'

'Were you behind on your rent when you were evicted?'

'A little.'

'How much?'

'Maybe one month.'

'Was that the reason you were evicted?'

'I don't know. They didn't give no reason. They just evicted everybody, all at once.'

'Did you know the other people in the warehouse?'

'I knew a couple. But we kept to ourselves. Each apartment had a good door, one that would lock.'

'This mother you mentioned, the one who fought with the police, did you know her?'

'No. I'd maybe seen her once or twice. She lived on the other end.'

'The other end?'

'Right. There was no plumbing in the middle of the warehouse, so they built the apartments on each end.'

'Could you see her apartment from yours?'

'No. It was a big warehouse.'

'How big was your apartment?'

'Two rooms, I don't know how big.'

'Electricity?'

'Yeah, they ran some wires in. We could plug in radios and things like that. We had lights. There was running water, but you had to use a community toilet.'

'What about heating?'

'Not much. It got cold, but not nearly as cold as sleeping on the street.'

'So you were happy with the place?'

'It was okay. I mean, for a hundred bucks a month it wasn't bad.'

'You said you knew two other people. What are their names?'

'Herman Harris and Shine somebody.'

'Where are they now?'

'I haven't seen them.'

'Where are you staying?'

'CCNV.'

Mordecai pulled a business card from his pocket and handed it to Lam. 'How long will you be there?' he asked.

'I don't know.'

'Can you keep in touch with me?'

'Why?'

'You might need a lawyer. Just call me if you change shelters or find a place of your own.'

Lam took the card without a word. We thanked Liza and returned to the office.

As with any lawsuit, there were a number of ways to proceed with our action against the defendants. There were three of them – RiverOaks, Drake & Sweeney, and TAG, and we did not expect to add more.

The first method was the ambush. The other was the serve and volley.

With the ambush, we would prepare the skeletal framework of our allegations, run to the courthouse, file the suit, leak it to the press, and hope we could prove what we thought we knew. The advantage was surprise, and embarrassment for the defendants, and, hopefully, public opinion. The downside was the legal equivalent of jumping off a cliff with the strong, but unconfirmed, belief that there was a net down there somewhere.

The serve and volley would begin with a letter to the defendants, in which we made the same allegations, but rather than sue we would invite them to discuss the matter. The letters would go back and forth with each side generally able to predict what the other might do. If liability could be proved, then a quiet settlement would probably occur. Litigation could be avoided.

The ambush appealed to Mordecai and myself for two reasons. The firm had shown no interest in leaving me alone; the two searches were clear proof that Arthur on the top floor and Rafter and his band of hard-asses in litigation were coming after me. My arrest would make a nice news story, one they would undoubtedly leak to humiliate me and build pressure. We had to be ready with our own assault.

The second reason went to the heart of our case. Hector and the other witnesses could not be compelled to testify until we filed suit and forced them to give their depositions. During the discovery period that followed the initial filing, we would have the opportunity to ask all sorts of questions of the defendants, and they would be required to answer under oath. We would also be allowed to depose anybody we wanted. If we found Hector Palma, we could grill him under oath. If we tracked down the other evictees, we could force them to tell what happened.

We had to find out what everyone knew, and there was no way to do this without using court-sanctioned discovery.

In theory, our case was really quite simple: The warehouse squatters had been paying rent, in cash with no records, to Tillman Gantry or someone working on his behalf. Gantry had an opportunity to sell the property to RiverOaks, but it had to be done quickly. Gantry lied to RiverOaks and its lawyers about the squatters. Drake & Sweeney, exercising diligence, had sent Hector Palma to inspect the property prior to closing. Hector was mugged on the first visit, took a guard with him on the second, and upon inspecting the premises learned that the residents were, in fact, not squatters, but tenants. He reported this in a memo to Braden Chance, who made the ill-fated decision to disregard it and proceed with the closing. The tenants were summarily evicted as squatters, without due process.

A formal eviction would have taken at least thirty more days, time none of the participants wanted to waste. Thirty days and the worst of winter would be gone; the threat of snowstorms or sub-zero nights would be diminished, along with the need to sleep in a car with the heater running.

They were just street people, with no records, no rent receipts, and no trail to be followed.

It was not a complicated case, in theory. But the hurdles were enormous. Locking in testimony of homeless people could be treacherous, especially if Mr. Gantry decided to assert himself. He ruled the streets, an arena I was not eager to fight in. Mordecai had a vast network built on favors and whispers, but he was no match for Gantry's artillery. We spent an hour discussing various ways to avoid naming TAG, Inc., as a defendant. For obvious reasons, the lawsuit would be far messier and more dangerous with Gantry as a party. We could sue without him, and leave it to his co-defendants – RiverOaks and Drake & Sweeney – to haul him in as a third party.

But Gantry was a contributing cause in our theory of liability, and to ignore him as a defendant would be to ask for trouble as the case progressed.

Hector Palma had to be found. And once we found him, we somehow had to convince him to either produce the hidden memo, or to tell us what was in it. Finding him would be the easy part; getting him to talk might be impossible. He quite likely wouldn't want to, since he needed to keep his job. He'd been quick to tell me he had a wife and four kids.

There were other problems with the lawsuit, the first of which was purely procedural. We, as lawyers, did not have the authority to file suit on behalf of the heirs of Lontae Burton and her four children. We had to be employed by her family, such as it was. With her mother and two brothers in prison, and her father's identity yet to be revealed, Mordecai was of the opinion we should petition the Family Court for the appointment of a trustee to handle the affairs of Lontae's estate. In doing so, we could bypass her

221

family, at least initially. In the event we recovered damages, the family would be a nightmare. It was safe to assume that the four children had two or more different fathers, and each one of those tomcats would have to be notified if money changed hands.

'We'll worry about that later,' Mordecai said. 'We have to win first.' We were in the front, at the desk next to Sofia's where the aging computer worked most of the time. I was typing, Mordecai pacing and dictating.

We plotted until midnight, drafting and redrafting the lawsuit, arguing theories, discussing procedure, dreaming of ways to haul RiverOaks and my old firm into court for a noisy trial. Mordecai saw it as a watershed, a pivotal moment to reverse the decline in public sympathy for the homeless. I saw it simply as a way to correct a wrong.

TWENTY-FOUR

Coffee again with Ruby. She was waiting by the front door when I arrived at seven forty-five, happy to see me. How could anyone be so cheerful after spending eight hours trying to sleep in the backseat of an abandoned car?

'Got any doughnuts?' she asked as I was flipping on the light switches.

It was already a habit.

'I'll see. You have a seat, and I'll make us some coffee.' I rattled around the kitchen, cleaning the coffeepot, looking for something to eat. Yesterday's stale doughnuts were even firmer, but there was nothing else. I made a mental note to buy fresh ones tomorrow, just in case Ruby arrived for the third day in a row. Something told me she would.

She ate one doughnut, nibbling around the hard edges, trying to be polite.

'Where do you eat breakfast?' I asked.

'Don't usually.'

'How about lunch and dinner?'

'Lunch is at Naomi's on Tenth Street. For dinner I go to Calvary Mission over on Fifteenth.'

'What do you do during the day?'

She was curled around her paper cup again, trying to keep her frail body warm.

'Most of the time I stay at Naomi's,' she said.

223

'How many women are there?'

'Don't know. A lot. They take good care of us, but it's just for the day.'

'Is it only for homeless women?'

'Yeah, that's right. They close at four. Most of the women live in shelters, some on the street. Me, I got a car.'

'Do they know you're using crack?'

'I think so. They want me to go to meetings for drunks and people on dope. I'm not the only one. Lots of the women do it too, you know.'

'Did you get high last night?' I asked. The words echoed in my ears. I found it hard to believe I was asking such questions.

Her chin fell to her chest; her eyes closed.

'Tell me the truth,' I said.

'I had to. I do it every night.'

I wasn't about to scold her. I had done nothing since the day before to help her find treatment. It suddenly became my priority.

She asked for another doughnut. I wrapped the last one in foil and topped off her coffee. She was late for something at Naomi's, and off she went.

The march began at the District Building with a rally for justice. Since Mordecai was a Who's Who in the world of the homeless, he left me in the crowd and went to his spot on the platform.

A church choir robed in burgundy and gold got organized on the steps and began flooding the area with lively hymns. Hundreds of police loitered in loose formation up and down the street, their barricades stopping traffic.

The CCNV had promised a thousand of its foot soldiers, and they arrived in a group – one long, impressive, disorganized column of men homeless and proud of it. I heard them coming before I saw them, their well-rehearsed marching yells clear from blocks away. When they rounded the corner, the TV cameras scrambled to greet them.

They gathered intact before the steps of the District Building and began waving their placards, most of which were of the homemade, hand-painted variety. STOP THE KILLINGS; SAVE THE SHELTERS; I HAVE THE RIGHT TO A HOME; JOBS, JOBS, JOBS. The signs were hoisted above their heads, where they danced with the rhythm of the hymns and the cadence of each noisy chant.

Church buses stopped at the barricades and unloaded hundreds of people, many of whom did not appear to be living on the streets. They were nicely dressed church folk, almost all women. The crowd swelled, the space around me shrunk. I did not know a single person, other than Mordecai. Sofia and Abraham were somewhere in the crowd, but I didn't see them. It was billed as the largest homeless march in the past ten years – Lontae's Rally.

A photo of Lontae Burton had been enlarged and mass-produced on large placards, trimmed in black, and under her face were the ominous words: WHO KILLED LONTAE? These were dispersed through the crowd, and quickly became the placard of choice, even among the men from the CCNV who'd brought their own protest banners. Lontae's face bobbed and weaved above the mass of people.

A lone siren wailed in the distance, then grew closer. A funeral van with a police escort was allowed through the barricades and stopped directly in front of the District Building, in the midst of the throng. The rear doors opened; a mock casket, painted black, was removed by the pallbearers – six homeless men who lifted it onto their shoulders and stood ready to begin the procession. Four more caskets, same color and

225

make but much smaller, were removed by more pallbearers.

The sea parted; the procession moved slowly toward the steps as the choir launched into a soulful requiem that almost brought tears to my eyes. It was a death march. One of those little caskets represented Ontario.

Then the crowd pressed together. Hands reached upward and touched the caskets so that they floated along, rocking gently side to side, end to end.

It was high drama, and the cameras packed near the platform recorded every solemn movement of the procession. We would see it replayed on TV for the next forty-eight hours.

The caskets were placed side by side, with Lontae's in the middle, on a small plywood ledge in the center of the steps, a few feet below the platform where Mordecai stood. They were filmed and photographed at length, then the speeches started.

The moderator was an activist who began by thanking all the groups that had helped organize the march. It was an impressive list, at least in quantity. As he rattled off the names, I was pleasantly surprised at the sheer number of shelters, missions, kitchens, coalitions, medical clinics, legal clinics, churches, centers, outreach groups, job-training programs, substance-abuse programs, even a few elected officials – all responsible to some degree for the event.

With so much support, how could there be a homeless problem?

The next six speakers answered that question. Lack of adequate funding to begin with, then budget cuts, a deaf ear by the federal government, a blind eye by the city, a lack of compassion from those with means, a court system grown much too conservative, the list went on and on. And on and on.

The same themes were repeated by each speaker, except for Mordecai, who spoke fifth and silenced the crowd with his story of the last hours of the Burton family. When he told of changing the baby's diaper, probably its last one, there wasn't a sound in the crowd. Not a cough or a whisper. I looked at the caskets as if one actually held the baby.

Then the family left the shelter, he explained, his voice slow, deep, resonating. They went back into the streets, into the snowstorm where Lontae and her children survived only a few more hours. Mordecai took great license with the facts at that point, because no one knew exactly what had happened. I knew this, but I didn't care. The rest of the crowd was equally mesmerized by his story.

When he described the last moments, as the family huddled together in a futile effort to stay warm, I heard women crying around me.

My thoughts turned selfish. If this man, my friend and fellow lawyer, could captivate a crowd of thousands from an elevated platform a hundred feet away, what could he do with twelve people in a jury box close enough to touch?

I realized at that moment that the Burton lawsuit would never get that far. No defense team in its right mind would allow Mordecai Green to preach to a black jury in this city. If our assumptions were correct, and if we could prove them, there would never be a trial.

After an hour and a half of speeches, the crowd was restless and ready to walk. The choir began again, and the caskets were lifted by the pallbearers, who led the procession away from the building. Behind the caskets were the leaders, including Mordecai. The rest of us followed. Someone handed me a Lontae placard, and I held it as high as anyone else.

Privileged people don't march and protest; their world is safe and clean and governed by laws designed to keep them happy. I had never taken to the streets before; why bother? And for the first block or two I felt odd, walking in a mass of people, holding a stick with a placard bearing the face of a twenty-two-year-old black mother who bore four illegitimate children.

But I was no longer the same person I'd been a few weeks earlier. Nor could I go back, even if I'd wanted to. My past had been about money and possessions and status, afflictions that now disturbed me.

And so I relaxed and enjoyed the walk. I chanted with the homeless, rolled and pitched my placard in perfect unison with the others, and even tried to sing hymns foreign to me. I savored my first exercise in civil protest. It wouldn't be my last.

The barricades protected us as we inched toward Capitol Hill. The march had been well planned, and because of its size it attracted attention along the way. The caskets were placed on the steps of the Capitol. We congregated in a mass around them, then listened to another series of fiery speeches from civil rights activists and two members of Congress.

The speeches grew old; I'd heard enough. My homeless brethren had little to do; I had opened thirty-one files since beginning my new career on Monday. Thirty-one real people were waiting for me to get food stamps, locate housing, file divorces, defend criminal charges, obtain disputed wages, stop evictions, help with their addictions, and in some way snap my fingers and find justice. As an antitrust lawyer, I rarely had to face the clients. Things were different on the street.

I bought a cheap cigar from a sidewalk vendor, and went for a short walk on the Mall.

228

TWENTY-FIVE

I knocked on the door next to where the Palmas had lived, and a woman's voice asked, 'Who's there?' There was no effort to unbolt and open. I had thought long and hard about my ploy. I'd even rehearsed it driving to Bethesda. But I was not convinced I could be convincing.

'Bob Stevens,' I said, cringing. 'I'm looking for Hector Palma.'

'Who?' she asked.

'Hector Palma. He used, to live·next door to you.'

'What do you want?'

'I owe him some money. I'm trying to find him, that's all.'

If I were collecting money, or had some other unpleasant mission, then the neighbors would naturally be defensive. I thought this was a nifty little ruse.

'He's gone,' she said flatly.

'I know he's gone. Do you know where he went?'

'No.'

'Did he leave this area?'

'Don't know.'

'Did you see them move?'

Of course the answer was yes; there was no way around it. But instead of being helpful, she withdrew into the depths of her apartment and probably called

229

security. I repeated the question, then rang the doorbell again. Nothing.

So I went to the door on the other side of Hector's last-known address. Two rings, it opened slightly until the chain caught, and a man my age with mayonnaise in the corner of his mouth said, 'What do you want?'

I repeated the Bob Stevens plot. He listened carefully while his kids romped through the living room behind him, a television blasting away. It was after eight, dark and cold, and I'd interrupted a late dinner.

But he was not unpleasant. 'I never knew him,' he said.

'What about his wife?'

'Nope. I travel a lot. Gone most of the time.'

'Did your wife know them?'

'No.' He said this too quickly.

'Did you or your wife see them move?'

'We weren't here last weekend.'

'And you have no idea where they went?'

'None.'

I thanked him, then turned around to meet a beefy security guard, in uniform, holding a billy club with his right hand and tapping it on his left palm, like a street cop in a movie. 'What are you doing?' he snarled.

'Looking for someone,' I said. 'Put that thing away.'

'We don't allow solicitation.'

'Are you deaf? I'm looking for someone, not soliciting.' I walked past him, toward the parking lot.

'We've had a complaint,' he said to my back. 'You need to leave.'

'I'm leaving.'

Dinner was a taco and a beer in a corporate bar not far away. I felt safer eating in the suburbs. The restaurant was of the cookie-cutter variety, a national chain getting rich with shiny new neighborhood watering holes. The crowd was dominated by young government workers, still trying to get home, all talking policy and politics while drinking draft beer and yelling at a game.

Loneliness was an adjustment. My wife and friends had been left behind. Seven years in the sweatshop of Drake & Sweeney had not been conducive to nurturing friendships; or a marriage either, for that matter. At the age of thirty-two, I was ill-prepared for the single life. As I watched the game, and the women, I asked myself if I were expected to return to the bar and nightclub scene to find companionship. Surely there was some other place and method.

I got dejected and left.

I drove slowly into the city, not anxious to arrive at my apartment. My name was on a lease, in a computer somewhere, and I figured the police could find my loft without too much trouble. If they were planning an arrest, I was certain it would happen at night. They would enjoy terrifying me with a midnight knock on the door, a little roughing up as they frisked me and slapped on the cuffs, a shove out the door, down the elevator with death grips under my arms, a push into the rear seat of a squad car for the ride to the city jail where I would be the only young white professional arrested that night. They would like nothing better than to throw me into a holding cell with the usual assortment of thugs, and leave me there to fend for myself.

I carried with me two things, regardless of what I was doing. One was a cell phone, with which to call Mordecai as soon as I was arrested. The other was a folded stack of bills – twenty hundred-dollar bills – to use to make bail and hopefully spring myself before I got near the holding cell.

I parked two blocks away from my building, and

watched every empty car for suspicious characters. I made it to the loft, untouched, unapprehended.

My living room was now furnished with two lawn chairs and a plastic storage box used as a coffee table/ footstool. The television was on a matching storage box. I was amused at the sparse furnishings and determined to keep the place to myself. No one would see how I was living.

My mother had called. I listened to her recording. She and Dad were worried about me, and wanted to come for a visit. They had discussed things with brother Warner, and he might make the trip too. I could almost hear their analysis of my new life. Somebody had to talk some sense into me.

The rally for Lontae was the lead story at eleven. There were close-ups of the five black caskets lying on the steps of the District Building, and later as they were marched down the street. Mordecai was featured preaching to the masses. The crowd appeared larger than I had realized – the estimate was five thousand. The mayor had no comment.

I turned off the television, and punched Claire's number on the phone. We had not talked in four days, and I thought I would show some civility and break the ice. Technically we were still married. It would be nice to have dinner in a week or so.

After the third ring, a strange voice reluctantly said, 'Hello.' It was that of a male.

For a second, I was too stunned to speak. It was eleven-thirty on a Thursday night. Claire had a man over. I had been gone for less than a week. I almost hung up, but then collected myself and said, 'Claire, please.'

'Who's calling?' he asked, gruffly.

'Michael, her husband.'

'She's in the shower,' he said, with a trace of satisfaction.

232

'Tell her I called,' I said, and hung up as quickly as possible.

I paced the three rooms until midnight, then dressed again and went for a walk in the cold. When a marriage crumbles, you ponder all scenarios. Was it a simple matter of growing apart, or was it much more complicated than that? Had I missed the signals? Was he a casual one-nighter, or had they been seeing each other for years? Was he some overheated doctor, married with children, or a young virile med student giving her what she'd missed from me?

I kept telling myself it didn't matter. We weren't divorcing because of infidelities. It was too late to worry if she'd been sleeping around.

The marriage was over, plain and simple. For whatever reason. She could go to hell for all I cared. She was done, dismissed, forgotten. If I was free to chase the ladies, then the same rules applied to her.

Yeah, right.

At 2 A.M., I found myself at Dupont Circle, ignoring catcalls from the queers and stepping around men bundled in layers and quilts and sleeping on benches. It was dangerous, but I didn't care.

A few hours later, I bought a box of a dozen assorted at a Krispy Kreme, with two tall coffees and a newspaper. Ruby was waiting faithfully at the door, shivering from the cold. Her eyes were redder than usual, her smile was not as quick.

Our spot was a desk in the front, the one with the fewest stacks of long-forgotten files. I cleared the top of the desk, and served the coffee and doughnuts. She didn't like chocolate, but instead preferred the ones with the fruit filling.

'Do you read the newspaper?' I asked as I unfolded it.

'No.'

'How well do you read?'

'Not good.'

So I read it to her. We started with the front page, primarily because it had a large photo of the five caskets seemingly adrift above the mass of people. The story was headlined across the bottom half, and I read every word of it to Ruby, who listened intently. She had heard stories about the deaths of the Burton family; the details fascinated her.

'Could I die like that?' she asked.

'No. Not unless your car has an engine and you run the heater.'

'I wish it had a heater.'

'You could die from exposure.'

'What's that?'

'Freezing to death.'

She wiped her mouth with a napkin, and sipped her coffee. The temperature had been eleven degrees the night Ontario and his family died. How had Ruby survived?

'Where do you go when it gets real cold?' I asked.

'Don't go nowhere.'

'You stay in the car?'

'Yes.'

'How do you keep from freezing?'

'I got plenty of blankets. I just bury down in them.'

'You never go to a shelter?'

'Never.'

'Would you go to a shelter if it would help you see Terrence?'

She rolled her head to one side, and gave me a strange look. 'Say it again,' she said.

'You want to see Terrence, right?'

'Right.'

'Then you have to get clean. Right?'

'Right.'

234

'To get clean, you'll have to live in a detox center for a while. Is that something you're willing to do?'

'Maybe,' she said. 'Just maybe.'

It was a small step, but not an insignificant one.

'I can help you see Terrence again, and you can be a part of his life. But you have to get clean, and stay clean.'

'How do I do it?' she asked, her eyes unable to meet mine. She cradled her coffee, the steam rising to her face.

'Are you going to Naomi's today?'

'Yes.'

'I talked to the director over there. They have two meetings today, alcoholics and drug addicts together. They're called AA/NA. I want you to attend both of them. The director will call me.'

She nodded like a scolded child. I would push no further, not at that moment. She nibbled her doughnuts, sipped her coffee, and listened with rapt attention as I read one news story after another. She cared little for foreign affairs and sports, but the city news fascinated her. She had voted at one time, many years ago, and the politics of the District were easily digested. She understood the crime stories.

A long editorial blistered Congress and the city for their failure to fund services for the homeless. Other Lontaes would follow, it warned. Other children would die in our streets, in the shadows of the U.S. Capitol. I paraphrased this for Ruby, who concurred with every phrase.

A soft, freezing rain began falling, so I drove Ruby to her next stop for the day. Naomi's Women's Center was a four-level rowhouse on Tenth Street, NW, in a block of similar structures. It opened at seven, closed at four, and during each day provided food, showers, clothing, activities, and counseling for any homeless woman who could find the place. Ruby was a regular, and received a warm greeting from her friends when we entered.

I spoke quietly with the director, a young woman named Megan. We conspired to push Ruby toward sobriety. Half the women there were mentally ill, half were substance abusers, a third were HIV-positive. Ruby, as far as Megan knew, carried no infectious diseases.

When I left, the women were crowded into the main room, singing songs.

I was hard at work at my desk when Sofia knocked on my door and entered before I could answer.

'Mordecai says you're looking for someone,' she said. She held a legal pad, ready to take notes.

I thought for a second, then remembered Hector. 'Oh yes. I am.'

'I can help. Tell me everything you know about the person.' She sat down and began writing as I rattled off his name, address, last known place of employment, physical description, and the fact that he had a wife and four kids.

'Age?'

'Maybe thirty.'

'Approximate salary?'

'Thirty-five thousand.'

'With four kids, it's safe to assume at least one was enrolled in school. With that salary, and living in Bethesda, I doubt if they'd go the private route. He's Hispanic, so he's probably Catholic. Anything else?'

I couldn't think of a thing. She left and returned to her desk where she opened a thick three-ring notebook and flipped pages. I kept my door open so I could watch and listen. The first call went to someone with the Postal Service. The conversation changed instantly to Spanish, and I was lost. One call followed another. She would say hello in English, ask for her contact, then switch to her native tongue. She called the Catholic diocese, which led to another series of rapid calls. I lost interest.

An hour later, she walked to my door and announced, 'They moved to Chicago. Do you need an address?'

'How did you . . . ?' My words trailed off as I stared at her in disbelief.

'Don't ask. A friend of a friend in their church. They moved over the weekend, in a hurry. Do you need their new address?'

'How long will it take?'

'It won't be easy. I can point you in the right direction.'

She had at least six clients sitting along the front window waiting to seek her advice. 'Not now,' I said. 'Maybe later. Thanks.'

'Don't mention it.'

Don't mention it. I'd planned to spend a few more hours after dark knocking on the doors of neighbors, in the cold, dodging security guards, hoping no one shot me. And she worked the phone for an hour and found the missing person.

Drake & Sweeney had more than a hundred lawyers in its Chicago branch. I had been there twice on antitrust cases. The offices were in a skyscraper near the lakefront. The building's foyer was several stories tall, with fountains and shops around the perimeter, escalators zigzagging upward. It was the perfect place to hide and watch for Hector Palma.

TWENTY-SIX

The homeless are close to the streets, to the pavement, the curbs and gutters, the concrete, the litter, the sewer lids and fire hydrants and wastebaskets and bus stops and storefronts. They move slowly over familiar terrain, day after day, stopping to talk to each other because time means little, stopping to watch a stalled car in traffic, a new drug dealer on a corner, a strange face on their turf. They sit on their sidewalks hidden under hats and caps and behind drugstore sunshades, and like sentries they observe every movement. They hear the sounds of the street, they absorb the odors of diesel fumes from city buses and fried grease from cheap diners. The same cab passes twice in an hour, and they know it. A gun is fired in the distance, and they know where it came from. A fine auto with Virginia or Maryland plates is parked at the curb, they'll watch it until it leaves.

A cop with no uniform waits in a car with no markings, and they see it.

'The police are out there,' one of our clients said to Sofia. She walked to the front door, looked southeast on Q, and there she saw what appeared to be an unmarked police car. She waited half an hour, and checked it again. Then she went to Mordecai.

I was oblivious because I was fighting with the food

238

stamp office on one front and the prosecutor's office on another. It was Friday afternoon, and the city bureaucracy, substandard on a good day, was shutting down fast. They delivered the news together.

'I think the cops might be waiting,' Mordecai announced solemnly.

My first reaction was to duck under the desk, but, of course, I did not. I tried to appear calm. 'Where?' I asked, as if it mattered.

'At the corner. They've been watching the building for more than a half hour.'

'Maybe they're coming after you,' I said. Ha-ha. Stone faces all around.

'I've called,' Sofia said. 'And there's a warrant for your arrest. Grand larceny.'

A felony! Prison! A handsome white boy thrown into the pit. I shifted weight from one side to another, and I tried my best to show no fear.

'That's no surprise,' I said. Happened all the time. 'Let's get it over with.'

'I have a call in for a guy at the prosecutor's office,' Mordecai said. 'It would be nice if they allowed you to turn yourself in.'

'That would be nice,' I said as if it didn't really matter. 'But I've been talking to the prosecutor's office all afternoon. No one's listening.'

'They have two hundred lawyers,' he said.

Mordecai did not make friends on that side of the street. Cops and prosecutors were his natural enemies.

A quick game plan was devised. Sofia would call a bail bondsman, who would meet us at the jail. Mordecai would try to find a friendly judge. What was not said was the obvious – it was Friday afternoon. I might not survive a weekend in the city jail.

They left to make their calls, and I sat at my desk, petrified, unable to move or think or do anything but listen for the squeaking of the front door. I didn't have to wait long. At precisely 4 P.M., Lieutenant Gasko entered with a couple of his men behind him.

During my first encounter with Gasko, when he was searching Claire's apartment, when I was ranting and taking names and threatening all sorts of vile litigation against him and his buddies, when every word uttered by him was met with a caustic retort from me, when I was a hard-charging lawyer and he was a lowly cop, it never occurred to me that he one day might have the pleasure of arresting me. But there he was, swaggering like an aging jock, somehow sneering and smiling at the same time, holding yet more papers, folded and just waiting to be slapped against my chest.

'I need to see Mr. Brock,' he said to Sofia, and about that time I walked into the front room, smiling.

'Hello, Gasko,' I said. 'Still looking for that file?'

'Nope. Not today.'

Mordecai appeared from his office. Sofia was standing at her desk. Everybody looked at everybody. 'You got a warrant?' Mordecai asked.

'Yep. For Mr. Brock here,' Gasko said.

I shrugged and said, 'Let's go.' I moved toward Gasko. One of the goons unsnapped a pair of handcuffs from his waist. I was determined to at least look cool.

'I'm his lawyer,' Mordecai said. 'Let me see that.' He took the arrest warrant from Gasko and examined it as I was getting cuffed, hands behind my back, wrists pinched by cold steel. The cuffs were too tight, or at least tighter than they had to be, but I could bear it and I was determined to be nonchalant.

'I'll be happy to take my client to the police station,' Mordecai said.

'Gee thanks,' Gasko said. 'But I'll save you the trouble.'

'Where will he go?'

'Central.'

240

'I'll follow you there,' Mordecai said to me. Sofia was on the phone, and that was even more comforting than knowing that Mordecai would be somewhere behind me.

Three of our clients saw it all; three harmless street gentlemen in for a quick word with Sofia. They were sitting where the clients always waited, and when I walked by them they watched in disbelief.

One of the goons squeezed my elbow and yanked me through the front door, and I stepped onto the sidewalk anxious to duck into their car: a dirty unmarked white one parked at the corner. The homeless saw it all – the car moving into position, the cops rushing in, the cops coming out with me handcuffed.

'A lawyer got arrested,' they would soon whisper to each other, and the news would race along the streets.

Gasko sat in the rear with me. I stayed low in the seat, eyes watching nothing, the shock settling in.

'What a waste of time,' Gasko said as he relaxed by placing a cowboy boot on a knee. 'We got a hundred and forty unsolved murders in this city, dope on every corner, drug dealers selling in middle schools, and we gotta waste time on you.'

'Are you trying to interrogate me, Gasko?' I asked.

'No.'

'Good.' He hadn't bothered with the Miranda warning, and he didn't have to until he started asking questions.

Goon One was flying south on Fourteenth, no lights or sirens, and certainly no respect for traffic signals and pedestrians.

'Then let me go,' I said.

'If it's up to me, I would. But you really pissed some folks off. The prosecutor tells me he's under pressure to get you.'

'Pressure from who?' I asked. But I knew the

answer. Drake & Sweeney wouldn't waste time with the cops; they would rather talk legalspeak with the chief prosecutor.

'The victims,' Gasko said with heavy sarcasm. I agreed with his assessment; it was difficult to picture a bunch of wealthy lawyers as victims of a crime.

Lots of famous people had been arrested. I tried to recall them. Martin Luther King went to jail several times. There were Boesky and Milken and other noted thieves whose names escaped me. And what about all those famous actors and athletes caught driving drunk and picking up prostitutes and possessing coke? They had been thrown into the backseats of police cars and led away like common criminals. There was a judge from Memphis serving life; an acquaintance from college in a halfway house; a former client in the federal pen for tax evasion. All had been arrested, led downtown, booked, fingerprinted, and had their pictures taken with the little number under their chins. And all had survived.

I suspected that even Mordecai Green had felt the cold clasp of handcuffs.

There was an element of relief because it was finally happening. I could stop running, and hiding, and looking to see if anyone was behind me. The waiting was over. And it was not a midnight raid, one that would certainly keep me in jail until morning. Instead, the hour was manageable. With luck, I could get processed and bailed out before the weekend rush hit.

But there was also an element of horror, a fear I had never felt in my life. Many things could go wrong at the city jail. Paperwork might get lost. Delays of a dozen varieties could be created. Bail could be postponed until Saturday, or Sunday, or even Monday. I could be placed in a crowded cell with unfriendly to nasty people.

Word would leak that I had been arrested. My

242

friends would shake their heads and wonder what else I could do to screw up my life. My parents would be devastated. I wasn't sure about Claire, especially now that the gigolo was keeping her company.

I closed my eyes and tried to get comfortable, which I found impossible to do while sitting on my hands.

The processing was a blur; surreal movements from one point to the next with Gasko leading me like a lost puppy. Eyes on the floor, I kept telling myself. Don't look at these people. Inventory first, everything from the pockets, sign a form. Down the dirty hall to Photos, shoes off, up against the measuring tape, don't have to smile if you don't want to, but please look at the camera. Then a profile. Then to Fingerprinting, which happened to be busy, so Gasko handcuffed me like a mental patient to a chair in the hall while he went to find coffee. Arrestees shuffled past, all in various stages of processing. Cops everywhere. A white face, not a cop but a defendant much like myself – young, male, handsome navy suit, obviously drunk with a bruise on his left cheek. How does one get plastered before 5 P.M. on a Friday? He was loud and threatening, his words garbled and harsh, and ignored by everyone I could see. Then he was gone. Time passed and I began to panic. It was dark outside, the weekend had started, crime would begin and the jail would get busier. Gasko came back, took me into Fingerprinting, and watched as Poindexter efficiently applied the ink and stuck my fingers to the sheets.

No phone calls were needed. My lawyer was somewhere close by, though Gasko hadn't seen him. The doors got heavier as we descended into the jail. We were going in the wrong direction; the street was back behind us.

'Can't I make bail?' I finally asked. I saw bars ahead; bars over windows and busy guards with guns.

243

'I think your lawyer's working on it,' Gasko said.

He gave me to Sergeant Coffey, who pushed me against a wall, kicked my legs apart, and frisked me as if searching for a dime. Finding none, he pointed and grunted at a metal detector, which I walked through, without offense. A buzzer, a door slid open, a hallway appeared, one with rows of bars on both sides. A door clanged behind me, and my prayer for an easy release vanished.

Hands and arms protruded through the bars, into the narrow hall. The men watched us as we moved past. My gaze returned to my feet. Coffey looked into each cell; I thought he was counting bodies. We stopped at the third one on the right.

My cellmates were black, all much younger than I was. I counted four at first, then saw a fifth lying on the top bunk. There were two beds, for six people. The cell was a small square with three walls of nothing but bars, so I could see the prisoners next door and across the hall. The rear wall was cinder block with a small toilet in one corner.

Coffey slammed the door behind me. The guy on the top bunk sat up and swung his legs over the side, so that they dangled near the face of a guy sitting on the bottom bunk. All five glared at me as I stood by the door, trying to appear calm and unafraid, trying desperately to find a place to sit on the floor so that I wouldn't be in danger of touching any of my cellmates.

Thank God they had no weapons. Thank God someone installed the metal detector. They had no guns and knives; I had no assets, other than clothing. My watch, wallet, cell phone, cash – and everything else I had with me – had been taken and inventoried.

The front of the cell would be safer than the rear. I ignored their eyes and took my spot on the floor, my back resting on the door. Down the hall, someone was yelling for a guard.

A fight broke out two cells away, and through the bars and bunks I could see the drunk guy with the white face and navy suit pinned in a corner by two large black men who were pounding his head. Other voices encouraged them on and the entire wing grew rowdy. It was not a good moment to be white.

A shrill whistle, a door opened, and Coffey was back, nightstick in hand. The fight ended abruptly with the drunk on his stomach and still. Coffey went to the cell, and inquired as to what happened. No one knew; no one had seen a thing.

'Keep it quiet!' he demanded, then left.

Minutes passed. The drunk began to groan; someone was vomiting in the distance. One of my cellmates got to his feet, and walked to where I was sitting. His bare feet barely touched my leg. I glanced up, then away. He glared down, and I knew this was the end.

'Nice jacket,' he said.

'Thanks,' I mumbled, trying not to sound sarcastic, or in any way provocative. The jacket was a navy blazer, an old one that I wore every day with jeans and khakis – my radical attire. It certainly wasn't worth being slaughtered over.

'Nice jacket,' he said again, and he added a slight nudge with his foot. The guy on the top bunk jumped down, and stepped closer for a better look.

'Thanks,' I said again.

He was eighteen or nineteen, lean and tall, not an ounce of fat, probably a gang member who'd spent his life on the streets. He was cocky and anxious to impress the others with his bravado.

Mine would be the easiest ass he'd ever kicked.

'I don't have a jacket that nice,' he said. A firmer nudge with his foot, one intended to provoke.

Shouldn't be a low-life street punk, I thought. He

couldn't steal it because there was no place to run. 'Would you like to borrow it?' I asked, without looking up.

'No.'

I pulled my feet in so that my knees were close to my chin. It was a defensive position. When he kicked or swung, I was not going to fight back. Any resistance would immediately bring in the other four, and they would have a delightful time thrashing the white boy.

'Dude says you got a nice jacket,' said the one from the top bunk.

'And I said thanks.'

'Dude says he ain't got no jacket that nice.'

'So what am I supposed to do?' I asked.

'A gift would be appropriate.'

A third one stepped forward and closed the semi-circle around me. The first one kicked my foot, and all inched closer. They were ready to pounce, each waiting for the other, so I quickly removed my blazer and thrust it forward.

'Is this a gift?' the first one asked, taking it.

'It's whatever you want it to be,' I said. I was looking down, still avoiding eye contact; thus, I didn't see his foot. It was a vicious kick that slapped my left temple and jerked my head backward where it cracked against the bars. 'Shit!' I yelled as I felt the back of my head.

'You can have the damned thing,' I said, bracing for the onslaught.

'Is it a gift?'

'Yes.'

'Thanks, man.'

'Don't mention it,' I said, rubbing my face. My entire head was numb.

They backed away, leaving me curled in a tight ball.

Minutes passed, though I had no concept of time. The drunk white guy two doors down was making an effort to revive himself, and another voice was calling for a guard. The punk with my jacket did not put it on. The cell swallowed it.

My face throbbed, but there was no blood. If I received no further injuries as an inmate, I would consider myself lucky. A comrade down the hall yelled something about trying to sleep, and I began to ponder what the night might bring. Six inmates, two very narrow beds. Were we expected to sleep on the floor, with no blanket and pillow?

The floor was getting cold, and as I sat on it I glanced at my cellmates and speculated as to what crimes they had committed. I, of course, had borrowed a file with every intention of returning it. Yet there I was, low man on the pole among drug dealers, car thieves, rapists, probably even murderers.

I wasn't hungry, but I thought about food. I had no toothbrush. I didn't need the toilet, but what would happen when I did? Where was the drinking water? The basics became crucial.

'Nice shoes,' a voice said, startling me. I looked up to see another one of them standing above me. He wore dirty white socks, no shoes, and his feet were several inches longer than mine.

'Thanks,' I said. The shoes in question were old Nike cross-trainers. They were not basketball shoes, and should not have appealed to my cellmate. For once, I wished I'd been wearing the tasseled loafers from my previous career.

'What size?' he asked.

'Tens.'

The punk who took my jacket walked closer; the message was given and received.

'Same size I wear,' the first one said.

'Would you like to have these?' I said. I immediately began unlacing them. 'Here, I would like to present you with a gift of my shoes.' I quickly kicked them off, and he took them.

What about my jeans and underwear? I wanted to ask.

Mordecai finally broke through around 7 P.M. Coffey fetched me from the cell, and as we made our way toward the front, he asked, 'Where are your shoes?'

'In the cell,' I said. 'They were taken.'

'I'll get them.'

'Thanks. I had a navy blazer too.'

He looked at the left side of my face where the corner of my eye was beginning to swell. 'Are you okay?'

'Wonderful. I'm free.'

My bail was ten thousand dollars. Mordecai was waiting with the bondsman. I paid him a thousand in cash, and signed the paperwork. Coffey brought my shoes and blazer, and my incarceration was over. Sofia waited outside with her car, and they whisked me away.

TWENTY-SEVEN

Strictly in physical terms, I was paying a price for my journey from the tower to the street. The bruises from the car wreck were almost gone, but the soreness in the muscles and joints would take weeks. I was losing weight, for two reasons – I couldn't afford the restaurants I'd once taken for granted; and I'd lost interest in food. My back ached from sleeping on the floor in a sleeping bag, a practice I was determined to pursue in an effort to see if it would ever become tolerable. I had my doubts.

And then a street punk almost cracked my skull with his bare foot. I iced it until late, and every time I awoke during the night it seemed to be expanding.

But I felt lucky to be alive, lucky to be in one piece after descending into hell for a few hours before being rescued. The fear of the unknown had been removed, at least for the present. There were no cops lurking in the shadows.

Grand larceny was nothing to laugh at, especially since I was guilty. The maximum was ten years in prison. I would worry about it later.

I left my apartment just before sunrise, Saturday, in a rush to find the nearest newspaper. My new neighborhood coffee shop was a tiny all-night bakery run by a rowdy family of Pakistanis on Kalorama, in a section of Adams-Morgan that could go from safe to treacherous in one small block. I sidled up to the counter and ordered a large latte. Then I opened the newspaper and found the one little story I'd lost sleep over.

My friends at Drake & Sweeney had planned it well. On page two of Metro, there was my face, in a photo taken a year earlier for a recruiting brochure the firm had developed. Only the firm had the negative.

The story was four paragraphs, brief, to the point, and filled primarily with information fed to the reporter by the firm. I had worked there for seven years, in antitrust, law school at Yale, no prior criminal record. The firm was the fifth-largest in the country – eight hundred lawyers, eight cities, and so on. No one got quoted, because no quotes were necessary. The sole purpose of the story was to humiliate me, and to that end it worked well. LOCAL ATTORNEY ARRESTED FOR GRAND LARCENY read the headline next to my face. 'Items taken' was the description of the stolen loot. Items taken during my recent departure from the firm.

It sounded like a silly little spat – a bunch of lawyers quibbling over nothing but paperwork. Who would care, other than myself and anyone who might know me? The embarrassment would quickly go away; there were too many real stories in the world.

The photo and the background had found a friendly reporter, one willing to process his four paragraphs and wait until my arrest could be confirmed. With no effort whatsoever, I could see Arthur and Rafter and their team spending hours planning my arrest and its aftermath, hours that no doubt would be billed to RiverOaks, only because it happened to be the client nearest the mess.

What a public relations coup! Four paragraphs in the Saturday edition.

The Pakistanis didn't bake fruit-filled doughnuts. I

bought oatmeal cookies instead, and drove to the office.

Ruby was asleep in the doorway, and as I approached I wondered how long she had been there. She was covered with two or three old quilts, and her head rested on a large canvas shopping bag, packed with her belongings. She sprang to her feet after I coughed and made noise.

'Why are you sleeping here?' I asked.

She looked at the paper bag of food, and said, 'I gotta sleep somewhere.'

'I thought you slept in a car.'

'I do. Most of the time.'

Nothing productive would come from a conversation with a homeless person about why she slept here or there. Ruby was hungry. I unlocked the door, turned on lights, and went to make coffee. She, according to our ritual, went straight to what had become her desk and waited.

We had coffee and cookies with the morning news. We alternated stories – I read one I wanted, then one that was of interest to her. I ignored the one about me.

Ruby had walked out of the AA/NA meeting the afternoon before at Naomi's. The morning session had gone without incident, but she had bolted from the second one. Megan, the director, had called me about an hour before Gasko made his appearance.

'How do you feel this morning?' I asked when we finished the paper.

'Fine. And you?'

'Fine. I'm clean. Are you?'

Her chin dropped an inch; her eyes cut to one side, and she paused just long enough for the truth. 'Yes,' she said. 'I'm clean.'

'No you're not. Don't lie to me, Ruby. I'm your friend, and your lawyer, and I'm going to help you see

Terrence. But I can't help you if you lie to me. Now, look me in the eyes, and tell me if you're clean.'

She somehow managed to shrink even more, and with her eyes on the floor, she said, 'I'm not clean.'

'Thank you. Why did you walk out of the AA/NA meeting yesterday afternoon?'

'I didn't.'

'The director said you did.'

'I thought they was through.'

I was not going to be sucked into an argument I couldn't win. 'Are you going to Naomi's today?'

'Yes.'

'Good. I'll take you, but you have to promise me you'll go to both meetings.'

'I promise.'

'You have to be the first one in the meetings, and the last one to leave, okay?'

'Okay.'

'And the director will be watching.'

She nodded and took another cookie, her fourth. We talked about Terrence, and rehab and getting clean, and again I began to feel the hopelessness of addiction. She was overwhelmed by the challenge of staying clean for just twenty-four hours.

The drug was crack, as I suspected. Instantly addictive and dirt cheap.

As we drove to Naomi's, Ruby suddenly said, 'You got arrested, didn't you?'

I almost ran a red light. She was sleeping on the office doorstep at sunrise; she was barely literate. How could she have seen the newspaper?

'Yes, I did.'

'Thought so.'

'How did you know?'

'You hear stuff on the street.'

Ah, yes. Forget papers. The homeless carry their own news. That young lawyer down at Mordecai's got himself arrested. Cops hauled him away, just like he was one of us.

'It's a misunderstanding,' I said, as if she cared.

They'd started singing without her; we could hear them as we walked up the steps to Naomi's. Megan unlocked the front door, and invited me to stay for coffee. In the main room on the first level, in what was once a fine parlor, the ladies of Naomi's sang and shared and listened to each other's problems. We watched them for a few minutes. As the only male, I felt like an intruder.

Megan poured coffee in the kitchen, and gave me a quick tour of the place. We whispered, because the ladies were praying not far away. There were rest rooms and showers on the first floor near the kitchen; a small garden out back where those suffering from depression often went to be alone. The second floor was offices, intake centers, and a rectangular room crammed with chairs where the Alcoholics Anonymous/Narcotics Anonymous chapters met together.

As we climbed the narrow stairs, a joyous chorus erupted from below. Megan's office was on the third floor. She invited me in, and as soon as I sat down she tossed a copy of the *Post* into my lap.

'Rough night, huh?' she said with a smile.

I looked at my photo again. 'It wasn't too bad.'

'What's this?' she asked, pointing to her temple.

'My cell partner wanted my shoes. He took them.'

She looked at my well-used Nikes. 'Those?'

'Yes. Handsome, aren't they?'

'How long were you in jail?'

'Couple of hours. Then I got my life together. Made it through rehab. Now I'm a new man.'

She smiled again, a perfect smile, and our eyes lingered for a second, and I thought, Oh boy! No wedding ring on her finger. She was tall and a little too thin. Her hair was dark red and cut short and smart,

253

above the ears like a preppie. Her eyes were light brown, very big and round and quite pleasant to gaze into for a second or two. It struck me that she was very attractive, and it seemed odd that I hadn't noticed it sooner.

Was I being set up? Had I wandered up the stairs for a reason other than the tour? How had I missed the smile and the eyes yesterday?

We swapped bios. Her father was an Episcopal priest in Maryland, and a Redskins fan who loved D.C. As a teenager, she had decided to work with the poor. There was no higher calling.

I had to confess I had never thought about the poor until two weeks earlier. She was captivated by the story of Mister, and its purifying effects on me.

She invited me to return for lunch, to check on Ruby. If the sun was out, we could eat in the garden.

Poverty lawyers are no different from other people. They can find romance in odd places, like a shelter for homeless women.

After a week of driving through D.C.'s roughest sections, and spending hours in shelters, and in general mixing and mingling with the homeless, I no longer felt the need to hide behind Mordecai every time I ventured out. He was a valuable shield, but to survive on the streets I had to jump in the lake and learn to swim.

I had a list of almost thirty shelters and kitchens and centers where the homeless came and went. And I had a list of the names of the seventeen people evicted, including DeVon Hardy and Lontae Burton.

My next stop Saturday morning, after Naomi's, was the Mount Gilead Christian Church near Gallaudet University. According to my map, it was the kitchen nearest the intersection of New York and Florida, where the warehouse had once stood. The director was a young woman named Gloria, who, when I arrived at nine, was alone in the kitchen, chopping celery and fretting over the fact that no volunteers had arrived. After I introduced myself and did a thorough job of convincing her that my credentials were in order, she pointed to a cutting board and asked me to dice the onions. How could a bona fide poverty lawyer say no?

I had done it before, I explained, in Dolly's kitchen back during the snowstorm. She was polite but behind schedule. As I worked the onions and wiped my eyes, I described the case I was working on, and rattled off the names of the people evicted along with DeVon Hardy and Lontae Burton.

'We're not case managers,' she said. 'We just feed them. I don't know many names.'

A volunteer arrived with a sack of potatoes. I made preparations to leave. Gloria thanked me, and took a copy of the names. She promised to listen harder.

My movements were planned; I had many stops to make, and little time. I talked to a doctor at the Capitol Clinic, a privately funded walk-in facility for the homeless. The clinic kept a record of every patient. It was Saturday, and on Monday he would have the secretary check the computer files against my list. If there was a match, the secretary would call.

I drank tea with a Catholic priest at the Redeemer Mission off Rhode Island. He studied the names with great intensity, but no bells went off. 'There are so many,' he said.

The only scare of the morning occurred at the Freedom Coalition, a large gathering hall built by some long-forgotten association and later converted to a community center. At eleven, a lunch line was forming by the front entrance. Since I wasn't there to eat, I simply ignored the line and walked directly to the door. Some of the gentlemen waiting for food

255

thought I was breaking their line, and they threw obscenities at me. They were hungry, and suddenly angry, and the fact that I was white didn't help matters. How could they mistake me for a homeless person? The door was being manned by a volunteer, who also thought I was being an ass. He stiff-armed me rudely, another act of violence against my person.

'I'm not here to eat!' I said angrily. 'I'm a lawyer for the homeless!'

That settled them down; suddenly I was a blue-eyed brother. I was allowed to enter the building without further assault. The director was Reverend Kip, a fiery little guy with a red beret and a black collar. We did not connect. When he realized that (a) I was a lawyer; (b) my clients were the Burtons; (c) I was working on their lawsuit; and (d) there might be a recovery of damages down the road, he began thinking about money. I wasted thirty minutes with him, and left with the vow to send in Mordecai.

I called Megan and begged off lunch. My excuse was that I was on the other side of the city, with a long list of people yet to see. The truth was that I couldn't tell if she was flirting. She was pretty and smart and thoroughly likable, and she was the last thing I needed. I hadn't flirted in almost ten years; I didn't know the rules.

But Megan had great news. Ruby had not only survived the morning session of AA/NA, she had vowed to stay clean for twenty-four hours. It was an emotional scene, and Megan had watched from the rear of the room.

'She needs to stay off the streets tonight,' Megan said. 'She hasn't had a clean day in twelve years.'

I, of course, was of little help. Megan had several ideas.

The afternoon was as fruitless as the morning, though

I did learn the location of every shelter in the District. And I met people, made contacts, swapped cards with folks I'd probably see again.

Kelvin Lam remained the sole evictee we'd been able to locate. DeVon Hardy and Lontae Burton were dead. I was left with a total of fourteen people who had fallen through the cracks in the sidewalks.

The hard-core homeless venture into shelters from time to time for a meal, or a pair of shoes, or a blanket, but they leave no trail. They do not want help. They have no desire for human contact. It was hard to believe that the remaining fourteen were hard core. A month earlier, they had been living under a roof and paying rent.

Patience, Mordecai kept telling me. Street lawyers must have patience.

Ruby met me at the door of Naomi's, with a gleaming smile and a fierce hug. She had completed both sessions. Megan had already laid the groundwork for the next twelve hours – Ruby would not be allowed to stay on the streets. Ruby had acquiesced.

Ruby and I left the city and drove west into Virginia. In a suburban shopping center, we bought a toothbrush and toothpaste, soap, shampoo, and enough candy to get through Halloween. We drove farther away from the city, and in the small town of Gainesville I found a shiny new motel advertising single rooms for forty-two dollars a night. I paid with a credit card; surely it would somehow be deductible.

I left her there, with strict instructions to stay in the room with the door locked until I came for her Sunday morning.

TWENTY-EIGHT

Saturday night, the first day of March. Young, single, certainly not as rich as I was not too long ago, but not completely broke, yet. A closet full of nice clothes, which were not being used. A city of one million people with scores of attractive young women drawn to the center of political power, and always ready, it was rumored, for a good time.

I had beer and pizza and watched college basketball, alone in my loft and not unhappy. Any public appearance that night could have ended quickly with the cruel greeting 'Hey, aren't you the guy who got arrested? Saw it in the paper this morning.'

I checked on Ruby. The phone rang eight times before she answered, and I was about to panic. She was enjoying herself immensely, having taken a long shower, eaten a pound of candy, and watched TV nonstop. She had not left the room.

She was twenty miles away, in a small town just off the interstate in the Virginia countryside where neither she nor I knew a soul. There was no way she could find drugs. I patted myself on the back again.

During halftime of the Duke-Carolina game, the cell phone on the plastic storage box next to the pizza squawked and startled me. A very pleasant female voice said, 'Hello, jailbird.'

It was Claire, without the edge.

'Hello,' I said, muting the television.

'You okay?'

'Just doing great. How about you?'

'Fine. I saw your smiling face in the paper this morning, and I was worried about you.' Claire read the Sunday paper only, so if she saw my little story, someone gave it to her. Probably the same hot-blooded doc who'd answered the phone the last time I'd called. Was she alone on Saturday night, like me?

'It was an experience,' I said, then told her the entire story, beginning with Gasko and ending with my release. She wanted to talk, and as the narrative plodded along I decided that she was indeed by herself, probably bored and maybe lonely. And perhaps there was a chance that she was really worried about me.

'How serious are the charges?' she asked.

'Grand larceny carries up to ten years,' I said gravely. I liked the prospect of her being concerned. 'But I'm not worried about that.'

'It's just a file, isn't it?'

'Yes, and it wasn't a theft.' Sure it was, but I was not yet prepared to admit that.

'Could you lose your license to practice?'

'Yes, if I'm convicted of a felony, it would be automatic.'

'That's awful, Mike. What would you do then?'

'Truthfully, I haven't thought about it. It's not going to happen.' I was being completely honest; I had not seriously thought about losing my law license. Perhaps it was an issue requiring consideration, but I had not found the time for it.

We politely inquired about each other's family, and I remembered to ask about her brother James and his Hodgkin's disease. His treatment was under way; the family was optimistic.

I thanked her for calling, and we promised to keep

259

in touch. When I laid the cell phone next to the pizza, I stared at the muted game and grudgingly admitted to myself that I missed her.

Ruby was showered and shined and wearing the fresh clothing Megan had given her yesterday. Her motel room was on the ground floor with the door facing the parking lot. She was waiting for me. She stepped into the sunlight and hugged me tightly. 'I'm clean!' she said with a huge smile. 'For twenty-four hours I'm clean!' We hugged again.

A couple in their sixties stepped from the room two doors down and stared at us. God knows what they were thinking.

We returned to the city and went to Naomi's, where Megan and her staff were waiting for the news. A small celebration erupted when Ruby made her announcement. Megan had told me that the biggest cheers were always for the first twenty-four hours.

It was Sunday, and a local pastor arrived to conduct a Bible study. The women gathered in the main room for hymns and prayer. Megan and I drank coffee in the garden and worked out the next twenty-four hours. In addition to prayer and worship, Ruby would get two heavy sessions of AA/NA. But our optimism was guarded. Megan lived in the midst of addiction, and she was convinced Ruby would slide as soon as she returned to the streets. She saw it every day.

I could afford the motel strategy for a few days, and I was willing to pay for it. But I would leave for Chicago at four that afternoon, to begin my search for Hector, and I wasn't sure how long I would be away. Ruby liked the motel, in fact she appeared to be quite fond of it.

We decided to take things one day at a time. Megan would drive Ruby to a suburban motel, one I would pay for, and deposit her there for Sunday night. She would retrieve her Monday morning, and we would then worry about what to do next.

Megan would also begin the task of trying to convince Ruby she had to leave the streets. Her first stop would be a detox center, then a transitional women's shelter for six months of structured living, job training, and rehab.

'Twenty-four hours is a big step,' she said. 'But there is still a mountain to climb.'

I left as soon as I could. She invited me to return for lunch. We could eat in her office, just the two of us, and discuss important matters. Her eyes were dancing and daring me to say yes. So I did.

Drake & Sweeney lawyers always flew first-class; they felt as if they deserved it. They stayed in four-star hotels, ate in swanky restaurants, but drew the line at limousines, which were deemed too extravagant. So they rented Lincolns. All travel expenses were billed to the clients, and since the clients were getting the best legal talent in the world, the clients shouldn't complain about the perks.

My seat on the flight to Chicago was in coach, booked at the last minute and therefore in the dreaded middle. The window seat was occupied by a hefty gentleman whose knees were the size of basketballs, and on the aisle was a smelly youngster of eighteen or so with jet-black hair, cut into a perfect Mohawk, and adorned in an amazing collection of black leather and pointed chrome. I squeezed myself together, closed my eyes for two hours, and tried not to think about the pompous asses sitting up there in first-class, where I once rode.

The trip was in direct violation of my bail agreement – I was not to leave the District without permission of the Judge. But Mordecai and I agreed that it was a minor violation, one that would be of no consequence as long as I returned to D.C.

From O'Hare, I took a cab to an inexpensive hotel downtown.

Sofia had been unable to find a new residential address for the Palmas. If I couldn't find Hector at the Drake & Sweeney office, then we were out of luck.

The chicago branch of Drake & Sweeney had one hundred and six lawyers, third highest after Washington and New York. The real estate section was disproportionately large, with eighteen lawyers, more than the Washington office. I assumed that was the reason Hector had been sent to Chicago – there was a place for him. There was plenty of work to do. I vaguely recalled some story of Drake & Sweeney absorbing a prosperous Chicago real estate firm early in my career.

I arrived at the Associated Life Building shortly after seven Monday morning. The day was gray and gloomy, with a vicious wind whipping across Lake Michigan. It was my third visit to Chicago, and the other two times it had been just as raw. I bought coffee to drink and a newspaper to hide behind, and I found a vantage point at a table in a corner of the ground floor's vast atrium. The escalators crisscrossed to the second and third levels where a dozen elevators stood waiting.

By seven-thirty the ground floor was crawling with busy people. At eight, after three cups of coffee, I was wired and expecting the man at any moment. The escalators were packed with hundreds of executives, lawyers, secretaries, all bundled in heavy coats and looking remarkably similar.

At eight-twenty, Hector Palma entered the atrium from the south side of the building, stepping hurriedly inside with a swarm of other commuters. He raked his fingers through his wind-tossed hair and went straight for the escalators. As casually as possible, I walked to another escalator, and eased my way up the steps. I caught a glimpse of him as he turned a corner to wait for an elevator.

It was definitely Hector, and I decided not to press my luck. My assumptions were correct; he had been transferred out of Washington, in the middle of the night, and sent to the Chicago office where he could be monitored, and bribed with more money, and, if necessary, threatened.

I knew where he was, and I knew he wouldn't be leaving for the next eight to ten hours. From the second level of the atrium, with a splendid view of the lake, I phoned Megan. Ruby had survived the night; we were now at forty-eight hours and counting. I called Mordecai to report my finding.

According to last year's Drake & Sweeney handbook, there were three partners in the real estate section of the Chicago office. The building directory in the atrium listed all three on floor number fifty-one. I picked one of them at random: Dick Heile.

I rode the nine o'clock surge upward to the fifty-first floor, and stepped off the elevator into a familiar setting – marble, brass, walnut, recessed lighting, fine rugs.

As I walked casually toward the receptionist, I glanced around in search of rest rooms. I did not see any.

She was answering the phone with a headset. I frowned and tried to look as pained as possible.

'Yes sir,' she said with a bright smile between calls.

I gritted my teeth, sucked in air, said, 'Yes, I have a nine o'clock appointment with Dick Heile, but I'm afraid I'm about to be sick. It must've been something I ate. Can I use your rest room?' I clutched my stomach, folded my knees, and I must have convinced her that I was about to vomit on her desk.

The smile vanished as she jumped to her feet and began pointing. 'Down there, around the corner, to your right.'

I was already moving, bent at the waist as if I might blow up at any second. 'Thanks,' I managed to say.

'Can I get you something?' she asked.

I shook my head, too stricken to say anything else. Around the corner, I ducked into the men's rest room, where I locked myself in a stall, and waited.

At the rate her phone was ringing, she would be too busy to worry about me. I was dressed like a big-firm lawyer, so I did not appear to be suspicious. After ten minutes, I walked out of the men's room, and started down the hall away from the receptionist. At the first empty desk, I grabbed some papers that were stapled together and scribbled as I walked, as if I had important business. My eyes darted in every direction – names on doors, names on desks, secretaries too busy to look up, lawyers with gray hair in shirtsleeves, young lawyers on the phone with their doors cracked, typists pecking away with dictation.

It was so familiar!

Hector had his own office, a small room with no name anywhere in sight. I saw him through his half-open door, and I immediately burst in and slammed it behind me.

He jerked back in his chair with both palms up, as if he were facing a gun. 'What the hell!' he said.

'Hello, Hector.'

No gun, no assault, just a bad memory. His palms fell to his desk, and he actually smiled. 'What the hell?' he said again.

'So how's Chicago?' I asked, resting my butt on the edge of his desk.

'What are you doing here?' he asked, in disbelief.

'I could ask you the same question.'

'I'm working,' he said, scratching his head. Five hundred feet above the street, tucked away in his nondescript little room with no windows, insulated by layers of more important people, Hector had been found by the only person he was running from. 'How'd you find me?' he asked.

'It was very easy, Hector. I'm a street lawyer now, savvy and smart. You run again, I'll find you again.'

'I'm not running anymore,' he said, looking away. It was not entirely for my benefit.

'We're filing suit tomorrow,' I said. 'The defendants will be RiverOaks, TAG, and Drake & Sweeney. There's no place for you to hide.'

'Who are the plaintiffs?'

'Lontae Burton and family. Later, we'll add the other evictees, when we find all of them.'

He closed his eyes and pinched the bridge of his nose.

'You remember Lontae, don't you, Hector? She was the young mother who fought with the cops when you were evicting everyone. You saw it all, and you felt guilty because you knew the truth, you knew she was paying rent to Gantry. You put it all in your memo, the one dated January twenty-seventh, and you made sure the memo was properly indexed into the file. You did this because you knew Braden Chance would remove it at some point. And he did. And that's why I'm here, Hector. I want a copy of the memo. I have the rest of the file, and it's about to be exposed. Now I want the memo.'

'What makes you think I have a copy?'

'Because you're too smart not to copy it. You knew Chance would remove the original to cover his ass. But now he is about to be exposed. Don't go down with him.'

'Then where do I go?'

'Nowhere,' I said. 'You have nowhere to go.'

265

He knew it. Since he knew the truth about the eviction, he would be forced to testify at some point, and in some manner. His testimony would sink Drake & Sweeney, and he would be terminated. It was a course of events Mordecai and I had talked about. We had a few crumbs to offer.

'If you give me the memo,' I said, 'I will not tell where it came from. And I will not call you as a witness unless I am absolutely forced to.'

He was shaking his head. 'I could lie, you know,' he said.

'Sure you could. But you won't because you'll get nailed. It's easy to prove your memo was logged into the file, then removed. You can't deny writing it. Then we have the testimony of the people you evicted. They'll make great witnesses before an all-black jury in D.C. And we've talked to the guard who was with you on January twenty-seventh.'

Every punch landed flush on the jaw, and Hector was on the ropes. Actually, we had been unable to find the guard; the file did not give his name.

'Forget lying,' I said. 'It will only make things worse.'

Hector was too honest to lie. He was, after all, the person who had slipped me the list of the evictees, and the keys with which to steal the file. He had a soul and a conscience, and he couldn't be happy hiding in Chicago, running from his past.

'Has Chance told them the truth?' I asked.

'I don't know,' he said. 'I doubt it. That would take guts, and Chance is a coward. . . They'll fire me, you know.'

'Maybe, but you'll have a beautiful lawsuit against them. I'll handle it for you. We'll sue them again, and I won't charge you a dime.'

There was a knock on his door. It scared both of us;

our conversation had taken us back in time. 'Yes,' he said, and a secretary entered.

'Mr. Peck is waiting,' she said, sizing me up.

'I'll be there in one minute,' Hector said, and she slowly backtracked through the door, leaving it open.

'I have to go,' he said.

'I'm not leaving without a copy of the memo.'

'Meet me at noon by the water fountain in front of the building.'

'I'll be there.'

I winked at the receptionist as I passed through the foyer. 'Thanks,' I said. 'I'm much better.'

'You're welcome,' she said.

From the fountain we went west on Grand Avenue to a crowded Jewish deli. As we waited in line to order a sandwich, Hector handed me an envelope. 'I have four children,' he said. 'Please protect me.'

I took the envelope, and was about to say something when he stepped backward and got lost in the crowd. I saw him squeeze through the door and go past the deli, the flaps of his overcoat around his ears, almost running to get away from me.

I forgot about lunch. I walked four blocks to the hotel, checked out, and threw my things into a cab. Sitting low in the backseat, doors locked, cabbie half-asleep, no one in the world knowing where I was at that moment, I opened the envelope.

The memo was in the typical Drake & Sweeney format, prepared on Hector's PC with the client code, file number, and date in tiny print along the bottom left. It was dated January 27, sent to Braden Chance from Hector Palma, regarding the RiverOaks/TAG eviction, Florida warehouse property. On that day, Hector had gone to the warehouse with an armed guard, Jeff Mackle of Rock Creek Security, arriving at 9:15 A.M. and leaving at 12:30. The warehouse had three levels, and after first noticing squatters on the ground floor, Hector went to the second level, where there was no sign of habitation. On the third level, he saw litter, old clothing, and the remnants of a campfire someone had used many months earlier.

On the west end of the ground level, he found eleven temporary apartments, all hastily assembled from plywood and Sheetrock, unpainted, but obviously built by the same person, at about the same time, with some effort at order. Each apartment was roughly the same size, judging from the outside; Hector couldn't obtain entry to any of them. Every door was the same, a light, hollow, synthetic material, probably plastic, with a doorknob and a dead bolt.

The bathroom was well used and filthy. There had been no recent improvements to it.

Hector encountered a man who identified himself only as Herman, and Herman had no interest in talking. Hector asked how much rent was being charged for the apartments, and Herman said none; said that he was squatting. The sight of an armed guard in a uniform had a chilling effect on the conversation.

On the east end of the building, ten units of similar design and construction were found. A crying child drew Hector to one of the doors, and he asked the guard to stand back in the shadows. A young mother answered his knock; she held a baby, three other children swarmed around her legs. Hector informed her that he was with a law firm, that the building had been sold, and that she would be asked to leave in a few days. She at first said she was squatting, then quickly went on the attack. It was her apartment. She rented it from a man named Johnny, who came around on the fifteenth of each month to collect a hundred dollars. Nothing in writing. She had no idea who owned the building; Johnny was her only contact.

She had been there for three months, couldn't leave because there was no place to go. She worked twenty hours a week at a grocery store.

Hector told her to pack her things and get ready to move. The building would be leveled in ten days. She became frantic. Hector tried to provoke her further. He asked if she had any proof that she was paying rent. She found her purse, under the bed, and handed him a scrap of paper, a tape from a grocery store cash register. On the back someone had scrawled: Recd frm Lontae Burton, Jan 15, $100 rent.

The memo was two pages long. But there was a third page attached to it, a copy of the scarcely readable receipt. Hector had taken it from her, copied it, and attached the original to the memo. The writing was hurried, the spelling flawed, the copying blurred, but it was stunning. I must have made some ecstatic noise because the cabdriver jerked his head and examined me in the mirror.

The memo was a straightforward description of what Hector saw, said, and heard. There were no conclusions, no caveats to his higher-ups. Give them enough rope, he must have said to himself, and see if they'll hang themselves. He was a lowly paralegal, in no position to give advice, or offer opinions, or stand in the way of a deal.

At O'Hare, I faxed it to Mordecai. If my plane crashed, or if I got mugged and someone stole it, I wanted a copy tucked away deep in the files of the 14th Street Legal Clinic.

TWENTY-NINE

Since Lontae Burton's father was a person unknown to us, and probably unknown to the world, and since her mother and all siblings were behind bars, we made the tactical decision to bypass the family and use a trustee as a client. While I was in Chicago Monday morning, Mordecai appeared before a judge in the D.C. Family Court and asked for a temporary trustee to serve as guardian of the estates of Lontae Burton and each of her children. It was a routine matter done in private. The Judge was an acquaintance of Mordecai's. The petition was approved in minutes, and we had ourselves a new client. Her name was Wilma Phelan, a social worker Mordecai knew. Her role in the litigation would be minor, and she would be entitled to a very small fee in the event we recovered anything.

The Cohen Trust may have been ill-managed from a financial standpoint, but it had rules and bylaws covering every conceivable aspect of a nonprofit legal clinic. Leonard Cohen had been a lawyer, obviously one with an appetite for detail. Though discouraged and frowned upon, it was permissible for the clinic to handle an injury or wrongful death case on a contingency-fee basis. But the fee was capped at twenty percent of the recovery, as opposed to the standard one third. Some trial lawyers customarily took forty percent.

Of the twenty percent contingency fee, the clinic could keep half; the other ten percent went to the trust. In fourteen years, Mordecai had handled two cases on a contingency basis. The first he'd lost with a bad jury. The second involved a homeless woman hit by a city bus. He'd settled it for one hundred thousand dollars, netting the clinic a grand total of ten thousand dollars, from which he purchased new phones and word processors.

The Judge reluctantly approved our contract at twenty percent. And we were ready to sue.

Tip-off was at seven thirty-five – Georgetown versus Syracuse. Mordecai somehow squeezed two tickets. My flight arrived at National on time at six-twenty, and thirty minutes later I met Mordecai at the east entrance of the U.S. Air Arena in Landover. We were joined by almost twenty thousand other fans. He handed me a ticket, then pulled from his coat pocket a thick, unopened envelope, sent by registered mail to my attention at the clinic. It was from the D.C. bar.

'It came today,' he said, knowing exactly what it contained. 'I'll meet you at our seats.' He disappeared into a crowd of students.

I ripped it open and found a spot outside with enough light to read. My friends at Drake & Sweeney were unloading everything they had.

It was a formal complaint filed with the Court of Appeals accusing me of unethical behavior. The allegations ran for three pages, but could have been adequately captured in one good paragraph. I'd stolen a file. I'd breached confidentiality. I was a bad boy who should be either (1) disbarred permanently, or (2) suspended for many years, and/or (3) publicly reprimanded. And since the file was still missing, the matter was urgent, and therefore the inquiry and procedure should be expedited.

There were notices, forms, other papers I hardly glanced at. It was a shock, and I leaned on a wall to steady myself and contemplate matters. Sure, I had thought about a bar proceeding. It would have been unrealistic to think the firm would not pursue all avenues to retrieve the file. But I thought the arrest might appease them for a while.

Evidently not. They wanted blood. It was a typical big-firm, hardball, take-no-prisoners strategy, and I understood it perfectly. What they didn't know was that at nine the following morning, I would have the pleasure of suing them for ten million dollars for the wrongful deaths of the Burtons.

According to my assessment, there was nothing else they could do to me. No more warrants. No more registered letters. All issues were on the table, all lines drawn. In a small way, it was a relief to be holding the papers.

And it was also frightening. Since I'd started law school ten years earlier, I had never seriously considered work in another field. What would I do without a law license?

But then, Sofia didn't have one and she was my equal.

Mordecai met me inside at the portal leading to our seats. I gave him a brief summary of the bar petition. He offered me his condolences.

While the game promised to be tense and exciting, basketball was not our top priority. Jeff Mackle was a part-time gun at Rock Creek Security, and he also worked events at the arena. Sofia had tracked him down during the day. We figured he would be one of a hundred uniformed guards loitering around the building, watching the game for free and gazing at coeds.

We had no idea if he was old, young, white, black,

fat, or lean, but the security guards wore small nameplates above their left breast pockets. We walked the aisles and portals until almost halftime before Mordecai found him, hitting on a cute ticket clerk at Gate D, a spot I had inspected twice.

Mackle was large, white, plain-faced, and about my age. His neck and biceps were enormous, his chest thick and bulging. The legal team huddled briefly and decided it would be best if I approached him.

With one of my business cards between my fingers, I walked casually up to him and introduced myself. 'Mr. Mackle, I'm Michael Brock, Attorney.'

He gave me the look one normally gets with such a greeting and took the card without comment. I had interrupted his flirting with the ticket clerk.

'Could I ask you a few questions?' I said in my best homicide detective impersonation.

'You can ask. I may not answer.' He winked at the ticket clerk.

'Have you ever done any security work for Drake & Sweeney, a big law firm in the District?'

'Maybe.'

'Ever help them with any evictions?'

I hit a nerve. His face hardened instantly, and the conversation was practically over. 'Don't think so,' he said, glancing away.

'Are you sure?'

'No. The answer is no.'

'You didn't help the firm evict a warehouse full of squatters on February fourth?'

He shook his head, jaw clenched, eyes narrow. Someone from Drake & Sweeney had already visited Mr. Mackle. Or, more than likely, the firm had threatened his employer.

At any rate, Mackle was stonefaced. The ticket clerk was preoccupied with her nails. I was shut out.

'Sooner or later you'll have to answer my questions,'
I said.

The muscles in his jaw flinched, but he had no
response. I was not inclined to push harder. He was
rough around the edges, the type who could erupt
with a flurry of fists and lay waste to a humble street
lawyer. I had been wounded enough in the past two
weeks.

I watched ten minutes of the second half, then left
with spasms in my back, aftereffects of the car wreck.

The motel was another new one on the northern fringe
of Bethesda. Also forty bucks a night, and after three
nights I couldn't afford any more lockdown therapy
for Ruby. Megan was of the opinion it was time for her
to return home. If she was going to stay sober, the real
test would come on the streets.

At seven-thirty Tuesday morning, I knocked on her
door on the second floor. Room 220, per Megan's
instructions. There was no answer. I knocked again
and again, and tried the knob. It was locked. I ran to
the lobby and asked the receptionist to call the room.
Again, no answer. No one had checked out. Nothing
unusual had been reported.

An assistant manager was summoned, and I convinced her that there was an emergency. She called a
security guard, and the three of us went to the room.
Along the way, I explained what we were doing with
Ruby, and why the room wasn't in her name. The
assistant manager didn't like the idea of using her nice
motel to detox crackheads.

The room was empty. The bed was meticulous; no
sign of use during the night. Not a single item was out
of place, and nothing of hers had been left behind.

I thanked them and left. The motel was at least ten
miles from our office. I called Megan to alert her, then
fought my way into the city with a million other

274

commuters. At eight-fifteen, sitting in stalled traffic, I called the office and asked Sofia if Ruby had been seen. She had not.

The lawsuit was brief and to the point. Wilma Phelan, trustee for the estates of Lontae Burton and her children, was suing RiverOaks, Drake & Sweeney, and TAG, Inc., for conspiring to commit a wrongful eviction. The logic was simple; the causal connection obvious. Our clients would not have been living in their car had they not been thrown out of their apartment. And they wouldn't have died had they not been living in their car. It was a lovely theory of liability, one made even more attractive because of its simplicity. Any jury in the country could follow the rationale.

The negligence and/or intentional acts of the defendants caused the deaths, which were foreseeable. Bad things happened to those living on the streets, especially single mothers with little children. Toss them out of their homes wrongfully and you pay the price if they get hurt.

We had briefly considered a separate lawsuit for Mister's death. He too had been illegally evicted, but his death could not be considered foreseeable. Taking hostages and getting shot in the process were not a reasonable chain of events for one civilly wronged. Also, he had little jury appeal. We put Mister to rest, permanently.

Drake & Sweeney would immediately ask the Judge to require me to hand over the file. The Judge might very well make me do it, and that would be an admission of guilt. It could also cost me my license to practice law. Further, any evidence derived from anything in the stolen file could be excluded.

Mordecai and I reviewed the final draft Tuesday, and he again asked me if I wanted to proceed. To

275

protect me, he was willing to drop the lawsuit entirely. We had talked about that several times. We even had a strategy whereby we would drop the Burton suit, negotiate a truce with Drake & Sweeney to clear my name, wait a year for tempers to cool, then sneak the case to a buddy of his on the other side of town. It was a bad strategy, one we ditched almost as soon as we thought of it.

He signed the pleadings, and we left for the courthouse. He drove, and I read the lawsuit again, the pages growing heavier the farther we went.

Negotiation would be the key. The exposure would humiliate Drake & Sweeney, a firm with immense pride and ego, and built on credibility, client service, trustworthiness. I knew the mindset, the personality, the cult of great lawyers who did no wrong. I knew the paranoia of being perceived as bad, in any way. There was guilt for making so much money, and a corresponding desire to appear compassionate for the less fortunate.

Drake & Sweeney was wrong, though I suspected the firm had no idea how very wrong it was. I imagined Braden Chance was cowering behind his locked door praying fervently that the hour would pass.

But I was wrong too. Perhaps we could meet in the middle somewhere, and cut a deal. If not, then Mordecai Green would have the pleasure of presenting the Burton case to a friendly jury one day soon, and asking them for big bucks. And the firm would have the pleasure of pushing my grand larceny case to the limit; to a point I didn't care to think about.

The Burton case would never go to trial. I could still think like a Drake & Sweeney lawyer. The idea of facing a D.C. jury would terrify them. The initial embarrassment would have them scrambling for ways to cut their losses.

Tim Claussen, a college pal of Abraham's, was a reporter for the *Post*. He was waiting outside the clerk's office, and we gave him a copy of the lawsuit. He read it while Mordecai filed the original, then asked us questions, which we were more than happy to answer, but off the record.

The Burton tragedy was fast becoming a political and social hot potato in the District. Blame was being passed around with dizzying speed. Every department head in the city blamed another one. The city council blamed the mayor, who blamed the council while also blaming Congress. Some right-wingers in the House had weighed in long enough to blame the mayor, the council, and the entire city.

The idea of pinning the whole thing on a bunch of rich white lawyers made for an astonishing story. Claussen – callous, caustic, jaded by years in journalism – couldn't suppress his enthusiasm.

The ambushing of Drake & Sweeney by the press did not bother me in the least. The firm had established the rules the prior week when it tipped a reporter that I had been arrested. I could see Rafter and his little band of litigators happily agreeing around the conference table that, yes! it made perfect sense to alert the media about my arrest; and not only that but to slip them a nice photo of the criminal. It would embarrass me, humiliate me, make me sorry, force me to cough up the file and do whatever they wanted.

I knew the mentality, knew how the game was played.

I had no problem helping the reporter.

THIRTY

Intake at CCNV, alone, and two hours late. The clients were sitting patiently on the dirty floor of the lobby, some nodding off, some reading newspapers. Ernie with the keys was not pleased with my tardiness; he had a schedule of his own. He opened the intake room and handed me a clipboard with the names of thirteen prospective clients. I called the first one.

I was amazed at how far I'd come in a week. I had walked into the building a few minutes earlier without the fear of being shot. I had waited for Ernie in the lobby without thinking of being white. I listened to my clients patiently, but efficiently, because I knew what to do. I even looked the part; my beard was more than a week old; my hair was slightly over the ears and showing the first signs of unkemptness; my khakis were wrinkled; my navy blazer was rumpled; my tie was loosened just so. The Nikes were still stylish but well worn. A pair of horn-rimmed glasses, and I would have been the perfect public interest lawyer.

Not that the clients cared. They wanted someone to listen to them, and that was my job. The list grew to seventeen, and I spent four hours counseling. I forgot about the coming battle with Drake & Sweeney. I forgot about Claire, though, sadly, I was finding that easier to do. I even forgot about Hector Palma and my trip to Chicago.

278

But I couldn't forget about Ruby Simon. I somehow managed to connect each new client to her. I wasn't worried about her safety; she had survived on the streets far longer than I could have. But why would she leave a clean motel room with a television and a shower, and strike out through the city to find her abandoned car?

She was an addict, and that was the plain and unavoidable answer. Crack was a magnet, pulling her back to the streets.

If I couldn't keep her locked away in suburban motels for three nights, then how was I supposed to help her get clean?

The decision was not mine to make.

The routine of the late afternoon was shattered by a phone call from my older brother Warner. He was in town, on business, unexpectedly, would've called sooner but couldn't find my new number, and where could we meet for dinner? He was paying, he said before I could answer, and he'd heard about a great new place called Danny O's where a friend had eaten just a week earlier – fantastic food! I hadn't thought about an expensive meal in a long time.

Danny O's was fine with me. It was trendy, loud, overpriced, sadly typical.

I stared at the phone long after our conversation was over. I did not want to see Warner, because I did not want to listen to Warner. He was not in town on business, though that happened about once a year. I was pretty sure my parents had sent him. They were grieving down in Memphis, heartbroken over another divorce, saddened by my sudden fall from the ladder. Someone had to check on me. It was always Warner.

We met in the crowded bar at Danny O's. Before we could shake hands or embrace, he took a step backward to inspect the new image. Beard, hair, khakis, everything.

'A real radical,' he said, with an equal mixture of humor and sarcasm.

'It's good to see you,' I said, trying to ignore his theatrics.

'You look thin,' he said.

'You don't.'

He patted his stomach as if a few extra pounds had sneaked on board during the day. 'I'll lose it.' He was thirty-eight, nice-looking, still very vain about his appearance. The mere fact that I had commented on the extra weight would drive him to lose it within a month.

Warner had been single for three years. Women were very important to him. There had been allegations of adultery during his divorce, but from both sides.

'You look great,' I said. And he did. Tailored suit and shirt. Expensive tie. I had a closet full of the stuff.

'You too. Is this the way you dress for work now?'

'For the most part. Sometimes I ditch the tie.'

We ordered Heinekens and sipped them in the crowd.

'How's Claire?' he asked. The preliminaries were out of the way.

'I suppose she's fine. We filed for divorce, uncontested. I've moved out.'

'Is she happy?'

'I think she was relieved to get rid of me. I'd say Claire is happier today than she was a month ago.'

'Has she found someone else?'

'I don't think so,' I said. I had to be careful because most, if not all, of our conversation would be repeated to my parents, especially any scandalous reason for the divorce. They would like to blame Claire, and if they believed she'd been caught screwing around, then the divorce would seem logical.

'Have you?' he asked.

'Nope. I've kept my pants on.'

'So why the divorce?'

'Lots of reasons. I'd rather not rehash them.'

That was not what he wanted. His had been a nasty split, with both parties fighting for custody of the kids. He had shared the details with me, often to the point of being boring. Now he wanted the same in return.

'You woke up one day, and decided to get a divorce?'

'You've been through it, Warner. It's not that simple.'

The maître d' led us deep into the restaurant. We passed a table where Wayne Umstead was sitting with two men I did not recognize. Umstead had been a fellow hostage, the one Mister had sent to the door to fetch the food, the one who'd barely missed the sniper's bullet. He didn't see me.

A copy of the lawsuit had been served on Arthur Jacobs, chairman of the executive committee, at 11 A.M., while I was at the CCNV. Umstead was not a partner, so I wondered if he even knew about the lawsuit.

Of course he did. In hurried meetings throughout the afternoon, the news had been dropped like a bomb. Defenses had to be prepared; marching orders given; wagons circled. Not a word to anyone outside the firm. On the surface, the lawsuit would be ignored.

Fortunately, our table could not be seen from Umstead's. I glanced around to make sure no other bad guys were in the restaurant. Warner ordered a martini for both of us, but I quickly begged off. Just water for me.

With Warner, everything was at full throttle. Work, play, food, drink, women, even books and old movies.

281

He had almost frozen to death in a blizzard on a Peruvian mountain, and he'd been bitten by a deadly water snake while scuba diving in Australia. His post-divorce adjustment phase had been remarkably easy, primarily because Warner loved to travel and hang-glide and climb mountains and wrestle sharks and chase women on a global scale.

As a partner in a large Atlanta firm, he made plenty of money. And he spent a lot of it. The dinner was about money.

'Water?' he said in disgust. 'Come on. Have a drink.'

'No,' I protested. Warner would go from martinis to wine. We would leave the restaurant late, and he would be up at four fiddling with his laptop, shaking off the slight hangover as just another part of the day.

'Candy ass,' he mumbled. I browsed the menu. He examined every skirt.

His drink arrived and we ordered. 'Tell me about your work,' he said, trying desperately to give the impression that he was interested.

'Why?'

'Because it must be fascinating.'

'Why do you say that?'

'You walked away from a fortune. There must be a damned good reason.'

'There are reasons, and they're good enough for me.'

Warner had planned the meeting. There was a purpose, a goal, a destination, and an outline of what he would say to get him there. I wasn't sure where he was headed.

'I was arrested last week,' I said, diverting him. It was enough of a shock to be successful.

'You what?'

I told him the story, stretching it out with every detail because I was in control of the conversation. He

282

was critical of my thievery, but I didn't try to defend it. The file itself was another complicated issue, one neither of us wanted to explore.

'So the Drake & Sweeney bridge has been burned?' he asked as we ate.

'Permanently.'

'How long do you plan to be a public interest lawyer?'

'I've just started. I really hadn't thought about the end. Why?'

'How long can you work for nothing?'

'As long as I can survive.'

'So survival is the standard?'

'For now. What's your standard?' It was a ridiculous question.

'Money. How much I make; how much I spend; how much I can stash away somewhere and watch it grow so that one day I'll have a shitpot full of it and not have to worry about anything.'

I had heard this before. Unabashed greed was to be admired. It was a slightly cruder version of what we'd been taught as children. Work hard and make plenty, and somehow society as a whole would benefit.

He was daring me to be critical, and it was not a fight I wanted. It was a fight with no winners; only an ugly draw.

'How much do you have?' I asked. As a greedy bastard, Warner was proud of his wealth.

'When I'm forty I'll have a million bucks buried in mutual funds. When I'm forty-five, it'll be three million. When I'm fifty, it'll be ten. And that's when I'm walking out the door.'

We knew those figures by heart. Big law firms were the same everywhere.

'What about you?' he asked as he whittled on free-range chicken.

'Well, let's see. I'm thirty-two, got a net worth of

five thousand bucks, give or take. When I'm thirty-five, if I work hard and save money, it should be around ten thousand. By the time I'm fifty, I should have about twenty thousand buried in mutual funds.'

'That's something to look forward to. Eighteen years of living in poverty.'

'You know nothing about poverty.'

'Maybe I do. For people like us, poverty is a cheap apartment, a used car with dents and dings, bad clothing, no money to travel and play and see the world, no money to save or invest, no retirement, no safety net, nothing.'

'Perfect. You just proved my point. You don't know a damned thing about poverty. How much will you make this year?'

'Nine hundred thousand.'

'I'll make thirty. What would you do if someone forced you to work for thirty thousand bucks?'

'Kill myself.'

'I believe that. I truly believe you would take a gun and blow your brains out before you would work for thirty thousand bucks.'

'You're wrong. I'd take pills.'

'Coward.'

'There's no way I could work that cheap.'

'Oh, you could work that cheap, but you couldn't live that cheap.'

'Same thing.'

'That's where you and I are different,' I said.

'Damned right we're different. But how did we become different, Michael? A month ago you were like me. Now look at you – silly whiskers and faded clothes, all this bullshit about serving people and saving humanity. Where'd you go wrong?'

I took a deep breath and enjoyed the humor of his question. He relaxed too. We were too civilized to fight in public.

284

'You're a dumb-ass, you know,' he said, leaning low. 'You were on the fast track for a partnership. You're bright and talented, single, no kids. You'd be making a million bucks a year at the age of thirty-five. You can do the math.'

'It's already done, Warner. I've lost my love for money. It's the curse of the devil.'

'How original. Let me ask you something. What will you do if you wake up one day and you're, let's say, sixty years old. You're tired of saving the world because it can't be saved. You don't have a pot to piss in, not a dime, no firm, no partners, no wife making big bucks as a brain surgeon, nobody to catch you. What will you do?'

'Well, I've thought about that, and I figure I'll have this big brother who's filthy rich. So I'll give you a call.'

'What if I'm dead?'

'Put me in your will. The prodigal brother.'

We became interested in our food, and the conversation waned. Warner was arrogant enough to think that a blunt confrontation would snap me back to my senses. A few sharp insights from him on the consequences of my missteps, and I would ditch the poverty act and get a real job. 'I'll talk to him,' I could hear him say to my parents.

He had a few jabs left. He asked what the benefit package was at the 14th Street Legal Clinic. Quite lean, I told him. What about a retirement plan? None that I knew of. He embraced the opinion that I should spend only a couple of years saving souls before returning to the real world. I thanked him. And he offered the splendid advice that perhaps I should search for a like-minded woman, but with money, and marry her.

We said good-bye on the sidewalk in front of the restaurant. I assured him I knew what I was doing, that I would be fine, and that his report to our parents should be optimistic. 'Don't worry them, Warner. Tell them everything is wonderful here.'

'Call me if you get hungry,' he said in an effort at humor.

I waved him off and walked away.

The pylon grill was an all-night coffee shop in Foggy Bottom, near George Washington University. It was known as a hangout for insomniacs and news addicts. The earliest edition of the *Post* arrived each night just before twelve, and the place was as busy as a good deli during lunch. I bought a paper and sat at the bar, which was an odd sight because every person there was buried in the news. I was struck by how quiet the Pylon was. The *Post* had just arrived, minutes before me, and thirty people were poring over it as if a war had been declared.

The story was a natural for the *Post*. It began on page one, under a bold headline, and was continued on page ten where the photos were – a photo of Lontae taken from the placards at the rally for justice, one of Mordecai when he was ten years younger, and a set of three, which no doubt would humiliate the bluebloods at Drake & Sweeney. Arthur Jacobs was in the center, a mug shot of Tillman Gantry was on the left, and on the right was a mug shot of DeVon Hardy, who was linked to the story only because he'd been evicted and got himself killed in a newsworthy fashion.

Arthur Jacobs and two felons, two African-American criminals with little numbers across their chests, lined up as equals on page ten of the *Post*.

I could see them huddled in their offices and conference rooms, doors locked, phones unplugged, meetings canceled. They would plan their responses, devise a hundred different strategies, call in their public relations people. It would be their darkest hour.

286

The fax wars would begin early. Copies of the trio would be sent to law offices coast to coast, and every big firm in the world of corporate law would have a laugh.

Gantry looked extremely menacing, and it scared me to think we had picked a fight with him.

And then there was the photo of me, the same one the paper used the Saturday before when it announced my arrest. I was described as the link between the firm and Lontae Burton, though the reporter had no way of knowing I'd actually met her.

The story was long and thorough. It began with the eviction, and all the participants therein, including Hardy, who surfaced seven days later at the offices of Drake & Sweeney where he took hostages, one of whom was me. From me it went to Mordecai, then to the deaths of the Burtons. It mentioned my arrest, though I had been careful to tell the reporter little about the disputed file.

He was true to his word – we were never referred to by name, only as informed sources. I couldn't have written it better myself.

Not a word from any of the defendants. It appeared as if the reporter made little or no effort to contact them.

THIRTY-ONE

Warner called me at 5 A.M. 'Are you awake?' he asked. He was in his hotel suite, hyper, bouncing off the walls with a hundred comments and questions about the lawsuit. He'd seen the paper.

Trying to stay warm in my sleeping bag, I listened as he told me exactly how to proceed with the case. Warner was a litigator, a very good one, and the jury appeal of the Burton case was more than he could stand. We hadn't asked for enough in damages – ten million wouldn't cut it. The right jury, and the sky was the limit. Oh, how he'd love to try it himself. And what about Mordecai? Was he a trial lawyer?

And the fee? Surely we had a forty percent contract. There might be hope for me after all.

'Ten percent,' I said, still in the darkness.

'What! Ten percent! Are you out of your mind?'

'We're a nonprofit firm,' I tried to explain, but he wasn't listening. He cursed me for not being greedier.

The file was a huge problem, he said, as if we had not thought about it. 'Can you prove your case without the file?'

'Yes.'

He howled with laughter at the sight of old man Jacobs sitting there in the paper with a convict on each side. His flight to Atlanta left in two hours. He'd be at his desk by nine. He couldn't wait to pass around the

288

photos. He would start faxing them to the West Coast immediately.

He hung up in the middle of a sentence.

I'd slept for three hours. I turned a few times, but further sleep escaped me. There had been too many changes in my life to rest comfortably.

I showered and left, drank coffee with the Pakistanis until sunrise, then bought cookies for Ruby.

There were two strange cars parked at the corner of Fourteenth and Q, next to our office. I drove by slowly at seven-thirty, and my instincts told me to keep going. Ruby was not sitting on the front steps.

If Tillman Gantry thought violence would somehow help his defense of the lawsuit, he wouldn't hesitate to use it. Mordecai had cautioned me, though no warning was necessary. I called him at home and told him what I had seen. He would arrive at eight-thirty, and we agreed to meet then. He would warn Sofia. Abraham was out of town.

For two weeks my primary focus had been on the lawsuit. There had been other significant distractions – Claire, moving out, learning the ropes of a new career – but the case against RiverOaks and my old firm was never far from my mind. There was a prefiling frenzy with any large case, then a deep breath and a pleasant calmness after the bomb hit and the dust settled.

Gantry didn't kill us the day after we sued him and his two co-defendants. The office was quite normal. The phones were no busier than usual. The foot traffic was the same. With the lawsuit temporarily set aside, my other cases were easier to concentrate on.

I could only imagine the panic in the marbled halls of Drake & Sweeney. There would be no smiles, no gossip by the coffeepot, no jokes or sports talk in the hallways. A funeral parlor would be rowdier.

In antitrust, those who knew me best would be especially somber. Polly would be stoic, detached, and forever efficient. Rudolph wouldn't leave his office except to huddle with the higher-ups.

The only sad aspect of slandering four hundred lawyers was the inescapable reality that almost all of them were not only innocent of wrongdoing but completely ignorant of the facts. No one cared what happened in real estate. Few people knew Braden Chance. I was there seven years before I met the man, and then it was only because I went looking for him. I felt sorry for the innocent ones – the old-timers who'd built a great firm and trained us well; the guys in my class who would carry on the tradition of excellence; the rookies who had awakened to the news that their esteemed employer was somehow responsible for wrongful deaths.

But I felt no sympathy for Braden Chance and Arthur Jacobs and Donald Rafter. They had chosen to go for my jugular. Let them sweat.

Megan took a break from the rigors of keeping order in a house filled with eighty homeless women, and we went for a short drive through Northwest. She had no idea where Ruby lived, and we didn't really expect to find her. It was, however, a good reason to spend a few minutes together.

'This is not unusual,' she said, trying to reassure me. 'As a rule, homeless people are unpredictable, especially the addicts.'

'You've seen it before?'

'I've seen everything. You learn to stay level. When a client kicks the habit, finds a job, gets an apartment, you say a little prayer of thanks. But you don't get excited, because another Ruby will come along and break your heart. There are more valleys than mountains.'

'How do you keep from being depressed?'

'You draw strength from the clients. They are remarkable people. Most were born without a prayer or a chance, yet they survive. They trip and fall, but they get up and keep trying.'

Three blocks from the clinic, we passed a mechanic's garage with a collection of wrecked vehicles behind it. A large, toothy dog with a chain around its neck guarded the front. I had not planned on poking around rusty old cars, and the dog made the decision to keep going an easier one. We figured she lived in an area between the clinic on Fourteenth and Naomi's on Tenth near L, roughly from Logan Circle to Mount Vernon Square.

'But you never know,' she said. 'I'm constantly amazed at how mobile these people are. They have plenty of time, and some will walk for miles.'

We observed the street people. Every beggar came under our scrutiny as we drove slowly by. We walked through parks, looking at the homeless, dropping coins in their cups, hoping we would see someone we knew. No luck.

I left Megan at Naomi's, and promised to call later in the afternoon. Ruby had become a wonderful excuse to keep in touch.

The congressman was a five-termer from Indiana, a Republican named Burkholder who had an apartment in Virginia but liked to jog in the early evenings around Capitol Hill. His staff informed the media that he showered and changed in one of the seldom-used gyms Congress built for itself in the basement of a House office building.

As a member of the House, Burkholder was one of 435; thus virtually unknown even though he'd been in Washington ten years. He was mildly ambitious, squeaky clean, a health nut, forty-one years old. He served on Agriculture and chaired a sub-committee of Ways and Means.

Burkholder was shot early Wednesday evening near Union Station as he jogged alone. He was wearing a sweat suit – no wallet, no cash, no pockets with which to carry anything valuable. There appeared to be no motive. He encountered a street person in some manner, perhaps a collision or a bump or a harsh word given or received, and two shots were fired. One missed the congressman, the other struck him in the upper left arm, then traveled into his shoulder and stopped very near his neck.

The shooting occurred not long after dark, on a sidewalk next to a street filled with late commuters. It was witnessed by four people, all of whom described the assailant as a male black homeless-looking type, almost a generic description. He vanished into the night, and by the time the first commuter could stop, leave his car, and rush to the aid of Burkholder, the man with the gun was long gone.

The congressman was rushed to the hospital at George Washington, where the bullet was removed during a two-hour surgery, and he was pronounced stable.

It had been many years since a member of Congress had been shot in Washington. Several had been mugged, but with no permanent damage. The muggings typically provided the victims with wonderful pulpits to rail against crime and the lack of values and the general decline of everything; all blame, of course, being laid at the feet of the opposing party.

Burkholder wasn't able to rail when I saw the story at eleven. I'd been napping in my chair, reading and watching boxing. It was a slow news day in the District, slow until Burkholder got shot. The news anchorperson breathlessly announced the event, giving the basics with a nice photo of the congressman in the

292

background, then went Live! to the hospital where a reporter stood shivering in the cold outside the ER entrance, a door Burkholder had passed through four hours earlier. But there was an ambulance in the background, and bright lights, and since she could not produce blood or a corpse for the viewers, she had to make it as sensational as possible.

The surgery went well, she reported. Burkholder was stable and resting. The doctors had released a statement which said basically nothing. Earlier, several of his colleagues had rushed to the hospital, and somehow she had been able to coerce them into appearing before the camera. Three of them stood close together, all looking sufficiently grave and somber, although Burkholder's life had never been in danger. They squinted at the lights and tried to appear as if it was a major invasion of their private lives.

I had never heard of any of them. They offered their concerns about their buddy, and made his condition sound far worse than the doctors. Without prompting, they gave their assessments of the general decline of Washington.

Then there was another live report from the scene of the shooting. Another goofy reporter standing on the Exact Spot! where he fell, and now there was really something to see. There was a patch of red blood, which she pointed to with great drama, right down there. She squatted and almost touched the sidewalk. A cop stepped into the frame and offered his vague summary of what went on.

The report was live, yet in the background there were flashing red and blue lights of police cars. I noticed this; the reporter did not.

A sweep was under way. The D.C. police were out in force cleaning the streets, shoveling the street people into cars and vans and taking them away.

Throughout the night, they swept Capitol Hill, arresting anyone caught sleeping on a bench, sitting in a park, begging on a sidewalk, anyone who obviously appeared to be without a home. They charged them with loitering, littering, public drunkenness, panhandling.

Not all were arrested and taken to jail. Two van loads were driven up Rhode Island, in Northeast, and dumped in the parking lot next to a community center with an all-night soup kitchen. Another van carrying eleven people stopped at the Calvary Mission on T Street, five blocks from our office. The men were given the choice of going to jail or hitting the streets. The van emptied.

THIRTY-TWO

I vowed to get a bed. I was losing too much sleep
floundering on the floor, trying to prove a point to no
one but myself. In the darkness long before dawn, I sat
in my sleeping bag and promised myself I'd find
something softer to sleep on. I also wondered for the
thousandth time how people survived sleeping on
sidewalks.

The Pylon Grill was warm and stuffy, a layer of
cigarette smoke not far above the tables, the aroma of
coffee beans from around the world waiting just inside
the door. As usual it was filled with news junkies at
4:30 A.M.

Burkholder was the man of the hour. His face was
on the front page of the *Post*, and there were several
stories about the man, the shooting, the police investigation. Nothing about the sweep. Mordecai would
give me those details later.

A pleasant surprise was waiting in Metro. Tim
Claussen was evidently a man on a mission. Our
lawsuit had inspired him.

In a lengthy article, he examined each of the three
defendants, beginning with RiverOaks. The company
was twenty years old, privately held by a group of
investors, one of whom was Clayton Bender, an East
Coast real estate swinger rumored to be worth two
hundred million. Bender's picture was in the story,

295

along with a photo of the corporate headquarters in Hagerstown, Maryland. The company had built eleven office buildings in the D.C. area in twenty years, along with numerous shopping centers in the suburbs of Baltimore and Washington. The value of its holdings was estimated at three hundred fifty million. There was also a lot of bank debt, the level of which could not be estimated.

The history of the proposed bulk-mailing facility in Northeast was recounted in excruciating detail. Then, on to Drake & Sweeney.

Not surprisingly, there was no source of information from within the firm. Phone calls had not been returned. Claussen gave the basics – size, history, a few famous alumni. There were two charts, both taken from *U.S. Law* magazine, one listing the top ten law firms in the country by size, and the other ranking the firms by how much the partners averaged last year in compensation. With eight hundred lawyers, Drake & Sweeney was fifth in size, and at $910,500, the partners were number three.

Had I really walked away from that much money?

The last member of the unlikely trio was Tillman Gantry, and his colorful life made for easy investigative journalism. Cops talked about him. A former cellmate from prison sang his praises. A Reverend of some stripe in Northeast told how Gantry had built basketball hoops for poor kids. A former prostitute remembered the beatings. He operated behind two corporations – TAG and Gantry Group – and through them he owned three used-car lots, two small shopping centers, an apartment building where two people had been shot to death, six rental duplexes, a bar where a woman had been raped, a video store, and numerous vacant lots he'd purchased for almost nothing from the city.

Of the three defendants, Gantry was the only one

willing to talk. He admitted paying eleven thousand dollars for the Florida Avenue warehouse in July of the previous year, and selling it for two hundred thousand to RiverOaks on January 31. He got lucky, he said. The building was useless, but the land under it was worth a lot more than eleven thousand. That was why he bought it.

The warehouse had always attracted squatters, he said. In fact, he had been forced to run them off. He had never charged rent, and had no idea where that rumor originated. He had plenty of lawyers, and he would mount a vigorous defense.

The story did not mention me. Nothing was said about DeVon Hardy and the hostage drama. Very little about Lontae Burton and the allegations of the lawsuit.

For the second day in a row, the venerable old firm of Drake & Sweeney was maligned as a conspirator with a former pimp. Indeed, the tone of the story portrayed the lawyers as worse criminals than Tillman Gantry.

Tomorrow, it promised, there would be another installment – a look at the sad life of Lontae Burton.

How long would Arthur Jacobs allow his beloved firm to be dragged through the mud? It was such an easy target. The *Post* could be tenacious. The reporter was obviously working around the clock. One story would lead to another.

It was twenty minutes past nine when I arrived with my lawyer at the Carl Moultrie Building, on the corner of Sixth and Indiana, downtown. Mordecai knew where we were going. I had never been near the Moultrie Building, home of civil and criminal cases in the District. The line formed outside the front entrance, and it moved slowly as the lawyers and litigants and criminals were searched and scanned for

297

metal devices. Inside, the place was a zoo – a lobby packed with anxious people, and four levels of hallways lined with courtrooms.

The Honorable Norman Kisner held court on the first floor, room number 114. A daily docket by the door listed my name under First Appearances. Eleven other criminals shared space with me. Inside, the bench was vacant; lawyers milled about. Mordecai disappeared into the back, and I took a seat in the second row. I read a magazine and tried to appear utterly bored with the scene.

'Good morning, Michael,' someone said from the aisle. It was Donald Rafter, clutching his briefcase with both hands. Behind him was a face I recognized from litigation, but I could not recall the name.

I nodded and managed to say, 'Hello.'

They scooted away and found seats on the other side of the courtroom. They represented the victims, and as such had the right to be present at each stage of my proceedings.

It was only a first appearance! I would stand before the Judge while he read the charges. I would enter a plea of not guilty, be released on my existing bond, and leave. Why was Rafter there?

The answer came slowly. I stared at the magazine, struggled to remain perfectly calm, and finally realized that his presence was merely a reminder. They regarded the theft as a serious matter, and they would dog me every step of the way. Rafter was the smartest and meanest of all litigators. I was supposed to shake with fear at the sight of him in the courtroom.

At nine-thirty, Mordecai emerged from behind the bench and motioned for me. The Judge was waiting in his chambers. Mordecai introduced me to him, and the three of us settled casually around a small table.

Judge Kisner was at least seventy, with bushy gray hair and a scraggly gray beard, and brown eyes that burned holes as he talked. He and my lawyer had been acquaintances for many years.

'I was just telling Mordecai,' he said, waving a hand, 'that this is a very unusual case.'

I nodded in agreement. It certainly felt unusual to me.

'I've known Arthur Jacobs for thirty years. In fact, I know a lot of those lawyers over there. They're good lawyers.'

They were indeed. They hired the best and trained them well. I felt uncomfortable with the fact that my trial judge had such admiration for the victims.

'A working file stolen from a lawyer's office might be hard to evaluate from a monetary point of view. It's just a bunch of papers, nothing of real value to anyone except the lawyer. It would be worth nothing if you tried to sell it on the streets. I'm not accusing you of stealing the file, you understand.'

'Yes. I understand.' I wasn't sure if I did or not, but I wanted him to continue.

'Let's assume you have the file, and let's assume you took it from the firm. If you returned it now, under my supervision, I would be inclined to place a value on it of something less than a hundred dollars. That, of course, would be a misdemeanor, and we could sweep it under the rug with a bit of paperwork. Of course, you would have to agree to disregard any information taken from the file.'

'And what if I don't return it? Still assuming, of course.'

'Then it becomes much more valuable. The grand larceny sticks, and we go to trial on that charge. If the prosecutor proves his case and the jury finds you guilty, it will be up to me to sentence you.'

The creases in his forehead, the hardening of his eyes, and the tone of his voice left little doubt that sentencing would be something I would rather avoid.

'In addition, if the jury finds you guilty of grand larceny, you will lose your license to practice law.'

'Yes sir,' I said, very much chastised.

Mordecai was holding back, listening and absorbing everything.

'Unlike most of my docket, time is crucial here,' Kisner continued. 'This civil litigation could turn on the contents of the file. Admissibility will be for another judge in another courtroom. I'd like to have the criminal matter resolved before the civil case progresses too far. Again, we're assuming you have the file.'

'How soon?' Mordecai asked.

'I think two weeks is sufficient time to make your decision.'

We agreed that two weeks was reasonable. Mordecai and I returned to the courtroom where we waited another hour while nothing happened.

Tim Claussen from the *Post* arrived with a rush of lawyers. He saw us sitting in the courtroom, but did not venture over. Mordecai moved away from me, and eventually cornered him. He explained that there were two lawyers in the courtroom from Drake & Sweeney, Donald Rafter and another guy, and perhaps they might have a word for the paper.

Claussen went right after them. Voices could be heard from the back bench where Rafter had been killing time. They left the courtroom and continued their argument outside.

My appearance before Kisner was as brief as expected. I entered a plea of not guilty, signed some forms, and left in a hurry. Rafter was nowhere in sight.

'What did you and Kisner talk about before I got back there?' I asked as soon as we were in the car.

'Same thing he told you.'

'He's a hard-ass.'

'He's a good judge, but he was a lawyer for many years. A criminal lawyer, and one of the best. He has no sympathy for a lawyer who steals the files of another.'

'How long will my sentence be if I'm convicted?'

'He didn't say. But you'll do time.'

We were waiting for a red light. Fortunately I was driving. 'All right, Counselor,' I said. 'What do we do?'

'We have two weeks. Let's approach it slowly. Now is not the time to make decisions.'

THIRTY-THREE

There were two stories in the morning *Post*, both prominently displayed and accompanied by photos.

The first was the one promised in yesterday's edition – a long history of the tragic life of Lontae Burton. Her grandmother was the principal source, though the reporter had also contacted two aunts, a former employer, a social worker, a former teacher, and her mother and two brothers in prison. With its typical aggressiveness and unlimited budget, the paper was doing a splendid job of gathering the facts we would need for our case.

Lontae's mother was sixteen when she was born, the second of three children, all out of wedlock, all sired by different men, though her mother refused to say anything about her father. She grew up in the rough neighborhoods in Northeast, moving from place to place with her troubled mother, living periodically with her grandmother and aunts. Her mother was in and out of jail, and Lontae quit school after the sixth grade. From there, her life became predictably dismal. Drugs, boys, gangs, petty crime, the dangerous life on the street. She worked at various minimum-wage jobs, and proved to be completely unreliable.

City records told much of the story: an arrest at the age of fourteen for shoplifting, processed through juvenile court. Charged again three months later for public drunkenness, juvenile court. Possession of pot at fifteen, juvenile court. Same charge seven months later. Arrested for prostitution at the age of sixteen and handled as an adult, conviction but no jail. Arrested for grand larceny, stealing a portable CD player from a pawnshop, conviction but no jail. Birth of Ontario when she was eighteen, at D.C. General with no father listed on the birth certificate. Arrested for prostitution two months after Ontario arrived, convicted but no jail. Birth of the twins, Alonzo and Dante, when she was twenty, also at D.C. General, also with no father listed. And then Temeko, the baby with the wet diaper, born when Lontae was twenty-one.

In the midst of this sad obituary, a glimmer of hope sprang forth. After Temeko arrived, Lontae stumbled into the House of Mary, a women's day center similar to Naomi's, where she met a social worker named Nell Cather. Ms. Cather was quoted at length in the story.

According to her version of Lontae's last months, she was determined to get off the streets and clean up her life. She eagerly began taking birth control pills, provided by the House of Mary. She desperately wanted to get clean and sober. She attended AA/NA meetings at the center, and fought her addictions with great courage, though sobriety eluded her. She quickly improved her reading skills, and dreamed of getting a job with a steady paycheck to provide for her little family.

Ms. Cather eventually found her a job unpacking produce at a large grocery store; twenty hours a week at $4.75 an hour. She never missed work.

One day last fall she whispered to Nell Cather that she had found a place to live, though it must be kept a secret. As part of her job, Nell wanted to inspect the place, but Lontae refused. It wasn't legal, she explained. It was a small, two-room squatter's apartment with a roof and a locked door and a bathroom nearby, and she paid a hundred dollars a month in cash.

I wrote down the name of Nell Cather, at the House of Mary, and smiled to myself at the thought of her on the witness stand, telling the Burtons' story to a jury.

Lontae became terrified at the thought of losing her children, because it happened so often. Most of the homeless women at the House of Mary had lost theirs, and the more Lontae heard their horror stories, the more determined she became to keep her family together. She studied harder, even learned the basics of a computer, and once went four days without touching drugs.

Then she was evicted, her meager belongings tossed into the street along with her children. Ms. Cather saw her the next day, and she was a mess. The kids were hungry and dirty; Lontae was stoned. The House of Mary had a policy forbidding the entry of any person obviously intoxicated or under the influence of drugs. The director was forced to ask her to leave. Ms. Cather never saw her again; not a word until she read about the deaths in the paper.

As I read the story, I thought of Braden Chance. I hoped he was reading it too, in the early morning warmth of his fine home in the Virginia suburbs. I was certain he was awake at such an early hour. How could a person under so much pressure sleep at all?

I wanted him to suffer, to realize that his callous disregard for the rights and dignities of others had caused so much misery. You were sitting in your nice office, Braden, working hard by the golden hour, shuffling papers for your rich clients, reading memos from paralegals you sent to do the dirty work, and you made the cold, calculated decision to proceed with an eviction you should have stopped. They were just squatters, weren't they, Braden? Lowly black street people living like animals. There was nothing in writing, no leases, no papers, thus no rights. Toss 'em. Any delay in dealing with them might hinder the project.

I wanted to call him at home, jolt him from his morning coffee, and say, 'How do you feel now, Braden?'

The second story was a pleasant surprise, at least from a legal point of view. It also meant trouble.

An old boyfriend had been found, a nineteen-year-old street tough named Kito Spires. His photo would frighten any law-abiding citizen. Kito had a lot to say. He claimed to be the father of Lontae's last three children – the twins and the baby. He had lived with her off and on over the last three years; more off than on.

Kito was a typical inner-city product, an unemployed high school dropout with a criminal record. His credibility would always be questioned.

He had lived in the warehouse with Lontae and his children. He had helped her pay the rent whenever he could. Sometime after Christmas, they had fought and he had left. He was currently living with a woman whose husband was in prison.

He knew nothing about the eviction, though he felt it was wrong. When asked about conditions in the warehouse, Kito gave enough details to convince me he had actually been there. His description was similar to the one in Hector's memo.

He did not know the warehouse was owned by Tillman Gantry. A dude named Johnny collected rent, on the fifteenth of each month. A hundred bucks.

Mordecai and I would find him soon. Our witness list was growing, and Mr. Spires might well be our star.

Kito was deeply saddened by the deaths of his children and their mother. I had watched the funeral

305

very carefully, and Kito was most certainly not in attendance.

Our lawsuit was getting more press than we could have dreamed of. We only wanted ten million dollars, a nice round figure that was being written about daily, and discussed in the streets. Lontae had sex with a thousand men. Kito was the first prospective father. With that much money at stake, other fathers would soon appear and claim love for their lost children. The streets were full of prospects.

That was the troubling part of his story.

We would never get the chance to talk to him.

I called Drake & Sweeney and asked for Braden Chance. A secretary answered the phone, and I repeated my request. 'And who's calling, please?' she asked.

I gave her a fictitious name and claimed to be a prospective client, referred by Clayton Bender of RiverOaks.

'Mr. Chance is unavailable,' she said.

'Tell me when I can talk to him,' I said rudely.

'He's on vacation.'

'Fine. When will he return?'

'I'm not sure,' she said, and I hung up. The vacation would be for a month, then it would become a sabbatical, then a leave of absence, and at some point they would finally admit that Chance had been sacked.

I suspected he was gone; the call confirmed it.

Since the firm had been my life for the past seven years, it wasn't difficult to predict its actions. There was too much pride and arrogance to suffer the indignities being imposed.

As soon as the lawsuit was filed, I suspected they got the truth from Braden Chance. Whether he came forth on his own, or whether they pried it out of him, was immaterial. He had lied to them from the beginning, and now the entire firm had been sued. Perhaps he showed them the original memo from Hector, along with the rent receipt from Lontae. More than likely, though, he had destroyed these and was forced to describe what he had shredded. The firm – Arthur Jacobs and the executive committee – at last knew the truth. The eviction should not have occurred. The verbal rental agreements should have been terminated in writing, by Chance acting for RiverOaks, with thirty days' notice given to the tenants.

A thirty-day delay would have jeopardized the bulk-mail facility, at least for RiverOaks.

And a thirty-day delay would have allowed Lontae and the other tenants time to survive the worst of winter.

Chance was forced out of the firm, undoubtedly with a generous buy-out package for his partnership share. Hector had probably been flown home for briefings. With Chance gone, Hector could tell the truth and survive. He would not, however, tell of his contact with me.

Behind locked doors, the executive committee had faced reality. The firm had enormous exposure. A plan of defense was devised with Rafter and his litigation team. They would defend vigorously on the grounds that the Burton case was based on materials stolen from a Drake & Sweeney file. And if the stolen materials couldn't be used in court, then the lawsuit should be dismissed. That made perfect sense, from a legal perspective.

However, before they were able to implement their defense, the newspaper intervened. Witnesses were being found who could testify to the same matters protected in the file. We could prove our case regardless of what Chance had concealed.

Drake & Sweeney had to be in chaos. With four

hundred aggressive lawyers unwilling to keep their opinions to themselves, the firm was on the verge of an insurrection. Had I still been there, and been faced with a similar scandal in another division of the firm, I would have been raising hell to get the matter settled and out of the press. The option of battening down the hatches and riding out the storm did not exist. The exposé by the *Post* was only a sample of what a full-blown trial would entail. And a trial was a year away.

There was heat from another source. The file did not indicate the extent to which RiverOaks knew the truth about the squatters. In fact, there was very little correspondence between Chance and his client. It appeared as though he was given instructions to close the deal as soon as possible. RiverOaks applied the pressure; Chance steamrolled ahead.

If we assumed RiverOaks did not know the evictions were wrongful, then the company had a legitimate claim for legal malpractice against Drake & Sweeney. It hired the firm to do a job; the job was botched; and the blunder was to the detriment of the client. With three hundred fifty million in holdings, RiverOaks had sufficient clout to pressure the firm to remedy its wrongs.

Other major clients would also have opinions. 'What's going on over there?' was a question every partner was hearing from those who paid the bills. In the cutthroat world of corporate law, vultures from other firms were beginning to circle.

Drake & Sweeney marketed its image, its public perception. All big firms did. And no firm could take the hammering being inflicted upon my alma mater.

Congressman Burkholder rallied magnificently. The day after his surgery, he met the press in a carefully staged exhibition. They rolled him in a wheelchair to a makeshift podium in the lobby of the hospital. He stood, with the aid of his pretty wife, and stepped forward to issue a statement. Coincidentally, he wore a bright red Hoosier sweatshirt. There were bandages on his neck; a sling over his left arm.

He pronounced himself alive and well, and ready in a few short days to return to his duties on the Hill. Hello to the folks back home in Indiana.

In his finest moment, he dwelt on street crime, and the deterioration of our cities. (His hometown had eight thousand people.) It was a shame that our nation's capital was in such a sorry state, and because of his brush with death he would from that day forward devote his considerable energies into making our streets safe again. He had found a new purpose.

He blathered on about gun control and more prisons.

The shooting of Burkholder had put immense, though temporary, pressure on the D.C. police to clean up the streets. Senators and representatives had spent the day popping off about the dangers of downtown Washington. As a result, the sweeps started again after dark. Every drunk, wino, beggar, and homeless person near the Capitol was pushed farther away. Some were arrested. Others were simply loaded into vans and transported like cattle to the more distant neighborhoods.

At 11:40 P.M., the police were dispatched to a liquor store on Fourth Street near Rhode Island, in Northeast. Gunshots had been heard by the owner of the store, and one of the sidewalk locals had reported seeing a man down.

In a vacant lot next to the liquor store, behind a pile of rubble and cracked bricks, the police found the body of a young black male. The blood was fresh, and came from two bullet holes to the head.

He was later identified as Kito Spires.

THIRTY-FOUR

Ruby reappeared Monday morning with a ferocious appetite for both cookies and news. She was waiting on the doorstep with a smile and a warm hello when I arrived at eight, a bit later than usual. With Gantry out there, I wanted the extra daylight and the increased activity when I got to the office.

She looked the same. I thought perhaps I could study her face and see the evidence of a crack binge, but there was nothing unusual. Her eyes were hard and sad, but she was in a fine mood. We entered the office together and fixed our spot on Ruby's desk. It was somewhat comforting to have another person in the building.

'How have you been?' I asked.

'Good,' she said, reaching into a bag for a cookie. There were three bags, all bought the week before, just for her, though Mordecai had left a trail of crumbs.

'Where are you staying?'

'In my car.' Where else? 'I sure am glad winter is leaving.'

'Me too. Have you been to Naomi's?' I asked.

'No. But I'm going today. I ain't been feeling too good.'

'I'll give you a ride.'

'Thanks.'

The conversation was a little stiff. She expected me

to ask about her last motel visit. I certainly wanted to, but thought better of it.

When the coffee was ready, I poured two cups and set them on the desk. She was on her third cookie, nibbling nonstop around the edges like a mouse.

How could I be harsh with one so pitiful? On to the news.

'How about the paper?' I asked.

'That would be nice.'

There was a picture of the mayor on the front page, and since she liked stories about city politics, and since the mayor was always good for some color, I selected it first. It was a Saturday interview in which the mayor and council, acting together in a shaky and temporary alliance, were asking for a Justice Department investigation into the deaths of Lontae Burton and family. Had there been civil rights violations? The mayor strongly implied that he thought so, but bring in Justice!

Since the lawsuit had taken center stage, a fresh new group of culprits was being blamed for the tragedy. Fingerpointing at City Hall had slowed considerably. Insults to and from Congress had stopped. Those who'd felt the heat of the first accusations were vigorously and happily shifting blame to the big law firm and its rich client.

Ruby was fascinated with the Burton story. I gave her a quick summary of the lawsuit and the fallout since it had been filed.

Drake & Sweeney was battered again by the paper. Its lawyers had to be asking themselves, 'When will it end?'

Not for a while.

On the bottom corner of the front page was a brief story about the Postal Service's decision to halt the bulk-mail project in Northeast Washington. The controversy surrounding the purchase of the land, the

311

warehouse, the litigation involving RiverOaks and Gantry – all were factors in the decision.

RiverOaks lost its twenty-million-dollar project. RiverOaks would react like any other aggressive real estate developer who'd spent almost a million dollars in cash purchasing useless inner-city property. River-Oaks would go after its lawyers.

The pressure swelled some more.

We scanned world events. An earthquake in Peru caught Ruby's attention, and we read about it. On to Metro, where the first words I saw made my heart stop. Under the same photo of Kito Spires, the same except twice as large and even more menacing, was the headline: KITO SPIRES FOUND SHOT TO DEATH. The story recounted Friday's introduction of Mr. Spires as a player in the Burton drama, then gave the scant details of his death. No witnesses, no clues, nothing. Just another street punk shot in the District.

'You okay?' Ruby asked, waking me from my trance.

'Uh, sure,' I said, trying to breathe again.

'Why ain't you reading?'

Because I was too stunned to read aloud. I had to quickly scan every word to see if the name of Tillman Gantry was mentioned. It was not.

And why not? It was obvious to me what had happened. The kid had enjoyed his moment in the spotlight, said too much, made himself too valuable to the plaintiffs (us!), and was too easy a target.

I read the story to her, slowly, listening to every sound around us, watching the front door, hoping Mordecai would arrive shortly.

Gantry had spoken. Other witnesses from the streets would either remain quiet or disappear after we found them. Killing witnesses was bad enough. What would I do if Gantry came after the lawyers?

In the midst of my terror, I suddenly realized the

story was beneficial to our side of the case. We had lost a potentially crucial witness, but Kito's credibility would have caused problems. Drake & Sweeney was mentioned again, in the third story of the morning, in connection with the killing of a nineteen-year-old criminal. The firm had been toppled from its loftiness and was now in the gutter, its proud name mentioned in the same paragraphs as murdered street thugs.

I took myself back a month, before Mister and everything that followed, and I pictured myself reading the same paper at my desk before sunrise. And I imagined that I had read the other stories and had learned that the most serious allegations in the lawsuit were indeed true. What would I do?

There was no doubt. I would be raising hell with Rudolph Mayes, my supervising partner, who likewise would be raising hell with the executive committee, and I would be meeting with my peers, the other senior associates in the firm. We would demand that the matter be settled and laid to rest before more damage was inflicted. We would insist that a trial be avoided at all costs.

We would make all sorts of demands.

And I suspected most of the senior associates and all the partners were doing exactly what I would be doing. With that much racket in the hallways, very little work was being done. Very few hours were being billed. The firm was in chaos.

'Keep going,' Ruby said, again waking me.

We raced through Metro, in part because I wanted to see if perhaps there was a fourth story. No such luck. There was, however, a story about the street sweeps being conducted by the police in response to the Burkholder shooting. An advocate for the homeless was bitterly criticizing the operation, and threatening litigation. Ruby loved the story. She thought it

313

wonderful that so much was being written about the homeless.

I drove her to Naomi's, where she was greeted like an old friend. The women hugged her and passed her around the room, squeezing and even crying. I spent a few minutes flirting with Megan in the kitchen, but my mind was not on romance.

Sofia had a full house when I returned to the office. The foot traffic was heavy; five clients were sitting against the wall by nine o'clock. She was on the phone, terrorizing someone in Spanish. I stepped into Mordecai's office to make sure he had seen the paper. He was reading it with a smile. We agreed to meet in an hour to discuss the lawsuit.

I quietly closed my office door and began pulling files. In two weeks, I had opened ninety-one of them, and closed thirty-eight. I was falling behind, and I needed a hard morning fighting the phone to catch up. It would not happen.

Sofia knocked, and since the door would not latch, she pushed it open while still tapping it. No Hello. No Excuse me.

'Where is that list of people evicted from the warehouse?' she asked. She had a pencil stuck behind each ear, and reading glasses perched on the end of her nose. The woman had things to do.

The list was always nearby. I handed it to her, and she took a quick look. 'Bingo,' she said.

'What?' I asked, rising to my feet.

'Number eight, Marquis Deese,' she said. 'I thought that name was familiar.'

'Familiar?'

'Yes, he's sitting at my desk. Picked up last night in Lafayette Park, across from the White House, and dumped at Logan Circle. Got caught in a sweep. It's your lucky day.'

314

I followed her into the front room, where in the center Mr. Deese sat next to her desk. He looked remarkably similar to DeVon Hardy – late forties, grayish hair and beard, thick sunshades, bundled heavily like most homeless in early March. I examined him from a distance as I walked to Mordecai's office to give him the news.

We approached him carefully, with Mordecai in charge of the interrogation. 'Excuse me,' he said, very politely. 'I'm Mordecai Green, one of the lawyers here. Can I ask you some questions?'

Both of us were standing, looking down at Mr. Deese. He raised his head, said, 'I guess so.'

'We're working on a case involving some people who used to live in an old warehouse at the corner of Florida and New York,' Mordecai explained slowly.

'I lived there,' he said. I took a deep breath.

'You did?'

'Yep. Got kicked out.'

'Yes, well, that's why we're involved. We represent some of the other people who were kicked out. We think the eviction was wrongful.'

'You got that right.'

'How long did you live there?'

''Bout three months.'

'Did you pay rent?'

'Sure did.'

'To who?'

'Guy named Johnny.'

'How much?'

'A hundred bucks a month, cash only.'

'Why cash?'

'Didn't want no records.'

'Do you know who owned the warehouse?'

'Nope.' His answer came without hesitation, and I had trouble concealing my delight. If Deese didn't know Gantry owned the building, how could he be afraid of him?

Mordecai pulled up a chair, and got serious with Mr. Deese. 'We'd like to have you as a client,' he said.

'Do what?'

'We're suing some people over the eviction. It's our position that you folks were done wrong when you got kicked out. We'd like to represent you, and sue on your behalf.'

'But the apartment was illegal. That's why I was paying in cash.'

'Doesn't matter. We can get you some money.'

'How much?'

'I don't know yet. What have you got to lose?'

'Nothing, I guess.'

I tapped Mordecai on the shoulder. We excused ourselves and withdrew into his office. 'What is it?' he asked.

'In light of what happened to Kito Spires, I think we should record his testimony. Now.'

Mordecai scratched his beard. 'Not a bad idea. Let's do an affidavit. He can sign it, Sofia can notarize it, then if something happens to him, we can fight to get it admitted.'

'Do we have a tape recorder?' I asked.

His eyes shot in all directions. 'Yeah, somewhere.'

Since he didn't know where it was, it would take a month to find it. 'How about a video camera?' I asked.

'Not here.'

I thought for a second, then said, 'I'll run get mine. You and Sofia keep him occupied.'

'He's not going anywhere.'

'Good. Give me forty-five minutes.'

I raced from the office and sped west toward Georgetown. The third number I tried from my cell phone found Claire between classes. 'What's wrong?' she asked.

316

'I need to borrow the video camera. I'm in a hurry.'

'It hasn't been moved,' she said, very slowly, trying to analyze things. 'Why?'

'A deposition. Mind if I use it?'

'I guess not.'

'Still in the living room?'

'Yes.'

'Have you changed the locks?' I asked.

'No.' For some reason, this made me feel better. I still had a key. I could come and go if I wanted.

'What about the alarm code?'

'No. It's the same.'

'Thanks. I'll call you later.'

We placed Marquis Deese in an office empty of furniture but crowded with file cabinets. He sat in a chair, a blank white wall behind him. I was the videographer, Sofia the notary, Mordecai the interrogator. His answers could not have been more perfect.

We were finished in thirty minutes, all possible questions served up and answered. Deese thought he knew where two of the other evictees were staying, and he promised to find them.

Our plans were to file a separate lawsuit for each evictee we could locate; one at a time, with plenty of notice to our friends at the *Post*. We knew Kelvin Lam was at the CCNV, but he and Deese were the only two we'd been able to locate. Their cases were not worth a lot of money – we would gladly settle them for twenty-five thousand each – but their filing would heap more misery upon the beleaguered defendants.

I almost hoped the police would sweep the streets again.

As Deese was leaving, Mordecai warned him against talking about the lawsuit. I sat at a desk near Sofia and typed a three-page complaint on behalf of our new

317

client, Marquis Deese, against the same three defendants, alleging a wrongful eviction. Then one for Kelvin
Lam. I filed the complaints in the computer's memory. I would simply change the names of the plaintiffs
as we found them.

The phone rang a few minutes before noon. Sofia
was on the other line, so I grabbed it. 'Legal clinic,' I
said, as usual.

A dignified old voice on the other end said, 'This is
Arthur Jacobs, Attorney, with Drake & Sweeney. I
would like to speak to Mr. Mordecai Green.'

I could only say, 'Sure,' before punching the hold
button. I stared at the phone, then slowly rose and
walked to Mordecai's door.

'What is it?' he said. His nose was buried in the U.S.
Code.

'Arthur Jacobs is on the phone.'

'Who is he?'

'Drake & Sweeney.'

We stared at each other for a few seconds, then he
smiled. 'This could be the call,' he said. I just nodded.

He reached for the phone, and I sat down.

It was a brief conversation, with Arthur doing most
of the talking. I gathered that he wanted to meet and
talk about the lawsuit, and the sooner the better.

After it was over, Mordecai replayed it for my
benefit. 'They would like to sit down tomorrow and
have a little chat about settling the lawsuit.'

'Where?'

'At their place. Ten in the morning, without your
presence.'

I didn't expect to be invited.

'Are they worried?' I asked.

'Of course they're worried. They have twenty days
before their answer is due, yet they're already calling
about a settlement. They are very worried.'

THIRTY-FIVE

I spent the following morning at the Redeemer Mission, counseling clients with all the finesse of one who'd spent years tending to the legal problems of the homeless. Temptation overcame me, and at eleven-fifteen I called Sofia to see if she had heard from Mordecai. She had not. We expected the meeting at Drake & Sweeney to be a long one. I was hoping that by chance he had called in to report everything was proceeding smoothly. No such luck.

Typically, I had slept little, though the lack of sleep had nothing to do with physical ailments or discomfort. My anxiety over the settlement meeting outlasted a long hot bath and a bottle of wine. My nerves were jumping.

As I counseled my clients, it was difficult to concentrate on food stamps, housing subsidies, and delinquent fathers when my life was hanging in the balance on another front. I left when lunch was ready; my presence was far less important than the daily bread. I bought two plain bagels and a bottle of water, and drove the Beltway for an hour.

When I returned to the clinic, Mordecai's car was parked beside the building. He was in his office, waiting for me. I closed the door.

The meeting took place in Arthur Jacobs' personal

conference room on the eighth floor, in a hallowed corner of the building I'd never been near. Mordecai was treated like a visiting dignitary by the receptionist and staff – his coat was quickly taken, his coffee mixed just right, fresh muffins available.

He sat on one side of the table, facing Arthur, Donald Rafter, an attorney for the firm's malpractice insurance carrier, and an attorney for RiverOaks. Tillman Gantry had legal representation, but they had not been invited. If there was a settlement, no one expected Gantry to contribute a dime.

The only odd slot in the lineup was the lawyer for RiverOaks, but it made sense. The company's interests were in conflict with the firm's. Mordecai said the ill will was obvious.

Arthur handled most of the talking from his side of the table, and Mordecai had trouble believing the man was eighty years old. The facts were not only memorized but instantly recalled. The issues were analyzed by an extremely sharp mind working overtime.

First they agreed that everything said and seen in the meeting would remain strictly confidential; no admission of liability would survive the day; no offer to settle would be legally binding until documents were signed.

Arthur began by saying the defendants, especially Drake & Sweeney and RiverOaks, had been blindsided by the lawsuit – they were rattled and reeling and unaccustomed to the humiliation, and to the battering they were taking in the press. He spoke very frankly about the distress his beloved firm was suffering. Mordecai just listened, as he did throughout most of the meeting.

Arthur pointed out that there were a number of issues involved. He started with Braden Chance, and revealed that Chance had been expelled by the firm. He did not withdraw; he was kicked out. Arthur spoke candidly about Chance's misdeeds. He was solely in charge of all RiverOaks matters. He knew every aspect of the TAG closing, and monitored every detail. He probably committed malpractice when he allowed the eviction to proceed.

'Probably?' Mordecai said.

Well, okay then, beyond probably. Chance did not meet the necessary level of professional responsibility by proceeding with the eviction. And he doctored the file. And he attempted to cover up his actions. He lied to them, plain and simple, Arthur admitted, with no small amount of discomfort. Had Chance been truthful after Mister's hostage crisis, the firm could have prevented the lawsuit and its resulting flood of bad press. Chance had embarrassed them deeply, and he was history.

'How did he doctor the file?' Mordecai asked.

The other side wanted to know if Mordecai had seen the file. Where, exactly, was the damned thing? He was not responsive.

Arthur explained that certain papers had been removed.

'Have you seen Hector Palma's memo of January twenty-seventh?' Mordecai asked, and they went rigid.

'No,' came the response, delivered by Arthur.

So Chance had in fact removed the memo, along with Lontae's receipt, and fed them to the shredder. With great ceremony, and relishing every second of it, Mordecai removed from his briefcase several copies of the memo and receipt. He majestically slid them across the table, where they were snatched up by hardened lawyers too terrified to breathe.

There was a long silence as the memo was read, then examined, then reread, then finally analyzed desperately for loopholes and words which might be lifted out of context and slanted toward their side of

321

the table. Nothing doing. Hector's words were too clear; his narrative too descriptive.

'May I ask where you got this?' asked Arthur politely.

'That's not important, at least for now.'

It was obvious they had been consumed with the memo. Chance had described its contents on his way out the door, and the original had been destroyed. But what if copies had been made?

They were holding the copies, in disbelief.

But because they were seasoned litigators they rallied nicely, laying the memo aside as if it were something they could handle effectively at a later date.

'I guess that brings us to the missing file,' Arthur said, anxious to find more solid footing. They had an eyewitness who had seen me near Chance's office the night I took the file. They had fingerprints. They had the mysterious file from my desk, the one that had held the keys. I had gone to Chance demanding to see the RiverOaks/TAG file. There was motive.

'But there are no eyewitnesses,' Mordecai said. 'It's all circumstantial.'

'Do you know where the file is?' Arthur asked.

'No.'

'We have no interest in seeing Michael Brock go to jail.'

'Then why are you pressing criminal charges?'

'Everything's on the table, Mr. Green. If we can resolve the lawsuit, we can also dispose of the criminal matter.'

'That's wonderful news. How do you propose we settle the lawsuit?'

Rafter slid over a ten-page summary, filled with multicolored graphs and charts, all designed to convey the argument that children and young, uneducated mothers are not worth much in wrongful-death litigation.

With typical big-firm thoroughness, the minions at Drake & Sweeney had spent untold hours spanning the nation to survey the latest trends in tort compensation. A one-year trend. A five-year trend. A ten-year trend. Region by region. State by state. City by city. How much were juries awarding for the deaths of preschoolers? Not very much. The national average was forty-five thousand dollars, but much lower in the South and Midwest, and slightly higher in California and in larger cities.

Preschoolers do not work, do not earn money, and the courts generally do not allow predictions about future earning capacity.

Lontae's estimate of lost earnings was quite liberal. With a spotty employment history, some weighty assumptions were made. She was twenty-two, and she would one day very soon find full-time employment, at minimum wage. That was a generous assumption, but one Rafter was willing to grant. She would remain clean, sober, and free of pregnancy for the remainder of her working life; another charitable theory. She would find training somewhere along the way, move into a job paying twice as much as minimum wage, and keep said job until she was sixty-five. Adjusting her future earnings for inflation, then translating to present dollars, Rafter arrived at the sum of $570,000 for Lontae's loss of earnings.

There were no injuries or burns, no pain and suffering. They died in their sleep.

To settle the case, and admitting no wrongdoing whatsoever, the firm generously offered to pay $50,000 per child, plus the full sum of Lontae's earnings, for a total of $770,000.

'That's not even close,' Mordecai said. 'I can get that much out of a jury for one dead kid.' They sank in their seats.

He went on to discredit almost everything in

323

Rafter's pretty little report. He didn't care what juries were doing in Dallas or Seattle, and failed to see the relevance. He had no interest in judicial proceedings in Omaha. He knew what he could do with a jury in the District, and that was all that mattered. If they thought they could buy their way out cheaply, then it was time for him to leave.

Arthur reasserted himself as Rafter looked for a hole. 'It's negotiable,' he said. 'It's negotiable.'

The survey made no allowance for punitive damages, and Mordecai brought this to their attention. 'You got a wealthy lawyer from a wealthy firm deliberately allowing a wrongful eviction to occur, and as a direct result my clients got tossed into the streets where they died trying to stay warm. Frankly, gentlemen, it's a beautiful punitive damages case, especially here in the District.'

'Here in the District' meant only one thing: a black jury.

'We can negotiate,' Arthur said again. 'What figure do you have in mind?'

We had debated what number to first place on the table. We had sued for ten million dollars, but we had pulled the number out of the air. It could've been forty or fifty or a hundred.

'A million for each of them,' Mordecai said. The words fell heavily on the mahogany table. Those on the other side heard them clearly, but it took seconds for things to register.

'Five million?' Rafter asked, just barely loud enough to be heard.

'Five million,' boomed Mordecai. 'One for each of the victims.'

The legal pads suddenly caught their attention, and all four wrote a few sentences.

After a while, Arthur reentered the fray by explaining that our theory of liability was not absolute. An intervening act of nature – the snowstorm – was partly responsible for the deaths. A long discussion about weather followed. Mordecai settled the issue by saying, 'The jurors will know that it snows in February, that it's cold in February, that we have snowstorms in February.'

Throughout the meeting, any reference by him to the jury, or the jurors, was always followed by a few seconds of silence on the other side.

'They are horrified of a trial,' he told me.

Our theory was strong enough to withstand their attacks, he explained to them. Either through intentional acts or gross negligence, the eviction was carried out. It was foreseeable that our clients would be forced into the streets with no place to live, in February. He could convey this wonderfully simple idea to any jury in the country, but it would especially appeal to the good folks in the District.

Weary of arguing liability, Arthur moved to their strongest hand – me. Specifically, my actions in taking the file from Chance's office, and doing so after being told I couldn't have it. Their position was not negotiable. They were willing to drop the criminal charges if a settlement could be reached in the civil suit, but I had to face disciplinary action on their ethics complaint.

'What do they want?' I asked.

'A two-year suspension,' Mordecai said gravely.

I couldn't respond. Two years, non-negotiable.

'I told them they were nuts,' he said, but not as emphatically as I would have liked. 'No way.'

It was easier to remain silent. I kept repeating to myself the words *Two years. Two years.*

They jockeyed some more on the money, without closing the gap. Actually, they agreed on nothing, except for a plan to meet again as soon as possible.

The last thing Mordecai did was hand them a copy

of the Marquis Deese lawsuit, yet to be filed. It listed the same three defendants, and demanded the paltry sum of fifty thousand dollars for his wrongful eviction. More would follow, Mordecai promised them. In fact, our plans were to file a couple each week until all evictees had been accounted for.

'You plan to provide a copy of this to the newspapers?' Rafter asked.

'Why not?' Mordecai said. 'Once it's filed, it's public record.'

'It's just that, well, we've had enough of the press.'

'You started the pissing contest.'

'What?'

'You leaked the story of Michael's arrest.'

'We did not.'

'Then how did the *Post* get his photograph?'

Arthur told Rafter to shut up.

Alone in my office with the door closed, I stared at the walls for an hour before the settlement began to make sense. The firm was willing to pay a lot of money to avoid two things: further humiliation, and the spectacle of a trial that could cause serious financial damage. If I handed over the file, they would drop the criminal charges. Everything would fold neatly into place, except that the firm wanted some measure of satisfaction.

I was not only a turncoat, but in their eyes I was responsible for the entire mess. I was the link between their dirty secrets, well hidden up in the tower, and the exposure the lawsuit had cast upon them. The public disgrace was reason enough to hate me; the prospect of stripping them of their beloved cash was fueling their hunger for revenge.

And I had done it all with inside information, at least in their collective opinion. Apparently, they did not know of Hector's involvement. I had stolen the file, found everything I needed, then pieced together the lawsuit.

I was Judas. Sadly, I understood them.

THIRTY-SIX

Long after Sofia and Abraham had left, I was sitting in the semi-darkness of my office when Mordecai walked through the door and settled into one of two sturdy folding chairs I'd bought at a flea market for six bucks. A matching pair. A prior owner had painted them maroon. They were quite ugly, but at least I had stopped worrying about clients and visitors collapsing in mid-sentence.

I knew he had been on the phone all afternoon, but I had stayed away from his office.

'I've had lots of phone calls,' he said. 'Things are moving faster than we ever thought.'

I was listening, with nothing to say.

'Back and forth with Arthur, back and forth with Judge DeOrio. Do you know DeOrio?'

'No.'

'He's a tough guy, but he's good, fair, moderately liberal, started with a big firm many years ago and for some reason decided he wanted to be a judge. Passed up the big bucks. He moves more cases than any trial judge in the city because he keeps the lawyers under his thumb. Very heavy-handed. Wants everything settled, and if a case can't be settled, then he wants the trial as soon as possible. He's obsessive about a clean docket.'

'I think I've heard his name.'

'I would hope so. You've practiced law in this city for seven years.'

'Antitrust law. In a big firm. Way up there.'

'Anyway, here's the upshot. We've agreed to meet at one tomorrow in DeOrio's courtroom. Everybody will be there – the three defendants, with counsel, me, you, our trustee, everybody with any interest whatsoever in the lawsuit.'

'Me?'

'Yep. The Judge wants you present. He said you could sit in the jury box and watch, but he wants you there. And he wants the missing file.'

'Gladly.'

'He is notorious, in some circles I guess, for hating the press. He routinely tosses reporters from his courtroom; bans TV cameras from within a hundred feet of his doors. He's already irritated with the notoriety this case has generated. He's determined to stop the leaks.'

'The lawsuit is a public record.'

'Yes, but he can seal the file, if he's so inclined. I don't think he will, but he likes to bark.'

'So he wants it settled?'

'Of course he does. He's a judge, isn't he? Every judge wants every case settled. More time for golf.'

'What does he think of our case?'

'He kept his cards close, but he was adamant that all three defendants be present, and not just flunkies. We'll see the people who can make decisions on the spot.'

'Gantry?'

'Gantry will be there. I talked to his lawyer.'

'Does he know they have a metal detector at the front door?'

'Probably. He's been to court before. Arthur and I told the Judge about their offer. He didn't react, but I don't think he was impressed. He's seen a lot of big verdicts. He knows his jurors.'

'What about me?'

There was a long pause from my friend as he struggled to find words that would be at once truthful yet soothing. 'He'll take a hard line.'

Nothing soothing about that. 'What's fair, Mordecai? It's my neck on the line. I've lost perspective.'

'It's not a question of fairness. You took the file to right a wrong. You did not intend to steal it, just borrow it for an hour or so. It was an honorable act, but still a theft.'

'Did DeOrio refer to it as a theft?'

'He did. Once.'

So the Judge thought I was a thief. It was becoming unanimous. I didn't have the guts to ask Mordecai his opinion. He might tell me the truth, and I didn't want to hear it.

He shifted his considerable weight. My chair popped, but didn't yield an inch. I was proud of it. 'I want you to know something,' he said soberly. 'You say the word, and we'll walk away from this case in the blink of an eye. We don't need the settlement; no one does really. The victims are dead. Their heirs are either unknown or in jail. A nice settlement will not affect my life in the slightest. It's your case. You make the call.'

'It's not that simple, Mordecai.'

'Why isn't it?'

'I'm scared of the criminal charges.'

'You should be. But they'll forget the criminal charges. They'll forget the bar complaint. I could call Arthur right now and tell him we would drop everything if they would drop everything. Both sides walk away and forget it. He would jump at it. It's a piece of cake.'

'The press would eat us alive.'

330

'So? We're immune. You think our clients worry about what the *Post* says about us?'

He was playing the devil's advocate – arguing points he didn't really believe in. Mordecai wanted to protect me, but he also wanted to nail Drake & Sweeney.

Some people cannot be protected from themselves.

'All right, we walk away,' I said. 'And what have we accomplished? They get away with murder. They threw those people in the street. They're solely responsible for the wrongful evictions, and ultimately responsible for the deaths of our clients, yet we let them off the hook? Is that what we're talking about?'

'It's the only way to protect your license to practice law.'

'Nothing like a little pressure, Mordecai,' I said, a bit too harshly.

But he was right. It was my mess, and only fitting that I make the crucial decisions. I took the file, a stupid act that was legally and ethically wrong.

Mordecai Green would be devastated if I suddenly got cold feet. His entire world was helping poor folks pick themselves up. His people were the hopeless and homeless, those given little and seeking only the basics of life – the next meal, a dry bed, a job with a dignified wage, a small apartment with affordable rent. Rarely could the cause of his clients' problems be so directly traced to large, private enterprises.

Since money meant nothing to Mordecai, and since a large recovery would have little or no impact on his life, and since the clients were, as he said, either dead, unknown, or in jail, he would never consider a pretrial settlement, absent my involvement. Mordecai wanted a trial, an enormous, noisy production with lights and cameras and printed words focused not on him, but on the declining plight of his people. Trials are not always about individual wrongs; they are sometimes used as pulpits.

331

My presence complicated matters. My soft, pale face could be the one behind bars. My license to practice law, and thus make a living, was at risk.

'I'm not jumping ship, Mordecai,' I said.

'I didn't expect you to.'

'Let me give you a scenario. What if we convince them to pay a sum of money we can live with; the criminal charges are dropped; and there's nothing left on the table but me and my license? And what if I agree to surrender it for a period of time? What happens to me?'

'First, you suffer the indignity of a disciplinary suspension.'

'Which, unpleasant as it sounds, will not be the end of the world,' I said, trying to sound strong. I was horrified about the embarrassment. Warner, my parents, my friends, my law school buddies, Claire, all those fine folks at Drake & Sweeney. Their faces rushed before my eyes as I saw them receive the news.

'Second, you simply can't practice law during the suspension.'

'Will I lose my job?'

'Of course not.'

'Then what will I do?'

'Well, you'll keep this office. You'll do intake at CCNV, Samaritan House, Redeemer Mission, and the other places you've already been to. You will remain a full partner with the clinic. We'll call you a social worker, not a lawyer.'

'So nothing changes?'

'Not much. Look at Sofia. She sees more clients than the rest of us combined, and half the city thinks she's a lawyer. If a court appearance is necessary, I handle it. It'll be the same for you.'

The rules governing street law were written by those who practiced it.

'What if I get caught?'

332

'No one cares. The line between social work and social law is not always clear.'

'Two years is a long time.'

'It is, and it isn't. We don't have to agree on a two-year suspension.'

'I thought it was not negotiable.'

'Tomorrow, everything will be negotiable. But you need to do some research. Find similar cases, if they're out there. See what other jurisdictions have done with similar complaints.'

'You think it's happened before?'

'Maybe. There are a million of us now. Lawyers have been ingenious in finding ways to screw up.'

He was late for a meeting. I thanked him, and we locked up together.

I drove to the Georgetown Law School near Capitol Hill. The library was open until midnight. It was the perfect place to hide and ponder the life of a wayward lawyer.

THIRTY-SEVEN

DeOrio's courtroom was on the second floor of the Carl Moultrie Building, and getting there took us close to Judge Kisner's, where my grand larceny case was awaiting the next step in a cumbersome process. The halls were busy with criminal lawyers and low-end ham-and-eggers, the ones who advertise on cable TV and bus stop benches. They huddled with their clients, almost all of whom looked guilty of something, and I refused to believe that my name was on the same docket with those thugs.

The timing of our entry was important to me – silly to Mordecai. We didn't dare flirt with tardiness. DeOrio was a fanatic for punctuality. But I couldn't stomach the thought of arriving ten minutes early and being subjected to the stares and whispers and perhaps even the banal pregame chitchat of Donald Rafter and Arthur and hell only knew who else they would bring. I had no desire to be in the room with Tillman Gantry unless His Honor was present.

I wanted to take my seat in the jury box, listen to it all, and not be bothered by anyone. We entered at two minutes before one.

DeOrio's law clerk was passing out copies of the agenda. She directed us to our seats – me to the jury box, where I sat alone and content, and Mordecai to the plaintiff's table next to the jury box. Wilma

334

Phelan, the trustee, was already there, and already bored because she had no input into anything about to be discussed.

The defense table was a study in strategic positioning. Drake & Sweeney was clustered at one end; Tillman Gantry and his two lawyers at the other. Holding the center, and acting as a buffer, were two corporate types from RiverOaks, and three lawyers. The agenda also listed the names of all present. I counted thirteen for the defense.

I expected Gantry, being an ex-pimp, to be adorned with rings on his fingers and ears and bright, gaudy clothing. Not so. He wore a handsome navy suit and was dressed better than his lawyers. He was reading documents and ignoring everyone.

I saw Arthur and Rafter and Nathan Malamud. And Barry Nuzzo. I was determined that nothing would surprise me, but I had not expected to see Barry. By sending three of my fellow ex-hostages, the firm was delivering a subtle message – every other lawyer terrorized by Mister survived without cracking up – what happened to me? Why was I the weak sister?

The fifth person in their pack was identified as L. James Suber, an attorney for an insurance company. Drake & Sweeney was heavily insured against malpractice, but I doubted if the coverage would apply. The policy excluded intentional acts, such as stealing by an associate or partner, or deliberately violating a standard of conduct. Negligence by a firm lawyer would be covered. Willful wrongdoing would not. Braden Chance had not simply overlooked a statute or code provision or established method of practice. He had made the conscious decision to proceed with the eviction, in spite of being fully informed that the squatters were in fact tenants.

There would be a nasty fight on the side, out of our

335

view, between Drake & Sweeney and its malpractice carrier. Let 'em fight.

At precisely one, Judge DeOrio appeared from behind the bench and took his seat. 'Good afternoon,' he said gruffly as he settled into place. He was wearing a robe, and that struck me as odd. It was not a formal court proceeding, but an unofficial settlement conference.

He adjusted his microphone, and said, 'Mr. Burdick, please keep the door locked.' Mr. Burdick was a uniformed courtroom deputy guarding the door from the inside. The pews were completely empty. It was a very private conference.

A court reporter began recording every word.

'I am informed by my clerk that all parties and lawyers are now present,' he said, glancing at me as if I were just another rapist. 'The purpose of this meeting is to attempt to settle this case. After numerous conversations yesterday with the principal attorneys, it became apparent to me that a conference such as this, held at this time, might be beneficial. I've never had a settlement conference so soon after the filing of a complaint, but since all parties agreed, it is time well spent. The first issue is that of confidentiality. Nothing we say today can be repeated to any member of the press, under any circumstances. Is that understood?' He looked at Mordecai and then at me. All necks from the defense table twisted for similar scrutiny. I wanted to stand and remind them that they had initiated the practice of leaking. We'd certainly landed the heaviest blows, but they had thrown the first punch.

The clerk then handed each of us a two-paragraph nondisclosure agreement, customized with our names plugged in. I signed it and gave it back to her.

A lawyer under pressure cannot read two paragraphs and make a quick decision. 'Is there a problem?' DeOrio asked of the Drake & Sweeney crowd.

336

They were looking for loopholes. It was the way we were trained.

They signed off and the agreements were gathered by the clerk.

'We'll work from the agenda,' the Judge said. 'Item one is a summary of the facts and theories of liability. Mr. Green, you filed the lawsuit, you may proceed. You have five minutes.'

Mordecai stood without notes, hands stuck deep in pockets, completely at ease. In two minutes, he stated our case clearly, then sat down. DeOrio appreciated brevity.

Arthur spoke for the defendants. He conceded the factual basis for the case, but took issue on the question of liability. He laid much of the blame on the 'freak' snowstorm that covered the city and made life difficult for everyone.

He also questioned the actions of Lontae Burton.

'There were places for her to go,' Arthur said. 'There were emergency shelters open. The night before she had stayed in the basement of a church, along with many other people. Why did she leave? I don't know, but no one forced her, at least no one we've been able to find so far. Her grandmother has an apartment in Northeast. Shouldn't some of the responsibility rest with the mother? Shouldn't she have done more to protect her little family?'

It would be Arthur's only chance to cast blame upon a dead mother. In a year or so, my jury box would be filled with people who looked different from me, and neither Arthur nor any lawyer in his right mind would imply that Lontae Burton was even partially to blame for killing her own children.

'Why was she in the street to begin with?' DeOrio asked sharply, and I almost smiled.

Arthur was unfazed. 'For purposes of this meeting,

Your Honor, we are willing to concede that the eviction was wrongful.'

'Thank you.'

'You're welcome. Our point is that some of the responsibility should rest with the mother.'

'How much?'

'At least fifty percent.'

'That's too high.'

'We think not, Your Honor. We may have put her in the street, but she was there for more than a week before the tragedy.'

'Mr. Green?'

Mordecai stood, shaking his head as if Arthur were a first-year law student grappling with elementary theories. 'These are not people with immediate access to housing, Mr. Jacobs. That's why they're called homeless. You admit you put them in the street, and that's where they died. I would love to discuss it with a jury.'

Arthur's shoulders slumped. Rafter, Malamud, and Barry listened to every word, their faces stricken with the notion of Mordecai Green loose in a courtroom with a jury of his peers.

'Liability is clear, Mr. Jacobs,' DeOrio said. 'You can argue the mother's negligence to the jury if you want, though I wouldn't advise it.' Mordecai and Arthur sat down.

If at trial we proved the defendants liable, the jury would then consider the issue of damages. It was next on the agenda. Rafter went through the motions of submitting the same report on current trends in jury awards. He talked about how much dead children were worth under our tort system. But he quickly became tedious when discussing Lontae's employment history and the estimated loss of her future earnings. He arrived at the same amount, $770,000, that they had offered the day before, and presented that for the record.

338

'That's not your final offer, is it, Mr. Rafter?' DeOrio asked. His tone was challenging; he certainly hoped that was not their final offer.

'No sir,' Rafter said.

'Mr. Green.'

Mordecai stood again. 'We reject their offer, Your Honor. The trends mean nothing to me. The only trend I care about is how much I can convince a jury to award, and, with all due respect to Mr. Rafter, it'll be a helluva lot more than what they're offering.'

No one in the courtroom doubted him.

He disputed their view that a dead child was worth only fifty thousand dollars. He implied rather strongly that such a low estimation was the result of a prejudice against homeless street children who happened to be black. Gantry was the only one at the defense table not squirming. 'You have a son at St. Alban's, Mr. Rafter. Would you take fifty thousand for him?'

Rafter's nose was three inches away from his legal pad.

'I can convince a jury in this courtroom that these little children were worth at least a million dollars each, same as any child in the prep schools of Virginia and Maryland.'

It was a nasty shot, one they took in the groin. There was no doubt where their kids went to school.

Rafter's summary made no provision for the pain and suffering of the victims. The rationale was unspoken, but nonetheless obvious. They had died peacefully, breathing odorless gas until they floated away. There were no burns, breaks, blood.

Rafter paid dearly for his omission. Mordecai launched into a detailed account of the last hours of Lontae and her children; the search for food and warmth, the snow and bitter cold, the fear of freezing to death, the desperate efforts to stay together, the

339

horror of being stuck in a snowstorm, in a rattletrap car, motor running, watching the fuel gauge.

It was a spellbinding performance, given off the cuff with the skill of a gifted storyteller. As the lone juror, I would have handed him a blank check.

'Don't tell me about pain and suffering,' he snarled at Drake & Sweeney. 'You don't know the meaning of it.'

He talked about Lontae as if he'd known her for years. A kid born without a chance, who made all the predictable mistakes. But, more important, a mother who loved her children and was trying desperately to climb out of poverty. She had confronted her past and her addictions, and was fighting for sobriety when the defendants kicked her back into the streets.

His voice ebbed and flowed, rising with indignation, falling with shame and guilt. Not a syllable was missed, no wasted words. He was giving them an extraordinary dose of what the jury would hear.

Arthur had control of the checkbook, and it must've been burning a hole in his pocket.

Mordecai saved his best for last. He lectured on the purpose of punitive damages – to punish wrongdoers, to make examples out of them so they would sin no more. He hammered at the evils committed by the defendants, rich people with no regard for those less fortunate. 'They're just a bunch of squatters,' his voice boomed. 'Let's throw them out!'

Greed had made them ignore the law. A proper eviction would have taken at least thirty more days. It would have killed the deal with the Postal Service. Thirty days and the heavy snows would've been gone; the streets would've been a little safer.

It was the perfect case for the levying of punitive damages, and there was little doubt in his mind a jury would agree with him. I certainly did, and at that moment neither Arthur nor Rafter nor any other

340

lawyer sitting over there wanted any part of Mordecai Green.

'We'll settle for five million,' he said as he came to an end. 'Not a penny less.'

There was a pause when he finished. DeOrio made some notes, then returned to the agenda. The matter of the file was next. 'Do you have it?' he asked me.

'Yes sir.'

'Are you willing to hand it over?'

'Yes.'

Mordecai opened his battered briefcase and removed the file. He handed it to the clerk, who passed it up to His Honor. We watched for ten long minutes as DeOrio flipped through every page.

I caught a few stares from Rafter, but who cared. He and the rest were anxious to get their hands on it.

When the Judge was finished, he said, 'The file has been returned, Mr. Jacobs. There is a criminal matter pending down the hall. I've spoken to Judge Kisner about it. What do you wish to do?'

'Your Honor, if we can settle all other issues, we will not push for an indictment.'

'I assume this is agreeable with you, Mr. Brock?' DeOrio said.

Damned right it was agreeable with me. 'Yes sir.'

'Moving right along. The next item is the matter of the ethics complaint filed by Drake & Sweeney against Michael Brock. Mr. Jacobs, would you care to address this?'

'Certainly, Your Honor.' Arthur sprang to his feet, and delivered a condemnation of my ethical shortcomings. He was not unduly harsh, or long-winded. He seemed to get no pleasure from it. Arthur was a lawyer's lawyer, an old-timer who preached ethics and certainly practiced them. He and the firm would never forgive me for my screwup, but I had been, after all, one of them. Just as Braden Chance's actions had

341

been a reflection on the entire firm, so had my failure to maintain certain standards.

He ended by asserting that I must not escape punishment for taking the file. It was an egregious breach of duty owed to the client, RiverOaks. I was not a criminal, and they had no difficulty in forgetting the grand larceny charge. But I was a lawyer, and a damned good one, he admitted, and as such I should be held responsible.

They would not, under any circumstances, withdraw the ethics complaint.

His arguments were well reasoned, well pled, and he convinced me. The folks from RiverOaks seemed especially hard-nosed.

'Mr. Brock,' DeOrio said. 'Do you have any response?'

I had not prepared any remarks, but I wasn't afraid to stand and say what I felt. I looked Arthur squarely in the eyes, and said, 'Mr. Jacobs, I have always had great respect for you, and I still do. I have nothing to say in my defense. I was wrong in taking the file, and I've wished a thousand times I had not done it. I was looking for information which I knew was being concealed, but that is no excuse. I apologize to you, the rest of the firm, and to your client, RiverOaks.'

I sat down and couldn't look at them. Mordecai told me later that my humility thawed the room by ten degrees.

DeOrio then did a very wise thing. He proceeded to the next item, which was the litigation yet to be commenced. We planned to file suit on behalf of Marquis Deese and Kelvin Lam, and eventually for every other evictee we could find. DeVon Hardy and Lontae were gone, so there were fifteen potential plaintiffs out there. This had been promised by Mordecai, and he had informed the Judge.

'If you're conceding liability, Mr. Jacobs,' His

342

Honor said, 'then you have to talk about damages. How much will you offer to settle these other fifteen cases?'

Arthur whispered to Rafter and Malamud, then said, 'Well, Your Honor, we figure these people have been without their homes for about a month now. If we gave them five thousand each, they could find a new place, probably something much better.'

'That's low,' DeOrio said. 'Mr. Green.'

'Much too low,' Mordecai agreed. 'Again, I evaluate cases based on what juries might do. Same defendants, same wrongful conduct, same jury pool. I can get fifty thousand per case easy.'

'What will you take?' the Judge asked.

'Twenty-five thousand.'

'I think you should pay it,' DeOrio said to Arthur. 'It's not unreasonable.'

'Twenty-five thousand to each of the fifteen?' Arthur asked, his unflappable demeanor cracking under the assault from two sides of the courtroom.

'That's right.'

A fierce huddle ensued in which each of the four Drake & Sweeney lawyers had his say. It was telling that they did not consult the attorneys for the other two defendants. It was obvious the firm would foot the bill for the settlement. Gantry seemed completely indifferent; his money was not at stake. RiverOaks had probably threatened a suit of its own against the lawyers if the case wasn't settled.

'We will pay twenty-five,' Arthur announced quietly, and $375,000 left the coffers of Drake & Sweeney.

The wisdom was in the breaking of the ice. DeOrio knew he could force them to settle the smaller claims. Once the money started flowing, it wouldn't stop until we were finished.

For the prior year, after paying my salary and

343

benefits, and setting aside one third of my billings for the overhead, approximately four hundred thousand dollars went into the pot of gold the partners divided. And I was just one of eight hundred.

'Gentlemen, we are down to two issues. The first is money – how much will it take to settle this lawsuit? The second is the matter of Mr. Brock's disciplinary problems. It appears as though one hinges on the other. It's at this point in these meetings that I like to talk privately with each side. I'll start with the plaintiff. Mr. Green and Mr. Brock, would you step into my chambers?'

The clerk escorted us into the hallway behind the bench, then down to a splendid oak-paneled office where His Honor was disrobing and ordering tea from a secretary. He offered some to us, but we declined. The clerk closed the door, leaving us alone with DeOrio.

'We're making progress,' he said. 'I've got to tell you, Mr. Brock, the ethics complaint is a problem. Do you realize how serious it is?'

'I think so.'

He cracked his knuckles and began pacing around the room. 'We had a lawyer here in the District, must have been seven, eight years ago, who pulled a similar stunt. Walked out of a firm with a bunch of discovery materials that mysteriously ended up in a different firm, which just so happened to offer the guy a nice job. Can't remember the name.'

'Makovek. Brad Makovek,' I said.

'Right. What happened to him?'

'Suspended for two years.'

'Which is what they want from you.'

'No way, Judge,' Mordecai said. 'No way in hell we're agreeing to a two-year suspension.'

'How much will you agree to?'

'Six months max. And it's not negotiable. Look,

Judge, these guys are scared to death, you know that. They're scared and we're not. Why should we settle anything? I'd rather have a jury.'

'There's not going to be a jury.' The Judge stepped close to me and studied my eyes. 'You'll agree to a six-month suspension?' he asked.

'Yes,' I said. 'But they have to pay the money.'

'How much money?' he asked Mordecai.

'Five million. I could get more from a jury.'

DeOrio walked to his window, deep in thought, scratching his chin. 'I can see five million from a jury,' he said without turning around.

'I can see twenty,' Mordecai said.

'Who'll get the money?' the Judge asked.

'It'll be a nightmare,' Mordecai admitted.

'How much in attorneys' fees?'

'Twenty percent. Half of which goes to a trust in New York.'

The Judge snapped around and began pacing again, hands clenched behind his head. 'Six months is light,' he said.

'That's all we're giving,' Mordecai retorted.

'All right. Let me talk to the other side.'

Our private session with DeOrio lasted less than fifteen minutes. For the bad guys, it took an hour. Of course, they were the ones forking over the money.

We drank colas on a bench in the bustling lobby of the building, saying nothing as we watched a million lawyers scurry about, chasing clients and justice.

We walked the halls and looked at the scared people about to be hauled before the bench for a variety of offenses. Mordecai spoke to a couple of lawyers he knew. I recognized no one. Big-firm lawyers did not spend time in Superior Court.

The clerk found us and led us back to the courtroom, where all players were in place. Things were

345

tense. DeOrio was agitated. Arthur and company looked exhausted. We took our seats and waited for the Judge.

'Mr. Green,' he began, 'I have met with the lawyers for the defendants. Here's their best offer: the sum of three million dollars, and a one-year suspension for Mr. Brock.'

Mordecai had barely settled into his seat, when he bounced forward. 'Then we're wasting our time,' he said and grabbed his briefcase. I jumped up to follow him.

'Please excuse us, Your Honor,' he said. 'But we have better things to do.' We started for the aisle between the pews.

'You're excused,' the Judge said, very frustrated.

We left the courtroom in a rush.

THIRTY-EIGHT

I was unlocking the car when the cell phone rattled in my pocket. It was Judge DeOrio. Mordecai laughed when I said, 'Yes, Judge, we'll be there in five minutes.' We took ten, stopping in the rest rooms on the ground floor, walking slowly, using the stairs, giving DeOrio as much time as possible to further pummel the defendants.

The first thing I noticed when we entered the courtroom was that Jack Bolling, one of the three attorneys for RiverOaks, had removed his jacket, rolled up his sleeves, and was walking away from the Drake & Sweeney lawyers. I doubted if he had physically slapped them around, but he looked willing and able.

The huge verdict Mordecai dreamed about would be lodged against all three defendants. Evidently RiverOaks had been sufficiently frightened by the settlement conference. Threats had been made, and perhaps the company had decided to chip in with some cash of its own. We would never know.

I avoided the jury box and sat next to Mordecai. Wilma Phelan had left.

'We're getting close,' the Judge said.

'And we're thinking of withdrawing our offer,' Mordecai announced with one of his more violent barks. We had not discussed such a thing, and neither

347

the other lawyers nor His Honor had contemplated it. Their heads jerked as they looked at each other.

'Settle down,' DeOrio said.

'I'm very serious, Judge. The more I sit here in this courtroom, the more convinced I am that this travesty needs to be revealed to a jury. As for Mr. Brock, his old firm can push all it wants on the criminal charges, but it's no big deal. They have their file back. He has no criminal record. God knows our system is overloaded with drug dealers and murderers; prosecuting him will become a joke. He will not go to jail. And the bar complaint – let it run its course. I'll file one against Braden Chance and maybe some of the other lawyers involved in this mess, and we'll have us an old-fashioned spitting contest.' He pointed at Arthur and said, 'You run to the newspaper, we run to the newspaper.'

The 14th Street Legal Clinic couldn't care less what was printed about it. If Gantry cared, he wouldn't show it. RiverOaks could continue to make money in spite of bad press. But Drake & Sweeney had only its reputation to market.

Mordecai's tirade came from nowhere, and they were completely astonished by it.

'Are you finished?' DeOrio asked.

'I guess.'

'Good. The offer is up to four million.'

'If they can pay four million, then they can certainly pay five.' Mordecai pointed again, back to Drake & Sweeney. 'This defendant had gross billings last year of almost seven hundred million dollars.' He paused as the numbers echoed around the courtroom. 'Seven hundred million dollars, last year alone.' Then he pointed at RiverOaks. 'And this defendant owns real estate worth three hundred and fifty million dollars. Give me a jury.'

348

When it appeared that he was silent, DeOrio again asked, 'Are you finished?'

'No sir,' he said, and in an instant became remarkably calm. 'We'll take two million up front, a million for our fees, a million for the heirs. The balance of three million can be spread over the next ten years – three hundred thousand a year, plus a reasonable interest rate. Surely these defendants can spare three hundred thousand bucks a year. They may be forced to raise rents and hourly rates, but they certainly know how to do that.'

A structured settlement with an extended payout made sense. Because of the instability of the heirs, and the fact that most of them were still unknown, the money would be carefully guarded by the court.

Mordecai's latest onslaught was nothing short of brilliant. There was a noticeable relaxing in the Drake & Sweeney group. He had given them a way out.

Jack Bolling huddled with them. Gantry's lawyers watched and listened, but were almost as bored as their client.

'We can do that,' Arthur announced. 'But we keep our position regarding Mr. Brock. It's a one-year suspension, or there's no settlement.'

I suddenly hated Arthur, again. I was their last pawn, and to save what little face they had left, they wanted all the blood they could squeeze.

But poor Arthur was not negotiating from a position of power. He was desperate, and looked it.

'What difference does it make?!' Mordecai yelled at him. 'He's agreed to suffer the indignity of surrendering his license. What does an extra six months give you? This is absurd!'

The two corporate boys from RiverOaks had had enough. Naturally afraid of courtrooms, their fear had reached new heights after three hours of Mordecai. There was no way on earth they would endure two weeks of trial. They shook their heads in frustration and whispered intensely to one another.

Even Tillman Gantry was tired of Arthur's nitpicking. With the settlement so close, finish the damned thing!

Seconds earlier, Mordecai had yelled, 'What difference does it make?' And he was right. It really made no difference, especially for a street lawyer like me, one whose job and salary and status would remain wonderfully unaffected by a temporary suspension.

I stood, and very politely said, 'Your Honor, let's split the difference. We offered six months; they want twelve. I'll agree to nine.' I looked at Barry Nuzzo when I said this, and he actually smiled at me.

If Arthur had opened his mouth at that point, he would've been mugged. Everyone relaxed, including DeOrio. 'Then we have a deal,' he said, not waiting for a confirmation from the defendants.

His wonderfully efficient law clerk pecked away at a word processor in front of the bench, and within minutes she produced a one-page Settlement Memorandum. We quickly signed it, and left.

There was no champagne at the office. Sofia was doing what she always did. Abraham was attending a homeless conference in New York.

If any law office in America could absorb five hundred thousand dollars in fees without showing it, it was the 14th Street Legal Clinic. Mordecai wanted new computers and phones, and probably a new heating system. The bulk of the money would be buried in the bank, drawing interest and waiting for the lean times. It was a nice cushion, one that would guarantee our meager salaries for a few years.

If he was frustrated by the reality of sending the other five hundred thousand to the Cohen Trust, he concealed it well. Mordecai was not one to worry about the things he couldn't change. His desk was covered with the battles he could win.

It would take at least nine months of hard labor to sort out the Burton settlement, and that was where I would spend much of my time. Heirs had to be determined, then found, then dealt with when they realized there was money to be had. It would get complicated. For example, the bodies of Kito Spires and those of Temeko, Alonzo, and Dante might have to be exhumed for DNA tests, to establish paternity. If he was in fact the father, then he would inherit from the children, who died first. Since he was now dead, his estate would be opened, and his heirs located.

Lontae's mother and brothers posed intimidating problems. They still had contacts on the streets. They would be paroled in a few years, and they would come after their share of the money with a vengeance.

There were two other projects of particular interest to Mordecai. The first was a pro bono program the clinic had once organized, then allowed to slip away as federal monies evaporated. At its peak, the program had a hundred lawyers volunteering a few hours a week to help the homeless. He asked me to consider reviving it. I liked the idea; we could reach more people, make more contacts within the established bar, and broaden our base for raising funds.

That was the second project. Sofia and Abraham were incapable of effectively asking people for money. Mordecai could talk people out of their shirts, but he hated to beg. I was the bright young Waspy star who could mix and mingle with all the right professionals and convince them to give annually.

'With a good plan, you could raise two hundred thousand bucks a year,' he said.

'And what would we do with it?'

'Hire a couple of secretaries, a couple of paralegals, maybe another lawyer.' As we sat in the front after

351

Sofia left, watching it grow dark outside, Mordecai began dreaming. He longed for the days when there were seven lawyers bumping into each other at the clinic. Every day was chaos, but the little street firm was a force. It helped thousands of homeless people. Politicians and bureaucrats listened to the clinic. It was a loud voice that was usually heard.

'We've been declining for five years,' he said. 'And our people are suffering. This is our golden moment to turn it around.'

And the challenge belonged to me. I was the new blood, the new talent who would reinvigorate the clinic and take it to the next level. I would brighten up the place with dozens of new volunteers. I would build a fund-raising machine so that we could lawyer on the same field as anyone. We would expand, even knock the boards off the windows upstairs and fill the place with talented advocates.

The rights of the homeless would be protected, as long as they could find us. And their voices would be heard through ours.

THIRTY-NINE

Early Friday I was sitting at my desk, happily going about my business as a lawyer/social worker, when Drake & Sweeney, in the person of Arthur Jacobs, suddenly appeared at my door. I greeted him pleasantly, and cautiously, and he sat in one of the maroon chairs. He didn't want coffee. He just wanted to talk.

Arthur was troubled. I was mesmerized as I listened to the old man.

The last few weeks had been the most difficult of his professional career – all fifty-six years of it. The settlement had given him little comfort. The firm was back on track after the slight bump in the road, but Arthur was finding sleep difficult. One of his partners had committed a terrible wrong, and as a result innocent people had died. Drake & Sweeney would be forever at fault for the deaths of Lontae and her four children, regardless of how much money it paid into the settlement. And Arthur doubted if he would ever get over it.

I was too surprised to say much, so I just listened. I wished Mordecai could hear him.

Arthur was suffering, and before long I felt sorry for him. He was eighty, had been contemplating retirement for a couple of years, but wasn't sure what to do now. He was tired of chasing money.

'I don't have a lot of years left,' he admitted. I suspected Arthur would attend my funeral.

He was fascinated by our legal clinic, and I told him the story of how I'd stumbled into it. How long had it been there? he asked. How many people worked there? What was the source of funding? How did we operate it?

He gave me the opening, and I slipped in. Because I couldn't practice law for the next nine months, the clinic had decided that I should implement a new pro bono volunteer program using attorneys from the big firms in town. Since his firm happened to be the largest, I was thinking of starting there. The volunteers would work only a few hours a week, under my supervision, and we could reach thousands of homeless people.

Arthur was aware of such programs; vaguely aware. He hadn't performed free work in twenty years, he admitted sadly. It was normally for the younger associates. How well I remembered.

But he liked the idea. In fact, the longer we discussed it, the larger the program grew. After a few minutes, he was talking openly of requiring all four hundred of his D.C. lawyers to spend a few hours a week helping the poor. It seemed only fitting.

'Can you handle four hundred lawyers?' he asked.

'Of course,' I said, without any idea as to how to even begin such a task. But my mind was racing. 'I'll need some help, though,' I said.

'What kind of help?' he asked.

'What if Drake & Sweeney had a full-time pro bono coordinator within the firm? This person would work closely with me on all aspects of homeless law. Frankly, with four hundred volunteers, we'll need someone on your end.'

He pondered this. Everything was new, and everything was sounding good. I plowed ahead.

'And I know just the right person,' I said. 'He doesn't have to be a lawyer. A good paralegal can do it.'

'Who?' he asked.

'Does the name Hector Palma ring a bell?'

'Vaguely.'

'He's in the Chicago office, but he's from D.C. He worked under Braden Chance, and got pinched.'

Arthur's eyes narrowed as he struggled to remember. I wasn't sure how much he knew, but I doubted if he would be dishonest. He seemed to be thoroughly enjoying his soul-cleansing.

'Pinched?' he asked.

'Yeah, pinched. He lived in Bethesda until three weeks ago when he suddenly moved in the middle of the night. A quickie transfer to Chicago. He knew everything about the evictions, and I suspect Chance wanted to hide him.' I was careful. I was not about to break my confidential agreement with Hector.

I didn't have to. Arthur, as usual, was reading between lines.

'He's from D.C.?'

'Yes, and so is his wife. They have four kids. I'm sure he'd love to return.'

'Does he have an interest in helping the homeless?' he asked.

'Why don't you ask him?' I said.

'I'll do that. It's an excellent idea.'

If Arthur wanted Hector Palma back in D.C. to harness the firm's newly acquired passion for homeless law, it would be done within a week.

The program took shape before our eyes. Every Drake & Sweeney lawyer would be required to handle one case each week. The younger associates would do the intake, under my supervision, and once the cases arrived at the firm they would be assigned by Hector to the other lawyers. Some cases would take fifteen

355

minutes, I explained to Arthur, others would take several hours a month. No problem, he said.

I almost felt sorry for the politicians and bureaucrats and office workers at the thought of four hundred Drake & Sweeney lawyers suddenly seized with a fervor to protect the rights of street people.

Arthur stayed almost two hours, and apologized when he realized he had taken so much of my time. But he was much happier when he left. He was going straight to his office with a new purpose, a man on a mission. I walked him to his car, then ran to tell Mordecai.

Megan's uncle owned a house on the Delaware shore, near Fenwick Island on the Maryland line. She described it as a quaint old house, two stories with a large porch that almost touched the ocean, three bedrooms, a perfect spot for a weekend getaway. It was the middle of March, still cold, and we could sit by the fire and read books.

She slightly stressed the part about three bedrooms, so there would be plenty of space for each of us to have privacy, without matters getting complicated. She knew I was limping away from my first marriage, and after two weeks of cautious flirting we had both come to realize that things would proceed slowly. But there was another reason for mentioning the three bedrooms.

We left Washington Friday afternoon. I drove. Megan navigated. And Ruby nibbled on oatmeal cookies in the backseat, wild-eyed at the prospect of spending a few days outside the city, off the streets, on the beach, clean and sober.

She had been clean Thursday night. Three nights with us in Delaware would make four. Monday afternoon we would check her into Easterwood, a small women's detox center off East Capitol. Mordecai had leaned heavily on someone there, and Ruby would have a small room with a warm bed for at least ninety days.

Before we left the city, she had showered at Naomi's and changed into new clothes. Megan had searched every inch of her clothing and bag looking for drugs. She found nothing. It was an invasion of privacy, but with addicts the rules are different.

We found the house at dusk. Megan used it once or twice a year. The key was under the front doormat.

I was assigned the downstairs bedroom, which Ruby thought odd. The other two bedrooms were upstairs, and Megan wanted to be near Ruby during the night.

It rained Saturday, a cold, blowing shower that came from the sea. I was alone on the front porch, rocking gently in a swing under a thick blanket, lost in a dream world, listening to the waves break below. The door closed, the screen slammed behind it, and Megan walked to the swing. She lifted the blanket and tucked herself next to me. I held her firmly; if not, she would've fallen onto the porch.

She was easy to hold.

'Where's our client?' I asked.

'Watching TV.'

A strong gust threw mist in our faces, and we squeezed tighter. The chains holding the swing squeaked louder, then faded as we became almost still. We watched the clouds swirl above the water. Time was of no importance.

'What are you thinking?' she asked softly.

Everything and nothing. Away from the city, I could look back for the first time and try to make sense of it all. Thirty-two days earlier I had been married to someone else, living in a different apartment, working in a different firm, a complete stranger to the woman I

357

was now holding. How could life change so drastically in a month?

I didn't dare think of the future; the past was still happening.

AUTHOR'S NOTE

Before writing this book, I had not worried too much about the homeless. And I certainly didn't know anyone who worked with them.

In D.C., I found my way to the Washington Legal Clinic for the Homeless, where I met Patricia Fugere, the Director. She and her colleagues – Mary Ann Luby, Scott McNeilly, and Melody Webb O'Sullivan – introduced me to the world of the homeless. Many thanks to them for their time and assistance.

Thanks also to Maria Foscarinis of the National Law Center on Homelessness and Poverty, and to Willa Day Morris at Rachael's Women's Center, and Mary Popit at New Endeavors by Women, and Bruce Casino and Bruce Sanford of Baker & Hostetler.

Will Denton once again read the manuscript and suggested changes to keep it lawyerly. Jefferson Arrington showed me the city. Jonathan Hamilton did the research. Thanks.

And to the real Mordecai Greens, a quiet tribute for your work in the trenches.